COUNCILOR

ALSO BY L. E. MODESITT, JR.

L.E. MODESITT JR.

COUNCILOR

TOR

A TOM DOHERTY
ASSOCIATES BOOK
NEW YORK

This is a work of fiction. All of the characters, organizations, and events portrayed in this novel are either products of the author's imagination or are used fictitiously.

COUNCILOR

A Tor Book
Published by Tom Doherty Associates
120 Broadway
New York, NY 10271

www.tor-forge.com

Tor® is a registered trademark of Macmillan Publishing Group, LLC.

Library of Congress Cataloging-in-Publication Data

Names: Modesitt, L. E., Jr., 1943– author.
Title: Councilor / L. E. Modesitt, Jr..
Description: First Edition. | New York : Tor, a Tom Doherty Associates Book,
    2022. | Series: The grand illusion ; 2
Identifiers: LCCN 2022008303 (print) | LCCN 2022008304 (ebook) |
    ISBN 9781250814456 (hardcover) | ISBN 9781250814463 (ebook)
Classification: LCC PS3563.O264 C68 2022 (print) | LCC PS3563.O264 (ebook) |
    DDC 813/.54—dc23
LC record available at https://lccn.loc.gov/2022008303
LC ebook record available at https://lccn.loc.gov/2022008304

Our books may be purchased in bulk for promotional, educational, or business use.
Please contact your local bookseller or the Macmillan Corporate and Premium
Sales Department at 1-800-221-7945, extension 5442, or by email at
MacmillanSpecialMarkets@macmillan.com.

First Edition: 2022

Printed in the United States of America

0 9 8 7 6 5 4 3 2 1

FOR JACQUELINE

MAJOR CHARACTERS

Steffan Dekkard   Isolate and Councilor, Former Security Aide for Premier Obreduur

Avraal Ysella-Dekkard   Empath, Former Security Aide for Premier Obreduur, wife of Dekkard

Emrelda Roemnal   District Patroller, sister of Avraal

Axel Obreduur   Premier of Guldor and Councilor from Oersynt (Craft)

Ingrella Obreduur   Legalist and wife of Axel Obreduur

Isobel Irlende   Security Empath for the Premier

Laureous XXIV   Imperador of Guldor

Guilhohn Haarsfel   Craft Party Floor Leader, Councilor from Kathaar

Saandaar Vonauer   Landor Party Floor Leader, Councilor from Plaatz

Hansaal Volkaar   Commerce Party Floor Leader, Councilor from Uldwyrk

Kaliara Bassaana   Councilor from Caylaan (Commerce)

Fredrich Hasheem   Security Committee Chair, Councilor from Port Reale (Craft)

Breffyn Haastar   Councilor from Brekaan (Landor)

Erskine Mardosh   Military Affairs Committee Chair, Councilor from Siincleer (Craft)

Kharl Navione   Councilor from Seibryg (Landor)

Pohl Palafaux   Councilor from Point Larmat (Commerce)

Gerhard Safaell   Waterways Committee Chair, Councilor from Enke (Craft)

Harleona Zerlyon   Justiciary Committee Chair, Councilor from Ondeliew (Craft)

Oskaar Ulrich   Former Premier (Commerce), Associate Vice-Presidente, Suvion Industries

Jaime Minz   Isolate, Former Security Aide for Ulrich, Assistant Security Director for Northwest Industrial Chemical

Izaak Trujillo   Guard Captain, Council Guards

COUNCILOR

PROLOGUE

Findi
24 Fallfirst 1266

ON Findi morning, Dekkard was up early, thinking about the day ahead, and that by noon he and Avraal would be married, little more than a week after he'd proposed. They'd not had much choice about the timing, not after he'd been suddenly selected to fill the Council seat left open by Haasan Decaro's untimely death.

He glanced around the small staff bedroom, musing that, after more than two years, he'd spent his last night in the Obreduur house. Avraal had left the night before, when she and Dekkard had used their newly purchased gray Gresynt to carry the last of her clothes to her sister Emrelda's house, where she spent the night . . . and where Dekkard and Avraal would be living after the wedding.

Another necessary accommodation to reality.

Recognizing that the last thing he needed was to be late, Dekkard quickly shaved and washed up, then threw on a set of old security grays to wear to breakfast. He hurried down to the staff room, where the normal Findi breakfast platter was already laid out, and poured his café and took two croissants, with his usual quince paste.

He ate quickly and had just stood to leave when Hyelda and Rhosali appeared.

"You're leaving already?" asked Hyelda.

"Not quite. I have to load a few things in the steamer, then change into my formalwear for the wedding. You're both going to be there, I trust?"

Rhosali grinned. "I wouldn't miss it. You're both good people, and I'll be able to tell the family and everyone that I was at a councilor's wedding."

"I'll be there." Hyelda offered an amused smile. "Someone has to settle Rhosali."

"Good." Dekkard smiled, then turned and walked into the back hall and up to his room, where he packed his few remaining clothes, then dressed in white formalwear and carefully made his way downstairs, carrying the case, and out to the gray Gresynt.

After loading and lighting off the steamer, he waited for full pressure before starting down the drive. Since it was well before third bell, he had plenty of time. Still, he worried. Because it was a Findi, and because the New Meritorists had often created demonstrations on endday, especially at Imperial University, which was on the way to Emrelda's and the Hillside Trinitarian Chapel, he wanted to have time to avoid any disruption. Fortunately, the university was quiet, and less than a third of a bell later he pulled the Gresynt into the chapel's parking area, where there were only two steamers, that of Presider Buusen and another Realto he didn't recognize.

He locked the Gresynt and walked toward the chapel with its gray stone walls and gold-tinted side windows that turned the greenish-white sunlight into a golden hue—when the sun shone through the green haze that suffused the atmosphere most days when it didn't rain. When he entered the chapel, he could hear the harmonium, suggesting that the other Realto belonged to the organist. He vaguely recognized the music. At least, he thought he'd heard it before, but since he'd been raised in a household essentially of lapsed Solidans, his only exposure to Trinitarian hymns and music had been at the Institute and when he had accompanied the Obreduurs to chapel.

Presider Buusen's study door was open, and Dekkard looked in and saw Buusen, clad in a simple green cassock, standing and looking out the half-open window.

The presider, a slender man, slightly taller than average height, possibly four digits shorter than Dekkard, with short-cut sandy and silver hair, turned and gestured for Dekkard to enter. "You're a little early, Steffan."

"More than a little," admitted Dekkard. "I didn't want to be late, and delays always occur when it's most inconvenient. I also wanted to thank you, again, for being so accommodating."

"I was free at this time." Buusen smiled as he went on. "Emrelda's been a good parishioner, and since you and Avraal will be living with her for a time, how could I resist the opportunity to have another young couple become part of the ward? Especially such a distinguished young couple."

"We may not be quite so faithful in attending as Emrelda," Dekkard replied. "I'll have to spend time in Gaarlak, since that's now my district."

"I understand. There have been other councilors attending during my time here." The presider gestured to the chairs in front of his desk. "We might as well sit."

"Thank you. How did you come to be a presider, might I ask?"

"I actually trained as a chemist, and there were questions that science couldn't answer. Not to my satisfaction. Science is good at explaining how. I found it lacking in answering why. Perhaps it's my weakness, but why do we think . . . or think we think . . . better than other creatures? Some believe that seabears are as intelligent as children, but they have no voices and no hands. Is it just random that we have hands and voices? Science so far cannot answer that question. There are fossilized bones that suggest we developed from arboreal creatures . . . but why us and not mountain ursinoids . . . or seabears." Buusen shrugged. "Those questions led me here. How did you get here?"

Dekkard smiled. "It's a very long and simple story . . . but the mostly simple fact was that I wasn't a very good artisan and I turned out to have some ability as a security aide, where I slowly fell in love with my partner, who let me discover that by myself."

"What about her?"

"We're both reserved, Avraal more than I am, although most people wouldn't see that."

"How are you finding being a councilor?"

"Very carefully," replied Dekkard wryly.

While Dekkard summarized how he'd gone from being a security aide to a councilor, what he didn't mention was that, while he knew the routine and outward duties of a councilor, if only from observation, he had no firsthand political experience. There was also the added fact that councilors had become targets of either Commercer-linked interests or of New Meritorist demonstrators. Over the four months before the recent election, five councilors from the Council of Sixty-Six had been assassinated, and there had been four attempts on Premier Obreduur when he'd still been a councilor, attempts that Dekkard and Avraal had thwarted.

So you have to not only worry about learning how to be a councilor, but also deal with possible assassination attempts . . . and being married.

Dekkard pushed those thoughts away—for the moment—and finished his summary. Before long, the organist stopped practicing and began playing what Dekkard would have called prelude music. Then Emrelda appeared, wearing an ankle-length teal dress with matching gloves, shoes, and nearly transparent headscarf.

"Avraal's ready, Presider Buusen."

"So am I," said Dekkard as he stood, followed by Buusen.

The presider smiled. "I won't be the one to hold up the ceremony. We'll give you a few minutes to get back to the bride, and then we'll take our places."

"She looks so beautiful," said Emrelda, her voice catching just slightly. "You'll see."

Then she turned and walked back toward the main entry to the chapel.

A minute or so passed before Buusen said, "It's time."

Dekkard handed the two rings to the presider. "I imagine you'll need these."

"It will make the ceremony go a little easier."

Dekkard and Buusen left the study, then walked along the corridor paralleling the nave, before entering the chapel proper. Dekkard stopped just short of the middle of the center aisle and turned to face the rear of the chapel. Buusen took the low step up to the sanctuary and also turned, looking down the center aisle.

Behind them was the usual golden-edged tapestry, hung from a shimmering brass rod that extended nearly the width of the sanctuary wall. Against a pale green background three golden orbs formed an arc. Within the orb on the left was a silver-edged green maple leaf, while the middle and highest orb held a silver-edged ray of golden sunlight splitting a green waterspout, and the orb on the right portrayed the outline of an antique four-masted ship haloed with the reddish-gold light of sunset on a calm sea. Though the tapestry changed each season, only the background color varied, currently a pale golden red for autumn.

Dekkard surveyed the small group in the five front pews—Premier Obreduur and Ingrella, as well as Gustoff and Nellara, although the Obreduurs' oldest child, Axeli, was in his second year at the Military Institute; Isobel Irlende, the security empath who was replacing Avraal; Hyelda and Rhosali; the office staff members of Obreduur's office and the few staffers from Dekkard's office; and in the back of the chapel, two Council Guards in their green-and-black uniforms, there to protect the Premier.

Svard Roostof, seated beside Ivann Macri and his wife, flashed a warm smile at Dekkard, and then the organist began playing the bridal processional.

Not that it was really a procession, just Emrelda, followed by her younger sister. Avraal wore a long-sleeved, high-necked, and ankle-length bright emerald-green dress, which suited her trim, petite, but slightly muscular figure far better than the more traditional pale green flowing gown. Her gloves and shoes matched the dress, as did her veil, although the veil was also more transparent than traditional, revealing more clearly her shimmering bobbed black hair. She did carry the traditional bridal bouquet of white and green gardenias.

Her gray eyes were on Dekkard, and his eyes were on her.

When Emrelda neared Dekkard, she smiled and stepped to the side, watching Avraal, as was everyone in the small assemblage of friends and guests. Suddenly, or so it seemed to Dekkard, Avraal was beside him, and the two turned to face Presider Buusen.

"Today, we are gathered here to witness and acknowledge the marriage of Steffan Delos Dekkard and Avraal Mikaila Ysella and to grant their union the blessing of the Three."

Buusen turned first to Avraal. "Is this indeed your wish and intent, freely given?"

"It is."

Then he turned to Dekkard and repeated the question.

"It is."

Buusen's eyes went to those in the pews. "As we acknowledge before the Three, our days are but fleeting threads in the fabric of time, yet in this transitory existence, one buffeted by the storms of fate and chance, the ties we make and hold enable us to weather the storms of life. Among the strongest of these ties is the commitment of a man and a woman to each other. So powerful and meaningful is this tie that it is specially blessed by the Three."

The presider turned his eyes back to Dekkard and Avraal. "Marriage is a commitment not to be taken lightly. While it can afford the greatest of rewards, it is not a commitment to abandon in times of trouble or temptation. For, like threads that are stronger when woven together, remaining bound together in times both of triumph and tribulation leads to the greatest of rewards." Buusen turned to Avraal and nodded.

She handed the wedding bouquet and her gloves to Emrelda, then turned to face Dekkard.

Buusen lifted the two rings and said, "These rings symbolize your decision and commitment to each other. In the sight of the Three and those gathered here, you pledge that commitment." He handed one ring to Avraal.

She accepted the ring and slipped it onto Dekkard's finger, saying as she did, "With this ring, I pledge my faith and love to you and to us both."

Buusen handed the second ring to Dekkard.

As had Avraal, he placed it on her finger, saying, "With this ring, I pledge my faith and love to you and to us both." In a murmur, he added, "With thanks and gratitude for your patience and love." He squeezed her fingers gently before releasing them.

They turned back to face the presider.

"In the sight of the Three, you have affirmed your love and commitment. May it always be so."

1

NEW PREMIER VOWS PROSPERITY FOR ALL

At the opening business session of the new Council, Premier Axel Obred-uur was direct and forceful in declaring that "The people of Guldor have spoken. They want prosperity for all, not just the wealthy and fortunate." Premier Obreduur went on to attack indirectly the policies of the previous government by claiming that the people wanted "meaningful work in Guldor, not cheap goods produced by impoverished susceptibles in other lands." Only after those points did he address the concern felt by most Guldorans, the need for a "return to stability and order" after the demonstrations and violence mounted by the extremist New Meritorists in recent months.

The Premier claimed that the demonstrations resulted from a failure of government to understand that destroying Guldoran jobs to increase short-term corporacion profits only meant that most Guldorans suffered immediately and that such increased profits would be short-term and temporary . . .

Gestirn, 24 Fallfirst 1266

2

O N Unadi morning, when Dekkard settled himself behind the wheel of the gray Gresynt, he wore one of his new gray suits, with the red cravat of a councilor. Avraal sat beside him as he eased the steamer down the narrow drive at Emrelda's house.

As he turned onto Florinda Way, he couldn't help but hope that most of the administrivia and personal changes that had occupied much of the previous week and a half were largely past. With Premier Obreduur's suggestion and blessing, he'd hired Svard Roostof as his senior legalist and Margrit Pettit as his personal secretary, and after bells of interviews settled on a junior legalist named Luara Colsbaan, who'd been highly recommended by Ingrella Obreduur, and two typists. All of the staff had been at the wedding and the reception following, hosted by Emrelda.

"It was quite an endday, dear, or should I say, 'Ritten Ysella-Dekkard'?" he asked playfully, reaching out to squeeze his wife's hand.

Calling it quite a day was an understatement. After all the changes—especially from security aide to councilor and from being single to being married—the simple act of driving to the Council Office Building left Dekkard with a sense of the surreal, a sense heightened by the early-morning mist too light to be rain and too transparent and warm to qualify as fog.

"It's been quite a year," she pointed out, ignoring his use of the title.

"But yesterday . . . was special."

"Yesterday . . . or last night?"

"Both," he managed, with only the slightest of hesitations.

"Last night," she said with an impish smile, squeezing his hand in return.

Dekkard flushed, but kept his eyes out for other steamers as he turned south on Jacquez.

"The last few days have been busy and different," he finally said as he turned onto Camelia Avenue. "But I've been thinking. We haven't talked about what you should be doing. I don't see you sitting around waiting for me or Emrelda to come home. Maybe you could take Isobel Irlende's place working for Carlos Baartol, at least for a while."

"Obreduur mentioned that possibility last week. I also thought about looking into working for the Guilds' Advisory Committee directly."

"Do they have any empaths?"

"Isobel said they didn't, but they used to. Carlos hired her, and they never replaced her."

"Then he obviously pays more."

"I want to work," Avraal replied, "but pay isn't everything."

"Then talk to them both."

"I set up appointments last Quindi."

"You didn't mention that," he said with a smile.

"That's because I wanted to see if you brought it up." She paused, then added, "I'm glad you did."

If likely almost too late. "So am I."

The rest of the drive was much like that of most mornings over the past two years. Dekkard watched the streets and the steamers on them. Avraal kept sensing emotions of anyone who neared the Gresynt. Yet neither of them worked for Obreduur anymore. Dekkard was a councilor in his own right, and Avraal couldn't work for either. Neither wore the gray security uniforms they'd donned for years, but gray suits, his with the appropriate councilor lapel pin, and hers still showing her as a staff aide, a matter they needed to take care of as soon as possible.

After Dekkard parked the Gresynt in the covered parking reserved for councilors, the two made their way across the drive to the Council Office Building. He carried a heavy gray leather folder holding various forms and papers.

As they neared the bronze doors, a Council Guard greeted them. "Good morning, Councilor."

"Good morning," replied Dekkard warmly.

Once inside, they took the central staircase to the second level, turning east toward Dekkard's office.

Except for Margrit, the outer office was empty, but she immediately said, "Good morning, Councilor, Ritten."

"Good morning," replied Dekkard, then called out, "Svard?"

"Here." Roostof hurried out through the open door from the staff room, where he'd likely been talking to Illana Zullt and Bretta Soike, the two clerktypists hired the previous Quindi . . . or possibly Luara Colsbaan, the newly hired junior legalist.

"Come on into my office."

In little more than moments, Roostof and Avraal were seated in front of Dekkard's desk.

"How are you coming with Illana and Bretta?" Dekkard asked.

"So far so good. You chose well."

Dekkard grinned. "*You* selected them, because you'll be the one supervising them. Avraal and I just approved your choice. You can take some credit, you know." He paused. "Now . . . there's one other thing. We've put off considering a technical or economic specialist. We need someone with an engineering background, preferably who comes from a hands-on family background and has been overlooked by the big engineering corporacions like Siincleer or Haasan Design." Dekkard hadn't wanted to make the decision on the position until his committee assignments on the Security Committee and the Workplace Administration Committee had been confirmed late the previous week.

"Bright, but without high-level corporacion connections," added Avraal.

Roostof offered a puzzled frown.

"You might recall that, just before the election," replied Dekkard, "there were some newssheet stories about how small engineering firms had unlikely, unfortunate circumstances befall them—rather consistently—and how the costs of government procurement have increased enormously. Now, with as many as fifteen possible Security buildings to repair or replace . . ."

"You think that's going to come before the Security Committee?"

Dekkard smiled wryly. "I'm going to do my best to see that it does." Particularly since the corruption of the engineering companies had led to the disappearance and likely death of Markell, Emrelda's husband. "Do you have any contacts where you could put out the word?"

"I know a few people . . ."

"Do what you can. It will be a while before it comes up." *And it will come up, before one committee or another, if not several.* Dekkard looked to Avraal. "We'll have to go before long. Is there anything else?"

"Not right now."

Dekkard stood. "Then I'll see you later, Svard. Avraal and I need to take care of her paperwork and spousal passcard."

Once Roostof had gone back to the larger staff office, Dekkard turned to Avraal. "Are you ready to go?"

"I am. But it feels strange not to be a staff aide anymore."

"You'll have the same access." *And a little bit more.* "Or is it because the access comes from me and not from your qualifications?"

"I'm glad you understand."

"The sooner we get you your spousal pin and passcard, the sooner you can talk to Carlos and the Guilds' Advisory Committee." Dekkard picked up his leather folder and gestured toward the door.

As they left his personal office, Dekkard turned to Margrit. "We're headed to administration. I'll be back as soon as I can." Not that he expected anyone to be looking for him at the moment, since very few even knew who he was—except job hunters and influencers.

On the walk to administration, the halls were mostly empty, unlike at midday or just before the Council was in session.

Once Dekkard presented all the forms to the head clerk, she looked up and said, "This won't take long. The Premier already told us to have Ritten Dekkard's lapel pin and passcard ready. Just have a seat."

As they seated themselves, Dekkard said, "An additional wedding present to you."

"And to you, in a way."

Dekkard nodded. "I suppose so, but the chance to meet you was the greatest gift." After a slight pause, he smiled sheepishly and added, "Even if it almost took me too long to realize it."

"I wouldn't have been ready for you before. You can ask Emrelda."

"She'd tell me the same thing, I'm sure."

"You won't mind my working somewhere else?"

"Of course, I mind. I'll miss having you close." He grinned. "But now I'll have you closer at night and when we're not working. You need to do something meaningful, just like Ingrella. I've known that almost from the time we first met."

In less than a sixth of a bell, the clerk returned, and Avraal turned in her staff pin and passcard and received a spousal pin and passcard. Then Dekkard walked her to the west doors of the Council Office Building, where he handed her the keys to the Gresynt. "Take the position that suits you best, not for the marks."

"You're assuming I'll be offered a position."

"You'll get offers from both." There was no way she wouldn't, Dekkard knew. Not with her being an extremely strong empath, *and* her experience working for the new premier as well as being the wife of a councilor.

"I'll let you know." She smiled again before leaving the building, heading across the drive to the covered parking.

When Dekkard returned to the office, he started in on the contents of the two inboxes on his desk, into which Margrit had sorted the day's letters and messages. Heliograms, infrequent as they were, just went on the desk. That system couldn't last, he knew, but since he'd never seen everything that had come into Obreduur's office, he wanted a better idea of what came into his own before letting it go through Roostof first.

He pulled out a letter from the Textile Millworkers of Gaarlak, frowning as he did. It was likely from Gretna Haarl, the recently chosen guildmeister. She had reportedly played a key role in the Gaarlak Craft Party's decision to recommend Dekkard as the replacement for the deceased Haasan Decaro. Despite assurances from Obreduur, Dekkard had doubts about that report, given that in his last—and only—conversation with Haarl, she had been acrimoniously critical of him.

He opened the envelope, extracted the letter, and began to read.

Dear Steffan,

The Guild would like to congratulate you on your becoming the Councilor for the Gaarlak District. As you may have heard, the Guild felt that you would be a far better choice to represent us than any other candidate suggested.

Your selection does present certain future problems, however. We hope that you will take steps to remedy them as you can. Some commitment to a residence or property on which a residence might be built would be an excellent beginning.

We look forward to seeing you and meeting with you on your next trip to Gaarlak, which we trust will be as soon as practicable. We also hope that you will retain the counsel and advice of Avraal Ysella.

The signature was, indeed, that of Gretna Haarl.

At least you can reassure her that you're definitely retaining Avraal's counsel. Except, given Haarl's prickly insistence on the equality of women in all spheres, Haarl might well regard their marriage as minimizing Avraal. Dekkard decided he needed to think on how to respond . . . and get Avraal's advice. But the fact that Haarl had indeed still supported him remained a puzzle . . . and a potential problem over time.

As he set that aside, the address on an expensive parchment-paper envelope caught his eye—Northwest Industrial Chemical—located on West Council Avenue, but that had to be a local office, because the corporacion's main plant and headquarters were in Chuive. He slit open the envelope and extracted the single sheet, immediately glancing to the signature line:

Jaime Minz
Assistant Director of Security

Shaking his head, he began to read.

Dear Steffan—
  Congratulations on being selected as Councilor from Gaarlak.
  While I shouldn't have been surprised, given your abilities and those of the Premier, I have to admit that it was masterfully done, although you must have mixed feelings about having to part ways with your partner. I'm most certain she'll be successful with whoever her next isolate may be.
  As you noted in our last conversation, the corporacion will likely face inquiries concerning the presumed theft of the dunnite used by the New Meritorist terrorists in their destruction of Security Ministry buildings. I can assure you that Northwest Industrial Chemical's records show a complete and unbroken chain of custody dealing with all sales of dunnite to government ministries and other corporacions, and that the corporacion will be completely forthcoming in providing such documentation should the Council or any Committee of the Council require such.
  Once more, my congratulations.

When he finished reading, Dekkard smiled wryly, especially considering the words about Avraal. *Even in a letter announcing his influencing intents, Minz can't resist throwing in a few words to undermine you.*

Minz, even if he was no longer a senior Security Committee staffer, was not someone to be ignored or minimized, especially with his new position and his long-standing connections to powerful Commercer councilors, past and present, including the previous premier. Dekkard continued reading the letters and messages, but less than a bell later, Margrit rapped on the door and eased it open.

"Svard and Luara would like a few minutes with you."

"Have them both come in." Dekkard straightened behind the desk and waited.

Moments later, Roostof entered the inner office with a mahogany-haired woman of medium height and the dark-honeyed skin more common among those from the southwest of Guldor, particularly those with a Landor or professional family background. That wasn't surprising, since Colsbaan was from Brekaan, but had received her degree in law from Imperial University prior to working as a legalist for the Women's Clerical Guild. She was also a good ten years older than Dekkard, and married with two children.

Dekkard motioned to the chairs in front of his desk.

After both were seated, Roostof said, "Luara and I were discussing the difficulty of proceeding without the records of issues and problems facing the district."

Dekkard turned to Colsbaan. "You found it hard to believe that there were no records, I take it?"

"Years ago, I worked briefly for Councilor Marrass, in a temporary position just before he stood down. He was most insistent that the office records went to his successor."

"I understand that has usually been the practice," replied Dekkard, "but my predecessor was ordered to destroy all records by the Landor Party leadership. One way or the other, we don't have any records. The Premier told me that was true in all the districts where Craft councilors replaced Commerce or Landor councilors."

A look of surprise appeared on Colsbaan's face and then immediately vanished.

"The Commercers don't take being defeated or thwarted very well, and they clearly exerted pressure on former Landor councilors as well," added Dekkard.

"I'd heard rumors, but I'm sad to have it confirmed that the Commercers aren't any more ethical in the Council than in practicing law, not that I expected otherwise."

"Is there anything else?"

"No, sir. It was just so unexpected, even after the . . . abuses by the Special Tactical Force."

Dekkard definitely had the feeling that Colsbaan was finding it hard to believe that any legalist would destroy records, possibly because guild legalists were always under scrutiny from the Justiciary Ministry, unlike corporacion legalists.

"The previous government engaged in a number of unexpected practices," Dekkard said dryly, "including the attempt of the recently deceased Treasury Minister to kill the Premier . . . or the situations where Security agents shot unarmed female demonstrators in the back. While Premier Obreduur has restricted the use of firearms by Special Agents and the STF, that's only a partial and temporary measure. We can only hope he can address some of the larger problems before the New Meritorists stage more demonstrations. If you have any thoughts along those lines, write them up. I'll be happy to look at them."

Colsbaan looked somewhat surprised.

"I mean it." *I'll need everyone's best ideas . . . and then some.*

"Yes, sir."

After Roostof and Colsbaan left his office, Dekkard continued going through the letters and Council notices, but the only one of immediate interest was about the backgrounds of Obreduur's proposed ministerial appointments, since Dekkard had never heard of most of the proposed appointees, and votes were scheduled on several of the appointees on Duadi. After he finished reading the letters, he turned them over to Margrit to give to Roostof for response, except for those from Gretna Haarl and Jaime Minz.

By then, it was time for him to leave for the floor and the Council session. The Premier had called a vote on a resolution modifying emergency appropriations legislation passed by the previous Council to defer any spending on rebuilding Security buildings damaged by the Summerend New Meritorist demonstrations.

Although Obreduur hadn't mentioned the reasons behind that exception clause, it was clear to Dekkard that the Premier felt voting to rebuild Security buildings without first looking into the abuses of Security agents and the Special Tactical Force would be politically catastrophic. It would send a message to the New Meritorists that the new Council was no different from the old Council. While Dekkard had been appointed to the Security Committee, the new chair of the committee, Fredrich Hasheem, had held off having the committee meet until Duadi, likely to give himself time to plan out his strategy for the coming year.

"I'm walking over to the Council Hall. I'll likely be back in a bell or less," Dekkard told Margrit as he left the office.

He'd just reached the central staircase when he saw Amelya Detauran and Elyssa Kaan escorting a dark-haired councilor almost as tall as the imposing Amelya, and a good fifteen years older than Dekkard. That councilor had to be Kaliara Bassaana, the Commercer councilor from Caylaan, whom Dekkard had never met.

"Councilor Bassaana," Dekkard said politely as he neared the three.

Amelya immediately said something to Bassaana.

The councilor smiled politely and turned. "Councilor Dekkard . . . Amelya has told me so much about you."

"Alas," replied Dekkard, "she's told me almost nothing about you, except that you respect Premier Obreduur and have considerably less respect for Eastern Ironway."

Bassaana offered an amused laugh, then said, "We might as well chat on the way to the floor." She paused before starting down the central staircase. "Do you still carry throwing knives?"

"I do, since a councilor carrying a gladius and truncheon is likely to be frowned upon."

"Then I'm certainly secure, with two armed isolates and an excellent empath around me. I understand you're to be married soon . . . to your former security partner."

"Actually, we were married yesterday."

"Congratulations. It must be quite a change for both of you, isn't it?"

"Only for me. Ritten Ysella merely became Ritten Ysella-Dekkard."

Dekkard thought Bassaana paused just for an instant before she said, "I don't believe many people know that."

"Most don't, but her father is descended from the last king of Aloor. Her brother, of course, is the heir to the lands."

"You chose well."

Dekkard laughed softly as he and Bassaana stepped out of the Council Office Building and onto the covered walk to the Council Hall. He also noticed

Bassaana's hand signal for Amelya and Elyssa to give them more space. "Avraal never told me. I found out from Ingrella Obreduur after I'd asked Avraal to marry me." That wasn't quite true, but it was true in spirit and close enough. He glanced around, but saw no sign of anything untoward, unlike the times during summer when there had been armed demonstrators. "The selection as councilor forced us to schedule the ceremony much earlier than we'd anticipated."

"You had no idea you were to be selected?"

Dekkard shook his head ruefully. "Even the Premier and the regional Craft Party coordinator were stunned."

"How did anyone even know who you were?"

"The Premier toured Gaarlak during Summerend. Avraal and I accompanied him. We stopped another assassination attempt, and there was a rather large news story about his tour and about how Avraal and I caught Councilor Aashtaan's assassin. We talked with local Guild officials, legalists, and others as part of his efforts in support of the Craft Party. He never said, but I surmised that was because Emilio Raathan had not been that visible and had to stand down in the election."

"Did he ever mention anything about your becoming a councilor?"

"He told me several times that in years to come, if I kept working and learning, I should think about it. He also said that I had a great deal to learn."

Bassaana chuckled, then asked, "Why do you think you were selected?"

Dekkard had thought about it a great deal. Still, he wondered whether it was wise to offer his opinion, but decided that Bassaana either knew or would find out. "Because I'm reasonably intelligent, mostly personable, necessarily loyal to the party, and one of the few suggestions that would block whoever else Obreduur had in mind in a way that he couldn't object to."

For a moment, Bassaana said nothing.

Dekkard said, "You already surmised that. There was no reason not to confirm it."

"To a Commercer?"

"To one of the five Commercers who voted for Obreduur."

"I can see why Amelya said I should talk to you."

"She's why I approached you," replied Dekkard pleasantly.

"For what purpose?"

"For mutual benefit . . . although I have no specific end in mind, except to preserve the Great Charter before it's effectively destroyed by the excesses of the New Meritorists or the previous premier."

"You'd equate the two?" Bassaana's voice was cool, but not edged.

"Only in their inability or unwillingness to understand that absolute power vested in either complete popular rule or complete rule by an elite would destroy Guldor."

"You're advocating moderation, Steffan. Moderation is not popular in troubled times."

"What's popular, especially in its extremes, is seldom best. At least, that's what history indicates. That's why the Great Charter shields councilors from the worst of popular opinion."

As Dekkard and Bassaana neared the bronze doors of the Council Hall, she said, "It's been a pleasant conversation. I look forward to meeting your wife."

Dekkard understood and stepped aside, opening and holding the door for Bassaana, Elyssa, and Amelya. As Amelya passed, he murmured, "Thank you."

She gave a quick smile and nod, but did not pause.

Dekkard waited for a minute or two before entering the Hall and walking toward the entrance to the floor of the Council chamber. The pair of Council Guards standing just inside the doorway to the councilors' lobby glanced at Dekkard just a moment longer than at the Craft councilor preceding him, Harleona Zerlyon, from Ondeliew, the chair of the Justiciary Committee. Dekkard headed for his desk at the far-left end of the back row. He was standing beside it when Councilor Hasheem approached him.

"Steffan . . . I'm so glad you've been assigned to the Security Committee . . . Axel mentioned that you had an interesting suggestion for dealing with the problems with the Security Ministry. We should meet in the dining room . . . say, at noon, tomorrow?"

"I'd be more than happy to, sir."

"Just Fredrich, please."

"I look forward to it . . . Fredrich."

"Excellent . . . excellent."

As Hasheem moved toward his own desk, Dekkard considered the implications of the brief conversation. Given the reactions of *Gestirn* and *The Machtarn Tribune* to Obreduur's views—that the New Meritorists were a symptom of a problem and not the problem itself—Hasheem's conversation strongly suggested that, while Obreduur agreed with the Security Ministry reforms Dekkard had proposed, the Premier didn't want to be seen as the one pushing those ideas. *Especially right now.*

At that moment, the lieutenant-at-arms appeared and thumped his gold and black ceremonial staff. "The Council is now in session."

Guilhohn Haarsfel, as Craft Party floor leader, and thus the majority floor leader, stood on the dais and announced, "The legislation having been read and discussed in the previous session, the Council is in session to vote on the amended emergency appropriations legislation. All councilors have a third in which to register their vote and deposit a plaque."

As Haarsfel finished speaking, Obreduur gestured, and the deep gong sounded once.

Dekkard waited as the more senior councilors walked to their party's plaque box and picked up two colored tiles, one signifying yes, one no, and tinted on one side to show party affiliation. Then each walked to the voting box set on the front of the dais, where one tile went into the ballot slot and the other into the null slot.

He recognized only a handful of councilors by sight, generally those few he'd been introduced to or met in passing through Obreduur, such as Hasheem or the three floor leaders.

Finally, as one of the more junior councilors, he went to the Craft plaque box and picked up his tiles and took his turn, placing the yes tile in the ballot slot and the no tile in the null slot. Finally, the deep chime rang again.

"The vote is closed," declared Obreduur. "Floor leaders, do your duty."

The three floor leaders watched as each voting tile was removed from the ballot box and placed in one of two columns in the counting tray, each column separated by party. Then the clerk wrote the vote totals on the tally sheet, and each of the three floor leaders signed the sheet.

As the majority floor leader, Haarsfel carried the tally sheet as he stepped onto the dais. "Those councilors approving the amended emergency appropriations legislation, twenty-nine Craft councilors, eight Landor councilors, and three Commerce councilors, for a total of forty. The legislation is hereby passed and will be enrolled and sent to the Imperador."

After another pause, Obreduur announced, "There being no other business, the Council is adjourned until the first afternoon bell of Duadi, the twenty-sixth of Fallfirst."

Dekkard looked to see if Obreduur might gesture to him, but the Premier left the floor with Haarsfel.

When Dekkard returned to his office, Margrit immediately said, "Did anything interesting happen?"

"We voted for an emergency spending measure, but one that did not include marks for repairing Security buildings until the Council can look into all the problems with Security."

"Someone should. I still can't believe they shot all those unarmed people."

"The problem is that the New Meritorists aren't that much better," replied Dekkard, "and the Premier and the Council are caught in the middle." *And it might not be very long before there are more demonstrations . . . if not worse.* Dekkard offered a wry smile before he entered his office and closed the door.

Once behind his desk, he took out several sheets of paper and began to write out specific points for the reform of the Security Ministry, based on what he'd mentioned to Obreduur. He hadn't had time to work out the details earlier, not with all the work setting up the office . . . and getting married.

In some ways, it's still hard to believe. The son of Argenti immigrant artisans marrying the descendant of royalty . . . and such a brilliant and talented descendant. His single regret was that neither his sister nor his parents had been there, but there hadn't been time to wait, and the cost of an ironway ticket was not insubstantial for one person, let alone three, and to come that distance for such a short time . . .

He pushed those thoughts away and went back to drafting his Security-proposal outline. Almost a bell later, he looked at a sheet of basic points.

1. Rename the Ministry of Security as the Ministry of Public Safety.
2. Restructure Ministry of Public Safety to remove Special Agents from the chain of command and to require senior officers to have served at least ten years as patrollers or patroller officers.
3. Transfer the Special Tactical Force from the Ministry of Security/Public Safety to the Army.

4. Restrict the powers of Special Agents to investigation and information collection, authorized in writing and approved by the Justiciary Minister.

5. Rename Special Agents as Information Officers and prohibit their carrying and use of firearms.

Then he left the sheet on his desk and walked out into the staff office, where Roostof was talking with Colsbaan. "Svard . . . I need a moment. Close the door when you come in."

"Yes, sir." Roostof followed Dekkard into the private office.

Dekkard did not sit, but handed the single sheet of paper to Roostof. "Svard, you're the legalist. Take a look at this and tell me the best way you know to accomplish it. You'll have to do this on your own, because no one else should know about it yet."

Roostof began to read, and his eyes widened, but he finished reading and looked up. "I can see why you want this kept quiet. Is this . . . a possibility?"

"It's definitely a possibility." *Whether it's a stalking horse for Obreduur, a veiled threat, or something more is another question.* What wasn't a question was that current high-level Security officials would oppose it any way that they could, and at present, Security agents were armed and would follow any order. "Treat it like it's a realistic legislative possibility . . . and one you don't want Security or Commercers to see or hear about. I need the best you can do by fourth bell tomorrow morning."

"Yes, sir."

After Roostof left, Dekkard checked his watch. Another bell to go, at the earliest, before he could expect Avraal. That gave him time to go over the background material on the proposed ministerial appointments.

A VRAAL returned a sixth after fourth bell, just as he was wondering what was taking her so long and was getting ready to close the office.

"I'm sorry," she said as she stepped into his office. "Everything took longer. By the time I could have sent a message, I realized I'd get here before the messenger."

"What happened?"

"Why don't I tell you on the way home?" She smiled brightly. "Unless there's some reason for you to stay later."

"No. Not this afternoon. Once people in Gaarlak discover I'm their councilor, that might change." He paused, then said, "I assume that means it's good, whatever it is."

"You can tell me." She looked guilelessly at him.

Dekkard shook his head. "On the way home, then."

Before he left his office, he checked the wall lamp to make certain it was off. Then he picked up the gray leather folder holding the papers on the ministerial appointments, as well as the letters from Jaime Minz and Gretna Haarl.

Once in the antechamber, he looked to Margrit. "Time to close up and for you to leave as well. I'll see you in the morning."

"Yes, sir."

"Good afternoon, Margrit," added Avraal.

"Good afternoon, Ritten." Margrit smiled cheerfully with the word "Ritten."

Svard appeared in the doorway to the main staff room. "I'll be working a little longer on that proposal."

"It doesn't have to be perfect," replied Dekkard. "Just make sure that I didn't propose something stupid or impossible under the Great Charter."

"I'm fairly certain you didn't do either of those. I just wanted to check on one or two possibilities. I let Luara, Bretta, and Illana go at fourth bell. There wasn't any reason for them to stay past the normal bell."

"Thank you. I appreciate it." Dekkard paused. He was fairly certain Svard wasn't married or deeply romantically involved. "I don't want to keep you from . . ."

Roostof laughed. "Katrina broke the engagement about the time of the Summerend upheavals. She said I was more in love with the law than with her."

Dekkard winced.

"You had nothing to do with that, sir."

"I can still be sorry."

"Don't be," replied Roostof cheerfully. "It wouldn't have worked out. Either another legalist or a scholar would probably be better. Not that I'm looking at the moment."

"Still . . . don't stay too late."

Roostof just smiled.

On the walk from the office to the central staircase, and then down to the main level, the corridor was almost empty.

Once they were in the Gresynt and headed south on Imperial Boulevard, Dekkard asked, "Can you tell me now?"

"I talked with the assistant director of the Advisory Committee. Timon Peres. I wasn't that impressed. He would have offered me a position, but likely just because I'm married to you. I didn't even let it get that far."

"I can see why that didn't impress you. What about Carlos Baartol?"

"He wants me to work for him. He really does . . . even when I told him that any information about you or your office had to come from you. He'll also pay me half again as much as I made working for Obreduur."

"Did you accept his offer?"

"I did. I start tomorrow."

"Good."

Avraal frowned slightly. "Do you mean that?"

"I do. I'm also glad you didn't say you had to check with me . . . and that you'll be making more marks."

"Why?" Avraal offered an impish smile, then asked, "So you don't feel guilty about my having to give up my position to marry you?"

"Partly," admitted Dekkard. "But also because you're worth more than Obreduur was allowed to pay you."

"That was true of you as well."

"But I ended up with a better position. Until you accepted Carlos's offer, you ended up with no position and no marks. Except for your savings, that is."

"You must have saved some, too."

"I did, over half my pay for the last two years." Dekkard smiled sardonically and added, "All of six hundred marks."

Avraal offered an amused laugh. "Spendthrift!"

"It might pay for a run-down cot in the poorest quarter of Gaarlak. Maybe."

"I still have well over a thousand marks left."

"After paying Emrelda for the Gresynt?"

Avraal nodded.

"Then we might afford a not-run-down cot in the poorest quarter of Gaarlak."

"We should be able to save more than that before long."

"I might have something left out of my transition allowance." While Dekkard had close to two thousand marks left in his one-time transition allowance from the Council, he didn't yet know how many more unexpected but required expenses might come up. *Still . . . if you save most of what's left . . .* He'd just have to see, but that reminded him of something else he needed to discuss with Avraal. "I got a letter of congratulations from Gretna Haarl—as guildmeister of the Textile Millworkers Guild. I would appreciate your thoughts."

"She'll want something."

"She does, but you need to read it before I say anything more. I also got a letter from Jaime Minz. He's now an assistant director of security for Northwest

Industrial Chemical. Since he's staying in Machtarn, that suggests he's really been hired as an influencer. I brought both letters home."

"Good."

Dekkard turned east on Camelia Avenue and approached the Imperial University, dominated by the central bell tower that dated back more than three centuries. He immediately looked for signs of trouble as they neared, but nothing looked amiss, unlike during the summer demonstrations. Before long, he turned uphill on Jacquez and, a little more than a mille farther along, made a left on Florinda Way.

As he turned off Florinda and eased the Gresynt up the narrow drive on the east side of Emrelda's house, Dekkard saw that the door on the side of the garage used by their larger gray Gresynt was open. "Emrelda must be home already."

"She should be. She's usually on the day shift."

Dekkard let Avraal out under the roofed east portico and then garaged the Gresynt. He quickly wiped it down and refilled the water and kerosene tanks before closing the garage door and making his way to the east portico door and from there to the kitchen.

"We're celebrating," announced Emrelda, still in her patroller's uniform and pointing to the tray with the two glasses of wine—Silverhills white—and the beaker of Kuhrs. "Your first full day as a married couple. And no, there wasn't anything to celebrate at the patroller station, but nothing to complain about, either, and that's almost enough to celebrate."

"We can also celebrate because I have a new job," said Avraal.

"The one with Carlos Baartol?"

"The very same. And we can also celebrate because we don't have to fix dinner," continued Avraal, "or rather Emrelda doesn't, because there's more than enough left in the cooler from yesterday."

"There's enough for a week," declared Emrelda. "Some will likely spoil before we can eat it, but we'll have to see. I thought there'd be a few more at the wedding, but Silvy and Pietr couldn't come at the last minute."

"And both of Luara's children were ill. That meant her husband couldn't come." After a pause, Dekkard grinned, then added, "But it also might be that someone wanted to make sure that there was enough of everything for everyone."

Emrelda looked directly back at Dekkard. "How would it have reflected on a new councilor if he—or his wife's sister—couldn't even feed his staff and the Premier and his staff? I just wanted to make sure." Then she smiled.

"I'm glad you did," replied Dekkard. "It was all outstanding, and that means we'll all be well-fed for the week." He was also glad that he and Avraal had paid for the two serving women . . . especially for the cleaning up.

He held up the leather case. "Over our celebration beverages, there are two matters I'd like your advice on. Both of you."

Avraal offered a mock grimace. "Only married a day, and it's back to politics."

Dekkard replied with a mournful look. "Only because I wanted to get them out of the way so we could enjoy the rest of the evening."

"Should we believe that?" Avraal looked to her sister, trying to keep from smiling.

"This time," replied Emrelda.

Dekkard shook his head, tucked the folder under his arm, and picked up the tray with the two wineglasses and beaker. Then he walked toward the hallway and from there turned toward the veranda. Both sisters followed him out into the late-afternoon sunlight that the veranda roof did not block.

He eased the tray onto the low table, followed by the folder. He took off his suit jacket, carefully folding it, and laid it over the back of the vacant white wicker chair before seating himself in the chair beside Avraal.

As he reached for his beaker, Avraal said, "You said we'd take care of politics first."

Dekkard caught the smile in her eyes and answered, as pompously as he could, "A sip or two of Kuhrs or Silverhills will make the politics less onerous, but . . ."

Both sisters laughed.

He took a sip of the lager, then opened the folder and extracted the letter from Gretna Haarl, handing it to Avraal.

She read it and passed it to Emrelda, after which she took a sip of wine.

Emrelda finished reading the letter and returned it to Dekkard, who laid it on top of the folder and looked to Avraal.

"I could either be flattered or annoyed," she said dryly. "Either way, it's a delicate matter."

"You just made it easier, I think," replied Dekkard. "Now I can write her back that not only are we married, but that you're now working for one of the principal consultants to the Guilds' Advisory Committee."

"I'm not sure anything will totally mollify her," said Avraal quietly.

"If I just thank her for her kind words and support, she'll think I'm dismissing her concerns, and that won't help." Dekkard paused. "It might help to mention one of my legalists is a woman recommended by Ingrella who has experience as a guild legalist."

"It might, especially if you don't mention she's the junior legalist."

"Is she that prickly?" asked Emrelda.

"More rather than less," said Avraal.

"And what about the suggestion that you buy a house or property?"

Dekkard quickly explained about the requirement that a councilor have a property or residence tie to his district.

"So you two will have to buy something in or near Gaarlak?"

Dekkard nodded. "We'll have a little time to figure out the finances, because there won't be any breaks in the Council sessions for at least a month, or longer, depending on what happens. Houses there, from what I understand, are quite a bit less expensive than here in Machtarn. Also, since we're young, people will expect something nice, but not huge."

"Now that you're a councilor couldn't you borrow some marks?" asked Emrelda.

"Only from one of the Guild banques," said Dekkard, "preferably one in Gaarlak."

"That's enough of that for this evening," said Avraal. "Let's see the other letter."

Dekkard replaced the Haarl letter in the folder and took out the one from Jaime Minz, handing it to Avraal, who read it and passed it along to Emrelda, who, in turn, read it, and handed it back to Dekkard.

"Well?" he asked.

"There's no need to reply to it, and you shouldn't," declared Avraal. "He'd use any reply against you, showing that you responded to an influencer."

"I hadn't planned to, but I thought I should show it to Obreduur and Hasheem."

"Just because Hasheem's the Security Committee chairman?"

"The dunnite issue isn't going away. I thought I'd only show him the letter, but not provide a copy."

"Do you think the dunnite for all those explosions in Security buildings came from Minz's new employer?" asked Emrelda.

"It had to come from either Northwest Industrial Chemical or from Suvion Industries," replied Dekkard. "Either that or the New Meritorists impersonated Navy personnel and showed up with forged papers and invoices, since the Navy doesn't seem to be aware of any theft."

"How could they not know?" pressed Emrelda.

"Because a fleet of several hundred warships uses a lot of ammunition and the amount planted in those fifteen buildings was a tiny percentage of total usage. I may be giving the New Meritorists too much credit."

Emrelda shook her head.

"Let that lie for now," suggested Avraal. "Just show the letter to Obreduur and Hasheem and don't mention it to anyone else."

"I hadn't thought otherwise," declared Dekkard, replacing the letter in the leather folder and closing it. He lifted his beaker. "Now . . . shall we begin the celebrations?"

4

ON Duadi morning, both Dekkard and Avraal were up earlier than when they had been at Obreduur's house, because now they had to fix their own breakfast, especially given that, on most days, Emrelda had to be at the patrol station a good bell before Dekkard had to be at his office. Not that fixing breakfast was that time-consuming, given that neither ate elaborately, since Avraal often only had café and at most one croissant. It helped that Emrelda had made café earlier, and that Dekkard found quince paste in the cooler.

Dekkard managed not to smile as he sandwiched a slice of quince paste between the two halves of his croissant as he sat across the breakfast room table from Avraal. After several sips of café and a bite of the croissant, he asked, "Are you sure I can just drop you off at Carlos's offices?"

"That makes the most sense. His office times are flexible, and they tend to run later than the Council offices do." Avraal took another sip of café. "So . . . if you need to work a little later, that won't be a problem."

"Not now."

"We'll deal with later when it comes," said Avraal. "Do you think Hasheem has more in mind for you than your idea about reforming the Security Ministry?"

"I doubt it. I suspect that both he and Obreduur like the idea, but they don't want to be responsible for it. That also allows Obreduur to declare in front of any empath that it wasn't his idea. Since I'm a former Council security aide, with a documented record of dealing with these problems, it will be much harder for anyone to claim my proposal is Obreduur's doing."

"That could make you a target."

"As if we haven't been already?"

"Just be careful, dear."

"I will, especially when you're not around."

Before long, the two were walking out to the Gresynt—Dekkard in another gray suit, and Avraal in a gray jacket, teal blouse, and trousers. Both wore their lapel pins.

Once in the steamer and headed toward Jacquez on Florinda, Dekkard said, "Where am I going?"

Avraal laughed, an expression between amusement and embarrassment. "That's right. You've never been there. His office isn't far from the Guildhall, where the Advisory Committee is, on the Avenue of the Guilds, a block closer to Imperial Boulevard, on the north side."

"When we get closer, you can show me the right building." That definitely would make the drive to the Council longer. *But it's time when we can talk . . . alone.*

"Did Carlos say anything about what you'll be doing?"

Unless you and all the other councilors take action to reform the Council so that every vote of every councilor is made an open and public record, we will have no choice but to take steps to change the government of Guldor, however long it may take and at whatever cost necessary to return the government to the people.

There was no signature, just the words "For the New Meritorists."

Dekkard was unsurprised. The only thing that did surprise him was that the New Meritorists had actually refrained from any demonstrations for two weeks before the election and two weeks after. *But then, that conveys a message that they're trying to be "reasonable," as if threatening revolt unless their demands are met is exactly reasonable.*

Dekkard was still considering the letter and what, if anything, he could do, when Roostof knocked on his door.

"Sir . . . ?"

"Come on in, Svard. If you'd close the door . . ." Dekkard motioned to the chair closest to his desk.

Roostof took it, then looked at Dekkard, who said nothing but instead handed the letter to the senior legalist.

After reading it, Roostof returned the single sheet. "Did they send one to every councilor?"

"I don't know, but it's likely."

"It seems like they think they won the election," said Roostof.

"They helped by pushing Security into unwise retaliation, especially against the unarmed demonstrators. The Council needs to do something, but I don't believe in granting what they're asking for. It hasn't worked before. We do need to address the university problems and the loss of good jobs to cheap overseas sussie labor . . . and, of course, reforming Security."

"It sounds like they want more than that, sir."

"There's no doubt that they do. But most people don't care all that much how councilors vote. Most people care about whether they have shelter and enough food, a good job, whether their lives will be better, and whether government is honest and evenhanded, which it currently isn't." Dekkard paused. "Even if the Council could grant their demand instantly, which it can't under the Great Charter, that still wouldn't come close to dealing with the conditions that worry most people, and before long it would make matters even worse."

"I can see that, sir."

"Since Security is something we might be able to improve . . . what are your thoughts on the Security Ministry proposal?"

The legalist offered a smile of wry amusement. "The more I thought about it, the more I thought it a very good and timely idea. I did make a few changes. They're only suggestions. The Commercers will oppose it in every way possible." He handed Dekkard several sheets. "I had Illana type some supporting points. They may duplicate your thoughts, but since you wanted my thoughts first thing this morning . . ."

"That's fine. I appreciate your work. I was caught off guard." At Roostof's

"For the first few days, I'll be learning more about his clients and mee
people . . . and accompanying him when necessary."

"We need to get a target and get back to practicing with knives," said Dekk

"We do, but we've only missed a few days."

"If things aren't too busy, I'll stop by Garlaand's on the way to pick you

"You've never liked putting off things that need to be done, have you?"

"You have to ask?" Dekkard grinned.

Avraal laughed.

The offices of Carlos Baartol turned out to be in a modest three-story
brick building, with a small steamer parking lot to one side. That was wl
Dekkard decided to let Avraal off, since it also would allow him to turn arou

"You can park in the visitor spot when you come back. That's if I don't
you first." She leaned over and kissed him on the cheek, then slipped ou
the steamer.

Dekkard watched as she walked to the building entrance and went in,
enjoying looking at her. Then he turned out of the parking area, but so
as he could tell, no one followed him to the covered parking for the Cou
Office Building, which had more guards than before the demonstrations ;
elections. He locked the Gresynt, crossed the entry drive to the west do
carrying his gray leather folder, and made his way to his office.

Margrit immediately offered a warm, "Good morning, sir."

"Good morning, Margrit. Is there anything urgent I should know?"

"There are several messages on your desk . . . and the letters in your inb
Besides that . . . no, sir."

Dekkard left the door to his inner office ajar, then took out the letter
Gretna Haarl that he and Avraal had drafted and handed it to Margrit to h
typed. After that, he settled behind his desk to open and read the two m
sages. The first was from Fredrich Hasheem, confirming a noon meeting
the councilors' dining room. The second was a form message from Obredu
to all councilors stating that the vote on ministerial appointees would begin
first bell, and would be without debate.

Then he began to open and quickly scan the letters in his inbox. The thi
one wasn't from Gaarlak . . . or anywhere near, but from Machtarn. The
turn address was simply the initials "RTC" and a street address. Dekka
frowned, wondering whose initials those might be, then opened the envelo
and read the typed missive.

Councilor Dekkard—
    The initials on the outside address stand for Reform The Council.
    For too long, the Council of Sixty-Six has hidden its actions and mo-
tivations behind the veil of three ossified parties. None of you have a
personal accountability for how you vote . . .

Dekkard quickly read through the rest of the New Meritorist rhetoric, slov
ing as he reached the last lines.

slightly puzzled expression, Dekkard added, "I'd mentioned this to the Premier when I was working with him, just about the need for reform. He mentioned it to Councilor Hasheem . . ."

"The new chair of the Security Committee?"

"Exactly. I'm meeting with him at noon about it. I'll let you know where we go from here. Do you have any thoughts on the proposed ministerial appointees?"

"There aren't any names proposed for Security or Treasury . . . or Public Resources. Is that because . . . ?"

"All three ministries have significant problems," said Dekkard. "There will likely be more hearings on all three ministries in the next few weeks. What do you know about the nominee for the Justiciary Ministry—Serapha Marler Kuta?"

"Not a great deal. She was proposed as a regional justicer in Veerlyn three years ago, but the Commercers turned her down. It was a close vote, as I recall, and even some of the Landor councilors supported her."

"Do you remember why?"

"She was the lead legalist in a case that required female sanitation workers on the ironways to be paid the same as men. The women were called health aides and the men were sanitation specialists."

"I take it she won the judgment," said Dekkard.

"She did."

"Was the case, by chance, against Eastern Ironway?"

"As I recall."

Dekkard just nodded and listened to what Roostof had to say about the other ministerial appointments, wondering if that litigation just might have been something that Bassaana had been involved with, indirectly, of course.

After Roostof left, Dekkard went through the rest of the mail, but no petitions or letters needed his personal attention, and he turned to Roostof's comments on the Security Ministry proposal, which were terse, but to the point.

Then he took out the listing of all the Craft Party councilors that had been passed out at the initial party caucus the previous Furdi and went down through the names, concentrating especially on the newly elected councilors, since he knew most of the returning Craft councilors, at least by name.

In any event, Dekkard needed to know all their names and associate those names with faces. So he alternated going over the list, and reviewing the key points of his Security proposal . . . and thinking about what the Council should be doing in dealing with the New Meritorists, not that any other councilor would much care what he thought, except possibly Obreduur . . . and only if what Dekkard presented could be accomplished politically. Before he knew it, it was close to noon, and he needed to head out for his meeting with Councilor Hasheem.

He stepped out of his personal office and nodded to Margrit. "I'll be gone until at least third bell because of the Security Committee meeting after the floor vote."

Then he headed for the Council Hall. While he didn't have to worry about an empie assault, there was always the faint possibility of an armed attack, and he kept his eyes open on the way down the main staircase and on the walk across the courtyard.

He had to wait for several minutes inside the councilors' dining room before Hasheem appeared.

"Steffan. I'm sorry to be a little late. I hope you weren't waiting too long."

"Just a few minutes."

Hasheem gestured to the host, an older dark-haired man attired in black and gold livery. "Just the two of us."

The host replied, "This way, Councilors."

The thirty tables were spaced farther apart than in a normal restaurant. About half were already taken, but the host seated them between two vacant adjoining tables, although Dekkard doubted that would last. He glanced at the creamy gold-streaked polished marble walls, and down at the ivory table linens, still halfway amused that he was seated in a dining room to which he had escorted Obreduur scores of times, but only eaten in once when he'd been an aide.

"The fare's the same as it always is," said Hasheem, setting his menu aside without looking at it.

"Then I take it you alternate between favorites," replied Dekkard, glancing at the listed entrées.

"The duck cassoulet, the three-cheese chicken, sometimes the cold spiced tomato soup, and once in a while the veal milanesia or, if I'm not that hungry, the hummus and flatbread."

When the server came to take their order, Dekkard decided on the three-cheese chicken and Hasheem on flatbread and hummus. Both ordered café.

Once the server departed, Hasheem lowered his voice slightly. "Did you receive a typed letter this morning with the initials 'RTC' on the outside?"

"Yes. I suspect every councilor did. We also might see handbills demanding change from the Council. Might I ask your thoughts on the matter?"

Hasheem shook his head. "They'll just make reforming the government even harder, and we're going to have enough difficulty even without their demands. You've had to deal with them more directly. What do you think?"

"They're highly talented zealots who've already done a lot of damage and will likely do more if they don't get their way."

"How would you handle them?"

"Allow peaceful demonstrations. Try not to shoot them," replied Dekkard dryly. "Every person who gets shot creates more followers. In the meantime, get the Council to address other problems first."

Hasheem fingered his chin.

Dekkard had the feeling he'd said enough. "What do you think?"

"I can see you've worked for Axel." Hasheem cleared his throat. "As I mentioned, Axel said you had suggested a legislative proposal to deal with the Security Ministry."

"More like a detailed outline," replied Dekkard, "but I've had my legalist look at it, and he feels it can be done under the scope of the Charter and existing case law. Basically, it splits Security three ways . . ."

When Dekkard finished his brief explanation, the older councilor nodded. "That makes sense. It also addresses the guild concerns and some of the issues raised by the New Meritorists. Still . . ."

"Most Commercers and some Landors won't like it?" suggested Dekkard.

"They won't like the idea of *any* reduction in the power of the Security Ministry."

"Will there be hearings on Security's abuses of power?"

"Those will start next week." Hasheem offered a wry smile. "I'm afraid they won't reveal much."

"Then," suggested Dekkard, "if individuals aren't to blame or can't be held accountable, that might suggest that changes are in order."

"It's a matter of timing, Steffan."

Dekkard understood that. "In short, certain shortcomings have to surface before anyone will consider fixing problems we already know exist. But to offer a solution before there's more awareness among the Council—and the people—will let the Commercers claim that we exaggerated the problem to justify the solution."

"Exactly."

"It just might take a little while to consider and perfect a possible solution, at least publicly."

"That might be best held tightly for a while." Hasheem leaned back slightly in his chair. "How does it feel to be a new councilor and newly married all exactly at the same time?"

"It still feels a little surreal, more so from the perspective of being a councilor. Avraal and I worked closely together for two years . . ." Dekkard knew that the rest of the conversation would be pleasantly personal, and that was fine with him, since he could see a server coming with their orders.

Just after Dekkard finished his chicken and was sipping his café, he saw a very familiar figure heading his way, accompanied by Harleona Zerlyon, the Craft legalist who was the new chair of the Justiciary Committee.

Both stopped at the table.

"Fredrich . . . Steffan . . . how was your meal?" Obreduur offered a knowing smile.

"As usual," replied Hasheem warmly.

Dekkard just nodded.

"And how is Avraal?" asked Obreduur.

"She's on the first day of her new position, sir," replied Dekkard. "I'll find out how that went tonight." He paused just slightly. "Since Legalist Kuta meets Ritten Obreduur's highest standards, is there anything else you can tell me, just in case anyone should ask me?"

Obreduur laughed, softly and warmly. "Just that she also meets Councilor Zerlyon's high standards as well. I'm glad you two enjoyed your meal." With a parting smile, Obreduur continued on his way out of the dining room, exchanging a few words with Zerlyon.

Clearly, Obreduur didn't want to dwell on the letter from the New Meritorists, but then, Dekkard reflected, he'd have to say something at the beginning of the Council session.

Hasheem glanced at the departing Premier then back at Dekkard. "I enjoyed the conversation, Steffan. It does look like we have a challenging time ahead." He eased his chair back. "If you'll excuse me. I do have a few quick matters to deal with before the committee meeting."

"I appreciate your thoughts and advice." Dekkard eased his own chair back and stood as Hasheem did. "Thank you."

"My pleasure, Steffan."

Dekkard inclined his head, and followed Hasheem, except Dekkard continued to the councilors' lobby because he wouldn't have even had enough time to return to his office before he'd have to turn back.

As he entered the lobby, a thin older female councilor immediately approached him—Elyncya Duforgue.

"Steffan, do you have a moment?" Contrary to her narrow face and severe dark blue jacket and trousers, Duforgue addressed Dekkard in a warm voice.

"As many as there are until we're in session," Dekkard replied in a friendly tone.

"I understand you hired Luara Colsbaan."

"I did." Dekkard wondered what the connection might be, since Colsbaan was from Brekaan and Duforgue was from Jaykarh, cities about as far apart as possible.

Duforgue smiled. "You're wondering at how I know her, aren't you?"

"Yes, I have to say."

"Ingrella asked me to consider her, but I'd already made commitments for legalists from Veerlyn. From what Ingrella said, I wish I could have hired her, but I asked her to let me know how her search went."

"I suspect I'll need her more than you do," replied Dekkard, "although she won't be working up to her abilities for a while. I'm still a little short of staff, and we have no records from the previous councilor."

"I understand that happened to all of us newly elected Craft councilors."

"Apparently, there were papers certain councilors didn't want to fall into Craft hands," said Dekkard. "Or they just wanted to make our success more difficult."

"Both . . . and more, most likely," replied Duforgue. "I noticed that you're on the Security and Workplace Administration Committees. With your background . . ."

"You understand the first, but not the second?"

"I had wondered."

"Besides doing security for Councilor Obreduur, a great deal of my other duties dealt with workplace problems, and I spent several years as an apprentice decorative plasterer, before I went to the Military Institute."

"You have packed a variety of experience into a few years."

"I once would have said that there weren't many other options, but there are always options. I have to admit I know as little about you, except that you've been a guild legalist."

For the next sixth of a bell or so, Dekkard listened to Duforgue, who was incredibly reserved about her accomplishments, but Dekkard surmised that she'd had a far harder early life than he had, and succeeding as a guild legalist in a small city based on timber, pulp, and paper couldn't have been easy.

The chimes rang, signaling that the Council was in session, and the two made their way to the floor and took their seats at their respective desks to listen to the Premier.

"Before we get to the votes on the ministerial nominees," Obreduur began, "it has come to my attention that the New Meritorists have attempted to contact every councilor with a letter that, in effect, demands that the Council immediately make the votes of all councilors known by their individual names. Since the Great Charter precludes such a procedure, and since any change in the Charter requires approval by a two-thirds vote by two successive Councils, any immediate change is not possible, even if it were advisable, which it is not." Obreduur paused for almost a minute before continuing.

"This Council will address the unmet needs of the people of Guldor because those needs have fueled support for the New Meritorists, but those needs can and will be met without the need to change the Great Charter or to accede to the demands of radicals who understand neither politics nor history. I have already begun to meet with all the floor leaders and with committee chairs to schedule hearings to address the most pressing needs.

"Now . . . the majority floor leader will call the vote for ministerial nominees." Obreduur took his seat behind the desk on the dais reserved for the Premier or the presiding councilor.

Guilhohn Haarsfel stepped forward. "As previously announced, at this time, there will be no nominees for the Ministry of the Treasury, the Security Ministry, and the Ministry of Public Resources. Nominees for those ministries will be presented after the conclusion of oversight hearings into irregularities in the operations of those ministries."

Over the next two bells, the nominees for the remaining seven ministries were approved by largely forty to twenty-six votes, roughly the same margins as those that had elected Obreduur as Premier, although only thirty-eight councilors voted to approve Serapha Marler Kuta as Minister of the Justiciary.

Because she was so effective in forcing Eastern Ironway to treat women workers equally with men? Although Dekkard had never met Kuta, he'd certainly liked what little he'd read and heard about her . . . although he did wonder why Ingrella Obreduur hadn't pushed for Namoor Desharra, who'd had similar legalistic success in Gaarlak.

Just after the chimes rang, signifying adjournment, the lanky and weathered Tomas Pajiin approached. Dekkard wondered what the former Lumber Guild steward had in mind. "Afternoon, Steffan."

"Good afternoon, Tomas. What can I do for you?"

"You might answer a question or two, if you don't mind."

"If I can," agreed Dekkard.

"How did you get selected? You're not from Gaarlak. You haven't worked that long for the Craft Party."

Dekkard understood the question Pajiin hadn't asked. "Obreduur didn't choose me. The Gaarlak Craft Party recommended me."

Pajiin frowned. "That really true?"

"It is. Obreduur received separate heliograms confirming it. He was as shocked as I was."

"Why in the world did you accept? You're too young . . ."

"Because it was clear that if I declined, he'd get a second choice he didn't like at all. Also, he told me in a way that made it obvious he wanted me to accept." Dekkard smiled politely and added, "I wouldn't even have thought about saying you were too old."

Pajiin stiffened. "If I were younger, I just might put you—"

"No . . . you couldn't. Not even then. Logging was your skill; security, physical and armed, is mine. I respect your skill. Don't disrespect mine."

"Might I ask," Pajiin said coolly, "if you've ever had to kill anyone?"

"More than I wanted," replied Dekkard.

"That's not an answer."

"Three . . . officially. That doesn't include the ones I stopped and didn't have to kill. You can ask the Premier."

Abruptly, Pajiin laughed. "I like you, Steffan. None of this polite evasion."

Dekkard grinned, as much in relief that his judgment of the former logger had been accurate. "I didn't think you wanted evasions. You don't strike me as the type."

"True that you worked as an apprentice plasterer before you got educated?"

"Very true. My father is a decorative-plaster artisan. I was very good at cleanup and prep. I just didn't have the higher skills." Dekkard could understand Pajiin's concern, since all Craft councilors had either worked with their hands at some point or had been legalists representing Crafters.

"You'll do." Pajiin paused. "Does that snooty expression ever leave Volkaar's face?"

"I don't know . . . but I've never seen the distinguished Commerce Party floor leader without it."

Pajiin shook his head. "Good talking to you. I need to get to committee meeting."

"Me, too."

The two walked off the floor and out through the councilors' lobby, turning left toward the committee rooms along the north wing of the Council Hall.

Dekkard suspected the Security Committee meeting would be short, since it was almost a pro forma organizational meeting, after which he'd return to the office and tell Roostof to draft the best legislation he could to reform the Security Ministry, because it was clear that Dekkard and Roostof would be on their own so far as either Hasheem or Obreduur was concerned, and letting anyone else know would just risk having the idea get out—and make it that much harder to get any reform.

5

D EKKARD was right. The Security Committee meeting was brief. Hasheem gave a short summary of the observed problems with Security and then informed the other six committee members that the Security Ministry oversight hearings would begin on Unadi afternoon with testimony from acting Security Minister Manwaeren and would continue for as long as necessary. Hasheem also noted that those testifying would be limited to current officials, since a vote of the full Council would be required to compel the testimony of former officials.

When Dekkard returned to his office, he corrected several letters, signed the remainder, then closed the office at fourth bell and made his way to the covered parking.

He drove to Harcel Garlaand's knife store, where he parked the Gresynt and walked inside. The wiry gray-haired Garlaand turned as Dekkard entered. He just stared and said nothing.

Dekkard smiled. "I'm still the same knife-thrower."

"But . . . it was in the newssheet . . . you're a councilor, and you're married."

"I married my partner. But that's why I'm here. We moved, and we need a new target."

"You married her? The one in the newssheet was the one who bought the knives?"

"She is."

Garlaand shook his head. "If it weren't in the newssheet . . ."

Dekkard grinned. "We still need a target . . . maybe more than ever." *We can't afford to get out of practice . . . not now.*

A sixth later, he had the target in the Gresynt and was on his way to pick up Avraal.

She'd obviously been watching, because he'd barely pulled into the parking area beside the building when she walked briskly to the Gresynt, sliding into the front seat next to him, and kissing him on the cheek.

"I got the target," he said as he pulled out onto the Avenue of the Guilds. "I also got a letter from the New Meritorists."

"I thought you would. They've circulated posters and broadsheets all across Machtarn saying that they've asked the Council to enact their voting reforms. I have a copy for you. Besides that, how was your day?" Her words held a wry undertone.

"I met with Hasheem . . ." Dekkard quickly summarized his day, then asked, "What about yours?"

"Mostly reading, and going through client files so that I know the background on what Carlos is working on. He actually has a substantial file on everything surrounding Markell, although I think you know most everything that's in it, not all the details, but those involved and what they've been up to . . ."

That was a polite way of suggesting he not ask about confidential files, Dekkard knew.

". . . and I escorted him over to the Advisory Committee for a meeting."

"You walked?"

"It's only a block . . . well, a little more than a block. I waited outside, but he had me check the room first. I saw Timon Peres."

It took Dekkard a moment to recall that Peres was the assistant director she'd talked to about a position. "How was that?"

Avraal grinned. "He wouldn't look at me. I had the feeling he was supposed to hire me."

"You never let him make an offer, you said."

"I don't like the feeling of being a trophy or a prize. With Carlos, at least I'm useful, and the pay is good . . . and that's something we'll need."

Dekkard nodded. *Especially since we need to buy a house in Gaarlak.* He turned north on Imperial Boulevard.

"What do you think the New Meritorists will do next?" asked Avraal.

"Not much for a few days . . . maybe even a week or so, but with what Obreduur said to the Council, it won't be long."

"Did he have to say that? Couldn't he just have said the first part—that there were problems?"

Dekkard shook his head. "He was already attacked for not putting the Meritorists at the top of the problems facing Guldor, but if he hadn't dismissed their demand, both the Landors and the Commercers—*and* all the newssheets in Guldor—would have been after his head. He can't afford that."

"I can see that, but I don't like it."

"Neither do I. That's another reason why I got the target."

"You don't think . . . ?"

"They've already targeted individual councilors. What makes you think they'll stop? Besides, they'd prefer to get their way by attacking individuals. Also, it took a lot of their resources to pull off the Summerend demonstrations, and they'll need time to rebuild them." Dekkard hoped it would take a while, but he doubted it would be long enough for Obreduur and the Council to address all the problems that had created support for the New Meritorists.

After a moment, he added, "Maybe we could just have a pleasant evening?"

"We should." Avraal reached out and squeezed his hand. "Along with some target practice."

Dekkard smiled.

6

NOTHING out of the ordinary occurred at work on Tridi, but when Dekkard entered the house after garaging the gray Gresynt, Avraal handed him an envelope, smiling. "It looks to be from your sister."

Dekkard looked at the names on the address: Ritter S. Dekkard & Ritten A. Dekkard. "You could have opened it. It's addressed to both of us."

"Not when it's from your family."

Dekkard slit the envelope open, using the sharpened tip of one of his throwing knives, extracted the letter, and held it so that Avraal could read along with him.

> Steffan . . . and Avraal!
>
> I'm so happy for the two of you. I can't tell you how much I've worried that you'd both put duty ahead of each other, and that would have been such a tragedy. I almost danced up the steps to tell Mother and Father when I got the heliogram that your wedding had actually taken place on Findi.
>
> I also can't believe that you're a councilor, Steffan. Father and Mother have a very hard time not immediately telling everyone about you. It helps that they can say that their son the councilor just got married to a marvelous woman. I have no problem—or shame—at all in boasting about my little brother and his extraordinarily talented, intelligent, and beautiful wife.
>
> In time, you'll get something special, and I'll write a longer letter, but I just wanted you both to know how happy I am for the two of you.
>
> All my love.

The signature was that of Naralta.

"That's . . . a lovely letter." Avraal's voice broke slightly.

Dekkard immediately wrapped his arms around her. "She's as happy for you as for me. She loved you from the moment she met you."

"It's not . . . that."

"I know." And Dekkard did. Although Avraal had written letters and sent heliograms to her brother and family, she'd done so without much hope of a response, and certainly not an immediate one. He knew intellectually why Avraal and Emrelda's parents had effectively disowned both daughters, but emotionally it made no sense to Dekkard. Disowning daughters because they wanted to be more than Landor broodmares? Losing daughters because of stiff-necked pride?

After several moments, Avraal straightened. "There's no point in mourning what can't be. Your sister is a dear. Your whole family is."

"Your sister is also quite something, too," Dekkard pointed out. "By the way, where is she?"

"She left a note saying she'd be back in a bit. She's running some errands. She also said we're going to a local tavern tonight. It's likely Elfredo's. Suits are definitely overdressing. We'll need to change."

"I can help with that." Dekkard grinned.

"I'm sure you could . . . but we'd never get there, and I am hungry." Avraal turned and walked toward their bedroom.

Dekkard followed and made do by occasionally leering while Avraal changed into black trousers and a deep teal blouse. The thin black vest she threw on concealed her throwing knives adequately. He decided on a green barong with gray trousers. Given where they were headed, he did not wear his councilor's pin, nor did Avraal wear a pin signifying she was an empath. They'd barely finished changing when Dekkard heard Emrelda close the east portico door.

"Don't mention the letter to Emrelda."

"Salt in old wounds that still haven't healed?"

Avraal nodded.

The two made their way to the kitchen.

Emrelda looked up as she left the pantry. "Good. You're both ready to go. I didn't feel like cooking, or leftovers, and, besides, Steffan's never been to Elfredo's. We could walk, but it's been a long day. Would you mind driving, Steffan?"

"I can do that. I'll get the steamer."

Within minutes, Dekkard was driving down Jacquez.

Elfredo's was located three blocks east of the Erslaan omnibus stop that marked the end of the line, a simple square building constructed of gray brick with black shutters. The door was black as well, with a single porthole window set face-high. Inside, the taverna wasn't quite what Dekkard expected. The walls and floor were of the same gray brick as the exterior, but the screened windows were wider than he realized, providing a pleasant breeze. Straight-backed chairs faced round oak tables without linens.

"Just take any table with napkins and cutlery," said Emrelda, heading for a corner table flanked by windows on both sides. She pointed to a blackboard on the wall where several entrées were chalked, along with the price.

"How good is the chicken piccata?" asked Dekkard.

"Not bad. The crayfish and mushroom ravioli are also good," replied Emrelda.

The three had only been seated for a few minutes when the server, an older woman, appeared. She looked to Emrelda. "It's been a while since we've seen you."

"It was a busy summer, Lizbet. You might recall my sister Avraal, and this is her husband Steffan."

"Pleased to meet you. Do you know what you'll have?"

"The ravioli special, with the red house wine," replied Emrelda.

"The chicken piccata," said Avraal, "with the house white."

"I'll try the ravioli," said Dekkard, "with the lightest pale lager you have."

"That'd be Elfredo's own."

Dekkard nodded.

"You're early," said Lizbet. "I'll have the drinks right back. Won't be that long for the fare." She looked to Emrelda. "It's good to have you back again."

Dekkard heard the definite softening in the older woman's voice.

"Thank you, Lizbet."

Once the server left, Emrelda said, "Most of the patrollers at the station come here now and again. I've probably been here more in uniform than not. The captain told me he'd told her about Markell so that I didn't have to explain. Elfredo and Lizbet are good people."

Lizbet returned with the two glasses of wine and Dekkard's beaker of pale ale. Then, after a moment, Dekkard lifted his beaker. "To a meal you two didn't have to cook."

Both sisters lifted their glasses in return.

Less than a sixth later, Lizbet returned with their entrées.

The three had just started to eat when two patrollers in uniform entered the taverna and looked around. Then the shorter of the pair waved to Emrelda, and the two walked over to the table.

The patroller who had waved stopped beside Emrelda. "Good to see you here, Emrelda." He looked quizzically at Dekkard.

"You may have seen my sister Avraal a while back, and this is her husband Steffan. I think it's fair to say they're newlyweds. Avraal, Steffan, this is Sammel, and his partner Georg."

"Pleased to meet you both," replied Dekkard, standing.

Georg looked at Dekkard. "How good are you with those knives?"

"Until just before he and Avraal were married," said Emrelda, "he was a security aide to the Premier. He's very good with them."

Georg frowned, then asked, "Were you one of the ones who caught that empie who killed the councilor right in the Council Hall?"

"Yes, Avraal and I were the team that did it. When we got married, though, we couldn't stay as a team. So we ended up with other jobs."

Georg looked puzzled, but Sammel smiled in amusement and quickly said, "It's good to meet both of you, and to see you with Emrelda. We won't keep you from your meal, but I didn't want Emrelda to think we'd ignore her."

"You'd never do that, Sammel. Georg, either." Emrelda smiled warmly at the two.

As the patrollers headed for a table on the other side of the room, Emrelda said, "You know, Sammel figured out who you are."

"I thought he had, but I hate the idea of announcing I'm a councilor. I'd rather be introduced as your sister's husband."

"Sammel was amused and pleased you handled it that way," added Avraal. "So am I."

"It just seemed better that way," said Dekkard. But then he'd never liked councilors who flaunted their position. The fact that neither Obreduur nor Emilio Raathan had done so had impressed him about both, although Dekkard doubted he would have agreed with most of Raathan's votes in the

Council. He took another bite of the ravioli. "This is better than 'not bad,' much better," he said to Emrelda.

"That's why . . . I thought we should come here."

Dekkard managed to say, "It was a very good choice," even though he felt that Emrelda had almost said, "Markell and I came here often," or words to that effect.

"The chicken piccata is also quite good," added Avraal. "Thank you for suggesting that we come here."

"It's not pretentious. It's just good."

"Sometimes, those are the best places," said Dekkard, thinking of the councilors' dining room, which tended to be on the pretentious side, but with dishes not quite so good as what he was eating.

"Often," agreed Avraal.

Dekkard decided just to enjoy the food, and the lager, which was every bit as good as Kuhrs, and the company.

7

NO excitement or anything out of the ordinary occurred on Furdi, except that Roostof started drafting the proposed Security legislation. He also informed Dekkard that it might be another few days before he had a list of possible candidates for an engineering specialist.

Fredrich Hasheem had also sent a list of the witnesses who would appear at the morning hearings of the Security Committee for the coming week, scheduled from third bell to noon for at least two days, but longer if necessary. Because Dekkard knew very little about the official operations of the Security Ministry, he spent several bells on both Tridi and Furdi afternoon in the committee room reading the confidential briefing books on the ministry's operations and budget.

He couldn't help but notice that the Intelligence Office had a budget that comprised almost a sixth of the ministry's annual expenditures, but that there was only the sketchiest outline of the budget components. A quarter went to criminal intelligence, a quarter to foreign intelligence, and half to civic intelligence. More study revealed that the civic intelligence section looked into corporacion illegalities, guild illegalities, and illegalities by other groups and organizations. There were no examples of what such illegalities might be.

When he left the committee room on Furdi afternoon, he wondered how long it would take him to gain more than a passing understanding of what was involved in Security.

After dinner on Furdi, as they had on Tridi, Dekkard and Avraal practiced with their knives.

Quindi wasn't any different, except Dekkard had to attend the organizational meeting of the Workplace Administration Committee. He knew several of the committee members, particularly Kaliara Bassaana, and the chair, who was Guilhohn Haarsfel. The third Craft councilor was Eduardo Nortak, whom Dekkard had never met and who didn't have a reputation for brilliance. Then, after that meeting, Dekkard spent another bell going over Security files.

That evening, Emrelda, Avraal, and Dekkard attended services at the Hillside Trinitarian Chapel, not because Dekkard was all that faithful, or even a Trinitarian, but primarily because Presider Buusen had been kind enough to marry him and Avraal, and, secondly, nonbelieving, or nonattending, councilors tended to be viewed with suspicion.

Even though the week hadn't been that demanding, Dekkard felt tired by the time he and Avraal went to bed on Quindi night, possibly because it seemed that the only thing he'd been able to accomplish during the entire day was getting his knives into the new target.

He definitely looked forward to having Findi off.

When he woke the next morning, Avraal was still asleep, and Dekkard just lay there, looking at her, still amazed that she was beside him.

"What were you thinking?" she asked a moment after she opened her eyes.

"How fortunate I was that you agreed with Obreduur to hire me. Otherwise . . ." He shook his head. "I never expected . . ."

"Neither did I." She reached out and touched his cheek. "But I've told you that . . ."

Dekkard kissed her hand, then slowly sat up. "And you need some café."

"How did you ever guess?"

He laughed softly, then pulled on the bathrobe that Emrelda had given him when she'd learned he didn't have one, then made his way to the kitchen, where he poured two mugs of café and put them both on the breakfast table.

Emrelda set down the newssheet and said, "Good morning."

"Thank you. She'll be here shortly. How are you? You looked a little tired last night when you came in."

"The afternoon shift on a Quindi night isn't slow in a patroller station. Yesterday afternoon was busier than most Quindis. Nothing too serious, except for a large brawl at Fernando's."

"Local tavern?"

Emrelda nodded. "Southtown area."

"You didn't mention that last night."

"You two looked as tired as I felt." Emrelda looked up as Avraal eased her way into the kitchen and sat down in front of her café, with a murmured "Thank you" to Dekkard.

"Is there anything in *Gestirn*?" asked Dekkard.

"Nothing except a story asking when the new premier is going to address all the problems he's facing."

Dekkard shook his head. "It's a new Council, and its first business meeting was little more than a week ago. It's the first real change of power since the last century."

"The article did mention that in passing at the end," replied Emrelda sardonically.

"If that's what *Gestirn* said, I dread what the *Tribune* might say," muttered Dekkard. He took a swallow of café and smiled at Avraal.

She offered a faint smile in return.

"Can either of you tell me what's new in your lives?" asked Emrelda. "Our schedules haven't exactly matched lately."

Dekkard glanced at Avraal, who'd barely had a few sips of café, then smiled. "I'd better start. She hasn't had enough café yet." He reached for one of the croissants on the platter in the middle of the table, then split it and inserted a slice of quince paste.

Avraal raised a single eyebrow, but did not speak.

"Every councilor got a letter from the New Meritorists." From there, he summarized the few other meaningful events. "Other than that, and getting a knife target, my work life is routine, drafting and signing correspondence, meeting people and trying to learn and remember names and more names. Matters will get more involved this coming week when the Security Committee starts oversight hearings on the Security Ministry." Dekkard took a swallow of café, followed by a bite of his croissant, then asked, "What's happening with the patrollers?"

"Everyone's worried about more demonstrations," replied Emrelda.

"Obreduur issued orders to Security, especially to Special Agents, not to fire at unarmed demonstrators, and for the STF not to be used unless there were large numbers of organized and armed demonstrators."

"Everyday patrollers don't trust the higher-ups in the Security Ministry," Emrelda pointed out.

"Given that quite a few of those higher-ups will be testifying before the Security Committee this coming week, I'll keep that in mind. Are there any questions that the patrollers you know would like answers to?"

"Let me think about that."

"There's a great deal I don't know about patrollers, but is there anything other councilors have said that destroyed their credibility with patrollers? I don't want to say something stupid and undo our attempts to improve things. Remember, I'm the most junior councilor and definitely the youngest."

Emrelda smiled. "I'll need to think about that as well."

Dekkard looked to Avraal. "Are you ready for a croissant?"

"In a minute."

"More café?"

"If you wouldn't mind?"

Dekkard got up and poured more café into her mug.

"Enjoy the service while you're still newly wed," said Emrelda in a warm tone of voice.

Avraal offered a mock scowl to her sister.

"I have a question for the two of you," said Dekkard. "Are either of you aware of any Landor groups that the Security Ministry might have been interested in?"

"Does this have to do with your being on the Security Committee?" asked Avraal.

"It does. I was studying the committee records. There's a part of Security called the Intelligence Office, and half their budget goes to something called civic intelligence. I can understand criminal intelligence and foreign intelligence, but 'civic intelligence'? That could justify anything. There was just one vague statement about illegalities by corporacions, guilds, and other groups and organizations."

"I have this feeling that you're going to be on duty even when you're not," Emrelda said to her sister.

"You don't think Security is going to be happy with Steffan?" replied Avraal. "I can't imagine why you'd think that."

"Neither of you answered my question," said Dekkard dryly.

"There aren't that many Landor groups," replied Emrelda. "Landors tend not to be joiners."

Because they view themselves as rulers over their lands? Dekkard did not voice that thought.

"What about the Heritage Society?" asked Avraal.

"They just meet and moan over how Guldor needs to go back to the good old days when Landors ran things and everything was truly golden," said Emrelda.

"Back before the Silent Revolution?" asked Dekkard.

"Well before," declared Avraal.

"What do they do besides, as you put it, 'moan and groan'?"

"They don't *do* anything."

"How do you know?" asked Dekkard.

"Cliven belongs," replied Emrelda. "Our dear brother wouldn't be caught dead in anything that advocated any political activity."

"Are there any others?" asked Dekkard.

"Oh, there are local hunt clubs . . . but those are just an excuse to kill boars and panthers . . . and to drink and boast a lot afterwards." Emrelda's words were definitely dismissive.

"Why do you want to know?" asked Avraal.

"We know Security has been following Obreduur and Carlos . . . as well as the guilds. I just wondered what Landors or Landor groups the Commercers in Security might be following. There are millions of marks going to the Intelligence Office. I'd like to know how they're being used. I also wonder if Security is also involved in protecting corporacions like Siincleer Engineering from competition."

"That would explain a lot," said Emrelda, bitterness creeping into her voice. "Security higher-ups just shut down cases or make sure evidence gets misplaced. They don't get involved directly."

"That's just a surmise on my part," said Dekkard. "I could be totally wrong, but there seems to be an enormous amount of marks going into civic intelligence without much description . . . or much oversight."

"But Security couldn't discover that the New Meritorists had planted explosives in fifteen regional headquarters buildings?" asked Avraal sarcastically.

"That thought did occur to me," replied Dekkard dryly.

Emrelda shook her head. "We're both going to have to watch out for you."

"Now that we've planned out tomorrow for Steffan," said Avraal, turning to her sister, "what would you like to do today?"

Emrelda smiled. "Actually, I'd like to start learning to throw knives."

8

THE rest of Findi was quiet, and Dekkard finally had enough time to write a letter back to Naralta. Later, Dekkard and Avraal enjoyed practicing with knives and teaching Emrelda, after which they cleaned up and had an early dinner at Octavia's.

As far as Dekkard was concerned Unadi came far, far too early, but he did manage to get himself washed and dressed before waking Avraal. He then went downstairs to the kitchen and saw Emrelda off, before setting out breakfast for himself and Avraal.

While he waited for her, he quickly read the morning edition of *Gestirn*, but the only story of immediate interest was one speculating on the fact that Obreduur hadn't proposed ministerial appointments for Public Resources, Security, or Treasury and what that might foreshadow. At that moment, he heard Avraal's footsteps, so he poured her café and set it at her place.

"Good morning, lovely lady," he said as she stepped into the breakfast room in her robe. He gestured to her café.

"Lovely? In this?"

"You look lovely in anything." *As well as in nothing.*

"I know what you're thinking, lecherous husband."

"It's not lecherous because it's you I'm thinking about."

She smiled. "That's a good recovery, but it's too early." She slipped into her chair and took a small sip of café.

Dekkard sat down across from her and split two croissants, then quietly began to eat while she slowly sipped more café.

After a while she asked, "Is there anything I should know in the newssheet?"

"They're guessing about why Obreduur didn't propose ministers for Treasury, Public Resources, and Security. I'd guess it's a Commercer ploy—raising doubts when any smart person should know. The reasons were announced in open session almost a week ago."

"That didn't make it into the newssheets," said Avraal, adding dryly, "I wonder why."

"The growers in the southwest are worried that there's been too much rain, and they've lost too much of their harvests, but the Landors still oppose any reduction in the tariff levels. Vonauer claims that Sargassan grain exporters will use a temporary shortage as an excuse to flood Guldor with inferior low-cost swampgrass rice or emmer wheat-corn, not to mention other grains."

"Cliven would agree with that, I'm sure. Not that he'll be writing any time soon."

Dekkard decided to change the subject, quickly. "On another matter, we should be getting some interest in the engineering staff position this week. Could you confirm with Carlos about taking a morning off to help me with interviews? It won't be until Furdi or later. It might not be until next week . . . or possibly later."

"I will. I'm sure it won't be a problem. He already agreed that I can have time off to help you, just so that it's not last moment . . . unless it's an emergency of some sort. That's in his interest as well." Avraal smiled.

"I'll try to avoid emergencies. I'm still a little worried about the Security oversight hearings."

"You'll be fine. Just make sure you're comfortable with anything you say or ask."

"That might be difficult. Anything associated with Security makes me uneasy." Dekkard finished his second croissant, and took a swallow of café.

Before long, the two had cleaned up the breakfast room and kitchen, and then finished dressing, and headed out the east door to the covered portico. More than a third later, after dropping Avraal off at Baartol's office, he parked the Gresynt in the Council covered parking, and, studying the area carefully, walked toward the Council Office Building.

Ahead of him, two men entered the building, one a tall figure in a gray suit with a bear-like gait he recognized, and he realized it had to be Jaime Minz. The other man he couldn't identify from behind. For a moment he wondered what Minz was doing, then realized that Minz was probably visiting a councilor, if not more than one.

Dekkard decided to hang back as the two stopped by the visitors' desk. The guard checked the visitors' log, then motioned, and a second guard appeared to escort the pair. When the second man turned slightly, Dekkard recognized him as well—Fernand Stoltz, the former committee legalist for the Public Resources Committee.

Still thinking about the appearance of Minz and Stoltz, Dekkard posted the letter to Naralta, climbed the center staircase to reach his office. Once there, he went to Roostof's desk.

The senior legalist looked up. "Sir?"

"How are you coming on that legislation?"

"I'll have a draft for you in the morning."

"Good. Do we have any interest in the technical position yet?"

"We have four inquiries so far. There might be a few more today or tomorrow."

Dekkard nodded. "Thank you." He headed for his desk, settled himself, and began to go through the messages and mail. After reading through it all, he turned them over to the senior legalist.

Then he said to Margrit, "I'll be at the Security Committee hearings until noon. I don't know if I'll stop to eat after that, but I should be back no later than a little after first bell."

"Yes, sir."

Dekkard passed two councilors he knew only by name and face on the way to the Council and nodded politely to both. They did the same.

Dekkard neared the committee room a good sixth before third bell to discover Laurenz Korriah and Shaundara Keppel, the two security aides for

Councilor Kharl Navione, waiting outside, a pair with whom he'd often talked in the staff cafeteria or elsewhere. "Good morning, Laurenz, Shaundara."

"Good morning, Councilor," replied Korriah, smiling from ear to ear.

"Only in public," replied Dekkard.

"So you're a councilor and you were the last to know? You do have a way," said Korriah, still grinning. "Where's Avraal?"

"We got married a week ago last Findi. She's working for a consultant, but she'll be helping me as she can."

"You don't do things by thirds." Korriah shook his head.

"Neither does Avraal," replied Dekkard. "I take it your councilor's inside?"

"He is."

"Then I'd better introduce myself."

"He's a good man, but he's very formal," said Korriah in a lower voice.

"Thank you. I appreciate the advice."

"Give our best to Avraal," added Keppel.

"I will." Dekkard smiled, then entered the committee room, where the only other councilor was Navione, who stood just below the dais holding a long, curved desk with seven seats behind it, each place marked with a bronze nameplate. Dekkard's place was the last on the left, while the center place was Hasheem's, with Navione to Hasheem's left.

Dekkard walked up to the older Landor councilor. "Councilor Navione, I'm Steffan Dekkard. We haven't been introduced, formally or otherwise."

"Thank you, Steffan." Navione replied pleasantly, but not effusively. "I'm glad to meet you face-to-face. Can you tell me anything beyond the general purpose of the hearings?"

"I'd only be guessing. Neither Chairman Hasheem nor the Premier has said a word to me. I do know that the Premier was concerned about how Security could have allowed the New Meritorists to infiltrate fifteen Security buildings without being discovered. Other than that . . ." Dekkard shrugged.

"That's a very good question. I have some doubts that Security will have a satisfactory explanation. I believe he earlier raised the issue of how they obtained that much dunnite."

"He may have. I know Kaliara Bassaana did as well."

Navione stiffened slightly as Hasheem entered the committee room, then said, "It is a pleasure to meet you, Steffan. Perhaps we should ready ourselves."

"My pleasure as well," answered Dekkard, who then moved to the dais, where he stood behind his place.

Over the next several minutes, the other committee members arrived, first Erik Marrak, the Commercer who had briefly been chair after Ivaan Maendaan's assassination during the Summerend demonstrations; along with the other Commercer, Jaradd Rikkard; then Breffyn Haastar, the other Landor councilor besides Navione, followed by Tomas Pajiin, seated at the far end of the long, curved desk opposite Dekkard.

As the Council Hall bells chimed three times, a stocky man in a security-blue suit, white shirt, and slightly lighter blue tie walked into the room followed by two uniformed Security agents.

"Welcome, Deputy Minister Manwaeren," said Hasheem. "Since we will be discussing confidential Security materials and action, this is not an open hearing. Your escorts can wait outside. The only others who will be joining us will be Premier Obreduur, who will only observe, along with his security empath." Hasheem smiled politely.

Manwaeren nodded to the Security agents, who departed, passing Obreduur and Isobel Irlende as they entered.

Hasheem waited until Obreduur seated himself in the row of chairs behind the table reserved for those appearing before the committee. Then he looked to Manwaeren. "Deputy Minister Manwaeren, we'll dispense with your reading your statement, but it will be entered into the record."

Manwaeren nodded, offering a perfunctory smile.

"The committee is well aware of the public events," continued Hasheem, "involving the New Meritorists and Security over the past several months. Our interest is to look into precisely why Security chose to react as it did and why it was so unprepared." Hasheem paused. "Prior to the first large demonstration here at the Council, just how much information did the ministry have on the group?"

"Chairman Hasheem, at that time, all information on the 'New Meritorists' was being gathered and evaluated by the Intelligence Office. The group had circulated a few broadsheets and held several public meetings almost two years ago. Then the meetings stopped. So did the broadsheets. Dissident groups have come and gone for decades. This group appeared to be no different. In hindsight, it is clear that they decided to minimize their public presence . . ."

Dekkard listened as Manwaeren spent more than half a bell explaining why Security had been caught off guard. His explanation seemed to make sense— but only superficially. Yet from studying Isobel Irlende, Dekkard was fairly certain that Manwaeren was telling what he believed to be the truth.

Manwaeren's explanation of lack of devoted resources and lack of knowledge also chilled Dekkard, because, if Security had no idea until events literally exploded, matters were far worse than he'd realized. *Was that because Security was more interested in investigating political opponents and small businesses who threatened larger corporacions?*

After Manwaeren finished, Hasheem nodded, then asked, "Who made the decision to deploy the Special Tactical Force to deal with the last demonstration at the Square of Heroes?"

"That was Minister Wyath's decision, Councilor."

"Was it also his decision to have them fire on armed protestors and then try to plant weapons on them to justify the shootings? Or was that *your* decision?"

Manwaeren stiffened slightly. "The STF commander was ordered not to shoot unless the patrollers or Palace Guards were threatened. It's clear that he misjudged the degree of threat and overreacted. Neither Minister Wyath nor I had any knowledge of his orders to plant weapons until well after the fact. STF Commander Orsken was immediately relieved and faces criminal charges before the High Justiciary. The preliminary hearing was held last Furdi."

Dekkard couldn't help but frown. He'd read nothing about the charges or hearing, but clearly Manwaeren was telling the truth about that, given Irlende's slight nod to Obreduur.

"Thank you. I have two final questions. How in the world was it possible for the New Meritorists to plant dunnite in fifteen regional Security headquarters buildings undetected? And how did they obtain that quantity of dunnite?"

"I'll answer the second question first. After the explosions, we investigated and discovered a report that a steam lorry carrying bulk dunnite belonging to the Navy had been involved in an accident en route to the Navy munitions facility in Uldwyrk. It went into the river near Tryar. The bodies of the driver and guards were never found, but the bulk of the dunnite was still in the lorry . . . if ruined by water. At the time, the Navy assumed that while the lorry was in the river, the water washed away or destroyed some of the dunnite because the rear doors were presumably jolted open by the impact. In retrospect, it's likely that the lorry was taken at some point, part of the cargo removed, and at a later time pushed off the bridge into the water."

That certainly fit with what Dekkard had surmised after talking to Macri and Roostof immediately after the Summerend explosions.

"As for the first question, we can only surmise that during routine maintenance work, the stolen dunnite was reshaped and planted in the stations over the course of more than a year. To date, we have found no indications of how this was accomplished or by whom specifically."

"Thank you." Hasheem turned to Councilor Marrak, the Commercer from Suvion, who would have been the committee chairman if the Crafters had not won the election. "Councilor Marrak, do you have any questions for Deputy Minister Manwaeren?"

"I do, Sr. Chairman." Marrak smiled warmly and looked at Manwaeren. "Was any information or evidence that the New Meritorists were considering violent actions ever brought to the attention of the ministry?"

"None that I am aware of."

"Was there any way that the ministry could have pursued these miscreants at that time?"

"No, Councilor. It was as though they disappeared into the green."

Dekkard sat, listening and watching, as Marrak asked more questions, inquiries designed to let Manwaeren effectively excuse what Dekkard felt had been a careless, if not willful, decision to expend marks following political enemies, instead of the more difficult task of investigating the New Meritorists.

Navione was next and his questions were more focused.

"Did the ministry take into account the disruption and deaths caused by the original Meritorists?"

"Why didn't you believe that this group could potentially be as dangerous, or more so, as it turned out?"

"Who was ultimately responsible for those decisions?"

"Did you express any reservations about those decisions?"

By the time Navione finished his questions, Dekkard was convinced that

Manwaeren had his position because he never disagreed with former Security Minister Wyath.

The questions asked by Haastar and Rikkard merely rephrased earlier questions. Pajiin simply stated that he had no questions at present.

"Councilor Dekkard, do you have any questions for the deputy minister?"

"I do, Chairman Hasheem. I'll forgo those already brought by more experienced councilors, but I do have a few inquiries."

"You may proceed."

"Deputy Minister Manwaeren, you mentioned that the Intelligence Office lost sight of the New Meritorists for almost two years. From what I've been able to determine, almost a sixth of the Security budget goes to the Intelligence Office, and half of that goes to civic intelligence. I may be missing something, but if those marks weren't spent on tracking down the New Meritorists, exactly what investigations, specifically, were they spent on?"

"Councilor, I really couldn't speak to specifics. Those are a matter for the Intelligence Office to address."

"Then, in *general* terms, what sorts of activities fall under 'civic intelligence'? I'm asking, as a new councilor, because I've been unable to find a definition of what the Civic Intelligence section does investigate, which seems a bit unusual for a section that receives almost a tenth of the entire Security budget."

"We provide a detailed budget—"

"I read the budget. It provides a breakdown for information gathering, analysis, and for enforcement. There are numbers for personnel, for equipment, and for operational costs. There is only a general statement that possible illegalities may be found in corporacions, guilds, and other organizations or groups. Nowhere does it explain exactly *who* the office is investigating . . . for example, how much of that budget went to investigate the New Meritorists or Foothill Freedom."

"Revealing actual investigations would jeopardize public safety," replied Manwaeren stiffly.

"Another question, then. Did the subject matter of the broadsheets and posters from two years ago differ markedly from those recently disseminated? In particular, did the earlier broadsheets call for changing the basis of the Great Charter?"

"As I recall, there was no great change—"

"So, two years ago the New Meritorists advocated overthrowing the Great Charter, and when they quit having open or public meetings, Security decided that they were no longer a threat?"

"There was no apparent immediate threat, Councilor."

"Was there an immediate apparent threat from the guilds whose officials you tracked?"

"Councilor, I object—"

"Deputy Minister Manwaeren," interjected Hasheem. "Councilor Dekkard has raised a valid point. Why did Security decide not to pursue the New Meritorists, who advocated overthrowing the Great Charter, but did continue to track and surveil individuals from groups offering no direct threat to the Council or the government of Guldor?"

Manwaeren looked across the faces of the councilors. "That decision was made by former Minister of Security Wyath. In retrospect, it was obviously incorrect."

"One last question," Dekkard said quickly, "what person or office is the operational supervisor of Special Agents?"

"Obviously, the ultimate authority is the Security minister, but the supervisor of Special Agents is the director of special projects, who reports directly to the minister."

"Thank you, Deputy Minister," said Hasheem strongly. "That will conclude the hearing for today. We appreciate your appearance and responses. The hearing tomorrow will deal with the operational choices made by the Intelligence Office. We would appreciate, as we have informed you, the presence of the director of that office and the heads of each of the three branches. We will expect specific answers."

"They will be here, Sr. Chairman."

To Dekkard, Manwaeren sounded anything but pleased.

The deputy minister rose from the small desk, turned and nodded politely to Obreduur, then made his way from the committee room. Obreduur and Irlende followed almost immediately.

Only then did Hasheem stand, turning to Navione and saying, "I appreciated your questions, Kharl." Then he turned to Marrak, and added, "And yours as well, Erik."

By then, Rikkard and Haastar were on their way out, and Dekkard eased toward Hasheem. "I hope my questions weren't too presumptive."

Hasheem shook his head. "You asked just enough. That way, the honorable deputy minister can't say that he didn't know of the committee's interest."

"That was also why you ended the hearing where you did, wasn't it?" *That . . . and that you didn't want to reveal further Manwaeren's ignorance of what was happening in his own ministry.* Since Hasheem had no love of Commercer appointees, such as Manwaeren, and definitely no love of the Security Ministry, the slightly early termination of the deputy minister's testimony was likely because Hasheem had far more interest in what those actually supervising the intelligence operations had to say. Dekkard also realized, belatedly, that Hasheem could summon Manwaeren before the committee because Obreduur had allowed the acting minister to remain as such until the Council approved a new Minister of Security.

"Exactly," replied Hasheem. "It will be interesting to see how honest those who appear tomorrow will be. I'll see you then, Steffan."

Dekkard nodded politely in return. When he left the committee room, he immediately scanned the area, but the only person nearby was Pajiin, who stepped toward Dekkard, as if he'd been waiting.

"Would you like to join me for lunch, Steffan?"

"That would be good." Dekkard kept his eyes moving as he walked beside the older councilor.

The two ended up seated at a table for two in the councilors' dining room. Both ordered café and the duck cassoulet.

"Something's going on in that committee," said Pajiin quietly. "It's more than just the New Meritorists. Did you come up with those questions yourself?"

"I did. I spent a few bells reading though committee files."

"You went to a lot of work just to dig out enough to ask those questions. Or did Hasheem put you up to it?"

Pajiin's direct bluntness concerned Dekkard, but he nodded, and said, "Hasheem had nothing to do with it." *Although he probably thought I would.* "Call it professional interest. Security has been tailing Craft guild officials for years. Three security aides to Craft councilors have been attacked in the last year. Councilor Mardosh's empath vanished without a trace. Former Landor Councilor Freust was assassinated, although it was reported as heart failure . . . I could go on. Security has enough resources to look into these, but so far as I can tell, they didn't, yet they can't protect their own buildings?"

Pajiin's laugh was hard. "You think you'll live long enough to even look into this mess?"

"I'm already looking into it, and I'm still here." *So far.* There was something about Pajiin that reminded him of someone, but Dekkard couldn't place who it was.

"Your questions made Manwaeren admit that he was a toady. He didn't like your questions. Navione's, either. Is Marrak always that stupid?"

"I've never heard him speak before." Dekkard stopped as the server returned with their platters.

Once the server left, Pajiin went on. "Hasheem let Marrak ask all those easy questions. They were supposed to show that Security did its duty. Marrak didn't even see that every answer Manwaeren gave showed how little he knew. Either that, or he was lying."

"The Premier's empath was watching him." Dekkard took a quick bite of the cassoulet, warm and filling.

"You know she's an empath? She the one who was your partner?"

Dekkard offered an amused smile. "My partner took another job. That was her replacement."

"Sold out for more marks, did she?"

"Not really. She's still working for the Craft Party, if less directly." Before Pajiin could ask another question, Dekkard went on. "You were a Lumber Guild steward, I understand. How did that lead to your running for the Council?"

"The guild put me up." Pajiin smiled coolly. "No one else was willing to try on just a few weeks' notice. Had a few friends in the Newssheet Guild who were willing to point out the lack of interest in Eshbruk by the previous councilor."

"You mean, Demarais Haaltf, one of those killed by the New Meritorists?"

"Thing is . . . Haaltf wasn't even as bad as his predecessor, and there were a few stories about that suggesting that one rotten councilor might just be that, but two in a row wasn't just the councilor. Enough people felt that way, but it was still close."

"What do you think about the New Meritorists?"

Pajiin barked a laugh. "They're smart folks who don't understand people."

"They seem to understand that people aren't happy."

"Who's unhappy, Steffan? It's lazy young people who don't know how to work. It's beetles who come here because they can't make it in Atacama."

"It's also millworkers who lost their jobs to the punch-card steam looms, fieldworkers who aren't needed because of steam tillers and tractors . . ."

"How long did you really work with your hands, Steffan?"

"Five years as an apprentice plasterer, Tomas, until I won the competition for a spot at the Military Institute."

"Not many like you left among the younger people. Not that I've seen in Eshbruk." Pajiin cleared his throat, then said, "The cassoulet's not bad."

Dekkard nodded, recognizing that Pajiin didn't want to talk politics any longer. "I've been told that most everything here is decent or better, except for something called the burgher's delight."

"What is it?"

"Fried ground beef topped with cheese and stuffed between two halves of a plain roll."

"Sounds terrible. Have you ever tried it?"

"With that description?" Dekkard shook his head.

After another third of eating and small talk, the two councilors left the dining room and went their separate ways, with Dekkard walking back to the Council Office Building.

He saw Jareem Saarh at a distance and half smiled, recalling how he'd thought Saarh would have trouble getting elected—since he'd been selected as a replacement after his predecessor had suffered an unfortunate "heart attack"—but apparently the anti-Commercer feeling had been great enough for Saarh to win.

Once back in his office, he went through the mail, and the typed responses Roostof had approved, signing most, occasionally adding a note in his own hand, and making changes to one or two. Then he headed back to the Council Hall and the Security Committee room, where he spent more than a bell going through committee records and previous hearing transcripts. He found nothing about specific operations conducted by the Intelligence Office.

Dekkard turned to the head clerk. "Why aren't there any records about the Intelligence Office, except a summary description and budget and personnel numbers?"

"Sir, the previous Premier had them turned over to the Security Ministry."

"For what reason?"

"We weren't told, sir. They just came and collected them."

"Was that something that Jaime Minz supervised?" Dekkard asked.

The clerk didn't answer.

"Do I have to have Chairman Hasheem ask the question?"

"No, sir. Sr. Minz was one of them."

"And the other?"

"I didn't know him. He was from the ministry."

"Thank you."

"Yes, sir."

After that, Dekkard walked into the adjoining staff office, looking for Frieda Livigne, since she was the only remaining professional Security Committee staffer he knew. Her desk was in the corner. He walked toward her, then said quietly, "Frieda?"

Livigne looked up politely. "Yes, Councilor."

"Steffan will do in private. Why aren't there any records of Intelligence Office operations? Nothing beyond general references and budgets?"

She gave the smallest of headshakes. "Jaime told me it wouldn't be long before you were asking questions."

"He was right about that. Intelligence Office operations?"

"The staff has always been under orders not to write down or transcribe any specific operations."

Dekkard could see that, in a fashion. "But there's nothing beyond budgets and some general descriptions. Why did Jaime turn them over to the Security Ministry?"

"Because he was ordered to, I imagine."

"Did Premier Ulrich offer any reason for the action?"

"Jaime said that Security needed them."

Dekkard raised his eyebrows. "To substitute for all the Security records that were incinerated by the New Meritorists?" *And a great excuse for getting them out of easy reach.*

"Steffan, any councilor could access the committee records. Councilor Hasheem often did."

"Except that Navione and Hasheem are the only ones left who could have. Everyone else on the committee is new."

"Those things happen, Councilor."

"Oh, I'm very aware that they occur. I'm even more aware of the circumstances when they occur." He smiled politely. "By the way, would you happen to know what Premier Ulrich happens to be doing these days? I'm sure you know, if anyone does."

Livigne paused, as if debating how to answer, then said, "I heard that he has a position as vice-presidente for political relations at Suvion Industries."

"Thank you. I appreciate the clarification and the information."

"It's my pleasure, Councilor."

"That," replied Dekkard, with an amused smile, "I'm quite sure of." He thought he saw the trace of a satisfied smile before he turned and left the staff office.

Ulrich . . . in a high position at Suvion Industries . . . the other major manufacturer of dunnite . . . and the same corporacion from which Wyath came. Dekkard doubted that either was a coincidence. He also wondered if Minz's appearance that morning was also just a coincidence, and what Minz and Stoltz were doing together.

On the way back to his own office, he was especially alert, but saw nothing suspicious or out of the ordinary. There was one message on his desk. He opened it and read the short note.

Steffan—
   You had some good questions. As usual, you were prepared.
   There were no knowing lies told.
   If you can, stop by the regular office on your way out. Don't reply by message. I likely won't get to it. Just come if you can.

The signature was just "Axel."

Dekkard couldn't say he was surprised. Obreduur had always tried to be as circumspect as possible in his dealings with other councilors. He slipped the note into the gray leather folder he used to carry papers to and from work, not that there were many—*so far*—then leaned back in his chair and concentrated on what approach he wanted to use in questioning the Security officials that would appear before the committee, both on Tridi and later in the week.

Before he knew it, it was past fourth bell, and he was walking south in the main second-floor corridor toward Obreduur's office. When he entered it, he saw that Isobel focused on him immediately, then smiled and said, "It's good to see you, Councilor."

"I'm very glad you're here, Isobel."

"So are we," added Karola from her desk beside the door to the inner office. "He said that you could go right in."

"Thank you." Dekkard stepped into the office and closed the door.

Obreduur looked up from the papers in stacks around him and gestured to the chair nearest to him.

Dekkard grinned as he sat down. "What did I miss?"

Obreduur chuckled. "Yes, I wanted to see you, but not because you missed anything. You met with Tomas Pajiin. He asked you, I assume?"

"He did. He seems rather direct. He's also approached me twice. Perhaps I'm cynical, but that doesn't seem like a coincidence, given that we have nothing in common and that I'm also at least twenty years younger . . . and that I'm a very junior councilor. So far, I've only told him what's appeared in the newssheets here in Machtarn." *And not even that.*

"That caution is probably advisable. He's known for directness, according to the Advisory Committee. He doesn't lie. He also isn't particularly well-liked."

Dekkard frowned. He abruptly recalled who it was that Pajiin reminded him of. "I know that it's just a feeling, but Pajiin feels to me like a rougher and less polished version of Haasan Decaro."

Obreduur offered a rueful but amused smile. "I don't think he's corrupt in the way Decaro was. At least, there's no evidence to that effect . . . and no rumors . . . and there were always rumors about Haasan, although I was the only one who even came close to knowing even a part of what he was doing. But I'd judge Pajiin could be just as ruthless in using people." After the slightest pause,

Obreduur said pleasantly, "I understand you've been studying the Security Committee records."

"What's left of them. Did you know that Ulrich had what committee records there were about the Intelligence Office turned over to the Security Ministry?"

"Hasheem told me that. You're likely the only other councilor who knows that. Navione has enough experience that he wouldn't need to look at committee records, and none of the others would care or would know enough yet to think about it."

"Then there's no point in bringing it up."

"No, there's not."

"How hard do you want me to question the Intelligence officials?"

"You're the councilor."

"You're the Premier," replied Dekkard.

"What do you think?"

Dekkard laughed softly, then said, "Just enough to make them wary. We won't get any answers beyond generalities, or words to the effect that they don't know the details or that those details are part of something ongoing that they'll be happy to reveal in the future. Not that they'll do it then, either."

"So why is Hasheem holding hearings?"

"To prove that the ministry is unresponsive and ineffective and needs reform. That would be my guess. *And* to prove that a Craft government isn't ignoring the problem while being able to point out to Commercers that we're not rushing to act without getting the facts straight . . . as well as trying to buy time from the New Meritorists." Dekkard paused then asked, "Did I leave anything out?"

"You covered all the major points."

"I assume you want me to be friendly to Pajiin, but not too friendly. Cordial, if you will."

"That might be useful."

"Is Nellara still practicing with the throwing knives?"

"She is. I suspect she's more devoted to them than Gustoff is."

"Is there anything else I should know?" asked Dekkard.

"I can't think of anything. How is Avraal doing?"

"She's still getting settled with Carlos. Have you heard anything more that might bear on Markell or Siincleer Engineering?"

"I don't know of anything new. I suspect that anyone investigating Siincleer Engineering won't find a thing."

"We already knew that. We'll have to find another way. Perhaps an investigation of the failure of small competitors?"

"That's possible, but it won't be quick or easy."

Dekkard had never thought that it would be.

Obreduur stood. "I look forward to the hearings tomorrow."

"They're likely to be more interesting for what's not said."

"Of course. That can suggest where to look, though."

"Or where the Commercers want us to look," returned Dekkard.

"That, too. Until tomorrow, Steffan."

Dekkard inclined his head. "Until tomorrow, sir."

"Leave the door open, I'll be right behind you."

Dekkard did so. Although he needed to consider what Obreduur hadn't said, that could wait until he got back to the house. Until then, he needed to act like a security aide.

9

WHEN Dekkard reached the parking area beside the office of Carlos Baartol, he had waited almost a sixth of a bell, and was about ready to get out of the Gresynt when Avraal hurried out.

"I'm sorry. I was in a meeting with Carlos and a client and it ran much longer," said Avraal as she slipped into the seat beside Dekkard.

"Because the client wasn't being as truthful as he or she might have been?"

"There was that, too. But it's a complicated matter. We can talk about it later. Carlos says I can share anything with you so long as you promise not to tell anyone."

"That's thoughtful of him."

"Rather pragmatic, I'd say," replied Avraal. "We're on the same side, and we both need each other." She leaned over and kissed his cheek. "Tell me how your day went on the way home."

Dekkard did just that, expressing his concerns about Pajiin and the considerations Obreduur and Hasheem were dealing with in holding oversight hearings on the Security Ministry.

When he finished, just about the time he turned off Camelia Avenue and north on Jacquez, Avraal said, "The missing records might be another reason why Hasheem and Obreduur wanted you on the Security Committee. You have some understanding and experience. What was Pajiin's reaction to what you told him, besides the snide comment about me selling out for more marks?"

"He wasn't particularly astonished by my comments about Security. He was also rather dismissive of the New Meritorists."

"He sounds like an old-style Craft Guilder."

"He comes across as a rougher, somewhat more honest version of Haasan Decaro, at least to me, although I'd have my doubts about how honest."

"Trust your doubts. I'll see if Carlos has any information on him."

"That could be helpful." Dekkard turned off Jacquez and onto Florinda Way, and in minutes he had the Gresynt up the narrow drive. As he stopped to let Avraal out under the portico roof, he noticed that the adjoining house was unshuttered, and he wondered when the neighbors, with their susceptible child, had returned. They hadn't just before the last day of Summerend, as he recalled. *But you weren't here often in the early weeks of Fallfirst, and your mind was definitely elsewhere.*

After Avraal got out, Dekkard eased the steamer into the garage, noting Emrelda's teal steamer in the other garage bay. He wiped the steamer down, then refilled the tanks before closing the garage and walking back to the house.

Both Avraal and Emrelda were in the kitchen.

"We're having spicy chilled tomato soup tonight," declared Emrelda.

"That's fine with me," replied Dekkard. "I had a heavy lunch with an overly inquisitive Craft councilor. How was your day?"

10

ON Duadi, Dekkard woke to the sound of rain, and the comparative coolness of the air told him that the rain had moved in from the north, and that it heralded the coming of true fall—by the weather and not the calendar—and possibly the beginning of the waterspout season.

"We might even have a week of cooler weather," he said, leaning over and kissing Avraal.

"Optimist," she replied, after returning the kiss.

With a smile he sat up. "I'll hurry."

"You always do," she replied with a smile that was faintly sleepy and mischievous.

Dekkard winced. "Not in everything."

"That's true." She smiled again, warmly.

Dekkard showered, shaved, and dressed quickly—except for cravat and jacket—then said, "I'll have your café ready."

"Thank you."

When he reached the kitchen, he saw that Emrelda was already in full uniform and about to leave.

"You're up earlier," she observed.

"The rain."

She raised her eyebrows. "It's been raining since before midnight."

Knowing any explanation would just invite more comment, he just shrugged, then said, "At least it will be cooler for a while. This has been a hot fall."

Emrelda grinned. "Especially for you two. I'll see you tonight." Then she turned and headed for the portico door.

Dekkard shook his head, then took a quick look at *Gestirn*. The only directly political story was on page three and stated that the Council was holding closed oversight hearings on certain questionable policies of the Treasury and Security Ministries.

That had to come indirectly from Obreduur. It also had to be part of the Premier's tactics to buy time before the New Meritorists returned to more demonstrations . . . or worse. Dekkard set the newssheet aside.

He had the café and croissants ready well before Avraal entered the kitchen, wearing a gray skirt and a pale cream blouse, but not the jacket that matched the calf-length skirt. "Working grays, I see."

"It's easier to conceal the knives . . . and we need to leave a little earlier." She sat down and took a sip of café.

Translated loosely, you don't want to tempt me by showing up in a robe. Dekkard smiled. "You look very good in the teal and gray."

"I could wear ragged security grays, and you'd say that."

"You look good in everything."

"That's not true . . . but thank you."

"I got a letter from a patroller in Siincleer. At least, I think it was from a patroller. It was typed on patroller stationery but unsigned. It had a clipping from the *Siincleer Star* . . . a short story about how a patrol chief was fatally shot from a distance as he entered his patrol station."

"Don't tell me it was the patrol chief you talked to," said Avraal.

"It was Karell Troyan. I doubt that there are two patroller officers with that name."

"Shot from a distance?" asked Dekkard. "No heart attack, no accident?"

"He was incredibly careful, from what I saw," replied Emrelda. "That might have been the only way to get to him. The letter also listed two other names of patrollers who have died suspiciously over the past five years. One was another station chief, and the other a deputy chief, both at stations in Siincleer."

"How did they have your address?" asked Dekkard.

"They didn't. I only left my station address, and that was the address on the letter."

"Did you show it to other patrollers?"

"Absolutely. The station chief made copies to send to a few other senior patrollers he knows and trusts, and he gave me an extra copy for you. He thought you might find it useful."

"Gelatin print copies?" asked Avraal. "Those aren't cheap."

"The station has the facilities."

"What did your station chief think?" asked Dekkard.

"He wasn't surprised. He said that there have always been rumors about things happening to senior patrollers who looked too closely at strange events around big corporacions, especially where the Navy was involved. The letter, however, seemed to stun him. He also suggested that I not return to Siincleer any time soon."

"I agree," said Avraal.

"There's no point in it. There won't be any evidence, and anyone who was involved directly in . . . what happened to Markell . . . has long since left." After a moment, Emrelda added, "Are we practicing with the knives before dinner . . . or after?"

"Which would you prefer?" asked Dekkard.

"Before."

"Then I'll change and set up the target now." Dekkard turned and headed for the upstairs bedroom that had become his and Avraal's quarters.

Dekkard sat down across from her. "Would you like a croissant?"

"Please."

Avraal actually ate the entire croissant, almost immediately, which told Dekkard that she anticipated a long day and was serious about leaving earlier. They quickly cleaned up, finished dressing, and were in the Gresynt in little more than a third of a bell.

As he headed off Florinda and onto Jacquez, Dekkard asked, "Which project needs you there early?"

"All of them, but especially the Eastern Ironway investigation. One of Carlos's sources has located several people who may have leads to the mysterious Amash Kharhan."

"The one who received the twenty-thousand-mark bribe for the illegal coal lease?"

"It's still legally a commission unless we can prove that those marks were paid contrary to law or that they induced someone to break the law or were paid in return for an illegal act."

Not for the first time, Dekkard was glad he wasn't a legalist, until he recalled what Macri had told him several months earlier—that he was already close to being a legalist. He smiled wryly, then said, "It would be helpful if you could tie that to the Commercers."

"Do you think anyone except the New Meritorists will really care?"

"You might be right."

"Might be?"

Dekkard laughed. "You're right. Most people won't care at all, even if it is another example of Commercer corruption." He couldn't help thinking that the tendency of people to ignore corruption or illegalities so long as it didn't seem to affect them was exactly why the Commercers had gotten away with so much for so long. It was only when their policies started to squeeze more from the really poor segments of Guldor that unrest began to grow, along with New Meritorist support.

Dekkard dropped Avraal off and drove to the Council Office Building without incident.

There were no important messages—sent by Guldoran Heliograph or otherwise—waiting for Dekkard at his office. The mail and petitions were all matters that Roostof could handle or delegate to Luara Colsbaan. So, after putting it all in Roostof's inbox, he asked, "How are you coming on the draft legislation?"

"I do have a draft."

"Bring it into the office. We need to talk about it before you come up with a final version."

Roostof followed Dekkard into the inner office and closed the door.

Dekkard sat down behind the desk. "To what degree are Special Agents shielded from criminal law and prosecution? Under current law, that is?"

"Theoretically, they're not," replied Roostof. "Practically though, that's another matter."

"You mean if someone falls down a set of steps, and there's no evidence found, or if someone's shot in dim light and no one saw the shooter . . . that sort of thing?"

The legalist nodded.

"How can we make them more accountable?"

Roostof offered an amused smile. "The best way is what you proposed. Put the STF under Army control, and put the Special Agents into an information ministry or office without any authorization to carry weapons. I added a provision that gives the new information office the ability to request patroller assistance in specific instances if there is reason to believe it's necessary." The legalist paused. "We didn't talk about this, but I'd suggest the information function be moved to the Justiciary or Treasury Ministry or, if you'd prefer, the Ministry of Health and Education."

Dekkard thought for a moment. "Justiciary and Treasury would be better for all the Special Agents." *And politically more acceptable.*

After going through the draft legislation and suggesting some changes, but mostly appreciating what Roostof had fleshed out from his bare-bones outline, Dekkard had to leave for the Council Hall. He crossed the courtyard under the covered portico with cool rain falling on both sides, the most comfortable walk to the Council Hall in months.

On reaching the Security Committee room, he saw that Hasheem and Navione were already there, talking quietly behind the conference table.

By a sixth before the third morning bell, all the Security Committee members were in the hearing chamber—except Erik Marrak—along with four Security officials, one of whom was seated behind the witness desk, and three others in chairs to the left, who were dressed in suits of differing shades of blue. Only the man at the desk—black-haired and slightly older—wore true security blue. Three committee clerks occupied a table to one side.

Just before the Council Hall bells chimed three times, Premier Obreduur and Isobel Irlende entered the chamber and sat to one side.

Marrak followed them, almost sauntering to his place at the long, curved desk on the dais.

Hasheem did not even look in Marrak's direction as he tapped the gavel and spoke. "Welcome, Director Mangele. As Deputy Minister Manwaeren should have informed you, the committee requested your presence to determine how your office was taken so unaware by the suddenness and the scope of the destruction created by the New Meritorists this past summer. I would also like to inform you that the nonconfidential portions of your testimony and that of your aides will be released to the newssheets." Hasheem smiled politely. "Let's make this simple. Why didn't your office see this coming?"

"Thank you for your directness," replied Mangele in a deep voice that carried a touch of irony. "The simple answer is that the New Meritorists provided no reason for the Intelligence Office to believe that they constituted a danger. They committed no crimes. In the past two years, prior to the very recent disturbances, they printed no manifestoes. They posted no posters and distributed no broadsheets. What would the committee have had the Intelligence

Office do? Our job is not to look into the private lives of people who have shown no intent of criminality or civil unrest."

"That's a very well-crafted response, Director Mangele," replied Hasheem. "I assume that the legalists of the Security Ministry have reviewed that statement?"

"Of course." Mangele smiled warmly.

"I think we would both agree that your statement represents how the Security Ministry *should* handle intelligence investigations. That still leaves several questions. Acting Minister Manwaeren testified that the broadsheets and posters of the New Meritorists publicly available two years ago clearly advocated the abolition of the Great Charter, by force, if necessary. Did you not see this as a potential threat to be investigated?"

"As I said before, there was no evidence of such a threat."

"Is that the usual practice of the Intelligence Office?" asked Hasheem pleasantly. "Not to investigate individuals or organizations unless there is some evidence of a threat?"

Dekkard noted Mangele's slight hesitation before replying.

"That is the usual practice, yes."

"Are there exceptions to that practice?"

"There may be, but I'm not aware of any."

Hasheem nodded, then asked, "Do you recall the judgment of the High Justiciary in the Guildmeister Andreas Bergstyn case?"

Mangele hesitated again. "I don't recall the details."

"In that case, over a period of three months, intelligence agents continually followed the guildmeister. Guildmeister Bergstyn gathered enough evidence and witnesses to bring the matter to the High Justiciary, which issued an order to the Security Ministry to provide evidence of any wrongdoing. Security failed to do so, and was enjoined to discontinue surveillance. You testified before the High Justiciary, and claimed privilege. The Justiciary viewed the documentation in camera and dismissed your claim. Are you sure that you don't remember?"

"That was an unusual case," said Mangele.

"What about the assault on Leistyr Abhram . . ."

Dekkard watched and listened over the next third of a bell as Hasheem cited eight more instances of Security "surveillance" efforts that had been found improper or illegal.

Then Hasheem said, "I have here another sixteen instances of improper and excessive surveillance practices by the Intelligence Office over the past five years. I see little point in citing the particulars of each. What I want to know, however, is exactly how you and your assistant directors could have decided in good conscience to undertake detailed surveillance of individuals for whom there was absolutely no evidence or even hint of wrongdoing, and yet, you could not justify further surveillance of a group that had openly declared its intent to change the government of Guldor by force."

Mangele did not answer.

"I'm waiting, Director. Why did you investigate these individuals and not the New Meritorists?"

Mangele remained silent.

Hasheem reached down, and a chime sounded. Dekkard assumed there was a hidden bellpull, but he'd never seen or heard of that.

The committee room doors opened, and three Council Guards appeared, followed by the Council lieutenant-at-arms.

For the first time, Mangele looked surprised.

"Since you have refused to answer a legitimate inquiry of the Council, you will be incarcerated in the Council gaol until such time as you are willing to answer truthfully and completely."

"You can't do this," Mangele protested.

"I can and will," said Hasheem. "That power is clearly invested in the Council. And don't tell me that you don't know or some other non-answer. Nor can you take refuge in non-incrimination. That provision does not apply to matters involved with official duties of government, as you well know."

Mangele paled, slumping slightly in his chair. The silence drew out.

To Dekkard, it seemed as though a sixth of a bell had passed, but it couldn't have been more than a minute.

Finally, Mangele cleared his throat. "In all of those instances you cited, I was ordered to carry out those investigations by the former Minister of Security, Lukkyn Wyath. I cannot speak to the instances you have not cited."

Dekkard looked to Erik Marrak, who was clearly stunned, as was Jaradd Rikkard. Pajiin seemed amused, Navione's face remained impassive, while Haastar actually looked bored.

"Were those orders relayed to you through Deputy Minister Manwaeren? Or did former Minister Wyath give them directly to you?"

Before Mangele spoke, Hasheem's eyes went to Isobel Irlende.

Mangele moistened his lips, then said, "To the best of my recollection, those orders were given to me directly."

Isobel Irlende nodded slightly.

"Thank you, Director. You will remain for a few minutes while I ask a few questions of your assistant directors." Hasheem looked to the man closest to Mangele. "Assistant Director Schoonover, in your capacity as the head of Criminal Intelligence, were you ever given orders to investigate someone for whom there was no hint or evidence of wrongdoing?"

"Not that I am aware, Sr. Chairman," replied Schoonover.

Irlende nodded slightly once more.

"What about you, Assistant Director Elberto, in your capacity as head of Foreign Intelligence?"

"Sr. Chairman, the office of Foreign Intelligence is charged with reporting on all activities of foreign corporacions and organizations that may impact on Guldor, either favorably or unfavorably. Any criminal activities we discern are referred to the Office of Criminal Intelligence. We have referred a few potential criminal instances, but there was definite evidence."

"Thank you." Hasheem nodded and looked to the third Security assistant director. "And you, Assistant Director Oostyr?"

"The Office of Civic Intelligence was tasked by Director Mangele to investigate the instances you cited. There were other cases as well where evidence of criminality was lacking."

Oostyr's voice was calm, but resigned.

"Thank you, Director and Assistant Directors. The material revealed in these hearings will be provided to the Minister of the Justiciary and to the Premier and, at his discretion, to the newssheets. You may go." Hasheem lifted the gavel and hit the wooden base twice. "Because of the legal limitations of the evidence provided, today's hearing is over."

Marrak turned to Hasheem. "No one else—"

"What else do you need to know, Erik?" asked Hasheem quietly. "There's been more than a little bending and breaking of the law, and we will be referring it to the Justiciary. Do you really want to say that it didn't happen?"

Marrak closed his mouth, then after several moments, said, "The proceeding was rather abrupt, and every councilor should have a chance to question the witnesses."

"If this had been a normal hearing, you'd be right. But when a hearing reveals criminal activity, the matter has to go to the Justiciary Ministry for possible prosecution. Any further questions might compromise their rights to an unbiased trial."

"They're going to be charged as criminals?" Marrak's voice was almost incredulous.

"That's up to the Minister of the Justiciary."

Dekkard doubted that either the assistant director for Criminal Intelligence or for Foreign Intelligence would be charged, but it was likely Mangele and Oostyr would be—possibly the acting minister as well.

"But they were just following orders."

"That excuses nothing," interjected Navione. "We're the government, not a corporacion."

Dekkard noticed that, during the brief conversation, Obreduur and Irlende had departed, as had the Security Ministry functionaries, along with Rikkard and Haastar. Pajiin remained, standing just off the dais.

Navione nodded to Hasheem. "Deftly done, Fredrich, without theatrics or histrionics."

"Thank you, Kharl."

Navione smiled briefly and then stepped away.

Hasheem moved closer to Dekkard. "Frieda Livigne resigned this morning. I understand you spoke with her yesterday, and that she was visibly disturbed after you left."

"I asked why Jaime Minz had ordered certain committee records turned over to the Security Ministry. She told me she presumed Minz was carrying out orders from Premier Ulrich."

"That was all?"

"I asked why the records weren't more extensive, and she said that was because staff was ordered not to take notes."

Hasheem just nodded, then said, "I'd hoped to keep one professional staffer for continuity purposes."

"I had no idea my questions—"

"You couldn't have known. Now, if you have anything the committee might consider, you could bring it up at the meeting tomorrow when we discuss the hearing results. Drafts for the committee members would be useful."

"I'll see what I can do, sir." Dekkard knew Hasheem didn't want him to mention specifics. He'd made that clear earlier.

"Good. Until tomorrow, Steffan."

"Until tomorrow."

Dekkard stood and then stepped off the dais onto the hearing room floor, then waited as he saw Pajiin moving toward him.

"Did you know what Hasheem was going to do?" asked the older councilor.

"I knew he wanted to find out how the New Meritorists got the dunnite. I had no idea that he had all those dossiers and citations." Dekkard had a good idea who was likely behind that documentation—most likely Carlos Baartol and Ingrella Obreduur. He began to walk slowly toward the door.

Pajiin laughed, quietly but harshly, as he kept pace. "Commercers don't know what tough is."

But will tough be enough to deal with both angry Commercers and rebellious New Meritorists? "They think they do, and more than a few corporacions aren't likely to be dissuaded by hearings." As he stepped through the door, Dekkard studied the corridor, but no one seemed interested in either him or Pajiin.

"Not until Hasheem and the Premier make sure that various corporacion presidentes are held personally accountable, one way or another."

"That will require some significant changes to corporacion law," Dekkard pointed out, stopping just outside the door, his eyes on the corridor, not the other councilor, whom he kept at a slight distance.

"Or using their tactics against them," suggested Pajiin.

"Fixing the legal frailties would be harder," admitted Dekkard, "but the social damage would be a lot less." *And so would the body count.*

"Good fortune with that," snorted Pajiin.

"We'll just have to see. I've seldom outthought the Premier, and I don't know any who've outmaneuvered him in the long run."

"We live in the short run, Steffan."

"Only because that's often the only option." Dekkard smiled. "I need to go. I'll see you in committee tomorrow—unless I run across you sooner."

"Until then," replied Pajiin cordially.

Dekkard walked toward the courtyard doorway, wondering how long it would be before the New Meritorists resumed their demonstrations, and how long it would take Bretta and Illana to type up the necessary copies of the proposed Security reform legislation, not that the final version to go to the full Council would look anything like Roostof's draft.

If it even gets that far.

Dekkard shook his head.

11

TRIDI morning, Dekkard was up and in the kitchen, and then the break-fast room, early, but not so early as Emrelda, who immediately handed him the newssheet.

"It's not bad," she said. "It just confirms what all the patrollers in the station already knew."

Dekkard nodded and began to read, picking out the key sections of the *Gestirn* front-page story.

> . . . in closed hearings yesterday morning, Security Ministry officials revealed two shocking facts. The first was that the Ministry ignored New Meritorist threats to overthrow the government for almost two years and was caught totally by surprise by last summer's demonstrations, destruction, and deaths. The second was that, while ignoring the New Meritorists, Security investigators trailed and watched Guild officials and several prominent Landors, despite the lack of evidence, and continued to do so until ordered to cease by the High Justiciary . . .
>
> . . . Premier Obreduur confirmed that the transcript of the hearings has been sent to the Minister of the Justiciary for evaluation and possible prosecution.

Dekkard finished the story and set the newssheet on the table next to where Avraal would sit. After pouring Avraal's café, he said to Emrelda, "You're right, but very few people know that except patrollers and some New Meritorists. People need to know, or they won't understand the need to reform Security."

"You think you can do that?" Emrelda's voice carried doubt.

"We won't know unless we try."

"Try what?" asked Avraal as she stepped into the breakfast room.

"To reform Security," replied Dekkard, gesturing to the newssheet.

Avraal took a quick look at the story. "The *Tribune* story will be different."

"I know," replied Dekkard. "Something about 'a few transgressions don't merit harsh punishment or changes in Security at a time when Guldor is threatened by radical extremists.'"

"You forgot the part about the financial stability provided by years of Commercer governments," added Avraal sarcastically before lifting her café mug and sipping from it.

"How will your patrollers take the story, do you think?" asked Dekkard.

"They'll wait and see. They'll hope things will get better, but they won't say anything until it's certain . . . if then. Right now, the captain's more worried about Southtown than about politics."

"What about Southtown?" Dekkard knew that the area to the southeast of

Erslaan was far less affluent than Hillside, and that parts of it were overcrowded, housing workers forced off the marginal agricultural lands east of Machtarn.

"It used to be just a place for poorer workers and their families, but it's gotten more crowded in the last year or so. Girls—not women—on the street, offering themselves for a few marks. Some of them just skin and bones. The Trinitarian outreach program helps some, but . . . there's never enough." Emrelda shook her head. "That's a problem you don't need. Have a good breakfast. I'm off."

As Emrelda headed for the portico door, Dekkard frowned. *Young girls on the streets? In Machtarn?*

He was still thinking about that when he sat down at the breakfast table and offered a croissant to Avraal.

"Just half, please."

Rather than leave half a croissant, which would get stale, Dekkard cut one in half, and gave half to his wife. Then he split the remaining half croissant and another one and sandwiched the quince paste into the middle of each.

Just about the moment he finished, Avraal asked, "Have you had any decent applicants for your engineering staff position?"

"Roostof said we have almost a dozen, but he's not impressed with most. I'll look over the applications after the Security Committee meeting. I'm not looking forward to presenting that proposed legislation."

"It won't be as bad as you think," she said quietly.

"No, it will likely be worse. Marrak will be outraged, and so will Rikkard. Navione will likely think no proposal will pass the Council. Haastar won't understand it or the need for it, and Pajiin will think that, if it goes before the Council, it's likely a warrant for my death."

"He hasn't said that, has he?"

"No, but it's clear that's the way he thinks."

"Is he right?"

"Partly. If I were a more senior councilor, it would be worse. I'm so junior that most Commercers will think, if the legislation is enacted, that I'm a front for Craft leadership. That's also why Obreduur and Hasheem, in particular, don't want to see or talk about my draft before I present it. That way, they can truthfully say that I developed it on my own, and that they're just trying to make it more reasonable, while pointing out that something has to be done to keep the New Meritorists from gaining more support from working people and blowing up more buildings and targeting more councilors.

"Whatever I present will be amended, and some amendments will likely be by Commercers." Dekkard shrugged. "That's the only possible way to legislate change. Even that may not be possible." He took a bite of the whole croissant, and then another, followed by some café.

"That's sad."

"That's politics . . . as we both know."

The two finished breakfast, dealt with the few dishes, and in less than a sixth were on their way to drop Avraal off. As he turned south on Jacquez,

Dekkard glanced toward the magnificent old oak tree that stood slightly back from the southeast corner of the intersection, a tree tall enough that he could even see it from the rear yard of Emrelda's house.

He couldn't help but be concerned as they neared Imperial University, given the number of demonstrations staged there over the summer, but he saw no sign of difficulties, nor were there any posters or flags flying from the parapets below the massive clock face on the tower that dominated the campus.

Little more than a third of a bell later, he walked into his office, where Margrit offered a cheerful, "Good morning, Councilor."

"Good morning to you," replied Dekkard. "Is there anything new?"

"No, sir. There weren't any messages, and there's not that much mail."

"Good." Dekkard walked to the staff office doorway. "Good morning, everyone. Svard? If you'd join me . . . with all the copies of the draft legislation?"

"Yes, sir."

Once the two were settled in the inner office, Dekkard read through the draft to make sure that what he had before him was what he recalled.

When he looked up, Roostof handed him a single sheet. "Sir, this has the points we talked about and answers to questions that I thought might come up."

Dekkard studied that sheet for several minutes. "There's one question we haven't discussed. What if Marrak or Rikkard says that more time is needed for implementation?"

"You could say that Security had two years to deal with the New Meritorists and wasted that time, or you could point out that the bill basically shifts units to other ministries with no internal reorganization required. In addition, the Army is definitely better suited to handle the STF, and that shouldn't be delayed."

"Not considering how badly the STF handled the demonstrations," agreed Dekkard.

After more than a third of a bell discussing the proposed legislation, Dekkard let Roostof go. Then he quickly read through the mail before putting it in Roostof's inbox on his way out of the office. Inside the gray leather folder he carried were the copies of the draft law and his notes.

Pajiin was waiting outside the Security Committee room. "Good morning. Do you know what Hasheem intends to do this morning? Besides continuing to set himself up for an untimely death?"

"I have no idea, Tomas. I'd guess that he'll either tell us the future agenda for the committee or possibly spend some time mollifying Marrak, Rikkard, and Navione."

"Nothing will mollify Marrak. He has to be from wealth. He couldn't be that arrogant at his age, otherwise."

Dekkard managed not to smile at Pajiin's calling Marrak arrogant. Instead, he said, "His family holds controlling interests in Eastern Ironway and Marrak Manufacturing."

"How do you know all that?" asked Pajiin.

"Many people think of security aides as part of the décor," replied Dekkard dryly. "You can learn a lot if you listen." That was true, but not how Dekkard had learned about Marrak's background. "We'd better go in. I'd rather not saunter in late the way someone else did."

"Go ahead," said Pajiin. "I'll be there in a moment."

Dekkard nodded, although he suspected Pajiin simply didn't want to walk in with him.

When he entered the chamber, he saw Hasheem, along with Navione and Haastar. As Dekkard stepped up onto the dais, he nodded to the others.

Hasheem looked to Dekkard. "You have something you want to bring up?"

"When it's appropriate."

"After we discuss the hearings."

Haastar walked behind Hasheem and Navione toward Dekkard, offering a surprisingly shy smile. "We haven't really talked. I wanted to say I appreciated your questions the other day."

"Thank you. It's a bit different being the one asking the questions, rather than the one drafting them."

"It doesn't show, but you'll get used to it." Haastar paused. "I got a letter the other day. Emilio Raathan said to convey his best."

For a moment, Dekkard was stunned. Emilio Raathan—the Landor who'd held his seat and had to step down? He'd only met Raathan once, when the former councilor had invited the Obreduurs, Avraal, and Dekkard to his enormous estate for "refreshments." "That was very thoughtful of him. How is he?"

"He wrote that he's enjoying not being a councilor. Patriana is enjoying it even more."

Dekkard couldn't help but smile. "She was rather definite about that."

"He also said," continued Haastar in an amused tone, "that if there had to be a Crafter councilor from Gaarlak, he couldn't think of anyone better."

"That was kind of him."

Haastar chuckled. "He's quiet, but he's never kind just to be polite. I have the feeling that you're much the same." He looked toward Hasheem, who was taking his place. "The chairman looks about ready to begin."

"Thank you, again."

"You're most welcome." Haastar moved easily back toward his place.

Pajiin arrived just after Dekkard exchanged words with Haastar, while Marrak and Rikkard, both stone-faced, silently took their places.

Hasheem gaveled the committee to order and announced, "The first order of business is a discussion of the testimony before the committee on the past two days. Once that is concluded, I will entertain other motions or matters from committee members." He paused, then said, "That testimony has revealed serious concerns about the effectiveness of the Security Ministry as well as a notable lack of concern for ethics and legality." He turned to Marrak. "You seemed rather perturbed that I unilaterally referred the matter to the Justiciary."

"There should have been a vote on such a referral." Marrak's words were clipped, as if he was having trouble being civil.

"Do you think the committee shouldn't have referred such breaches of legality to the Justiciary?" asked Hasheem, his voice mild.

"That isn't the question," declared Marrak.

"I'm glad you agree that Security should be bound by the law." Hasheem paused, then asked, "You do believe that, don't you?"

"Of course, but as a matter of procedure—"

"As a matter of procedure, votes are only required for legislative matters," Hasheem interjected. "Since there were no legislative matters involved, no vote was required. Also, I might note that I followed the precedent set by the previous chairs of this committee, all of whom were Commercer councilors." Hasheem smiled politely. "In the future, out of courtesy, and a respect for demonstrated agreement, I will endeavor to remember to ask for a vote on matters not necessarily requiring a vote."

Dekkard saw that Pajiin was having difficulty concealing what looked to be a smirk.

"Outside of procedure, Councilor," continued Hasheem, "do you have any other thoughts on what you heard over the past two days?"

"It seems that we're giving in to the rabble," countered Marrak. "They blew up buildings and blocked water lines and sewer pipes. They shot councilors of the Sixty-Six and regional councilors. Yet we're concerned that Security bent a few rules in trying to protect the public."

"Shooting lumbermen who refused to load an unsafe ironway log hauler wasn't just bending the rules, Councilor," said Pajiin coldly. "That never came before the Council, I'd wager."

"People need to do their jobs," returned Marrak.

"People have the right to refuse when equipment kills them. Two men died, and Eastern Ironway called in Special Agents. They shot ten men. Three died. One will never walk again." Pajiin held up his right hand. "I was fortunate. Unsafe loading equipment cost me those fingers. Used to be that the ironways listened. Back then, they fixed the log haulers. Last year, they didn't. They called in Special Agents instead. Security has no business using firearms to break up groups protesting unsafe work practices."

"There were demonstrations everywhere," added Rikkard. "Security had to do something."

"They didn't have to shoot unarmed women who were fleeing," said Navione, "especially not in the back."

Hasheem used the gavel twice. "We clearly have a problem, and it has several sides. All sides need to be addressed. That is one of the mandates the Premier has laid upon the committee. Dealing with the obvious illegalities of Security is only the first step. There will be others."

After that, the "discussion" was less heated. In fact, most of the words were cool—if not cold—with Marrak and Rikkard insisting that most of the fault was the result of workers who wanted to be paid more than they were worth and whom the New Meritorists were inciting and exploiting. Navione stated that only Commercers seemed to use Security agents against people who had grievances, at which point Marrak declared that Landors' use of steam machines had resulted in a glut of poor landless people flooding the cities.

Dekkard just listened.

After a time, Hasheem gaveled the "discussion" to a halt. "I think each of you has made his points clear. The committee will deal with those issues at the appropriate time." He looked to Dekkard. "Councilor Dekkard, you indicated that you had a matter to bring before the committee."

"Yes, Sr. Chairman, I do." Dekkard stood and handed a draft to Rikkard, then passed one out to each of the other committee members. When he finished, he returned to his seat. "Over the past several months, we have seen illegality and a lack of competence in the Security Ministry. The STF has murdered hundreds of unarmed protestors and then tried to plant weapons on the bodies to justify those murders. At the same time, Security failed to protect the water and sewage systems serving the Council and the Palace. Nor could it even protect its own buildings. Those are far from all the problems that have surfaced.

"In order to address these problems, my staff and I have drafted legislation to reform the Security Ministry. The main thrust of the proposed legislation is to return Security to its primary purpose of maintaining civil law and order. To do this will require the transfer of the Special Tactical Force to the control of the Imperial Army, because the STF has clearly become a military unit more concerned with using force than keeping order. As such, the Army possesses the ability, traditions, and discipline to assure that the STF is properly focused and directed.

"Likewise, the continued abuses of armed Security Special Agents have demonstrated the problems created by investigators with unlimited access to firearms. For this reason, the intelligence functions of security would be moved and split. Civic investigations would be handled by agents not empowered to carry firearms as part of the Justiciary, as would criminal investigations. Investigations of foreign criminality, including tariff fraud and foreign commercial crime, would be handled by the Treasury Ministry, in coordination, if necessary, with the Justiciary Ministry . . ."

Over the next few minutes Dekkard added explanations, then nodded to Hasheem. "I'd be happy to answer questions, or let you all read the draft and discuss the matter later."

"Such a proposal is a total overreach," declared Marrak, even before Hasheem could reply.

"Councilor Marrak," stated Hasheem firmly, "I think the hearings have demonstrated that some restructuring and reform of Security is necessary. That is not the question. The question is how much of each is necessary. Councilor Dekkard has provided a draft proposal. As we all know, drafts are just that. They are a starting place. Since the councilor has put in what appears to be considerable thought and work, and since he has, I daresay, much more experience in this field than anyone else on the committee, his draft is as good as any from which we can work to create a piece of legislation that will address the difficulties facing Security. I don't see much point in discussing this draft until we all have had a chance to study it and come up with questions, suggested changes, or even differing approaches. Does anyone have any disagreement with that approach?" Hasheem looked from councilor to councilor.

The only one who disagreed was Marrak. "Why can't we start with the law and make modest changes to that?"

"Would you care to address that?" Hasheem looked to Dekkard.

"In fact, that was exactly where we did start," replied Dekkard. "The problem is that the legislation establishing—reestablishing, really—the Ministry of Security was written almost fifty years ago, and there is no actual authorization for Special Agents or the STF. There was an amendment to the basic law made twenty-two years ago which empowered the Minister of Security to authorize the use of firearms by Security personnel 'as necessary,' but there are no guidelines and no requirement for such. I could go through the draft and show you, point by point, why each provision addresses specific problems, but we'd be here a very long time, and until you read the draft, my explanations would have no context."

"That should address your question, Councilor Marrak," said Hasheem. "If you have an alternative proposal, and care to put it in ink, the committee will certainly consider it. Given your concerns, and the need for each committee member to read the draft and come up with any other proposals, the committee will not meet on the issue of legislation reforming the Ministry of Security until next Tridi." Hasheem paused. "Are there any other questions?" After another pause, he finished, "There being none, this meeting of the committee is concluded."

Dekkard was gathering his papers and his two remaining copies of the proposed legislation when Erik Marrak approached. "Yes?"

"Who really drafted this?"

"My two legalists and I did," replied Dekkard. "No one else has seen it."

Navione appeared at Marrak's shoulder. "From what I read, it's technically well drafted."

"Both my legalists are very experienced," Dekkard said blandly.

"*You* drafted this?" asked Marrak.

"I drafted the provisions. They turned it into the proper language and made suggestions to improve it."

Marrak shook his head, then turned away, stepping off the dais and heading for the door.

"You know the Commercers will fight you on all the major provisions," said Navione.

"I had not thought otherwise," replied Dekkard.

"I've heard that you and your wife are a very effective security team. For your sake, I hope so."

"It's only a draft," Dekkard pointed out.

"Some people would rather kill the infant boar than deal with the full-grown animal." Navione glanced in the direction of the departing Marrak.

"Thank you. I'll keep that in mind."

Navione smiled and said, "Take care, Steffan." Then he headed toward the door.

Why would he tell me that right now? Is Marrak really that ruthless?

Dekkard doubted that the councilor would dirty his own hands, but he likely knew people who would. *But over a preliminary legislative draft?*

He was even more careful on his way back to the Council Office Building, still pondering Navione's words when he reached his office.

He stopped in the open doorway to the side office. "Svard . . . would you and Luara come into the office? Bring the applications we have so far." Then he walked into his office and sat down.

Colsbaan entered first, followed by Roostof, who closed the door. Both sat slightly forward in their chairs.

"First, I'd like to thank you both for all the work on the Security draft. Chairman Hasheem has scheduled a hearing on it next Tridi." Dekkard went on to brief them, in general terms, on what had happened. He did not mention Navione's warning.

"How much of it will remain after the committee gets through with it?" asked Colsbaan. "Do you have any feel for that?"

"Not really. As I told you, Hasheem said it was a good place to start. That could mean anything. If they had any sense, at the least, they'd agree to moving the STF to the Army and disarming Security agents, but the Commercers don't want to give up the influence they have with the Security agents."

"I know it exists," said Colsbaan, "but how does it work in practice?"

Roostof managed to conceal, mostly, a startled expression.

Dekkard nodded to the senior legalist.

"All the large corporacions have security departments," Roostof began. "They can pay more than average patroller and Security agent wages. So the patrollers and agents who want marks get recruited by the corporacions. Those recruits stay in touch with their former comrades. Sometimes, they ask for 'favors.' Those who give the favors are more likely to be hired when they have more experience."

"And some stray beyond favors," added Dekkard, thinking of his own encounters. "They're essentially freelance operatives and sometimes killers who get hired when a corporacion wants someone erased without corporacion fingerprints."

"I thought it was something like that," replied Colsbaan, "but it's better to make sure."

"Spoken like a true legalist," said Roostof dryly.

"Now," said Dekkard, "let's go over the applications. I'd like your comments."

By the first afternoon bell, Dekkard, Roostof, and Colsbaan had agreed on the best applications, although Dekkard suspected that they might rank them differently.

"Svard . . . I'd appreciate it if you'd set up the interviews first thing on Duadi morning."

"Yes, sir."

Once the two left, Dekkard took out the calendar for the Workplace Administration Committee, but the next hearing wasn't until Unadi afternoon.

12

W HEN Dekkard picked up Avraal outside Carlos Baartol's building, she slipped into the front seat, and he pulled out onto the Avenue of the Guilds.

"How did your day go?" asked Avraal.

Dekkard quickly related what had happened at the committee meeting, and what Navione had said.

"Frig! Turn around. We need to talk to Carlos. This isn't something we should even try to handle by ourselves, you especially."

"What do we need to handle?" asked Dekkard.

"Emrelda sent me a message. Something came up at the station. But the wording was strange. She said she'd have to work until around midnight, and to take care, but not to spoil anything by going to bed too early. She'd never say it that way. It's a warning."

"You think Marrak went to Security? The Special Agents? Even after the hearings?"

"Who else? I'd guess he told them that your proposal will remove their power and guns unless you're stopped."

"Frig!" Dekkard could see the rest all too clearly. Even if he and Avraal were successful in dealing with renegade Special Agents, it would come out that he'd proposed cutting their powers . . . and if any of the Specials were hurt—or killed—he'd face a hearing in front of the Council . . . if not worse. Under any circumstances, his acting directly against Special Agents would at the least make reform more difficult, if not impossible. "I see what you mean."

He decided against making a U-turn and pulled into the next parking area, where he turned the steamer and headed back to Carlos's office. "Can Carlos and his people handle it?"

"The security business is how he started. It's only a small part of what he does now, but it's an important part."

That made Dekkard feel a little better. Not much, but some.

He parked the Gresynt in the first open space he saw in the parking area, and the two walked into the building, tastefully floored in polished gray stone, with light teal plaster below the chair rail, and pale cream above.

Avraal led the way up the wide gray stone staircase, with its polished brass bannister, and into the second-floor anteroom, nodding to the woman seated at the desk. "This is important. Oh, Elicya, this is my husband."

"I'm pleased to meet you, sir."

"And I you."

Avraal knocked on the half-open door.

The dark-haired and pleasant-faced Baartol looked up from the papers on his desk. "Avraal . . . I thought you'd gone."

"So did I. We may have a serious problem."

The two walked in and Dekkard closed the door, while Avraal began to explain. Then Dekkard added what had happened at the Security Committee.

When he finished Carlos said to Avraal, "You and your sister know each other well, I take it. So, if something's wrong in Security, why did they let her send a message?"

"The regular patrollers, even the officers, think highly of her. Also, they might have been trying to allow her to alert us. They don't think much of Special Agents, and they despise the STF. But anytime a patroller goes against a Security agent, at least directly, bad things happen."

"Interesting. I'd guess that they're planning some sort of unfortunate domestic . . . incident . . . possibly a gas leak, but most likely a fire, because fires destroy most, if not all, of the evidence. It's happened more than once. Does your sister have a coal-gas cooler?"

"Yes . . . a fairly new one. It's in the pantry off the kitchen."

"That makes it easier for them. Fiddling with gas stoves is more obvious and more easily detected, even in a fire." Carlos rummaged in his desk and took out a single sheet of paper and looked to Avraal. "You both need to sign this. It's a standard home security contract. You took it out a few days after you were hired. The very nominal fee will be deducted monthly from your pay."

Both signed.

"And I'll need a door key."

Dekkard took out his key ring and slipped his key off. "That's to the east portico entrance."

"Excellent. I'm going to have to hurry on this," said Carlos. "I'm very glad you didn't try to handle it yourself. It would have been messy. It still will be, but, if it goes right, I can solve several problems at once." He smiled coolly. "You two go over to Obreduur's house. Tell him I sent you. Stay until I get there. You need to be somewhere where lots of people can vouch for you, both important people and staff. That might not be necessary, but we try to plan for all the likely possibilities."

Neither Dekkard nor Avraal said anything until they were in the steamer.

Little more than a sixth of a bell passed until Dekkard arrived at the Obreduurs'. Since the gates to the drive were open, he drove to the portico and parked there.

Axel Obreduur opened the side door just before Dekkard and Avraal reached it.

"What did you do now, Steffan?" asked the Premier in a tone that was mostly humorous.

Dekkard told him, including Carlos's instructions.

"You might as well have dinner with us. There will be plenty. There always is. Hyelda makes sure of that. I'll tell Ingrella what happened later. I'd rather not have Nellara worrying. She's quite fond of you. I'm quite certain that Carlos can take care of the matter."

"Do you have any idea how?" asked Dekkard.

"No. We seldom discuss inner details of complex matters. It works better that way. Now, it's a little early for dinner. Why don't you join Ingrella in the sitting room. I'll join you shortly."

"Thank you."

Ingrella did not rise from her armchair but set aside the thin volume she was reading, gestured for the two to sit down, and then said, "I would judge that you two are facing a difficulty."

"We are," said Avraal. "Axel said he'd tell you later."

"It's a serious difficulty, then. I suppose that's not unexpected. The Commercers are having a hard time adjusting to a position of less power."

At that moment, Nellara came down the steps. "I thought I heard your voices. What are you doing here?"

"We stopped to get some advice," said Dekkard.

"Could you please help me, Steffan? We really didn't have time to work much on that underhanded cast. I can get the knife to the target, but it doesn't hit with much force."

Ingrella raised her eyebrows.

"Please? It won't take that long."

"If you're willing," said Ingrella, looking to Dekkard.

"I'd be happy to."

"Avraal and I haven't talked in some time," said Ingrella, "but no more than a sixth."

"Then let's go out and see what we can do," said Dekkard to Nellara, who smiled happily.

When they entered the garage, Dekkard noticed that the target was already set up. *Except it's more likely that she and Gustoff never take it down.* "Show me what you're doing."

Nellara picked up one of the knives that Avraal had brought back from the Obreduurs' house in Malek. She made the underhand cast. The knife wobbled but stuck.

"Let's see your grip."

Nellara picked up a second knife, then showed Dekkard.

"You need to have the end of the hilt in your palm, like this." Dekkard adjusted her grip. "Now try it."

The knife bounced off the target.

"That didn't work." Nellara's voice was doleful.

"Your grip is fine, but you're swinging your arm. You need more of a snapping release." Dekkard recovered the two knives. "Watch how I release it."

Dekkard's knife was slightly off-center. *You could use more practice.* "Now you try it."

Nellara's knife bounced again.

"You almost had it that time. Just a little more snap at the end . . . like when you want to silence Gustoff."

The next knife stuck firmly, if at the edge of the target.

Dekkard smiled. "That's a start."

Close to a third of a bell had passed when Dekkard led the way back to the sitting room.

Both Obreduurs were with Avraal.

"I did it!" exclaimed Nellara. "Steffan helped me so I could get the knives to really stick."

"She'll need to practice more for accuracy," said Dekkard.

"But at the end they all hit the target and stuck."

"That's often not good enough if you're threatened," Dekkard said mildly. "That's why you need to work on accuracy. You might get only one chance."

"That's true of more than a few things," commented Obreduur.

"You often get more than one chance in law, but it gets costlier and costlier," said Ingrella.

"There's a definite similarity between law and politics," replied Obreduur. "The more personal you make anything, the more expensive it becomes. Remember that, Steffan."

Dekkard grinned. "I'll certainly try."

Hyelda appeared in the archway to the dining room. "Dinner is ready." Then she turned to Dekkard and Avraal. "Welcome back, Councilor, Ritten." Her voice was genuinely warm.

"Steffan, please, except when I have to be very formal, and this isn't one of those times."

"The Ritter . . . he always said you two were going places."

"I also said I didn't know where," replied Obreduur. "I never would have guessed he'd be a councilor so young. Later, I thought."

Ingrella led the way into the dining room, and several moments later, Gustoff hurried in after the others. His mouth opened, then closed.

"Yes, Gustoff," said Ingrella, "we have dinner guests."

"I'm sorry. I didn't know."

"It was unplanned," said Obreduur. "They stopped by, and we invited them to stay for dinner."

The dinner consisted of small veal cutlets sautéed in butter and wine, with mushrooms, brown rice, and green beans. There were more than enough of the lime tarts laid out for dessert.

Ingrella and her husband steered the conversation into a variety of topics, except law and politics.

After the leisurely dinner, Nellara and Gustoff were excused.

Nellara abruptly turned in the archway. "Steffan, thank you so much." Then she was gone.

For the next two bells, the four gathered back in the sitting room, where, with some prompting by Dekkard, Ingrella discussed some of her more influential cases, including the one where she had met her husband.

Dekkard tried not to fidget, but he found his eyes going to the front hall.

"Looking to the door," said Obreduur, "isn't going to bring Carlos here any faster. Some things take time."

"If they're to be done right," added Ingrella.

More than another bell passed before the front door chimes rang.

Obreduur answered the chimes and led Carlos Baartol back to the sitting room.

"Everything's settled," declared Carlos. "They planned a fire, but the false repairman apparently didn't understand the pressure requirements for the gas line, and he asphyxiated himself. That happened to one of the Security Special Agents as well."

"He was an isolate?" asked Avraal.

Carlos nodded. "The other two agents were a little confused, but the regular station patrollers—especially your sister—were happy to take their confessions. Of course, the Special Agent subcaptain had no idea who issued the orders. He just gets them by typewritten message and then destroys them. They've done that for years. It makes finding who's behind anything difficult. The other patrollers really didn't like the idea of Special Agents trying to burn down your sister's house." Carlos offered an open smile. "It did take a while to air everything out. The sussie boy next door was fascinated by it all. His parents weren't. Not so late at night."

"Now what?" asked Dekkard.

"The house is fine, including the coal-gas cooler. There might be a few things disarranged because the local patrollers were very thorough. Everything else should be fine by tomorrow," said Carlos. "There are a few loose ends we need to address."

Dekkard had a feeling that he might know what one of those was, but that was definitely a question left unasked.

Avraal grinned. "I'm very glad we took out that security contract on the house."

"So am I," replied Carlos. "A pleasant good night to you all."

Once Carlos left, Dekkard turned to the Obreduurs. "Thank you for hosting us at a difficult time, and more important, for putting Avraal in touch with Carlos."

"With your tendency to stir things up, I thought Carlos could be useful."

"All I want to do is reform Security."

Obreduur smiled ironically. "All? If your proposal follows what you mentioned to me a while back it would destroy an enormous amount of the Commercers' hidden and illegal power. You don't think they'll do anything they can to stop it?" The Premier paused. "I just thought that they'd stay closer to the law. But we all learn."

Dekkard stiffened inside at Obreduur's casual brushing off of attempted murder, yet, at the same time, he had the feeling that Obreduur had left something unsaid.

"Be careful on your drive home," said Ingrella.

"We will," said Avraal.

"And I'll dig out that book I mentioned for the next time I see you. Both of you might enjoy it," added Ingrella.

Once they were outside, Dekkard shook his head. He'd known that trying to reform government would be difficult. *But not potentially fatal. And not over a mere draft.*

Dekkard concentrated on driving, because a light mist cut down how far he could see with the acetylene headlamps. He could almost feel Avraal tense up as he turned off Jacquez onto Florinda.

"It does surprise me that Special Agents would do that in uniform," said Avraal.

"It's a combination of practicality and arrogance. Who in Guldor would question a Security agent? They've gotten away with it for years. Look what happened to Markell. I'd wager they were in uniform."

When Dekkard drove up the drive to the house, he saw that all the lights were on.

"The only one I can sense is Emrelda," said Avraal.

So Dekkard garaged the Gresynt, and he and Avraal walked to the portico.

Emrelda was waiting at the portico door. "Are you two all right? What happened? I didn't know you'd hired a private security firm."

"It was a last-minute necessity," said Avraal, following Emrelda inside. Dekkard turned off the portico light, closed the door, and followed them inside to the kitchen. He could smell the barest hint of coal gas.

"Tell me everything," Emrelda demanded.

Alternatingly, Dekkard and Avraal did, and then Avraal said to Emrelda, "Now it's your turn."

"I worried about the sudden schedule change, especially when three Security Special Agents and a Special Agent subcaptain showed up. The captain was the one who suggested that I write the note so you wouldn't be worried. He didn't tell me what to write, but you two obviously got the message. The Special Agents all disappeared when it got dark, but the subcaptain stayed at the station. My captain was definitely surprised when one of your security people arrived at the station to report a failed attempt at either burglary or destruction. He strongly suggested the Special Agent subcaptain accompany him and the patrollers investigating the house. The Special Agent subcaptain wasn't thrilled about that.

"The two Special Agents who survived happily turned in the subcaptain. He insisted that they were merely on a protective detail. Augusta shredded him on that," said Emrelda. "Protective detail for a saboteur?"

"Augusta?" asked Avraal.

"The station empath. I suspect she had a little help from your security team's empath. Oh, and when I told Captain Narryt you were on the Council Security Committee, he smiled and said he'd have a copy of the crime report for you. Apparently, you have the clearances to see those."

Or at least he can assume that I do. Or he just really wanted to get a copy into Dekkard's hands.

Emrelda shook her head. "How did we all get here?"

"By trying to do things right," suggested Dekkard.

13

E MRELDA was still seated at the breakfast room table when Dekkard got there on Furdi morning, wearing her uniform trousers and shirt, but not the uniform blouse.

"I didn't expect you to still be here," he said.

"Because I worked so late, the captain said he wouldn't need me until between fourth and fifth bell. He likely wants me out of the way for a while."

"So that you wouldn't be considered part of the effort to embarrass Special Agents?"

"Partly. He's documented one or two other cases, but I don't think he ever sent them anywhere. I got the feeling that he doesn't want me to know what he's doing in his effort to show how corrupt the Special Agents are."

"Everyone knows they're corrupt," said Avraal, both bitterly and with a yawn as she trudged to the table in a robe and sat down.

"No," replied Emrelda. "Poor people do. Small businesses like Engaard Engineering do."

Dekkard managed not to wince at the mention of Engaard, the company Special Agents and corporacion freelancers had destroyed by disappearing and likely killing Emrelda's husband and then killing the head of the company. "Students do, and so do most artisans. And, of course, the New Meritorists. Commercers and even some Landors remain willfully blind to it. There's an old idea that the truth can set you free." Dekkard shook his head. "Not so long as people's truths are rooted more in what they want to believe than the verified facts before them."

"I suspect the captain is going to send a copy to every patroller captain warning them that this was an example of renegade Special Agents and that they need to be aware of such possibilities."

"That just minimizes the fact that most of them are doing it," protested Avraal.

"The captains all know it," replied Emrelda. "They just haven't been able to do much. This might give some of the braver ones a few ideas. Also, I doubt that Obreduur will muzzle the newssheets, at least not as much as the Commercers have."

Dekkard sipped his café. He definitely had the feeling that he might be sitting on a powder keg. He was also irritated for another, much more personal reason.

"Why the sour look?" asked Emrelda.

"We haven't been married even two weeks, and everyone's messing with our sleep."

"Sleep?" asked Emrelda playfully.

Dekkard offered a mock grimace.

Avraal smiled cynically. "The Commercers don't care."

"They will."

The two sisters exchanged looks.

"And how do you like being the leader of the Craft Party Reform movement?" asked Emrelda.

"It could get a little uncomfortable."

"Could?" asked Emrelda, not quite acidly.

Then both sisters laughed.

"I didn't plan on being quite so exposed. I'm not a party leader like Obreduur. I'm not a committee chair like Aashtaan or Maendaan. I'm just a junior councilor. The most junior of all. I thought that everyone would attack the proposed bill, that they'd offer delays, legal questions, and amendments, and that we'd have to fight to get just some of the provisions."

"That's exactly what will happen. If we can keep you alive for the next few weeks," replied Avraal. "You need a full-time Council-paid empath with a longer range—besides me."

Emrelda nodded.

"Do you have any ideas?" asked Dekkard dryly. "They're not exactly common as rain."

"No one is even going to try to get close to you. You need an emotional-pattern sensor. They can pick out patterns from a greater distance, but only in general areas. That would work fine in the Council grounds and buildings, which are limited. Most of the time, pattern sensors make terrible security aides, but someone like that might be just what we need for a while. I'll write a message to Carlos and have Emrelda send it."

At Dekkard's surprised look, she added, "After last night, do you think I'm letting you out of my sight? Or that Carlos would let me?"

Before they left the house, both wearing their knives under their jackets, Avraal wrote a message to Carlos Baartol and gave it to Emrelda.

"I'll send it out of Erslaan before I get to the station."

Out of well-deserved caution, Dekkard took a roundabout route to the Council buildings and to the covered parking. He and Avraal didn't sprint, but they moved swiftly across the drive and into the office building.

"So far, no one's even noticed we're here," said Avraal as they took the narrower and more secure staff staircase—more secure against an attack from a distance at least.

When Dekkard and Avraal reached the office, Margrit immediately handed him a message. "It's from Chairman Hasheem."

Dekkard took the envelope, wondering what was in the message.

The text was short.

There will be an urgent but brief Security Committee meeting at fourth bell this morning.

Dekkard looked at the words again. They didn't change. He handed the message back and said quietly to Margrit, "Have everyone join us in my office. That includes you, and the door needs to be shut."

"Yes, sir."

As he and Avraal entered the office, he shook his head.

"What?" asked Avraal.

"It's just . . . I'll tell you later." He remained standing, since there weren't enough seats for everyone.

"Sir?" said Svard as he entered.

"You'll hear soon enough. No one's done anything wrong." *Except possibly me.*

Once everyone was in the office, Dekkard smiled wryly. "As most of you know, I wanted to make a change in the way Guldor is governed, particularly to rein in Security, especially the Special Agents and the STF. I presented the proposal to the committee yesterday morning. Chairman Hasheem said it was a starting point. One other councilor warned me to be careful. Apparently, he was right. Security and some Commercers didn't want me starting anything like that . . ." Dekkard very briefly described what had happened the night before, and the results. Then, he said, "I seriously doubt that this will have any impact on any of you. Past Security abuses have targeted councilors or their security aides. But I wanted all of you to be aware of it. I would prefer that you not be the ones to spread this information. Do any of you have any questions?"

"They tried to kill you both just because you're trying to reform Security?" blurted Illana.

"What world have you been living in?" asked Bretta, the clerk-typist Dekkard had hired on the recommendation of Gloriana Saffel. "Reform's the last thing they want."

Luara Colsbaan nodded at that.

"I just thought you all should know. That's why you'll be seeing a great deal more of Ritten Dekkard, at least until this sorts out." *Which could be months—if not years.* "Thank you."

Once the staff left the inner office, Avraal asked, "What were you going to tell me later?"

"Until yesterday, I hadn't realized—really realized—one aspect of being a councilor, and it's an aspect I don't much like."

"Don't make me guess."

"It means that I'm going to have to depend on others much more, just as we had to depend on Carlos. As security staffers, we could do what was necessary, within the law, and we didn't have to worry that much about other repercussions. If we, especially me, had handled last night, however it turned out, even if everything we did was legal, it could have crippled, if not destroyed, the chance for Security reform."

"Isn't that politics?"

"It is," Dekkard admitted. "But it feels different when you come up against it personally and directly."

"It's better you're seeing that now." Avraal smiled wryly. "You might as well go through the mail and notices before the committee meeting. I'll be right outside with Margrit."

The only notice in the pile of mail and petitions was notification of an afternoon meeting of the Workplace Administration Committee the following Duadi. He finished reading the mail well before he and Avraal had to leave. They stepped out early and used the staff staircase.

It was a good sixth before the bell when Dekkard entered the committee room. Both Haastar and Pajiin were there.

Pajiin immediately moved to Dekkard's side of the dais, where he said laconically, "No Commercers."

"Did you expect them to be early?"

"Might be best that way. Marrak didn't like your draft. Not at all."

"You talked to him after the committee meeting?" asked Dekkard.

"No. He and Rikkard had lunch together afterwards." Pajiin laughed. "Didn't even have to strain to hear what he was saying."

"What was that, if I might ask?" Dekkard smiled winningly and added, "Besides imprecations at me and my lack of a noted ancestry and wealth?"

"Not that much about you. More about how stupid Crafters didn't understand that workers didn't make Guldor great. Marks invested in new and better equipment mattered. Workers were just another tool. Also said the New Meritorists were book-smart idiots."

"From what I've seen, he's right on that." Dekkard broke off as Hasheem and Navione moved to the dais. "Later."

At the last moment, Rikkard walked to the dais, but mounted on Pajiin's side and took the long way to his place between Navione and Dekkard while avoiding any eye contact.

At precisely fourth bell, Hasheem gaveled the committee into order. "This meeting will be brief. As at least one of you knows . . ."

As Hasheem spoke, Dekkard thought he saw the chairman offer a quick glance toward Rikkard.

". . . but most do not, roughly two bells ago, an armored Security steamer, driven by what appeared to be a Security Special Agent, rammed the side of a steamer carrying Councilor Erik Marrak. He died instantly. So did his driver and security aide. The driver of the armored steamer has not been located. I do not have any more information. When more is known, you will be informed by the Office of the Premier. That is all." Hasheem gaveled twice.

Dekkard just sat there—stunned. Carlos had mentioned loose ends, but handling a loose end that quickly and brutally—that was a shock. Dekkard remained at his place, unmoving, for what felt like several minutes. When he rose, only Hasheem remained in the committee room.

Dekkard walked slowly out of the chamber to where Avraal waited.

Hasheem and his isolate security aide, Erleen Orlov, moved to join Dekkard and Avraal. Hasheem said quietly, "If you'd lead, Erleen."

"Yes, sir."

Hasheem said nothing more until they were in the courtyard, where Dekkard found himself evaluating any position from which he might be targeted.

"You looked at least as surprised as anyone when I announced the news about Marrak, and certainly not pleased."

"That just might be because last night, while we had dinner and spent the evening with the Obreduurs, we were informed that four Special Agents, under the direct orders of a Special Agent subcaptain, were apprehended by patrollers after trying to sabotage our house. Two didn't survive, but the survivors implicated the subcaptain."

"How did you manage that?" asked Hasheem skeptically.

"I work for Carlos Baartol," said Avraal. "A home security package is an additional benefit I chose to pay for."

"As I hope you understand, sir," said Dekkard, "we were rather occupied until late last night. There was the need to vent the house, and the patrollers' investigation, and trying to put everything back together. There was still the faintest odor of gas this morning."

"I see." Hasheem paused. "Would you mind if I conveyed that to Commerce Floor Leader Volkaar?"

"I have no problem with that. It's what happened."

"Is there a patrol report on the matter?"

"The station captain said it would be ready sometime today."

"The Special Agents were moved," added Avraal, "to an undisclosed location. The captain felt that his station patroller staff might be subjected to . . . undue pressure."

Dekkard hadn't known that, but Emrelda must have mentioned it to Avraal sometime when he'd been out of the breakfast room.

Hasheem smiled tightly. "I see why you're accompanied."

As the four entered the Council Office Building, Hasheem added, "I'm sure you'll be in the chamber this afternoon."

"Of course," replied Dekkard.

When Hasheem turned toward his office, Orlov looked back and flashed a wide grin—one that immediately vanished.

"An armored Security steamer," murmured Dekkard.

"That just might convey Security displeasure, or muddy the waters," returned Avraal.

"Likely both."

As soon as he and Avraal returned to the office, Dekkard gathered his staff and relayed the circumstances of Councilor Marrak's death. For a long moment, there was silence.

Finally, Margrit asked, "What do you think will happen now, sir?"

"I have no idea," replied Dekkard. "As I see it, the Commercers have gone beyond the law for years, using Special Agents and illegal means to increase the power of the larger corporacions and to decrease the power of workers and the guilds, as well as keeping smaller businesses from competing with the larger corporacions. The first public awareness of this came with the Kraffeist Affair and Eastern Ironway. At the same time, the corporacions have been using more steam-powered equipment and cutting back on the number of workers, and the large Landors have been using more steam tractors and using fewer farmworkers. Educated young people who aren't from well-connected families aren't getting good jobs and are having trouble getting accepted by the better universities. At least some of them have turned to the New Meritorists. The New Meritorists are also gathering followers from unemployed workers.

"With the finding on the Kraffeist Affair, the High Justiciary has indicated that it isn't going to bend the law, at least not as much, with a Craft Minister of the Justiciary, and the Commercers are suddenly realizing that a lot of their abuses are coming to light, and they're trying to stop that from happening." Dekkard cleared his throat. "The Commercers still have a great deal of power, and they're getting scared, and a whole lot of Guldoran workers and artisans are angry about how badly they've been treated . . . and that was even before what's likely to come out. So far, the regular patrollers have behaved well, but no one trusts the Special Agents or the STF, and that means the Premier doesn't dare use them, because they'll make any public demonstration worse."

"Could it really get that bad?" asked Roostof.

"I think it could, but I honestly can't tell. I thought you all ought to know."

"Thank you, sir," said Luara Colsbaan. "Is there anything we can do?"

"Just your jobs." Dekkard grinned. "And keeping me from saying legalistic things I shouldn't."

Both legalists offered amused, if brief, smiles.

After the staff left the office, Avraal looked to Dekkard. "You're more direct than Obreduur would have been."

"These are more direct times." Dekkard paused. "That means they'll likely keep targeting me . . . in some way."

Avraal's laugh was soft and bitter. "How else can they send the message that opposing or stopping Commercer abuses is likely fatal? Even if we keep you safe, most councilors won't want to risk what you already have."

"Then the only thing to do is to keep attacking by pushing Security reform." Dekkard also suspected he would still have to be cautious in terms of self-defense. Except the odds were that no one was going to attempt a close-in attack. *But you never know.*

Dekkard half expected it when, a bell later, two uniformed patrollers appeared at the office, accompanied by a Council Guard, and insisted on seeing him.

One handed him a sealed envelope. "With Captain Narryt's compliments, sir."

"I accept with gratitude," replied Dekkard.

"As well as with mine," added Avraal.

"We delivered a copy each to the Premier and the Security Committee chairman. The captain thought you should know that as well."

"Tell the captain I appreciate that, and everything he and all of you are doing."

"Thank you, sir."

When the two patrollers and the Council Guard left, Margrit looked at Dekkard.

"If I'm not mistaken, it's the patrol report on the attempted destruction of our house."

"Delivered here, sir?"

"As a courtesy. The copy to the Premier and the one to Chairman Hasheem will provide documented evidence of Security Special Agent malfeasance."

"That way," added Avraal, "it's less likely some unfortunate occurrence might befall the councilor or the captain, and that, even if such occurred, the evidence would still survive."

Margrit shook her head.

Dekkard carried the envelope into the office, where he opened and read the detailed report. Then he handed it to Avraal.

When she finished, she said, "Very thorough. Quite a condemnation. There's nothing to point back to Marrak, though."

"There wouldn't be. Just like there's nothing to point back to Siincleer Engineering in Markell's case. We have a good chance of reforming Security. There's almost no hope of holding individuals accountable for past abuses because there won't be any direct links."

"I didn't think there would be," replied Avraal dryly.

Just before the first bell of the afternoon, she accompanied Dekkard from the office to the Council Hall. Once he was in the councilors' lobby, Dekkard knew she could go to the spouses' lounge. He'd no sooner entered the lobby than Harleona Zerlyon joined him.

"Councilor," acknowledged Dekkard.

"Harleona, Steffan," she replied with a smile. "I understand you got a rather strong reaction to your Security reform proposal. An attack by Special Agents, no less." Before Dekkard could ask where she'd heard that, she added, "Axel told me. Keep pushing. Hasheem won't press hard enough. We can't change the past, but it would be a disaster not to change the future." With a nod, she continued toward the floor.

Dekkard understood the practicality, but he still was going to see if he could find a way to make certain corporacions pay. *One way or another.*

"For a councilor whose worst enemy just got taken out, you're looking pretty grim," said Pajiin, appearing almost from nowhere.

"It's the opening skirmish of a long war," replied Dekkard.

"Even if you pass that reform proposal, the next Council will repeal it."

"Not if they don't want a revolt, they won't. The Commercers and Security have gotten away with a lot because there have been no restrictions set in law. Once there are restrictions protecting people, people tend to get nastier when they're broken. You made that point in committee the other day about workplace rules . . ."

Pajiin had looked to say more, but stopped, then said, "You might have something there." The warning bell sounded, and he added, "We'd better go on in."

Dekkard made his way into the Council Hall and sat at his desk. The only vote scheduled was for a small supplemental to pay for rubble removal from the damaged Security buildings, a concession to practicality, since Obreduur opposed any additional funding until investigations into the damage and Security legislation were completed.

The vote was quick and largely perfunctory, with forty-seven for the funding and eighteen opposed, and one councilor not voting, since the Commerce

Party had yet to decide on a replacement for Marrak. After the vote was announced, and the Council adjourned, Dekkard stood and walked toward the lobby. He halted as Hasheem stepped up beside him.

"Did you tell that patroller captain to send me a copy of that report?" asked the older councilor coolly.

"Except for being the victim, I had nothing to do with that, nor did Ritten Dekkard. The captain said there would be a written report. I did not ask for a copy. I did not suggest anything. I was certainly caught off guard when two patrollers delivered a copy to me. I do know that the captain has been displeased by the excesses of Security for some time. I believe, but am not absolutely sure, that he was one of the patrol captains behind the message to the Premier that regular patrollers would shoot to kill Special Agents or STF forces who fired on unarmed demonstrators."

Hasheem's eyebrows lifted. "There was such a message?"

"You can ask Premier Obreduur," replied Dekkard pleasantly, adding, "The best way to stop personal attacks by the Commercers might well be a relatively quick passage of strong Security reform measures. It also might buy time with the New Meritorists. I am certain that whoever replaces Marrak on the committee will do his best to drag out the process, hoping that the New Meritorists will create more demonstrations, supporting the idea that Security needs to remain unfettered to deal with such rebels. As chairman, of course, you will determine how the committee will proceed."

"Steffan, I wasn't suggesting—"

You could have fooled me. "Nor was I, but you can see how I might be a little out of sorts after all the attacks on both the Premier and me, and why I feel addressing immediate reform is in the best interests of everyone—except for certain Commercers."

"Some Landors might prefer a more deliberate approach."

"I'm sure some might, but I doubt that Kharl Navione or Breffyn Haastar are among them, and neither is Tomas Pajiin." Dekkard managed a warmer smile.

"I see. Then working out a final bill might not prove as difficult as I feared."

"I think not, but, as you have pointed out, one never knows until all the votes are tallied."

"Do you have other projects?"

Dekkard shook his head. "Having Council control of Security strikes me as the most important and immediately necessary legislation."

"We'll talk . . . as necessary." With a nod, Hasheem eased away.

Dekkard could tell that Hasheem wasn't completely pleased, but then, Dekkard wasn't exactly pleased, either, especially with the suggestion that he'd sent the patrol report to Hasheem. If that had been his intention, he would have delivered the report personally.

Avraal waited for him outside the councilors' lobby, and he immediately asked, "Did you see Hasheem when he came out?"

"I did. He was slightly irked and yet somehow pleased. Why?"

"I'll tell you on the way back to the office."

They had almost reached the Council Office Building when Dekkard finished explaining.

Avraal nodded. "He's not used to someone with your focus, and this is the first time in his political career when he doesn't have to be cautious and indirect."

"Should I have been more placating and indirect?"

"It would have made him feel better, but no. The Craft Party is running out of time, and I'm not certain that even Obreduur realizes it."

Once they returned to the Council Office Building, while Avraal remained in the outer office, Dekkard dealt with the letters Roostof had prepared for him.

Just after third bell, Roostof and Avraal entered his office. The senior legalist handed a broadsheet to Dekkard.

"Thank you, Svard." Dekkard began to read.

SECURITY REFORM NOW!
Secret Hearings Just a Cover-Up!
A month after the Heroes Square massacre, still no action from the new Council . . .

After reading the entire broadsheet, Dekkard looked up and said cynically, "What a surprise. But there's a danger that the Council won't act because some councilors don't want to be seen as giving in to the New Meritorists, especially Commercer councilors."

"They might go along with your reform ideas," countered Avraal. "Then when the next demonstrations take place, they'll claim that shows the weakness of giving in to the radicals."

"Not reforming Security will only make matters worse, but the process could be painful."

"It isn't already?" said Avraal sardonically.

Dekkard gave an acidic chuckle, then handed the broadsheet back. "Svard, have Margrit file this with the others. We have a little more time."

Roostof frowned. "Sir?"

"The New Meritorists want to see what they can get from the new government before they resort to violence again. Getting reforms quickly would be useful, because that will justify Obreduur using force. I hope Hasheem will speed the process in the Security Committee."

"Will he?" asked Roostof.

"Obreduur will likely have to persuade him." Dekkard shrugged. "We'll just have to see." And he had always disliked depending on others—except Avraal—necessary as it often turned out to be.

14

WHEN Dekkard reached the breakfast room on Quindi morning, Emrelda had already left, not surprisingly, since, the night before, she had informed Dekkard and Avraal that she would work the early shift. Dekkard noticed *Gestirn* was folded to the second page and laid out at an angle, suggesting that Emrelda had wanted to call attention to something. He immediately picked up the newssheet and began to read.

> Premier Axel Obreduur announced yesterday that Lukkyn Wyath, the former Minister of Security, and Maartyn Manwaeren, the acting Minister of Security, have both been placed under house arrest, pending an investigation of certain violations of the Criminal Code. In addition, Josef Mangele, Director of the Office of Intelligence at the Ministry of Security, resigned abruptly late yesterday afternoon, citing severe personal health issues . . . Since the Security Committee's investigation of the Security Ministry is ongoing, it appears unlikely replacements will be named in the immediate future . . .

What else has Obreduur uncovered? Or was the Justiciary Ministry using what surfaced in the hearings?

Dekkard's eyes took in the next lines.

> . . . prior to his time in the Security Ministry, Sr. Wyath was the Director of Security for Suvion Industries . . .

Suvion Industries? While a security background made sense for Wyath, it still bothered Dekkard.

Below that story was a smaller one that noted that Stannel Orsken, former commander of the Special Tactical Force, had pled guilty to two counts of misfeasance in office, and had accepted voluntary statelessness in lieu of three years in a work camp.

Why would he accept exile? And why didn't the prosecutors ask for a longer sentence? Dekkard thought for a moment, realizing that the only illegal thing that Orsken ordered was to plant weapons, which wasn't a capital crime. He'd certainly used bad judgment in having the STF troopers fire on the demonstrators, but proving criminal intent would be difficult.

Before starting to fix breakfast and café, he scanned the rest of the newssheet and found a short story about Erik Marrak's death, mentioning the "presumably stolen" armored Security steamer, but little more than a two-sentence summary of his background. Dekkard almost missed the story on the last page about more than twelve hundred Atacaman men, women, and children swarming across the Rio Doro thirty milles north of Port Reale, all of them ill-nourished and some close to starving. Several hundred appeared to be escapees from the Atacaman penal and "reeducation" complex northwest of Port Lenfer. He frowned. Atacama wasn't known for humane prisons, and Lenfer was supposed to be the worst.

So how did they escape? And how many others will follow?

Dekkard doubted he'd ever know, but he had to wonder as he prepared the cafés.

By the time Avraal trudged into the breakfast room, he had everything ready, and the newssheet folded as Emrelda had left it.

"You might read the story Emrelda left the newssheet open to," he suggested.

Avraal took several sips of café before picking up *Gestirn*. Her eyes widened. "He must have some very solid evidence."

"I wonder what the story in the *Tribune* says."

"Either that the new premier is overreacting and encouraging violence by the New Meritorists, or there isn't a story at all. Likely the latter, because they know he has the facts."

Avraal set *Gestirn* aside and went back to sipping her café.

Abruptly, he remembered something he'd meant to ask Avraal. "Ingrella mentioned a book the other night?"

"It's something called *The City of Truth*. She called it a forgotten classic and very well written. She said she'd get it to one of us before long."

Dekkard offered an amused smile. "I wonder what surprise it holds. The last book she recommended told me that I was marrying the descendant of royalty."

Avraal grinned. "I don't think it's that kind of book."

"With Ingrella, you never know."

"She said it was gently thought-provoking."

"I'll reserve judgment," said Dekkard before eating half of a quince-filled croissant in one large bite.

"Considerate of you," said Avraal dryly.

Dekkard winced. "I didn't mean it that way. It will be thought-provoking; it just might not be gently so."

"*That*—you would know."

Dekkard smiled and shrugged helplessly.

Avraal laughed.

Once they finished breakfast, including cleaning up, dressing, and getting into the gray Gresynt, Dekkard decided to take yet another route to the Council Office Building.

As he pulled up to the guard post at the covered parking entrance, Avraal said, "How did you come up with that scenic route? Not that varying the way here isn't an excellent idea."

"I looked at Emrelda's city maps while I was waiting for you. I assume she has them because she needs to know all that as a dispatcher. You're both alike in that respect." *And in more than a few others.*

Avraal only shook her head as the Council Guard waved them through the gate, her senses clearly turning to the area close to the steamer as Dekkard eased it into his assigned space.

As soon as Dekkard reached the office and neared Margrit's desk, she handed him two messages. The first was a notice that the Council would meet briefly at first afternoon bell to swear in Councilor-select Villem Baar.

Dekkard handed the notice to Avraal, who read it and gave it back.

That has to be Marrak's replacement. Dekkard had no doubt that Baar would be sharper and more politically astute than Marrak, but he wondered what other abilities the new councilor might have.

The second message was from Fredrich Hasheem, announcing that the Security Committee would begin addressing Security Ministry reform legislation on Unadi, beginning at third morning bell, and that the committee would meet every morning until a legislative proposal was agreed upon. Dekkard smiled wryly as he handed that one to Avraal.

She smiled and returned it.

Dekkard gave both notices back to Margrit. "Thank you." Then he walked to the open doorway to the staff office. "Svard, we'll have to start the interviews earlier on Duadi. Chairman Hasheem will be holding Security Committee meetings at third morning bell all next week. See if you can work out half before second bell."

"I don't think that will be a problem, sir, but I'll let you know if it is."

"Thank you."

Avraal remained in the outer office while Dekkard went through the mail and petitions, then signed or changed the replies that Roostof and Colsbaan had composed. After that, he asked Colsbaan and Avraal to join him.

Once they were both seated, Dekkard said to Colsbaan, "I called you in here because you need to be working on more than legalist explanations for constituents and because I need you to follow up on something that came up several months ago, when I was working for Councilor Obreduur. He gave me a letter from the junior legalist with the Working Women Guild in Gaarlak. She asked for support of legislation to allow women of the streets to be represented by legalists from the nearest Working Women Guild. I wasn't aware of any legislation to that effect then, but if there was, it died when the Imperador dissolved the previous Council." Dekkard looked to Colsbaan. He could also see the hint of a faint smile on Avraal's face.

"I take it you want me to look into that, sir?"

"More than that. I want you to draft that legislation in a way that's suitable to go through the Workplace Administration Committee. Find as many legal precedents as you can to support the idea. Some Commercer legalists claim that guild legalists can't represent people in a trade who aren't official guild members, but that's not a uniform practice. I know, for example, that if artisans pay dues to the local artisans' guild, they're members of the guild. On the other hand, by law, sex workers can't be guild members unless they work in a licensed brothel or massage parlor. That law was enacted to make sure that sex workers complied with the health codes, but it effectively means that they have no legal standing or protection."

"That's true," Colsbaan said slowly. "Sir, might I ask your thoughts on how you would justify such a change in law?"

"I'd think that women of the streets might be far likelier to adhere to the guild's and the government's guidelines and health practices, as well as to know their legal rights and responsibilities."

"From what I've seen, some wouldn't want to pay guild dues, and some couldn't," Colsbaan pointed out.

"If they don't pay at least reduced dues, then they wouldn't get guild legalist services, unless they agreed to pay dues for at least the subsequent year."

"They might promise and not pay," Colsbaan pointed out.

"Perhaps," agreed Dekkard. "But many might. In any case, that's what I'd like you to work on. Oh, you also should send a letter to Myram Plassar, the regional steward for the Working Women Guild in Gaarlak. Tell her that I'm looking into this and see if she can offer any assistance."

"Have you met her, sir?"

"Just once, but we didn't talk about legislation. It wouldn't be wise to introduce something like this without contacting the guild there." Dekkard turned to Avraal. "Can you think of anything I might have forgotten?"

"You might want to talk to the street patrollers to see what they think."

"You're right." Dekkard looked back to the junior legalist. "For now, keep all of this between us and Svard until I can get some answers from patrollers."

"I can do that, sir. Is there anything else?"

"Not at the moment. You don't have to rush, but don't put it off, either."

"I won't, sir."

After the junior legalist left the office, Dekkard asked, "She's good at not showing much. What was her reaction?"

"She was definitely surprised, I think as much about what you knew as about the request for draft legislation. She was also pleased."

"Most likely to have some real legalist work."

"A little more than that."

"Good. What do you say we go over to the councilors' dining room and have something to eat before the Council session?"

"It's better than the staff cafeteria."

"Meaning not that much better."

"The décor is better."

"Since there is no décor in the cafeteria . . ." Dekkard kept his words light and stood.

Outside his personal office, he stopped and said to Margrit, "We're going to get something to eat at the councilors' dining room. We'll be back after the floor session. It should be well before second bell."

"Yes, sir."

From the office, Dekkard and Avraal walked to the center staircase and down to the first level. As they moved toward the polished bronze doors leading into the courtyard, a slender councilor, sandy-colored hair shot with silver, accompanied by a single female security aide, likely an empath, moved toward them.

"Breffyn Haastar," murmured Dekkard, saying more loudly, "Good day, Breffyn."

"It's good to see you healthy and well, Steffan."

"The same to you. I don't believe you've met my wife, Avraal. Dear, this is Councilor Breffyn Haastar, from Brekaan."

"You're from the Sudaen Ysella family, I believe," said Haastar, inclining his head politely.

"I am, but how did you know?"

Haastar smiled, shyly. "Family, and most recently Emilio Raathan mentioned it in a letter."

Dekkard managed not to frown. Raathan had known of Avraal and her family, but how had the former councilor known they were married?

Haastar's security aide opened the door, and Dekkard and Avraal followed the other councilor into the courtyard.

"There was quite a story about you two getting married in the Gaarlak newssheet," added Haastar. "Emilio sent me a clipping."

Dekkard laughed softly. "We didn't know about that story."

"I can understand that. From what Kharl Navione said, you two were rather occupied, and being selected as councilor came as a great surprise."

"A very great surprise to both of us," said Avraal pleasantly.

Dekkard kept looking for anyone, particularly at a distance, who didn't seem to belong in the courtyard, but the scattered individuals he saw were either Council Guards, staffers with no interest beyond themselves, or two councilors with aides far ahead of them and about to enter the Council Hall.

"I think we'll all be surprised in one way or another over the next few months," replied Haastar. "I just hope the results are worth it."

"Isn't that up to us?" asked Dekkard, almost gently.

"It is," agreed Haastar, "but we both know that some councilors can't conceive of change at a time when change is inevitable, while others reject any change unthinkingly."

"So how should the Council approach dealing with those changes?" asked Dekkard.

"Let younger councilors like you propose the unthinkable, complain loudly, modify the most objectionable features, and then declare that we've preserved the spirit of the Great Charter against radical onslaughts."

"You think that my reform proposal is unthinkable to some?"

"Only to Commercers and a handful of truly conservative Landors, while others won't want to oppose Security and its Commercer allies." Haastar chuckled and added, "But some are realizing that they also don't want to oppose the Premier and you two."

"The two of us?" asked Avraal.

"It's been a long time, if ever, since the Council held an isolate councilor married to a powerful empath from a regal lineage, both of whom are experienced security aides."

"There can't be that many people who know all those details," Dekkard pointed out.

Haastar shook his head. "Most of the Council knows a great deal. Ritten Ysella-Dekkard's background isn't quite that well known, but it will be."

"What do you suggest?" asked Dekkard amiably.

"Do what needs to be done." Haastar offered an amused smile. "You will anyway."

"Why are you telling me this?" asked Dekkard casually.

"So you know absolutely where I stand. I'd prefer not to be in the line of fire. Your aim is known to be deadly." Haastar paused. "And the Ysellas never forget."

"I'd prefer not to be in the line of fire, either," replied Dekkard, "but that's not an option."

"You understand that. The Commercers don't, especially those like Schmidtz and Palafaux." As they neared the Council Hall, Haastar added, "I appreciated getting to meet you in person, Ritten, and talking to both of you. Just take care of yourselves." Then he gestured to his security aide, who moved ahead and opened the door to the Council Hall.

Dekkard took the door from her and nodded to her to rejoin Haastar.

Once they were inside and walking toward the councilors' dining room, Dekkard said quietly, "That was quite a conversation for a short walk. How truthful was he?"

"I don't think he said a word that was untrue. That doesn't mean he'll support everything you propose, but I don't think he'll oppose it, either. We'll talk more about it later."

Meaning not here. Dekkard nodded.

They'd no sooner stepped into the entry of the councilors' dining room than a tall dark-haired woman stepped toward them.

"Kaliara Bassaana," Dekkard murmured.

"Ritten Dekkard, I've been so looking forward to meeting you, as I'm sure your husband has told you." Bassaana nodded toward Dekkard.

"He mentioned it," replied Avraal warmly. "And I'd hoped to meet you, since Steffan respects you and your integrity."

"That's kind of you, Steffan."

"Not kind," replied Dekkard. "Honest and practical. Integrity is what makes meaningful legislation and its necessary compromises possible. I suspect neither of the previous premiers fully understood that."

"There was much neither understood," replied Bassaana dryly.

"Would you care to join us?" asked Avraal.

"That would be delightful, but I'll have to decline *this* time. I'm supposed to eat with Councilor Volkaar. But thank you for the invitation." Bassaana's smile was warm and seemed genuinely regretful, which made Dekkard suspect it was not.

"Until the next time, then," replied Avraal.

"Until then." Bassaana moved toward Hansaal Volkaar, who had just entered.

Dekkard waited until the Commercer floor leader and Bassaana had been seated before stepping forward.

"Just the two of you?" asked the thin functionary in black and gold livery. "This way, Councilor, Ritten." He led them to a table for two, the table linens the usual light ivory that stood out against the dark green marble floor.

Once they were seated and had ordered—Dekkard opting for the three-cheese fowl and Avraal for chilled tomato soup—he asked, "What do you think of Kaliara Bassaana?"

"She doesn't know quite what to make of you, and she's definitely wary of me."

"In her boots, I'd definitely be wary of you," said Dekkard.

"She doesn't strike me as the kind who'd put a knife in your back—more the kind who will profess more support than she'd actually give."

"A relatively honest politician, then?"

Avraal offered a faint smile. "Something like that."

Just then, Tomas Pajiin entered, accompanied by Daffyd Dholen, the Crafter councilor from Actaan, and the two were seated against the opposite wall. Almost without looking, Dekkard could see that Pajiin's eyes kept drifting to Avraal, although Dholen's did not.

"Is the covert scrutiny annoying?" he asked in a low voice.

"It's not exactly covert, but it's not lecherous. He's puzzled."

"What? That a beautiful woman agreed to marry me?"

She shook her head. "It's not that."

"Should I introduce you?"

"No. Let's see what happens."

At that moment, their entrées arrived, along with iced cafés for each of them, and Pajiin turned his attention exclusively to Dholen, a graying and slightly paunchy councilor close to Pajiin's age. Dekkard still wondered about Pajiin's scrutiny of Avraal, but decided not to ask more. "How is the soup?"

"Better than adequate."

"But not as good as yours or Emrelda's?"

"Not as good as Emrelda's. What about the chicken?"

"Good, but not great. Any further thoughts on the councilor from your region of Guldor?"

"He'll vote for your proposals so long as he's not the deciding vote. He *might* be the deciding vote, but I'm not sure you should count on it."

"That's better than I'd initially hoped. I still can't believe that Emilio Raathan said nice things about us."

"Haastar was definitely telling the truth about that."

"I need to send a nice, if slightly vague, letter to Raathan."

"You do," agreed Avraal.

Pajiin and Dholen ate relatively quickly and left the dining room without so much as looking in Dekkard's or Avraal's direction.

Before all that long, or so it seemed to Dekkard, it was time for him to go to the floor.

"The session will be short," he said.

"I'll watch from the spouses' gallery. Take your time leaving so that I can get down to the lobby entrance."

"I will."

Once he was in the Council chamber, Dekkard glanced around, noting that only fifty or so councilors were present. That wasn't unexpected, given that the only business was to swear in Marrak's replacement. Dekkard wondered why the swearing in couldn't have been held on Unadi, or at the next scheduled Council session. *But then, Obreduur got you sworn in as early as possible.* And Obreduur had despised the way the Commercers had delayed and manipulated procedures and had as much as said he wouldn't do the same.

After the chimes rang, the lieutenant-at-arms appeared and thumped the ceremonial staff.

Then Obreduur stood and declared, "The only order of business for this session of the Council is the swearing in of Councilor-select Villem Baar of Suvion. Lieutenant-at-Arms, please escort the councilor-select to the floor."

The same uniformed figure who had opened the Council session walked to the door from the Premier's floor office and opened it, then led Baar to the dais.

Obreduur read the oath of office, while Baar repeated each phrase.

"I solemnly swear that as a councilor of the Sixty-Six, I will uphold the Great Charter and all of its provisions, in both letter and spirit, that I will by word and deed defend those provisions, and that I undertake my sacred duties and responsibilities of my own free will, without reservation or hesitation."

After the swearing in, Obreduur said, "There being no other business, the Council stands adjourned until its next meeting." He gave two solid thumps with the gavel.

Several Commercers joined Hansaal Volkaar in congratulating Baar.

Dekkard moved closer, just so that he could get a better impression. Baar looked to be around ten years older than Dekkard. He was also slender and several digits shorter, with longish, slicked-back blond hair above a round face and a nondescript nose. His eyes seemed to change color as he moved, but looked to be predominantly pale, watery green.

After a few moments, Dekkard turned and headed for the councilors' lobby.

Back in his office, there would be mail responses to review, among other things, and he really did need to compose and dispatch a thoughtful letter to Emilio Raathan.

15

ON Findi morning, Dekkard, Avraal, and Emrelda ended up in the breakfast room at close to the same time, although Avraal immediately retreated into sipping her café.

"How is Captain Narryt doing?" asked Dekkard. "It took a lot of courage to send those reports to the Premier and Chairman Hasheem."

"He decided that he'd have a better chance not ending up dead or missing if he sent the reports, especially since the Craft Party controls the Council. He also persuaded several other captains to send in older reports that suggested Special Agent interference."

"I hope his judgment is accurate," replied Dekkard.

"The Justiciary minister's charges against Wyath and Manwaeren may help," suggested Avraal, "especially after the Security Committee hearings." She took another sip of café, then asked, "Could we not start the day talking about work?"

"We could and should," said Dekkard, even though he'd wanted to ask Emrelda about what most patrollers thought about working women. "What would you like to do today?"

"Nothing except take it easy and fix a good dinner," said Avraal. "We will need to go to the grocers for a few things."

"And practice with knives some," added Emrelda.

In fact, that was exactly how the day went, and after a repast of lemon-orange chicken with sautéed orange and yellow peppers, accompanied by lemongrass rice and a seasonal green salad, which Dekkard helped prepare—mainly by chopping and cutting and cleaning up various pans and utensils—the three found themselves sitting on the veranda in the late twilight. Dekkard sipped a beaker of Kuhrs, while the sisters each nursed a glass of Silverhills white.

"Have you heard anything from Cliven or Mother?" Avraal asked Emrelda. "I sent them each a letter and a heliogram about the wedding and explaining why we had to get married so quickly. I didn't expect an immediate response, but . . ."

"You hoped," Emrelda finished for her. "I wrote them both as well. I haven't heard, either. I would have thought that at least Mother would have been pleased. She thought you'd never get married."

"Perhaps the idea that you married a Craft councilor was somewhat of a shock," suggested Dekkard. He wasn't about to suggest that they might have felt that Avraal's marrying a Craft councilor was beneath her, just as Emrelda's marriage to a distinguished engineer had been.

"They're more likely hurt that we didn't inform them well in advance," replied Avraal. "Or suspicious that we had to get married for reasons unsuited to a spinster Landor daughter."

"I doubt Father would have thought you had to get married. Not you," said

Emrelda. "Even if you'd given them notice, they wouldn't have come anyway. They didn't come for Markell and me. Cliven and Fleur sent a lovely silver tray a month later. They'll probably do something like that. I wrote Mother every month. It was a year before she wrote back."

"I've been writing her every few weeks," said Avraal flatly. "She answers once every month or two. Mostly with platitudes and hints that I really should return to Sudaen and a more suitable life for a Ysella."

Dekkard doubted that their mother would never change, even though it seemed more than clear the sisters would never be accepted for what they were. *You're just incredibly fortunate to have the family you have even if it took a little while for them to understand who you are.*

"What are you thinking, dear?" asked Avraal.

"About people."

"That's rather vague. Are you thinking uncharitable thoughts about our parents and trying to avoid saying anything? Or wondering why we even care after so long?"

Dekkard shook his head. "I understand why both of you care. What I don't understand is why they don't support your being the best at what you can be."

"Tradition is sometimes stronger than those who embrace it," said Avraal.

"Those in my family have been artisans for generations—"

"Your family has brains and courage," snapped Avraal.

"So do you and Emrelda," countered Dekkard. "It's a shame your parents don't."

"They have brains," said Emrelda, "and courage. What they don't have is perception. They still see the world as it was a generation ago."

"They're trying to maintain old ways in a changed world, and it isn't going to change back," added Avraal. "They tried to instill the old values, and some of them were good. Father insisted that we be able to kill and butcher our own livestock, and do it well, and pretty much every other task on the land. Don't ask someone else to do something you won't, he always said. But they think that we've betrayed them. In their terms, we have."

"How? If either of you had married a Landor, none of his lands or marks would have come back to your family. You'd have had to bear children, likely more than you'd want, and the children would face what you faced with even fewer choices and less marks."

"You are a dear," said Avraal gently. "You put it so succinctly. If you said those words to Father, or even Cliven, they wouldn't have any meaning. Father would say that you couldn't possibly understand. Cliven would nod politely and say that you lived in a different world."

That's because they both live in the past. But Dekkard only said, "I can see that. There's a long tradition in your family. Sometimes, that tradition doesn't suit everyone. I suspect something like that was why my parents fled Argental. They wanted to do more than the limited, functional art that was allowed."

"They had great courage," said Avraal.

"You and Emrelda also have great courage."

"So we all have courage," said Avraal wryly. "Who cares?"

"We do," replied Dekkard. "We have to live our dreams, not the dreams of others. Trying to live out others' dreams will destroy a person." He laughed, adding sardonically, "Of course, living out our dreams might do the same, but . . ."

"But what?" asked Emrelda.

"I was going to say that it's more honest, but it's probably not. Dreams are illusions unless and until you realize them." He shrugged. "And even if we do, that could be an illusion as well."

"You're so cheerful," said Avraal, adding cheerfully, "Do you think you could be a little darker?"

"No. That's about as dark as I get."

"Good," said Emrelda, lifting her glass. "That's enough darkness." She stood and refilled her wineglass and Avraal's. "One more round, and that should be enough for brighter dreams or dreamless sleep."

Dekkard hoped so, and that he hadn't said too much.

16

WHEN Dekkard woke up on Unadi morning, the first day of Fallend, he opened his eyes to find Avraal looking at him.

"You were quite eloquent last night." Her voice was gentle.

"I talked too much. I shouldn't have had that last beaker of Kuhrs," Dekkard returned apologetically.

"I'm glad you did. Sometimes . . . sometimes, I think you hold back when you shouldn't."

"I'm still learning."

"Just keep being you." She reached out and touched his face. "I liked how you said Emrelda was special, too."

"You two are different, but, as the oldest, it took incredible courage to defy your parents."

"It made it easier for me. I've told her that, but it was good that you saw how hard it was for her." Avraal sat up. "We need to eat."

Dekkard grinned. "I need to eat. You need your café."

Avraal offered a faux grimace, then replied, "No more than you need that sickly-sweet quince paste."

Dekkard just shook his head as he got out of bed.

Emrelda had already left for work, and Dekkard fixed café and fetched croissants from the pantry cooler, then scanned *Gestirn*, noting another story about harvest difficulties, this time in the southeast of Guldor where the excessive summer heat and dryness had combined with heavy and early fall rains to decimate the maize and wheat-corn harvests.

That's not good . . . and that will likely mean more people moving into Southtown. But he didn't dwell on it, because he and Avraal both had to hurry through breakfast and finish getting ready so they wouldn't arrive late at the Council Office Building, particularly since a cool fall rain was falling. *And you'll have to be in the office much earlier tomorrow.*

Even so, it was only a sixth past second bell when Dekkard stepped through the door into his office, the cuffs of his trousers slightly damp after crossing from the covered parking to the Council Office Building.

Margrit had messages and mail waiting for him on his desk. When he finished reading through them, none requiring immediate response or instructions to Roostof on his part, it was nearly time to leave for the Security Committee meeting.

Carrying the gray leather folder with Roostof's notes in it, Dekkard didn't say much as he and Avraal took the main staircase down to the first level, nor when they started along the covered walkway to the Council Hall.

"You're worried about the committee meeting, aren't you?" asked Avraal.

"I feel like I'm going to be a target, or rather that my proposal will be. I'm not a legalist, no matter what Macri said about my being close. If I can't defend the proposal well, we'll lose the chance to rein in Security for this Council and maybe forever."

"Hasheem's behind you, isn't he?"

"He is, but he's not a legalist."

"Don't argue the law. Argue the facts. The facts show that Security needs to be reined in. The STF shot unarmed demonstrators and got caught planting weapons. The law should enable justice, not obstruct it."

Dekkard smiled wryly. "You should be there arguing."

"It's what you've been saying all along, just in a different way."

As they neared the committee room, Dekkard saw Pajiin standing by the door, talking to Daffyd Dholen. He wondered why, since Dholen was chair of the Public Resources Committee, but before he and Avraal neared, Dholen turned and headed farther down the long corridor, presumably to a committee meeting of his own, while Pajiin entered the Security Committee chamber.

"How long, do you think?" asked Avraal.

"I doubt we'll adjourn early. The Commercers will stall and try to amend things, and the session will likely last until noon. If I'm not here, I'll be in the councilors' dining room."

"Don't go anywhere else."

"I won't." Dekkard reached out, quickly squeezed her hand, and headed into the committee room. He immediately saw the seating on the dais had been changed to reflect seniority, with Hasheem flanked on his right by Haastar and on his left by Navione. Rikkard remained in the same position beside Navione, but the new committee member—Villem Baar, as Dekkard had suspected— now sat where Dekkard had been positioned, while Dekkard's place was at the far right, where Pajiin had been, and Pajiin had moved one seat closer to the center, between Dekkard and Haastar.

Dekkard took his new seat beside Pajiin, noting that Navione was already seated.

The older Craft councilor asked quietly, "Do you know anything about Baar?"

"Only that he'll be sharper and more dangerous, in a subtler way, than Marrak ever was. The Commercer leadership will likely be happier with Baar, but that's a guess on my part."

Pajiin nodded to Breffyn Haastar as the Landor councilor stepped up on the dais and seated himself. Rikkard and Baar took their seats perhaps three minutes before third bell, followed by Hasheem.

The moment the third chime died away, Hasheem gaveled the committee to order.

"Before we begin the business of the day, I'd like to recognize the newest member of the Security Committee, Villem Baar. Councilor Baar has a solid and extensive background as a legalist for the noted firm of Barthow, Juarez and Whittsyn. I'm certain he will add expertise in drafting a solid Security reform proposal."

Dekkard tried to watch Baar without being too obvious, by looking generally in Hasheem's direction, but it was harder than he thought. Baar, as the junior councilor, was seated at the far left and Dekkard, seated opposite Baar, couldn't see Baar clearly if he looked directly at Hasheem, and he didn't want to appear overly interested.

"Welcome to the committee, Councilor."

Baar nodded politely.

"The committee is hereby in session to consider the proposed Security reorganization act. As determined at the previous meeting, the reform proposal presented by Councilor Dekkard has been accepted as the draft framework from which the committee will work. We will begin discussion of the proposal by allowing each committee member to make brief comments on the draft and to address questions to Councilor Dekkard. I will defer my questions and comments until all other committee members have completed theirs." Hasheem turned to Navione.

The senior Landor councilor looked down at a sheet of paper, then at Dekkard. "We're all well aware of the range of abuses committed by the Security Ministry's Special Tactical Force. At the same time, transferring the STF to the Army would place all military forces under the Imperador. What do you say to that, Councilor Dekkard?"

Dekkard wanted to take a deep breath. Instead, he smiled. "I'd say that it's a step toward restoring the spirit of the Great Charter. The Great Charter vested a certain amount of control in the Imperador by granting him the power to appoint the two most senior military leaders. The STF has effectively become a domestic military force that is not subject to military control or tradition. Nor has it been truly under the control of the Council, as the previous hearings revealed. Such a force was clearly not envisioned by the framers of the Great Charter."

"Wouldn't that increase the power of the Imperador?"

"I'd say it would reduce past overreaches by the Security Ministry and by past premiers without markedly increasing the power of the Imperador."

"Wouldn't reducing the power of the Security Ministry at this time enable demonstrators such as the New Meritorists to create even greater problems?"

"The proposal doesn't eliminate the STF. It places it under Army authority. It could still be used. The only force that would be changed would be the Special Agents, and they were never trained to deal with crowd control or to operate as a unified force."

Navione then asked several more technical questions dealing with timing and implementation. By the time Dekkard had done his best to answer Navione's questions, almost a bell had passed.

After Navione, the next questioner was Breffyn Haastar. "Why do you believe such a significant restructuring of the Security Ministry is necessary, particularly at this time?"

"The very nature of society and business in Guldor has changed enormously in the last century. The improvements in machinery and transportation have increased the powers available to government, particularly to the Security Ministry, but, as the committee's recent hearings have revealed, the Security Ministry has not used those increased powers wisely. They have, in fact, ignored pressing problems while pursuing political and commercial aims of the party controlling the Council.

"This proposal would be one step toward returning the ministry to dealing with public safety, rather than spending public funds and personnel to pursue political aims. I would point out that, without this legislation, there would be nothing in law to prevent the current government from using the ministry in the same fashion as previous governments have, but for very different aims."

"That is a good point, Councilor," replied Haastar, "and a point I don't see anyone else considering. I have no other questions."

"Councilor Rikkard?" said Hasheem.

Rikkard looked squarely at Dekkard. "You make this sound so idealistic. One of the functions of government is to protect private property. How can this 'Ministry of Public Safety' protect property when it would disarm two out of three branches of the Security Ministry?"

"This proposal is not so much idealistic as practical, Councilor. As the previous hearings demonstrated, the Special Agents, lacking any training in crowd control, simply made matters worse. With this same lack of discipline, so did the STF. The STF is essentially a military unit without military discipline or control. Placing it under the Army would strengthen its discipline and usefulness. The STF would still be available to deal with large unruly demonstrations, should they continue, *after* being retrained by the Army. In the meantime, Army units could be used, as they were this past summer. I refer to early demonstrations in Oersynt."

"What if Special Agents don't want to give up their weapons?" asked Rikkard.

"If they refuse, they become lawbreakers, and they'll be treated like any other lawbreaker. If they feel that strongly, they could request a transfer to the STF." Dekkard thought he caught a hint of an amused smile from Hasheem.

"Won't the lack of firearms cripple criminal investigations?" Rikkard continued. "An unarmed investigator would be an easy target for an armed criminal."

"The proposal grants investigators the right to use firearms on a specific case-by-case basis or to request armed patrollers to accompany them."

"That would just add bureaucratic delays," said Rikkard tartly.

"Not if they request patrollers to accompany them. The only bureaucratic delay is if they want to carry firearms themselves. This committee discovered a great deal about Security, and no one here had any firearms. As an economic and a security specialist, I encountered a few situations involving criminality and managed to resolve them without firearms even when confronted with firearms."

Rikkard appeared likely to say something, then closed his mouth.

"Do you have any further questions, Councilor?" asked Hasheem.

"Not now."

"Councilor Pajiin?"

Pajiin smiled pleasantly. "I have no questions at this time, but I would like to agree with the point that reform of the Security Ministry is long overdue.

I also support the disarming of Special Agents. Their principal use in my district has been to break up lawful protests about violations of work safety rules. In effect, they have supported illegal corporacion actions."

"Thank you, Councilor. Councilor Baar?"

Villem Baar offered an almost sleepy smile that Dekkard immediately distrusted, then said, "There were reports that the regular Security patrollers threatened to shoot the Special Tactical Forces. Wouldn't this proposal empower those patrollers to ignore the authority of the Council?"

"In case you weren't aware, Councilor," replied Dekkard politely, "the civic patrollers threatened to do that if, and only if, the STF continued to shoot unarmed demonstrators, including shooting women, who were fleeing the demonstrations, in the back. There was no evidence that such use of firearms actually took place. In addition, the STF tried to cover up its misdeeds by planting weapons on the bodies of unarmed people."

"There's still the question of authority."

"No," replied Dekkard. "As I noted previously to the committee, there is no authority in law for the Special Tactical Force. Nor did the Security Ministry ever codify procedures or rules for either Special Agents or the STF."

"Then perhaps we should consider that," said Baar smoothly.

"That's exactly what this proposal does. It limits the use of firearms to those who need them. It places a paramilitary force under military authority and discipline, and it returns Special Agents to investigation, relying on legal processes, rather than permitting unsupervised investigation of political opponents while ignoring the very real dangers of the New Meritorists."

"Those are unfounded allegations—"

Hasheem rapped the gavel sharply. "Councilor, they are not unfounded. If you wish to check the transcripts of the prior hearings, you will find several instances of such abuse, and those abuses were testified to by some of the highest officials in the Security Ministry."

Baar's mouth opened, as if he couldn't believe the reprimand Hasheem had delivered.

"Do you have any other questions for Councilor Dekkard, either legal or factual?"

Baar did not speak immediately, then finally said, "Not at this time, Sr. Chairman."

"That being the case, the committee will proceed to discussing the specific provisions of the proposal."

"Sr. Chairman, I must protest," declared Baar. "I have not had enough time to study the proposal."

"Councilor, you were provided a copy of the proposal only slightly later than the other councilors. Unlike most members of this committee, you are a highly trained and experienced legalist. This legislative proposal is straightforward. Therefore, with your superior abilities and training, you should have no difficulty in understanding the language and should certainly be able to discuss the specific provisions."

"This is most irregular."

"No, Councilor, it is not. We have been tasked by the Premier to recommend reforms as soon as practical. You may raise factual or legal objections to provisions or language. You may suggest changes or improvements. What you may not do is ask for delays."

"Writing legislation in haste cannot be wise, Sr. Chairman."

"Councilor, no one said anything about writing legislation in haste. We will take whatever time is necessary to consider and discuss each provision of the proposal. You and indeed all members of the committee will have every afternoon and as late into the evening as you wish to review the transcripts of the hearings and go over the documents obtained from Security. As much of that material is confidential, only councilors on the committee and committee staff will have access, of course, but that should prove no hindrance to you with your extensive experience."

"I understand, Sr. Chairman." While Baar's tone was pleasant, Dekkard had no doubt that the councilor was fuming.

"Now, we'll begin with the statement of purpose," said Hasheem.

Dekkard had no doubt that the next bell would be long and tedious, and that Baar would attempt to soften or eviscerate anything that he could.

When Hasheem gaveled the Security Committee meeting to an end exactly at noon, Dekkard felt as though Villem Baar had objected or argued, smoothly and politely, over almost every noun and verb in the opening section of the proposed bill, and even a few of the indefinite articles. Although, in the end, the language remained substantially the same, Dekkard knew the committee meetings would be brutal for the next week or for however long it took to go through the entire proposal.

Baar and Rikkard left the committee room immediately, followed by Navione.

As Dekkard stood, so did Pajiin, who shook his head slowly. "Baar's one of those who gives legalists a bad name."

Dekkard laughed softly. "That's why they selected him. They knew that the Premier wanted to reform Security."

"That's why the Premier put you on the committee, wasn't it?"

"He never said a word about it. He did know that I wasn't happy with Security."

"He's good about reading people. You think he's a hidden empie?"

Dekkard shook his head. "He understands people, and he's worked with all sorts."

"You'd know, or your wife would." Pajiin smiled. "Baar underestimated both you and Hasheem."

"He'll have Commercer researchers digging up every bit of legalese and evidence against what's in the proposal. It's going to be a very long week."

Pajiin nodded. "Until tomorrow." Then he turned and left the dais.

Dekkard realized that he was the last councilor, besides Pajiin, in the room, and he made his way toward the door, where Avraal waited.

"The two Commercer councilors were fuming."

"How did you know they were Commercers?"

"I remembered Villem Baar because I was in the spouses' gallery when he was sworn in on Quindi. They were together."

"The other one was Jaradd Rikkard. Shall we get something to eat?"

"A little something."

"That's fine. I need to calm down. I spent three long bells explaining and defending the proposed legislation, and we only got through the opening statement of purpose."

"Did you give up anything important or lose your temper—openly?"

"No."

"Then you're winning. Now, let's go eat."

The two went to the councilors' dining room, where Dekkard had the moderately spicy chilled tomato soup, because he discovered that he really wasn't all that hungry. The remainder of the day at the office was busy, if uneventful, with Dekkard spending a bell at the Workplace Administration hearing, then returning to the office to deal with correspondence. He followed that with a good bell of reviewing the next sections of his Security reform proposal, trying to pick out provisions or words where Baar would raise objections and thinking over how best to counter them.

At a sixth before fourth bell, Avraal stepped into his office and closed the door.

"Is it bad news or worse news?" asked Dekkard dryly.

"Neither. We just got this message from Carlos." She handed Dekkard an envelope addressed to Councilor Steffan Dekkard and Ritten Avraal Ysella-Dekkard.

"He's emphasizing that you're a double Ritten," said Dekkard dryly.

"One's only honorary, as I told you. But Carlos loves to use titles for all they're worth."

"I suspect that's to make fun of them."

"Of course." Avraal smiled.

Dekkard opened the envelope and read the words written on the plain white formal card. "If we can stop by his office on the way home, he has someone we can interview for suitability as an emotional-pattern sensor." He handed her the card. "We might as well stop by."

"Might as well?"

Dekkard flushed. "We should. Can you tell how good this empath is?"

"We'll see. We'll have to drive around the city a bit to tell what they sense." She paused. "There's one other thing."

"Oh?"

"You're likely to be at the biggest risk traveling to and from the Council, or on enddays. That means . . ."

"Lodging? Even if I can get a stipend, the way Obreduur did for us—that's asking a lot of Emrelda. The house isn't that big. That's quite an imposition."

"Having you dead would be an even greater imposition, and she was quite clear about not having me go through what she's been through."

"It sounds like you've already talked this over with her."

"Of course. Besides, you shouldn't mind having three women looking out for you." Avraal smiled mischievously.

"Three?"

"Almost all emotional-pattern sensors are women."

Dekkard nodded. That figured. Female empaths outnumbered male empaths by four to one, just as male isolates outnumbered females by about the same ratio.

By the time fourth bell chimed, even if it happened to be less than ten minutes later, he was more than ready to leave the office, especially since he knew he and Avraal would have to be back at work early on Duadi morning, and he hadn't planned on stopping to see Carlos. *But if this empath can sense hostility or purpose at a distance, it will be worth it. More than worth it.*

Neither he nor Avraal saw or sensed anything out of the ordinary as they made their way to the covered parking. The traffic on Imperial Boulevard and the Avenue of the Guilds wasn't bad. Dekkard parked in an open space next to the building, and at a third before fifth bell, the two walked up the stairs and into Carlos Baartol's office.

Elicya looked up from her desk. "He thought you'd be here about now. Go on in. I'll get Nincya."

Dekkard left the door open as he and Avraal walked into Baartol's private office.

Baartol looked up, then stood. "I found someone who's a pattern sensor of sorts."

"But?" asked Dekkard.

Baartol offered an amused smile. "You'll see. She doesn't have security credentials, but she can read both people and books, unlike some from her background. You won't be able to hire her as a security type, but as a junior clerk or personal messenger or something like that. She's the best I could find, and you'll be better off with someone now than waiting."

"What you're saying is that my life expectancy is rather short if I don't have someone now as opposed to the perfect someone after I'm dead."

"It might not be quite that bad," replied Baartol.

At that moment Elicya ushered another figure into the office, then withdrew and shut the office door.

Baartol gestured and said, "Nincya, I'd like you to meet Councilor Steffan Dekkard and Ritten Avraal Ysella-Dekkard. Steffan, Avraal, this is Nincya Gaaroll."

Gaaroll was a good three digits shorter than Avraal, but blocky and muscular. Her hair was an unruly mop of short auburn curls. Her mouse-brown eyes held intensity. The lines in her face showed that she was probably older than either Dekkard or Avraal. She wore what resembled a blue messenger's tunic and trousers without any insignia. Her polished black boots still looked worn. She studied the two. "You two are pretty young to be a councilor and a Ritten."

"So far as we know, we're the youngest in quite some time," replied Dekkard.

"Isolate and empath. Is all that blather in the newssheets about you true?"

"What's in there is true," replied Avraal.

"Why do you want someone like me?"

"Because we can mostly handle threats close to us," said Dekkard. "That means the danger is going to come from far enough away that we can't see it until the last moment, if then."

"Even for an empie strong as you?" Gaaroll looked to Avraal.

"I'm afraid so."

"Who's after you?" Gaaroll snapped her head back to look at Dekkard.

"Quite a few Commercer types as well as some former Special Agents."

Gaaroll smiled. Her expression was almost anticipatory, in a predatory way. "Most Special Agents are easy to sense. Commercer bullyboys aren't much harder. Money types, bankers . . . real professional assassins . . . most of them are a lot harder. You have to know what to feel . . . or not feel."

"Can you do it?" asked Avraal.

"Better than most."

"Can you project emotions?"

Gaaroll shook her head. "Maybe just a little. Doesn't seem to register with most people."

"Why are you available?"

"Because I don't put up with airs and shit."

"I can only afford to pay you like a junior clerk." Dekkard looked to Avraal.

"But you'll get room and board," she added.

"I don't know . . ."

"One of the times the councilor is at the greatest risk is going to the Council and coming home."

"Snipers, then. That sort of thing."

"It's a possibility."

Gaaroll nodded almost dismissively. "What would I be doing while he's working?"

"Odd chores . . . also accompanying him when he leaves the office."

"You're a junior councilor. Why do people want to kill you?"

"Because he's leading the effort to reform the Security Ministry, disarm the Special Agents, and break the ties between the large corporacions and Security," said Avraal. "Possibly because several corporacion contract assassins have vanished when attempting to kill the Premier while we were his security aides."

"You two do know how to make enemies. What can you pay?"

"No more than forty marks a month," replied Dekkard. "The same as the other junior clerks, but they don't get room and board, and the food's quite good."

"I'm interested."

"Then we need to take a drive," said Avraal. "You can tell us what you sense and where."

"That's fair."

"What sort of emotional patterns can you sense, from how far away?" Dekkard asked.

"I don't sense patterns," Gaaroll replied. "I just sense focused emotions, or shielded ones. I can't tell you what they're feeling or why. I can only sense that they're strong. Around tall buildings with lots of people, a little more than a third of a mille. In other parts of the city, about half a mille. Over open ground, sometimes a mille."

"I'll be working for a while yet," said Baartol. "Let me know how your sensing test turns out."

"That part won't be the problem," said Gaaroll.

Dekkard saw why Gaaroll was available, but he just nodded. He and Avraal led the way out of the office and to where the Gresynt was parked.

"Fab steamer," observed Gaaroll.

"It was paid for in blood," said Dekkard coolly, as he turned to Avraal. "How do you want to do this?"

"We'll sit in back for now."

"If I decide to work for you, will it be that way?"

"No," said Dekkard. "To and from the Council we'll be in front. You'll be in the second row. That way fewer people will know about you." *And the last thing I want is a flippant distance empie sitting next to me.*

"Suits me."

Avraal raised her eyebrows, but said nothing.

Once everyone was in the steamer, Dekkard pulled out of the parking area and turned south on Imperial Boulevard, heading toward Commerce Circle and the harbor. Sooner or later, they'd run across something, especially near the piers.

"There's not much going on here," said Gaaroll.

"Just let us know if and when you sense anything."

As they neared Commerce Circle, Gaaroll said, "Some sort of fight or argument on the south side of Commerce Circle, maybe three people."

When Dekkard drove around the circle to where the north and south lanes merged, he caught sight of three people, gesturing at each other—two women and a man, most likely over territory for the coming evening. He only caught a glimpse, because the late-afternoon traffic going north was heavy.

"There's something at the piers."

"Which ones? The main passenger piers, the ferry pier, the freight piers, or the river piers?"

"The freight piers . . . the second long one . . . Someone died."

The access to the pier was blocked, but from what Dekkard could see, a steam lorry lay on its side, with a ship's crane halfway through the cab. Crates were strewn everywhere. "You called that one. Can you always pick out deaths?"

"No. If someone gets hurt first, most times I can. Someone gets shot, doesn't expect it, wouldn't feel the poor sap who got it. Killer maybe. Some of them get a rush."

Dekkard had to wonder just where Gaaroll had picked up her experience.

He managed a U-turn and headed back north, past Harbor Way. He turned west on the next street—the one that ran past Rabool's, one of Carlos Baartol's favorite bistros. "Tell me anything you sense on this street."

"There's a place up on the left. The bouncer did something, maybe ran off a beggar. There's a steamer trying to park in front. Bouncer's feelings are strong."

Dekkard saw a gray Realto a good block and a half away.

"Steamer coming toward us. Feels like trouble."

Dekkard immediately turned down the next alley.

The Realto ignored the Gresynt, but Avraal said, "Special Agent types. Probably looking for someone."

Obreduur had mentioned that Security spent a great deal of time scouting Rabool's, but Dekkard hadn't expected to run into a Security steamer when it wasn't quite evening.

He drove for another third around the harbor and warehouse areas of Machtarn before Avraal said, "You can head back to Carlos's office."

Gaaroll had impressed Dekkard, but that wasn't the question. What Avraal thought was what mattered.

As they got out of the Gresynt in the parking area, Dekkard said, "Do you have any other questions?"

"You don't carry one of those short-swords or a truncheon."

"No," said Dekkard, drawing back his coat to reveal the throwing knives. Avraal did the same.

"You any good with them?"

"You can watch us practice and decide for yourself," said Avraal.

"Have—"

"Yes," said Dekkard. "More than you want to know, and that's the last time we'll talk about it. Unless you want to learn how to use a throwing knife."

"You'd teach me?" For the first time, the flippant hardness softened.

"If you're willing to work at it. Now, are you interested in the position? If you agree, it starts here and now. You'll be on the Council payroll by sometime tomorrow."

"It sounds interesting. Yes."

"There's one other thing, Gaaroll," said Dekkard. "You *will* be polite when you're on duty, both to me and the Ritten, but also to the other staffers. Not subservient, just polite."

"And you will call him 'sir.'" Avraal's voice was like cold iron.

Gaaroll shivered slightly, suggesting to Dekkard that Avraal had reinforced her words with a healthy emp projection.

"Yes, Ritten."

"Let's go up and tell Carlos that you have a job, and then we'll head home. Do you have enough clothes and things for the next day, or do we need to stop somewhere?"

"Sr. Baartol told me to bring clothes for the week." Gaaroll snorted. "That's all I've got."

"There's a cleaning woman who comes once a week. She does laundry, but you have to take it down to the basement," said Avraal. "Call that another perquisite of being an untitled security aide. The only personal weapons you can carry are short-bladed knives."

Dekkard gestured toward the building door, then followed Avraal and Gaaroll inside and upstairs.

Elicya had left, but Baartol was waiting for them. He just looked to Avraal.

"Yes. She has the abilities we need," replied Avraal.

And the right attitude about Special Agents and Commercer toughs. But Dekkard only nodded.

Baartol smiled pleasantly and looked to Gaaroll. "Nincya, this is a great opportunity for you. There won't be another."

"Yes, sir. I understand."

So did Dekkard, but he just said, "If you'd get whatever you're bringing."

"My case is in the outside office, behind the desk."

Dekkard gestured for Gaaroll to head out and get it.

As soon as Gaaroll stepped into the outer office, Baartol smiled sardonically and said, barely above a murmur, "She's good, but . . ."

"We'll work it out," replied Avraal quietly, but coldly firm.

It's going to be interesting. Especially with three strong-willed women in the same house.

Once in the parking area, Dekkard and Avraal got in the front seat, while Gaaroll and her stained and battered canvas-covered suitcase were in the second row of seats.

"You're on duty now," said Dekkard. "Let us know about any strong emotions, even if they don't seem to be approaching."

"Yes, sir."

On the way to Emrelda's, Gaaroll located from four blocks away a man who felt strongly. By the time they could see him, the reason was clear. The man, barely more than a youngster, was cuffed and walking between two patrollers. Gaaroll said, "He feels a lot."

As they passed the patrollers and their captive, Avraal added, "He'd kill both of them right now, if he could."

"That type never lasts on the streets," said Gaaroll.

Or anywhere else, unless they're sons of extremely wealthy Commercers or Landors.

Before that long they were on Camelia Avenue, passing Imperial University, and in another sixth, they reached Erslaan, where Dekkard turned north on Jacquez.

When they passed the Hillside sign, Gaaroll murmured, "Swells . . . never thought."

"We'll turn left two streets up, on Florinda," said Dekkard.

"There's strong feelings from the second house from the corner on that street," said Gaaroll.

"They have a sussie son, and a low-level empie nanny," replied Avraal. "Is it more than that?"

"Probably not. But the feelings are strong." Gaaroll paused. "They're fading now. Empie shouldn't need to use that much force. Not on a sussie."

Dekkard looked to Avraal.

"That's a little too far for me. I've wondered about that before."

Dekkard nodded. Left unsaid was the fact that interfering in others' family life was frowned upon unless one knew for certain that someone was physically endangered.

Dekkard turned on Florinda and drove right up past the portico into the garage that Emrelda had thoughtfully opened.

"You live here?" asked Gaaroll.

"We do, along with my sister. It's her house. Now, let's go in and have you meet her."

"You're bringing me in, and she doesn't know?"

"She knows that we have to bring someone in, just not who," replied Avraal.

The three made their way inside and to the kitchen, where Emrelda stood, still in her uniform.

Gaaroll's mouth opened slightly, just for a moment, when she saw Emrelda.

"This is my sister, Emrelda," said Avraal. "She's a patrol dispatcher. Her husband was an engineer who disappeared after he discovered a large engineering company was sabotaging the project he was working on. Emrelda, this is Nincya Gaaroll. She's an emotional sensor who can locate strong emotions much farther away than I can."

"I can't tell what they are," interjected Gaaroll. "Just that they're strong. I'm not a security type."

"I thought this might be why you were late," said Emrelda, nodding slowly. "Welcome, Nincya. We're both counting on you to keep Steffan safe."

"The three of us ought to be able to do that," replied Gaaroll.

"We hope so," replied Emrelda. "Now, let me show you to your room. It's a bit small, but it's on the main level. It has a half bath next to it, but you'll have to use the tub or shower in the center upstairs bathroom, preferably at night, since all of us shower in the morning. Once you get your things put away, you can join us in the kitchen. Dinner tonight will be simple—it's cold potato soup, but I'll fry up some skillet bread. There are also some lemon tarts I picked up on the way home."

"Sounds good . . . I mean very good."

From the instant look of surprise that vanished more quickly than it had appeared Dekkard had the feeling that Gaaroll didn't have dinner all that often—if at all.

Emrelda left with Gaaroll, but returned to the kitchen in minutes. "We'll have to do something about her wardrobe. How good is she?"

"From what I can tell," replied Avraal, "she's very good at sensing strong emotional patterns at a distance. But we'll have to see."

"She's had a hard life," said Emrelda, "but I suspect some of that is her own doing."

Both Dekkard and Avraal nodded.

In less than a sixth, Gaaroll was back in the kitchen. "Can I do anything?"

"Not right now. You can help Steffan clean up."

For just a moment, Gaaroll stiffened, as if she couldn't believe Dekkard cleaned up.

"I spent five years as an apprentice plasterer, before I won a place at the Military Institute," Dekkard said dryly.

"You're not a swell?"

"I've had to learn. Avraal and Emrelda have also helped. Now, let's enjoy dinner."

17

O N Duadi morning, Dekkard had to struggle to get himself up a good bell earlier than usual for the long day ahead. He did notice that Gaaroll, who had showered the night before, had left the bathroom neat, which was a good sign. *If it continues.*

Gaaroll was already in the kitchen with Emrelda, who stood, ready to leave, when Dekkard arrived.

Emrelda smiled at Dekkard. "We had a nice chat." Then she turned to Gaaroll. "I'll see you late this afternoon."

Once Emrelda left, Dekkard asked, "Would you like more café?"

"Please."

Dekkard refilled her mug and then poured his own café. "Have you had anything to eat?"

"I ate with—" She gestured to where Emrelda had exited. "Is she a Ritten, too?"

"You can call her Emrelda, except on formal occasions, and there won't be many of those."

"It's strange. I mean, one day I'm in a women's bunkhouse, and now I have a room to myself."

"So long as you keep Steffan safe," said Avraal as she entered the breakfast room, dressed except for her jacket and throwing knives.

Dekkard filled Avraal's mug and set it at her place. Avraal seated herself and took a slow sip of café.

"How did you sleep?" Dekkard asked Gaaroll.

"Took a little to get used to the quiet. Good after that."

"What was your last position?"

"Wasn't a position. Stevedores Guild called me in to check cargo ships. Piecework . . . see if they were smuggling people inside big crates or iron containers. Usually from Noldar or Atacama. Most empies have trouble sensing through a lot of metal."

Dekkard had a number of ideas why Gaaroll's working for the Stevedores Guild wouldn't have lasted. Rather than say anything, he split his two croissants, and filled each with a slice of quince paste.

"You *like* that?"

"I do, but you and Avraal share the same feeling about my preferences." Dekkard smiled and took a large bite out of the first croissant.

Gaaroll shook her head.

When they finished eating, Dekkard and Avraal took care of their dishes and instructed Gaaroll on what to do with hers.

Less than a sixth later, the three were in the Gresynt heading down the drive, with Dekkard and Avraal in front, and Gaaroll in the middle of the bench seat that composed the second row.

"Empie next door is beating emotions at the sussie," said Gaaroll.

"I know," replied Avraal, "but we can't exactly prove it, and it hasn't gone to physical abuse."

"Sometimes . . ."

"Emotional abuse is worse than physical abuse," Avraal finished bleakly.

"It's stopped. For now," said Gaaroll.

Thank goodness. Dekkard had a feeling that the empie next door was going to be a problem over time. "We'll take the standard way to work this morning," he said as he turned south on Jacquez. "Not that we'll be doing that often. It's too obvious, but Nincya should know it. I've figured out a number of other ways to get from here to the Council Office Building, but we'll be alternating routes every morning."

Within another few minutes Dekkard had turned onto Camelia Avenue.

As they neared Imperial University, Gaaroll said urgently, "There's someone hiding in that big tower up ahead. He's trying to remain calm. Feelings real strong."

"Frig!" snapped Dekkard, waiting for a space in the oncoming traffic before he made a U-turn to head back toward Erslaan. He ignored the angry gestures of the driver who'd had to slow down.

"He's really pissed," said Gaaroll. "That's a guess. He just spiked his feelings."

"The one in the bell tower or the driver I cut off?" asked Dekkard.

"Both," replied Gaaroll.

"Could the one in the tower have been angry about something else?" asked Avraal.

"Don't think so. The moment you turned, that was when his feelings spiked."

"Besides," said Dekkard, "who would be up there this early in the morning and get angry the moment I turned?" He'd considered the possibility of snipers. *But so soon?* That made sense. Whoever wanted to get at him was trying to get to Dekkard before he realized how much danger he was in and took steps to try to avoid them. "We won't be coming this way any time soon."

"The bell tower is one of the few places where a shooter has an unobstructed view of the avenue," said Avraal. "He must have been watching for you with field glasses. They could find out that we have a gray Gresynt with a councilor's emblem welded to the bumper. You always drive, and likely no other councilors come this way."

Because they all live in more prosperous areas.

Dekkard took an even more circuitous route to the Council Office Building because he didn't want to go back up Jacquez—just in case whoever was behind the assassin had someone waiting near the house.

As a result, the three of them barely made it to the office by half before second bell.

"We had to make an unplanned detour, Svard. Nincya, Svard is the senior legalist and staff director. Svard, this is Nincya Gaaroll. She goes on the payroll as a junior clerk, but she's really a distance emotional-pattern reader. No security credentials, but I'll need her and Avraal close for a while." *Maybe a long while.* "Now, we need to get started on the interviews." Dekkard turned. "Margrit, can you help Nincya with the paperwork for her appointment as a junior clerk? Leave blank anything Svard or I have to fill in."

"Yes, sir."

The first interview was with Aensyn Mychels, a tall, well-built, dark-haired young man. His degree, from Imperial University, was in structural engineering. He settled easily into the chair directly across the desk from Dekkard, with Avraal on his right and Roostof on his left. His eyes went mostly to Dekkard and Roostof.

After the largely perfunctory questions about his studies and his degree, asked mainly by Svard, Dekkard asked, "Why do you want to work as what amounts to an engineering consultant for one of the most junior members of the Council?"

Mychels smiled warmly. "From what I've seen, the Council appropriates vast sums for engineering projects, and it seems that many of those projects, for one reason or another, don't get built. I think I could be helpful in reducing some of that unnecessary spending."

Dekkard was well aware of excessive appropriations, but the reason wasn't the one Mychels named. It was the fact that the excesses were returned to the Treasury and could be redirected to councilors' pet projects with minimal, if any, oversight.

"There have been recent stories about large engineering corporacions using unethical methods to squeeze out small and more efficient businesses through, shall we say, dubious methods. What do you think about that, Aensyn?" asked Dekkard.

"That may be true," replied Mychels, "but I've done work internships with two of them, and I never saw anything that would suggest that."

"You never saw anything that would suggest that?" asked Avraal pleasantly. "Not the slightest hint of pressuring suppliers? Or the corporacion suddenly obtaining a project after another company's failure? Or overhearing senior engineers saying, after a contract went to another smaller business, 'Don't worry. We'll get it back'? Or similar instances?"

Mychels stiffened.

Avraal looked to Dekkard.

"You can go, Aensyn, I'm afraid that your talents aren't what we're looking for." Dekkard stood and smiled pleasantly.

After Mychels left, Avraal said, "He was lying. He saw plenty of that."

The second interview was with Shuryn Teitryn, a thin young man with almost whitish skin, and pale blond hair, suggesting that there was more than a strain of Atacaman in his background. He had degrees in civil engineering and mechanical engineering, but from Ondeliew University, rather than from Imperial University or even Siincleer University.

From the largely perfunctory opening questions, Dekkard got the impression that Teitryn had struggled to finish his degrees, not from his transcripts, or from the fact that it had taken him six years.

". . . and I knew, with my background, one degree, especially one from a less than prestigious university, wasn't even going to get me in the door of the large companies. So, I started going to the smaller companies. Most of them aren't hiring at the moment. I was set up for an interview with Engaard Engineering, but the founder died of a heart attack and one of the senior engineers vanished. I guess the business just fell apart."

"Do you know any names of people at the company?" asked Avraal.

"I sent in my papers, transcripts, and the draft of an engineering project I did at the university. It was all I had, because I couldn't get an internship. I got a message from the receptionist to show up for an interview, last summer."

"When?" asked Avraal.

Teitryn frowned. "It was on a Unadi, the nineteenth of Summerfirst, I think. I'm pretty sure it wasn't the twenty-fifth. When I got there, the woman at the office told me that Sr. Engaard had been called to look into a problem with a project in Siincleer and to stop by on Tridi. But when I did, she told me that Sr. Engaard had died of a heart attack in Siincleer, and that one of his senior engineers was missing. She said, under the circumstances, that it was unlikely that they would be hiring. She gave me back my papers."

"Did she tell you the name of the senior engineer?" Avraal pressed.

"No. She just said he was a talented senior engineer." Teitryn paused. "That was disappointing. I know it had to be hard on both the families, but that was the only engineering outfit that seemed interested. That was why, when I saw the announcement on the board at the professional engineers hall about your job, I thought maybe I could still use my expertise." He looked at Avraal. "Did I say something wrong?"

She shook her head.

"I have an engineering question for you," said Dekkard. "It might not be in your field, but I'd appreciate the best answer you can provide. Do you think a parabolic solar mirror could be built that was large enough and with a narrow enough focus to cut metal?"

Teitryn frowned. "That's not my field, but I think you'd have terrible difficulty with the tolerances because a mirror that could concentrate that much energy might be so big it would deform. Also, I don't see how you could easily move the mirror or the metal to get a straight cut. The best use of mirror like that might be to concentrate it on a boiler to generate steam. That might make a good emergency source of steam for a warship—"

Dekkard smiled and held up his hand. "You've more than answered the question."

Dekkard and Svard asked several more questions before Dekkard stood. "I'd appreciate it if you'd wait in the outer office, Shuryn."

The thin engineer stood. "Yes, sir. I'll be there."

Once Teitryn had left, Dekkard turned to Avraal. "Was he telling the truth?"

"He was. I'm not sure that he could do otherwise. If you hire him, you'll have to have Svard and me coach him on how to say nothing without lying."

"Then you think he's a possibility?"

"He's awfully green, but if Halaard saw potential in him, enough to grant him an interview, that puts him ahead of most."

Dekkard nodded and walked to the door, opening it. "Sr. Siinjin, if you'd come in."

Fitzhugh Siinjin was broad-shouldered, with tight-curled, dark hair and slightly darker skin that suggested a Landor background in the southwest, possibly near Surpunta.

"It's a pleasure to meet you, Councilor." Siinjin focused immediately on Dekkard, who merely gestured for the other to seat himself before settling behind the desk.

Again, Dekkard let Svard do the first questions before he asked, "You said that you thought working on engineering matters in a political setting would be fascinating. In what way?"

"Well, sir, the Council decides all the funding for Army and Navy construction, and if I could provide expertise to give you more insight . . ."

"How would you deal with the fact that many of these decisions are made because of political considerations?"

"Isn't that the nature of politics, sir? I could help make it a little less political."

"What do you think about the fact that more significant Council-funded building projects are going to the largest engineering corporacions?"

"Unless I knew something to the contrary, I'd have to assume that's because they have the expertise to build those projects."

Dekkard smiled and stood. "You have very impressive credentials, Sr. Siinjin, but they're not quite what we're looking for. Thank you for your time."

When Siinjin had left the outer office, Dekkard looked to Avraal.

"Mealymouthed corporacion type. His credentials are too good to be applying for this job. I suspect one of the engineering corporacions asked him to apply. I didn't ask him that, because, if they did, I don't want to alert them, and if they didn't it would just make him angrier. He was angry enough when he left. He's the kind who gets personally affronted when rejected."

Dekkard turned back to Svard. "These were the best?"

"Most good engineers don't want to work in politics. The others had obvious problems."

"Then we'll go with Teitryn and see how it works." Dekkard made a mental note to himself to have a talk with Teitryn in the next few days, including giving him some limited background on what had happened with Engaard Engineering, but without names.

Dekkard barely had enough time to sign and seal the appointment papers for Gaaroll and Teitryn, who was clearly amazed that he had been chosen, before he and Avraal had to leave for the Security Committee meeting. He carried the gray folder with Roostof's notes.

They reached a point on the far side of the main hallway when Dekkard stopped and turned to Avraal. "I want you to walk right up to the door to the committee room with me and wait. Try to sense if anyone is surprised to see me."

Avraal nodded. "I can do that. Do you think the Commercer councilors would be that stupid? Usually assassinations are done through intermediaries."

"I doubt it, but it certainly can't hurt."

At about two minutes before third bell, Rikkard and then Baar entered. Dekkard followed, taking his time so that he was inside the committee room and halfway to the dais as the chimes rang third bell.

"How kind of you to join us, Councilor," said Hasheem sardonically.

"My apologies, Sr. Chairman," replied Dekkard. He laid the leather folder on the surface of the desk, hoping he wouldn't have to scramble to look at Roostof's notes.

"The committee is now in session." Hasheem tapped the gavel. "Today we will be dealing with section one of the proposed legislation to restructure the present Security Ministry. Section one lays out the structure of the new Ministry of Public Safety, the transfer of the Special Tactical Force to the Army, and the restructuring of Special Agents as unarmed investigative agents within either the Justiciary or Treasury Ministries."

"A point of order, Sr. Chairman," began Baar. "How can the legislation be called a restructuring when there was no formal structure for the Special Agents?"

"Would you care to address that, Councilor Dekkard?"

Dekkard could tell it would be a long morning. "If the honored councilor from Suvion would look at part three of section one, the proposal clearly states that while the Security Ministry indirectly, but never formally, established Special Agents as part of the ministry by authorizing them to carry firearms, the test of whether a subpart of a ministry exists as an entity is whether that subpart operated in the same fashion for a continuing period. Since the directive authorizing the use of firearms was issued in 1244, twenty-two years ago, the Special Agents, by fact and act, compose a discrete part of the ministry and are thus a transferable entity."

"I believe that addresses the issue," said Hasheem. He tapped the gavel once. "Point of order denied."

Dekkard knew that more of the same would come, but one factor in his favor was that the Commercers had been in power so long that in many cases, especially in Security, they'd seldom sought specific legislative authority. By the time the committee meeting ended at noon, Dekkard felt sweaty, and they'd only covered the introduction and section one. Baar had managed to insert some "clarifications" and word changes. But the structure remained close to what Roostof had drafted and Colsbaan had reviewed. Unfortunately, changes in the implementing details in the next three sections could easily weaken the bill. Dekkard also knew that without all the briefing papers by Roostof and Colsbaan, he never could have managed to mostly hold his own against Baar.

As Dekkard stood, so did Pajiin, who said, "It's going to be a long and interesting week."

"Long, yes, I don't know how interesting."

"It's interesting to watch Baar. You ever do anything to him?"

"I never knew who he was until he was selected to replace Marrak, and I never really even knew Marrak."

"The Commercers don't care much for you."

"It might be because I worked for Obreduur. He's hardly their favorite."

"He's the Premier."

"I know. I'm just a junior councilor." *And far more vulnerable.* Dekkard let Pajiin leave first. He also noticed that Hasheem avoided him.

Avraal was waiting by the committee room door.

"Was anyone surprised this morning?"

"Not when you walked in. Hasheem was slightly annoyed, and Pajiin was amused. Baar seemed resigned, but not in any lasting sense or with deep feelings. Rikkard didn't seem to care at all."

"That's interesting. Rikkard seemed bored, as if it didn't matter."

"Maybe it doesn't to him."

"There's something more there. But we need to think about it. Let's get something to eat. I have a Workplace Administration Committee meeting at two."

"Do you know what it's about?"

"Safe handling of ironway ties—that was what was on the committee notice."

"Are ironway ties that dangerous?"

"They're big and heavy. I imagine stacking them wrong could be a problem, but if Haarsfel is holding a hearing, there must be more. I don't happen to know what it is." Except in the back of his mind, there was . . . something . . . but he couldn't remember what.

Dekkard had the duck cassoulet, but Avraal turned that down when he suggested it, saying, "Even dry duck is greasy. I'll have a half order of the three-cheese chicken."

After that, she walked with him to the Workplace Administration Committee room and said, "I'll be back in a bell. Wait for me if you finish early."

Dekkard made his way into the committee room, where Kaliara Bassaana was talking to Yordan Farris, the other Commercer councilor, who cut a handsome figure. Eduardo Nortak, the Craft councilor reputed to be less than brilliant, appeared. Then the two Landor councilors—Quentin Fader and Elskar Halljen—sauntered in. Only then did Chairman Haarsfel take his place.

"Today's hearing will deal with reports from the Ironway Maintenance Guild that ironway crosstie shops are not complying with the required ventilation standards . . ."

At that, Dekkard finally recalled the meeting with Obreduur and the ironway workers where one of them had said something similar. Almost a bell later, several guild officials had testified and presented evidence, leaving Dekkard slightly puzzled. The problem didn't seem to be with the law requiring ventilating, but with proving the lack of compliance, since whenever inspectors appeared, miraculously everything was vented. *The ironways paying off the inspectors to be notified? Or do they just have people watching the inspectors?*

More than two bells after the hearing had begun, as the other committee members straggled out, Kaliara Bassaana followed Dekkard, then turned as Dekkard joined Avraal.

"Acting like newlyweds?" offered Bassaana.

"Of course," replied Dekkard. "We're still quite newly wed."

"That's sweet," said Bassaana warmly.

When the two moved away, Avraal said quietly, "That's not what she meant."

"I know. How did she feel?"

"Amused, mainly. Certainly not irritated."

"Well, let's get back to the office so that I can deal with the correspondence and petitions."

18

THERE were no difficulties getting home on Duadi night, although Dekkard wasn't about to take Camelia Avenue any time soon. Not that Gaaroll didn't sense some strong feelings at a distance, but they were all momentary spikes or in places from where there was no possibility of a clear shot. The lack of strong emotional outbursts from next door was also a relief.

At breakfast on Tridi, after Emrelda had left, and after Avraal had finished two mugs of café and half a croissant, she turned to Gaaroll. "This endday we're taking you shopping for better working clothes."

"What's wrong with these? They're clean. No patches or holes."

"There are two reasons. First, your clothes would be acceptable if you only worked in the office, but before long you'll have other duties. Those will put you in the public eye, particularly in the eyes of the Council Guards, and they'll stop you more. You'll get angry, and that won't be good for anyone. Second, you're going to have to accompany Steffan to other places besides the office where you'll need to fit in as an aide. Since we can't hire you as a security aide, you need to dress as an office aide."

"Can't afford fancier clothes."

"You don't have to. Steffan has a one-time allowance for expenses like that."

Dekkard managed not to wince. *There goes more of what's left of my transitional allowance as a new councilor.* And he knew that there were far too many expenditures to come.

Gaaroll frowned.

"We're not talking fancy, Nincya. Something similar to what you already wear, except with better fabric, slightly cleaner lines, and greater variation in color."

"You sure about that?"

"You're going to be there," replied Avraal.

"If that's all." Gaaroll's words were grudgingly accepting.

In one sense Dekkard understood, but he'd certainly had to pay for upgrading his own wardrobe, outside of quite a few excellent cravats Avraal had given him. "We'll need to leave a little earlier," he said. "I'm going to try some backstreets to see if we can get close to the university bell tower."

"You don't think they've given up on that after your acrobatic U-turn yesterday?" asked Avraal sardonically.

"I have no idea, but I'd like to see if they're still posting someone there, and see if you can sense something as well as Nincya."

"If there was a shooter, he might want to collect more pay," said Gaaroll. "Could have reported you never got in range."

"Well, we'll see what we find," said Dekkard. "If anything at all."

Before long, the three were in the Gresynt, headed west on Florinda until it intersected Ortez Way, which angled toward the university.

From what Emrelda's maps showed, Wisteria Street, three blocks north of Camelia Avenue, wound through the small park just outside the east gates of Imperial University and dead-ended into North University Way, which eventually became West University Way, and ended at Camelia Avenue. When he saw the route, he wondered why more people didn't take it. He soon found out. Within the park, Wisteria was dotted with unmarked bitumen speed rises, which delivered a jolt any time Dekkard exceeded the speed of a fast walk. North University Way was narrow and crowded with parked steamers—those of students. From the number of newer Gresynts and Kharlans, many of those students were wealthy indeed. There was little traffic. Three- and four-story buildings lined the space on the south side of the stone walls, and while Dekkard could sometimes see the bell tower, it was difficult.

"Someone's up there," said Gaaroll laconically. "Feels the same, best I can recall."

Dekkard kept the Gresynt moving slowly. The watcher in the bell tower would barely be able to see the Gresynt, and on North University Way, it certainly wouldn't have stood out. "Can you slow down some more for a bit?" asked Avraal.

Dekkard slowed, checking his rearview mirrors, but the closest steamer was more than a block back.

"All right," said Avraal, after a time. "He's definitely been posted to look for something, but what I can't tell."

"I can't get any more, either," said Gaaroll.

"That really doesn't tell us much."

"It's enough that we don't use Camelia Avenue anytime soon, and never without Nincya," said Avraal.

Dekkard was glad he'd allowed extra time. Even so it was almost a sixth past second bell when the three of them entered the office.

As soon as Dekkard had checked the messages to see if there was anything urgent—there wasn't—he asked Roostof and Teitryn to join him and Avraal. Once the door closed, Dekkard turned to Teitryn. "I'm sorry I didn't have time to brief you on what your specific duties entail earlier, but yesterday was particularly hectic. I take it that Svard briefed you on all the administrivia. Since I see a staff pin, I assume you have your passcard as well."

"Yes, sir."

"Good. You'll need it. Now, here's the outline of what we need you to find out. Just before the election there was a lengthy article in *Gestirn* about a number of strange coincidences like the one you experienced with Engaard Engineering, where a smaller and newer engineering firm underbid one of the larger firms, and then suffered strange events and reverses."

"Then that wasn't the only one?"

"We don't believe so. We need you to build up a file on all of those occurrences. To begin with, you're not to contact anyone personally. You're to build up as great a compilation as you can from purely documentary sources. You'll probably have to go to the Imperial University Library to view newssheets from other cities. Ostensibly, you're looking into the change in historical costs of construction funded by the Council and what media and public reaction has been in the past ten years. Svard will draft a statement authorizing your document search, and I'll sign and seal it. You can show the authorization to anyone, but don't relinquish it. If they won't grant you access, don't protest. Just get their name and position and give it to Svard. After you've done all you think you can that way, we'll move on to step two. Gather the news stories on Engaard Engineering and anything you can easily find. We already have some information."

"How long do you think this should take?"

"I have no idea, but be prepared to go over what you've been able to find by around Unadi the thirteenth."

"Yes, sir!"

"Do you have any other questions, Shuryn?"

"Not at the moment. Sr. Roostof has been most helpful."

After Roostof and Teitryn had left the office, Dekkard walked to the window and looked out. The sky to the west and north was clear, but wind was out of the northeast, suggesting the possibility of rain later. Then he looked to Avraal. "What were their reactions?"

"Just about what you saw. Svard was a bit concerned. Shuryn's just excited to have a real position with any engineering in it. I get the feeling he's the kind who won't let go."

"That's good if he doesn't take it to extremes." At Avraal's raised eyebrows, he added, "Immediately, and all at once, that is." *Since you do intend to take it to the extremes the bastards deserve, if you can possibly manage it.*

With an amused smile, she nodded.

"I need to read through all messages and mail before the Security Committee markup, and then go over the notes Svard gave me about what Baar will likely try today."

"I'll leave you to it. I'll spend some time working with Gaaroll."

"That would be very good. Thank you."

Avraal slipped out of the inner office.

Somewhat more than a sixth before third bell, Dekkard and Avraal left the office for the Council Hall and the markup session, Dekkard carrying the gray leather folder with his notes.

"Someone's tracking us," said Avraal as they stepped out of the Council Office Building and into the courtyard leading to the Council Hall.

"How close?"

"Fifty yards back. Empath. Strong. A little unsteady. Relatively new, I'd guess, since she's accompanying a councilor and an isolate."

"Any idea who?"

"I'd guess that Hasheem finally got someone to replace Arthal Shenke. That would be a great relief for Erleen."

"It would be. Arthal left her in the lurch," Dekkard pointed out.

"That New Meritorist empie almost killed him as well as Aashtaan. Do you blame him?"

"I suppose not."

"You do blame him. I can hear it in your voice." Avraal added in a slightly bemused tone, "Not everyone is as duty-driven as you, dear."

"Nor you," returned Dekkard with a smile. "We'll see soon enough."

In fact, Avraal's assessment was verified when Dekkard stopped briefly at the committee room door and glanced back to see Erleen Orlov and another woman in security grays flanking Hasheem. The new security aide looked as though she'd barely finished training.

Dekkard turned back, made his way into the committee room, took his seat, and waited for Hasheem to follow him into the chamber.

The markup session on the Security and Public Safety Reorganization Act— the title provisionally agreed to by the committee—was every bit as difficult and tedious as Dekkard had feared, with Baar trying to eliminate or, if not successful, restrict the impact of every change. As Dekkard expected, the committee agreed to a few changes, one of which was to allow reassigned Special Agents to carry arms on dangerous assignments if authorized by their director, rather than by the Justiciary minister, as Dekkard's original words had proposed. Dekkard countered by insisting that that would amount to carte blanche in no time at all, as had happened before, and that such permits be limited to two weeks, and that no more than two agents in any one section be allowed such permission, except by specific authority of the minister. Dekkard's amendment to Baar's amendment passed 4–3.

Dealing with every line of the bill was similar.

Still, by the end of the third day of markup, the proposal remained remarkably close, all things considered, to the original proposal.

Rikkard remained almost disinterested, while Navione and Haastar occasionally asked questions or made comments. Pajiin said little, but voted to support Dekkard on every issue, while Hasheem supported several of Baar's amendments, but also supported Dekkard's modifications. Navione's and Haastar's votes tended to follow those of Hasheem.

Furdi would be even more brutal, Dekkard knew, because the last section dealt with timetables and implementation dates. A long implementation period would be exactly what the Commercers wanted, because it would goad the New Meritorists into more violence.

Except for broadsheets, the letter to all councilors, and posters scattered around Machtarn, the New Meritorists had been quiet. *Too quiet.* And that worried Dekkard.

He had the strong feeling that they wanted a Security reform act, but that was just the beginning of their demands. The next would be the wide-scale change of Council voting procedures, a change that would require totally altering the basis of the Great Charter, changes that couldn't be accepted because, as both Dekkard and Obreduur knew, they would eventually destroy Guldor, just as such changes had once destroyed the Grand Democracy of Teknold. Yet the New Meritorists seemed determined to settle for nothing less.

"The markup's over," said Pajiin. "What are you thinking about?"

"That tomorrow will be worse," said Dekkard dryly.

"You'll do fine tomorrow," said Pajiin, rising from his seat behind the dais.

"Thank you." As Pajiin moved away, Dekkard stood and stretched, then began to walk toward the rear of the committee room, leather folder in hand.

"Councilor?" ventured one of the committee clerks, Sohl Hurrek, as he recalled.

Dekkard slowed and turned, his eyes scanning the clerk, alert for anything that might be wrong. "Yes?"

"Nothing really, sir." The clerk stepped back.

Dekkard saw the red mist seeping from a pouch Hurrek held—and moved, dropping his folder, kneeing the clerk in the groin and following with an elbow to the throat. The clerk staggered and went down, while the now-open pouch flew backward in the direction of the second clerk, who fled toward the chamber door.

Dekkard dashed sideways, trying to escape the reddish mist that had to be Atacaman fire pepper dust. Even so, by the time he reached the chamber door, where the second clerk had halted, he could feel his legs burning from the moments they'd been in the mist.

Avraal stood just outside the door. "Out! Into the hall!" she snapped at the second clerk, throwing knife in hand, adding to Dekkard, "You, too."

"The other clerk?"

"He's good as dead. He took several gasps of the fire pepper dust." Avraal yelled, "GUARDS! GUARDS!"

The second clerk started to bolt, and Dekkard slammed him into the wall. "You frigging move, and I'll gut you."

The clerk looked at Dekkard, then collapsed against the wall and slid down it to the floor, ending up in a heap.

The scattered passersby in the hall looked toward the pair in gray suits, one a man wearing the red cravat of a councilor—with a crumpled figure on the floor against the wall to one side.

"GUARDS!" bellowed Dekkard.

From somewhere appeared a Council Guard, then two.

"Sir?"

"A frigging clerk attacked me with Atacaman fire pepper dust," snapped Dekkard. "He's still in the committee room. This one's just a witness, I think. Get me the Guard captain."

Avraal sneezed.

"Move away from me," Dekkard told her. "There's likely dust clinging to my trousers."

Avraal did.

Two of the guards remained, looking stunned, while a third sprinted off.

The faint but potent acrid scent of the Atacaman fire pepper kept that area of the Council Hall largely empty as people scurried away. Avraal was a good five yards from Dekkard, and he could see that her eyes were still watering, as were his.

As far as Dekkard was concerned, it took forever before he spied the Guard captain—Izaak Trujillo—and several guards hurrying toward him. He doubted that even a sixth had passed.

"Guard Captain Trujillo."

"Councilor Dekkard, I might have guessed."

"No offense, Guard Captain, but can we go somewhere that I can get these trousers off? I was attacked with Atacaman fire pepper. I can already feel blisters forming. The clerk who did it is likely dead in the committee room. I knocked him down, and he ended up breathing his own dust." Dekkard gestured at the clerk at the base of the wall. "I have no idea whether he was involved, but he tried to run. He's definitely an important witness. Possibly the only one."

"He was trying to escape in front of Steffan," added Avraal, still holding her throwing knife. "This and an empblast persuaded him otherwise, but when he saw Steffan coming he didn't want to stay around. Steffan changed his mind."

Trujillo gestured to the Council Guards and pointed to the clerk on the floor, who was beginning to stir. "Keep him under tight guard." Then he said to Dekkard and Avraal, "We'll go to the Premier's floor office. It's next door to mine, but he's got a sink there, and you can wash any of the dust off your legs. One of the kitchens should have some maize oil, and you can put that on your skin afterward. That will help with the burns and the blisters."

Getting Dekkard to the Premier's office and washing and drying his legs and feet thoroughly and then slathering them with maize oil took well over a third of a bell. During the latter part of that time Guard Captain Trujillo left with the committee clerk. Dekkard ended up in a straight-backed wooden chair in the small inner floor office of the Premier. He looked at his oil-coated legs. There were scattered red spots on his lower thighs and knees, but those didn't itch or burn. Below his knee were more red spots, many of which simultaneously burned and itched, along with several raised welts that definitely itched and burned, although he had to admit the worst of it had begun to subside.

Dekkard's damp trousers were in a leather bag borrowed from the Council Guards, and pale green Guard trousers were draped over the small bookcase.

Obreduur sat behind the desk. He said dryly, "I must say, Steffan, that over the past few months, your presence has made the Council a far more exciting place."

"A clerk throwing Atacaman fire pepper?" said Dekkard. "That makes no sense." Actually, it might, but Dekkard wanted someone else to explore that.

"It might," replied the Premier, "but I've sent for the Guard captain, and we should hear what he has to add before we speculate."

Dekkard nodded. So did Avraal.

Obreduur picked up a stack of papers and began to read.

Dekkard tried to ignore the itching and burning.

Another sixth passed before Trujillo stepped into the small office, where Obreduur gestured him to the remaining chair. Trujillo handed a gray leather folder to Dekkard. "I believe this is yours, Councilor. We cleaned it."

"Thank you. I must have dropped it in trying to get away."

"It was on the floor near Hurrek, the dead clerk."

"Have you found out anything we don't know, Guard Captain?" asked Obreduur.

"I talked to the other clerk," offered Trujillo, "with a Guard empath present. He knew nothing. All that Hurrek said to him was that junior councilors should know their place, and someone should teach them. According to the surviving clerk, Hurrek said that just before he tried to attack Councilor Dekkard."

"Someone put him up to it," said Avraal.

Someone who wagered I'd kill him so no one would know who was behind it. Dekkard wasn't about to say that. "Is it possible that the dead clerk didn't even know the pouch held pure Atacaman fire pepper? That he might have thought it held something less potent?"

"That was my suspicion," said Trujillo. "The pouch was three layers of waterproofed leather, with twin seals. The attack wasn't meant to be seen as fatal. Whoever set it up likely hoped it might be, but Atacaman fire pepper dust isn't the most certain of weapons."

Dekkard nodded. "I suspect they wanted me out of the way for a few days, especially tomorrow."

Obreduur looked to Dekkard.

"The last day of markup for the Security reform bill."

"That's still quite a risk," said Obreduur. "The chairman could have postponed the markup."

"That might not have been it at all," offered Trujillo, almost apologetically. "You still carry throwing knives, Councilor Dekkard. You responded to the attempt by pushing the attacker to the floor and trying to get away from the dust. You used no weapon. While it was unfortunate that the clerk died of inhaling the dust, if you *had* used the knives . . ."

"It could have been very messy," said Dekkard bleakly.

"We would have had to hold an inquiry as to whether the use of the knife was justified, because Atacaman pepper dust is not considered, by nature, a lethal weapon of attack."

"So it appears that your instincts were essentially correct, Steffan," said Obreduur.

"As it is, the attack will be reported as a disgruntled clerk's attempt to chastise a junior councilor gone fatally wrong. Since Hurrek was a holdover from the previous government, that makes a sad sort of sense. All the witnesses say the same thing. That part of the corridor and the committee room won't be bearable until this evening, and the councilor suffered painful pepper burns. We will be looking into who might have paid him." Trujillo shook his head, then looked to Obreduur. "Is there anything else you need, Premier?"

"No, there isn't, Guard Captain. I appreciate your taking care of it, as always, professionally."

"Thank you," said Dekkard. "I also appreciate it, and I'll return the pants."

Trujillo rose. "Thank you, sir, for keeping your head. Could have been a lot worse."

That, Dekkard understood.

After the Guard captain departed, Dekkard donned the borrowed pants, a digit or so short, but the pale green didn't clash too much with his gray jacket. *Unless you look closely.* Then he inclined his head to Obreduur. "Thank you, sir."

"You handled it well enough that you didn't need much help." Obreduur paused. "Do you have any idea?"

"Besides the usual suspects? No."

Obreduur nodded thoughtfully.

Dekkard opened the folder and checked the contents, but nothing seemed to be missing. Then he and Avraal left the small floor office, Dekkard carrying his leather folder and the sealed leather bag that held his peppered trousers.

As they walked along the main corridor toward the courtyard doors, Avraal asked, "How are your legs?"

"Better. Not great."

One of the Council Guards at the entrance to the Council Office Building studied Dekkard for several moments as he approached, frowning, then nodded as he apparently recognized the councilor.

Most others in the corridors either didn't notice the slightly mismatched trousers or didn't think much about it.

Or they just saw what they thought they saw. Which was what most people did anyway, Dekkard suspected.

Neither Gaaroll nor Margrit were most people.

"What happened?" demanded both, not simultaneously, but nearly so.

"An unhappy committee clerk tried to attack me with Atacaman pepper powder," replied Dekkard. "Someone put him up to it."

"Who?" demanded Gaaroll.

"That may be hard to find out," said Dekkard dryly. "He suffocated on his own powder. The other clerk knew nothing about it." He raised his voice. "Svard! Everyone in the front office."

Once everyone was there, Dekkard gave a quick summary of the Atacaman pepper incident, ending with, "It was an unfortunate incident, especially for the clerk, but he was clearly misguided. I'd appreciate it if you'd keep it to yourselves for the immediate future."

Luara Colsbaan nodded at that.

"Now, I have a few things to catch up on." Dekkard managed a pleasant smile, although he wanted to scratch several places on his lower legs. He wouldn't because the scratching would be painful. So he kept smiling until he and Avraal were alone in his office.

"Who do you think was behind this?" asked Avraal. "Rikkard or Baar?"

Dekkard shook his head. "The Atacaman pepper was 'cute' at best and sadistic at worst. It was designed to get me in trouble, one way or another, either covered in painful welts or facing an inquiry and possible dismissal from the Council, if not a murder charge, if I'd been stupid enough to use a throwing knife. That's much more the sign of a twisted mind."

"Who?" Then Avraal's mouth opened.

"Exactly," said Dekkard. "Someone like the new assistant director of security for Northwest Industrial Chemical."

"Jaime Minz . . . he thinks that way, and he has that snarky charming manner." She paused. "But why?"

"I'm guessing, but it might be the most basic of all motives. Jealousy. He's intelligent and capable, and served as an aide far longer, but I'm the one who's a councilor and married to you. His letter as much as said that Obreduur strong-armed everyone to get me selected. And, finally, if I can get the Security reform proposal to the floor, Obreduur will get it passed, and before long the Commercers will begin to lose power as the Army takes over the STF and the Special Agents can't carry weapons and intimidate the regular patrollers."

"What do you plan to do now?"

"Survive. Somehow." Dekkard had the feeling that most of the Commercers wouldn't like the Security reform bill. How the Imperador would receive it was another question, but he hadn't been pleased with the massacres by Security, and the transfer of the STF to the Army strengthened his position as Imperador. Laureous still might veto the legislation, unless Obreduur managed forty-four votes on passage.

That's thinking a bit too far ahead. He smiled wryly. "I might as well get down to the mundane details of correspondence."

"I'll leave you to that." Avraal smiled and eased her way out, closing the door quietly.

Dekkard picked up the first typed response, which addressed a complaint about excessive freight charges for produce by Guldoran Ironway, something which no councilor could address directly—only through the Rate Bureau of the Transportation Ministry. The letter that had been drafted for Dekkard's signature by Colsbaan stated that Dekkard was forwarding the complaint to the Rate Bureau with a recommendation that the bureau look into the high rate differential between produce and manufactured goods. Dekkard signed the letter, adding a note at the bottom.

> *This has been a problem for years, and I'll be working with others in the new Council to address it.*

Both of which were true.

Still thinking about all the problems created by decades of Commercer governments, he picked up the next draft response.

Right at third bell Avraal opened Dekkard's door. "There's someone here you should see."

Dekkard hurried out—only to find Karola Mayun, the personal secretary for Premier Obreduur, standing there. "What are you doing here? Not that it's not good to see you."

"Ritten Obreduur asked me to bring this to you. She said that she'd promised it some time ago, but that you weren't crossing paths much anymore. She said you could take your time." Karola handed Dekkard a small cloth bag wrapped tightly around what had to be a book. "I have to run. The Ritten didn't want to trust it to the messenger service. Anna still isn't all that comfortable at the front desk with all the important people we seldom saw before." Karola's smile was definitely amused.

"Thank you for bringing it," said Avraal, "and thank Ritten Obreduur as well."

"I will." Then Karola headed out the door.

Gaaroll looked up from the small desk by the main door that she'd been assigned with a puzzled expression. Avraal had moved another small desk to the other side of Dekkard's door and used it when she was in the office and didn't want to bother Dekkard.

"You look confused, Nincya. What is it?" said Margrit kindly.

"She's the Premier's personal secretary, and you all know each other?"

Dekkard smiled. "You know that Avraal and I worked for the Premier, but so did Margrit and Svard. He let them come work for me because they had no chance of being promoted. So, of course, we all know each other. Just like you'll come to know everyone here." Dekkard started to hand the book to Avraal. "It was really for you."

"I know. But keep it in your office until we leave."

Dekkard understood that. Given Ingrella's taste and inclination for not only rare books, but those of a nature not always politically acceptable, especially to Commercers, the book was better on his desk for the next bell or so.

During the last bell of the workday, Dekkard managed to sign or correct all the correspondence, as well as spend a sixth or so going over Roostof's notes on the last section of the Security reform legislation. By then, more of the itching and burning had subsided.

Dekkard again took a different route back to the house, and Gaaroll didn't discern any strong emotions located where they presaged danger.

Emrelda had a chicken and mushroom casserole almost ready to eat when the three entered the house. Dekkard quickly filled in Emrelda on the Atacaman pepper attack while Gaaroll and Avraal did what they could to help.

"Do you have any idea who?"

"We have an idea," replied Dekkard, "but at the moment, it's just an idea. The Council Guard captain is still looking into it, even if it's been reported as an unfortunate misadventure."

"It could have been very unfortunate for you," said Emrelda with a barely concealed bitterness.

"It's better that way for *now*," Avraal said, with the slightest emphasis.

Gaaroll, looking at Avraal, stiffened slightly for a moment.

"Yes," said Emrelda to Gaaroll, clearly having seen the other's reaction, "we're very protective."

"They might sometimes forgive," added Dekkard, "but they never forget. Anything."

"It's time to eat," declared Emrelda, "and, Steffan, you look like you need that Kuhrs."

Dekkard just grinned. He still didn't even sip the lager until the sisters touched their wine. Gaaroll had lager.

He thought about asking Emrelda about patrollers and working women, but decided against it.

In the end, neither Avraal nor Dekkard even looked at the cloth-wrapped book until they were alone in their bedroom, when Dekkard handed it to her.

"She said we both should read it." Avraal eased the small leather-bound volume out of the cloth bag and looked at the cover, without title on either the front or the spine. Then she opened to the title page. She looked at the words, then turned the book in the dim light of the single wall sconce so that Dekkard could also read them.

AVERRA
The City of Truth
Johan Eschbach
377 TE

"What sort of date is that?" asked Dekkard.

"It's a Teknold date. I don't know how it equates exactly to Guldoran dating, but it has to date back over a thousand years."

"Is the book that old? It doesn't look that old."

"It might be a copy, but it's still old. I've never seen that kind of binding, not even the oldest volumes in Father's library, and some of those dated back to when Aloor was independent."

Avraal turned to the first page, and they began to read.

I.

I once walked the ways of a city where the names of the streets changed every few blocks, although I discerned little difference from block to block. Was that change in nomenclature a matter of wistful thinking on the part of the inhabitants, or a perception of differences invisible to me as a mere outsider? Or, perhaps, had the inhabitants merely failed to realize that names describe, at best, but a fraction of a street, or an individual, and in frustration or desperation, named the most salient feature of each segment, thus creating chaos in a vain quest for accuracy? I could not say then which it might have been, nor could I now, these many years later.

Here in Averra, no street is exactly the same as it was the last time I trod it, whether the pavement be brick or stone, nor will it ever be the same. For that is the nature of cities and their streets and, indeed, of those who inhabit them, since each of us, in passing, leaves an ephemeral yet lasting mist on each way along which we have passed in the course of our days. That mist, which those of science dismiss, is as real as the world itself, although it cannot be measured with calipers or poured into a beaker and weighed, for it is the accumulation of all the mists of all the passersby that imbue each boulevard, avenue, street, or even each narrow alleyway with its character, and, if the mists are strong enough, pervasive enough, even wisps of stories . . .

Avraal closed the book, slowly, but carefully. "I've never heard of Averra. Have you?"

Dekkard shook his head. "It might be a place that never existed. Or one that disappeared long ago. But why would Ingrella want us to read this book? Especially now?"

"She always has her reasons, and they've never failed Obreduur—or us. We'll read it, bit by bit, together." Avraal replaced the book in the cloth bag, and then slipped both into the single drawer of the bed table.

As he undressed, Dekkard's mind lingered over the title. A city of truth that he'd never heard of? Yet the book didn't seem one of fancy or fanciful tales.

He stifled a yawn. It had been a long day.

19

O N Furdi, Dekkard took yet another route to the Council Office Building, and neither Avraal nor Gaaroll sensed anything untoward.

As the three entered the Council Office Building, Avraal said, "While you're at the committee markup, I'll write a note to Ingrella thanking her for the loan of the book."

"I still wonder about why she picked that particular book," returned Dekkard.

"I'm sure we'll find out," said Avraal, sweetly enough that Dekkard had to suppress an instinctive wince, since that excessively sweet tone usually meant "you idiot" or something similar, though Avraal had never used such words with Dekkard.

She hasn't had to . . . yet.

Once in the office, Dekkard quickly checked the mail, noting the gradual increase in volume, no doubt as his constituents in Gaarlak discovered who their new councilor happened to be. He still finished reading through all the letters and petitions before leaving for the Security Committee markup of the reform proposal. There were no messages, which reminded Dekkard that Obreduur was as prone to sending messages as the Commercers had been.

But then, you've only been a councilor less than a month.

He and Avraal left the office for the committee meeting a little less than a third before third bell, while Margrit taught Gaaroll the comparatively simple office filing system. Dekkard again carried the gray leather folder with the notes he hoped he wouldn't need. It still bore the faintest hint of the scent of Atacaman fire pepper.

As Dekkard and Avraal approached the committee room, Hasheem and his two security aides moved toward them. Dekkard turned toward the three.

"How are you feeling this morning, Steffan?"

"Much better than yesterday. Several of the welts haven't healed, but I imagine they'll be gone in a few days."

"Do you know who might have been behind it?" Hasheem asked evenly, but quietly.

"It had to be someone associated with the Commercers, possibly someone close to a former committee member, but I couldn't say who, since I never knew any of the previous Commercer councilors on the committee." Dekkard paused. "Didn't all of the professional investigative staff resign following the elections, except for Frieda Livigne?"

"They did. That's customary when party control changes."

Even if it's a "custom" that hasn't been practiced in decades.

"Did you know any of them?" asked Hasheem.

"Just in passing. I talked occasionally with Jaime Minz. He sent me a letter informing me that he is now assistant director of security for Northwest Industrial Chemical. I didn't reply, since it was an announcement. The only other one was Frieda, but I've heard nothing from her since the day I asked her a few questions."

Hasheem nodded. "That's interesting." He gestured toward the committee room.

Avraal lingered by the door as Dekkard entered, followed by Hasheem.

Dekkard took his seat as Pajiin entered the chamber, then Haastar.

Once the councilors were all seated, and the three bells chimed, Hasheem rapped the gavel once, then said, "Before we begin the official meeting, I have one brief announcement. You all may recall that, after the new Council was seated, I hired one new clerk and retained one clerk—that was Sohl Hurrek—in the hopes of having a certain continuity of staff expertise. Unhappily, Hurrek took umbrage at a councilor's expertise and tried to use a squeeze pouch filled with Atacaman fire pepper powder on the councilor. The councilor knocked Hurrek aside in his efforts to avoid the worst of it. The remaining clerk also managed to escape. Hurrek fell into the powder and suffered respiratory failure. The Council Guards verified that he suffered no wounds or bruising." Hasheem's eyes drifted in the direction of Rikkard and Baar, and paused, if momentarily. "The chair finds such inconveniences tiresome and beneath Council standards, and trusts that nothing of the sort will reoccur."

From what Dekkard could tell, the only councilors who looked surprised were Haastar and Pajiin, not that the lack of reaction from the others meant anything a day later.

Hasheem cleared his throat. "The committee will now consider section three of the Security reform proposal. Part one of section three sets forth the implementation dates for the transfer of the Special Tactical Force to the Army."

Immediately, Baar said, "The proposal mandates an immediate transfer of the Special Tactical Force to the Army upon approval of the legislation by the Imperador. I submit that three months is far more suited and propose an amendment to that effect."

"The amendment is offered," noted Hasheem. "Councilor Dekkard, would you care to respond before a vote is called on the amendment."

"I would, Sr. Chairman. The proposal does not require the immediate physical transfer of the STF. It requires that the command authority over the STF be transferred immediately. Any physical transfer of forces would then be undertaken as the Marshal of the Army sees fit. Since the STF is physically separate from other Security forces, any delay in the change of authority would merely delay the integration of the STF into the Army with no benefit to either its soldiers or to the Army. The reason for the transfer, I might remind the committee, was that the STF found itself unable to maintain standards and discipline and massacred hundreds of unarmed Guldorans. The sooner the STF is placed under military authority, and proper discipline is restored, the better for all of us."

"The vote is on the amendment."

Dekkard didn't quite hold his breath, but only Baar and Rikkard voted for it, and it was defeated.

Baar's next amendment was to delay the disarming and transfer of Special Agents by two months beyond the two weeks in the legislation. That also failed, but not without lengthy debate, lasting close to a full bell, but the vote was four against and three in favor. Baar's third amendment was to extend the effective date to a month. That passed, four to three.

Baar then offered a series of amendments dealing with the dates establishing the Ministry of Public Safety. Debate and votes took another bell.

Finally, Hasheem announced, "This is the final vote on the approval of the Security and Public Safety Reorganization Act. Councilor Baar?"

"I vote nay."

In the end, Dekkard was surprised that both Landors actually supported the amended form of the bill.

"The vote being five in favor, two opposed, the committee approves the bill and refers it to the majority floor leader for debate and vote. The next meeting of the committee will be at fourth bell on Duadi to discuss possible security measures dealing with foreign vessels docking at Guldoran ports. The committee stands adjourned."

Most surprising was the fact that Villem Baar crossed from his end of the dais to approach Dekkard.

"Councilor Dekkard, I have to say that you likely would have done exceedingly well as a courtroom legalist."

"Thank you, but I'm not sure I have the temperament for it. Much of what you suggested resulted in a better piece of legislation."

"I appreciate your saying that. We both will have to live with the results." Baar inclined his head and left.

"He's saying that it's likely going to become law," said Pajiin.

"I suspect so." *And that's when the troubles will resume.*

Pajiin smiled crookedly. "Going to be some real unhappy Special Agents."

"And the regular patrollers will have their hands full for a while," replied Dekkard, standing and gathering his papers, then easing them into the leather folder.

Pajiin was still smiling as he left the committee room.

Dekkard realized that Hasheem had not left the dais, but was walking toward him. So he turned and waited.

"That was very well done, Steffan, especially given the . . . distractions aimed at you. I'm sure that the Premier will call on you during the debate over the proposal in the full Council. I would guess that the proceedings and vote will consume all of the session next Tridi, but that's up to the Premier and Floor Leader Haarsfel."

"I assume that the Commercers will strongly oppose the bill."

"I doubt it. Security isn't that well liked anywhere. Some of them may vote against it out of necessity."

"But they're hoping the ensuing problems will discredit the Craft Party?"

Hasheem nodded. "I can see you've already thought that through."

"I'm worried about the Special Agents' implementation. A month gives them time to make trouble."

"I'll make sure the Premier knows of your concerns. What do you think will happen?"

"After the act becomes law, and implementation begins, the New Meritorists will start to demonstrate for change in the Council's voting procedures. Various Commercer groups will attack the demonstrators, making it difficult to keep the peace without casualties. After that, matters will escalate, and the Commercers will want the Army to use the STF." Dekkard shrugged. "That's just a feeling, though."

Hasheem shook his head. "With that, you still think your proposal is a good idea?"

"Without it, the demonstrations and riots would already have started, I think."

"Axel said something like that. I hope you're both wrong, but he's seldom that far off." Hasheem offered a wry smile, then turned toward the door.

Dekkard picked up his leather folder and followed.

Avraal had stepped inside the committee room door and stood waiting for him.

"Did you sense anything when I entered the committee room?"

"There wasn't any reaction from either Baar or Rikkard."

"That definitely makes Minz more likely. Did Hasheem have any reaction when I mentioned him or Frieda Livigne?"

"Minz caught his interest. Frieda not so much. With Hasheem it's hard to tell. He keeps his feelings close."

"We'll have to assume that we're on our own, then."

"Isn't that always the safest assumption?" asked Avraal dryly, turning toward the main corridor.

Dekkard laughed softly, then said, "Do you think you could get Carlos to look into Sohl Hurrek and see if he could find out anything about him?"

"When I next see him, I'll ask. It can't hurt."

Left unsaid was the fact that Baartol would likely find little or nothing.

The rest of Furdi at the office was routine. Dekkard wondered if he'd hear anything more from Trujillo, but the Guard captain didn't come to the office, nor did he send a message.

Dekkard was more than ready to leave at slightly after fourth bell.

As Dekkard, Avraal, and Gaaroll headed from the office to the central staircase, Dekkard saw Kaliara Bassaana walking swiftly and not looking back. He nodded politely to Yordan Farris as they passed, out of courtesy, because they were both on the Workplace Administration Committee. Farris returned the nod with a pleasant smile.

As the three left the building, Gaaroll said abruptly, "Four men beyond the back wall of the covered parking. Real strong emotions."

As she finished speaking, Dekkard heard shots.

"Someone's dead," Gaaroll said flatly.

"Two Council Guards are running that way," added Avraal.

"Could you tell if the feelings were directed toward us?" asked Dekkard.

"More like they were all tied in a circle."

"Whoever was in the bell tower? What about those feelings?"

"They were . . . stretched, long."

"I wonder if those indications might help," mused Dekkard.

"Hadn't thought of it that way," said Gaaroll. "I'll remember that."

"Didn't anyone ever ask you anything like that?" said Avraal.

Gaaroll shook her head. "Just asked if there were people in holds or cargo boxes."

"You need to work on that," said Avraal. "If you'd tell us more."

"I can do that."

Dekkard thought that Gaaroll actually sounded pleased. He still took a different route home and was particularly careful as he neared Florinda Way. Both Avraal and Gaaroll were as well, but neither discerned any danger.

Emrelda was in the kitchen, preparing something, when the three entered the house and joined her. "What happened today?" she asked, in a sardonically amused tone. "Shots? More Atacaman fire pepper dust?"

"Nothing like that, not at me, anyway," replied Dekkard dryly. "The Security Committee approved the Security reform act and sent it to the full Council. It's looking like the Council might pass it."

"Did the Commercers on the committee postpone everything, the way you feared?"

Dekkard shook his head. "They tried, but didn't have the votes. It's close to what I told you. The bad news is that regular patrollers will have to handle any New Meritorist demonstrations."

"Can I tell Captain Narryt that?"

"With one qualification. That's if there aren't any floor amendments to the bill. There could be, and they could be anything."

"Do you think there will be?" asked Avraal.

"There *could* be, but since floor amendments are in open session, a Commercer councilor might not want his name on anything that crippled or delayed reform. I have the feeling that their strategy now is to watch the demonstrations and unrest that are bound to happen and blame the Crafters because we weakened Security."

"What happened to that idealistic isolate who just wanted to make things better?" asked Emrelda in a cheerfully sarcastic tone.

"Nothing more than a handful of attempts on his life and getting selected as a councilor," replied Dekkard in a tone that he hoped was equally cheerful.

Gaaroll's eyes widened slightly at Dekkard's response.

"Cheer up," bantered Emrelda. "Things could be worse."

"I did—and things got worse."

Avraal groaned and rolled her eyes. "That's so old it has moss on it."

Emrelda shook her head. "Steffan, if you'd get everyone drinks, dinner's about ready."

"What is it?" asked Gaaroll.

"You'll see."

Dinner turned out to be paprika chicken strips and chunks with diced peppers and onions over fried rice, with skillet bread on the side. Dekkard ate every bit that was on his plate.

20

SINCE he had no committee meetings on Quindi morning, as soon as he got to the office Dekkard turned the keys to the Gresynt over to Avraal, and promised he'd stay put while she went to meet with Baartol. Then, after she left, he asked Shuryn Teitryn to join him. The nervous young engineering aide entered and took the seat to which Dekkard had gestured.

"Yes, sir?"

"I just thought I'd ask you about your efforts in finding information about abuses of power by large engineering firms."

"Sir, as you must know, outside of the newssheet story in *Gestirn* and a more detailed version of the same story in the Ondeliew *Daily News* and, well . . . the *Gestirn* stories about Engaard Engineering . . . there's very little with much detail."

"That's why you were hired. Your job is to find tidbits, stories that hint at something larger, as many of them as you can. Some will turn out to be impossible to track further, but once you have assembled as much as you can then we'll decide where to go. Now, what indefinite hints have you discovered?"

"Yes, sir. Some aren't much. There was a reference to night heliographs installed on Imperial warships by Siincleer Engineering. The installation began later than planned by the Navy, as a result of contractual difficulties with the business that designed them before Siincleer bought it out. I haven't found any other references to those difficulties. There was a story about the Navy being pleased with the performance of the night heliographs, but not the cost overruns. The Neewyrk *Reporter* ran a single story last spring about procurement irregularities for the Naval Yard, but nothing else."

When Teitryn finished his short list of discoveries, Dekkard nodded. "You've got the right idea. Keep at it. And have Illana type up a duplicate of what you've found and give it to Svard. Tell him I said he needs to keep it in a safe place."

"Yes, sir." Teitryn paused. "I do have a question, sir. I've come across one or two stories that suggest corporacion malfeasance of the sort we're looking for in engineering, but in other fields."

"Don't search for those, but if you run across them, document them and put them in a separate file. They'll be useful later." Dekkard stood and smiled. "Keep at it. It's likely going to get harder."

Once Teitryn left, Dekkard turned his attention to the letters and petitions. He finished reading through all of them, turned them over to Roostof, and began to think about how he might speak to the merits of the Security reform act when it came before the full Council.

If you have to speak? Who else would Obreduur ask?

Margrit knocked on the door. "Guard Captain Trujillo would appreciate a moment, sir."

"Have him come in." Dekkard stood and waited.

Trujillo entered the office, and Margrit quietly shut the door behind him.

"Councilor, I trust you're feeling better."

"I am." Dekkard gestured to the chairs, then seated himself. "I wondered if I might see you again."

"The Premier asked me to brief you on our discoveries concerning the clerk, Sohl Hurrek. Do you have any idea why Hurrek might have disliked you to such an extent?"

"I have no idea. I only had professional dealings with him in obtaining access to past committee transcripts and records. I was pleasant, and so was he. I can only surmise that someone else persuaded him to act against me."

The Guard captain nodded. "Hurrek deposited ten thousand marks in his account in the Imperial Banque of Guldor. The account was opened recently, only two weeks ago."

"Almost as if he planned not to remain as a committee staffer," said Dekkard musingly.

"He was carrying a second pouch of Atacaman fire pepper dust."

"Two? What on earth for?"

"There's no indication of what he planned to do with the second pouch. We may never know. I doubt what he had in mind would have benefitted anyone." Trujillo smiled sardonically.

"Perhaps someone wanted to discredit the committee, although I don't see how another pouch would do that."

Trujillo shook his head. "You're known to be good with knives. Deadly, in fact. Someone wanted you to use those knives to kill Hurrek. That way, you'd be in trouble, possibly even be forced to resign, and Hurrek couldn't say a word." Trujillo again smiled sardonically. "Whoever set it up didn't know you well enough. I went over the report of Councilor Aashtaan's murder. You used a truncheon in a way that minimized harm to the attacking empie, even with Atacaman fire pepper dust flying around. I've inquired and studied. You only use lethal weapons when there's no other possible option. That's where the plotter made his mistake. That still doesn't answer who it might be."

"No, it doesn't. By protecting the Premier, I've doubtless thwarted the ambitions of some former Commercer councilors, but I don't see them as taking it that personally. I might even have annoyed a Commercer staffer or two inadvertently, but enough to plot out something like this? It doesn't make sense."

"That's what we've discovered." Trujillo shrugged. "But if you think of anything . . . ?"

"I'll certainly let you know," Dekkard finished.

"That's all I have, Councilor."

Dekkard stood. "Thank you for sharing your findings. I truly appreciate it."

"My pleasure, sir."

Dekkard thought Trujillo actually meant it, and he walked to the outer office door with the Guard captain.

Dekkard was still musing over Trujillo's visit, noting that the Guard captain hadn't pressed him to name any "annoyed" staffers, when Avraal returned. He immediately related what Trujillo had conveyed.

"It's looking more and more like Jaime Minz," she declared.

"Could Carlos find out if Northwest Industrial Chemical has any accounts with the Imperial Banque of Guldor?"

"We could ask him, but it wouldn't prove anything. Besides, that deposit had to have been made with mark notes. Minz wouldn't be stupid enough to write a cheque. Neither would anyone at Northwest."

"Minz can't have that much in marks, and that means Northwest had to be behind it."

"Or some other Commercer interest," Avraal pointed out. "Ulrich is now with Suvion Industries."

"I'm still inclined to think it's Northwest, and it has to be connected to the missing dunnite that the New Meritorists used to destroy the regional Security buildings. Minz's letter mentioned that Northwest's records would show no discrepancies. Why would he write a letter addressing that one way or another?"

"Maybe that wasn't the point of the letter."

"A veiled warning?" Dekkard nodded. "He was always giving veiled warnings."

"Do you think someone at Northwest allowed the New Meritorists to obtain the dunnite?"

"Why would anyone?" Dekkard paused. "To turn the New Meritorists into a threat dangerous enough that the Council would back giving Security even greater powers?"

"It might have worked," suggested Avraal, "if the STF hadn't massacred hundreds at the Square of Heroes."

"No," corrected Dekkard. "It still might have worked if the regular patrollers hadn't discovered them planting weapons on the bodies. That's one reason I structured the reform act the way I did."

"Because you trust the regular patrollers more?"

"Someone has to be in charge, and I wouldn't want Special Agents or the STF in charge. Would you?"

"No, but don't you think that the Commercers will immediately work to find weak patrollers to corrupt?"

"I'm sure they will—if we let them. That's another reason why I hired Teitryn. If we can come up with more and more examples of that, it just might force them to be a bit less corrupt."

"Optimist."

"The other night you and Emrelda thought just the opposite."

"That was the other night." Avraal smiled.

"Did you talk to Carlos about looking into Sohl Hurrek?"

"He said he'd see what he could find."

Dekkard nodded. "That's all we can ask."

The afternoon was taken up largely with correspondence and writing a few notes about the Security reform act.

Dekkard inadvertently took a longer route home, due to far more stops than the map indicated, but at least there were no hints of snipers.

As he drove up the drive to the portico, Avraal said, "Leave the Gresynt out. We'll be going to services tonight. You, too, Gaaroll."

"Emrelda?" asked Dekkard quietly.

Avraal nodded.

When the three entered the house, Emrelda met them in the hallway, still in her security blues.

"You're going to services in uniform?" asked Gaaroll.

"Why not?" asked Emrelda.

Dekkard knew that Emrelda never would have worn her uniform to services if Markell were still alive, and he suspected that her decision to wear the uniform was part of her deciding to move on with her life. "You always look good in uniform."

"Are you humoring me?"

Dekkard caught the glint in her eye and replied, "It's too dangerous to humor or patronize any woman in your family, but especially when they're in uniform."

Both sisters laughed. Even Gaaroll smiled.

"I brought some pastries so we don't starve. They're on the table in the breakfast room."

None of the pastries survived the next bell, and both Avraal and Gaaroll were alert as Dekkard pulled out of the drive and turned toward Jacquez on the way to the Hillside Trinitarian Chapel.

Again, he noted the tall and massive oak tree that dominated the southeast corner of the intersection of Jacquez and Florinda, so large that he couldn't even see the upper stories of the house east of it.

Less than a sixth of a bell later he pulled the Gresynt into the chapel's parking area, moderately crowded but not packed. After Dekkard locked the Gresynt, the four walked toward the gray stone chapel, whose gold-tinted side windows reflected the late-afternoon sun.

Inside the chapel, the four took a pew near the rear, the same one that Emrelda had always taken. The harmonium played a hymn that Dekkard vaguely recognized, but could not name. During the short processional, the slender Presider Buusen, clad in a plain green cassock, moved to the front of the sanctuary, a simple raised platform with a lectern on each side. A golden-edged tapestry, backed with the red-gold of autumn and depicting the three orbs of love, power, and mercy, dominated the wall behind the sanctuary.

The music ended; the congregation stood, and Presider Buusen intoned, "Let us offer thanks to the Almighty for the day that has been and for the nights and days to come, through His love, power, and mercy."

"Thanks be to the Almighty, for His love, power, and mercy."

The presider lowered his hands; the congregation seated itself, and the small choir struggled through the anthem, followed by the Acknowledgment, and then Presider Buusen's homily, which centered on the difference between blind faith and enlightened faith, although Dekkard would have made the distinction between blind faith and thoughtful faith.

When the thankfully short service concluded, Dekkard mused on faith, and the grounds for having faith in people and institutions, although he knew he didn't put much faith in organized religion.

"You're looking thoughtful," said Avraal as they walked toward the Gresynt.

"I was thinking about why we put faith in people or institutions."

"Because it's impossible to exist for long, or well, without putting faith in at least a few people."

"That's true, but some people definitely trust the wrong individuals. Others choose more wisely."

"I'd say," replied Avraal, "that misplaced trust, or faith, often reflects what someone wants to believe. Some people are more careful than others in that respect."

"You took your time in deciding about me."

Avraal laughed softly. "I liked and trusted you from the beginning, but I didn't trust my feelings."

"And she didn't want to get hurt," added Emrelda from behind them.

"Who asked your opinion?" replied Avraal in a tartly humorous tone.

"I don't have to be asked. I'm your older sister."

"You sound like my older sister as well," replied Dekkard dryly.

"For that," said Emrelda, "you can chop and cut and get the drinks while we fix dinner."

Dekkard smiled. He had no doubt that he'd have been doing both anyway.

As he began to chop the onions and peppers, he said to Emrelda, "I've been meaning to ask you a professional question for almost a week, and there never seemed to be the right time for it. But, since I'm chopping onions . . ."

"What is it, Steffan?"

"When we were campaigning for Obreduur, he had a meeting with a legalist for the Working Women Guild of Oersynt . . ." Dekkard went on to explain the issue of allowing guild legalists to represent women working the streets.

Emrelda smiled sardonically. "I haven't heard a question."

"How would most patrollers feel about that?"

"Most wouldn't care one way or the other. Some wouldn't like it because they couldn't take liberties with street women. Some would prefer it because they'd feel better knowing a legalist was representing the woman. If it turned out to result in more women following the hygiene requirements, most patrollers wouldn't have a problem, and most wouldn't have much sympathy for the patrollers who didn't like such a law."

"You'd mentioned the other day about girls walking the streets in Southtown."

"What you're proposing won't help them. There's not even a brothel or a massage parlor there. The single men are too poor for that, and the married ones make do with their spouses."

Dekkard had no trouble detecting the sardonicism. "A lot of abuse?"

"No one reports it, but I've seen the bruises. They slipped and fell. They walked into a door. We can't help them if they won't talk to us. They won't talk to us because they have nowhere to go but the streets."

"Is it that bad in other workers' neighborhoods?"

"From what I've heard, Southtown's better than many. In Rivertown, patrollers go in threes—and only in daylight."

"You've got your answer, dear," said Avraal. "Are you finished chopping those onions?"

"In just a minute or two. My words got ahead of my hands." Dekkard grinned.

"For once," murmured Avraal.

Emrelda failed to smother a snort.

Dekkard managed not to shake his head.

21

FINDI morning found Emrelda, Gaaroll, Avraal, and Dekkard all at the breakfast table at the same time.

"Remember, Nincya," Avraal said, looking up from her café, "today, we're taking you shopping."

"How could I forget?" replied Gaaroll glumly.

"The only woman in the house who doesn't want to shop? Amazing," said Dekkard dryly.

"I suppose you like to shop, too," said Gaaroll.

At that, both Emrelda and Avraal both laughed.

"Steffan's required some persuasion on more than one occasion," said Avraal.

"The councilor?"

"I've only been a councilor for a month," replied Dekkard. "Before that, I was a security aide."

"Who could persuade you? You're an isolate."

"They persuaded me with good food, drink, and good company." *And the hope of a great deal more.*

"Just like you'll get a good meal after shopping," said Avraal.

"If there's a meal . . ." said Emrelda.

"You're definitely included," said Dekkard. If Emrelda wanted to join the shopping expedition, Dekkard wasn't about to exclude her, not with all she'd provided. *And after all she's been through.* He looked to Avraal. "Should we plan to leave around fourth bell?"

"No later than fourth bell," she replied.

Before long, the four finished eating and cleaning up the kitchen and breakfast room, then headed to their rooms.

Dekkard was the first dressed, wearing the blue barong.

Avraal smiled. "I've always liked that on you."

"Why do you think I wore it today?"

"Dear, there's something else you should wear."

Dekkard frowned.

"From now on, I'd feel more comfortable if you'd carry your personal truncheon, all the time. I know it's not customary, but it's within the law, and when you're at the Council your jacket will mostly conceal it."

"It won't be much use against firearms."

"No, but I'd still feel better."

Dekkard wasn't about to argue, especially given how accurate her instincts were. He retrieved the truncheon and changed belts.

"It doesn't show that much."

Dekkard just smiled, then made his way to the garage and readied the gray Gresynt, driving it under the portico, where he got out, deciding that waiting outside was better than standing around inside and getting in the way.

Gaaroll joined him, sitting on the steps. After several minutes, she looked up. "How long will this all take?"

"A fair part of the day, but you'll get some new clothes and a very good meal." He smiled wryly. "Besides, did you have anything more interesting planned?"

"Not really." Gaaroll stiffened. "The empie next door is using too much force on the boy."

"Even I can feel it," said Avraal as she stepped out onto the side portico.

"Feel what?" asked Emrelda as she followed her sister.

"Emping violence," replied Avraal.

Abruptly, the front door of the house next door flew open, and a dark-haired boy ran out and down the front steps. A red-haired older woman appeared on the front stoop and said, "Tomas! Get back inside! Now!"

The boy staggered, and then began to sob as he turned back toward the empie, who was doubtless his nanny.

Avraal winced, then stiffened.

This time, the red-haired nanny staggered, grabbing the iron railing on the west side of the stoop. She turned toward Avraal, her face twisted in anger.

"Don't!" snapped Avraal. "I could smash your shields, and your mind."

The empie/nanny's eyes went to Avraal's blue linen jacket and the gold brooch with the red stone in the center—the informal sign of a professional empath.

"You're using too much force on the boy," said Avraal, her voice strong. "When we can detect it through walls, that constitutes excessive use of emping, especially on a child, susceptible or not. I don't think you want to lose your job over it, but that's your choice."

"No patroller would bother."

"No," said Emrelda. "Most wouldn't, but since I live next door, and since I'm a dispatcher at the Erslaan Patrol Station, I would."

Dekkard watched the color drain from the nanny's face. He had the feeling that Avraal had sent reassurance to the boy.

"We can tell if you've been using too much," added Emrelda. "Don't think you can get away with it when we're not around. You'll still leave traces."

"Especially if you take your anger out on the boy," added Avraal.

The nanny glared at Avraal.

"Don't tempt me," said Avraal.

The nanny turned away, then said quietly to the boy, "Tomas, we need to go inside."

The boy followed her into the house.

Dekkard looked to Avraal inquiringly.

"Just a gentle suggestion—what she *should* have been using all along."

"It won't last," said Gaaroll flatly.

"Probably not, but, at the moment, there's not much else we can do," said Emrelda. "If there are more instances with witnesses—that's another story."

The four got into the steamer, Dekkard and Avraal up front, and Emrelda and Gaaroll in the second row of seats.

"Still quiet over there," said Gaaroll as Dekkard turned onto Florinda Way.

"It will be for a while," replied Avraal.

"Only for a few days," said Gaaroll. "That kind forgets quick."

Dekkard had the feeling Gaaroll had more than a little experience with "that kind," but only asked, "Where should we start?"

"Julieta, I think," replied Avraal. "We'll be closer to Octavia's when we finish."

"Octavia's?" asked Gaaroll.

"It's a very good bistro."

Dekkard took an indirect route, heading south of Camelia Avenue before turning west toward Imperial Avenue. He parked the Gresynt behind Julieta and followed the others into the women's store, knowing he only had one function.

Three bells and two thirds later, Gaaroll had six sets of work clothes in vaguely similar styles, but in different colors, as well as a single gray suit, albeit all with trousers—the one aspect of attire about which Gaaroll was adamantly steadfast. Dekkard spent more marks out of his transition allowance than he wanted to think about, not that the costs were excessive, but he'd been hoping to hold on to as many marks as he could.

As they neared the Gresynt, he turned to Avraal and asked, hopefully, "Octavia's now?"

"Well, I had thought we might stop by Esperanza," Avraal grinned, then added, "but headscarves aren't something that Nincya would wear."

Once the three women were in the Gresynt, Dekkard turned toward Octavia's Bistro, eventually parking half a block from the older building. Tall and narrow windows of grayed or silvered glass framed by the black brick accentuated alternating courses of red and black bricks. When they reached the bistro, Dekkard opened the black door for the others, following them into a much lighter space with walls of a light silver-gray, and floors of a similar stone. The tables and chairs were all of wood bleached to a pale gold.

In moments, the four were seated at a round corner table.

Dekkard thought about having the basil-cream shrimp pasta, but since he'd had that before, he decided on almond-cream pasta with roasted chicken slices and seasonal greens, with a chilled Kuhrs. Avraal decided on plain almond-cream pasta, also with the seasonal greens, but with wine. Dekkard didn't hear what Emrelda or Gaaroll ordered because he thought a woman leaving the bistro was Frieda Livigne, until she turned. He still wondered what had happened to her, even though he had no doubts that she'd never been anywhere close to him politically.

After everyone had ordered, Emrelda looked to Gaaroll and asked in a cheerfully humorous tone, "Now, that wasn't too painful, was it?"

Gaaroll flushed slightly. "It was . . . all right."

"Perhaps even a little better than that?" suggested Dekkard, who'd seen at least a few hints of pleasure from the distance empath over the course of the shopping expedition.

"Maybe," conceded Gaaroll.

The two sisters raised their eyebrows almost simultaneously, and Avraal said dryly, "Just maybe?"

Gaaroll flushed more, but the server's arrival interrupted the moment, as he provided the sisters each with a glass of Silverhills white and Dekkard and Gaaroll each with a beaker of Kuhrs.

Dekkard lifted his beaker. "To the successful conclusion of the great shopping expedition."

The others joined him, and everyone sipped or drank. Then Avraal looked at Dekkard. "Successful? You didn't get anything."

"Sometimes that's successful." *Especially if I'm paying.*

"Oh?"

"You thought several of my shopping trips were successful even when you didn't buy anything." Then he added, "Or much."

"Good emendation," Emrelda said with a smile.

"Do you shop much?" asked Gaaroll.

"Some," said Emrelda, grinning at her sister, "but not as much as Avraal. She has to look good all the time. I just wear a patroller's uniform."

"I admit it," said Avraal. "I like clothes, but only the right kind."

Gaaroll looked to Dekkard. "And you, sir?"

"I didn't worry too much about clothes until this year. I got promoted, and then I got . . . involved with someone who wanted me to look good, and then I got selected as councilor, which meant buying more clothes than I ever owned in my life."

"You see," said Emrelda almost wickedly, "those two will get you addicted to clothes. A year ago, Steffan had maybe three barongs and a single gray suit. Now . . ."

Dekkard managed not to choke on the mouthful of Kuhrs he'd just swallowed.

The remainder of the meal was lighthearted, and Dekkard liked the almond-cream chicken, but not so much as the basil-cream shrimp pasta he'd had before.

Almost two bells later, Dekkard drove up the drive to the house, and let the women off before garaging the Gresynt and then checking the water and kerosene levels and wiping the Gresynt down.

When he walked up the steps to the east portico, Gaaroll stood there waiting.

"Councilor," she said quietly. "Thank you. No one has ever done anything like this for me."

"You're welcome. I'm glad you like them." Dekkard smiled. "We still have to pick them up once they're tailored."

"On Tridi?"

"If some disaster doesn't occur," agreed Dekkard.

"Thank you. Again."

Dekkard gestured to the side door, then followed her inside.

He and the others hadn't been in the house more than a sixth before there was a pounding on the front door.

"They could have used the chimes," muttered Emrelda.

"That's trouble," said Gaaroll.

"I'll get it," insisted Emrelda.

Avraal followed her sister, but stood well back from the door. Dekkard came up beside Avraal.

The tall and slightly paunchy man who stood at the door was unfamiliar to Dekkard, but Emrelda said politely, "Sr. Waaldwud, what can I do for you?"

"Enough is enough, Sra. Markell. First, the patrollers are here at all bells of the night, and now one of your lodgers—and you shouldn't be allowed lodgers—has insulted my son's nanny."

"Sr. Waaldwud, I have no lodgers. The woman who addressed your nanny was my sister Ritten Ysella-Dekkard. She's married to Councilor Dekkard, councilor of the Council of Sixty-Six. She's also a certified security empath, and she caught your nanny using excessively violent empathic projections on your son. She told your nanny that sort of force was illegal. Your nanny took offense."

"And what's this nonsense about your being a patroller?"

"Oh, that." Emrelda smiled. "I am. I'm a patroller second, dispatcher at the Erslaan station. I've been a patroller for more than five years. I've just never said much about it."

For several long moments, Waaldwud was silent. "I see."

Avraal stepped forward. "I don't think you do, Sr. Waaldwud. I'm not only a certified security empath; I'm a certified parole screener as well. There's no patroller who will deny my credentials and findings. Your nanny needs to be more gentle with her use of empath projection. When I can sense that level of violence through walls, it's far too much. She can change; she can find another position; or she can face charges. Those are your choices and hers."

"You *women* are telling *me* . . ."

Much as Dekkard wanted to get involved, he decided against it. Instead, he watched Avraal and waited.

"No, I'm telling you *the law.*" Avraal's voice was pleasant, but Dekkard noticed that Emrelda eased to the side.

Abruptly, Waaldwud swallowed, then said, "I'll speak with her."

"That might be for the best, Sr. Waaldwud. Good evening," said Emrelda, closing the door.

Once the door was closed, Dekkard asked Avraal, "What did you project?"

"Just the feeling of the full might of the law, with the sense of iron bars closing around him. I haven't used that much since I was a parole screener, but he clearly needed a reminder about the law."

Emrelda shook her head. "There will definitely be neighborhood gossip. There probably was already, but there certainly will be now."

"I'm sorry," said Avraal.

"I worried about Tomas," replied Emrelda, "but I couldn't sense what you and Nincya did. It just makes me wish I could have done something earlier."

"We did what we could when we could," said Avraal, "and I think we all could use a drink on the veranda."

Dekkard immediately headed for the pantry to get the wine and lager. He'd just poured two glasses of wine when Avraal appeared behind him, putting her arms around him and saying, "Thank you."

"For what?"

"You know. For letting me handle Waaldwud."

"It seemed prudent," Dekkard said, "although I was tempted."

She let go of him, stepped forward, and took the two wineglasses. "I suspected."

Dekkard smiled. "I'll be there in a minute."

"We're not going anywhere."

22

O N Unadi morning, Dekkard took yet another route to the Council Office Building, and neither Gaaroll nor Avraal discerned anything unusual, even next door. Dekkard knew that sooner or later, probably sooner, the assassin, or assassins, would move closer to Emrelda's house, or to Council Avenue, and position themselves where Dekkard couldn't avoid them—and where his truncheon wouldn't be of much use. But he wasn't about to ignore Avraal's suggestion to carry a personal truncheon. He didn't see whoever directed the assassins giving up, although he still held a faint hope that they might—*if* he survived long enough for the Council to pass the Security reform act and have it approved by the Imperador.

The entire morning and early afternoon were routine. The hearing before the Workplace Administration Committee dealt with the processes by which Aaken Industries produced coal tar dyes, and the failures in using loading chutes that had resulted in continual poisoning of loaders.

The process manager at Aaken contended that the problem lay with the sloppiness of the loaders, while the Chemical Workers Guild contended that Aaken had refused to replace square loading chutes with chutes that had semi-circular lower sides so that the coal tar had less of a tendency to stick. Because Aaken hadn't changed the chutes, the loaders had to open the chutes continually to clear them, which exposed them to the raw coal tar, creating injuries and deaths. According to the safety standards promulgated by the Ministry of Health and Education, covered loading chutes were required, but there were no specifications for the construction of the chutes. At the end of the meeting, as chair of the committee, Haarsfel announced that there would be another hearing on Furdi afternoon, dealing with the log-handling practices of several timber corporacions. Dekkard couldn't help but wonder if Pajiin might have had something to do with that, given his earlier remarks, even though Pajiin obviously wasn't on the Workplace Administration Committee.

When he returned to the office, Margrit handed him a thick envelope, which held a printed copy of the Security and Public Safety Reorganization Act as it had been reported out of the Security Committee, with the notation that all councilors had received a copy.

Dekkard spent the remainder of the afternoon in his office, while Avraal worked at Baartol's. She returned slightly after fourth bell for an uneventful drive home. The evening was also unremarkable, including almost a bell of throwing-knife practice.

Duadi was even quieter with only a short Security Committee meeting, during which the Treasury security director testified about foreign powers' past attempts to use vessels from other countries to smuggle spies into Guldoran ports.

There was more correspondence to sign and correct, and since Dekkard didn't like leaving things undone, he stayed another third to finish it. Because matters had been so quiet, Dekkard felt even more concern when Avraal, Gaaroll, and he left the Council Office Building that afternoon. The route he took connected with Jacquez some six blocks north, and uphill of Florinda Way. He'd barely started south on Jacquez when Gaaroll spoke.

"There's someone—no—two people on Florinda Way. They're on the east side of Jacquez. Near the corner. Might be in a steamer."

"Strong emotions?" asked Dekkard.

"From one. Almost nothing from the other."

Dekkard glanced to Avraal and mouthed, "Professional?"

"Most likely," she murmured.

"Let's turn east at the next corner and circle behind them."

"And then?" asked Avraal.

"We watch and see what they do," replied Dekkard.

"That could be a while," Avraal pointed out.

"Do you have a better alternative? No matter how we approach the house, if one of them has a rifle, they'll have a clear shot, at least until dark."

"Is either of them an isolate?" Avraal asked Gaaroll.

"I can sense both their feelings."

"Why wouldn't they use an isolate?" asked Avraal. "They have to know I'm an empath."

"An isolate near the house? The moment you detected that lack of detectable emotion, we'd know it had to be an assassin. That suggests there's an assassin somewhere nearby, but not too close, possibly even closer to the house."

"So the two are decoys. Otherwise, they wouldn't be so obvious."

"We'll have to move closer and see if you or Nincya can sense an isolate." As he spoke, Dekkard turned left off Jacquez. He headed east for three blocks, then turned south, slowing as he neared Florinda Way. "Do either of you sense anything?"

"Not yet," said Avraal.

"Only the two," said Gaaroll. "One of them's throwing off strong feelings."

Dekkard eased the steamer around the corner and onto Florinda Way, moving barely above a walking pace, which was easy enough, since there was never much traffic on Florinda. Given the slight slope, he couldn't yet see the intersection with Jacquez.

As the Gresynt neared the end of the tree-lined block, Gaaroll said quietly, "There's someone up high across the street from the two in the steamer. I can't sense anything except his presence. That means he's an isolate."

"Not in a house?"

"No, sir."

Dekkard thought for a moment, before he remembered. "There's a large oak just back from the corner."

"That's the big oak. From there he'd have an open shot at any steamer in the intersection of Jacquez and Florinda," said Avraal. "With all the trees to the east, no one in that block would see much. They might not even hear much."

"What do you have in mind?" asked Dekkard.

"Getting close enough to create a panic attack in the decoy who already feels strongly. Then we can see what the man in the tree does."

Dekkard parked the Gresynt almost a block away from Jacquez, behind an older and larger Kharlan. Then he turned in the seat and said to Gaaroll, "You stay with the steamer. If you sense someone else with strong feelings moving in, honk the steamer's horn."

"I could help."

"Doing that will be help enough." *For now, at least.* "The last thing we need is to be surprised by someone else." Dekkard eased out of the Gresynt, then crossed the pavement to the south side, with Avraal beside him as they walked slowly toward Jacquez.

The older trees, mostly stately elms planted in the two-yard-wide strip between the sidewalk and the curb, not only shaded the sidewalk, but also made it difficult for the possible sniper in the tree to see or hear them until they were within a few yards of the oak.

Dekkard found his hand fingering the truncheon, even as he wondered how useful it would be against an armed sniper.

Still, there were plenty of large-trunked trees along the way, and, once they got closer, Avraal could sense where the assassin was without revealing herself. *Once she panics the two in the steamer.*

"There's a steamer coming up from Jacquez," Avraal said. "Just keep walking. I'll distract the driver, if necessary."

The blue Realto drove past the two.

"Just the driver, and he didn't even notice us," said Avraal.

Dekkard could just make out the gray Realto parked some ten yards east of Jacquez—as well as the massive trunk of the oak ahead. "What about the two in the steamer up ahead?"

"Their feelings haven't changed."

"Can you locate the isolate?"

"He's definitely in the oak tree, about five yards up. We'll duck behind the next elm, and I'll see what I can do with the two in the Realto."

As they neared the elm Avraal had mentioned, Dekkard studied the area to the left of the oak, where a high stone wall stood only a yard back from the sidewalk, with bushes sculpted into shapes filling most of the space between the wall and the sidewalk. Between the wall, the topiary bushes, and the oak, it would be difficult for anyone in the house or anyone driving by to see much, another possible reason why the presumed sniper picked that location.

Once Avraal and Dekkard moved into position, shielded from the view of the sniper and the two in the Realto, all Dekkard could do was to wait and hope no one decided to walk by, although he had noticed that very few people walked anywhere in the "better" residential districts.

But until you act, there's nothing to worry about. After that was another question.

Abruptly, the Realto lurched forward, then halted short of Jacquez, before turning in front of another steamer and accelerating downhill toward Erslaan.

"Now we wait," murmured Avraal.

Dekkard and Avraal remained in the shadows behind the elm tree. Almost a sixth passed, and a single steamer turned off Jacquez and headed east on Florinda Way, seemingly oblivious to Avraal and Dekkard.

Several minutes more went by before Avraal murmured, "He's coming down. He's got the rifle in a shoulder sling. He'll come down the back side where he can't be seen from the street. I'll distract him. Don't argue." She pointed. "Over there."

Dekkard moved silently past the oak and behind the neatly trimmed topiary she'd indicated—that of a spout-maid—knowing that, if the sniper looked hard in his direction, he'd immediately detect Dekkard.

Remaining motionless, Dekkard waited, watching as a lean figure in a nondescript mottled gray and brown jacket and trousers swung down from the lowest limb, almost two yards above the ground. Before the sniper could scan the area thoroughly, Avraal stepped from behind the elm, took several steps and stopped, throwing knife in hand. Her voice was even and calm as she said, "I wouldn't reach for the rifle, if I were you, especially since I'm not your target."

With the sniper's eyes on Avraal, Dekkard edged closer.

"Can you really use that knife?"

"Do you want to risk finding out?"

Dekkard saw the fractional tensing of the sniper and moved, his truncheon striking with all the force he could muster.

The sniper's hand went toward his belt, but with Dekkard's second strike the pistol the sniper had been reaching for hit the ground. Dekkard's third strike sent the man to the ground facedown, his hands groping for the pistol, but before he could grasp it, Dekkard brought his boot heel down hard on the back of the man's neck with enough force that there was a barely audible snap.

Pinlights comprising an image of an unfamiliar face flashed in front of Dekkard's eyes, then vanished.

"He's dead," said Avraal, confirming what Dekkard already knew, as she replaced her knife in the sheath under her jacket.

"Has anyone seen us?"

"Not yet. Between the wall, all the topiary, and the oak, it would be hard to see much, and we're both in gray."

"Just leave the body."

The two walked back up the block to the Gresynt.

"No one seems to be watching or noticing," she said quietly.

"That's a risk we'll have to take." Dekkard opened the driver's-side door, slid into the seat, and lit off the Gresynt, waiting for the pressure to build.

"What happened?" asked Gaaroll. "That Realto left in a hurry."

"The driver must have panicked when the assassin fell out of the tree," Dekkard said mildly, easing the Gresynt into a tight U-turn to head east on Florinda Way.

"He fell out of the tree?" asked Gaaroll.

"He might have had a little help. He broke his neck."

Gaaroll swallowed, then asked, "What about the patrollers?"

"They'll find a man with a pistol and a sniper's rifle with a broken neck on the ground beneath a tree. If they look further, they'll find hints that he climbed the tree. His body might have a bruise or two, but he clearly died of a broken neck."

The question Dekkard couldn't answer was whether the two in the car would mention their panic attack. But if they were questioned by an empath that would come out. Still, there was little proof.

The bigger problem was that it might be even harder to detect the next possible assassin.

For the moment, Dekkard didn't want to think about that.

23

WHEN Dekkard and Avraal finally reached the house and garaged the Gresynt, Avraal turned to Gaaroll. "Nincya, we'll tell Emrelda about the assassin first."

"I didn't see anything. All I sensed was that he died."

"Which is what happened," said Dekkard sardonically, deciding that he'd deal with the Gresynt later. He did close the garage door, though.

When the three reached the kitchen, Emrelda looked up with an expression of annoyance and relief. "I was getting a little worried."

"Part of that was my fault," said Dekkard. "There were a lot of letters to sign and some to correct, and I stayed late to finish them. That wouldn't have been too bad, but, as we were headed down Jacquez, Nincya sensed two possible assassins on the east side of Florinda Way. We investigated and found another up in the big oak tree at the end of the block, the one back from the intersection—"

"An assassin?" asked Emrelda.

"We weren't sure," said Dekkard. "We left Nincya in the steamer and we walked down close enough for Avraal to sense the three." Dekkard looked to Avraal.

"The man in the tree was an isolate."

"Do I want to hear more?" asked Emrelda.

"It's better that you do," said Dekkard.

"I managed to panic the two in the Realto," said Avraal. "They drove off in a hurry. We waited for the third man. He must have been worried, because he slipped and fell headfirst. He broke his neck. We left the body where he fell."

"Oh," added Dekkard. "He had a rifle in a sling and pistol."

"I haven't heard any patroller whistles," replied Emrelda, frowning.

"We thought it might be better if someone else discovered the body," said Dekkard.

"That was rather convenient," said Emrelda, dryly.

"After everything so far," replied Avraal, "I'm not about to turn down a convenient occurrence, especially when we have no real idea who might be behind these attacks. All it means is that someone is still after Steffan and they'll likely try again."

"Whoever's behind it is linked to the Commercers," said Dekkard, "most likely to a large corporacion."

"You think . . . Siincleer Engineering?"

Dekkard shook his head. "I think it's linked to me and possibly to the Security reform act. All of this started after I introduced the proposed legislation. The full Council is supposed to debate and vote on it tomorrow. I may be called upon to defend the act before the Council."

"Who else supports it?" asked Emrelda.

"Quite a few councilors, possibly because Security has been doing the bidding of the major corporacions, if quietly, for decades."

"What a surprise," interjected Emrelda with a sardonic bitterness.

"Many will likely vote for it, but won't want to speak in favor of it."

"Will you still be a target even after it becomes law?" asked Gaaroll.

"Of course," replied Avraal. "If Steffan's killed, that will warn other councilors not to take on the corporacions, because they never forget."

Gaaroll looked to Emrelda. "Is that true?"

"It's true." Emrelda's voice was like cold iron.

"What can we do?"

"Keep him from getting killed, and discover and prove who's behind it," said Avraal. "Not just who's hiring the assassins, but who's behind them."

"And possibly who's behind them," added Emrelda.

"You think you can?" Gaaroll's voice trailed off.

"Why not?" asked Avraal. "Besides, if we don't, who will? It can't be that much worse than what you've already lived through, can it?"

Gaaroll offered an amused smile. "When you put it that way."

"Now that we've settled that," said Emrelda, "could we have dinner?" Then she stopped. "I almost forgot. Steffan, you've got a letter from Oersynt. Since the return address is N. Dekkard . . ."

"It's from your sister," finished Avraal.

"Thank you. I'll read it a little later. Right now, I'm going to get the drinks," offered Dekkard. He could definitely use a Kuhrs, and he suspected Avraal could use a glass of Silverhills.

In the end, Dekkard had two hefty beakers of Kuhrs with dinner, which was spicy-hot rice and chicken fry-up with a green salad.

After they ate, Dekkard and Avraal retreated to the sitting room, where he opened the letter. He glanced at the first few lines and smiled. "I'm going to read this aloud.

"Thank you for your letter. I'm sorry to be a little late in replying, but I had a family portrait commission that had to be finished by yesterday.

"I still find it hard to believe that my younger brother—I almost wrote 'little brother'—is a councilor and married to someone as beautiful and remarkable as Avraal—"

"She really wrote that?"

"Word for word.

"You two really are a golden couple. I do worry that you will become targets. I mean real targets, not just political targets. I've overheard enough in doing portraits to see how marks corrupt people, especially Commercers. Maybe it's just that people who can be corrupted tend to be Commercers, or that the talents that make someone a success in business, and sometimes politics, lead more easily into corruption.

"I will paint a wedding portrait for you two, even if I have to take the ironway to Machtarn to do it, but I'll let you get settled before I show up. From what I read in the newssheets, just being a councilor right now is unsettling enough. The other unsettling thing is the weather. We had ice rains last week that pretty much destroyed all the late crops and the fall fruit. Sheralla's husband is a produce factor, and he says that with the weather damage prices are bound to go up . . ."

From there the letter went into news about their parents and a few friends. When Dekkard finished reading, he looked to Avraal.

"I love your sister. She thinks a lot of you."

"I think highly of your sister, and she thinks highly of you."

"Now that we've agreed on that," said Avraal, "and that everyone agrees that we're targets, it might be a good idea to head for bed."

Dekkard smiled. Avraal hadn't mentioned sleep.

And after that tomorrow would come, no matter what.

24

ON Tridi morning, Dekkard immediately scanned *Gestirn,* but the paper had no mention of a mysterious body being found in the Hillside area. Then again, the body might have been discovered too late to make the morning edition.

Or the other two came back and found the body and removed it. That had both upsides and downsides.

After reading yet another story about poor crop yields, not only in Guldor but in Noldar as well, Dekkard set aside the newssheet and poured café for himself and Avraal, who looked at the newssheet when she arrived.

Dekkard shook his head, and Gaaroll said nothing.

The three left the house a sixth earlier than usual and avoided Jacquez on another circuitous route to the Council Office Building. Even so, they arrived just after Margrit and Roostof had opened the office.

"You're early, sir," said Margrit cheerfully.

"It might be a long day with the debate on the Security act," replied Dekkard.

Margrit handed him two messages. "These just arrived."

"Thank you." Dekkard gestured for Avraal to enter his personal office, then followed her in, closing the door. He set the gray leather folder on the desk, opened the first message, from Obreduur, and began to read.

Steffan—

Fredrich has suggested that you give the opening statement on the background for the Security and Public Safety Reorganization Act, including the abuses that the Act is designed to remedy and the provisions that address those abuses. I agree with his recommendation. No one knows the Act better than you, and you speak well.

Dekkard handed the message to Avraal, then opened the second one, which, unsurprisingly, was from Hasheem, saying that he'd recommended Dekkard to do the introduction to the bill and that the Premier had agreed. "The second one is from Hasheem. It says the same thing."

"So you're the councilor who's the voice of Security reform." Her voice was cool.

"Otherwise known as the designated target," he replied dryly. "As Naralta predicted."

"Did you have any idea it would be this bad?"

"Not until they attacked the house." Dekkard paused. "But I should have realized that it could get that way after what happened to Markell. I just didn't think it would happen over a legislative proposal." He shook his head. "There's nothing you can do here at the moment. You could come back and meet me for lunch." He extended the keys to the Gresynt.

"You won't leave the office?"

"Not until you return."

"Promise?"

"Only if Obreduur and Isobel Irlende escort me to the floor."

"I'll be back in time to go to lunch with you." She leaned forward and took the steamer keys.

Once she left, Dekkard quickly read through the letters and petitions, then gave them to Roostof. After that, he took out the background material, including Roostof's notes, and settled down to create a set of talking points to summarize the act and the reasons why the Council needed to pass it. Coming up with something he was comfortable with took over two bells.

He'd just finished a few minutes before Avraal returned.

"Did you learn anything new from Carlos?"

"Not much beyond what we already know. Obviously, I didn't mention last night. I did mention the possible assassin in the university bell tower. That bothered him. He said that political struggles usually didn't end in attacks on councilors."

"It just might be that his removal of Marrak escalated the struggle," Dekkard said.

"But that was essentially in return for an attack on us."

"For Commercers, that doesn't count," replied Dekkard dryly. "Only attacks on them matter."

"Enough," declared Avraal. "You need to eat before you face the mountain cats."

"They're more like Atacaman desert serpents."

She shook her head. "We're leaving."

No one noticed as they walked from the office, although Dekkard thought he saw Saarh entering his office. When they reached the Council Hall and the councilors' dining room, Dekkard opted for the three-cheese chicken and Avraal had the chilled spicy tomato soup. After that, she escorted him to the councilors' lobby before making her way to the spouses' gallery.

Carrying the gray leather folder that he hoped he wouldn't need, Dekkard entered the Council chamber a good sixth before first bell, and seated himself at his desk at the rear.

Other councilors filed in, one of whom was Pajiin, who stopped beside Dekkard's desk and asked, "Are you going to speak?"

"I've been asked to give the opening statement on the act before it's opened to debate."

"Aren't you the fortunate one?"

"The Premier's likely trying to keep Craft targets to a minimum."

"Why don't they target him?"

Dekkard managed not to frown, thinking, surely, Pajiin understood that. After the slightest hesitation, he replied, "Too obvious. Besides, they need a strong Craft Premier that they can vilify in the future."

"You think they're thinking that far in the future?"

"Do you think they're not?" asked Dekkard, his voice low, but sardonic.

Pajiin offered a soft bark of a laugh, then moved to his desk and sat down.

Several minutes passed before the single long chime sounded, and the lieutenant-at-arms thumped his ceremonial staff, followed by Obreduur's statement that the Council of Sixty-Six was in session.

Haarsfel moved to the lectern on the left side of the dais. "The matter before the Council is the Security and Public Safety Reorganization Act, as reported from the Security Committee and presented to the Council. Offering the opening statement for the committee is Councilor Dekkard, who offered the original version of the act. Councilor Dekkard."

Dekkard walked to the dais and stood beside, not behind, the lectern to the right of the Premier's—or presiding councilor's—desk, then inclined his head. "Thank you, Floor Leader Haarsfel."

For a moment, Dekkard said nothing, just surveyed the chamber. "As all of us know, over the past several months, we have seen illegality and a pronounced lack of competence in the Security Ministry. I won't list all the problems; they should be familiar to everyone. In order to address these issues, the Security Committee accepted a draft proposal, which the committee then debated and amended, and I have to give credit to the honorable Councilor Villem Baar for the improvements he especially made to the legislation. The main thrust of the Security and Public Safety Reorganization Act is to return Security to its primary purpose of maintaining civil law and order . . ."

Dekkard took less than a sixth to introduce the act, then inclined his head to Haarsfel.

"Thank you, Councilor Dekkard, for a concise summary of the need for the act and its basic provisions. The Council has two bells for debate on the bill itself, followed by two bells, if necessary, for debate and vote on the five amendments registered with the majority floor leader." Haarsfel turned to Hansaal Volkaar, the Commercer floor leader. "You requested time to speak against the bill."

"I did. We have a number of concerns about the proposed act, in particular, the speed required for implementation . . ."

The statements, by Commercer councilors and two Landors, largely repeated the issues raised by Baar in the Security Committee hearings on the bill, and, after each, Haarsfel requested that Dekkard reply.

Given what Dekkard had learned in dealing with the issues in the Security Committee, his responses, he felt, were better and more concise.

Little more than a bell passed before Saandaar Vonauer, the Landor floor leader, turned to Haarsfel and said, "We have no more requests to speak."

"Then open debate on the proposed act is closed, and the Council will address the amendments registered for debate and consideration. The first amendment registered is to strike paragraph B of section one, and all the language dealing with the transfer of Special Tactical Force to the Army. Councilor Baar, you registered this amendment. Would you care to explain the rationale for the amendment?"

"Thank you, Floor Leader Haarsfel. I would." Baar moved to stand behind the right lectern. "The Special Tactical Force was created to deal with levels of unrest beyond the capabilities of everyday Security patrollers. With the rise of the New Meritorists and the level of violence they have brought to the streets of Guldor, we find it neither timely nor wise to remove the STF from the Security Ministry. Perhaps in times to come, it could be considered, but at present it is unwise and ill-considered."

When Baar finished, Haarsfel looked to Dekkard. "Would you care to respond, Councilor Dekkard?"

"Thank you, Floor Leader, I would." Dekkard moved to where he stood beside the right lectern. "The honorable councilor from Suvion has conveyed the impression that the transfer of the Special Tactical Force from the Security Ministry to the jurisdiction and discipline of the Army removes the ability of the government to use force against large demonstrations. That was never the purpose of the act. The purpose was to turn an undisciplined force that fired on women and unarmed demonstrators into a better-disciplined force. There is nothing in the act that prohibits the use of the STF against large-scale and armed demonstrators, once the Army deals with the deficiencies manifested by past STF behavior. In the interim, the Army is perfectly capable of dealing with such contingencies. The unspoken reason behind this amendment is to maintain an armed force effectively controlled by the party in control of the government, and that reason goes against the letter and spirit of the Great Charter."

Dekkard thought he actually saw a nod or two when he finished.

Following the vote to adopt the amendment, which failed with only twenty-eight councilors supporting it and thirty-eight opposing it, Baar then spoke, in turn, on the remaining three amendments: to retain armed Special Agents as part of the new Ministry of Public Safety; to disallow criminal charges against Special Agents if they acted under the orders of a lawful superior; and to extend the implementation date of the act by four months.

The debate and votes on the amendments took more than a bell, and, in the end, all three additional amendments were rejected. The one vote that surprised Dekkard was the one on granting immunity to Special Agents, because only ten Commercers and one Landor voted for it.

Did Baar offer that just so that the Commercer leadership could claim they tried to protect rogue Special Agents? Not that they'd ever admit they ever used rogue agents.

Although Haarsfel had allotted four bells for debate and for the vote, it was only a third past third bell when he announced, "There being no other amendments registered with the clerk, and no pending requests for time, the question before the Council is on the passage of the Security and Public Safety Reorganization Act. The vote is for or against the proposed legislation. All councilors have a third in which to register their vote and deposit a plaque."

As Haarsfel finished speaking, Obreduur gestured, and the deep gong rang once.

Dekkard waited until most of the councilors had voted, then walked to the Craft Party's plaque box. There he picked two of the colored tiles, one signifying yes, one no, then walked to the double box set on the front of the dais, where he placed the yes tile into the ballot slot and the other into the null slot.

Villem Baar was one of the last to vote, and as he turned from the ballot box, he looked to Dekkard and gave the slightest of nods.

Finally, the deep chime rang again.

"The vote is closed," declared Obreduur. "Floor leaders, do your duty."

The three floor leaders watched as each voting tile was removed from the ballot box and placed in one of two columns in the counting tray. Then the clerk wrote the vote totals on the tally sheet, and each of the three floor leaders signed the sheet. As the majority floor leader, Haarsfel carried the tally sheet as he stepped onto the dais.

"Those councilors approving the passage of the Security and Public Safety Reorganization Act, twenty-nine Craft councilors, ten Landor councilors, and five Commerce councilors, for a total of forty-four."

Forty-four? Dekkard had never expected that kind of margin, but that just might be so that the Commercers could later claim—when the troubles began—that the Craft Party had been given support on the first major legislation and that the Commercers certainly hadn't obstructed the Crafters.

Dekkard was still sitting at his desk as Obreduur announced, "There being no other matter to be considered, the Council is hereby adjourned."

Dekkard stood slowly, then turned.

As he walked toward the councilors' lobby, Hasheem joined him. "Congratulations, Steffan. It's not often a junior councilor drafts a bill, successfully guides it though committee, and gets it passed with enough votes to override a possible veto by the Imperador." The older councilor smiled and asked humorously, "What do you plan next?"

"The committee could investigate how the New Meritorists obtained the several tonnes of dunnite it took to destroy fifteen regional Security offices."

"Isn't that almost irrelevant now? Without the STF and the Special Agents, the new Ministry of Public Safety won't need those buildings."

Dekkard shrugged. "Possibly. What if the New Meritorists have more? Or they try again? If we don't know how they obtained that dunnite, how can we stop them from getting more?"

Hasheem's brow wrinkled into a frown. "Minister Manwaeren explained that at the Security hearings, and he was telling the truth."

"He was certainly telling what he *believed* to be the truth, but the so-called investigation took place months after the theft. The New Meritorists had to have obtained that dunnite months earlier, if not more than a year. Why didn't the Navy report the accident? *Was* there even an accident or only a written report of the accident, slipped into the files well afterward to cover someone's tracks? Minister Wyath resigned as soon as Obreduur became acting Premier. He certainly wasn't asked those questions, and certainly not with an empath present."

"What do you suggest?" asked Hasheem. "That's hardly a subject for a hearing."

"Just ask Security to produce the report. Then contact the Navy officials who ostensibly made the report. Ask them to provide the report they made to Security about dunnite on those dates. If the report they supply matches, that ends the inquiry. If they deny the existence of the report, then there's a problem—and a need for a hearing."

"I'll have to think about it."

You mean, talk it over with Obreduur. "And if we don't look into it, and the New Meritorists blow up something else?"

"You make a very good point, Steffan. For now, enjoy the moment."

When assassins are still after me? "We'll do what we can, Fredrich. Thank you."

Avraal was waiting just outside the councilors' lobby. "You were magnificent!"

"Not that good," he protested. "All the facts were on my side."

"You made that obvious. Not everyone could. Obreduur was pleased. So was Hasheem."

"Hasheem congratulated me. Then he asked me, almost humorously, what I planned next. I suggested looking into how the New Meritorists got all that dunnite. He didn't seem pleased."

"I'm not sure I am, either. We'll talk about that later." Avraal motioned in the direction of the courtyard.

Meaning that worries her more than a little. As he walked beside Avraal, he decided to change the subject. "I did promise Gaaroll we could pick up her clothes on the way home."

"That's probably a good idea. Then she can run more errands so that Bretta and Illana don't have to."

"Is anyone concentrating on us?"

"Not that I can discern."

On the walk back to the Council Office Building, while they saw several councilors at a distance, those they saw were little more than faces to Dekkard.

Dekkard had barely stepped into the anteroom of his office when Roostof appeared, an anxious expression on his face. "Sir, what happened?"

Dekkard smiled. "The Council passed the act with forty-four votes. Thank you for drafting it so well."

"Luara helped. She tightened up the legal language better than I could have."

Dekkard walked to the doorway to the main staff room, looked to Colsbaan, and said, "Thank you for what you added to the Security reform act. The Council passed it with forty-four votes."

"Svard did most of it, sir."

"He said you made it better. For that, you deserve thanks as well."

"He's kind."

"He is," replied Dekkard, "but he doesn't give credit where it's not due. So thank you."

Colsbaan smiled, if shyly.

Dekkard turned his attention back to Margrit. "I'll go through the responses as quickly as I can, but I promise to be out of here by a third past fourth bell."

"I'll stay out here," said Avraal.

Dekkard hurried into his office and began to go through the typed responses drafted by Roostof and Colsbaan. As usual, most were acceptable, if not better, and he added personal notes to more than a few. Three others he made more extensive corrections and changes to, and those would have to be retyped.

He actually stepped out of the inner office at a sixth past fourth bell, handing the stack of responses to Margrit and saying, "I did promise."

She smiled and handed a large envelope to Dekkard. "This just arrived by messenger from the Premier."

A message from Obreduur wasn't totally unexpected, but Dekkard was surprised that it had come so quickly and in such a large envelope. He opened it, only to discover two smaller envelopes—one addressed to "Steffan" in a hand that Dekkard recognized as that of Obreduur, and a second one addressed to "Avraal and Steffan" in a second hand.

Dekkard handed the jointly addressed missive to Avraal and opened the one addressed to him. As he had half suspected, it contained a note card engraved with the emblem of the Council and the words "Office of the Premier" beneath. The handwritten message was short.

> *Steffan—*
> *From beginning to end, you created and managed the Security and Public Safety Reorganization Act with an expertise rarely seen in the Council, guiding it through the various hazards—in and out of the Security Committee—to successful passage.*
> *My heartfelt thanks and appreciation for your skill and perseverance.*

It was signed "Axel."

Dekkard nodded. *A note of appreciation and praise that could appear on the front page of* Gestirn *without adverse repercussions.*

His eyes returned to one of the phrases in the handwritten note—"guiding it through the various hazards—in and out of the Security Committee." He handed the note card to Avraal and pointed to the phrase.

"Interesting," she replied.

Meaning that we'll talk about that later. "What was in the other envelope?"

"An invitation from Ingrella to an early dinner on Findi at fourth bell. I'll write an acceptance when we get home, and we can send it by messenger tomorrow morning."

Dekkard turned back to Margrit. "We're leaving now."

At those words, Gaaroll immediately rose from her small desk, and followed Dekkard and Avraal out of the office. Since it was after fourth bell, the second-level hallway contained only a few scattered handfuls of people, mostly staffers, although Dekkard thought he glimpsed Breffyn Haastar and an aide heading down the main staircase.

When they stepped out of the west doors of the Council Office Building, under the sheltered entry roof, Dekkard turned to Gaaroll. "Do you sense anything?"

"No, sir, not any real strong feelings."

Dekkard still found himself scanning every possible place that might harbor a sniper. He saw that Avraal was concentrating as well. Neither said much until Dekkard was driving south on Imperial Boulevard.

"Aletina's first?" he asked.

"Unless you want to double back," replied Avraal sweetly.

Dekkard winced, but said, "I was just thinking about dragging out the process."

"Be our guest."

Dekkard didn't even shake his head. When the time came he turned right off Imperial Boulevard and then into the small parking area behind the shop. Then he looked to Gaaroll.

"Do you want either of us to come in with you?"

"I'll come get you if I have trouble," she replied.

Dekkard fretted, but in less than a sixth Gaaroll returned with the first sets of tailored garments.

"You didn't have any trouble, did you?" asked Avraal.

"Not after I showed my Council passcard and staff pin." Gaaroll grinned shyly. "They make a difference."

Dekkard then drove to Julieta, where, again, Gaaroll had no difficulties, emerging with the remainder of the garments Dekkard had purchased for her.

Rather than go by Imperial University, Dekkard turned east on Altarama Drive past the Obreduurs' house and then wound his way through East Quarter and farther east until he came to Jacquez, where he turned north.

As he crossed Camelia Avenue, he asked, "Nincya, do you sense anyone with strong emotions?"

"Not ahead of us. Over to the left a few blocks, though."

"The Erslaan Patrol Station, most likely," said Avraal.

Two blocks south of Florinda Way, Dekkard turned west for a block then north before turning east on Florinda. Once he had the steamer in the garage, he took a slow deep breath.

"It gets to me, too," said Avraal, her voice barely above a murmur.

Gaaroll carefully gathered her garments and led the way into the house.

"I'm in the kitchen!" called out Emrelda, adding, even more loudly, "Great surprise."

The three hurried into the kitchen.

"You're a little late," said Emrelda from where she stood at a side counter. "How did your day go?"

"The Council passed Steffan's Security reform act with enough votes to override a veto by the Imperador," Avraal replied immediately. "He was brilliant in explaining and defending it. The Premier sent him a note congratulating him, and Ingrella sent another inviting us to an early dinner on Findi."

"The dinner means more than the note," said Emrelda.

"We're a little late because we stopped to pick up Nincya's new clothes," added Dekkard.

Gaaroll looked down at the garments she still held, but Dekkard thought he caught a trace of a smile.

"Well, nothing at all happened at the station today. No bodies or brawls in Southtown. No reports of missing people. Rather interesting, I thought."

"That might suggest other implications," said Dekkard.

"Take your blessings where you can," suggested Emrelda dryly. "Dinner's a chicken mushroom casserole. Nincya, go hang those up. By the time you do, dinner should be ready."

"I'll get drinks," volunteered Dekkard.

Once Gaaroll left, Emrelda said quietly, "I meant it. Erslaan is well patrolled, and people in Hillside report everything. Unlike Southtown, where the first person to 'find' a body is a sanitation shovelhand."

"Then someone removed him before anyone could report the body," said Dekkard. "They don't want Security patrollers involved."

"That's the way I see it," answered Emrelda.

"Go get the drinks," added Avraal gently.

Dekkard did, and the casserole turned out to be excellent and filling, but then, Dekkard knew, almost anything either sister prepared was that way.

After dinner, while Gaaroll modeled her new office garb for Avraal and Emrelda, Dekkard went out to the veranda. A light and cold rain had begun to fall, and he sat there, thinking.

After a time, Avraal appeared.

"How were the clothes?"

"She almost looks like a different person."

"Is she pleased?"

"She doesn't say much, but yes."

"Good."

Avraal sat in the wicker chair next to Dekkard. "Do you think it was wise to mention investigating the dunnite so quickly?"

"We need to know. Hasheem will doubtless talk it over with Obreduur. It's up to them, but I think the New Meritorists had some help. I still think Minz is involved, but the fact that Suvion Industries hired Ulrich bothers me as well."

"With both of them involved, that could make you even more of a target."

"If Minz is behind the assassins, do you think it will make any difference?"

"Probably not, but we don't know for certain if he's the one." Avraal shivered. "It's getting cool out here."

"We don't have to stay here." Dekkard immediately rose.

"We do have to do something else, though."

"Oh?" Dekkard looked intently at Avraal as she stood.

"Not that." She smiled gently. "Or—not just yet."

"What?"

"We need to read a little more of Ingrella's book, so we can talk about it on Findi."

Dekkard nodded, not quite glumly.

"It's still early," said Avraal, an amused tone in her voice.

25

Can cities be said to be constructed of falsehood; or duplicity; or deception; or faith? Certainly, many call Averra a city of truth. I would not claim such. Rather, I would suggest that Averra is of itself, partaking neither of the grand cosmopolitanism of Teknar, nor of the studied insolence of Argo, nor of the ice-blue, frozen character that infuses Cimaguile, nor even of the naïve barbarian pride of Aloor.

Averra being of itself, its name will vanish when the city does. Historians, mythologists, writers of fact and fiction, all will forget Averra because it is but itself. Most great cities take on aspects in excess of reality, and when they fall—and all cities fall—they are recalled by their mythical excesses, or more properly by the illusions of their excesses, and not by what existed in actuality for so long. For this reason, if not for others, there will be no grand epics of Averra, no tragic tales of rulers' offspring stolen or bought or bartered.

The truth of mere existence carries little weight in the ballads of the bards or in the tomes of history or the romances re-created from vagrant scraps of discarded history. The tellers of tales and singers of songs whose art endures are recalled because of the excesses they depicted beyond the recounting of mere existence or accurate portrayal. Whether we recognize it or not, all beings prefer excess to accuracy. Averra has never devoted itself to excess, except perhaps to an excess of accuracy, and that is why the city and its artists will be forgotten far sooner than those who glorified the varied excesses of other cities.

AVERRA
The City of Truth
Johan Eschbach
377 TE

26

WHILE Dekkard slept well, he still woke early and worried on Furdi, but since Avraal was still sleeping he did his best to shower, shave, and dress quietly, then made his way downstairs.

Emrelda was mostly in uniform, and sat at the breakfast room table finishing her café. "You're up early."

"I had a few things on my mind."

"Imagine that."

Dekkard poured his café and sat down.

Emrelda gestured to the copy of *Gestirn* at the end of the table. "There are two stories you both need to read. The first is about the corrupt former Security ministers. The other's a version of the attack on the house here. It's more about the coming trial of the three perpetrators who survived, and doesn't mention any of us by name. You're a highly placed government official. Oh, and there's also a story about your Security reform act. A very small story."

Dekkard shook his head. "I'm sorry. You had no idea what you were getting into when Avraal and I got involved with each other."

Emrelda smiled. "I wouldn't have it any other way. I've worried about her for years." The smile faded. "You two both want to save the world, or at least Guldor, and you've made a fair start. The problem is that too many people don't like having their cozy corrupt privileges destroyed. It doesn't help that Obreduur is using you."

"I knew that well before all this happened. So did Avraal."

"Knew what?" asked Avraal, yawning, as she entered the breakfast room, followed by Gaaroll.

"That Obreduur is using us and our idealism."

"I warned you." Avraal put a hand to her mouth to cover another yawn.

"You did. Very thoroughly," Dekkard replied as he got up to pour Avraal's café. While he was at it, he poured a mug for Gaaroll.

"Thank you, sir."

"You're welcome, but the 'sir' isn't necessary in private." Dekkard paused and studied Gaaroll, who wore a dark maroon tunic and trousers. "You look stylishly professional in that outfit. I like it."

Gaaroll looked slightly embarrassed. "I do, too."

"That's good," said Dekkard cheerfully as he seated himself and reached for the newssheet.

"Is something in there?" asked Avraal.

"Just three stories, Emrelda told me." Dekkard began to read. The first story, and the largest, dominated the front page.

Justiciary Minister Serapha Marler Kuta announced yesterday the indictments of three former officials of the Security Ministry. Lukkyn Wyath, the former Minister, was charged with five violations of the Criminal Code, along with Maartyn Manwaeren, recently the acting Minister of Security, and Josef Mangele, who recently resigned as Director of the Office of Intelligence . . .

Dekkard quickly read the story, which essentially stated that all three had used their offices to provide illegal surveillance services to commercial and corporacion interests while neglecting their duties under the Great Charter. The story detailed much of what had come out in the Security Committee oversight hearings.

The second story was just as Emrelda had summarized it, with the addition that Mangele had authorized the attack, according to unnamed sources, and that two Special Agents and a subcaptain Special Agent had been indicted for attempted murder, conspiracy to commit murder, and breaking and entering, and malfeasance in office.

Dekkard frowned. Marrak had been moved to the Security Committee after Councilor Maendaan's death in the Summerend demonstrations, and had briefly been chair. He would have been again—if the Commercers had won the election. But that was comparatively recent, while Jaime Minz had been a committee staffer for former Premier Ulrich for years. *Minz likely knew enough to blackmail Mangele into ordering the attack.* That would also mean that Minz knew enough that Mangele would likely never reveal that Minz had pressured him.

The third story, on the bottom of page two, was about the passage of the Security reform act. It did not mention Dekkard. He didn't know whether to be annoyed or relieved.

He put down the newssheet and quickly summarized what he'd read.

"None of that would have been reported a year ago," offered Emrelda.

"That's because none of them would ever have been caught, and the previous Council never would have held hearings," replied Avraal.

"Will that stop them from trying to kill you?" asked Gaaroll.

"I don't think we can count on that, Nincya," replied Dekkard as he reached for the croissants and the quince paste.

"Why do they hate you that much?"

"I doubt that any of them"—*with one possible exception*—"hate me at all. I'm just someone who's upset their plans for the Commercer plutocracy to take over Guldor, and they want to remove me as expeditiously as possible."

"Plutocracy?"

"Rule by the very rich," supplied Avraal.

"They already rule," said Gaaroll.

"Not as much as they'd like," countered Emrelda as she stood. "I'll be late if I don't get going." She looked first at Avraal. "I'll messenger your note before I go to the station."

"Thank you. Ingrella will get a quicker response that way."

Then Emrelda turned to Dekkard, and added cheerfully, "Try to have a less exciting day."

"I'll do my best, and we'll see you tonight," said Dekkard.

Emrelda picked up her patroller's cap and left the breakfast room.

Dekkard passed a croissant to Avraal, and then cut his own croissants, quickly filling them with quince paste.

Little more than two thirds later, the three were on their way to the Council Office Building, with Dekkard taking another variation on one of the many routes he'd worked out, one which brought him to Imperial Boulevard three blocks north of Camelia Avenue.

As he turned onto the boulevard, Gaaroll said, "Really strong feelings west of here, sir."

"How far west?"

"I'm guessing close to the river."

"That's a good mille, maybe farther," said Dekkard. "Right in the middle of the Rivertown area."

"Have to be strong for me to sense that far."

Dekkard could believe that. "Are they moving this way?"

"No, sir. Just sort of boiling up."

"I wonder what that's all about," mused Dekkard to Avraal. "Can you sense anything?"

"No. That's way too far for me." She turned her head. "But there's a lot of smoke billowing up. It looks like it's about where Nincya's sensing feelings."

"Maybe it's a big fire. That would get people's emotions running strong. Still. Nincya, let me know if it heads this way."

"Don't think it will, sir. Feels like lots of feelings all jumbled together. Might be because it's so far."

Or because it's a huge fire.

Dekkard was still wondering about what sort of fire could get that large in Rivertown when he reached the Council Office Building. He pulled up in front of the west doors, then got out of the Gresynt so that Avraal could take it to work at Carlos Baartol's.

As she eased behind the wheel, she smiled. "I'll be back before noon. That way we can have something to eat before you go to your Workplace Administration Committee meeting."

Dekkard watched her drive away before he and Gaaroll walked to the doors, entered the building, and made their way to the office, where he immediately began to read the mail and petitions. When he finished, he asked Colsbaan to come into the office.

"Luara, how are you coming on the working women's project?"

"I've gone through all the relevant laws, both dealing with guilds and with legalist counsel, and I'm fairly sure that I've determined where and what changes need to be made. I've started researching the case law on representation of non-guild members by guild legalists. That's going to take some time."

"Have you heard anything from Myram Plassar?"

"Yes, sir. She replied almost immediately expressing support. She said it would take a week or so to gather the material that might be helpful. I'd estimate that it will be Unadi at the earliest before I get anything."

"Is there anything you need from me right now?"

"No, sir. Not now. When I get farther along, I'll give you the options for how we can approach it legislatively. I can see several possibilities, but I need to do some more work to see if case law precludes any of them."

"I've made some inquiries of my own, and it appears that most patrollers won't have a problem with such a law."

"Some will."

"I know," replied Dekkard. "That's one reason why those women need the law. If there's nothing else?"

"No, sir."

Dekkard stood. "Then I won't keep you. If you'd tell Svard I need a minute with him."

Moments after Colsbaan left, Roostof entered the inner office.

Dekkard motioned for him to close the door and take a seat. "How do you think Shuryn is doing?"

"Well enough. I've had him handling some of the correspondence dealing with engineering and practical matters. He writes well enough. A little too technical at times, but better than I did when I started."

"How is his engineering research coming?"

"Faster, now. Initially, he had to find out where a lot of the material was. He was excited the other day to discover that he could access the national library of the Guldoran Engineers Guild. He told me that there's very little there directly involving corporacions, but that by going through some of the papers he gets leads to other stories."

"That sounds promising." Dekkard's words were cautious.

"More promising than either of the other two applicants." Roostof snorted.

"How are Bretta and Illana doing?"

"Bretta's a little sharper, but they both work hard. Illana knows more about Gaarlak."

"I'd hope so. That was one of the reasons I hired her." Dekkard paused, then asked, "Did you read this morning's *Gestirn*?"

"Yes, sir. What story are you asking about?"

"None—directly. All three stories got me thinking about something else." *If indirectly because of Jaime Minz.* "How do you think the New Meritorists really obtained all that dunnite?"

Roostof frowned. "I thought that was explained at the Security hearings."

"Acting Minister Manwaeren was certainly telling what he believed to be the truth, but the so-called investigation took place months after the theft." Dekkard explained what he'd already told Hasheem. "I suggested Hasheem look into the matter yesterday. He said he'd think about it. That the report might be missing by now."

Roostof smiled. "Then the Justiciary minister can charge Wyath with destroying government records or something similar. His explanation before the High Justiciary could be very interesting, especially since the self-incrimination provision of the Great Charter doesn't apply to ministry appointees in regard to their duties."

"What if the report is real and the Navy corroborates it?" asked Dekkard.

"Then there's the question as to why the Navy never made it public, and why they kept it from Security until Security asked. Either the Navy or Security is covering up something."

Dekkard nodded. "I'd like you to write up how the Security Committee should approach the dunnite problem. Keep it between us. It could be more explosive than the Security reorganization act."

"I can see that, sir." Roostof paused. "Are you sure you want to pursue this *now*?"

"If it's just between us, I'm not pursuing anything. But I'd like the option, and something like this needs to be handled carefully. You're very thorough."

"Yes, sir."

After Roostof left, Dekkard considered the points that his senior legalist had brought up.

Avraal arrived at a third before noon.

"How's Carlos?"

"He's worried about you. He inquired about you twice, in different ways. I asked him if he'd heard anything from his contacts, but he said he hadn't and that bothered him."

"Meaning that something's going on, and someone's trying to keep it from getting to him?"

"Or that someone's doing this on the corporacion side, completely with corporacion contacts, most likely people reserved for important matters."

"Important removals, you mean," said Dekkard sarcastically. "Except why is it so important to remove me? I'm just the second-most-junior councilor."

"Do you want a list, dear? You had the nerve to draft and pass an act that everyone in the Council knew was necessary, but that everyone also knew that every large corporacion in Guldor would oppose. You've survived at least five assassination attempts, and are thought to be behind a well-connected councilor's death. You somehow got selected over whoever Obreduur wanted to replace Decaro. You embarrassed the entire Security Ministry more than once, and, by passing your reform act, you've kept the New Meritorists relatively quiet. And finally, by that and by your very continued existence, you've made it difficult for the Commercers to concentrate on dealing with Obreduur, and that enabled him to put Wyath and the other top Security thugs on trial in a way that will further hurt and embarrass the Commercers." Avraal paused. "It also galls many of them that you're handsome and dangerous."

"When you put it that way . . ."

"Is there any other way?"

Before Dekkard could respond, she added, "And some of them suspect you're anything but done. Which you're not."

"Do I have a choice with Minz and Northwest Chemical likely after me?"

"Not really. Not now," she replied. Then she offered an amused smile, one slightly forced, Dekkard thought, and said, "But don't ask questions like a clueless little boy who's just thrown a hornets' nest into the middle of the table at a formal dinner."

Dekkard managed a sheepish grin. "No more stupid questions." *At least, I'll try.* "Now, we'd better get something to eat."

The two walked quickly, but did not rush, to the councilors' dining room. There, as they entered, Kaliara Bassaana appeared.

"Good day," said Dekkard politely.

"The same to you, Steffan, Avraal. Since you were so kind to invite me to eat with you might I prevail upon you two to join me?" Bassaana looked directly at Avraal.

"Of course," Avraal replied. "We'd be delighted."

"Three, please," said Bassaana to the host, a thin man attired in black and gold livery, who escorted them to one of the circular tables for four.

Bassaana moved her chair slightly before seating herself, so that she was equidistant from Avraal and Dekkard.

As the server appeared at the table, Bassaana asked Avraal, "Do you know what you want?"

Avraal nodded.

"Then we'll order everything now." Bassaana inclined her head to the younger woman.

"Café, the chilled tomato soup, and a small side of greens."

Dekkard gestured to Bassaana, who offered a small amused smile, but said, "Café, and the chicken salad."

"Café also, and a half of the duck cassoulet with a small side of greens."

"Very good, Councilors, Ritten."

Once the server left, Bassaana said, "I'm so glad we had a chance to get together. You two are by far the most interesting couple of any in the Council."

"Only for the novelty," replied Dekkard dryly. "Someone like the Premier has accomplished far more. I also suspect it took you far more effort to get elected than it did me."

"That's very kind of you—"

"And truthful," said Avraal. "Steffan doesn't have that many illusions, and, except when referring to me, he's definitely not given to flattery."

Bassaana laughed gently. "I think you just made my point." She paused, then said, "Before I forget, Steffan, I must congratulate you on the passage of the Security and Public Safety Reorganization Act. Something like it was long overdue, and the way you structured it was masterful."

"That's quite a compliment from you," replied Dekkard. "I just tried to be practical."

"I heard that you actually drafted it. Is that true?"

"Half true. I gave my legalists the structure and the basic provisions and then asked them to make it as legally solid as they could."

"Why did you say the act was masterful?" asked Avraal.

"Because Steffan destroyed nothing. The STF remains intact, but under tighter control, which was definitely necessary. The Special Agents lost only the ability to carry firearms, which they'd abused, but not their jobs or their functions, placing them where they might actually be useful, and the regular patrollers can now concentrate on keeping the peace. No one could really complain that much. Well, except for a few who felt duty-bound to do so. And the vote was such that the Imperador will have to sign it, if he hasn't already."

"I was fortunate." Dekkard could see the political rationale she'd described, even if he hadn't thought of it that way. *Was that accident, good fortune . . . or maybe what happens when you look at form and function first?* Dekkard would have liked to have thought the latter, but suspected the first two—and Roostof's care in drafting the language—also had a lot to do with the act getting passed.

"More than merely fortunate," said Bassaana. "Effective. Hasheem was fortunate you took on the problem. Not all committees work that smoothly. Some don't work at all, you'll find."

"Sometimes they get bypassed, as in the Kraffeist Affair," said Dekkard, knowing that Bassaana had been outmaneuvered by Ulrich when she'd wanted to get at Eastern Ironway.

"That's true," agreed Bassaana, "but look where it got Ulrich."

At that moment, the server returned with their drinks, entrées, and salads.

After taking a sip of café, Bassaana continued, "Speaking of committees, do you have any idea where Haarsfel is headed with these hearings?"

"He hasn't shared anything with me," replied Dekkard.

Bassaana smiled. "That wasn't the question I asked, Steffan."

Dekkard smiled. "I know, Kaliara, but I'm not about to speculate on what senior councilors in my party might be thinking. For a junior councilor, that's not wise." He paused, just slightly, and added, "I do have a thought, but it's only my thought."

"What might that be?"

"I've noticed that while the past Councils have passed some workplace safety rules affecting a number of occupations, they don't seem to be enforced. In some cases, there's actually no way to do so. It will be interesting to see the workplaces discussed in future hearings."

"And you've not talked to the committee chairman?"

"Not once about anything concerning the Workplace Administration Committee."

"That was most carefully said."

Dekkard laughed softly. "I've talked briefly with him, in his capacity as majority floor leader, on two occasions, once before I became a councilor, and once after I was sworn in."

"That's all?" Bassaana sounded genuinely surprised.

"That's all. I've been working hard to learn what I didn't know about being a councilor. Outside of security and workplace matters, my knowledge in other areas is limited."

"I assume you have more contact with the Premier."

"A bit more, but not that much. We've had one dinner together, and he's asked me to come by his office for a brief talk twice." Dekkard offered an amused smile. "I did use his floor office to wash off the Atacaman pepper."

Bassaana's mouth opened, so quickly that Dekkard doubted the surprise was feigned. "Someone in the Council Hall attacked you with Atacaman fire pepper?"

"Inside the committee room. The one Security Committee clerk retained by Chairman Hasheem. Apparently, he thought I wasn't deferential enough to the more senior Commercer councilors."

"I assume Hasheem released him or had him charged with assault." There was a touch of the righteous in the older councilor's tone.

Dekkard shook his head. "He tripped trying to get away and inhaled the remainder of the dust in the pouch he held. He had some sort of respiratory failure. That was what Guard Captain Trujillo told me." He hesitated. "You didn't know?"

"Hasheem and the Premier obviously didn't want anyone to know. The clerk wasn't otherwise injured, was he?"

"The Guard captain said there wasn't a mark on him."

"I'm sure there wasn't. It sounds like someone wanted you to overreact."

"I'm glad I didn't," said Dekkard, "but I really didn't think at all. I just wanted to avoid the pepper dust."

"You were carrying your knives, weren't you? You always do. I noticed that you're carrying a personal truncheon now, too."

"I have been since the committee incident. I wasn't then."

"Do you have any ideas?"

"It struck me as a more personal attack rather than a, shall we say, professional one. I know I've upset various interests professionally, but who could I have offended personally? Obreduur is the only councilor I even knew on a personal basis, and I didn't and don't know any ministers, corporacion senior officials, or others of power. Most of my acquaintances have been other security aides, and security aides don't have the power and connections to set up something like that."

"That's an interesting point," observed Bassaana.

"As you pointed out," said Avraal, "Steffan's Security reform act didn't affect anyone personally, and he had nothing to do with the indictments of Minister Wyath and the others."

"These things often work out over time," said Bassaana.

"One way or another," replied Dekkard. "We'll just have to see. Is there anything interesting coming before the Transportation Committee?"

"Chairman Waarfel appears to be taking his time. We've only had an organizational meeting and a hearing about the abuse of excess appropriations. Something your former employer addressed in an amendment during the last days of the previous Council."

For a moment, Dekkard was surprised, not only about the "supplemental" ironway appropriations, but also because he'd forgotten that Waarfel had become chair of the Transportation Committee, a position Bassaana would have assumed if the Commercers had won the election. The other surprise was that Haarsfel had chosen to chair Workplace Administration and let the undistinguished Waarfel chair the Transportation Committee. "Waarfel's from Aloor, and his growers have never been treated well by the ironways. I can't believe he has any great love of them. Have you talked with him?"

"Only in generalities. Like many councilors who've been here awhile, he's cautious."

"Is that an observation or a recommendation?" asked Dekkard, looking down at his plate to realize he'd already eaten most of the cassoulet.

"Every councilor has to discover what works for her or him. I'd judge that you're careful, but neither patient nor cautious."

"Whereas you're careful, and only as patient and cautious as necessary?" asked Dekkard, keeping his tone light.

"Those are all necessities for women in politics or with power."

"I'd say that they're necessities for everyone in politics or power," interjected Avraal, "except that many men don't realize it."

Bassaana laughed, then said to Dekkard, "She might save you yet."

Dekkard let an amused smile cross his lips. "She already has."

"Then you've learned more than most male councilors." Bassaana took a small bite of chicken from the salad, then set her fork on the plate, as if to signify she'd had enough, even though more than a third of the salad remained, and turned to Avraal. "I'm curious, and I hope you'll indulge me. You're from a very old Landor family. Were you tutored, or sent off to school?"

Avraal smiled politely. "All of us were largely taught by my mother, but had occasional tutoring in advanced subjects until we reached the university level. My brother was sent to Imperial University. I studied at Sudaen Women's Seminary, and then at the Empath Academy in Siincleer."

Bassaana nodded. "Do you think you're typical?"

"No," replied Avraal with a smile. "No more than you are."

"Point taken," replied Bassaana cheerfully. "No woman with political position is typical."

"Whereas there are enough men with power, political or otherwise," said Dekkard, "that those who resemble each other are said to be typical."

"And those who don't are considered dangerous, as are all women with power." Bassaana's smile showed sardonic amusement. "That might be why the three of us are eating together."

"To what end?" Avraal asked Bassaana.

"I have no end, except political survival, which will become increasingly difficult over the next year, especially once the demonstrations and riots resume."

"Why do you think that will happen?" asked Avraal.

"Don't you?"

"I'd be interested in why you think so," said Avraal.

"The New Meritorists won't be satisfied until they've destroyed the Great Charter or until they're effectively destroyed. Either way, that will create unrest and more demonstrations. Avraal, you never did tell me how you ended up working for Obreduur."

Bassaana's abrupt shift back to Avraal told Dekkard that there would be no more political talk.

"I thought it would be interesting, and I applied. He interviewed me and hired me. That was five years ago. How did you get into politics?"

"It was the only way I could keep my independence, do something halfway meaningful, and avoid domestic politics."

Marriage as merely domestic politics? "You never thought about marriage? Not ever?"

"Not as anything other than servitude." Bassaana turned back to Avraal. "You were careful and fortunate." She smiled. "This has been a most interesting conversation, and I'm sure there will be others. Now, if you will excuse me."

Dekkard stood as she did, replying, "Most interesting."

Once Bassaana was well out of earshot, Dekkard just looked at Avraal.

"She evaded but never lied. You didn't know she wasn't married?"

"How would I know?" Dekkard frowned. Amelya Detauran had always referred to Bassaana as Kaliara. He shook his head.

"What?"

"I wondered about her relationship with Amelya Detauran. I've gotten the impression that they're closer than usual."

"If there is a relationship it's secondary to being a councilor. Everything is, I'd guess."

"What does she want from us?"

"I think, from what I gathered, she truly thinks we're dangerous, and she doesn't want to be a target. That would fit with her indirect approaches to Obreduur and her backdoor assurances of support. Also, it's clear from what happened in the last Council that she can't trust the Commercer leadership."

Dekkard recalled how she'd been sidelined during the Kraffeist Affair, when she'd tried to have the Transportation Committee look into Eastern Ironway. "How far can we trust her, if at all?"

"Only when it's in her interest, but you already knew that, and there's no doubt that she knows that you know."

"Or that you've told me," replied Dekkard.

"Either way."

Dekkard nodded.

When Dekkard tried to sign for Avraal's meal, the server informed him that Bassaana had already taken care of it.

"She can afford it," Avraal pointed out.

As they walked from the councilors' dining room to the Workplace Committee hearing room, Dekkard still wondered what else Bassaana had in mind. What Avraal said about Bassaana made sense, but she didn't strike him as someone who'd merely settle for survival.

The hearing was long, almost three bells, and dealt with the log-handling practices of three separate corporacions: Jaykarh Logging, Eshbruk Timber and Milling, and Nolaan Wood Products. From what Dekkard heard, none of them were exactly distinguished by workplace safety.

When he returned to his office, he signed all the letters that didn't require notes or corrections, and put aside the others for the morning. He also couldn't help thinking about the fact that, sooner or later, he and Avraal needed to think about going to Gaarlak and finding a small property of some sort to satisfy the requirement of a physical tie to the district he'd been selected to represent.

The drive back to the house was nerve-racking, but thankfully without incident.

27

BECAUSE he wondered about the possible fire in the Rivertown area, on Quindi morning Dekkard checked *Gestirn* closely as soon as he reached the breakfast room. He finally found a small story near the back of the newssheet.

A local disturbance near Rivertown escalated into violence and then into a fire that burned an entire block, killing at least fifteen people trapped on the upper floors of a condemned structure. The cause of the disturbance is not known at this time, but is believed to have started at a local grocery shop. When patrollers intervened, the disputants turned on them, claiming that the patrollers helped keep the area poor. One patroller was badly injured.

"What are you finding so interesting?" asked Emrelda.

"Yesterday on the way to the Council . . ." Dekkard went on to explain briefly, then added, "I don't see how burning down an entire block and attacking patrollers solves anything."

"It doesn't," replied Emrelda. "But a lot of them have little or nothing. They're hungry, and food prices are going up. I'd wager that someone got angry over what the grocer was charging, and matters went from there. On Duadi, two patrollers from our station ran into that at a produce cart in Southtown. They had to stop a man from beating up the vendor."

"Does that happen often?"

"All the time," said Gaaroll. "Some places, anyway."

"More than we'd like," added Emrelda.

"You're a dispatcher, but you don't always stay in the station, do you?" asked Gaaroll.

Emrelda smiled wryly. "No. I get called in more than a few times on cases involving women or children. I never told Markell that, though. He would have worried."

"And we don't?" asked Dekkard.

"It's not the same. You and Avraal had—and still do, it appears—jobs even more dangerous than being a patroller. Sometimes, I can make a difference. Why wouldn't I want that? You understand."

"We do." Dekkard nodded. Markell had obviously wanted to protect Emrelda, more than she wanted to be protected. *But there's no point in saying that now.*

As he heard Avraal's steps on the stairs, he hurried into the kitchen to get their cafés.

From that point on, breakfast was routine. Before long, the three once more headed off to the Council Office Building.

Because Quindi looked to be a comparatively uneventful day for Dekkard, he sent Avraal off to her official job, after promising to be very careful, then spent the morning catching up on correspondence, the volume of which seemed to grow weekly, if not daily, along with complaints that also increased, from those about ironway freight rates and barge rates, to others as esoteric as wanting to know whether Dekkard had any way to arrange for a constituent's son to become an imperial page.

Thankfully, Roostof knew about that—would-be pages applied to the Imperador's chamberlain.

Just after noon, Dekkard received a moderately thick package from Hasheem with a note informing him that the Imperador had signed the Security and Public Safety Reorganization Act, and that, as a result, the budget for the former Ministry of Security had to be refigured for the newly established Ministry of Public Safety, and some of funding shifted to Treasury and Justiciary for the Special Agents and functions transferred to those ministries.

Dekkard read the last lines of the note again.

> . . . *in view of your work in creating the Ministry of Public Safety, I thought you should look over the budgetary proposals for the coming year. The professional staff will need your comments by Unadi afternoon in order to address them before presenting the staff recommendations to the committee for a vote or amendments on Tridi.*

He hadn't even thought about budgets, but with the new calendar year beginning in little more than four weeks, the final budget and appropriations legislation would be coming before the Council in less than two weeks.

Dekkard looked at the pages of tables and numbers, then slowly began to read the comparisons prepared by the professional Security Committee staff, none of whom he had met, except in passing.

It's another way of learning about Security—or Public Safety. Even if he hadn't planned on learning that aspect of the new ministry. He also wondered if the request from Hasheem was a way of postponing dealing with the issue of the stolen dunnite.

By a third after third bell, Dekkard had drafted a rough response and made several suggestions, based on the fact that the new ministry would need to hire more patrollers. He handed the draft to Roostof with a request to make suggestions and changes, as well as any mathematical corrections, by midmorning on Unadi.

By the time he finished discussing that with Roostof, Avraal arrived. "You look exhausted. What have you been doing?"

"Wrestling with appropriations for the new Ministry of Public Safety."

"I thought the professional staff did that and presented the numbers to the committee."

"They do. Except Hasheem asked me to look over their figures before they go to the committee. It seems to me the staff underfunded the regular patroller budget. Whether they'll take my recommendations, who knows? Roostof's looking over my numbers and draft." Dekkard massaged his forehead. "That was something I didn't plan on."

"There will always be something you didn't plan on. We need to get you home and fed. I think we can skip services tonight."

That was just fine with Dekkard.

28

EMRELDA had to work on Findi, and Dekkard and Avraal slept in, so that they didn't get to the kitchen for breakfast until after the second morning bell. Dekkard wore old grays, while Avraal wore a robe over her nightclothes. They found Gaaroll, wearing one of her older outfits, sitting at the breakfast room table with an old deck of pastecards, dealing out what looked to be a game of impatience.

"How long have you been up?" asked Dekkard.

"Had breakfast with Emrelda. She offered to drop me off in the Erslaan area. Said I could look around there."

"Obviously, you didn't go." Dekkard began to fix café for himself and Avraal.

"No point in it. I don't have many marks, and I've got good clothes now." She smiled. "Thank you again. Margrit said I looked stylish. Probably not, but it's nice to be able to fit in in a swell office."

"You're learning," said Avraal.

Gaaroll looked at Dekkard. "You were really a plasterer?"

"An apprentice to a decorative plasterer."

A frown crinkled her forehead.

"My parents are artisans. I didn't have the talent. After they realized that, my mother suggested I compete for a place at the Military Institute. I was fortunate enough to get one. I went into security after graduation and applied for a position with the Council. Obreduur hired me. Working security for a councilor fulfills the service requirement." *If barely.* Dekkard filled two mugs with café and placed one in front of Avraal and the other across from her, then went to the pantry cooler, from which he extracted three croissants and the quince paste, placing them on two plates and bringing them back to the table.

Avraal sipped her café while Dekkard split his croissants and filled them.

"What are you two doing today?" asked Gaaroll.

"We're going to dinner early at the Obreduurs'," said Avraal. "We need to run some errands before that."

Dekkard managed not to frown. Avraal hadn't mentioned errands.

"Would you like to come with us?" asked Avraal.

"I'll need to change."

"As if we don't?" asked Dekkard dryly.

A hint of a smile crossed Gaaroll's face, but vanished quickly.

"Just a few small things," explained Avraal. "I'd thought perhaps we might gift them with some wine, or anything else that might be appropriate, and we really should get some wine for the house. Emrelda's done more than her share of that."

Dekkard and Avraal didn't hurry, and it was close to fourth bell before they left the house by the east portico door.

"Trouble's coming," said Gaaroll. "Next door."

Dekkard glanced to the adjoining house to see Sr. Waaldwud walking toward them.

Waaldwud stopped at the edge of the drive and glared. "I hope you're all happy. Clare just gave me notice. She said she couldn't work here with an empath looking over her shoulder."

"I'm sorry she felt that way," replied Avraal pleasantly. "Some people have difficulty meeting professional and legal standards."

"That's easy enough for you to say. You don't know how hard it is to find a decent nanny." Then Waaldwud turned abruptly and stalked back toward his front door.

"The boy deserves better," said Avraal quietly.

"Better nanny and better father," said Gaaroll.

"Most likely," said Avraal, "but we don't control either."

"Is there any other trouble around?" asked Dekkard sardonically.

"Just him," replied Gaaroll.

Gaaroll didn't sense any other strong emotions during the various errands, in the middle of which the three stopped at Elfredo's, where Avraal and Dekkard ordered various light plates. Gaaroll ate the largest share, which was what Avraal had in mind, Dekkard suspected.

After eating, Avraal and Dekkard picked up two cases of assorted wines, most for the house, as well as two special bottles for the Obreduurs and a decorative basket for the wine. Even so, the three were back at the house by slightly after second bell.

Dekkard and Avraal thought about sitting on the veranda, but decided against it, given the arrival of a chilly wind out of the northeast. Instead they repaired to the sitting room.

"What are you going to say about the Eschbach book?" Dekkard asked.

"What will you say?" she returned with a smile.

"I haven't thought about it. I have had a few other matters on my mind recently."

"You didn't think about the book or what you'll say?"

"I thought about the book. I'd be interested to know just who Johan Eschbach was. If he was just a writer or . . . something more."

"Just a writer?" asked Avraal. "Does a writer have to be something more? How would you feel if someone asked if you were just a councilor or if you were something more?"

Dekkard winced. "I didn't mean it quite that way. I wondered if his words were based on observation or experience or both."

"That's not much better," Avraal pointed out, again smiling.

Dekkard shook his head. Finally, he asked, "What do you think?"

"I've enjoyed what we've read so far, and I'm looking forward to reading more. I like the way he writes. For him, Averra is alive."

"I'm not sure that I'd think of Machtarn in that way. Gaarlak, maybe."

"That could be because Gaarlak grew slowly. Machtarn has more than doubled in size in the last generation."

"So . . ." Dekkard drew out the word. ". . . you're saying that rapid growth destroys a city's character?"

"Makes it different anyway." Avraal stood. "I need to change for dinner."

"I thought . . . ?"

"There's informal, and there's informal."

Dekkard smiled, then stood. "You can pick what I'm wearing. I'm obviously not good at distinguishing between shades of informal."

"I'll be happy to choose something for you," said Avraal, in a tone both amused and verging on the overly sweet.

In the end, Dekkard wore a rich green barong with deep gray trousers, and Avraal a green mid-calf-length dress with three-quarter sleeves and a sleeveless vest of a lighter green.

"You two look good," said Gaaroll. "You're sure you don't need me?"

"You don't sense any strong emotions nearby, do you?" asked Dekkard.

"No, sir."

"We'll chance it," said Dekkard. "No one was watching this morning. You don't sense anyone, and it's unlikely anyone beside the Obreduurs knows where we're going or when."

Even so, Dekkard didn't take Jacquez or Camelia Avenue on the way, and he approached the Obreduur house from the east on Altarama Drive. The gates were open, and he drove up under the portico, where he parked the Gresynt. Avraal carried the small basket that held two bottles of Silverhills Red Reserve.

Axel Obreduur stood at the top of the steps waiting, wearing a silver-trimmed black barong, one of the few times that Dekkard had seen him not wearing a jacket.

"Greetings, Avraal, Steffan. That's a handsome steamer."

"We were fortunate to find one this good," replied Dekkard, definitely not wanting to explain, "especially since I got to know about Gresynts here."

"Come in, come in." Obreduur led them into the sitting room, where Ingrella stood beside the chair that was her favorite.

Avraal handed her the basket. "Just a small token."

"You two didn't have to," replied Ingrella, who then turned to her husband and gave him the basket.

"You really didn't," added Obreduur. "I assume you're ready for refreshments. Silverhills white and Kuhrs?"

"Please," replied Dekkard, while Avraal nodded.

After Obreduur left the room, Ingrella said, "I'm so glad you could come. Our life has been crowded, especially now, with the possible food shortages. Axel's had to invite committee chairs here, ministers—people who might be ministers." She paused and offered a smile that Dekkard would have called quietly wicked. "And some who, after coming, will never be."

"I have to say that I was impressed by Serapha Marler Kuta," said Dekkard. "Was she one of those you favored?"

"She was, although I leaned more toward Elyncya Duforgue, but since Elyncya decided to run for councilor and was elected, I was certainly happy with Serapha."

Dekkard nodded. *Another example of how far out they planned matters.* After the years of working for Obreduur, that didn't surprise him. "I'm assuming the indictment of Wyath and the others will lead to a trial. It will be interesting to see how that goes."

"You wouldn't have heard, but Mangele hanged himself in his cell sometime this morning. We got the word around midday."

"Will that make convictions more difficult?" asked Dekkard, finding himself strangely unsurprised, almost as if he'd known something like that might happen.

"On some counts, those involving conspiracy to commit murder, it will weaken the case. That's just my opinion. I don't see how Wyath can escape the charge of high treason, though."

"In case you haven't already noticed," declared Obreduur, returning with a tray that he set on the side table, "it's unwise to wager against her opinions, especially in legal matters."

"I take it that there was a mountain of evidence against Mangele," said Dekkard. "Even though the Security Committee hearings didn't go into matters deeply, I got that impression." He paused. "Was Fredrich instructed not to allow too much in the way of specifics, but enough to justify an investigation?"

"Steffan," said Obreduur, "you don't miss much." He handed a wineglass of Silverhills white to Avraal, then a second to Ingrella.

"Usually," replied Dekkard, "that means I missed something even more important. What is it this time?"

Obreduur laughed and handed a beaker of Kuhrs to Dekkard. "There isn't something more this time. You're missing less and less."

"I'm likely missing more than I should."

"That's true of all of us." Obreduur raised his beaker. "To friends and a pleasant evening."

"To friends," replied the other three, not quite simultaneously.

"That was quite a 'token' in that basket," said Obreduur. "Silverhills Red Reserve?"

"Well," replied Dekkard, "since we'll never be able to truly repay all we've learned, I thought our token ought to be slightly more than token."

"It was his idea," said Avraal, "but I agreed, especially after everything, not to mention the loan of certain books."

"Have you started reading *The City of Truth*?" asked Ingrella.

"We have," said Avraal. "We're reading it together. It seemed better that way."

Ingrella shot an amused glance at her husband.

"She wagered you would," explained Obreduur.

"How are you finding it?"

"Provoking enough that I'll have to reread it," said Dekkard. "The language is beautiful, but I have to confess I've never heard of Averra, and I studied a fair amount of history."

Ingrella smiled enigmatically. "You need to finish it, and don't skip to the end, because that won't answer your question unless you read what's in between."

"I thought it might be something like that," said Avraal.

Dekkard didn't disagree, but only said, "It may be a while before we finish it."

"There's no hurry," replied Ingrella. "It's better savored than hurried through."

"As are many things," added her husband.

"It has to be rare and valuable," said Dekkard. "We appreciate your letting us read it."

"Axel trusted his life to you both for years," said Ingrella dryly. "I think we can trust you to care for a moderately rare book."

"I will say," Dekkard said, "that I've never read anything quite like it, but that was the point, wasn't it."

Ingrella nodded. "One of them."

"She seldom has a single point or objective," said Obreduur. "I learned that very quickly."

"Almost not quickly enough," Ingrella replied playfully.

"I definitely understand that," said Dekkard.

"Unlike many men," commented Avraal.

"As a woman and an empath," replied Obreduur, "you would know."

Ingrella turned slightly to Avraal. "Have you decided what to wear to the Council's Yearend Ball?"

Avraal looked to Dekkard.

Dekkard shrugged helplessly. "I didn't know there was one."

Ingrella then looked to her husband.

"The reminders will go out tomorrow. We have been a little busy."

"When is it?" asked Dekkard.

"It's always the evening of the last Quindi of the year," replied Ingrella. "It's held in the Council Hall building. They turn the main corridor outside the councilors' dining room into a ballroom of sorts. Each councilor can invite one other couple, and only one couple."

"What about just one person?" asked Dekkard, thinking of Emrelda.

"That's fine," replied Obreduur. "The invitation is only good for a single couple or a single individual."

"If I might ask," said Avraal, "how formal an occasion is it?"

"There's no requirement—" began Obreduur.

"In practice," declared Ingrella, "it's as formal as you can manage. There are no exceptions to the one additional invitation per councilor. Invitations are coveted. Even corporacion presidentes can only come by invitation. Ministers and their spouses are invited, but they don't get additional invitations. The Imperador is invited, always, and he always regrets, but he gets two additional invitations. Occasionally, over the years, someone from the Imperial family has attended."

"For those few such as I," asked Dekkard, "is deep gray formalwear acceptable?"

"Absolutely!" declared Ingrella.

Obreduur smiled and nodded.

"Is any color of gown frowned upon?" asked Avraal.

"I was going to mention that," said Ingrella. "It's never spoken of, and a few wives or women accompanying single councilors have been—discomfited—but brilliant scarlet would not be the best choice."

"The Scarlet Daughter?" asked Dekkard.

"Since it's a long-standing custom," replied Ingrella with an amused smile, "no one has ever spoken of it to me, but I'd surmise that there might be some connection."

"Just scarlet, or most bright reds?" asked Dekkard.

Both women just looked at him.

Dekkard got the message.

Ingrella turned back to Avraal. "Men often forget that we need time to prepare for such events."

Obreduur flushed and said, "The reminders and the additional invitations will be sent by messenger to every councilor tomorrow."

"Thank you, dear," said Ingrella, adding to Avraal, "I'm certain you and Steffan will look stunning. You have excellent taste."

Dekkard got that message as well.

The conversation returned to a lighter mode for the next third of a bell, when Hyelda appeared in the archway. "Dinner is ready for all you distinguished people."

"Three out of four, anyway," said Avraal.

"Four out of four, and you know it." Dekkard grinned even as he stood, then followed Ingrella and Avraal into the dining room.

There was no blessing, but Dekkard knew the Obreduurs were religious only out of public necessity, as he and Avraal had also become.

Once everyone was seated, with Silverhills white wine in every wineglass, dinner began with a light salad of greens, followed by chicken Suvion, roasted boneless chicken breast filled with a sharp melted Encoran cheese, and topped with a butter basil sauce and accompanied by starburst noodles, also topped with the butter basil sauce, with green beans amandine.

"This is definitely special," said Dekkard after a single bite of the chicken. "I've never had anything like it."

"It's new for us, too," replied Ingrella. "It was in a cookbook that Elyncya Duforgue gave us, and it looked good. I asked Hyelda if she would try it. She said it's fairly easy to fix."

"Easy or not," said Avraal, "it's delicious."

Dessert for each person was a slice of orange chiffon cake topped with orange slices lightly drizzled in Goldlund orange brandy. Dekkard didn't leave a morsel, and neither, he noticed, did Obreduur.

Dekkard finished just savoring what had been an excellent dinner when Obreduur began to speak, his voice pleasantly conversational.

"You might be interested to know that the Imperador definitely knows who you are. He mentioned you when I met with him yesterday after he signed your Security reform act."

"In what context?" asked Dekkard warily. He wasn't aware that Obreduur met regularly with the Imperador, but supposed that was a necessity.

"He knew that you'd drafted and championed the bill, and he knew the circumstances of your being selected as councilor. He wanted to know how you managed it."

"What did you tell him?" Dekkard smiled pleasantly. "That Gretna Haarl insisted on me to keep you and Jens's choice from becoming councilor? Or was Jens your choice?"

Ingrella offered an amused smile, while Obreduur chuckled, then said, "You're right on both counts. But I didn't tell Laureous that. I just said that the district party had made up its mind, and it would have created lasting hard feelings to ignore their choice in a district that we barely won. He understood."

"He may not have understood that rejecting you would have eventually undermined Axel," added Ingrella.

"Especially with women?" asked Avraal.

"That was a consideration," said Ingrella.

Meaning that it was a strong consideration. That meant Dekkard owed Gretna Haarl even more than he'd realized. In turn, that definitely meant they'd have to go to Gaarlak before long.

"Fredrich mentioned your concerns about the Commercers' amendment to extend the implementation of transferring Special Agents. You're right about that, *but* there are political considerations. He also mentioned your interest in pursuing the dunnite issue, and your suggestion for inquiring about a certain report. I suggested he make the inquiry. Even if the report turns out to be spurious, as it well might, do you think that's wise right now?"

"Wise? I don't know if it's politically wise. If what I suspect is so, it's absolutely necessary."

Obreduur sighed softly, but not theatrically. "I thought it might be something like that." Then he smiled wryly. "I've learned that it's not a good idea to disregard your suspicions. What is it that you suspect?"

"That certain Commercer interests, quite possibly Northwest Industrial Chemical, or even Suvion Industries, indirectly provided the dunnite used by the New Meritorists in order to create a greater threat to law and order in Guldor as part of the effort to strengthen the Ministry of Security and give Commercers even more power over prominent Crafters and Landors."

"I've wondered about that, but it seemed a stretch even for Ulrich."

"It is rather interesting," said Dekkard, "that he's now an associate vice-presidente of Suvion Industries, which is the other major producer of dunnite besides Northwest."

"Interesting, but it doesn't prove that he's involved, only that the likelihood is greater."

"Speaking of Ulrich," said Dekkard, "I ran across something interesting. You may recall that he was very interested in the night heliographs used by the Navy. Apparently, some smaller business designed the heliographs, then ran into contractual difficulties, and was bought out by Siincleer Engineering.

The heliographs work fine, but the installations were behind schedule with significant cost overruns."

Obreduur frowned. "Siincleer Engineering? Are you looking for information on them?"

"No. I have someone looking into possible instances where large corporacions lost bids to smaller corporacions, that then suffered strange reversals that resulted in the large corporacion getting the contract or taking over the smaller business—if not both."

"That's not something that the Council's likely to be able to do much about, not through legislation."

"I've thought as much," replied Dekkard. "But I've thought it might be interesting to see how much more the government ministries ended up paying as a result of such occurrences, particularly if there happened to be an ongoing pattern of 'unfortunate circumstances' only befalling smaller competitors."

"That might better be handled by the Justiciary."

"I'd definitely agree with that, sir, once there's evidence to pursue, as has occurred in the cases of former Minister Wyath and acting Minister Manwaeren."

"He does have a point, Axel," said Ingrella, with a smile that was definitely mischievous. "And you did say that too many Craft councilors tend to be overly cautious."

Obreduur's laugh was both amused and rueful. "I suppose I deserved that." He paused. "I appreciate the insights and initiative you have both demonstrated, but I have to caution you. Trying to change a Commercer subculture that has dominated Guldoran politics for more than half a century will take time. Trying to change it overnight will create as much unrest as the New Meritorists, if not more." He held up a hand, as if to forestall any objection. "I understand. Not changing it will also doom Guldor. Picking which changes need to be made first is critical, and you were right in picking Security reform. That goes hand in hand with the prosecution of Wyath and Manwaeren and the prosecution of Special Agents who clearly exceeded their authority."

"Then what do you think is the next priority?" asked Avraal.

"To implement the Security reforms as the first step in dealing with the New Meritorists."

What if they don't want to deal? Dekkard decided against asking the question, and said instead, "That could be a challenge."

"But necessary."

Dekkard nodded.

"Now that you two have decided the priorities of the Council, just how many mysterious books do you have?" Avraal asked Ingrella. "Ones like that banned history or rare ones like *The City of Truth*?"

"She has only a few shelves like that," said Obreduur. "The rest are more normal histories, legal commentaries, and more than a few novels."

For the next bell or so, the conversation revolved around books, and it was close to the second bell of night when Dekkard backed the Gresynt down the drive and headed west on Altarama toward Imperial Boulevard.

"You didn't want us talking any more politics. Was that making Obreduur uneasy?"

"Not so much Obreduur as Ingrella. I think she has some doubts about his priorities. Also, I don't think it's in your interest for him to know everything you have in mind."

"You're right about that," agreed Dekkard, "especially since matters aren't going to work out the way he wants. Not with the New Meritorists, particularly if they're being supplied by Commercer interests. I have to wonder if they didn't get the semi-automatic pistols from Commercer sources as well."

"How could you trace that?" asked Avraal.

"I have no idea, but Carlos Baartol said that one shipment from Atacama was on a barge on the Rio Doro. At the time, I didn't think about it, but the word 'shipment' suggests more than a few pistols."

"That's another reason why you need to keep your own counsel more now," said Avraal.

"Our counsel," corrected Dekkard.

"Thank you."

Dekkard was more than happy to get to the house and garage the steamer. Unadi would come too soon, and he had no idea what the day might bring—if anything—other than the routine of correspondence, reading, and meetings and worrying. And then there was that comment by Ingrella about possible food shortages. And, unfortunately for his banque balance, there was also the need to purchase formalwear.

29

FOR the next three days, Dekkard's life was busy, but uneventful, except that he received a reminder of the Yearend Ball, along with a single black and gilt-edged invitation for a guest. He saw no mentions of food shortages in *Gestirn,* and the sole newssheet article dealing with the Council was a small story on Unadi noting that the Imperador had signed the Security and Public Safety Reorganization Act into law. At the very bottom of the story a single line stated that the law was based on a legislative proposal by first-term Councilor Dekkard from Gaarlak.

Dekkard couldn't help but wonder how that ended up in the newssheet and why.

Other than that, nothing notable occurred, until he turned onto Council Avenue toward the Council Office Building on Furdi morning, and Gaaroll declared, "Lots of feelings ahead. Some sort of strong."

Dekkard slowed the Gresynt slightly and said, "Not one strong set of feelings?"

"No, sir."

"It might be a demonstration." Even as he spoke, he could see scattered demonstrators flanking the avenue.

When he drove closer, he could see that most were dressed in Meritorist blue, and most held up large signs.

"ENACT VOTE ACCOUNTABILITY!"

"PUT YOUR NAME WITH YOUR VOTE!"

"REFORM THE COUNCIL!"

"VOTE BY NAME, NOT PARTY!"

"DOWN WITH PARTY TYRANNY!"

Every sign was slightly different, and Dekkard quickly lost track of all the variations.

"You were right, dear," said Avraal. "Once they got Security reform, they turned to their next demand."

"They all say something different," said Gaaroll.

"No, they all say the same thing in a different way," replied Dekkard. "They want every vote every councilor makes made public. For example, we passed Security reform last week. They want a listing of how each councilor voted. They want that sort of list for every vote taken in Council, for motions, amendments, whatever. That's explicitly forbidden by the Great Charter. What they're demanding would require repealing the very basis of the Charter, but they don't want to say that."

"Why not?" pressed Gaaroll.

"Because it's more appealing to say every councilor should publicly have to stand behind and justify every vote. The problem is that before long every councilor would be voting either for what's popular or for what Commercers with marks want. Taxes and tariffs aren't popular. So before long, there wouldn't be enough revenue to pay for the popular things, and even less funding for unpopular, but necessary, services and programs like roads or canals. It's more complicated than that, but that's the general idea."

Dekkard was grateful that the Council Guards had either cleared or prohibited the demonstrators from gathering close to the Council Office Building. He also wondered if Obreduur had given instructions to let the New Meritorists demonstrate peacefully if they didn't pack the area around the Council buildings.

He slowed the Gresynt for the guard at the gate to the covered parking to check the steamer, then drove to his reserved space.

"There's another set of strong feelings, but they aren't that close," said Gaaroll.

"Where are they?" asked Avraal.

Gaaroll pointed to the north, in the direction of Heroes Square and the Palace of the Imperador.

"There's likely another demonstration there," said Dekkard. *And the Palace Guards might not be so forbearing.*

"I think I'll stay here today," said Avraal firmly.

"I'd appreciate that," replied Dekkard. He also wondered if she'd already decided that, since she was wearing a dark gray jacket and trousers with a lighter gray blouse, set off by a striking green scarf.

The three walked quickly from the Gresynt to the Council Office Building and then up to Dekkard's office.

"Sir," asked Margrit politely, "what do the demonstrators want now?"

"Just for the Council to throw out the Great Charter and turn the government over to popularly elected councilors who will promise the most to the people and plutocrats."

Margrit didn't succeed in trying not to wince at Dekkard's cutting, sardonic tone.

"You can't tell that I think it's a bad idea, can you?"

"Not at all, sir," Margrit replied cheerfully.

"Are there any messages?"

"Just two." She handed him the envelopes.

"Thank you. I'm sorry if I was a bit sharp. I wasn't angry at you."

"I could tell that, sir." Margrit paused, then asked, "If it's such a bad idea, why do they want the Council to do it?"

"They don't understand human nature. Most people always want more. They'll support a councilor who promises more over one who says that the government can't afford it without raising taxes. If corporacions and wealthy individuals can find out how a councilor votes, they can find ways to remove councilors who disagree with their views and support those who agree. And the wealthy always have more marks than the working people and the poor. That's why so-called personal accountability will turn into a contest between those councilors who are the most popular and those who can be bought by the wealthy."

"People should understand that," said Margrit.

"It took me several minutes to give you a short, incomplete answer. The New Meritorists just shout about the need for personal accountability. Who can be against holding someone accountable? Even when it won't work and never has?"

Margrit frowned. "If it hasn't worked . . ."

"The answer they give is that it failed elsewhere a long time ago, and it's later, and Guldor is different. Unfortunately, basic human nature doesn't change." Dekkard smiled ruefully and added, "You see? Trying to refute their simple, reasonable-sounding statement takes time and a knowledge of history, and most people don't want to listen or hear what they don't want to hear. Since you work for me, you have to listen, and I've harangued enough for so early in the day."

He carried the messages into his office, then stood there, looking out the window.

Avraal followed him and closed the door. "Those signs really upset you."

"They did. People want to believe simple truths. But people have many differences, and differences require a government based on compromise and complexity . . . but since complexity bothers people, it's shielded here in Guldor by a little illusion." *Perhaps more than a little.* He opened the envelope and read the short message on the card.

"Is that another problem?"

He shook his head. "Just a reminder from Haarsfel about the Workplace Committee meeting this afternoon. Let's see what the second one portends." The handwritten note was somewhat longer, and he nodded.

"Well?"

"Hasheem apologizing for being late in thanking me for the work I did on the appropriations and telling me he appreciated my recommendations. He didn't say that he or the staff accepted them, though."

"Would he put that in writing?"

"Probably not." Dekkard looked at the stack of letters and petitions in the two boxes on his desk.

"I'll be outside." With a faint smile, Avraal turned and made her way from the office, gently closing the door.

The first three letters dealt with subjects that kept coming up—working conditions at the linen mills, ironway freight rates, and the tax treatment of relatives who worked for family businesses that weren't corporacions. The fourth letter was entirely different.

Councilor Dekkard—
   I'm writing to offer a belated word of congratulations. I honestly didn't think I'd ever see an artisan councilor from Gaarlak, even if you were trained and raised in Oersynt . . .

Who in Gaarlak would know that and write about it? Dekkard's eyes dropped to the neat signature at the bottom of the single sheet of plain, but quality, notepaper:

—Hrald Iglis

Iglis? After a moment, he placed the name and the man—the cabinetmaker that Obreduur had quietly suggested should run for councilor. *But why would he write?* They'd only met once, and for less than a third of a bell. Dekkard returned his attention to the remainder of the letter.

> *I also wanted to thank you for pushing the reform of the Security Ministry. Reducing the power of Special Agents was long overdue. As I am certain you know, that is only the first step of many necessary if Guldor is to survive as envisioned by the drafters of the Great Charter.*
>
> *Whenever you get back to Gaarlak, the shop is usually open. I hope you'll stop by. Even Jens will be happy to see you.*

The fact that Iglis knew Dekkard had drafted the basics of the Security reform act meant that the *Gaarlak Times* had either picked up the *Gestirn* story or had a correspondent in Machtarn, the latter being most likely, given that Emilio Raathan had sent Breffyn Haastar a clipping about Dekkard and Avraal.

Dekkard took a deep breath. *You're going to have to get to Gaarlak before long.*

He set aside the letter from Iglis and continued to read through the letters and petitions, finding nothing that either Roostof or Colsbaan couldn't handle. After turning the correspondence over to Roostof, Dekkard turned his thoughts to how he could persuade Hasheem to look into the dunnite issue. Was Ulrich's connection with Suvion why Hasheem was reluctant? *Or does he even know?*

Obreduur knew, but would he have told Hasheem? *Not necessarily.*

He hadn't made much progress on a strategy to persuade Hasheem when Avraal entered.

"It's a third before noon."

"You're right. We should go. In a minute. You need to see this first." He stood and handed her the letter from Iglis, then watched as she read.

Avraal finished and handed the letter back. "That's a side-door confirmation that Jens was Obreduur's choice. Do you think Jens had anything to do with Haasan Decaro's death?"

"If he did, it would have been so indirect that there'd be no way to trace it."

"You didn't answer the question, dear."

"I don't know. He's certainly capable of it. My feeling is that he made an observation to the effect that Gaarlak would suffer if Decaro actually became councilor, and the person to whom he made the suggestion took it as a suggested order. But if that's the case, why would he be happy to see me?"

"You're not to meet with Jens unless I'm there. With the knives he doesn't know about."

"That goes without saying." Dekkard paused. "Is it possible he didn't really want to be councilor?"

"Like you, I don't know what to think, except that we'd better leave if you don't want to rush lunch."

On the walk through the Council Office Building, the only other councilor Dekkard saw was Elskar Halljen, a Landor from Altaan who was also on the Workplace Administration Committee. Dekkard murmured the other's name to Avraal, then nodded. Halljen returned the gesture.

Just after they entered the Council Hall, another councilor approached. For a moment, Dekkard didn't recognize Jareem Saarh, accompanied by his two security aides—Micah Eljaan and Malcolm Maarkham—but then he inclined his head and said, "Good day."

Saarh looked to Dekkard, then Avraal, but replied with only the barest nod and kept walking. Eljaan looked to Avraal and mouthed, "Bad day."

At least that was what Dekkard thought he said.

Once they were well away from Saarh, he turned to Avraal. "What was Saarh's real reaction to my pleasantry?"

Avraal said nothing.

"That bad?"

"Not as bad as it might be. Landor contempt for you. Disgust when he looked at me."

"Because you're from a distinguished Landor family and you married me?"

"That and the fact that Emrelda rejected him."

"You never mentioned that." *Not that Emrelda rejecting suitors is exactly a surprise.*

"That was long before he became a councilor."

"Were you the one who filled in the background on Saarh in the book Obreduur keeps on councilors?"

"I told him what I knew from what I overheard when Saarh proposed to our father that Emrelda should marry him."

"He never looked at you the times he entered Obreduur's office," Dekkard pointed out.

"He didn't recognize me. Landor daughters are never security aides. Before that, the only time he saw me was when I was a girl. But with the news stories . . ."

"He finally realized you were the younger sister of the woman who rejected him for a mere engineer."

"He definitely was disgusted." She paused. "The Landor world can be very small, dear."

As they entered the councilors' dining room, a tall female councilor stepped up to Dekkard and said enthusiastically, "Steffan! I'm so glad to see you." Then she stopped and looked at Avraal, offering an embarrassed smile. "I'm sorry. That didn't come out right. I'm Harleona Zerlyon. You must be Avraal, or do you prefer Ritten Ysella-Dekkard?"

"Avraal is fine."

"I wanted to talk to Steffan because he wrote the Security reform act. The act transferred the Special Agents, or most of them, to the Justiciary Ministry, and I'm the chair of the Justiciary Committee."

"And you wanted his thoughts on what he had in mind?"

"They'd be very helpful."

"Then why don't you join us?" asked Avraal. "We didn't have anything special in mind."

"You're certain?"

"I'm with him not just as his wife, but as his security aide."

"I'd heard. Is it that bad?"

"We wouldn't call it good."

"I'm so sorry. Axel had said you'd both been attacked."

"Attacks on councilors seem to be getting more common," said Dekkard dryly, before turning to the host and saying, "Three, please."

Once the three were seated and had ordered, Avraal looked to Zerlyon. "You had some questions for Steffan?"

"I did." The older councilor paused, then said cautiously, "The Security and Public Safety Reorganization Act did solve one problem for the Justiciary Ministry."

"But created several more?" asked Dekkard. "Before I hear about the new problems, what old problem did the act solve?"

"For years, local and regional prosecutors complained that they didn't have enough experienced investigators to follow up on cases, and that the Special Agents assigned by Security were often less than helpful."

"That's likely because those Special Agents, or their friends, were often behind some of the matters being investigated," replied Dekkard. "That problem won't go away, not until the head prosecutors start firing new investigating agents for not doing their job. They might have to fire as many as half. Some will likely quit before their former associates kill them."

Zerlyon looked quizzically at Dekkard. "You actually thought about that?"

"That's a guess on my part. I didn't know how many, but it's much easier to get rid of someone by transferring them into a position they can't or won't do. I've never had much sympathy for Special Agents anyway."

"Do you know how Hasheem feels about that?"

"We never talked about it, because he never brought it up. Nor did anyone else. My guess is that everyone knew something had to be done quickly before the New Meritorists started demonstrating again, and, for various reasons, no one wanted to look too deeply into the ramifications. So, when all the problems surface, they can blame me and the Craft Party."

"No wonder people are after you. I had no idea."

"I take it that the new Justiciary minister isn't sure that the funding that came with the transferred agents will suffice."

"More than four hundred agents will be transferred in the Machtarn region, and the prosecutors had been asking for a hundred more investigators, but the funding won't support four hundred."

"I didn't have any say over the funding levels, but that still might work," said Dekkard. "I'd wager that a year from now, half those Special Agents will have been fired or quit, and with the increasing number of cases the prosecutors will be glad for the additional investigators." He shrugged. "If I'm wrong, blame me." *Everyone else likely will.* "Now, what are the other issues?"

"There's a certain amount of liability involved with the ruined regional Security buildings."

"They weren't transferred, and I didn't think about that. Wouldn't the liability rest with the successor ministry, the new Ministry of Public Safety?"

"Most likely, but it wasn't spelled out."

Dekkard managed not to sigh. It wasn't as though he and Roostof had gotten much help. "What else?"

"There are also potential liabilities with Special Agents who turn out to have committed illegal acts ordered by previous ministers or their appointees."

Dekkard offered a sardonic smile. "Why do you think I wrote the act that way? So that they'd largely end up under the Justiciary Ministry, and your committee." That hadn't been his primary reason in the slightest, but he wasn't going to admit it. "Besides," he added cheerfully, "I think that you, the Justiciary Committee, and the legalists at the Justiciary Ministry can find a way to deal with that far better than the Security Committee ever could."

"It's kind of you to say that."

"Not kind," Dekkard replied. "Accurate. I'm a security specialist, not a legalist."

"The act was well-written in the legal sense."

"We did our best."

"Who's putting pressure on you, Councilor?" asked Avraal sweetly.

For a moment, Zerlyon froze, before saying, "The senior Commercer justicer on the High Justiciary made a number of inquiries."

"Then I do hope my answers to those inquiries will prove helpful," said Dekkard. "I've told you what I did and what I know."

"I appreciate that. Both Palafaux and Baar have proved—"

"Less than helpful?"

Zerlyon nodded. "Gerhard Safaell is too deferential, and criminal law isn't Elyncya's forte. It isn't mine, either, but I'm learning."

"What about the Landors on the committee?" asked Avraal.

"They might as well be Commercers."

Zerlyon's response reminded Dekkard how fortunate he'd been that Navione and Haastar were the Landors on the Security Committee. "I don't envy you, especially in dealing with Baar. He's very bright and sharp."

"He is. You might be interested to know that he asked me if you had any training as a legalist."

"Only what I learned from Ivann Macri and Svard Roostof in Obreduur's office, and Svard works for me now."

The server appeared with their orders, and after that, the conversation turned to the differences Dekkard and Zerlyon saw in the Council as a result of the elections, and, of course, the weather, and how soon before Machtarn would begin to see waterspouts and spout-rains.

As they left the councilors' dining room, following Zerlyon, Dekkard noticed that the other councilor's security aides immediately appeared, but neither Chavyona Leiugan nor Tullyt Kamryn looked in his direction, although he and Avraal had often talked with the pair.

Dekkard understood the reasons it had to be that way, at least in the Council buildings, but it had taken years to become friendly with even a handful of staffers, and now he had to start all over becoming friendly with other councilors. *Whether you want to or not.*

As Avraal and Dekkard neared the committee room, Avraal said quietly, "Someone's following us, just at the edge of what I can sense."

"Another empath, trying to keep just beyond your senses?"

"Either that or someone knowledgeable about empaths. I'll try to locate and follow them after you enter the committee room."

When Dekkard walked into the chamber, Quentin Fader and Kaliara Bassaana stood on the dais, conversing, while Elskar Halljen spoke with one of the clerks.

Dekkard didn't recognize a number of men in the back of the chamber, most likely the witnesses scheduled to appear. Then Yordan Farris entered, followed by Nortak, and then by Chairman Haarsfel.

As soon as the chime of first bell struck, Haarsfel gaveled the committee into session. "Today, we will be hearing from representatives of the Glassworkers Guild of Ondeliew. I believe that your safety steward has a statement for the committee?"

"I do, Sr. Chairman." A thin and wiry man wearing an old, brown jacket and matching trousers, with a white shirt and a tan cravat, took a seat at the witness desk, facing the committee on the dais. He cleared his throat and began to speak. "The Glassworkers Guild appreciates the opportunity to bring our safety concerns to the attention of the committee. We understand that the committee is only beginning inquiries into workplace safety in Guldor.

"The guild has brought the problem of proper ventilation and control of milled sand dust to the attention of the management of Ondeliew Plate Glass Works time and time again. For a few days, or a week, conditions improve, then conditions return to where they were. The corporacion claims there's no way to make glass without making sand dust. What they're saying is that they won't spend the marks on proper seals for the ball mills.

"Breathing ground sand dust over time makes breathing harder and harder. The Glassworkers Guild has only been able to find fifteen former glassworkers who lived past the age of fifty-five. The others died of respiratory problems, usually classified as consumption . . ."

As the guild safety steward continued, his words recalled the time when Dekkard's father had dipped a bandana in water and wrung it out, then tied it so that it covered his nose and mouth and said, "Do this before you sand any surface, especially a painted surface or a dry plaster surface. If you don't you'll die before you're forty, coughing blood from your lungs."

Dekkard almost shuddered. *Breathing ground sand must be worse than plaster dust.* He forced his attention back to the witness. By the time the hearing ended just after third bell, Dekkard had two overarching thoughts. First, how many more abuses and evasions of workplace safety rules had Haarsfel lined up for the committee, and second, how could Fader and Farris both look so bored with all the examples and deaths recounted before the committee?

As the other committee members left the chamber, Dekkard walked over to the safety steward. "Thank you for coming. I started out as an apprentice plasterer, and one of the first things I was taught was how to avoid breathing plaster dust. I had no idea of how much worse your problem is."

"We're glad to have the opportunity. We usually find out about hearings *after* the managers come back and say everything's fine."

Dekkard could see that, and how it would take a long time to address all the safety problems—but he wasn't about to say so. Instead, he said a few words to each of the men before leaving the hearing room.

Avraal was waiting outside. "How was the hearing?"

"Very informative and ice-rain chilling. Glassworkers inhale ground sand dust all the time. That dust destroys their lungs. Almost none live past fifty-five." He paused, then asked, "Did you find out who was following us?"

She shook her head. "They backed off just before you got to the committee room."

Dekkard nodded. That wasn't a surprise. It had been that sort of a day, and he still had to write a response to Iglis.

30

ON Quindi morning, when he reached the breakfast room, Dekkard immediately read the *Gestirn* story on Furdi's demonstrations.

> Demonstrators thronged the Square of Heroes and Council Avenue yesterday morning carrying signs demanding that every councilor's vote be recorded by name on every issue. "They should be held personally accountable for every vote they cast!" declared one demonstrator.
>
> Even if the new Council agrees to such a change, it cannot be enacted in the timeframe demanded by the protestors because the present centuries-old voting system, which mandates only revealing total votes by party affiliation, can only be changed by a two-thirds majority of two successive Councils, and the second vote cannot occur any sooner than three years after the first. If a second vote is negative, the first vote is negated and the process must begin anew.

The rest of the story presented, simplistically, Dekkard thought, the arguments for and against the New Meritorists' demand. He shook his head.

"Is it that bad?" asked Gaaroll.

In response to Gaaroll's question, Emrelda rolled her eyes, possibly as much in anticipation of Dekkard's response as in reaction to Gaaroll's inquiry.

"The newssheet told both sides," replied Gaaroll, her tone slightly defensive.

"It gave the *appearance* of telling both sides," Dekkard finally said. "The problem with so-called accountability is that the New Meritorists want each councilor to be directly accountable to the people on every single vote. Over time, the people always want to get more and pay less. This is true in everyday life, and it would be true in politics. If the Great Charter allowed it—"

"Not at breakfast, please," declared Avraal as she entered the breakfast room.

"I know," said Dekkard. "Not before café." He immediately filled Avraal's mug and set it down before her, then poured his own café.

"I need to go," declared Emrelda. "Services tonight?"

Since her words weren't really a question, Dekkard nodded. Then he sat down and took two croissants from the platter, prepared and ate them, waiting for a time before asking Avraal, "More café?"

"If you would, please."

He refilled her mug and then put a single croissant on her plate.

Slowly, she ate half of it, then eased the plate away. "I'll feel better later."

From past experience, Dekkard knew she would. "I'd thought that I'd just work in the office today, and that you could do what you can for Carlos. There's really nothing for you to do, not today, and I suspect I'll need you a great deal more later."

"That sounds fine, *if* nothing's changed by the time we get to the office." She paused. "I forgot to mention that I got a nice note from Ingrella in response to my thank-you note to her."

"That's not customary. What tidbit did she add?"

Avraal smiled. "She told me to be grateful that you listen."

"You give very good advice."

"One of my many unofficial duties as Ritten-wife."

Dekkard was glad she followed the words with an amused smile, and he quickly said, "For which I'm most grateful."

While Dekkard drove to the Council Office Building by yet another round-about route, neither Avraal nor Gaaroll sensed any possible trouble, possibly because a cold autumn rain was falling. Even so, the lack of possible trouble bothered him almost as much as if there had been a problem, because he doubted that anyone who'd gone to as much effort, as evidenced by previous attacks, would just suddenly walk away. *Which means trouble will come when unexpected or in a totally unexpected manner. And your reactions may have to be constrained.* That was something he hadn't anticipated when he'd been selected.

Once Avraal left the office, Dekkard turned his attention to the correspondence. The first letters were more or less expected, one asking whether Dekkard could do anything about the closed and run-down Phanx mill, because it was becoming a danger, another from Craft District Councilor Mayherne asking if they could meet on his next visit to Gaarlak, a third complaining about the rates charged for heliograph messages.

He picked up the fourth envelope in the stack, slit by Margrit but not removed, as he'd instructed for all letters, absently noting the handwritten return address in Gaarlak, and took out the single sheet of plain paper and began to read.

> *Most Honorable Councilor Dekkard—*
>
> *Why is it Guldor continues with an antiquated governmental system designed well before there were ironways or steam power? The three-party system represents skilled labor and artisans, the land-owning aristocracy, and the rich and commercial professionals. More than half of the working people in Guldor don't fit into any of those categories, and so they effectively have no representation in the Council.*
>
> *Any councilor can claim that he or she supports or opposes something, but the people have no assurance that this is so, because there is no record with which such promises can be compared.*
>
> *Therefore, I strongly urge you to support an amendment to the Great Charter requiring the recording of each councilor's vote and the public distribution of such voting records. Your failure to support such an amendment will be distributed widely across your district.*

There was no signature as such, just a name: "The People's Committee for Public Accountability."

Dekkard looked at the envelope. While the return address and the Imperial postmark indicated it came from Gaarlak, all that meant was that it had been mailed from there and that there were at least some New Meritorists there. He set it aside to deal with later and continued through the letters and petitions. When he finished reading through them all, he took the stack to Roostof and set it in his incoming box, then said, "I'll need a moment with you now."

"Yes, sir."

When the two returned to Dekkard's office, he handed the New Meritorist letter to Roostof. "Read it, and then we'll talk."

Roostof read it, then looked up. "It reads like a New Meritorist wrote it, but I've never heard of this committee."

"I'm sure that one of them did, but the People's Committee for Public Accountability sounds better. I need you to draft the best possible reply to this letter that can fit on one page."

"You're not going to answer this . . . this trash, sir?"

"No. But I want a good reply ready when honorable citizens of Gaarlak start writing similar letters. Unless I'm mistaken, they will. Among those letters will be one from a true Meritorist. My reply will then be circulated all across Gaarlak, especially if it's a poor reply."

"You think that will really happen, sir?"

"I'll be amazed if it doesn't, but it could be that the next time I go to Gaarlak some newsie will ask a similar question—or someone else. In any event, I need a concise and precise answer, and you're better at that than I am. Much better."

"If you say so, sir."

"You're better at it, and you don't have to protest otherwise." Dekkard smiled. "And don't stay here too late tonight. You might think about finding a sympathetic or compatible woman legalist."

"I've found that seeking them out doesn't work," said Roostof dryly.

Thinking about Avraal, Dekkard nodded. "You're probably right." Then he added, "But you might try going places where they can find you."

Roostof laughed.

After the legalist left, Dekkard walked to the window and looked out at the rain before returning to his desk and sitting down to write out a response to Hrald Iglis.

It took Dekkard three revisions and most of a bell to write a reply that thanked Iglis for his supportive comments while promising to stop by the shop on his next visit to Gaarlak. In the end, he decided against mentioning Jens Seigryn.

Dekkard couldn't say that the rest of the day was that bad, or that long, but he was glad when fourth bell chimed and Avraal arrived. He didn't mind it that much that the rain had gotten colder and heavier, partly because it made it less likely that an assassin would be looking for him, or able to discern one Gresynt from another. One of the aspects of his situation was that he couldn't exactly actively pursue probable assassins, and, given that the only Security personnel theoretically able to investigate were the Special Agents, there wasn't anywhere else to turn, at least not until the Security act reforms were fully implemented.

As for the evening services at the Hillside Trinitarian Chapel, Dekkard endured them, but a few words of Presider Buusen's homily definitely did catch his attention.

"All too often we attribute motives of the Almighty to those occurrences that have no motives. The wife who plans an outdoor party and prays for sun, only to have it spoiled by a rainy afternoon, might say that the Almighty wasn't listening, while the farmer who worried that the dry weather might stunt his crop thanks the Almighty for that same rain. Did the Almighty chose the farmer over the woman? Why would a God of Love, Power, and Mercy choose one over the other? Or manipulate the weather because more people wanted sun or rain? Why can't we accept that the rain just fell because that is the nature of rain?"

Why indeed? Except most people wanted answers that applied to them personally, even when there weren't any.

31

AFTER breakfast on a cool, but clear, Findi morning, Dekkard went to work on both steamers. Beginning by going over fittings and fluids, he checked the pressure in the small acetylene tanks that fed the headlamps. He went on to check the boiler and hoses, and then the engine, followed by changing the filters on the water and kerosene tanks. He finished by cleaning and polishing both steamers, not that their exteriors would stay spotless with all the rain that usually fell in late autumn.

Then he got out the target and began to practice with throwing knives.

Gaaroll showed up immediately, and he gave her a short lesson, during which Avraal and Emrelda appeared. In turn, he worked with Emrelda, then Avraal, after which he watched and coached all three women.

While Emrelda retrieved the blades after a set of throws, Dekkard turned because he saw a movement from the corner of his eye. When he did, he saw a younger dark-haired woman with Tomas, the boy next door.

"I see you've noticed the new nanny next door," said Emrelda.

"Like most men," added Avraal, grinning.

Dekkard also saw a smile on Gaaroll's face. "Is she an empath?"

"Low-level. I'd guess she hasn't been a nanny long," replied Avraal. "She's gentler."

"Good thing," said Gaaroll. "Last one should have been your target. Wouldn't have lasted long, though. You and Ritten Dekkard almost never miss the center."

"He never does," said Avraal. "I still do sometimes."

"Not recently," corrected Dekkard.

"Have you ever missed when—" began Gaaroll.

"When it counted, I've never missed hitting an attacker. Sometimes, I couldn't strike where I *needed* to. So far, things have turned out, because I had help or could use my truncheon, but you can't count on luck. That's why we practice as much as we do. With knives, if you miss, you might end up dead."

"You ever thought about carrying a gun?" pressed Gaaroll.

"Not seriously. Firearms aren't legal for private citizens. They're not even legal for regular patrollers without permission. Just for the military, Special Agents, for now, and for the STF. If I got caught with one, even using it in self-defense, I'd lose my security certification. And now, I'd face a disciplinary hearing before the Council and could be ejected from the Council."

"Thrown out? For self-defense?"

Dekkard smiled. "No. For using a firearm. If I use a personal truncheon or a knife, and it's self-defense against a lethal threat, that's allowed."

"Seems like the laws work better for the law-busters."

"Not really. They get caught using a firearm, and it's death for a major crime or statelessness for a lesser offense." *If they're caught, and too many haven't been.*

"Statelessness?"

"Effectively, exile. They lose their citizenship. Usually, most of them end up indentured workers or dustsloggers in the army somewhere in Medarck or swamprats in Sargasso."

"They ought to do that to most of the Special Agents."

"In time, it just might happen to some," said Dekkard, thinking of the three on trial for attempting to kill Avraal, Emrelda, and him.

"You talking about the Special Agents?" asked Emrelda, turning back toward Dekkard and Gaaroll. "Captain Narryt's worried about them. Most of them aren't happy about your act." She smiled wryly. "I didn't tell him you wrote it. Most of them feel it's an insult to take their guns."

"Even if the act takes their guns because too many of their own misused them for too long? Avraal and I saw too much of that too close, especially during the student demonstration at Imperial University."

"They don't see it that way," Emrelda said.

"Most men with guns don't," said Avraal, "and that could be a problem."

"It could be," replied Dekkard. "I hope it's not."

"What will the Council do if it is?"

"It depends on what kind of problem it becomes, and what Obreduur feels that the Council can and should do."

"What would you do?" asked Gaaroll.

"I don't know. The Special Agents have been a huge part of Security abuses. They weren't going to like anything that dealt with the problem. I've never had any illusions about the Special Agents' dislike of being transferred and disarmed, but I hoped that keeping their jobs—or being able to transfer to the STF—would mute the dissatisfaction." He looked to Emrelda. "From what you say, though . . ."

"The captain's worried."

"Did he say more than that?"

Emrelda shook her head. "If we had something to eat at Elfredo's around a third after third bell, the captain or Lieutenant Kunskyn might be there."

"At least no one would have to fix dinner." Dekkard grinned, then shivered slightly. The wind had picked up, giving the air a cold bite. "And I'm definitely going to wear something warmer."

Emrelda turned to Avraal. "I really like your knives. They feel right, but then, we're built the same way."

"I like the councilor's better," said Gaaroll.

Dekkard just shrugged. That Gaaroll favored his knives wasn't surprising, he supposed, given that her hands were overlarge for her height, although there wasn't that much of a difference between their blades.

"If we're going to eat?" suggested Emrelda.

Dekkard immediately went to take down the target.

By the time everyone cleaned up and dressed, and traveled to the tavern, they walked in at slightly after a third past third bell, but only a third of the tables in the gray brick building were taken. Although the windows were closed because of the wind, Dekkard was still glad that he'd worn a jacket, even if it was one of his older ones.

Emrelda headed for one of the round oak tables in the corner, from where she could see most of the taverna.

Following Emrelda, Dekkard took a quick glance at the blackboard on the wall where the word "Specials" and several entrées were chalked, along with the price. As he sat down, he noted that the server who came to their table was slightly younger, meaning that she was likely a mere ten years older than he.

"Heard you made patroller first," the server said to Emrelda with a pleasant smile. "That mean you'll be head dispatcher?"

Dekkard glanced to Avraal inquisitively, but she looked as surprised as Dekkard felt.

"Only on endday or swing shifts." Emrelda gestured. "You remember my sister Avraal. The handsome fellow is her husband Steffan. They haven't even been married a month, and this is Nincya. She works for Steffan. Steffan, Nincya, this is Chellara. She's Elfredo's niece and can tell us what's really good today."

Chellara smiled warmly. "Uncle fixed some chicken rosara. It's really good, and the crayfish and mushroom ravioli are especially good today."

In the end, Dekkard ordered the chicken rosara, as did Gaaroll, while Avraal opted for chicken piccata, and Emrelda chose the crayfish-mushroom ravioli, suggesting to Dekkard that it might be her favorite dish, since she ordered it often.

Within two minutes, Chellara hurried back with the glasses of wine and Dekkard's and Gaaroll's beakers of pale ale.

Dekkard looked to Emrelda. "Patroller first? You didn't tell us, and that merits congratulations, I'd say."

Emrelda flushed slightly. "It's just . . . how could I . . . ?"

"Old Landor habits die hard? You can't announce your successes?" Dekkard shook his head, then looked at Avraal and added, "You don't get to say a word. You're almost as bad. I've had to drag your accomplishments out of you, and you usually minimize what you do when we've accomplished things together, even when I'd have been injured or dead without you."

Avraal looked to Emrelda. Then both sisters smiled guiltily.

"This dinner is definitely on me, and congratulations to you." He lifted his beaker in a toast. The others lifted their glasses as well.

The four had not gotten their entrées and were sipping their drinks when a pair of patrollers entered and took a wall table. Before sitting, the one facing Emrelda smiled and offered a pleasant wave, a gesture that she returned.

Chellara had just brought the entrées when a single uniformed patrol officer entered and began to survey those in the tavern, where most of the tables were filled. He caught sight of Emrelda and immediately walked over.

"That's Lieutenant Kunskyn," said Emrelda. "He might be able to tell us something."

The stocky, muscular officer stopped short of the table. "Emrelda, I never had a chance to congratulate you. If anyone deserved a promotion to patroller first, you did."

"Thank you. I appreciate those words." Emrelda then motioned. "Lieutenant, this is my sister Avraal and her husband Steffan."

"The councilor—"

Dekkard lifted a hand. "Until a month ago I was a security aide, doing many things similar to a patroller."

"I'd heard that." Kunskyn paused. "The captain said you were behind the Security reform act."

"I had a little to do with it. I felt it was necessary, but it's likely going to make your life more difficult for a time."

"Can't get good timber without felling trash trees," replied Kunskyn before turning back to Emrelda. "Have you seen the captain?"

"Not since we arrived, but we've only been here a third or so. I know he was worried about something to do with the Special Agents."

Kunskyn stiffened, then glanced apologetically at Dekkard. "With your background, sir."

"Steffan, please, and I won't say a word."

"With your background . . . anyway, all the Special Agents were called away this afternoon. No one knows why. Captain said he was going to look into it."

That's not good. "I could be very wrong, Lieutenant, but it sounds very much like a last-bell effort to prove the worth of the Special Agents, possibly raids of some sort."

"That's what the captain thought. I'd better get back to the station." Kunskyn smiled at Emrelda. "Congratulations."

"Thank you."

After Kunskyn was well away from the table, Gaaroll looked to Emrelda. "He's sweet on you."

"He's a good person, but not for me." Emrelda looked to Dekkard. "You mentioned raids. What sort of raids, do you think?"

"Something designed to provoke the New Meritorists, I'd wager." *And possibly to remove anyone who knows about cooperation between corporacions and the New Meritorists.*

"And an excuse for the Special Agents to take out their anger on people," added Avraal.

"There's not too much we can do now," said Dekkard, taking a bite of the chicken rosara and deciding it was every bit as good as Chellara had said it was. Then he added, "And we ought to celebrate a certain promotion."

"Definitely," agreed Avraal.

While Dekkard enjoyed the meal, and the conversation, his mind was very much on the Special Agents and what they might be doing—and to whom.

On the drive back to the house, he was alert, as was Avraal, but there were no signs of trouble. Not that Dekkard expected any from the Special Agents, but his one worry was that Minz, or whoever else was after him, might not know what the Special Agents had planned.

He dropped the other three off at the portico, then garaged the Gresynt and checked it over so that it would be ready in the morning.

As he was closing the garage, Avraal appeared. "I wondered why you were taking so long."

"I was just getting the steamer ready for tomorrow."

"You're worried, more than a little," said Avraal.

"Does it show?"

"Only because I know you. You weren't quite . . . you at Elfredo's. Not after what the lieutenant said."

"Whatever the Special Agents were or are doing, it isn't going to be helpful."

"What do you think they're doing?"

"Raiding every house where there's a suspected New Meritorist, shooting people, even planting weapons. They've probably been told that no one appreciated their going easy on the New Meritorists and that's why they're all being transferred—or something else to make them angry."

"Going easy? After all the unarmed people they shot?"

"For them, that's going easy."

"You don't think they'll come here, do you?"

Dekkard shook his head. "They're angry, but not stupid. If they come here, after the last attempt, that would show what they're doing was a move against me and the Craft Party. They'll do their best to set this up as a preemptive raid against the New Meritorists." He smiled cynically. "Unfortunately, they're also probably right, because it wouldn't have been that long before the New Meritorists resumed more violent activities—at least once it became clear that the Council isn't ready to tear up the Great Charter. This will make them angrier and more violent sooner. Some may even claim that the Security reforms were a ruse to catch them off guard."

"That's absurd, but I can see how some people might want to look at it that way." She took his arm. "Perhaps we should read a little more in Ingrella's book."

"It can't hurt." *And it just might get your mind off what's likely happening.*

When I walk along the sinuous paths that wind through the Woods of Dawn, a sense of impermanent eternity enfolds me, as solid and as transitory as the hint of pine resin that clings to the cones savaged by the baron jays drilling out the pine nuts to feed their ravenous nestlings . . . nestlings who will in turn seek out similar cones from which to pry out pine nuts for their nestlings.

The permanence of the Woods of Dawn differs from that of the city proper, and that difference consists not just of that between wood and stone, but of how each maintains itself. Each aspect of the Woods of Dawn contributes to its renewal. Younger pines replace older pines; baron jays replace baron jays. Renewal or maintenance in Averra requires thought; the stones do not replace themselves. The sewers, storm drains, and aqueducts do not unclog themselves. Yet the thoughts of those who have maintained Averra over the generations add to the ephemeral mists of thought and feeling that provide an unseen patina to the stones of the city, an invisible shimmer to walls already ancient.

Living in Averra gives another kind of life to the city, but that life depends on care . . . and thought. Perhaps trees think as well, but if they do, we can only see the outcome of such thoughts over years, even decades, not moments.

AVERRA
The City of Truth
Johan Eschbach
377 TE

WHILE reading from *The City of Truth* kept Dekkard from worrying too much, or at least reducing his worries enough for him to get to sleep, he woke early on Unadi and was in the breakfast room while Emrelda was still eating. Without a word, she handed him the morning edition of *Gestirn*.

Still standing, he immediately began to read.

> In a series of Findi afternoon raids in cities across Guldor, Security Ministry Special Agents targeted individuals suspected of involvement in the Summerend New Meritorist demonstrations. Early reports suggest that more than three hundred individuals in ten Guldoran cities were arrested and incarcerated. Reports also suggest that, as a result of armed resistance, close to sixty individuals were wounded in the operation, and twenty-three are known to be dead.
>
> Seven Special Agents were wounded, two fatally. Special Agents also searched more than a hundred business properties in the operation . . .
>
> . . . the head of Special Agents could not be reached for comment . . .

Dekkard lowered the newssheet, shaking his head.

"You thought something like this might happen," said Emrelda.

"I did. I tried to disband and transfer the Special Agents as quickly as possible, because I worried about something like this."

"I thought I'd go in early," said Emrelda as she stood and moved to the sink in the kitchen, where she quickly washed and racked her mug and plate. "I might find out more."

Avraal walked into the breakfast room wearing a robe, followed by Gaaroll. "How bad was it?"

"Raids in ten cities," replied Dekkard. "Three hundred suspected Meritorists incarcerated, sixty shot, more than twenty killed. A handful of Special Agents wounded, several killed, and more than a hundred small shops searched. So much for peaceful Security reform."

"Those friggin' bastards," muttered Gaaroll. "Never liked the Specials."

"Does it say who ordered the raids?" asked Avraal.

"The head of Special Agents couldn't be reached for comment, according to the *Gestirn* story." *There's something wrong . . .*

"But they knew how many had been shot and arrested?" Gaaroll snorted.

As Gaaroll spoke, Dekkard recalled what he'd been trying to remember. *Frig!* "The Special Agents are under the director of special projects, who reports directly to the Security minister."

"With Manwaeren removed as acting minister, that means no one's really been supervising them," said Avraal.

"It's not likely. I should have thought of that," replied Dekkard.

"No. Obreduur should have," said Avraal.

Dekkard shook his head. There were just too many aspects of the shift in power in the Council that neither he nor Obreduur, or the newly appointed ministers, knew enough about. That was hardly surprising, given that there hadn't been a meaningful shift in power in decades, if not longer.

Dekkard was still worrying over it when he eased the Gresynt out of the garage and down the drive toward Florinda Way. "Do you sense any strong feelings anywhere?"

"No, sir. Not even next door," replied Gaaroll. "That's good."

"One small thing that seems to have gone right," said Dekkard quietly.

The drive to work was uneventful, although Dekkard doubted that would last once he was in his office. He noticed that a few more Council Guards were posted around the entrance to the covered parking and the Council Office Building.

Roostof, not surprisingly, was waiting in the anteroom when Dekkard, Avraal, and Gaaroll entered.

"I assume you saw, sir?" said the senior legalist.

"The *Gestirn* story on the Special Agents? I did. I suppose it was too much to hope for a peaceful Security reform. I knew the violence would come after the act became law. I just didn't expect it to come from rogue Special Agents. I should have. The act took away their guns and a lot of their power."

"That was long overdue," said Luara Colsbaan from the door into the main staff room.

"Part of the problem, Svard," said Dekkard, "was something you pointed out. There really wasn't a structure or set of procedures for Special Agents. Manwaeren said Special Agents were in the Office of Special Projects, and the director reported to the Security minister. When Lukkyn Wyath and Manwaeren were indicted and removed, I should have realized that removed most supervision of the Special Agents."

"Why shouldn't others have realized it first, sir?" asked Roostof. "Such as Obreduur?"

"Most councilors, maybe all of them, clearly had no idea that there were few, if any, legal or procedural restraints on Special Agents. There was never any mention of it until we brought it up in the Security Committee hearings. *We* knew that, but I didn't think about how the Special Agents would react when faced with losing their guns and power, especially with the removal of the top leadership of the ministry. I don't think Obreduur even knew there weren't any procedural restraints, because you discovered that after you came to work for me. While the matter was discussed briefly in the committee hearings, I don't recall seeing it in the summary accompanying the proposal to the floor. The past lack of procedures and rules would have seemed irrelevant since those very people lacking them were transferred to ministries with such procedures."

"Sir," said Margrit, "you have a message, and what looks to be a large document from the Premier."

Large document? Dekkard frowned for a moment, then realized that it had to be his copy of the proposed combined appropriations legislation, which he needed to read and study before debate and possible amendments began before the full Council on Tridi.

"The message is likely from Chairman Hasheem calling an emergency meeting of the Security Committee," said Dekkard as he turned and took both the small envelope and the much thicker and heavier one from Margrit. He opened the small envelope quickly and read the short message, nodding as he did. "The Security Committee will meet at third bell." Then he looked to Roostof. "I'm going to go through the correspondence. If you think of anything else I should bring up, just let me know." Dekkard's eyes went to Colsbaan. "You, too, Luara."

"Yes, sir."

Avraal said, "I'll be out here."

"In a moment." He gestured to his office. "I need your thoughts on a few things."

Once the two were in the office with the door closed, Dekkard opened the heavy envelope and took a quick look. It was what he'd thought. He set it on the desk and turned back to Avraal. "The committee meeting will be short. You can walk me there and wait, then walk me back and drive to your office at Carlos's, an office that you're hardly even in, thanks to my vulnerabilities." He paused. "Maybe I need to hire an empath so that you can actually work."

"I'd rather quit working for Carlos. Isobel is about the only other empath who's as good as I am, and you need the best."

What she wasn't saying, Dekkard knew, was that even the best empath might not be good enough to save him.

"Besides, then I'd just worry all the time. I offered to quit last week. I told Carlos I wasn't earning what he was paying me. He laughed. He told me that keeping you alive was worth every mark."

"You never mentioned that."

She smiled sweetly. "I was saving it until you brought up hiring someone. I knew it would cross your mind sooner or later."

Worth every mark? "Did he say why?"

"Not exactly. I asked. What he said was that you're more important than you think, and people want access."

"So people are already paying Carlos to influence me through you?"

"They are, but all he tells them is that he'll see what he can do. He never even asks me what you're doing."

Dekkard couldn't blame Baartol for taking that approach, and certainly so far, he definitely owed Carlos. *And he's never asked for anything, but sooner or later he might.* "Nothing comes without a price."

"You knew that already."

"I still think you should see him after the committee meeting."

"Why don't we decide then?"

Dekkard smiled wryly. "You're right. After the committee meeting."

"And I'll be outside working with Nincya while you deal with the correspondence."

"More tips on security and what to look for?"

"It can't hurt to have her know. She learns quickly, and the more eyes watching out for you right now, the better. Besides, she's caught up on the filing. Margrit's letting her practice typing when her machine isn't being used. The way the number of letters is increasing, that might help, too."

"Did you mention this to Svard?"

"You mean, did I ask him? No. I told him what I just told you. He agreed."

Dekkard laughed softly, then said, "It's probably better with you two running the office."

"Probably?" asked Avraal.

"Let me cling to some small shred of illusion about my managerial abilities."

She grinned. "So long as it's just a small shred."

Dekkard winced. *Except that she's right.*

"Dear, you're a doer and a thinker. You're good at both. That's what you need to concentrate on. You don't have to do everything else, and you shouldn't."

"I haven't done the thinking part all that well. I didn't think through what the reaction of the Special Agents could be."

"Neither did anyone else. You just have to get on with other matters."

"It's hard to think about the other matters. I keep thinking about the fact that I should have realized."

"You've been a councilor a month. Obreduur's been one for years, and he didn't see it."

"That's not much consolation."

"How about the fact that it isn't your job to control the Premier's ministers and the appointees who work for them? You tried to make the transition as quick as possible so these sorts of things wouldn't happen."

"That point helps. A little."

"Good. You can't do anything more about it now, and you can take care of other matters."

"Yes. I'm very diligent with correspondence."

"Steffan. I'm not fond of either useless self-pity or self-flagellation. You missed something. So did everyone else. Are you the Almighty to be always perfect?"

The iron in Avraal's voice brought Dekkard up short.

"I should have—"

"Sowshit! If anyone should have seen it, it should have been Obreduur, and I don't want to hear any more. You've been more accurate than anyone, but you're not perfect, and you'll kill yourself trying to meet that expectation. All you can do now is learn from what happened."

Dekkard swallowed. After a long moment, he said, "You're right. I'm sorry."

Avraal smiled sweetly, but her voice was cool. "You can still go through the correspondence." She turned and left the office.

Dekkard just sat there for several minutes. He'd never seen Avraal so angry. *Have you been that difficult? Or is "useless self-pity" something that really angers her? Or is it useless self-pity in* you? *Or are you getting hung up on what you didn't foresee and going over and over it?* He glanced toward the door. *Likely all of them.*

After another few minutes, he picked up the top letter and began to read. He had to reread it twice, because he wasn't concentrating. He still had to force himself to concentrate on the next letter.

Given the likely subject of the Security Committee meeting, Dekkard didn't want to be late, and at a third before third bell he opened his office door.

Avraal looked up from the small table desk where she was writing something.

"I thought we should leave a little earlier." Then he turned to Margrit. "I finished reading through everything on my desk. If you'd give it all to Svard."

"Yes, sir," said Margrit pleasantly.

Avraal stood.

Dekkard wished he knew what she was feeling, but she looked perfectly composed, as she almost always did. *Is she still angry with me? Or my excessive self-pity?* He said nothing until they were out of the office and no one was nearby. "You were right. I still think I should have seen what might happen, but, as you so accurately pointed out, I'm not perfect and never will be. You were also absolutely right about the futility of obsessing over my failure. I am sorry."

"So am I," she said quietly, reaching out and squeezing his hand gently. "You've done so much, and you've done it well. It just made me so angry that you were beating yourself to death over something that no one else foresaw. Especially when they have so much more experience."

"They have experience in reacting. None of us have experience in anticipating the reaction to what we do when we're in power. Not even Obreduur." Dekkard smiled wryly. "That's something else that I just realized. It also shows how much anger we're facing in trying to undo what the Commercers have done. That's something we need to think about in the weeks and months ahead—who's going to get angry and about what. If you could think about that as well, I'd appreciate it."

"I can do that. And thank you for asking."

Dekkard *thought* Avraal was no longer angry, but, not for the first time, he wished he knew how she really felt. *But then, she likely feels the same way.* He reached out and took her hand, holding it until they headed down the main staircase.

It was slightly more than a sixth before the bell when Dekkard left Avraal at the door to the committee room and entered. Haastar, Navione, and Baar were already there, and Pajiin appeared only moments later.

The older Craft councilor immediately took his place beside Dekkard. "Did you know anything about those raids? Before, I mean?"

"No. I'm guessing that no one besides their director did, either."

"Why do you think that?"

"Every Council appointee senior to the director is in gaol." Dekkard might have said more, but Rikkard entered the chamber with an expression Dekkard felt reflected poorly concealed smugness. "We can talk later." He regretted those words even as he spoke them, since he wasn't sure he wanted to talk to anyone after the meeting. *Later could mean much later.*

Hasheem took his place at the center of the dais, and, even before the third chime, rapped the gavel and declared, "This meeting will be an open discussion of the Special Agent raids of yesterday. Just so you are all clear on the matter, the Premier did not authorize the raids. They seem to have been ordered by the director of special projects, Stuart Jebulon, without informing the Premier. At present, Jebulon's location is unknown.

"From the information I received from the Premier this morning, it appears that the Special Agents conducted raids in Machtarn, Oersynt, Ondeliew, Uldwyrk, Kathaar, Neewyrk, Port Reale, Siincleer, Nolaan, and Jaykarh. They arrested and incarcerated almost four hundred presumed New Meritorists for no reason other than being suspected of harboring sympathies. Even possessing a copy of the *Manifesto of the New Meritorists* was considered proof of being a lawbreaker. Also, some sixty were wounded, and some of those died overnight. The total number of dead is now over forty."

When Hasheem finished, he remained silent for almost a minute, before saying, "That is essentially all I know."

"How many Special Agents were wounded or killed?" asked Rikkard.

"As I told you, Councilor, four were killed, three wounded."

"I just wanted to make sure, Sr. Chairman."

"Are there any other questions?"

"Were all the raids in larger cities?" asked Haastar.

"If there were others, the Premier is not aware of them."

"Was the acting minister aware of the raids?" asked Navione.

"It appears that he was not."

After almost a minute when no one else asked any questions, Hasheem asked, "Do any members of the committee have any constructive suggestions?"

"The committee should commend the Special Agents," Rikkard immediately said.

"Commend them for a rather excessive use of force?" asked Haastar. "They killed or wounded more than sixty people in order to arrest four hundred."

"Those Meritorists wanted Security reform. We gave them that," returned Rikkard. "It wasn't enough. They started agitating to destroy the Council and the Great Charter. They got what they deserved."

"I've seen the Specials call loggers New Meritorists when the poor men didn't even know what a Meritorist was," declared Pajiin. "Likely half of those they arrested or killed weren't Meritorists at all."

While Dekkard definitely agreed with Pajiin, he hadn't expected the other to have spoken up so strongly.

"The Special Agents know. They always know," declared Rikkard.

"Like you," murmured Pajiin.

"Sr. Chairman," said Dekkard politely when no one else appeared likely to speak up, "until the reform of the Security Ministry takes effect, Special Agents remain under the authority of the director of special projects. I suggest that the committee issue an order for him to appear before the committee to explain the basis for the raids by the Special Agents—preferably as soon as possible."

"Thank you, Councilor. Are there any other suggestions?"

"Sr. Chairman," offered Villem Baar, "I second Councilor Dekkard's suggestion."

Baar's support initially surprised Dekkard, but then he wondered if Baar wanted to use a hearing to exonerate or justify the raids.

"Without hearing from the director," Baar continued, "the Council has no way of knowing whether he exceeded his authority, or whether the action was justified by the evidence and circumstances. The possibility also exists that the action was justified, but the way in which it was carried out was not. The committee and the Council need that information."

"Very well. Although Councilor Dekkard did not offer that as a motion, since you seconded it, Councilor Baar, I will take the suggestion as a motion and ask for a vote."

The only vote against the motion came from Rikkard. That didn't surprise Dekkard.

"The business of the committee having been completed," declared Hasheem, "the meeting is concluded."

Dekkard remained in his seat for several moments, thinking over Baar's support, and realizing that if the director of special projects didn't show up and couldn't be found, the blame would conveniently fall on the director, and it would be even more difficult to root out any connections between Commercers and the New Meritorists, if they existed. Dekkard remained convinced that there had to be such connections. *But what if there aren't?* That also was a possibility, but then how had the New Meritorists obtained all that dunnite?

He stood and made his way to the back of the committee room, where Avraal waited just inside the door.

"What are you thinking?" she asked.

"About the implications of what happened in the committee." As they walked back toward the courtyard doors, he told her what had happened and his subsequent thoughts.

"I think you're right. Jebulon is either fleeing and hiding on his own, or someone's paid to get him out of Machtarn." Avraal paused. "He has to be out of Guldor already. He likely left on a foreign freighter or passenger liner last night."

"I could send a message to Obreduur suggesting that Treasury might check the passenger manifests of any vessels that left Machtarn yesterday or early today to see if anyone who might be Jebulon was aboard. That is, if Treasury hasn't already done so."

"No more than that."

"And Gaaroll could run it over to his office."

"That would be best," said Avraal as they stepped out into the noticeably cooler air of the courtyard and onto the covered portico that led to the Council Office Building.

"Are you still upset with me?"

"No. I wasn't really angry at you. Well . . . maybe some." She paused. "I was mostly just angry. I was angry because Obreduur and Hasheem positioned you to write the Security reform act. I was angry because they gave you no guidance. I was angry because that meant the Commercers would attack you, when you were really doing what they had in mind. I talked to Isobel and Erleen. No one's even come close to attacking Obreduur or Hasheem. And I was a little angry at you for blaming yourself when you did so much for them—as if all the things that happened were your fault."

"When you put it that way . . . I'm sorry. I knew they were setting me up, but someone had to do it. I'm a good choice. I just didn't think the reaction would be that violent. I also didn't see how much more strain that put on you. You didn't want to tell me about it, either, because I'd just get more worried, but that also must have made you angry. And I'm sorry about that, too."

She stopped and looked at him. "Given just a hint . . . you see so much. I forget . . ." She shook her head. "You know, I checked with administration. You're the youngest councilor ever."

Dekkard smiled ruefully. "A truth wrapped in a compliment. I so often manage to act with the judgment of a slightly older man that you forget how young I really am."

"I admit it. You have more judgment and maturity than most men ten or fifteen years older."

"Not maturity. I have intelligence and training, and they help, but . . . sometimes, there's just no substitute for maturity, and that's when I make mistakes, I suspect."

"You don't make many." She smiled warmly at him. "I'll take you as you are."

Dekkard wrapped his arms around her for a long moment, even as he realized he had a very long appropriations measure to study, and he needed to think about what the New Meritorists might do next.

Not that there's likely much you can do about it.

34

ON Duadi morning there was a lengthy and detailed article about the raids in *Gestirn*. It quoted Obreduur extensively, but the basic point was that the Council hadn't authorized the raids, and those who did and participated would be charged under the criminal code. Dekkard was about to set the newssheet aside when a small article caught his eye, about the rapid rise in the cost of flour and breadstuffs, due to poor harvests and the high cost of imported emmer wheat-corn.

He recalled Ingrella's comment. *And she doesn't make idle comments. She wanted you to know that.*

"I didn't see anything new in it," said Emrelda, from where she sat, in uniform, at the breakfast room table finishing her café.

Dekkard forced his mind back to Emrelda's comment. "Neither did I." He set the newssheet aside and poured two mugs of café, because he heard Avraal's steps in the hall. He set hers at her place.

"Thank you." Avraal sat down and picked up the mug.

Dekkard turned back to Emrelda. "Last night you said that the patrollers in your station were angry about what the Special Agents did. Do you think that's representative?"

"Most patrollers I know feel that way. Most of the patrollers they know in other stations feel the same. How far that goes, or what it's like in other cities, I don't know."

"Most of the patrollers on the docks don't care for the Specials," added Gaaroll, who had been so quiet that Dekkard had hardly noticed her. "Think they're bastards."

"I wouldn't have put it quite that way," said Emrelda with an amused smile, "but it's not inaccurate."

"Will the Premier do what he says?" asked Gaaroll.

"He'll do what he can," replied Dekkard. "He can't question or put Director Jebulon on trial if he's left the country, but the Justiciary minister clearly wants to hold guilty agents responsible."

"That figures. Director skips, and gets off."

"Wyath and Manwaeren won't get off," Dekkard pointed out, as he sat down and then moved two croissants to his plate.

"Hate to see any of 'em get off," said Gaaroll.

So did Dekkard, but that was up to others at this point.

"I need to go," said Emrelda. "Just be careful."

"We'll do our best," said Gaaroll.

"We have to do better than that," said Avraal dryly, as Emrelda left the breakfast room.

"If you're going to do better than best, you'll need more than café," said

Dekkard, placing a croissant on her plate. "I won't insist on quince paste, though."

"Not if you want me to be effective, you won't." She cut a small piece off the end of the croissant and ate it, then returned to sipping her café.

Dekkard wisely said nothing more and concentrated on finishing his own breakfast, then returned to their room, put on one of the red cravats, and donned the dark gray suit jacket, while Avraal finished dressing in a gray suit with trousers, touched up with one of her teal scarves, this one absolutely brilliant.

"That scarf looks good on you."

"Thank you."

Dekkard appreciated her smile, especially after the turmoil of Unadi.

Once more, he took a different route to the Council Office Building, and neither Avraal nor Gaaroll sensed any danger until they neared the Council premises.

Even before Dekkard turned onto Council Avenue, Gaaroll said, "Strong feelings up by Heroes Square and near the Council. Feels like that last demonstration, but there are fewer of them."

"Are there any tightly focused?" asked Dekkard.

"Not that I can tell, sir."

Dekkard could feel Avraal tightening up and said, "If either of you sense anything . . ."

"We will," replied Avraal.

When Dekkard drew closer to the blue-clad demonstrators, he saw that they were more scattered, and the signs were far less professional in appearance and lettering. He caught several of the messages as he drove by.

MURDER FOR WANTING CHANGE?

WANTING CHANGE SHOULDN'T MEAN DEATH

EXECUTE THE SPECIALS!

SPECIALS = DEATH SQUADS

And, of course, REFORM THE COUNCIL!

After Dekkard turned in to the covered parking area and brought the steamer to a halt in his spot, he turned to Avraal. "I know you were worried that whoever's after me might use the demonstration as a cover to shoot me and create more violence, but I also had the feeling that this demonstration was spur of the moment, and that meant—"

"That those after you wouldn't have known quickly enough?"

"Also . . . neither of you sensed an intent or focus. If you had, I would have turned and sped away. In addition, this was a smaller demonstration. There were less than a hundred. An assassin would stand out in such a small group, and might get caught. That's not something they'd want. If there had been hundreds, I wouldn't have chanced it." The last reason had come to Dekkard after he'd parked, but he wasn't about to admit that he'd largely gone on feel and trust in Avraal and Gaaroll.

"They just may be waiting for us to let down our guard or to get careless," said Avraal.

"I've worried about that, too," replied Dekkard before opening the steamer door and getting out.

As they walked across the street toward the Council Office Building, Dekkard asked, "I'd like your thoughts about the demonstrators being out here this morning."

Avraal did not answer immediately. Finally, she said, "They organized this demonstration less than two days after an extensive series of raids. To me, that says that the Special Agents either didn't have very good information about the New Meritorists or that the raids were designed to incite more violence."

"What about being a last-chance strike at them?"

"That, too. That might have been what Jebulon used to motivate the agents. I still think the principal aim was to upset the Meritorists and to undermine the government."

"By showing that the Crafter government either can't be trusted or that it's not in control?"

"Both, most likely," she replied. "Either one is bad from Obreduur's point of view. The raids make it harder to deal with the New Meritorists, and would advance Commercer hopes of regaining control of the Council."

"That means more demonstrations and broadsheets against the Council and more pressure from corporacions to crack down even harder on the New Meritorists."

"Not immediately," she pointed out. "They need to create the illusion that he had time enough to deal with the problems and failed." She added, as they neared the bronze west doors to the Council Office Building, "Enough for now."

As soon as they reached the office, Margrit handed him four envelopes.

"The first one is from Premier Obreduur. Anna brought it."

Dekkard put Obreduur's envelope on the bottom and opened the second message. "A reminder about the Workplace Administration Committee meeting this afternoon." The next was another reminder, from Haarsfel as majority floor leader, that debates and discussion on the next year's budget and appropriations legislation would begin at fourth bell on Tridi, and that councilors could expect daily sessions to last until at least fifth bell every day until the appropriations were passed.

Dekkard showed that to Avraal, then handed it to Margrit. "Make sure everyone reads this. The office will be open until fifth bell until the appropriations pass."

The fourth envelope held a short note from Fredrich Hasheem on Security Committee stationery, which suggested that Dekkard drop by his office between fourth and sixth bell. Dekkard merely said, "Apparently, I have to meet with Chairman Hasheem later this morning, largely at my convenience. Also, I'll need to talk to Shuryn later this morning, if you'd tell him, probably around fifth bell."

"I can do that, sir."

"Thank you."

Then he and Avraal walked into his office, where he set his leather folder on the desk and opened Obreduur's envelope. He took out the single sheet and held it so that Avraal could read it as well.

Steffan—

The subject of your last message appears to have acted as you feared; although the names do not match, the description does.

I appreciate your speed and thoughtfulness in mentioning the possibility.

The signature was simply "Axel."

Avraal shook her head. "He's never liked to put much in writing."

"Unless he wants it to appear in the newssheets." Dekkard slipped the note into his gray leather folder. "So Jebulon is likely on a foreign vessel headed for a livable city in the Teknold Confederacy. I don't see him going to Medarck or Sargasso, because Obreduur could demand any country there return him and be assured that they would." While it had been almost a decade since the Guldoran fleet had bombarded Dreshaan into rubble, Dekkard doubted that any of the less industrialized countries would want to risk it—not over a demand to return a criminal.

"What do you think Hasheem wants?"

"To tell me that he got an answer from the Navy about the report that Manwaeren said existed about how the New Meritorists got the dunnite. Whatever he's found out, he doesn't want to put it in writing." Dekkard frowned. "Then again, he's cautious. He just might tell me that the Navy confirmed Manwaeren's story. I'll just have to see. He wrote that I should come by any time after fourth bell."

"That gives you time to go through your pile." Avraal's eyes went to the neat stack in the inbox and added, "Maybe." Then she smiled.

Dekkard shook his head in return. "I still need to study the appropriations bill as well."

Then he smiled and said, "Go work with Nincya. Or conspire with Svard to improve how the office works."

She grinned back at him. "Don't tempt me."

He gestured her toward the door. "We'll leave to see Hasheem at fourth bell."

Once Avraal closed the door, Dekkard sat down behind the desk, picking up the first letter, clearly from Guldoran Ironway, but postmarked from Gaarlak. He extracted the letter and began to read, his eyes focusing more on the words after the courteous opening.

I understand that you and my wife talked when you were here in Gaarlak last summer, and she conveyed to you my concerns about the lack of adequate supplemental funds for ironway right-of-way and track maintenance. With the restrictions on the last reallocation legislation, Guldoran Ironway's ability to maintain the track in the Gaarlak district will be greatly diminished, and I thought you would want to be aware of that . . .

The signature was that of Waaltar Haelkoch, district manager.

Dekkard couldn't help smiling, if ruefully, and wondering how many more letters referencing personal contacts would show up regarding the coming appropriations. *Probably not that many this year.* Next year would be a different matter.

He jotted down a brief note to Svard that he had met with Haelkoch's charming wife, but not to commit to more than thanking Haelkoch and promising to look into the matter.

The remainder of the correspondence and petitions were more routine. He even read through the opening section of the appropriations measure before he and Avraal left the office just after fourth bell for the short walk to Hasheem's office, which was one of the closest to the main staircase down to the main level.

When Dekkard and Avraal walked through the door, Hasheem's personal secretary looked slightly puzzled, but Erleen Orlov stood immediately, grinning. "Councilor Dekkard, Ritten, I wondered if we might see you both. I'd like you to meet my new partner, Myrenda Lestiig." Then she half turned to the very young-looking empath. "Myrenda, this is Councilor Steffan Dekkard and his wife, Ritten Avraal Ysella-Dekkard. They were once Premier Obreduur's security team."

"I'm very pleased to meet you both."

Dekkard could hear a hint of nervousness in Lestiig's voice. "We're glad to meet you and pleased that Erleen has a solid and dependable partner."

"And one who's a strong empath as well," added Avraal warmly.

"Not as strong as you are, Ritten," replied Lestiig.

"But close," replied Avraal, "and you're still learning."

"Thank you."

The secretary cleared her throat. "Councilor Hasheem said you could just go in, Councilor Dekkard."

Avraal looked to Dekkard with a smile. "We'll be fine here."

"I'm sure you will," replied Dekkard, who then turned and entered the inner office, closing the door.

Hasheem rose from the desk and stepped around it, gesturing to the chairs, then took the one that half faced to the window.

Dekkard took the one that faced Hasheem.

"Axel warned me that you were dangerous," said Hasheem, with a rueful smile. "He said you were dangerous because you see what others don't or don't wish to."

"Dangerous?" Dekkard asked lightly.

"When people don't wish to see something, they get angry, sometimes violent, when it's brought to their attention in a way where they can't ignore it." The older councilor paused. "I appreciate very much your suggestion that I look into that letter Manwaeren referenced. The letter does exist. It looks perfect. It's on the proper stationery with the proper format and references, and the correct names. It's also a forgery. The Navy was very unhappy to discover it existed. Admiral Jingao—he replaced Admiral Gorral—insisted on personally refuting the forgery before the Premier and his empath. He was somewhat mollified when the Premier assured him that former Security Minister Wyath would also be charged with aiding and abetting the fraudulent creation of government records. I've been led to believe that the Navy is not at all unhappy with the Security and Public Safety Reorganization Act—if for other reasons dealing with the former minister and his predecessors."

Dekkard nodded, waiting.

"I did not mention your name in connection with this matter to anyone but the Premier, and only in person. He did not use your name, either." Hasheem paused, then looked to the window, out at the darkening sky, before finally continuing. "This revelation presents a problem, as I'm sure you understand. Everyone would prefer that the matter remain as it is, with the blame primarily upon the New Meritorists and secondarily upon the corrupt leadership of the last Security minister. So, for the present, or unless more definitive evidence surfaces, the Premier would prefer that no hearings be held on the matter, since they could prove . . . unsettling at a time when there is already all too much unresolved." Hasheem paused again. "I'm certain you understand."

Dekkard definitely understood. "I can see the problem. Without absolute and irrefutable evidence, it would appear that the government would be trying to cover up or distract from ministerial malfeasance, and that would be very unwise."

"Precisely. I'm glad that we're clear on that. I trust you understand why I wanted to convey this in person."

"Absolutely." *So there are no paper trails anyone can find or use.* "And should any such evidence appear, I'll make certain that you and the Premier know immediately."

"We would both appreciate that greatly. Disruption within the Council and the government is to be avoided if at all possible."

"Especially since disruption is one of the tools being used by corporacions against the government."

"To date, however, there's little or no proof of that," Hasheem pointed out.

"That's true." *And it well may be too late when such proof is both visible and irrefutable.*

Hasheem stood. "That's all I wanted to say, Steffan."

"I appreciate it."

With two empaths outside the door, when Dekkard left the inner office, it scarcely surprised him that Avraal stood beside the personal secretary's desk.

Dekkard turned to Erleen. "It was good to see you. And to meet you, Myrenda," he added.

Both inclined their heads in return.

Once Avraal and Dekkard were out in the main corridor and away from Hasheem's office, she asked, "What exactly did Hasheem wish to tell you?"

"That an admiral told Obreduur that the letter Manwaeren referenced was a forgery, insisting on having an empath present, likely Isobel, and that they want the matter hushed up unless irrefutable evidence showed up. I agreed— mostly. I did promise that if such evidence appeared, I'd let them know first."

"None of that's going to help us, but you knew that before you stepped into his office."

"So did you. Did you find out anything of interest while you were waiting?"

"Hasheem is wary of you. He felt better at the end, at least somewhat. Myrenda is one of the strongest empaths I've run across in years, but her technique feels rough. She is strong enough to block any emp attack against Hasheem."

"That's good."

"It means that the three most important Craft councilors are protected against attacks."

"Three? Haarsfel doesn't even have an empath."

"I said important, not most senior. You're more important than Haarsfel, because you affect how things turn out."

Dekkard definitely had his doubts, but he wasn't about to argue, especially not after the day before. "Anything else?"

Avraal shook her head. "How do you feel about Obreduur and Hasheem's decision?"

"That it's wrong, but I can't call hearings."

"Maybe we should talk to Carlos."

"Won't he tell Obreduur?"

"If we merely talk to him about the decision and ask him for his opinion, that shouldn't upset Obreduur, and that's if Carlos even tells Obreduur. He might not, especially if he shares our concerns."

"What if he—" Dekkard broke off as he saw another councilor heading toward them—Villem Baar, accompanied by two security aides. "Villem Baar," he murmured, then said more loudly, "Good morning, Villem."

"The same to you, Steffan." Baar inclined his head to Avraal. "I presume this is the redoubtable Ritten Ysella-Dekkard?"

"I am, but not all that redoubtable," replied Avraal.

"Your accomplishments would say otherwise," replied Baar cheerfully, before looking to Dekkard. "Steffan, do you have any idea when there might be additional hearings in the Security Committee or what the subject might be?"

"The chairman hasn't said anything to me. He may be preoccupied with budget and appropriations measures, given the comparatively last-moment passage of the Security reform act and the changes it entailed for next year's budget and appropriations."

Baar looked slightly disconcerted. "You can tell I'm new here. I hadn't even considered that. Thank you. I won't keep you. A pleasant day to you both." With a smile he turned and continued toward the main staircase.

"Was he as disconcerted as he looked?" asked Dekkard.

"More so, I'd say."

Dekkard frowned, then thought for a moment. "He's only been a councilor for three weeks. I suppose he wouldn't have considered that."

"Why did they select him?"

"Because any legalist would have been better than Marrak, and someone thought they needed a legalist to water down or kill the Security reform act— and they needed someone quickly."

Avraal nodded. "What do you think of him?"

"I don't know, but I have the feeling he's not entirely what the Commercers would like. I can't tell you why, except he congratulated me on the way I handled the Security reform act, and it was without condescension."

"That alone suggests he's different."

"I didn't recognize either of the security aides. Did you?"

"No. They have to come from the corporacion or legalist field. The empath is moderately strong. You could take the isolate one-handed, but I got the impression that he doesn't know it. He may be used to carrying a pistol."

"That's not exactly legal."

"You're surprised," she asked sardonically, "when he comes from the corporacion security world?"

"You saw that when you were a parole screener?"

"Even before that, in Sudaen."

Dekkard opened the office door for her, then followed her in. "I take it nothing astounding happened?" he asked Margrit.

"No, sir."

"Excellent." Dekkard turned to Avraal. "Would you like—"

"No. I'd barely get there, and then I'd have to come back. Besides, I thought we were going to stop there on the way home."

"I need to talk to Shuryn. I should have earlier."

"I'll be here."

Dekkard reached out and squeezed her hand, then released it, and walked to the doorway to the staff room. "Shuryn?"

"Yes, sir?"

"Come on into the office."

Moments later, the extremely fair-skinned and blond junior engineer was seated in front of the desk, slightly on the front edge of his chair.

"How is your research coming?"

"I've found a few more instances, sir, but it's like there's a stone wall most of the time."

"A stone wall?"

"There are basic pieces of information in the newssheets, and sometimes I can find a bit more in the professional journals. If I'm fortunate, there might be a small reference months later that suggests the project or building or contract has been completed by the larger firm. But it's like there's a stone wall around anything between those points."

Dekkard nodded. "There probably is. For now, you've done enough research. Write it all up. Every instance you've found. Are there different cases for some corporacions?"

"Sometimes."

"Group them by corporacions. At some point, we may also need a chronological listing. Once Svard and I"—*and a few others*—"read your report, we'll see where we go from there."

"There's not much there on a number of them, sir."

"Don't worry, Shuryn. I expected that. But we have to start somewhere."

"Yes, sir. Is that all, sir?"

"For now, and until I read your report," replied Dekkard with a smile.

Once Shuryn left, Dekkard checked the notice for the Workplace Administration meeting, but all it said was "Testimony from the Paperworkers Guild of Eshbruk."

Something else that Pajiin helped set up? He'd just have to see.

After reading more of the appropriations measure and having a light lunch in the councilors' dining room, Dekkard walked to the committee room, escorted by Avraal.

Dekkard looked into the chamber and saw at least a dozen men and two women, who had to be testifying witnesses. He turned back to Avraal. "It's likely to be two bells, at least. If it's shorter, I can walk back with Kaliara Bassaana."

"I'm certain she won't mind that." Avraal's tone of voice was between dry and acid.

"I'll wait," Dekkard replied with an amused smile.

"*If . . . if* you finish that early, you should go back with her and learn what you can." Then she smiled in return, before turning to leave.

Dekkard walked into the chamber and sat down beside Yordan Farris. "Good afternoon, Yordan."

"Good afternoon, Steffan." Farris paused for a moment, then said, "I'd like to apologize."

Dekkard managed to conceal his surprise. "Whatever for?"

"I didn't realize that you and your wife were the ones who saved others when my predecessor was assassinated here in the Council Hall."

"I'm the one who ought to be sorry," replied Dekkard. "We didn't pick out the assassin in time to shield Councilor Aashtaan."

"I don't think anyone could fault you for that," replied Farris. "But you've been pleasant and even acknowledged me when it wasn't required, and no other Crafters do."

Dekkard almost shook his head. "Sometimes people don't think. I never sought this job. I didn't even know I was being considered. I often wondered if that might have been true for you."

Farris hesitated, then smiled sheepishly. "It was. I was a legalist in Hyarh, and chosen as a compromise. Then the Imperador called for new elections, and . . . well, let's just say that some things came out. I had nothing to do with them, and the party decided to stay with me."

Interesting. Dekkard nodded and said, "Similar circumstances."

Farris lowered his voice and asked, "What do you make of these hearings?"

"I'm guessing, but in the past, hearings in various industries always brought in corporacion officials. Seldom did the Council hear from guilds or workers. I'd guess that the chairman is redressing that lack of balance. What else he might have in mind, he hasn't said. Not to me, anyway."

Farris nodded slowly, then said, "Thank you."

Haarsfel taking his place and dropping the gavel spared Dekkard having to say more. "The committee is in session. We hear from representatives from the Paperworkers Guild of Eshbruk. Guildmeister Duerfeld, if you would begin . . ."

The graying and shadow-thin Duerfeld seated himself behind the small witness desk. "Thank you, Chairman Haarsfel. We deeply appreciate the invitation to appear before the Workplace Administration Committee . . ."

After a not quite lengthy opening, Duerfeld settled into a listing of dangers facing workers in the paper mills, beginning with those facing the rag girls who sorted the cloth used for the finer grades of paper.

After Duerfeld's statement, in which he summarized the hazards, each of the guild representatives who followed gave detailed descriptions of the difficulties in each area of papermaking. The first of two testimonies that hit Dekkard the hardest involved the wood chipping and pulping areas. A number of men had lost digits and limbs, and even their lives, including one unfortunate who had literally been chipped and his remains pulped.

The second striking testimony involved the skin lesions and early deaths for men who worked with the bleach tank slurry—the worker testifying opened his shirt and revealed the evidence.

Dekkard noticed that the revelation of the lesions didn't faze Bassaana at all, but seemed to unsettle both Halljen and Farris.

All in all, the hearing lasted until a third before fourth bell and confirmed, at least to Dekkard, what Haarsfel was doing—conducting week after week of hearings showing safety shortcomings by various corporacions. The only question, in Dekkard's mind, was what would follow the hearings. Would it be a report and the creation of a Workplace Safety Administration? Or extensive litigation against the corporacions by the Justiciary Ministry? Both? Neither? Something else?

It was too early to tell. *And it might not make any difference if Obreduur doesn't find a way to deal with the New Meritorists.*

When Haarsfel gaveled the hearing to an end, Dekkard knew Avraal would be waiting outside. He picked up his leather folder and timed his departure so that he ended up beside Kaliara Bassaana walking to the chamber door. "Another moderately long hearing."

"That's understandable. Haarsfel wants to give the workers their time."

"Do you think he'll summon any of the iron and steel guilds?"

"Kathaar Iron and Steel is possible. He and Vhiola don't get along that well."

Vhiola? Then Dekkard made the connection. Vhiola Sandegarde, the councilor from Nolaan who had been the chair of the Commerce Committee and who was also an heir to Kathaar Iron & Steel. "That seems unlikely."

"With him, you never know." Bassaana looked toward the open doors of the committee room. Avraal waited just beyond them, beside Amelya Detauran and Elyssa Kaan.

"It's too bad you can't hire your wife, since she's clearly acting as a security aide," said Bassaana.

"We're managing so far. I make more now than both of us did together before we were married. We'll just have to see how things turn out," said Dekkard with a cheerful tone he didn't fully feel.

"Do you really think matters will improve with the New Meritorists stirring up trouble?"

"Not soon. Between incidents like the unauthorized raids by disaffected Special Agents and the New Meritorists, I think we may be in for an interesting autumn and winter."

"Can you blame the Special Agents?"

"Oh, that's easy enough to do. I've seen far more misconduct on their part than just those raids. But all those behind the orders the agents followed? They should be executed."

"And the Meritorists rewarded?"

"Hardly," replied Dekkard. "I'm just as opposed to their goals as those behind the raids."

"You could end up with both sides firing at you, Steffan."

Dekkard ignored the bait. "Anything's possible, Kaliara. Have a pleasant evening."

"You as well." Dekkard let Bassaana leave the chamber first, then stepped out and joined Avraal.

"Whatever you said to Bassaana, I think I would have liked. She wasn't happy, although she smiled pleasantly at me." Avraal turned, and the two began the walk to the far end of the Council Hall and the doors to the courtyard.

Dekkard quickly related the exchange.

"You handled that well, especially with your answer about anything happening."

"Good. She has to know that some Commercers are behind the Special Agents."

"From her reactions, she has to know that you know, and that doesn't bother her."

"From what I see, very little bothers her. Her power and politics are a game. That might be because she doesn't need more power or marks."

"Dear, those are the very people who game politics to increase their power and marks."

"I keep forgetting that," he replied ruefully.

"You don't think that way."

"You don't either."

"Why do you think I left Sudaen? I understand how it all works, but I prefer not to operate that way." She paused, then added, "We may not have much of a choice, though."

"We're still going to see Carlos on the way home, then?"

"Do you think we shouldn't?" asked Avraal.

"You just pointed out that our choices are limited. I have to agree."

By the time Dekkard and Avraal returned to his office, fourth bell had already chimed, and Dekkard said to Margrit, "I'll deal with the correspondence in the morning. I have another appointment this afternoon."

After Dekkard spoke, he realized he really didn't have to explain, but he hadn't wanted to leave the impression that he was leaving work undone on a whim.

"Yes, sir." Margrit smiled, almost as if she understood.

She probably does. Dekkard gestured to Gaaroll, and he and Avraal headed out of the office, with Gaaroll close behind.

When the three left the Council Office Building, Dekkard saw no trace of the morning's demonstrators. Neither Avraal nor Gaaroll sensed any danger or emotional focus on Dekkard as they walked to the Gresynt, which Dekkard inspected before entering.

A sixth later, Avraal and Dekkard walked into Baartol's outer office, having left Gaaroll to watch the steamer.

The desk outside the inner office was vacant, and Dekkard knocked on the half-open door and asked, "Do you have a few minutes?"

"For you two, I'll always have time, but it will have to be less than a third of a bell, because I have a meeting at the Guildhall at fifth bell. While I can be a trace late . . ." Baartol nodded to Elicya, who slipped out of the inner office, and then motioned for Avraal and Dekkard to enter, although he did not rise from behind the desk.

"This won't be solved in a third," said Avraal, "but we can give you enough to consider in helping us with a solution."

"Or a course of action," added Dekkard, closing the door as he followed Avraal into the office.

Avraal looked at Dekkard.

"There's a very good possibility that the Commercers actually supplied the dunnite to the New Meritorists . . ." Still standing, Dekkard went on to outline the situation, including everything—*except* his suspicions about Jaime Minz, though he did mention the positions Ulrich and Minz now occupied. ". . . and given the political situation, neither Obreduur nor Hasheem wants any further Council investigations into the dunnite."

"Interesting. You're concerned, I take it, because you believe there's a connection between the dunnite and the attempts on your life?"

"More that those who facilitated the dunnite transfer may have larger plans to heighten the conflict between the government and the New Meritorists. I'm viewed as an obstacle—"

Avraal's harsh short laugh stopped Dekkard cold. "Right now, you are the only one who sees what's going on and is willing to do anything. Except we don't have the knowledge and power necessary to do much."

"And that's why you're here," said Baartol calmly.

Dekkard nodded.

"The two of you have enough power. What you don't have is the knowledge about how and where to apply it in a way that can't be traced back to you." He leaned forward slightly in his chair. "The other problem you have is that unless you do what is necessary yourselves, it can be traced back to you. With the right contacts and information, anything done through third parties can be traced."

For a moment, Baartol's words seemed paradoxical. Then Dekkard nodded. A strong and talented empath could track and discover anyone that he and Avraal talked to or asked to do something—except another isolate or an empath as strong as Avraal. "But that's allowed as part of a legal service, such as home security."

"True, *but* that's protecting one's own property, which is allowed under the law, so long as excessive force is not employed. There is also a third problem, which may be the greatest. Both of you have been disciplined and trained to defend—except in terms of political action. You've just told me that any immediate political action is foreclosed."

"So far as I can determine," replied Dekkard.

"Your judgment in that area is doubtless superior to mine. In the other area, I'd like to offer some observations. While the attempts at assassinating you, Steffan, are doubtless linked at the top to an individual or a few individuals in large and powerful corporacions, those individuals are likely not located in Machtarn. There also will be no discernible or provable link to those carrying out the attacks."

"Meaning that some corporacion vice-presidente tells an underling to take care of the problem so that he can deny ordering anything illegal, and so that the blame, if it's even discovered, falls on whoever organizes matters."

"That is the usual pattern." Baartol stood. "Please think all that over, and if you need additional advice, I'm always here."

"We appreciate the insights," said Avraal.

Dekkard did also, although he knew most of what Baartol had laid out. "Thank you."

"You're both more than welcome."

"Oh," added Dekkard. "One other thing. Have you had any luck in finding out anything about Sohl Hurrek, the committee clerk?"

"Not yet. I'll let you know immediately if we do."

"Thank you," Dekkard said again.

Baartol just nodded.

Neither Dekkard nor Avraal spoke until they were outside.

Then Avraal said, "We'll talk later."

"That's for the best."

Once they reached the house, Dekkard stopped under the portico to let Avraal and Gaaroll out, then drove the Gresynt to the garage. He closed the doors and walked toward the portico. As he did, he saw a woman about Emrelda's age talking to Avraal, and he tried to catch some of the words, but the other woman was talking so softly he couldn't make out what she said.

"We did what we could," said Avraal. "I'm sorry it was hard on you."

The other woman again spoke softly, then turned and walked back to the adjoining house, almost as if she were slinking.

"The lady of the Waaldwud house?" asked Dekkard.

"Ameena Waaldwud, Tomas's mother. She said that, no matter what her husband said, she appreciated what we did. Tomas is already happier and much better behaved."

"That he's better behaved doesn't surprise me. That she told you does."

"She's the kind that wants to do right, but she's trapped because she's married to the wrong man, and she never developed any marketable skills."

"And without skills . . ." Dekkard shook his head. There were few choices indeed for a woman without skills who left her husband.

Emrelda's first words when they entered the kitchen were, "Another long day?"

"There were New Meritorist pickets outside the Council buildings . . ." From there Dekkard recounted everything, except the details of their conversation with Baartol. He only mentioned that they'd stopped by his office to get Baartol's views on the current situation.

"Well, I'm glad that Ameena Waaldwud recognized the favor you did her," replied Emrelda. "I can't say that I'm exactly astonished that Obreduur doesn't want to look into the dunnite problem when he can leave it on the doorstep of the previous Commercer government."

"It's quite convenient," replied Dekkard dryly. "How was your day?"

"I got called out to help with a domestic-violence case." Emrelda smiled ruefully. "The man attacked me. I discovered I really enjoyed subduing him. He was stunned that a small woman could put him on the floor. Well, a small woman's truncheon correctly and swiftly applied. Because he attacked a patroller, he'll be spending some time in gaol." She shook her head. "Unless his wife leaves, though, it will just make her life harder when he gets out."

"I'd leave," said Gaaroll. "Will she?"

"I couldn't say. A few do leave. Those are the ones who have family that are willing and can help. The rest . . ." Emrelda shrugged. "Anyway, dinner's a mash-up of leftovers, but there should be plenty for everyone."

While there was enough for everyone, there also wasn't anything left, but since the leftovers included half of a small lemon pound cake, Dekkard was definitely satiated. The conversation revolved around speculations about what the New Meritorists would do next, and when that might be. The reluctant consensus being sooner than later, but not immediately, although Dekkard wondered if that might be what the Meritorists wanted everyone to think.

Once Avraal and Dekkard were alone in their bedroom, he turned to Avraal and said, "What do you make of what Carlos said?"

"What he basically told us." She held up a finger as she mentioned each point. "Whoever is behind the mechanics of the shooting attempts is here in Machtarn. There would be no evidence trail back to whoever ordered the attacks, *and* asking him to deal with it risked everything coming back to us."

"Then how did Marrak's death not come back to us?" asked Dekkard.

"We never asked him to do anything. If you recall, he said there were a few loose ends to take care of. I think he'd had difficulties with Marrak before. You might also recall that Carlos told me earlier that there wasn't any activity among the people he *knew*. That means outsiders."

"Among outsiders, he'd have difficulty erasing traces of his activity, and our involvement," added Dekkard. "That's why he limited what he said and told us to think things over."

"Except he was more than hinting that it was better that we do it ourselves."

"Why would he do that?"

"It might be that Commercer operatives are watching him."

"So what do we do? Follow Jaime Minz?"

"No. To begin with, I follow Minz. We don't have to ask about that. Gaar-oll stays with you. She can't sense what people feel, only how strongly they feel, but that should work well enough in the Council buildings. Also, that way, people won't comment about me being an unpaid security aide."

"At least, not as much. You don't care much for Kaliara Bassaana, do you?"

"How could you tell?"

Dekkard grinned.

"She's an opportunist, through and through. Right now, opportunity lies through the Craft Party, but that's only for now."

"She doesn't seem to think anything's going to change soon," said Dekkard. "I'd like to know why she thinks that."

"Because of you and Obreduur and some solid evidence of criminal misdeeds by Commercer politicians."

"There's something else," said Dekkard, musingly.

"If there is she'll want a high price for revealing it."

"I'm not interested in paying that kind of price. I'm just hoping I can figure out what it is." *And not engaging in unfounded wishful thinking.* "But there's one problem with you following Minz. Our steamer may be nondescript if elegant gray, but it has a moderately visible councilor's emblem rising from the front bumper."

"I can borrow a very nondescript Ferrum from Carlos without explaining." Avraal paused. "We should sleep on it, and see how we feel in the morning."

Dekkard looked at her.

"I said sleep." Then she smiled.

35

E VEN by Tridi morning, neither Dekkard nor Avraal had a better plan.
Once they were at the office, Dekkard copied the address of the Northwest Industrial Chemical's Machtarn office onto a blank note card—693 West Council Avenue, Suite Two—and handed it to Avraal. "You're sure Carlos won't ask about your borrowing the steamer, or what we've decided."

"If anything, he'll make a point of not asking."

"You think he doesn't want to get involved? I wonder about that. He didn't have a problem with the Special Agents."

"That was within the scope of home protection. I think he doesn't want us involved with him, and it's likely because of Marrak. I don't think Carlos realized how many Commercer interests were involved."

"I can see that," replied Dekkard, "especially with the trial of those three Special Agents coming up. Whoever is defending them—" He paused. "It might be useful to find out what legalist is defending them. That's not something I could have anyone in the office ask about. And Carlos would be another track back to us. What about Ingrella?" Dekkard paused. "No. That's too open, discreet as she is. What about Emrelda asking her captain?"

"That might be best. She could ask him about the trial because it was her house and she wants to know who would defend someone like that."

"I have the feeling this isn't going to be quick."

"Of course not," replied Avraal, "not when we need to find out soon." She paused. "There's another complication."

Dekkard frowned.

"Assistant director of security or not, Minz is an influencer. That means some of the time he'll be up here in the Council Office Building. Even if most councilors are on the floor for the budget debate and votes, he may visit senior staffers, and if I have to use Carlos's Ferrum . . ."

"You can't park close enough to follow him," Dekkard finished.

"I'd like to try tailing him far enough back with our steamer. If that doesn't work, I'll ask Carlos. Also, using the Gresynt keeps Carlos out of it."

"Everything gets more complicated," said Dekkard ruefully.

Avraal looked at him. "You just found that out?"

"No, but the stakes feel higher when I'm the target. I'm beginning to see why Obreduur was sometimes withdrawn. I wonder if that's why he concentrated on reading or writing something when we were taking him someplace."

"Partly, I'd guess. But you're different people as well."

Dekkard handed her the keys to the Gresynt.

"Thank you. I'll tell Gaaroll on the way out that she'll be escorting you to the floor at fourth bell. On your noon break, I'm assuming you'll go to the councilors' dining room."

"To see who stops by when there's no empath around?"

"It might be worth a try."

Dekkard nodded, then leaned forward and kissed her cheek, murmuring in her ear, "Just be careful."

"I'll be very careful, dear, but the same goes for you."

"I will. I promise." *And that definitely means not having lunch with Kaliara Bassaana.*

Once Avraal left, Dekkard began to read through and sign—or revise—the typed letters prepared for his signature on Duadi. Then he turned to reading the new letters and petitions. He was halfway through the stack when he came across another letter from Gaarlak with especially clear penmanship.

Most Honorable Councilor Dekkard—

You come from an artisan background. Surely you, more than so many councilors, can see just how antiquated Guldor's governmental system now is. How can a system designed well before ironways or steam power represent the working people of Guldor . . .

Another letter from a New Meritorist. Dekkard was right, because from there the letter repeated the same rhetoric, if in slightly different wording, as had appeared in the earlier letter.

Unlike the previous letter, however, the letter was signed, by one Hassaeu Dinarmyn, and there was a return address. There was no reference to either the New Meritorists or the People's Committee for Public Accountability. Dekkard had the feeling that the letter was the first of many, and he hoped Roostof had a solid response ready.

Since he had a little time left before he had to leave for the floor when he finished reading through the correspondence, he called Luara Colsbaan into the office.

"How are you coming on the legislative proposal for legal representation of all working women?" Dekkard frowned, then asked, "How did that term— 'working women'—ever get enshrined in law as applying to women in the massage and sex trades? Women have worked outside the home for centuries."

Colsbaan smiled wryly. "Almost all female legalists ask that question. Few men do. There are a number of stories, but they all date back to Delehya Detruro—"

"The Scarlet Daughter of Laureous the Great?"

Colsbaan looked surprised for a moment, then continued. "I never heard that, only that she was the wife of an early premier, who said that doing anything on your back for men was work, and, to spite her, once her husband had to stand down, his enemies passed one of the early laws on women of the street and called it the Working Women's Act. That was long before the Silent Revolution, but by then, the women in the trade declared that they were indeed working women." She paused. "She was really the daughter of Laureous the Great?"

"Her exploits and scandals—as you said, on her back—were at least partly responsible for the present form of the Great Charter. There's a historical novel about her—*The Scarlet Daughter.* When I read it, I thought it couldn't be true. Then I read some rare histories and discovered that the novelist understated her exploits. Both the novel and the histories are rare, for obvious reasons." Dekkard offered an embarrassed smile. "I'm afraid I got us off on a tangent. How are you coming on the proposal and the supporting material?"

"I just received the material from Myram Plassar yesterday. She cited two cases I hadn't seen and enclosed copies of the regional justicers' decisions, with the note that, despite an appeal to the High Justiciary, the High Justiciary re-affirmed the regional justicers."

"So we have to amend the basic language of the Working Women's Act?"

"Yes, sir. I should have a package together for you to look at in about a week."

"Good. Have Svard look at it first, please. He's a much better legalist than I am," said Dekkard dryly. "If you run into difficulty, let me know."

"Yes, sir."

"That's all I needed to know right now." Dekkard stood. "I appreciate all your work on this. It's not exactly a glamorous project."

"No, sir. It is necessary . . . and it's overdue."

Very overdue, like more than a few things.

As Colsbaan left the office, Dekkard smiled at the thought that the daughter of Laureous the Great had been responsible for the legal nomenclature of "working women," although it appeared that the Imperial family managed to assure her married surname was cited, in likely what was a form of quiet public repudiation of the daughter responsible for the last meaningful loss of power by the Imperador.

Dekkard walked out of his office and nodded to Gaaroll. "Time to go, Nincya."

Once they entered the main hallway and headed for the central staircase, Dekkard said quietly, "Just concentrate on strong feelings."

"Yes, sir."

As they reached the north side of the main staircase, Gaaroll said quietly, "Two men on the far side of the staircase. The one on the right looked at you. Immediately, his feelings got really strong."

"Thank you." Dekkard looked at the pair, partway down the far side of the split staircase. It took him a moment to identify Councilor Schmidtz. *But who is the other?* Then it came to him—Fernand Stoltz, who used to be the chief legalist for the Public Resources Committee. *Of course. Schmidtz had been chair. Stoltz must have moved to his personal staff.* Dekkard didn't have any idea why Stoltz would feel strongly at seeing him. *Unless he'd lost his job, and was talking to his former boss, or had to take a salary reduction. But why would Stoltz hold you responsible?* Dekkard had only met Stoltz once when, not quite in passing, he'd asked the legalist a pointed question about the differential in coal prices as a result of the Kraffeist Affair. But then, more recently, Dekkard had seen Stoltz entering the building with Minz. They hadn't acted like strangers, and Minz could easily have talked to Stoltz about Dekkard.

When Dekkard and Gaaroll reached the bottom of the staircase, Schmidtz was opening the bronze door to the courtyard, and Stoltz was out of sight, which meant that he wasn't headed for the Council Hall with Schmidtz.

"Where did the strong-feeling one go?"

"He's headed toward the west doors. His feelings are fading."

"Thank you."

Dekkard and Gaaroll crossed the courtyard in a cold, damp, and biting wind. He could see she was shivering by the time they stepped into the Council Hall, and he dug a five-mark note out of his wallet and handed it her. "After you drop me off, go get something hot to drink at the staff cafeteria."

"Sir?"

"You're shivering, and you don't get paid for another three weeks."

"Thank you, sir."

When they reached the councilors' lobby, Dekkard turned to Gaaroll. "Be back here at fifth bell."

"You won't be going anywhere to eat?"

"The councilors' dining room has an entrance to the Council floor." Before Gaaroll had the chance to feel embarrassed, Dekkard immediately added, "I asked the same question when I started with Councilor Obreduur. I'll see you later."

"Yes, sir."

Dekkard smiled, then turned and walked into the councilors' lobby. He'd taken no more than three or four steps when Schmidtz, who was only a digit or two shorter than Dekkard and whose thick black hair was turning white in places, stepped toward him.

"Councilor Dekkard. I don't believe we've met, not formally, anyway. I'm Gerard Schmidtz."

"Steffan Dekkard. We haven't met, but your name is most familiar. You were chairman of the Public Resources Committee." Dekkard decided to see if Schmidtz would ask more.

"In the previous Council, you were a staffer for the Premier, I understand?"

"Assistant economic specialist and security aide."

"You authored the Security reform proposal. Was that something you worked on for Obreduur?"

"I was concerned about the excesses of Security for some time, but we never talked about legislation, either before or after the election." Dekkard smiled politely, since what he said was literally true. "If you'd oblige me, in turn, were you caught off guard when Premier Ulrich kept the Public Resources Committee from holding hearings on the Kraffeist Affair? It was an abuse of public resources, first and foremost . . . at least it seemed that way to me. Or was I missing something?"

Schmidtz's smile seemed forced, but he said, "It was foremost an abuse of public resources, but the Imperador was greatly concerned about the impact on the Imperial Navy and suggested to Premier Ulrich that the issues might be best heard by the Military Affairs Committee." Schmidtz shrugged. "When the Imperador and the Premier agree . . ."

Dekkard nodded. "That makes it clear. Thank you."

"You're welcome. I'm very glad we had a chance to meet."

"I feel the same way." Dekkard inclined his head politely. After all, Schmidtz was senior.

"We'd best get to the floor," said the older councilor, nodding in turn to Dekkard. "It's almost fourth bell." Then he turned and walked toward the chamber entrance.

Dekkard followed, taking his seat behind his small desk. He glanced around, noticing the presence of most Crafters, and what looked to be the majority of Commercers. However, only half of the Landor councilors seemed to be there.

Several Landors entered just before the fourth bell rang, followed by the single long tone of the gong. As it died away, the lieutenant-at-arms thumped his ceremonial staff, followed by Obreduur's calling the Council of Sixty-Six into session.

Haarsfel moved to the lectern on the left side of the dais. "The matter before the Council is the passage of the combined appropriations bill. Each floor leader has one sixth of a bell to make a statement about the proposed legislation, beginning with the honorable Landor Party floor leader." Haarsfel stepped back from the lectern.

The pinch-faced Saandaar Vonauer stepped up and began to speak. "The appropriations measure before the Council is adequate but not outstanding. In our view there are areas with excessive spending, such as funding two dreadnoughts for the Navy, and areas significantly underfunded, such as canal and waterway improvement and maintenance . . ."

Dekkard understood why the Landors wanted more canal improvements, given the high ironway freight rates charged by all three Guldoran ironways. He listened as Vonauer spoke.

Some eight minutes later, the Landor floor leader concluded, ". . . and, at the appropriate time, we will be offering amendments to improve the measure before the Council."

Haarsfel stepped to the lectern and said, "The honorable Commerce Party floor leader."

Hansaal Volkaar stepped up to the lectern. "The Commerce Party concedes that the Craft Party made a valiant effort to create an effectively balanced appropriation package for the coming year. The appropriation measure before the Council, however, is less than adequate, especially in areas vital to the continuation of Guldor's economic obligations and the challenges to its world military position. Not only did the so-called Security and Public Safety Reorganization Act reduce the government's ability to deal with dissidents, but this budget also reduced the funding of its successor, the Ministry of Public Safety, as well as the funding for the Ministry of the Treasury. At a time when Guldor faces a growing threat of maritime piracy, and increases in the fleets of the Teknold Confederacy and the Polidoran Comity, the Navy ship-procurement budget received only a token increase. Despite the significant increase in ironway freight and passenger traffic, the ironway maintenance funds were not increased . . ."

Dekkard listened as Volkaar went on about the lack of increased funding,

funding that benefitted, as far as Dekkard could discern, primarily the largest corporacions in Guldor.

Volkaar's conclusion was similar to that of Vonauer. ". . . and we will be proposing amendments to rectify the considerable shortcomings in this budget."

Haarsfel again returned to the lectern. "The Craft Party supports the appropriation measure as drafted by the committees of the Council. It strikes a balance between the needs of the people and the funding available without enacting any additional revenue enhancing or reducing funding for vital needs. It recognizes the jobs created by corporacions by maintaining the basic structure enacted by the last five Commercer-controlled Councils, but rejected demands for additional funding for programs that appear to benefit primarily corporacions and their stockholders . . ."

In turn, Haarsfel took his full ten minutes, and concluded by saying, "And we believe that this measure, as drafted, represents a fair balance between competing needs and should be approved as it stands by the Council." After a long moment of silence, he went on. "The opening statements having been concluded, the Council hereby will consider the measure at hand, section by section. The question is on the approval of the preamble. If there is no objection—"

Volkaar immediately stood, and declared, "I object and request a vote on the preamble."

"A vote is requested. Is there a second?"

"I second the request," declared Pohl Palafaux, the Commercer from Point Larmat, who was rumored to be in the pocket of Siincleer Shipbuilding.

"There being a second, the vote is for or against approval of the preamble. All councilors have a third in which to register their vote and deposit a plaque."

As Haarsfel finished speaking, Obreduur gestured, and the deep gong sounded once.

Effectively, a vote against the preamble—or any section—would kill the proposed appropriations and require revision by the leadership. Dekkard doubted that any section would be disapproved, but the votes were likely to be largely party line for Crafters and Commercers, although there likely would be a few Commercer defectors.

As before, Dekkard waited until the more senior councilors voted before depositing his plaque—for—in the ballot box. The final vote was forty-four in favor, twenty-two opposed, those in favor being all twenty-nine Crafters, twelve Landor councilors, and three Commercers, while in opposition were six Landors and sixteen Commercers.

The debate and voting moved to section one, appropriations for Agriculture, and by the time Obreduur called the midday recess, there had been two votes called, one on increasing funding for the waterway overflow fund, which was defeated by a de facto coalition of Crafters and Commercers, and one on decreasing subsidies for growers engaged in melon misrepresentation—also defeated by roughly the same margin. Even after listening to the short debate on the second proposed amendment, Dekkard wasn't entirely certain what melon misrepresentation entailed, but figured that if the Landors wanted to retain subsidies even with misrepresentation, he was against it.

He stood after Obreduur gaveled the beginning of the break and was making his way toward the door that led to the councilors' dining room when he saw Elyncya Duforgue, who was hard to miss—a tall, lanky, and extremely graceful woman with black hair streaked with white. She was with a councilor he knew he should recognize—and didn't. He desperately tried to remember who the square-faced and black-haired councilor was when Elyncya said, "Steffan, would you like to join Erskine and me for lunch, such as it will be?" Her lips quirked into a rueful smile.

Erskine! That had to be Erskine Mardosh, the chairman of the Military Affairs Committee. "I'd be delighted." And he was, because he'd been impressed with what he'd learned about Elyncya right after the election.

"Excellent!" declared Mardosh warmly. "I requested that Elyncya ask you, because we've never crossed paths. I've heard a great deal about both of you, from most reliable sources, and I thought it would be good to spend a few minutes over a meal."

The three waited several minutes to be seated, given that quite a few of the councilors—but not all—had the same idea. Once they had ordered, Mardosh turned to Duforgue and said, "You have a most interesting background."

She offered an amused laugh. "You mean as a former legalist and guildmeister of the Working Women of Jaykarh? No, I didn't come up on my back, so to speak. I started after certification as an assistant to the previous guild legalist. I grew up as a farm girl in a tiny town north of Aaken, and no one else was interested in giving me a position. That may have been because my education wasn't from any distinguished institution, or because I was a woman or because I wasn't married. But I didn't want or need a husband, and I needed a job. So I took it. That was fifteen years ago. Eight years ago, I became the head legalist for the guild."

"You had to be very good," said Dekkard. "Some important people were thinking you'd make a good Justiciary minister."

For an instant Mardosh looked surprised, but Dekkard couldn't tell whether that was because of the fact or because Dekkard had known it.

"I'd heard that," replied Duforgue. "From what I've seen, I'd much rather be a councilor."

"Why did you decide to run?" asked Mardosh.

"I didn't." Duforgue smiled. "All the women's guilds, and a few others, put up my name. I was skeptical whether any woman could win, but I did my best, and it worked out."

"We're very glad you did," replied Mardosh. Then he turned to Dekkard. "I understand you graduated from the Military Institute. If I may say so, you look a little young to have completed a tour and then spent two or three years as a Council staffer."

"I am a bit young. I applied for security training after graduation. That counted toward my obligation. Then I was informed of several security aide positions here at the Council and learned that serving two years would discharge the remainder of my obligation. So, I applied and was accepted by Councilor Obreduur."

"You were informed?" Mardosh pressed.

"I had no idea that such a position even existed. I'd thought I'd be a better naval security officer than a junior fleet officer. So did the Institute. Apparently, they were correct."

"It's rather interesting," said Mardosh, "that neither of you sought to be councilors. The Premier didn't, either." He smiled wryly. "Perhaps more councilors should be selected that way." He stopped as the server returned with their meals.

Foreseeing a long afternoon, Dekkard had an order of the duck cassoulet with a side of seasonal greens and café, while Mardosh had a full cassoulet, and Duforgue the three-cheese chicken.

After the server departed and everyone had eaten several bites, Dekkard turned to Mardosh and asked, "How did you come to be a councilor?"

"Unlike you two, I sought the position. When I became an assistant guildmeister for the Shipfitters Guild, I'd thought about eventually becoming guildmeister until I realized that two things happened to guildmeisters in Siincleer. They either didn't do much and generally remained in that position, or they tried hard to improve conditions. Shall we say that untoward events occurred to those who persisted in such efforts."

"Siincleer Shipbuilding is headquartered there, as is its engineering subsidiary, as I recall."

"Yes, they are." Mardosh offered a mildly sardonic smile. "That had something to do with my decision to attempt to improve matters legislatively, rather than through the Guild."

"Is Siincleer Shipbuilding any more ruthless than other large corporacions?" asked Duforgue.

"I couldn't say, Elyncya," replied Mardosh. "I don't know enough about other corporacions to make comparisons."

"In other words," said Dekkard, "Siincleer is extremely ruthless and quietly effective, and you doubt that other corporacions are quite that ruthless, but you have no way of knowing."

"You said that. I didn't." Mardosh paused, then offered a cynical smile. "You offered that so quickly that I suspect you know something about the Siincleer corporacions."

"Not nearly what you do, I'm certain," replied Dekkard, "but I've been looking into corporacion practices." He shrugged, then went on, "I'm certain you've seen traces of that with both Siincleer and others, particularly in military construction and procurement."

Mardosh nodded. "I'm hoping to make some changes in government procurement and construction contracts that will preclude certain practices and increase safety rules. Needless to say, such changes have to be thought out carefully. Very carefully."

And designed to look far more modest than they will actually be. "I can see that. The Security reform act was perhaps too obvious." Dekkard didn't think so, but wanted to see their reactions, Mardosh's in particular.

Both Mardosh and Duforgue shook their heads.

Then Mardosh said, "That act reformed government ministries. You can't be indirect there. Unless it's spelled out, political appointees and bureaucrats will find a way to thwart change."

While Dekkard agreed with him about government ministries, he had the feeling that even more force—of some sort—would be necessary in reforming the subtle but pervasive corporacion corruption that had spread throughout Guldor. *And that might be even tougher than dealing with the New Meritorists.*

"That's certainly what I've seen," added Duforgue.

"We both know what's occupied Steffan the past few weeks," said Mardosh genially, "but how are you coming, Elyncya?"

Duforgue smiled pleasantly. "Unlike Steffan, I didn't even know my way around the Council buildings, and it's taken me a while to assemble a staff."

Dekkard could believe that. Emos Wersh, her predecessor, although a Crafter, had scarcely been interested in legal issues, particularly those affecting women, although he had met with Obreduur at least once that Dekkard could recall.

"My interests, obviously, look more toward making improvements in the legal code, particularly in clarifying the confusing welter of laws dealing with women's rights and the rights of all workers . . ."

Before all that long, it was time to return to the Council floor.

As Dekkard rose from the table, another thought crossed his mind. As Premier and majority floor leader, Obreduur and Haarsfel had largely made the committee assignments, and Obreduur had taken a seat on the Military Affairs Committee, but allowed Mardosh to become chair. *Because Obreduur deferred to Mardosh's seniority, or because he didn't think he could handle the additional workload? Or was it for some other reason?*

Not for the first time, Dekkard wished he had more experience.

Once the Council session resumed, Haarsfel continued with the consideration of amendments. Over the next four bells, the Council considered eight more agricultural amendments. After all the amendments on section one came the vote to approve that section, which passed on a vote of fifty to sixteen, all sixteen in opposition being Commercers.

Once that vote was announced, Obreduur recessed the Council until fourth bell on Furdi morning.

When Dekkard stepped out at a sixth after fifth bell, both Avraal and Gaaroll waited for him in the councilors' lobby.

"Long day?" asked Avraal, as the three began to walk toward the courtyard and the Council Office Building beyond.

"Very long, but I learned how much I don't know about agriculture."

"Such as?"

"Among other things, that misrepresentation of melons is a crime with a significant penalty, and that the shortage of ammonia from coal gasification plants makes fertilizer more expensive because the textile industry will pay more for ammonia for dyes. None of it exactly fascinating, but useful. How was your day?"

"Like yours," replied Avraal. "We can compare notes later."

After a quick stop by the office, where only Roostof and Margrit remained, according to Dekkard's earlier instructions, the three headed for the steamer.

As they crossed the street to the covered parking, Dekkard asked, "Are there any strong feelings around?"

"I could sense some in the Council Office Building," replied Gaaroll, "but not out here."

"I'm a little worried," Dekkard said quietly as they neared the Gresynt. "It's been too quiet."

"You mean, too long since the last attempt on you?" replied Avraal sardonically. "It's only been two weeks. They're likely working on another plan or waiting until a time of great turmoil."

"So that the death of a junior councilor will go largely unnoticed?"

"Of course."

Dekkard just snorted, but he did look over the Gresynt carefully, especially the acetylene cylinders for the headlamps. Nothing seemed amiss, and he got into the steamer.

At third of a bell later, he started up the drive to Emrelda's house.

"Just garage it," said Avraal. "We can walk."

Dekkard did just that, and when the three entered the house, they found Emrelda in the kitchen.

She turned and said, "We're having roast fowl. It'll be another bell."

"Is there anything we can do?" asked Avraal.

"No. The potatoes are roasting with the bird, and the salad's in the cooler."

"Then we should spend some time practicing with knives," suggested Dekkard.

"It sounds like you had a frustrating day," said Emrelda.

"Six bells of listening to appropriations amendments," replied Dekkard, "interspersed with quite a number of unnecessary votes."

"My day wasn't *that* dull," said Emrelda, "but I'll join you."

"There's a bit of a chill. You'll need a jacket," Emrelda said to Gaaroll. "I think I have one in here that should do. It's too short for me and too broad."

In moments, Emrelda returned with a plain security-blue jacket that she handed to Gaaroll. "Try it on."

Gaaroll looked at the jacket not quite dubiously, but took it and pulled it on. Then she smiled. "It fits perfectly."

"I thought it would," replied Emrelda. "You're shorter than I am, but broader across the shoulders. I got that as part of the uniform issue when I joined the patrollers, but it didn't fit right. They issued me another one and told me to keep that one, since it wouldn't fit anyone else, and there aren't that many women patrollers. Without insignia and shoulder patches, it's just a security-blue jacket. You could wear it anywhere."

"It's warm." Gaaroll paused, then said, "Thank you."

"You're welcome. Now, about knife throwing?"

Dekkard headed for the door. In less than five minutes, he had the target up against the brick sidewall of the garage. While the air beside the wall felt warm, once he stepped back several paces, he could definitely feel the strong cold wind out of the northwest.

He handed one of the knives to Gaaroll.

She barely managed to hit the edge of the target. "Frig! It's hard the way the wind gusts."

Dekkard just looked at her.

"I know, sir. Frigging likely that's when you'll most need the knife."

"Or when the light's bad," added Avraal, "or when you're caught off guard . . ."

Despite the strong, gusty, and cold wind, after less than a sixth, Dekkard felt better about his accuracy, and Gaaroll was definitely improving.

After another third, Emrelda said, "I need to see to the chicken."

"Gaaroll and I will put away the target," said Avraal. "Steffan, you can help Emrelda, and get the drinks ready."

For a moment, Dekkard wondered why Avraal had said that. Then he realized what she wanted. "Be my guest. Silverhills and Kuhrs?"

Both Avraal and Gaaroll nodded.

Once Emrelda and Dekkard were inside the house, Emrelda looked at Dekkard. "What are you supposed to tell me?"

"Nothing. I am supposed to ask you a question. You remember the three Special Agents who survived the attack on the house?"

"Yes." Emrelda's tone was wary.

"They're coming up for trial before one of the Machtarn regional justicers. I imagine some of the patrollers from the station may have to testify. If possible, we'd like to find out what legalist, or legalists, from what firm are representing them. Since it is your house they attacked, it's not improbable that you'd like to know."

"And better that neither of you has to ask."

"Just like Avraal, you can finish my sentences," Dekkard said lightly. "In the end, our wanting to know shouldn't matter, but it could right now."

Emrelda nodded slowly. "I can see that. I can also see that it's best I don't ask any questions."

"That's true."

"I should be able to find out, but it might take a few days."

"Thank you. Whatever you can do is better than what we could do."

"Not better. Less traceable." She smiled. "I need to get the chicken out of the oven."

"I'll get the drinks. Would you like me to bring in the salad from the cooler first?"

"If you would."

Dekkard had taken care of the salad and had just put the drinks on the table when Avraal and Gaaroll reentered the house.

"Getting even colder out there," said Gaaroll. "Cold enough for an ice rain."

"Wash up," said Emrelda. "By the time you do, I'll have dinner on the table."

The roast chicken and the roasted potatoes, along with Emrelda's milk gravy, were just the meal for a chill autumn night.

Much later, after they retired to their bedroom, Dekkard told Avraal about Schmidtz's approach and introduction. "It seemed more than a little forced. He must have a reason. I can't help wondering if it's because of something Minz told Fernand Stoltz. I saw them together earlier today."

"They had to have known each other for some time. I'm sure that we'll find out sooner or later why Schmidtz decided to approach you."

Dekkard still worried about how they might find out, but since he couldn't add much more, he asked what he'd wanted to know all evening. "Did you find out anything interesting about Minz?"

"Not much. He spent most of the morning in his office, then took a steamhack to the Council Office Building, where he spent a few minutes talking to a guard while they checked the visitor logs. He must be on Kuuresoh's access list, because no guard escorted him to the Councilor's office."

"Who was it on his staff you introduced me to—"

"Shayala Raeverte, the junior legalist for Erich Kuuresoh. I don't know her all that well."

"But since that was while votes were going on in Council, Minz had to be there talking to someone."

"I'd practically have to hang around there to encounter her 'accidentally.'"

"Unless you ran into her at the end of the day."

"I'll see what I can do over the next few days, depending on what else you and Minz are doing."

"Until the appropriations pass, I'll be sitting in Council voting on amendments," said Dekkard dryly.

"Anyway, I got a great deal of practice at empathically distracting people while I waited outside. Then Minz left the building. It took him a few minutes to get a steamhack. From there he went to the Imperial Banque of Machtarn, and from there to the Café Imperiale, where he had lunch with an older man I didn't recognize, but who turned out to be Duiran Keilleigh, a vice-presidente of Transoceanic Shipping."

"How did you find that out?"

"I charmed the maître d'hôtel and asked who the distinguished gentleman in the pin-striped black suit happened to be. He told me, and I thanked him for correcting me because I thought it might have been former Premier Ulrich."

"And then what?"

"He went back to his office, or the building at any rate, and he left at a sixth before fifth bell in what I presume was his own steamer, a newish blue Realto."

"Which he no doubt purchased after being hired by Northwest Chemical."

"Possibly."

"Security aides, even senior ones, can't afford even Realtos."

Avraal looked away for a moment, then said, "Did you ask Emrelda about the legalists? She never hinted anything to me."

"That's so that, if she's asked, she can say you never asked her. She said she thought that she could find out, but that it might take a few days."

"But she'll have to say you asked."

"If it's in conjunction with an attack on me, I'll already be involved. It's better that we're both not." *At least if we can keep it that way.*

"You really think you can limit what people know?"

"Not in the long run, but for now I'd like to."

Avraal smiled ruefully. "Optimist."

"Sometimes, things work out," replied Dekkard, smiling broadly. "We are together."

Her smile widened.

36

A COLD icy rain descended on Machtarn on Tridi night, stopping sometime during the night. When Dekkard woke on Furdi, it seemed darker
than normal, suggesting heavy clouds, but when he pulled back the curtains a
touch and looked outside he discovered everything shrouded in fog.

Most likely the warmer air from the ocean.

He reached the kitchen just in time to encounter Emrelda leaving. "You're
going early because of the fog?"

"What else? It'll be even thicker around the station, and I live closer than
most of the patrollers."

And you and your sister are the responsible types. But all Dekkard said was,
"Just be careful."

"What else?" replied Emrelda, with an amused smile.

Avraal, Gaaroll, and Dekkard didn't gulp down breakfast, but did eat
quickly, and left the house early.

While the drive to the Council Office Building was far slower, it was also
a surety that no one would be able to shoot him from any distance. Certainly,
neither Avraal nor Gaaroll sensed anything more than worried drivers of other
steamers trying to navigate through the fog, a fog that thinned as they neared
the Council buildings.

"There's no reason for me to come in," said Avraal. "Just pull up in front,
and I'll take the steamer. I'll be back at fifth bell. If I'm late, I'll meet you at
the office."

Dekkard did exactly what she suggested.

Once Avraal drove off in the Gresynt, Dekkard turned and walked toward
the west doors of the building, Gaaroll beside him.

As they neared the west doors, Dekkard asked, "Any strong feelings?"

"No, sir. Just a muddle."

"Good. Let's hope it stays that way."

The remainder of Furdi was uneventful, as was Quindi, although both days
were long. Dekkard listened to more amendments to the pending appropriation legislation, and voted on all of them, usually in opposition, while learning
about obscure problems. He dutifully read correspondence, and then signed or
changed the replies, later signing the revisions.

Avraal followed Jaime Minz, who visited no councilors' offices on either day,
but did visit the Machtarn offices of Transoceanic Shipping, Kathaar Iron &
Steel, Uldwyrk Systems, and Oostermein Products, a combination of corporacions that, at first glance, likely had minimal commercial connections with
Northwest Industrial Chemical, since Uldwyrk Systems built steam turbines
for naval ships and large passenger or commercial ships and since Oostermein
manufactured a range of home health products including sweet oils, liniments,
and several elixirs for tired blood and other tired organs. On reflection, Dekkard

realized that Northwest Industrial Chemical likely supplied all four corporacions with some chemical formulation or another. Even so, Minz was in security, not sales, and that suggested some form of sharing of security-related information—or a deeper collusion.

Because Captain Narryt had spent the past two days at Security Ministry headquarters as part of the team working on the transition from the Ministry of Security to the Ministry of Public Safety, Emrelda had not been able to talk to him about the legalists representing the Special Agents who had attacked the house.

On Quindi evening, once again, the four attended services at the Hillside Trinitarian Chapel, where Presider Buusen gave a homily on the virtue of patience, a virtue Dekkard appreciated in the abstract, but found unhelpful in his present circumstances, even if there was little he or Avraal could do—not prudently, at least—without more information. Yet it seemed like that information was getting harder and harder to come by.

Dinner was quiet, and, shortly thereafter, well before the first bell of night, Avraal and Dekkard sat in the sitting room talking.

"A long, tiring, and not terribly eventful or productive week," Dekkard said, finding himself yawning once, and then again.

"Sometimes, dear, uneventful is better."

"I know that, but unproductive isn't, not with Commercers like Minz wanting to remove me."

"We don't have a shred of real proof that it's Minz." Avraal yawned. "Now, you've got me doing it."

"That's because you worked harder this week." Dekkard yawned again, and he realized he was having trouble keeping his eyes open.

"Sitting here yawning isn't going to help either of us," said Avraal. "Sleep—and I mean sleep—might help us both."

Dekkard found he was even too tired for a comeback. "I think you're right." He stood, then followed Avraal from the sitting room.

37

DEKKARD did sleep somewhat later on Findi morning and was relieved that he didn't have to spend six bells listening to debate over amendments, section by section. He also had no idea what he and Avraal might do, except that it wouldn't include doing much outside, where the temperature was not quite cold enough to freeze water, but where a steady wind blew out of the north-northwest.

As Dekkard sat across the breakfast table from Avraal, having finished his croissants and quince paste, he wondered about the day.

"You're looking distracted, dear."

"I was thinking about what we should do today."

"We're going shopping. Rather, you are, and I'm coming with you. You've avoided getting formalwear, and you need some warmer suits for winter and a heavier and much better winter overcoat. Just the two of us."

"I can do with what I have. Well, except for the formalwear."

Avraal just looked at him.

Dekkard decided not to dispute that expression. "What about—"

"Emrelda has the noon-to-evening shift, and Gaaroll said she didn't want to go anywhere. We could even have an early dinner at Estado Don Miguel."

"Can we afford it?" he asked dryly.

"Since I'm paying . . ." she said with a warm smile.

He laughed softly. "That sounds like a good idea."

They didn't hurry in breakfasting and getting dressed. Dekkard wore one of his gray suits, with his councilor's pin, while Avraal wore a deep rich blue suit with a pale blue blouse and a translucent headscarf that matched the blouse. She also wore a gold lapel pin signifying her empath status.

They left the house at fifth bell, with Dekkard driving and heading up Jacquez on a slightly more roundabout route to Imperial Avenue. "Excellencia?"

"Of course."

Dekkard nodded.

"Side street! Now!"

Dekkard floored the accelerator, and the Gresynt skidded as he turned east onto the tree-lined street just below the top of the hill—and as something— likely a bullet—passed somewhere just behind his head. "Frig!" After an instant, he asked, "Are you all right?"

"Better than you," replied Avraal as she straightened in the front seat and leaned toward Dekkard. "I ducked. You couldn't. You've got a piece of something in your neck. Just a little splinter, it looks like."

Dekkard felt a twinge, and then Avraal pressed something against his neck. "Where to, now?"

"The moment you turned, I lost track of whoever it was. He was at the edge of my abilities. Just keep going east."

He kept driving east. "Should we double back?"

"No. After what we did to foil the last attempt, they just might have a secondary ambush set up just in case we repeated ourselves. Just take a longer route to Excellencia."

"After what just happened?"

"It's the best thing we can do. Who'd expect you to go shopping? Also, they might have another team watching the approach to the house just in case we returned."

"There's a bullet hole in the side of the steamer. Don't you think someone might notice?"

"Most people won't even see one hole or know what caused it." After a moment, she added, in a more humorous tone, "It will just increase your image. People will ask what councilor is so important that people shoot at him."

"Very amusing." At the same time, Dekkard realized that she was likely as shocked as he was and trying to make light of the situation. "I'm sorry. That . . . shot . . . just jolted me. And you're right. We need to make it a very long day." He paused. "If we come home after dark?"

"That would definitely be safer. At the least, they'd have to be close enough for me to sense them before they could determine if it's us."

After four blocks, Dekkard turned back north. He ended up going to Justiciary Avenue before he turned back west, because none of the other east-west streets went all the way through to Imperial Boulevard. Before that long, he parked in the lot behind Excellencia, then got out and inspected the Gresynt's exterior. Avraal had been right. The single bullet hole through the gray-finished sheet metal wasn't really that obvious.

After several moments, he shook his head.

"See?" asked Avraal as she stepped up beside him. "The hole isn't that big or that noticeable."

"I'm really glad you ducked. If you hadn't—"

"I know. How did you know to turn right?"

"It was closer." Dekkard grinned sheepishly. "Except I didn't think. I just reacted."

"I've always trusted your reactions." She gestured toward the store. "Shall we?"

"By all means."

Deep gray formalwear, with all the accessories, three heavier suits—all in various shades of gray—a winter overcoat, and two more dress shirts later, all of which he'd have to pick up after the following Tridi, Dekkard and Avraal left Excellencia and drove to Escher & Hill, where, after more deliberation about cravats than Dekkard ever contemplated when he was a security aide, they agreed on three—red, dark red, and scarlet—all in silk.

Then they proceeded to Julieta, where Avraal bought a black wool overcoat, telling Dekkard, "I need one that will give me easier access to my knives."

Given the events of the past several weeks, Dekkard wasn't about to argue with her explanation, and besides, she looked good in it.

Once they were back in the Gresynt, Avraal said, "It's still a little too early in the afternoon for dinner at Don Miguel's, even on Findi. Why don't we go to Garlaand's and look at knives?"

"Do you have something in mind?" asked Dekkard.

"Only looking at knives."

Dekkard had his doubts, but turned the Gresynt north on Imperial Boulevard. After driving not quite halfway to Council Avenue, he turned west and then, a block later, south on Regency Way, pulling into the small parking area adjacent to the three-story brick building that held Garlaand's blade emporium.

After leaving the steamer, they walked toward the store, stopping briefly to study the display window, which held not only an array of knives, but also axes, swords, machetes, and one lone cane knife. The gladius in a gilded scabbard Dekkard had seen the last time was missing.

"Are you ready to go in?" asked Avraal.

Dekkard started. He hadn't realized that he'd been standing there so long. "I'm sorry. I was wondering who would buy a gladius with a gilded scabbard."

"Someone who was never a security aide," replied Avraal.

Dekkard opened the store door and then followed Avraal inside.

The wiry gray-haired man who was walking out of the door behind the glass-fronted case holding various knives looked at Dekkard and then Avraal, then looked again.

"Yes, we're still the same people, Harcel," said Dekkard cheerfully. "You remember Avraal?"

"How could I possibly forget a woman who throws knives so well?"

"You're kind," said Avraal.

"Accurate, Ritten." Garlaand paused. "Are you still a security aide?"

"I can't be, not now that we're married."

"We're still partners," said Dekkard, "just in a different way for the last month." Abruptly, Dekkard realized that they'd been married exactly one month ago to the day. As he thought said that, it struck Dekkard that the idea for dinner at Don Miguel's had to be Avraal's way of assuring that they would celebrate that first month, since there definitely hadn't been much celebrating recently.

"I had thought about it when you came in for the target, but I've never had a councilor as a customer before."

"There's a first time for everything," said Dekkard. "You told me that you'd never had a security aide who used knives on duty before, either."

"I still don't have any others." After a pause, Garlaand asked, "You didn't break any blades, did you?"

"No," said Avraal, "but I wanted to buy another set like the ones you sold me. They're for my sister. She's almost exactly my size, and she's practiced with my knives and really likes them. I want them to be a surprise."

"I think I have another set like that. They even have the sharpened edges near the tip. Let me see." Garlaand turned and headed toward the back.

Dekkard looked to Avraal. "Spur of the moment or long consideration?"

She offered an embarrassed smile. "Spur of the moment that should have been long consideration. Emrelda's made comments more than once. And I've always had trouble surprising her with birthday gifts."

"When is her birthday?"

"The twenty-ninth of Fallend."

Garlaand returned with the blades. "They're exactly the same in weight, length, and balance. The hilt end is a touch fancier."

Avraal picked up one. "It feels the same. Can I throw one of them?"

"Be my guest." Garlaand motioned to the back room, which held not only his forge, but also a pair of targets.

After just a few throws—all close to the center of the target—Avraal said, "She should like these."

Dekkard suspected that what his wife hadn't said was that if Emrelda didn't like them, Avraal would certainly be happy to keep the knives.

Almost a bell after they entered the shop, Dekkard and Avraal left with the knives and a double sheath.

"Don Miguel's?" said Dekkard.

"I thought you'd never ask." She smiled warmly.

Once they were in the Gresynt, Dekkard drove the block and a half to Imperial Boulevard, where he turned south. Less than a third of a bell later, Dekkard parked the steamer in the area behind the Nordstar Building, which held Estado Don Miguel. Then they walked into the building and to the foyer of the restaurant, which appeared to be less than half full.

The maître d'hôtel looked at them for a long moment, his eyes taking in Dekkard's pin, before he spoke. "Councilor . . . ?"

"Dekkard. I know we didn't make reservations, but this early in the evening, we thought it wouldn't be too much of a problem."

"Not at all, sir. You've been here before?"

"Several times, but that was when I worked for Premier Obreduur."

"I thought you looked familiar. Will anyone be joining you?"

"No, just my wife and I."

"Very good, sir. This way."

The maître d'hôtel led them to a corner table for four, and Dekkard steered Avraal to one of the chairs facing out, then took the other. The maître d'hôtel presented them with menus, then departed, while a server appeared immediately.

"Ritter, Ritten . . . would you care for an aperitif?"

"Silverhills white."

"Karonin . . . if you have it, Kuhrs, if you don't," said Dekkard.

"We do have Karonin, sir."

"Excellent." Dekkard had heard more than a few mentions of how good a lager Karonin was, but had never sampled it, and the one-month anniversary of their wedding seemed a good time to try it.

Once the server left, Avraal smiled and murmured, "Show-off."

"I really wanted to try it. To see if it's as good as Kuhrs or Riverfall." As he spoke, he noticed three men seated several tables away. One was definitely Gerard Schmidtz. Then he recognized the other two—Pohl Palafaux and Jareem

Saarh. *Two Commercer councilors and a Landor. All on different commit-tees.* In the last Council, the Landor had been semi-officially supporting the Commercers, and Palafaux and Saarh had adjoining districts. Palafaux was indebted to, if not owned by, Siincleer Shipbuilding, and Schmidtz was on the Military Affairs Committee.

"Do you see the three men over there?"

"Saarh, Palafaux, and Schmidtz?"

"I don't have a good feeling about that combination, especially after Saarh's reaction the other day and the fact that Schmidtz made a deliberate introduc-tion to me, for no real reason."

"You don't think he was merely trying to be pleasant?" Avraal smiled wick-edly. "I can't imagine why you're skeptical." She paused. "I did tell you that Fernand Stoltz was the kind to hold a grudge."

"I only asked him a polite question that he didn't want to answer. Commer-cers hold grudges for the pettiest of reasons."

"Fernand might just be holding a grudge because we helped make Obred-uur Premier, and when the Crafters took power, most of the committee staff—especially on Public Resources—lost their positions."

"I doubt dear Fernand was terribly sympathetic when Craft staffers lost their positions when their councilor lost or had to stand down."

"As you've hinted before, dear, Commercers and their staffers believe they're above the indignity of losing their positions." She paused, then added, "Saarh just looked at us and then looked away, and he's not feeling very happy at all. Since he's talking to Schmidtz, it will be interesting to see how they all react."

Dekkard waited for several moments. "Well?"

"Saarh's upset, and a little angry. Schmidtz is amused and doesn't seem per-turbed. Palafaux feels slightly irked, more at Saarh, I suspect, but that's more guess than certainty. Both Commercers are holding pleasant expressions. Saarh is not." She lifted her menu. "We should consider what we're going to eat."

Dekkard turned his attention to the menu, first looking to see what Don Miguel's charged for the Karonin, then finally deciding on what he'd chosen the very first time he'd come to Estado Don Miguel—the breast of duck à la apricot with lemongrass rice and seasonal greens. Avraal opted for lime and cilantro veal piccata, with risotto, and the seasonal greens.

As they lowered their menus, their server returned, with their drinks, as if he'd been watching, which he probably had.

After they gave their order, before the server could leave, Dekkard asked, "I see two other councilors—Councilor Schmidtz and Councilor Palafaux. Are they regulars here?"

The server hesitated, his eyes going to Avraal's golden pin with the red star-burst that signified she was an empath, then said, "I wouldn't know how often he comes, but I've seen the one with the white-touched black hair more than once."

"Thank you," replied Dekkard, adding in a humorous tone, "Now I can reproach him for trying to keep Don Miguel's a secret."

When the server left, Avraal said, "Reproach him?"

"No, but if I see Schmidtz any time soon, I'll ask him how his meal was. I'm not going to pretend I never saw him. That's what Saarh does."

"And not well, either."

Dekkard lifted his beaker. "To a wonderful first month with you."

For a moment, Avraal looked momentarily stunned, then she shook her head. "All day you never said a word. Not one word."

"Then I wouldn't have been able to surprise you with the fact that I remembered. I've thought about it most of the day." That was only a slight exaggeration. Then he took a sip of the Karonin, then a second.

"Is it worth it?"

"All the time with you has been more than worth it."

"I'm glad." She smiled, then added, "But I was asking about the Karonin."

"Oh, I'd say it's just slightly better than Riverfall, which is a hair better than Kuhrs. It's definitely not worth what they charge, but I'm glad to know that for certain, and the cost of one beaker is certainly worth the knowledge. Sometimes, paying for honest, if overpriced, goods is the cheapest way to learn."

"So philosophical."

"Why not? I'm with a beautiful lady who will tell me when I've made an error, and I have, and you have, and we have the time at the moment."

"You don't make that many errors."

"That's because I have you, or if you prefer, you have me."

"How about, we have each other."

Dekkard smiled. "I can toast that as well." He lifted his beaker, and Avraal followed by lifting her wineglass.

After taking a small swallow of the Karonin, he glanced toward the table holding the three councilors, who were clearly preparing to depart. "They're leaving. That must have been a very long luncheon."

"Or a short early dinner, but it doesn't feel that way."

Dekkard could see that Schmidtz was talking to Saarh, apparently in a genial fashion. *But then Minz always talks in a genial manner.*

"How does it feel?"

"Saarh's still somewhat angry, and Schmidtz is trying to soothe him. Palafaux is totally detached from it all. Cool and removed, like he's thinking about something else."

"I wonder what."

As the other three councilors left, Schmidtz nodded and said something to the maître d'hôtel.

"From the maître d's reaction, Schmidtz slipped him a few marks."

"That suggests he's a regular here."

Both paused as the server returned with their entrées and salads.

"The duck looks as good as I remember from our first time here," said Dekkard. "You look even better."

"Flattery might get you somewhere—later."

If something else unpleasant doesn't happen. "I do hope so." Dekkard offered a lecherous smile.

Avraal shook her head, even as she smiled.

Dekkard cut and ate a morsel of the duck. It was as good as he recalled. After a few more bites, he said, "A week or so ago, you mentioned that Carlos might have some leads to the possibly mythical Amash Kharhan and the twenty thousand marks paid by Eastern Ironway as either commission or bribe."

"He hasn't mentioned anything, and I haven't asked . . . and before you ask about anything on Siincleer Engineering or anything related to Markell, nothing new has turned up."

"Then it might just be up to us to find a way for it to turn up."

"Do you think Shuryn can discover anything?"

"If he does, it's more likely to be matters that, when pursued, will lead back to the Siincleer corporacions. I doubt we'll be able to prove who was behind the scheme to destroy Engaard Engineering."

"We've known that from the beginning."

"That's the problem with corporacions. It's almost impossible to hold an individual responsible when they're acting in the corporacion's interest. I'd like to find a way to make senior officials liable."

Avraal just looked at him.

"I know, I know. Right now, I don't need any more corporacion enemies." He paused, then added, "But if they're all already after me . . . ?"

"Don't even think it," said Avraal.

While there was a hint of amusement in her statement, Dekkard also heard the underlying concern. "You're right. That should wait."

"Or you could find someone else to push it—like Harleona Zerlyon. It *is* a legal matter."

Avraal returned to addressing her lime veal piccata.

"I could try her or Elyncya Duforgue. They're both on the Justiciary Committee. Elyncya might be better because Harleona is the committee chair."

"While I haven't met Elyncya, I'd favor her, especially since Ingrella spoke favorably of her, and you mentioned that she wanted to change some of the laws dealing with corporacions."

And you did meet Harleona, and weren't excessively impressed. "When the time seems right, I'll broach the idea to Elyncya."

Avraal nodded and finished a small bite of seasonal greens. After a moment, she asked quietly, "Do you see the two couples who just came in?"

Dekkard turned his head slowly. "I don't recognize any of them. Should I?"

"No," Avraal replied with a smile, "but the black-haired heavyset one? That's Phillipe Sanoffre."

"The Minister of Health I drafted so many letters to? The one you saw when you accompanied Obreduur to warn about the New Meritorists possibly blocking the sewers?"

"The very same. He looks much happier now."

"Being a minister under Ulrich would have been trying for anyone," replied Dekkard. "I wonder what he's doing now."

"Making more marks, I'm certain." Avraal looked directly at him. "What do you want for dessert?"

"I thought about the lemon chiffon cake, but . . . would you like to split it?"

"Order it, and I'll have a bite or two."

Dekkard did, and she did.

As she set down her fork, Avraal said, "That was just right."

"I agree." He grinned. "You had four bites."

"It was good, and you offered to split it. I didn't even eat half." She smiled mischievously. "You're sounding like a Commercer, or even worse—a *Landor*."

Dekkard clutched at his chest. "That's a mortal wound."

They both laughed.

Somewhat later, when they left the Nordstar Building, Dekkard could see the sun had dropped well below the hills to the west of the Rio Azulete, but it was little more than early twilight.

"It's not dark yet," he said as they walked toward the Gresynt. "Would you mind if we took a short drive out of the way?"

"What do you have in mind?"

"I'd like to drive by the building where Jaime Minz works. Just so I have a better picture."

"You don't think he'd be there on a Findi?"

"I doubt it. He never worked late when he was a Security Committee aide, unless he was working for someone else, but that's forbidden by Council rules."

"Not if he was engaged in work for the committee elsewhere, or Ulrich told the committee that's what he was doing."

"That wouldn't surprise me." But then, after what he'd seen in the last year, he doubted that there was much left to surprise him. *Except, as soon as you think that, something will come up.* He opened the steamer door for Avraal.

"Thank you."

"Thank you—again—for the dinner. I quite thoroughly enjoyed it." *Especially after Schmidtz and the other two left.*

Once he had the steamer pressure up, not all that long with the flash boiler, Dekkard headed north on Imperial Boulevard. When he reached Council Avenue, he turned west, but when he neared the six hundred block, Avraal spoke up.

"Slow down. It's in the next block on the right."

Dekkard checked the mirrors, but there was no one near, and he slowed the Gresynt almost to a walk as they neared 693 West Council Avenue, a handsome five-story brick building with limestone corner quoins and two obvious entrances—the front entry and a side entry to the parking area, which boasted a gate and gatehouse. The gate was closed and presumably locked, and the gatehouse was vacant. A single steamer occupied the bitumen-paved lot, a blue Realto.

"Might that be the newish blue Realto of the assistant director of security for Northwest Industrial Chemical?"

"Unless it's identical."

"Could it be a corporacion steamer left locked up here on endday?" asked Dekkard.

"Most corporacions don't leave steamers out in the weather. Also, there's a lamp lit on the second floor."

"I don't suppose we should drop in unannounced," said Dekkard as the Gresynt crept past the building.

"The Council might frown on breaking and entering."

"The Commercers, especially." Dekkard eased up the Gresynt's speed as he continued west to the next cross street, where he turned left. At Justiciary Avenue he turned back east toward Imperial Boulevard.

"Rent in that area and in that building can't be cheap," he mused, "not that close to the Council and the Justiciary Ministry and the courts."

"It's worth every mark to corporacions." Avraal paused, then asked, "How do you plan to go home?"

"Past the Council and then head south and wind around to come up Florinda from the west. Do you have a better suggestion?"

"That was what I was going to suggest."

Despite the darkness by the time they reached Florinda, Dekkard scanned every possible ambush site as they neared the house. Once he eased the Gresynt into the garage, he took a deep breath and released it.

"I feel the same way," said Avraal.

How long can we keep doing this? But he didn't voice that thought as he got out of the Gresynt and then took the package containing his cravats from the middle seat.

Avraal retrieved the knives and sheath for Emrelda, and the two left the garage. Dekkard closed the door, and they walked to the portico.

Emrelda opened the portico door even before they reached it. "You were gone a long time. How was your day?"

"Interesting. Is Gaaroll around? I'd rather not explain twice."

"She's in the breakfast room. We were having something to eat. Do you need anything?"

"No. We're fine."

Dekkard and Avraal followed Emrelda along the short hall and then through the kitchen to the breakfast room. Gaaroll immediately looked up from where she sat at the table.

"Emrelda asked about our day," said Dekkard. "After the bullet went through the Gresynt, everything got better." He managed to keep his tone light as he related the attack.

"You weren't hurt, and you went shopping after that?" Emrelda's eyes went to the package that Dekkard carried containing the three different red cravats.

"My dear wife made the most valid point that no one would expect us to do so, and that someone might be waiting around here for us to return—and it would be safer to return after dark."

Gaaroll nodded in agreement, but did not speak.

"That makes sense," said Emrelda, "but it's well after dark."

"We didn't just go shopping for us," said Avraal, handing Emrelda a second package. "We got these for you. Call it a slightly early birthday present."

Emrelda's eyes widened as she unwrapped the brown paper and saw the knives. "They're almost like yours."

"They're just a touch more decorative, but they throw the same. I checked them out."

"You didn't have to."

"I wanted to, and you deserve a pleasant surprise."

"It's definitely a surprise . . . my own set of knives." Emrelda paused. "Are you sure you wouldn't like something to eat?"

"No, we're fine," said Avraal.

"Avraal treated us to dinner at Don Miguel's," added Dekkard. "A first month anniversary present."

"Shouldn't you be doing the treating?" asked Emrelda teasingly.

"Absolutely, but she asked first, and I wasn't about to argue."

All three women smiled.

38

UNADI morning, Emrelda, in full uniform, stopped Dekkard in the hall before he entered the kitchen. She kept her voice low as she said, "The captain stopped by the station yesterday while I was on duty. I talked to him briefly about the legalists representing the Special Agents. He'll see what he can find out."

"Thank you. I appreciate it."

"Steffan? Please be careful. I don't want Avraal . . ." Emrelda shook her head.

Dekkard knew what she wouldn't say—that Emrelda didn't want her sister widowed and definitely not under circumstances where Avraal might feel guilty for somehow not doing enough. "I know. I'm doing the best I can."

"If you can stop this hunt—and that's what it is—do it, and worry about the consequences later."

"I understand, but it's hard when you don't know who the hunter is."

"Maybe you should think about removing all the hunters." Emrelda stepped back. "I need to go."

Dekkard watched her leave. He'd certainly thought about just finding a way to remove Minz. *But what if it's someone else?*

He made café for himself and for Avraal almost mechanically, still thinking about the near miss of the day before and how little they both knew.

All too soon, the three of them headed out into a cold morning, Dekkard in just a suit, Avraal in a suit and an overcoat, left unbuttoned, and Gaaroll in the security-blue jacket she'd received from Emrelda. In minutes, they were in the gray Gresynt starting down the drive.

"Do you sense anything?" asked Dekkard.

"There aren't any strong feelings to the east," said Gaaroll.

"What about in the other direction?" asked Avraal.

"Nothing that I can sense so far."

"We'll go west on Florinda," said Avraal. "We'd likely have to stop at Jacquez, no matter which way we go." She turned to Dekkard. "Take the winding bumpy way behind the university. We haven't gone that way in weeks."

Dekkard drove down the drive as quickly as he dared, immediately turning west. He was approaching the first cross street with Florinda when Gaaroll said, "There's something another block to the west on the north side of Florinda."

"What about south on this cross street?"

"I don't sense anything."

While strong emotions didn't necessarily mean an assassin, and lack of emotion didn't necessarily mean no shooter, following what Gaaroll and Avraal sensed—or didn't sense—gave him the best odds. Dekkard turned left, then continued to Ortez Way, from there onto Wisteria Street, eventually ending up on the bumpy section of North University Way.

"There's lots of strong feelings south of here, maybe on Camelia Way," said Gaaroll.

When Dekkard reached a point just north of the university bell tower, Avraal said, "I can feel some anger below the tower."

"Someone just died. Farther south," said Gaaroll. "And another. People are getting hurt."

"Frig!" Dekkard shook his head. "It's got to be another student demonstration, and I'd wager there's an agitator among the students shooting at the patrollers." He kept driving.

"More hurt," added Gaaroll.

Avraal said nothing.

Instead of continuing on the street where it turned south to become West University Way, which would join Camelia Avenue in about three blocks, Dekkard turned north and then west, weaving through side streets to get to Imperial Boulevard.

"I'm glad we weren't caught in the middle of this one," Avraal finally said.

"There was another one?" asked Gaaroll.

"There were several last summer. We almost got trapped on an omnibus in the middle of one. Steffan got us out just in time."

"*We* got out together," said Dekkard.

The rest of the drive to the Council Office Building was without event, for which Dekkard was grateful.

When he brought the Gresynt to a halt before the west doors of the building, Gaaroll immediately spoke, her tone deferential. "Sir, it seems they're trying to pick you off from a distance, and that's hard."

"You want to know why someone doesn't just show up and shoot me. Because to get close enough would reveal to Avraal a great deal about the attacker, and they don't want to leave any tracks. Someone who's disposable isn't likely to want to get close to a strong empath, and they wouldn't want to risk someone more valuable. Not for me." Dekkard grinned ruefully. "Even so, it may come to that if we can't find out who's behind it. They don't know about you, and they may just be trying from a greater distance, believing that Avraal can sense considerably farther than other empaths."

Dekkard opened the door and got out, and Avraal slid behind the wheel. "Take care of him, Gaaroll, and don't let him do anything stupid."

"Yes, Ritten."

As Dekkard shut the steamer door, he glanced to Gaaroll.

She hurried out of the Gresynt, closing the door behind her. "No strong feelings anywhere near, sir."

"Good. Once we're inside, tell me what you do sense." Then he looked back at Avraal and nodded, watching for a moment as she drove away, then turned and walked swiftly toward the bronze doors of the building.

Gaaroll kept pace with Dekkard, and, possibly five yards inside, she said, "There are just little piles of feelings everywhere."

"So what you sense from each person is just a little pile of feelings?"

"Pretty much, sir. Strong feelings stand out because they're bigger piles."

"Do the piles have colors?"

"Mostly they're sort of gray. Strong feelings are dark gray. Really strong feelings are black. Except sometimes they're red."

"What do you think red is?"

"I don't know, sir. It might be anger, but I've never been able to tell for sure."

"What if you sense a small black pile?"

"It's farther away."

That made a sort of sense to Dekkard. "Are any piles white or light gray?"

"You and the Ritten usually are. So is Ritten Emrelda."

"Is that because you know us?"

"I don't know, sir."

"Think about it. It might be a way of improving your ability."

When Dekkard stepped into the office, he immediately looked to Margrit.

"No messages this morning, sir."

"Good. Hopefully, that means nothing has gone wrong, yet." He turned to Gaaroll. "Thank you. We'll be leaving for the floor at a third before fourth bell."

"Yes, sir."

Dekkard went through the letters and petitions on his desk. Most were routine, but two nearly identical letters followed the general thrust of the New Meritorist rhetoric on the need to hold councilors publicly and personally responsible for every Council vote. Dekkard shook his head as he thought about where that would lead.

The New Meritorists want to change the system to allow mob rule, and the Commercers have already corrupted it enough that it's close to a plutocracy. And at times, Dekkard felt no one, except himself and Obreduur, really wanted to go back to the principles and working practices that had served Guldor so well for so long. *Principles that allowed improvements without increasing the power of marks and personality.*

When Dekkard stepped out of his personal office at a third before fourth bell, Gaaroll stood by the anteroom door, waiting, wearing the security-blue jacket.

They had barely stepped out into the corridor when Gaaroll said, "There's someone going down the grand staircase with strong feelings."

"Dark gray or black?"

"Not quite dark gray."

"Could you tell if it was a man or woman?"

"Not for certain. If I had to guess, I'd say a woman."

"Why do you think that?" Dekkard was honestly curious.

"Women's feelings are sharper, but somehow . . . there's more there. I can't explain it. It's just the way it feels. Usually. A few men are like that, though."

Dekkard kept walking, and, as soon as he could see the staircase, he asked, "Is that person still on the steps?"

"No. I can't sense them. Maybe they calmed down, or maybe they walked toward the west doors."

Gaaroll sensed no other strong emotions on the walk to the Council Hall.

Dekkard was pleased that, despite the chill wind, she seemed comfortable in her new jacket.

He made it to the councilors' lobby well before fourth bell, where he immediately encountered Pajiin and Daffyd Dholen.

"Steffan," began Pajiin, "what do you think Chairman Hasheem is going to do next?"

Nothing, from what I see. Dekkard smiled wryly. "He seems to have focused exclusively on Security reform and the appropriations for the new Ministry of Public Safety. He's said nothing about anything the committee will be doing in the future."

"Have you said anything to him?" asked the slightly paunchy Dholen. "Recommended anything?"

For a moment, Dekkard was tempted to mention the dunnite issue—except that Dholen chaired the Public Resources Committee, on which Gerard Schmidtz served. Dekkard shook his head. He hadn't recommended anything. "I haven't heard what you and the Public Resources Committee have been looking into."

"Are you asking if we'll be looking more into the Eastern Ironway lease of the Eshbruk Naval Coal Reserve?"

"I did wonder," Dekkard admitted.

"There's not much we can do about what's past," Dholen said. "We've been holding hearings on the overall leasing procedures, for both the coal and timber reserves."

"A very good idea, given the recent abuses," replied Dekkard. *And politically likely more astute, given the Justiciary proceedings and the unusual death of former Public Resources Minister Kraffeist.* "Has Gerard Schmidtz been helpful?"

"Only in informing me that the existing procedures were developed for a reason. His attempted guidance has slowed progress somewhat, but we're proceeding. The Security Committee seems to have fared better in that respect."

"That might be because the senior Commercers on the committee in the last Council were Ulrich and Maendaan, and the only holdover was Erik Marrak."

"Who perished in an unfortunate accident several weeks ago, I understand. We didn't have that fortune. Councilor Sandegarde is of a mind similar to Gerard's."

"My condolences," said Dekkard.

"Thank you."

At that moment, the four bells began to ring out, and the three moved toward the Council chamber.

The debate and the vote on amendments to the annual appropriations continued with the section on Public Resources. By the time Haarsfel recessed the Council for the midday break, there had been votes on five Commercer amendments, all defeated, and a vote on the complete Public Resources section, which passed.

As he was about to leave the chamber, Dekkard caught sight of Yordan Farris, standing alone, and decided to approach him. "Yordan, if you don't have any meal plans, would you like to join me? Since we're likely to be sitting next to each other in committee hearings for some time, I thought . . . ?"

"Thank you." Farris offered a shy smile. "I'd like that."

Once they were seated in the councilors' dining room, Dekkard said, "I know almost nothing about you, except that you replaced Councilor Aashtaan in the previous Council, and then were elected in the last elections. That's it."

Farris gave an amused smile. "All I know about you, Steffan, is that most senior Commercer councilors are very wary of you." He paused. "Would you care to tell me why?"

"I didn't know that," replied Dekkard. "Some have been cool toward me, and others, like Gerard Schmidtz, have been quite cordial."

"Gerard is outgoing with everyone, from what I've seen, even with Saandaar Vonauer, and that takes some doing."

"He seems like the kind who wants to know something about everyone . . ." Dekkard broke off his words as the server approached.

Dekkard ordered café, a cup of white bean soup, and a side salad, while Farris chose the duck cassoulet and café.

"You were saying?" prompted Farris.

"Just that Gerard likely uses friendliness as a way to get information."

"He says it's more effective than intimidation." Farris's words were wry. "Why do you think the Premier and the floor leaders let you guide that Security reform legislation?"

Dekkard shrugged. "I doubt that it had much to do with the fact that I actually know something about security. It was more that everyone knew that Security was out of hand, and they wanted someone politically disposable to handle it in a practical matter."

"You have a strange definition of practical, Steffan. You came up with a radical restructuring. I still don't see why they let you get away with it."

"Because everyone knew it was necessary, and no one else wanted to be the one to offer a reform proposal."

"You make it sound so simple."

"I'm just a simple former security aide who did his best."

"Just like the Premier is a simple councilor who just happened to become Premier?"

"Of course." Dekkard smiled. "More important, doesn't everyone want simple and understandable solutions?"

Farris nodded. "But the reorganization disrupted the previous working arrangements."

Dekkard smiled. "I certainly hope so." *But that won't happen completely until the Special Agents are actually transferred.*

Both waited until the server finished delivering their meals and until they had each taken several mouthfuls.

"Where do you think Haarsfel is going with the Workplace Administration hearings?" asked Farris.

"He hasn't confided in me," replied Dekkard. "What do you think?"

"He's trying to turn sloppy worker practices into corporacion violations of safety standards. If he's successful, he'll use the hearings as the basis to impose stricter controls at ruinous costs."

Dekkard could see that Farris clearly discounted the evidence of the even more ruinous impact of corporacion workplace practices on worker health, but he saw no point in arguing and simply said, "If that's where he's headed, it seems a bit roundabout."

"He has to show all the so-called terrible things to build sympathy. He won't call corporacion safety officials to show that the workers are more at fault. They close windows that should be open. They don't wear their dust masks or protective aprons . . ."

When Farris finished, Dekkard said, "I can see you feel strongly about this."

"Someone has to. With those New Meritorists trying to tear down the Charter and workers wanting to be paid more than they're worth." Farris shook his head.

As Farris talked, Dekkard began to understand why Avraal had been dismissive of him when she'd heard he'd been selected to replace Aashtaan. *Farris leaves a second impression far less favorable than his first.*

"The New Meritorists are definitely a problem," agreed Dekkard. "What do you think they'll do next? Start more protests demanding every vote by every councilor be documented by name?"

"They protest, but they run away and don't give their names. They want to hold us accountable for what they don't understand, but they won't be accountable for their protests? They just want to control every councilor so that they can get more from the Council, and where will it come from? Not from them, that's for certain."

"That would take a two-thirds vote by two successive Councils," Dekkard said mildly. "I know the Premier is opposed to what they want. I don't see that happening any time soon."

"What happens if they start blowing up buildings again?"

"They only attacked Security buildings."

"They'll attack the Council if we don't give in, mark my words."

"How many other councilors feel that way? Do you know?"

"Gerard has said as much. As have Pohl Palafaux and Hansaal Volkaar. Erik Marrak said so, too, before the New Meritorists got him for opposing your Security reform act."

"I never heard anything about who or what was behind his death, only that someone rammed him with an armored Security steamer."

"Some Special Agents found links to the New Meritorists in the armored steamer."

"They must have had a reason for not making that known."

Ferris shrugged. "I wouldn't know."

"I certainly wouldn't either," said Dekkard. "It looks like it's getting close to the time to head back to the floor." He offered a wry smile. "I need to make a stop first. It's going to be a long afternoon." He stood and smiled warmly. "Thank you for joining me."

"You're welcome. Perhaps another time?"

"The way the debate and voting are going we could have a long week and possibly one after this."

Farris laughed. "I hope not."

"So do I." Dekkard let Farris leave first, because, in fact, he did have to use the facilities located between the dining room and the floor of the Council.

A few minutes after Dekkard returned to the floor, the afternoon debate and amendment votes to the annual appropriations continued with the Waterways section. In the end, two bells and a third later, after votes on five Commercer amendments, all defeated, there was a vote on the complete Waterways section, which passed.

The next section was Transportation, where the first Commercer amendment under consideration was to add five million marks to the existing ironway maintenance funds.

Dekkard had no doubt that the amendment was an effort to funnel more funding to the ironways, primarily to Guldoran Ironway. The vote on the amendment was a bit closer than on most of the others, with twenty-eight in favor—including all nineteen Commercer councilors—and thirty-eight opposed.

Next came an amendment proposed by Saandaar Vonauer and the Landors, proposing the elimination of all ironway maintenance funding on the grounds that, so long as the ironways charged higher rates for agricultural products, they should not receive governmental maintenance funds. From what he'd seen, Dekkard agreed, and he voted for the amendment, which was defeated by just two votes, thirty-two for and thirty-four against.

After votes on four more amendments, and the vote approving the Transportation section, at two thirds past fifth bell, Obreduur recessed the Council until fourth bell on Duadi morning.

Both Avraal and Gaaroll waited outside the councilors' lobby.

"Another long day?" asked Avraal.

"Very long, I had lunch with Yordan Farris."

Avraal winced.

"Yes, I know. In a way, you warned me. But it was interesting, in a painful way. What about your day?"

"About the same as yours."

In short, we'll talk about both later. "You remember the ironway supplemental funding I discovered? And Obreduur's amendment to last year's supplemental?"

"I do."

"The Commercers tried to amend the Transportation section of next year's appropriations to funnel another five million marks to the ironways, with most of it, from what I could make out from the language, going to Guldoran. The amendment failed."

"They never stop trying, do they?"

"It doesn't seem so. Unfortunately, so did one to cut all the supplemental funding."

Dekkard spent the time walking back to the office—where only Roostof and Margrit remained—telling Avraal about the various other amendments. After promising the two staffers that he'd handle the replies awaiting his signature in the morning, he and Avraal, and Gaaroll, made their way to the covered parking, largely empty.

Once more Dekkard managed a different route back to the house. There were no signs of attackers, which suggested that whoever hired them knew that for the next week or so Dekkard would be working a less predictable schedule.

When Avraal went to hang up her overcoat and Gaaroll to her room, presumably for the same purpose, Dekkard looked to Emrelda. "Anything from the captain?"

"Not yet. The day got a little scrambled. There was another disturbance at a grocery shop in the southeast, one of those places catering to the workers in Southtown. We had to send a whole squad there to keep it from getting out of control. The captain didn't want something like what happened in Rivertown."

"I imagine not." Although Emrelda didn't say more, Dekkard couldn't help wondering if matters were worse than he thought.

After dinner—a beef and vegetable pie—and some conversation, Avraal and Dekkard moved to the sitting room.

First, Dekkard filled her in on the details of his lunch with Yordan Farris, adding after the straight description, "I do wonder who told him that Marrak's killer was a New Meritorist. He's not the type to invent that."

"Or much of anything else," replied Avraal dryly. "I'd wager it was Schmidtz, but that's a guess based on what you told me."

"Schmidtz is the most likely, but Farris also mentioned Pohl Palafaux, and Palafaux was with Schmidtz and Saarh yesterday afternoon. We'll just have to see. So, how successful was your day?"

"Our friend Jaime spent most of the morning in his office, or at least in the building. I got there early enough to see him drive up in the blue Realto. So he was likely working there yesterday. At just before fifth bell, he went to the Imperial Banque of Machtarn for a good third. From there, he returned to his office. About a bell later, he walked across the street to the Council Avenue Bistro, where he had lunch with a man in a dark brown tweed suit who looked to be in his late thirties with brown hair and brush mustache. The lunch felt friendly, with no strain on either side, and lasted well over a bell.

"From there he walked to a building on Justiciary Avenue, less than three blocks from his own office, and a block from the Machtarn Regional Justiciary Building. I couldn't determine where in the building he went, but according to the building directory, all the offices held legalist firms. I wrote down all the names. Do you want to see them now?"

"No. They wouldn't mean anything now, and I wouldn't remember them." Dekkard stifled a yawn. "But keep the list safe. We'll see if any of the names match whoever's defending the Special Agents."

"You are tired. You always want to see everything." She smiled. "Do you want me to read you to sleep with a few pages from *The City of Truth*?"

Dekkard yawned again. "I wouldn't remember a word of that, either."

39

THE first thing on Dekkard's mind when he came downstairs on Duadi morning, again earlier than usual, was to see what was in the morning edition of *Gestirn*.

"There's nothing about the Council," said Emrelda.

"I wanted to see about the demonstration at Imperial University and whether they mentioned the trouble your station had with Southtown yesterday."

"The demonstration's on the front page. There's nothing about Southtown." Emrelda added dryly, "There wouldn't be, unless it killed someone important or they burned a whole block or more, like happened in Rivertown."

Dekkard could see that. He picked up the newssheet to read about the demonstration. A section of the lead paragraph summarized what he wanted to know:

> . . . was the latest in protests against policies designed to restrict admissions . . .
>
> Three Public Safety Patrollers were wounded, and one was killed when an unidentified person opened fire on the patrollers . . . patrollers returned fire and killed the man, who was not identified as a student. Five students were wounded, one seriously . . .

Dekkard laid the newssheet on the side table, shaking his head.

"That bad?" asked Gaaroll.

"Not as bad as it could have been. There's too much to fix, and not enough time."

"Not enough time to fix what?" asked Avraal as she entered the breakfast room.

"The university admission policies. Remember the student demonstrations after Minister Sanoffre capped admissions because he thought too many poorer students were competing with less-qualified richer ones?"

"He said that?" asked Gaaroll.

Dekkard snorted. "Hardly. It was indirect and politely said, but that was what he meant. Obviously, fixing that wasn't at the top of Obreduur's priorities."

"Dear," said Avraal quietly, "it's only been a little over a month since the new Council took office, and this year's admissions were already set."

"Apparently, the students didn't see it that way," Dekkard pointed out. "The new Minister of Health and Education could at least have announced that the admission caps would be looked at or removed for the next year."

"Did you think about it?" asked Avraal.

Dekkard took a deep breath, then looked at Avraal, and said quietly, "Someone told me that I wasn't responsible for everything."

Avraal dropped her eyes.

Emrelda laughed.

After a moment, Avraal looked at Dekkard, smiled sweetly, and said, "You're right. I was right."

Dekkard looked at the floor, then shook his head.

All three women laughed.

So did Dekkard.

The remainder of breakfast was quiet, because everyone needed to leave quickly.

Upstairs, while they were finishing dressing, Dekkard said, "If you wouldn't mind, I'd like to see that list."

Avraal smiled sweetly once more, then replied, "I thought you said it wouldn't mean anything yet."

"I was wrong. I was tired, and I wasn't thinking."

Avraal replied gently. "You're not sleeping well. I worry about you."

"I worry about me, too, but we're doing the best we can." Dekkard shook his head. "About the list. There's always the possibility that some Commercer legalist like Frieda Livigne might be working for one of those firms or set up their own office."

"I would have recognized one of those names."

"More likely than I would," Dekkard admitted, "but if I run across any of the names . . . ?"

Avraal took a folded sheet from her gray purse and handed it to him.

"Thank you." He unfolded it and began to read the names—Spaerse, Simmons & Haarka; Faegel and Cardenaez; Wheitz and Groebel; Strotherington and Suddeth; the Criminal Law Specialists; Hoover and Delver . . . He shook his head. There had to be thirty names on the list. "You wrote all these down?"

"He was somewhere upstairs for quite a while. The hard part was keeping the security guard distracted while I was writing."

"You are a wonder." He leaned over and kissed her cheek, then handed back the list.

"So are you."

"Wonderfully stupid when I'm tired. Do you have any more thoughts about Farris?"

"He's likely a Commercer placeholder until the next election. That suggests they don't think Obreduur can hold power that long."

"I'm sure they're working to ensure he doesn't. I just hope the New Meritorists don't have more dunnite stashed somewhere, but I have this feeling that they do—and that they'll use it at the worst possible time."

"For what?"

"Whatever will hurt the Council's control the most." Dekkard pulled back the bedroom curtains. The low clouds that covered the sky were greenish black. "Dark and cold. Perfect for spoutstorms off the shore and spout-rain. We need to get moving."

Avraal looked past him and nodded. "Definitely time for a winter slicker."

Dekkard didn't have one of the fancy wool-lined slickers. He just had a tacky gray oilskin, which he pulled on as he led the way out of the bedroom and down the stairs. Gaaroll waited by the portico door, also wearing a slicker, most likely from Emrelda.

Neither Avraal nor Gaaroll sensed any danger, possibly because they left the house almost half a bell earlier than usual, or possibly because even an assassin didn't really want to be caught out in a spout-rain—and shooting accurately was impossible in such a deluge. Even so, he still avoided taking Jacquez, but just as he turned onto Council Avenue a good mille east of the Council Hall, the spout-rain began, at first not quite the wall of water that it would become, but by the time Dekkard pulled up close to the Council Office Building, the rain was coming down in full force, and Dekkard could barely see the covered parking across the street.

He turned in the seat to Avraal. "Maybe you should just come to the office."

"I can't do anything here. I'll go to Carlos's and do what I can there until the rain lets up. If it doesn't, I'll come back here early and I'll see if I can 'accidentally' run into Shayala Raeverte late this afternoon."

Dekkard nodded. "Then we'll see you after the floor debate."

"Enjoy yourself," she said, her voice cheerfully sarcastic.

"The same to you," he answered with a smile.

Then, since there was no help for it, he opened the steamer door, and dashed around the front of the steamer and under the projecting roof that jutted out over the building entrance. Once he and Gaaroll dashed inside, he shook his head. His trousers were damp from mid-calf down.

The main corridor held almost no one, partly because he was early, and doubtless because of the weather. When Dekkard and Gaaroll reached the office, they found Margrit and Roostof there, as well as Illana.

There were no messages, and he didn't know whether to be relieved or worried. After deciding not to be either, Dekkard immediately went to work in reading and signing the various responses he hadn't dealt with on Unadi, setting aside the ones he changed for retyping, after which he read through the mail.

He finished dealing with all of that slightly less than a third before fourth bell, when he and Gaaroll left for the Council Hall. Not for the first time Dekkard appreciated the wide portico roof over the walkway between the two buildings, although he thought that the rain was lessening, and the sky to the northwest looked more greenish than black. He sat at his desk a few minutes before fourth bell, since no one had approached him in the councilors' lobby.

Precisely on schedule, Obreduur reconvened the Council, followed by Haarsfel's announcement that the Council would continue considering amendments to the annual appropriations for 1267 beginning with those dealing with Health and Education.

Two bells later, after votes on six amendments, Haarsfel recessed the Council for a one-bell break. Dekkard stood and glanced around, wondering who might be a pleasant luncheon companion, but anyone he considered seemed to be talking to someone else. So, he headed toward the archway leading to the councilors' dining room.

Halfway there, Gerhard Safaell appeared next to him. "Would you mind if I joined you for something to eat?"

Dekkard knew little about Safaell, except that he was a Crafter and a former guild legalist from Enke and that Harleona Zerlyon had found him "too deferential." After his meal with Yordan Farris, someone less strident certainly would be more welcome. "I'd like that. I'm not terribly fond of eating alone." He smiled. "And I confess I don't know all that much about you, even though we have adjoining districts."

"I suspect I know even less about you. Only that the Premier thinks highly of you."

"That may be because my wife and I protected him well for several years, not necessarily because of my abilities as a councilor." As the two neared the host, Dekkard said, "Just the two of us."

Once the two were seated, Safaell said, "Isn't your wife from an old Landor family?"

"One of the oldest," said Dekkard, "but she's not exactly traditional." He paused as a server appeared, then said, "Café and the duck cassoulet."

"Café and the three-cheese chicken for me," added Safaell. "I had the duck yesterday."

"I had the white bean soup. It wasn't bad."

"None of it's bad, but the best dishes are few, and that can get tiresome."

"I take it you're not fond of the burgher's delight?"

"Hardly. I'm not sure anyone is, except Hansaal. Do you know what the Premier thinks about it?"

"He mentioned it and suggested other items were better." Dekkard waited until the server poured his café, then took a sip. "I've found his recommendations on food to be helpful."

"And his other recommendations?"

"Since I became a councilor, he's made no recommendations. He did approve of my marrying Avraal."

"I've seen your wife several times, if not closely. I'd agree with the Premier. She also looks like she has a mind of her own."

"Very much so. Are you married?"

Safaell smiled sadly. "No. My wife died three years ago. Our son and one daughter live in Enke. The boy—well, he's definitely a man—he's a legalist, and our oldest daughter is a physician, a surgeon, actually. The youngest is in her last year here at Imperial University."

"As a legalist?" asked Dekkard.

Safaell grinned. "Absolutely."

"It sounds like they're all doing well. If I might ask, what did your daughter think about the demonstrations this past year at the university, especially yesterday?"

"She avoided the violence, but it shook her up some. I'm just glad she's living with us, I mean me. I still can't believe Elizabeta is gone." Safaell cleared his throat. "Bettina understands the anger, but she thinks the student activists and the New Meritorists are fools, as do I. She also thinks that of more than a few councilors. Frankly, she asked me to meet you. She liked your Security reform legislation."

"I can only take credit for the basic provisions, and my legalists drafted the document proper."

"Did Axel . . . ?"

Dekkard shook his head. "Neither he nor Fredrich Hasheem ever talked to me. Axel knew I wanted to reform Security, but we never talked about it." That wasn't precisely accurate, but reflected Obreduur's advice and approach.

"That's most interesting and promising. Grieg and Ulrich always meddled with legislation. They both thought they were experts in everything."

That the two previous Commercer premiers had meddled didn't surprise Dekkard. "Was it that—or were they trying to insert language fed to them by Commercer corporacions?"

Safaell offered an amused smile. "In a way, it's too bad you're married. Bettina would like you a lot. That's the sort of question she'd ask."

"I can't help you with that." Dekkard laughed softly, then asked, "What's she interested in . . . in legal matters, that is?"

"Everything. She's asked so many questions about waterways law she probably knows more than I do. I had her analyze your Security reform language for me."

"I hope she didn't find many flaws?"

"Neither of us did."

"Good. I can tell Svard that. He did most of the legal work."

At that moment the server returned with their entrées. The conversation for the rest of the meal consisted of pleasantries and noncontroversial observations. Dekkard found that he wasn't that hungry and left half the cassoulet.

When they returned to the Council floor, Haarsfel brought up the last amendments to the Health and Education section of the bill, and then the vote to approve the entire section. From there, he moved the Council on to consideration of various amendments to the Treasury and Commerce section of the appropriations. When Haarsfel announced that there were fifteen amendments registered, Dekkard could almost feel the entire Council sigh.

They got through votes on eleven amendments before Obreduur recessed the Council at a third past fifth bell.

On the walk back to the Council Office Building, Dekkard told Avraal and Gaaroll about his day on the floor, but not about his lunch with Safaell.

When they entered the office, where only Roostof and Margrit remained, Dekkard immediately addressed his senior legalist. "You got quite a compliment today, Svard. You know Councilor Safaell? From Enke? He's a former guild legalist, and his youngest daughter is in her last year in law at Imperial University. They were both impressed with the legal language and construction of the Security reform act. I emphasized that all the legal language came from you and Luara, but largely from you. I thought you should know that."

"Thank you, sir, and thank Councilor Safaell for me, if you would."

"You deserve the compliment." Dekkard grinned. "Just accept it, as someone once advised me."

Avraal laughed quietly.

Roostof couldn't help smiling. Neither could Margrit or Gaaroll.

After a moment, Dekkard said, "I'll be in early in the morning to deal with the responses, and I expect you both to be out of here right after we leave."

"Yes, sir."

Gaaroll quickly retrieved her slicker, as did Dekkard, and the three walked swiftly from the office. The main corridor was almost deserted as they walked toward the grand staircase, a sign that most of the staffers had already left the building.

As they stepped off the staircase on the main level, Gaaroll halted and said, "Someone died. Likely just beyond the covered parking."

"Can you sense anything else?" Avraal asked immediately.

"No. No other strong feelings."

The three kept walking down the long corridor, but Dekkard saw several staffers gathered by the west door. A man slightly taller than Dekkard with an aquiline face and gray hair cut short in the same military style that Dekkard preferred stood with them. It took Dekkard a moment to recall his name, but he did—Eyril Konnigsburg, the retired admiral who had replaced Oskaar Ulrich as the councilor from Veerlyn.

A Council Guard stood before the doors. "It shouldn't be more than a few minutes, Councilors, but one of the sentries spotted a man with a rifle on the west side of the covered parking. He resisted the guards, and they had to shoot him. They're sweeping the area to make sure he didn't have an accomplice."

Sentries? Dekkard turned to Avraal. "Do you recall sentries?"

She shook her head.

Dekkard certainly didn't recall sentries, but such a precaution certainly made sense, and if they were posted with lookouts on the third level or on the roof, they'd certainly have a good view. He also wondered if the shooter had been after him. Minz likely wouldn't have known about them, not if Dekkard didn't.

Less than a sixth later, after the arrival of a second guard, both guards stepped away from the doors.

"You can go now. The area's clear."

Konnigsburg was the first to leave, seemingly unperturbed.

Dekkard let a number of the staffers go next before following.

The pale green sky above Machtarn, cloudless and clearer than it had been in weeks, lacked even a trace of haze—one benefit of a spout-rain.

"Do either of you sense anything?"

"No," replied the two women, not quite simultaneously.

"Let's just hope it stays that way."

At least for the drive home, it did, and Dekkard garaged the Gresynt with relief, closed the garage door, and made his way to the house.

"There's a letter for Steffan on the front side table," Emrelda called from the kitchen, adding, "It'll be a third or so before dinner's ready."

Avraal stood beside the small table. She handed the letter to him. "It's from Naralta."

"We have time before dinner. Let's go into the sitting room. You can read it with me."

"I don't want to intrude."

Dekkard smiled. "You're not intruding." *Besides, you'll question me on it after I read it anyway.*

He walked into the sitting room and pressed the compression lighting plate for the wall lamp behind the loveseat. Then he gestured for Avraal to seat herself, after which he did the same. He slit the envelope carefully with one of his throwing knives before replacing it in its sheath, extracted the letter, and held it where they both could read Naralta's precise script.

Dear Steffan—

It was good to get your latest letter. I really appreciate it, especially hearing how busy you and Avraal are. So do Mother and Father. They're so proud of you, and they're happy you found someone as special as Avraal. Once the election was over, I'd hoped that you two could have some time together, without more trouble, but with more demonstrations by those New Meritorists, and there have been some here as well, I guess that won't happen. Some people are never satisfied.

Also, my belated congratulations. The newssheets here barely mentioned your name as the author of the act to reform the Security Ministry. Most of the credit went to the Premier, but that's not surprising since he's also the councilor from Oersynt and Malek. I know that must have taken a lot of work on your part . . .

The rest of the letter dealt with local news and the two new portrait commissions she'd received, and the fact that Oersynt had already had two light snowfalls.

When they finished reading, Dekkard looked to Avraal. "She still thinks you're special."

"And Emrelda thinks you're special."

Dekkard managed a frown. "Do you think they're both deluded?"

They both laughed softly.

Dinner was a simple roasted chicken with rice and onions. Dekkard only took small portions.

Avraal glanced at his plate.

"I'm not that hungry. It might be that I had the duck cassoulet for lunch."

The only work-related matter discussed was the possible sniper outside the Council Office Building, and when Dekkard mentioned it, Emrelda asked, "Do you think he was after you?"

Dekkard shrugged. "He could have been after either of us or someone else. Things are quiet now, but far from settled. When the trial of Wyath and Manwaeren starts, it will be interesting to see what develops."

"Very little," said Avraal sardonically. "The Justiciary prosecutors have likely already questioned them with their legalists and an empath present, but emotional reactions to questions aren't admissible as evidence. They can lead to conspirators *if* the prosecutor knows their names, and *if* the prosecutor has reasonable cause to ask about such a person."

"I know we need those limitations," said Emrelda, "but sometimes . . ." She shook her head.

Immediately after cleaning up, Emrelda asked Dekkard to go out with her and check the fittings on her steamer.

Once they reached the garage, she said, "Captain Narryt stopped by. The trial of the three Special Agents begins a week from today. The legalist firm representing them is Wheitz and Groebel." She handed him a sheet of paper. "I wrote it down to be sure. The captain doesn't know if I'll be called to testify. They could plead guilty, he said." Emrelda frowned, then asked, "Why would they do that when they have to know that the Justiciary wants to make an example out of them? Or is it because an open trial would reveal a great deal more to the newssheets? That way, they might fear that if they ask for a trial, their families may face all sorts of indirect retributions."

"They knew that already," replied Dekkard. "Thank you." He went over to the steamer and checked the fittings, particularly the headlamp fittings. "They're fine, but you knew that."

When they returned to the house, Avraal asked cheerfully, "How are the fittings?"

"They're fine," replied Dekkard, "but it won't be that long before she'll need to replenish the acetylene cylinders."

Later, when Dekkard and Avraal retired to their bedroom, Avraal said, "I take it that Emrelda wanted to tell you something, but felt Gaaroll was hanging too close?"

"Exactly. The Special Agents' trial begins a week from today, and their legalist firm is Wheitz and Groebel. If I recall correctly, that's one of the firms in the building Minz visited the other day."

"It definitely is, but given how many legalists are in the building . . ."

"Suggestive, but little more," said Dekkard disgustedly. "Like everything, it seems."

"Or everything in politics."

"Was your day more productive than mine?"

"First, finish telling me about your day. You never mentioned lunch, except for that bit about Safaell praising Svard's legal work. I assume there was more."

"There was." Dekkard related the rest of the lunch conversation. "I tend to believe his reasons, if only that they fit together."

"His daughter sounds like she's acting in place of his wife."

"She probably is. She's likely bright, possibly brighter than he is, and he knows it, and who else could he trust? Now your day."

"I spent the morning interviewing some young empaths with Carlos. He's definitely going to need someone before long, or he's looking for someone he can groom to work for Obreduur so that he can get Isobel back. He was honestly unsure about which, I could sense, only that he knows there's a need for another empath. Then when the rain finally stopped, I went looking for Jaime Minz. He was in his office, or in the building, until just about noon. He left the Realto and took a steamhack to the ironway station. He carried a leather case, the one he often carries, and a satchel, likely an overnight bag. I waited, but he didn't come out of the station."

"Taking a train at around first bell. That had to be a local," mused Dekkard.

"The closest place of any size is Point Larmat, and the next would likely be Obaan."

"He might have gone beyond Point Larmat to Siincleer, but he would have arrived there only a bell or two before midnight. What's interesting about that is that Point Larmat is Palafaux's district, and Obaan is Schmidtz's, but they were both here for all the votes. And Siincleer is obviously tied to military affairs, and Schmidtz is on that committee, while Palafaux has ties to Siincleer Shipbuilding."

"Again, as you put it," said Avraal, "suggestive, but hardly more than that."

Dekkard just shook his head.

"Since Jaime was on his way elsewhere, I did manage to run into Shayala this afternoon. She was pleasant, but she really didn't want to talk to me. So we spent a bit of time talking about how the Council had changed. She wanted to know what you were like behind your security façade. I told her you were wonderful, and how your staff liked and respected you. Then I told her about the Atacaman fire pepper incident. She was definitely shocked. I mentioned that it was sometimes a little strange talking to staffers we'd been friendly with, but we'd seen many of them, and that Amelya and Elyssa had been pleased, and so had Erleen, and that we'd met the new isolate working with her. But that neither of us had seen Jaime Minz, and I asked if she knew anything about him."

"And?" pressed Dekkard.

"She said that Minz was some sort of influencer with Northwest Chemical Industries and he'd been by the office several times to talk with Councilor Kuuresoh, but had missed him the last time. Minz offered to provide any background information on industrial chemicals if she ever needed anything. That was about it."

Dekkard frowned. "So Minz has been talking with Kuuresoh, who's on the Military Affairs Committee. Schmidtz is one of the other Commercers on that committee."

"That doesn't prove anything."

"I know, but Palafaux is tied to corporacions who get lots of contracts from the Navy, and he and Schmidtz are trying to persuade Saarh about something, and Saarh's district adjoins Schmidtz's. At the same time, dear Jaime keeps visiting Kuuresoh, without a Council Guard escort, which means that he's on Kuuresoh's access list."

Absently, Dekkard realized he ought to put his family on his access list, but doing so wasn't urgent, given how far away they lived. He also realized that it might be a good idea to see if he could work in another lunch with Erskine Mardosh.

"Where could Saarh fit in?" asked Avraal. "He's on the Agriculture and Commerce Committees."

"Maybe Siincleer Shipbuilding or Engineering needs something from the Commerce Committee. That's the only possibility I can think of. According to his profile in that book of Obreduur's, he definitely needs the marks he gets as a councilor because his lands don't generate that much income." Dekkard paused. "There are definite ways that corporacions can indirectly funnel marks to councilors, especially Landor councilors. They can just overpay for harvests or whatever."

"That thought depresses me." Avraal yawned. "We've done enough thinking for the night, and I need some sleep, and you certainly do." After just an instant, she added, "Sleep, dear man."

Dekkard kept his wry smile to himself. There would be other nights.

40

AGAIN, on Tridi morning, Dekkard needed to be up early, and he showered, shaved, and mostly dressed before hurrying down to the kitchen, where he poured two cups of café, then entered the breakfast room, where Emrelda was still seated.

"Another early morning?"

"For us. Until the appropriations are done. With luck, I thought that might be Quindi, but with all the amendments, I have the feeling that the votes will drag into next week."

"Aren't you fortunate." Emrelda gestured to the newssheet. "There are two stories there."

Dekkard set down the two mugs, one at Avraal's place, and picked up the morning edition of *Gestirn*.

Near the bottom of the front page was a story about a disturbance in Uldwyrk caused when almost a hundred women protested the price of flour at a grocer's and blocked access to the shop for much of the day before they were removed by local patrollers.

Dekkard wanted to shake his head. What good would blocking a grocery store do? *At least they didn't call in Special Agents.*

Then he turned to the political stories. Both were short. One concerned the opening of the trial of former Security Minister Wyath and former acting Minister Manwaeren. Besides the various charges of both malfeasance and misfeasance, and high treason for Wyath, the story mentioned that the various abuses with which the two were charged had led directly to the Security and Public Safety Reorganization Act. The second stated that, under the hand of Premier Obreduur, the annual appropriations legislation was moving more quickly than in previous years.

Five full days of near-continuous votes, with possibly four or five more to come, seemed unending enough to Dekkard. *And what's happening this year is considered fast?*

While he and Avraal had certainly escorted Obreduur to those endless votes in previous years, somehow they seemed longer when he was the one listening and voting. *But isn't that true of everything?* He set down the newssheet and seated himself as Gaaroll entered the breakfast room, followed by Avraal.

"Is there anything in the newssheet?" Avraal sat down and took a sip of café.

"Only a story about the Wyath and Manwaeren trial starting today, and a few words about the appropriation."

"Nothing about the shooter at the Council Office Building? Or anything more on the university demonstration?"

"I didn't see anything," said Dekkard, wondering if he'd missed something.

"Nothing," added Emrelda. "I read the whole newssheet closely."

"I wonder why it's not in the newssheet," mused Dekkard.

"It could be that the Council Guards aren't talking about it yet," said Avraal. "Maybe Obreduur doesn't want a news story yet. It happened late enough that there weren't many people around. The only witnesses would be the Council Guards. And I'm sure Guard Captain Trujillo doesn't want to say anything."

"One other thing, dear," said Avraal. "I'll need the Gresynt today."

"That's fine. I'm certainly not going anywhere, except to the Council floor."

Dekkard continued to wonder about the missing newssheet coverage when he, uneventfully, reached the Council Office Building and turned the Gresynt over to Avraal.

Once he and Gaaroll stepped into the main corridor inside the building, she said, "Strong feelings going up the main staircase."

"Let me know if they change direction or head toward us."

"Yes, sir."

As they neared the center grand staircase, Gaaroll said, "They're heading west on the second level. Might be wrong, sir, but it feels like anger."

"What makes you think that?"

"There's red mixed with the black. Feels that way, leastwise."

"If you feel things like that, keep letting me know."

When they reached the second level, she added, "Not so strong. They went into an office near the west end. Can't tell exactly which one."

Dekkard wondered who felt that strongly, but it could have been a councilor or a staffer. Anyone could have strong feelings of anger. The Almighty knew, he certainly had.

Roostof and Margrit were standing by her desk talking when Dekkard and Gaaroll walked into the outer office. They both turned immediately.

"Good morning, sir."

"The same to both of you. There aren't any messages, are there?"

"Not yet," replied Margrit. "The morning mail hasn't been delivered yet. But there's a heliogram on your desk."

"I'm also certain that there's a stack of responses for me to go over and sign."

"There are quite a few," said Roostof, with a slight grin.

"Then I'd better get to them." He glanced to Gaaroll. "We'll leave for the Council Hall at a third before fourth bell."

She nodded in reply.

Once he entered his personal office, he immediately settled behind his desk. He picked up the heliogram, wondering what was so important that someone had paid considerably extra to send such a message. He opened it.

> Councilor Dekkard—
> Reform The Council!
> Now!

The sender's name was that of Juan Todos.

What Dekkard wondered was how the sender had managed to get that message sent under an obvious pseudonym. But maybe the message had just been forged and added to a heliograph messenger's bag.

Either way, it was concerning.

After thinking about it and deciding there wasn't much he could do, he began to go through the responses awaiting his attention. It was close to third bell when he finished, and after he returned the signed letters, as well as the ones that he'd changed that needed to be retyped, Margrit delivered the morning mail.

A letter from Gaarlak topped the stack, set there because Margrit had clearly recognized the name of the sender—Emilio Raathan. Dekkard extracted the letter from the already-slit envelope and began to read.

Dear Steffan—

Thank you so much for your kind and thoughtful response. I know how little free time a councilor has, particularly in his first term. So I do appreciate the time you took to respond.

As you may have gathered, Breffyn Haastar has been kind enough to keep me apprised of some of what has transpired in the new Council. He is most impressed with your demeanor and your accomplishments, and your considerable courage in undertaking efforts at reform that are long overdue. While you have a very different background from Breffyn, there are doubtless areas where you two could come to an agreement, and it might be worthwhile for both of you. I've told him that as well.

I know that, even with your past experience, you must be spending bells at being the best councilor you can be. Nonetheless, it would be good if you could come to Gaarlak before long and take steps to establish a physical and legal presence here.

Dekkard nodded. Raathan echoed what others had said, but he didn't see how he could leave Machtarn until the Midwinter Council Recess, and that was more than a month away.

Patriana also sends her best. We both think you made an excellent decision in asking Avraal to marry you, and we offer our hopes that you two can make as happy a life together as we have.

The letter was just signed "Emilio."

He set that letter aside for a personal response, and began to read through the rest of the letters and petitions. He managed to read through all of them, and even draft a rough response to Raathan, before it was time to leave for the Council Hall. He needed to reply to Naralta, but that might have to wait a day or two.

Gaaroll detected no strong feelings on the walk to the Council Hall, and Dekkard exchanged passing greetings with Rikkard and Dholen in the corridor leading to the councilors' lobby. Once Dekkard entered the lobby, Pajiin gestured to him.

"I saw you eating with Farris."

"I was being sociable." Dekkard lowered his voice. "You can't change people's minds or votes if you don't talk to them."

"You'll never change his."

"That's possible." Dekkard grinned. "But you don't know if you don't try."

Pajiin shook his head.

"You've been spending time with Daffyd Dholen. Public Resources and logging?"

"What else?" Pajiin smiled pleasantly. "The other day you had lunch with Mardosh and the woman legalist Councilor Duforgue. What was that about?"

"He asked both of us. He said he just wanted to talk to get to know us better."

"For now."

"That's true for all of us, isn't it?" asked Dekkard gently.

The other grinned. "Of course."

With four bells about to chime, Dekkard made his way to the floor and sat down at his desk.

Promptly at four bells, Obreduur convened the Council, and Haarsfel announced the next amendment to the Treasury and Commerce section of the appropriations.

Authored by Hasheem, that amendment offered sought to increase Treasury appropriations to fund the payroll of transferred Special Agents, on the grounds that the initial appropriations had been inadequate. While Dekkard had some unease about any more funding for the soon-to-be former Special Agents, he voted for it, as did most of the Council, since it passed on a fifty-to-sixteen vote.

By noon, the Council had voted on four amendments, the only one passing being the first of them, and then voted to approve the entire section dealing with Treasury and Commerce.

When Obreduur recessed the Council for the midday break, Dekkard immediately looked for Mardosh, but could not see him. He hoped to find someone else he'd never talked to and whom he thought he might like to know better when someone spoke behind him.

"Steffan?"

At the feminine tone, Dekkard turned to find himself face-to-face with another councilor, a broad-shouldered, muscular woman in a blue pin-striped suit with a white blouse and scarf. She was a good five digits shorter than Dekkard, with brown hair in a precise bob, and looked possibly ten years older, although Dekkard knew she must be older than that. It took him a long moment to recognize the speaker. "Councilor Sandegarde, you surprised me."

"Good." The single word was humorously sharp. "And 'Vhiola' will do. Since you obviously haven't arranged lunch beforehand, we should take advantage of the situation."

Dekkard smiled warmly. "Since you already have, I agree." He gestured in the direction of the councilors' dining room, then walked beside Sandegarde.

Once seated, she smiled pleasantly. "You don't have that hard-edged personality that many security aides do. That's unusual, especially in a top ten graduate of the Military Institute. Then, it might come from your familial background and your early work as an artisan."

"You've obviously had my background researched. Isn't it unusual to do that for one of the most junior councilors?"

"You're unusual, and you'd be a fool not to know it. You're anything but a fool. Also, you could be quite the ladies' man, but you aren't. Then, once I saw your wife, I understood. You worked together for several years. Wasn't that difficult?"

"Not until the last few months. She's very determined and very reserved. I was slightly intimidated until she indicated she might be interested."

"Intimidated, or calculatedly careful."

"Definitely intimidated, which led to care."

"Ah. So romantic and so traditional." Sandegarde's words were just a shade too sweet. "When did you find out who she really was?"

"Not until after I proposed to her."

"You don't have to keep up appearances, you know. Now that you're a councilor and married, no one cares how you two carried on before you wed."

Dekkard laughed softly. "Some traditional things are actually true, Vhiola."

"Yet you're both radicals. Oh, I know you're not in favor of those idiotic New Meritorists, and you doubtless believe in Obreduur's futile dream of returning the Council to a more—shall we say—pristine time, which would make you reactionaries. You're anything but reactionaries. Absolutely masterful how you got yourself selected. Very few have succeeded in outmaneuvering the Premier, and you handled the Security reform impeccably. The only problem is that you're too young and you've been too successful too quickly. That's why you have enemies trying to kill you."

Dekkard easily maintained a pleasant expression. "What would be the point of that? Security reform was necessary. I was convenient."

"Councilors never get attacked, even with Atacaman pepper dust, in the Council spaces unless they have powerful enemies. Hasheem tried to hush it up, but that's impossible. Someone always finds out."

"I suspect you're always one of those someones."

"Usually, but not always. No one is always perfectly informed. That's also something never to forget."

"I won't. Advice from a woman of your background, education, and accomplishment should never be ignored." *Not necessarily followed, but never ignored.*

"Flattery, yet."

"I think not. You have knowledge of politics, industry, finance, and likely much more than that, and you've been chair of the Commerce Committee."

"Only for a few months."

Dekkard paused as the server arrived, and both ordered. Sandegarde chose the duck cassoulet with café, and Dekkard the three-cheese chicken, also with café.

Once the server left, Dekkard looked directly at Sandegarde. "Why did you ask me to have lunch, rather than a promising new councilor like Villem Baar?"

"Because you intrigue me. Most councilors don't."

"I'd say that the Premier would be far more intriguing."

"Obreduur is indeed intriguing, and everyone watches him."

"Whereas few consider with whom his former lowly security aide meets."

"That is something to be considered, but few councilors are lowly, and any-one trusted to develop a major piece of legislation? Hardly."

Dekkard offered an amused smile. "The fact that my legalists wrote a good piece of legislation was incidental, and we both know it. If my draft had been terrible, Hasheem would have had it amended into something reasonable, and my name still would have been on it."

"So what, Steffan, is your next project or objective?"

"That depends on what others do, especially the New Meritorists."

"As I said before, you don't strike me as a reactionary. And what if they're far weaker than they seem?"

"That's possible. It's also possible that they'll surprise everyone again."

"Everyone? You weren't surprised. From what you predicted, some might think you had access to their inner council."

Sandegarde's words suggested that she'd had sources high in certain minis-tries, and still might, either Security or Health and Education, because those were the ministries to which Obreduur had conveyed Dekkard's predictions.

"I don't know what their leadership structure is. I just pointed out obvious weaknesses. Someone else could easily have done so."

"Yet no one did. Why not?"

"I don't know that. Some midlevel official could easily have done so and been ignored or overruled. In fact, I'd be amazed if that didn't happen. I can't believe that someone in Security didn't know."

"That's possible," Sandegarde agreed pleasantly. "It does suggest that from whom a warning comes is as important as its accuracy. There's a danger there, though. If one is often accurate, the personal results when one is not can be severe, if not devastating."

"I imagine that's why many officials—or even councilors—hesitate to pre-dict."

"You could have a bright future, Steffan, especially if you don't reach too high too quickly."

"I'll keep that in mind."

"I imagine you will." Sandegarde turned her head toward the approaching server. "I do believe our orders are about to arrive. Tell me, how did you find life at the Military Institute after being an artisan?"

The abrupt shift told Dekkard that it was likely that Sandegarde had dis-covered what she most wanted to know, or to convey, and that the remainder of the lunch would be more pleasant. *Maybe, but you'll need to be cautious with every word.* "Not all that much different behind the superficial appear-ances. Everything had to meet standards and be accomplished on time. There was always something new to learn and then master. And there was a lot of plain hard work, much of it seemingly unnecessary."

Dekkard waited until Sandegarde began to eat before he took a bite of the chicken. It wasn't as tasty as usual. *Or is that you?* After a bite or two, he asked, "How do you see the difference between the iron and steel industry and Council politics?"

"That's an interesting question. My answer would be similar to what you just said. Both produce something necessary for Guldor. Steel supports every large building, every ship, every steamer or steam lorry. Laws and regulations support and hold society together. Weakness in either hurts people and society as a whole."

"Yet most people think of steel as more necessary than politics," Dekkard pointed out. "Even some councilors, I imagine."

"That's a necessary illusion, Steffan. Think about it."

"It's an illusion that the New Meritorists would destroy in their desire for personal accountability."

"That's why they need to be annihilated. Not merely stopped. Totally removed. Otherwise the issue will keep coming up."

"Their grand illusion is that personal voting accountability will solve everything."

"Won't it?" Sandegarde smiled sardonically. "What's it like, being a decorative plasterer?"

"Like everything else. A lot of work on a great deal of detail that most people don't even notice—unless it's done badly—and more time spent on preparation and cleanup than on the actual work."

From there the remaining conversation became more superficial, from how the weather seemed unseasonably cold far too early to how many entrées on the dining room menu were good enough to be eaten more than infrequently.

Dekkard returned to his desk on the Council floor just before the first bell. Obreduur immediately called the Council into session, and Haarsfel called up the next section of the proposed appropriation act—that of the Justiciary.

Throughout the voting, Dekkard mulled over the conversation with Sandegarde, but the only definitive items were her observation that someone wanted to kill him and her advice—or warning—not to reach too high too quickly.

As if you'd even reached, when being a councilor was something dropped on you. Yet clearly many on the Council believed that Dekkard had somehow orchestrated his selection. *Another illusion that they want to believe in? But why?*

Even before the session finished, at a third past fifth bell, Dekkard had located Erskine Mardosh and moved the moment the gavel came down. Since Mardosh paused for a moment, Dekkard reached him just as he turned to leave.

"Steffan, what brings you looking for me?"

"The hope that we could lunch tomorrow. I have a matter of possible interest, and even if it's not—particularly if it's not—your advice would be welcome." Seeing what he perceived as apprehension, Dekkard added, "I'm not trying to sell or influence anything except possibly your concern for Guldor."

"You could just come to my office, you know?"

"I could, but I'd rather it be seen as more casual."

"Then we'll have lunch. The Premier says you have interesting ideas."

"Thank you, sir."

"Erskine will do, Steffan. I can see respect without honorifics."

"Then, tomorrow."

"Tomorrow it is." The older councilor smiled and turned.

Dekkard slowly made his way to the councilors' lobby and then out into the main corridor, where Avraal and Gaaroll stood waiting.

"You're one of the last ones out," said Avraal. "What did you stop to arrange?"

"Lunch tomorrow." Dekkard offered a tired smile. "This afternoon was all about the Justiciary. How was your day?" Dekkard began to walk toward the courtyard.

Avraal kept pace with him. "I spent most of it listening as Carlos talked to various people about various matters. It was likely more interesting than voting on amendments."

Dekkard nodded. That meant that Minz wasn't back from wherever he'd gone. "My formalwear, suits, shirts, and overcoat should be ready, and so should your new overcoat. The way the weather's been, I think I'm going to need the heavier suits and the overcoat sooner than I thought." As he saw the hint of a smile, he added, "But not sooner than you did."

As they left the Council and entered the courtyard, Dekkard definitely felt the chill. "Nincya, do you sense anything?"

"Nothing that strong, sir."

When they reached the office, the only one there was Roostof.

"Holding the post, Svard?"

"Someone needed to," replied the legalist cheerfully, "and I have fewer commitments than most of the staff. It also gave me a chance to read through Luara's draft legislation. It's quite good."

"Excellent. I look forward to seeing it." Then Dekkard smiled warmly, and, for some reason finding himself thinking of Safaell's daughter Bettina, went on to say, "We really should do something about that lack of commitments— besides more work, that is." After he'd spoken, he wondered why he had, given he'd never even seen or met the young woman.

"You've got more than enough to deal with, sir," replied Roostof with a tone of amusement.

"More than likely," agreed Dekkard, "but shut off the lamps. You can walk out with us. That way, I'll know you're not working too late."

"Just a moment, then." Roostof ducked into the staff office, and then into Dekkard's. In moments, the only lit lamp was the one on the wall beside the entry door, and Roostof had donned a heavy brown overcoat.

Gaaroll opened the outer door, and Avraal and Dekkard stepped into the corridor. Roostof followed, after shutting off the last lamp, and then locked the office door.

"Where do you live, Svard?" asked Avraal.

"Westpark, in the Old Citadel. They turned it into flats several years ago. I bought one when they were cheap. That was when Westpark was a little . . . paler . . . than it is now. More space than I could have gotten anywhere, and it's only a short walk to Imperial Boulevard. One covered parking slot came with the flat. You could almost fit two of my little Ferrum in the slot."

"Citadel's getting close to turning swell," said Gaaroll.

"I was fortunate," admitted Roostof. "I couldn't afford what the flats go for now."

"I wouldn't say fortunate," said Avraal. "Prescient is more accurate."

When they reached the grand staircase, Dekkard saw two men near the bottom of the staircase, then realized that the two were Schmidtz and Fernand Stoltz. "There's Councilor Schmidtz with Fernand Stoltz. Svard, did you ever deal with Fernand?"

"When he was the chief legalist for the Public Resources Committee, I asked for some information about logging leases on Imperial lands. He was *less* than helpful. I managed to get what I needed from one of the clerks. I heard he had to go back to Councilor Schmidtz's personal staff as a junior legalist for a time. Now he's with a firm, Paarsens and something else. They represent Eastern Ironway. That's what I heard from Charmione Lundquist."

"From Councilor Sandegarde's office?" asked Avraal.

"Last time I heard, she was," replied Roostof.

Dekkard couldn't help but wonder at that seeming coincidence, right after his lunch with Vhiola Sandegarde, but with only sixty-six councilors, it wasn't surprising that staff legalists knew one another regardless of party. "What do you hear about Councilor Sandegarde?"

"Not much, really," replied Roostof. "She's supposed to be very sharp. She's an heiress to a big fortune, and that's about it."

Dekkard wouldn't have expected much more. Staffers who survived working for councilors tended not to offer much about those they worked for.

Outside, the wind had picked up, and, as Roostof headed for the staff parking area, Dekkard couldn't help but shiver. He definitely looked forward to getting his new heavy overcoat.

"A good night to sit before a fire and read," suggested Avraal as they crossed the street to the covered parking.

"After we pick up all my new clothes, and a hot meal," agreed Dekkard.

41

Every time I cross the Long Bridge of Asula, either way, in light or in darkness, although I seldom walk in the rain or snow, I cannot help but be reminded that it is not only the oldest bridge in the city of Averra, but that it contains no mortar, no wood, nothing but stone, and each stone is so finely fitted that one cannot place the thinnest of blades between those stones anywhere on the bridge or its roadway, even where the years of passage by carts and wagons have worn faint grooves in the stone.

That is one kind of strength, the solidity of form fitted so perfectly to function that no outside or foreign aids or supports are needed. So often we reinforce what does not need it. Or we under-design a bridge or building and then surround or infuse it with foreign supports or reinforcements. Or perhaps the design and construction are well-suited, but fears of inadequacy spur the addition of unnecessary appurtenances.

Both life and cities can be hampered by such thoughts and by superfluous supports that we convince ourselves are necessary. Some cities need walls. Some do not, but three layers of walls may weaken a city more than relying on one strong and well-built and perfectly designed wall. The extra walls will empty the Treasury, and those building them will be tempted to take shortcuts, feeling that no enemy will dare to attack a city with three walls. Yet building three walls may proclaim that the city possesses great wealth, enticing attacks that a single wall would not . . .

AVERRA
The City of Truth
Johan Eschbach
377 TE

42

ONCE again, on Furdi morning, Dekkard and Avraal woke early, although Dekkard wasn't that enthused about yet another day of seemingly unending votes.

"You were rather closemouthed about your upcoming lunch today," Avraal said as she adjusted the blouse she'd just donned.

"You thought we should read last night."

"You almost fell asleep."

"I meant to tell you when we were alone, but it slipped my mind."

Avraal smiled. "Other things didn't."

"You're right. Lunch is with Erskine Mardosh. He's the chair—"

"You don't have to explain who he is, dear. How much are you going to tell him, and to what end?"

"I had no intention of mentioning the assassination attempts. I was thinking about mentioning the trio at lunch on Findi and, if he seems interested, Markell's disappearance."

"What makes you think he might be interested?"

"What I told you about the earlier lunch, when he said that the reason he got involved—"

"—in politics was because it was too dangerous for a guild official to look into Siincleer Shipbuilding," continued Avraal. "He was cautious then. He may not have changed. Only talk about Markell in generalities. Not by name."

"You're right. He still might be willing to supply information we can use. That was one reason I wanted to meet him over lunch during voting, rather than going to his office."

"I'm sure at least a few councilors will notice, including Bassaana and Vhiola Sandegarde."

"Let's just hope they get the wrong idea." He started toward the bedroom door to head downstairs and ready Avraal's café, then turned back to look at her again.

She smiled. "You look good—and very distinguished—in that suit."

"I should. You essentially picked it out, and your taste is excellent, and I have enough sense to realize that." Dekkard grinned, then left the bedroom.

Emrelda was still at the breakfast room table, and Gaaroll entered just after Dekkard poured two mugs of café and set them on the table.

"Another early morning?"

"Not by your schedule," replied Dekkard amiably. "I'm so looking forward to sitting and waiting, voting, sitting and waiting, when almost all of the votes are already determined."

"Then why does the Council have all those votes?" asked Gaaroll.

"Because Council rules require recorded votes on appropriations and any amendments, and because the party or parties on the losing side want their positions on the record so they can bring up votes that are advantageous in the next election."

"Posturing." Gaaroll snorted.

"Also known as telling people where you stand," replied Dekkard.

"Most folks just want to be paid fair, eat well, and have a decent place to sleep."

"Some also want work that's meaningful," added Emrelda, after which she stood. "I'll have to work a little later, and I haven't had time to shop."

"Then why don't we go to Elfredo's tonight?" asked Dekkard, although the question was really rhetorical.

"I'm good with that," replied Emrelda.

"Good with what?" asked Avraal as she entered the breakfast room and glanced toward her sister.

"Eating at Elfredo's tonight," said Emrelda, "since everyone will be working late."

Avraal merely nodded, then sat down at the table and slowly took a sip of café.

Dekkard went to get the croissants and quince paste from the cooler.

Less than two-thirds of a bell later, Dekkard pulled on his new overcoat, and, thinking about his lunch with Mardosh, he remembered to retrieve the copy of the anonymous letter Emrelda had received, likely from a patroller in Siincleer, along with the article from the *Siincleer Star* and the letter from Jaime Minz. He slipped all three into his gray leather folder, then headed out to the garage.

Although the sky was clear, a cold wind blew out of the northwest. Dekkard was more than glad for his new overcoat and the new heavier dark gray wool suit he wore.

Neither Avraal nor Gaaroll sensed any significant emotions on the way to the Council Office Building, and that bothered Dekkard. He couldn't believe that whoever had been after him had just given up.

Except Minz is out of town. Did he decide to make it personal? Couldn't he get anyone to take it on after the sniper who "fell" out of the tree? Or is something else afoot?

When Dekkard neared the Council Office Building, he said, "I assume you'll be taking the Gresynt."

"That's a good assumption. Votes until fifth bell?"

"That's also a good assumption."

Dekkard drove up to the west entrance, where he stopped and turned the steamer over to Avraal. Then he and Gaaroll walked inside and up to the office.

"No messages, sir," said Margrit, "but there's a letter on top that looks like an invitation."

"Thank you."

The envelope on top of the others was indeed an invitation, one that Dekkard read carefully.

The Advisory Committee of the Guilds of Guldor
requests the honor of your presence at its
annual Yearend Reception
Findi, 36 Fallend 1266
2nd–5th Bells

Because he was a Craft councilor, he and Avraal definitely couldn't refuse the invitation. In a way he wondered why he hadn't seen any others, but then, why would he? Corporacions hosted most of the receptions and parties, and, except for Jaime Minz, Dekkard didn't know anyone in any corporacions.

After setting the invitation aside, he immediately set to work on reading and signing the replies to various letters and petitions, among which was his reply to Emilio Raathan. When he finished those, he began to read the letters that had just arrived. The first was yet another complaint about the excessive freight rates charged by Guldoran Ironway as a result of their formulae that incorporated both space and weight. The next letter protested the excessive message charges for heliograms, followed by one requesting higher taxes on imported cotton because cheap Sargassan cotton hurt the flax growers around Gaarlak.

Dekkard picked up the fourth letter warily, noting that it had a return address in Gaarlak and an Imperial postmark, but no name above the return address. He extracted the single sheet and began to read.

Councilor Dekkard—

As a recently selected member of the Council of Sixty-Six, you cannot but be aware that the three-party, hidden-vote system that decides the laws of Guldor is the remnant of an archaic approach to good government. Surely, the protests of the past year and the unbridled corruption of the previous Commercer government should give you pause, as well as the election of a Craft councilor from Gaarlak for the first time in more than three decades.

The people of Guldor demand change, fundamental change, a change that goes beyond a shift in which archaic party controls the Council. The present Council is running out of time if it wants a peaceful change to the Great Charter. The people will have change, and personal accountability by each and every councilor for all of their votes. This change can be peaceful—or otherwise.

The choice is up to you.

There was no signature.

Dekkard lowered the letter. While he agreed with the need for change, he still didn't see how the "personal accountability" of revealing individual votes would make any basic change. At best it would lead to a struggle between popularity and marks, with no real accountability.

He finished going through the incoming mail, then wrote a careful acceptance to the Advisory Committee, which he took with the invitation to Margrit. "If you'd message this reply to the Advisory Committee."

"I'll take care of it, sir."

"Thank you." Because he wanted a word with Roostof, he carried the mail to the senior legalist, then asked, "Did you finish going over Luara's draft?"

"I did, sir. There were a couple of little details. She's reworking the backup material for you now. It shouldn't be more than a day or so, unless you need it sooner."

"I'd like it, but there's no rush. It needs to be good to get Haarsfel even to look at it, and he likely won't until after we finish the appropriations."

After leaving Roostof, Dekkard departed for the Council floor with Gaaroll. He didn't wear his overcoat, but the heavier gray wool suit was warm enough that he didn't get more than mildly chilled crossing the courtyard to the Council Hall.

Almost precisely at fourth bell, Haarsfel brought the Council into session to finish votes on the last amendments to the Justiciary section of the appropriations proposal. Five amendments later, all proposed by the Commerce Party and all defeated, and the final vote on the Justiciary section as a whole, Obreduur recessed the Council for the midday break.

Dekkard stood, glancing around, then made his way toward Mardosh, who eased toward Dekkard. The two walked to the councilors' dining room.

After the two were seated and had ordered, Mardosh asked, pleasantly, "What was it you wanted to talk about?"

"A rather strange set of occurrences that might seem merely coincidental, but which I hoped you might be able to shed some light on. As you know, the New Meritorists obtained a rather substantial amount of dunnite in some fashion, which they used to destroy some fifteen regional Security offices. There are exactly three sources from which they could have obtained that much dunnite—the Navy, Northwest Industrial Chemical, and Suvion Industries. Given the Navy's paperwork and administrative structure, and the fact that the only place where dunnite is handled in large blocs is at the munitions plant—"

"You think it was stolen from one of the two corporacions? I'd agree they're more likely."

"What's rather interesting is that at the Security Committee hearings, Manwaeren testified that the Navy reported a stolen steam lorry of dunnite, and he thought he was telling the truth. Further committee investigation revealed that the letter and report were perfect forgeries, which incensed the Navy. Also interesting is that former Premier Ulrich is now an associate vice-presidente of Suvion Industries, and his former Security Committee isolate and security aide is an assistant director of security for Northwest."

"All that is rather curious, Steffan, but without more evidence—"

"I know that, but, if you'd bear with me, there's a bit more." Dekkard paused while the server delivered their cafés. Then he extracted the letter from Minz from his gray folder and handed it to the older councilor. "I received this immediately after I became councilor."

Mardosh read the letter and frowned. "That's rather odd. Why would he even mention dunnite?" He returned the letter to Dekkard, who replaced it in the folder.

"Because I'd once asked him where the New Meritorists might have gotten the dunnite, I suspect, but that was before the elections. There's yet another odd aspect of all this." Dekkard related his brief encounter with Schmidtz, and then went on, "Last Findi, Avraal and I went shopping. After we finished, we had an early dinner at Estado Don Miguel."

"I've been there once or twice. It's quite good, if expensive. I hope it was for something special."

"Special for us. We'd been married just a month, but I happened to notice three men dining there. In fact, the three were Pohl Palafaux, Gerard Schmidtz, and Jareem Saarh, and Saarh was very upset to recognize us."

"How could you . . . ? Oh, of course, your wife."

"He remained upset even after they finished and left. All of that ties into something else, the question of the degree of corruption in military procurement." Dekkard summarized what Shuryn Teitryn had pulled together, with the exception of what had happened to Markell. "That brings me to the last instance. In this case, the senior project engineer vanished after discovering that the site supervisor used different specifications, ones that would have likely caused structural failure. The engineer summoned the head of his company. Before the presidente arrived, the engineer vanished. So did the supervisor." Dekkard told most of the rest of the details, without names and only identifying Emrelda as a patroller related to the senior engineer. "Then, last month the patroller received these, or rather, the originals of these."

Dekkard handed the older councilor the two sheets.

Mardosh read the letter and then the clipping, then handed them back. "The letter's unsigned. It was typed, probably on a patrol station typewriter, duplicated on a patrol copier."

"Those are my copies. The original was unsigned as well, but on patroller letterhead."

"Obviously, Steffan, you're not just telling a story. This requires a criminal investigation, and there's not enough here even for hearings that might unearth more."

"Three moderately senior patroller station chiefs, all investigating unscrupulous acts involving government contracts, were killed in one way or another. A senior engineer vanished, and the head of his engineering firm suffers a dubious heart attack on site. Councilor Palafaux is known to have strong ties to Siincleer Shipbuilding and Siincleer Engineering, while Councilor Schmidtz—"

"—is the senior Commercer on the Military Affairs Committee and was briefly chairman."

Dekkard smiled pleasantly, then asked, "Was I wrong to bring all of this to your attention?"

Mardosh shook his head. "I appreciate your doing so quietly. Despite the highly suggestive evidence that you've presented, and with what you obviously know about the Siincleer corporacions, until there's more hard evidence and a clear path to hearings, keeping this sort of information out of the newssheets is the only practical and safe course."

"I'd thought as much," replied Dekkard. "I also wondered what you could tell me about Siincleer Shipbuilding, such as who in particular to be wary of, or of other incidents that might bear on what we've already discussed."

Mardosh frowned once more, then glanced past Dekkard. "I believe we're about to be served."

Once the server presented Dekkard with his bowl of white bean soup, accompanied by a large dinner roll, and Mardosh with his bowl of onion soup, and then departed, Dekkard said politely, "You were about to say?"

"The Premier has concerns about proceeding too quickly in dealing with abuses by certain corporacions. So do I. What you have discovered is not unknown, but investigating those abuses can be perilous." Mardosh paused and took several spoonfuls of soup, which also held toasted bread chunks covered in melted white cheese.

Dekkard decided to sample his own soup, after which he said politely, "I understand that, but that presents a conundrum. We agree that such abuses need to be curbed. Yet, proceeding toward hearings or criminal Justiciary action is unwise without more evidence, but seeking more evidence is also unwise. Or do I misunderstand?"

"At present, that is the situation. I doubt that will remain so."

"Because of what the trial of the former Security ministers may reveal? I'm skeptical that the trial will reveal much more than is currently in the newssheets. Director Mangele hanged himself, and the director of special projects is nowhere to be found, which suggests to me that he's fled Guldor. Wyath and Manwaeren can lie about everything without changing the sentences they're likely to receive."

"Nothing remains the same, Steffan." Mardosh went back to his onion soup.

"That's true." *But sometimes the changes are so small that they might as well not occur, or they're for the worse.* "Do you think the presidente of Siincleer Shipbuilding will make some fatal mistake?"

"That's unlikely. Juan del Larrano makes few mistakes. He's very good at insulating himself from anything sordid. From what I understand, Pietro Venburg is the most senior official in the Siincleer corporacions who might know the details of anything improper."

"I've not heard of him." But then Dekkard had only belatedly realized that he'd heard of del Larrano. "Is Venburg the director of security?"

Mardosh smiled. "No. Corporacions operate by the rules. Or they're supposed to. Pietro Venburg is the vice-presidente for legal affairs of the parent corporacion. He's said to be an excellent legalist."

"I take it you met with him when you were involved with the guild?"

Mardosh shook his head. "Sr. Venburg wouldn't deign to meet with a guildmeister, let alone an assistant guildmeister. Back then, I only met with his assistant, Wilhelm Burnneto."

"And since then?"

"I've met several times with Venburg, and I've passed polite words with del

Larrano, at a banquet or two, and some other events. We never talk politics. It's all very polite."

"You make it sound as though there's no point in talking substance with anyone from Siincleer. I assume that's because there isn't."

Mardosh smiled sardonically. "That's also a good assumption. Siincleer Shipbuilding will only do what it's required to do by the law and by the Navy inspectors. They're not about to change unless required by law. If the corporacion can cut corners, it will, but never on anything major for the military. Major flaws or unfair competition can get a business banned from even competing for contracts for ten years." Mardosh's smile returned, even more sardonic. "For some reason no one has ever been able to prove unfair competition."

"That explains a great deal." Especially why Markell had been so upset. Navy inspectors would have caught the lack of adherence to the basic specifications. If Halaard Engaard had been allowed to live and proved Siincleer had been sabotaging Engaard Engineering, that could have cost Siincleer ten years' worth of highly lucrative contracts. "I take it that the problem is coming up with proof."

"I've been looking for hard proof for years. There are always pieces, but never enough." Mardosh's expression turned somber. "Against the Siincleer corporacions, there aren't any second chances. They'll sacrifice anyone in the corporacion to make sure that another corporacion doesn't even get a first chance."

"The destruction of smaller corporacions and mysterious deaths that always work to the advantage of corporacions like Siincleer or Haasan Design don't count as proof?" Dekkard thought he knew the answer, but he wanted to hear what Mardosh had to say.

"There has to be hard evidence tying someone to a deliberate and documented action or policy to the disadvantaging of the unfortunate competitor. So far, no one has managed to clear that hurdle."

"So how do you plan to handle the matter? Or do you?"

"I'm not ready to reveal anything except to say that, if anyone wants to take on the problem, the remedy has to be legislative, because I don't see anyone ever proving what most of the engineering and construction industry knows. The number of bodies you cite is far from all of them, and none of them even came close to succeeding. I'd also prefer that you keep what I'm saying to yourself for now."

"I will. You do make a very convincing point."

"I hope so, Steffan. You need to be patient in some matters. Not all of them, as you proved with Security reform. You need to know when to act and when not to. In the meantime, keep your information in a safe place. The time will come when it will be most useful."

Dekkard nodded. "I appreciate your advice, and your cautions about even approaching anyone in the Siincleer hierarchy."

"They're generally safe to approach in a social setting, so long as you avoid politics."

"That's often true with most people." Dekkard took his last spoonful of the white bean soup. While it had been a good choice for a cold day, he didn't quite finish it.

"Is there anything else you wish to talk over before we return to the floor?"

"How is the onion soup?"

"It's almost as good as the white bean soup, but lighter." Mardosh smiled. The remaining conversation was more cheerful.

Once Dekkard returned to the Council chamber, the afternoon proceeded much like every other afternoon that week. Haarsfel called up the next section of the appropriations, Workplace Administration. Small as the total amount of funding was, there were ten amendments, all by Commercers, and all attempted to cut back funding for various aspects of workplace safety, beginning with funding for inspectors' salaries and travel. The last amendment eliminated funds for a study of unsafe practices in the timber industry.

Dekkard saw Pajiin shaking his head when Haarsfel announced the amendment designed to eliminate the study, but, in the end, it failed. Only an amendment to reduce funding for farm wagon safety inspections passed. Dekkard could see that, given the continuing replacement of horse-drawn wagons by steam lorries.

Obreduur recessed the Council at three minutes past fifth bell, right after the vote on the entire Workplace Administration section.

Even so, Dekkard found both Gaaroll and Avraal outside the councilors' lobby.

"You're earlier today," said Avraal. "That will make Emrelda happy."

"It makes me happy, too. How was your day?"

"Complicated. We can talk later."

"The same here. But there is one thing before I forget. We have to make an appearance on Yearend at the Guilds' Advisory Committee annual Yearend reception. It's in the afternoon. We haven't talked about Yearend."

"Neither have Emrelda and I. That shouldn't be a problem."

The walk across the courtyard back to the Council Office Building didn't seem so cold as it had on Tridi, but as they neared the doors to the Council Office Building, Gaaroll said, "Really strong feelings just inside the Council Hall."

Avraal immediately hurried forward and opened the bronze door.

Dekkard quickly strode inside, followed by the other two, then turned to Gaaroll. "What sort of feelings? Black or red?"

"Some of each, but mostly red. They're gone now."

"Did someone die?"

"Didn't feel that way, sir. Not strong enough for a serious injury, I think."

"I don't sense anything unusual nearby," added Avraal.

Both Roostof and Margrit were in the anteroom when Dekkard, Avraal, and Gaaroll entered.

"How did it go, sir?" asked Roostof.

"The appropriations and I both survived for now." Dekkard grinned wryly. "One other thing—I'll need to talk to you and Shuryn in the morning before the votes start."

"Yes, sir. I'll make sure he knows as soon as he comes in."

"Good. Close the office as soon as we leave."

"We can do that, sir."

"We'll see you in the morning." Dekkard retrieved his overcoat from his office and donned it, then made sure he had the gray leather folder with the letters in it before he left the office.

The walk to the covered parking was without event, but when they reached the Gresynt, Avraal waited until Gaaroll entered the steamer and closed the door before telling Dekkard, "Minz is still out of town. We can talk later."

Dekkard remained cautious on the drive back to the house, and definitely on edge for the last few blocks, but neither empath sensed anything suggesting an attack. Since they were going out to eat, he left the Gresynt under the portico roof.

Emrelda, still in uniform, greeted them in the hall. "We should go now. It'll get crowded later."

Dekkard smiled and turned around.

Less than a sixth later, the four walked into the gray brick building that was Elfredo's. Heavy curtains covered the windows, muting the outside light and leaving the tavern dim, given that half the wall lamps weren't lit.

Dekkard had wondered if he'd be overdressed, but uniformed patrollers filled four or five tables, and several waved or gestured to Emrelda, who returned the gesture. As she led the way to one of the few vacant tables, Dekkard glanced at the blackboard with the specials listed. He didn't see the chicken rosara there, but there was chicken Jeeroh, which he'd never heard of, and the crayfish and mushroom ravioli.

They'd barely seated themselves before Lizbet, the older server, appeared. "Good to see you again. You never mentioned that that handsome fellow married your sister was a councilor." The server grinned.

"I thought it was better to be her husband than a councilor," said Dekkard cheerfully.

"Aye, and you'd be right 'bout that."

"Two Silverhills white, and two house pale lagers," said Emrelda. "I'll have the ravioli."

"Chicken piccata," said Avraal.

Gaaroll looked uncertain. After a long moment, Dekkard said, "What's chicken Jeeroh?"

"Fowl's stewed in peppered ale, not Atacaman peppers, but sweet peppers, then browned and served with a sweet cream sauce over noodles."

"I'll try it."

Gaaroll chose the chicken piccata.

In moments after taking the orders, Lizbet returned with the two glasses of wine and the two beakers of ale.

"The Special Agents don't come here, do they?"

"Elfredo doesn't like them, and neither do most patrollers," replied Emrelda. "Would you come if you were one of them?"

"Not often, but the food is good."

"What they would get would be bland. Not bad, just bland."

Dekkard could see that. "Have you seen many of them lately?"

"Special Agents? Hardly."

"How do you think they're taking the coming change?"

"Who knows? They never talk around us regular patrollers, and now that they won't be special—just regular investigators without firearms—they're almost never in the station. We haven't seen one in the last week. That's fine with all of us." Emrelda paused. "When will they be gone?"

"If they adhere to the law, no later than the tenth of Winterfirst. It could be earlier, since the law reads no later than the tenth." Dekkard had the feeling that even those who chose to resign would wait until the last possible moment, just to make matters difficult for the three ministries involved.

"You don't think they'd disobey, do you?" asked Emrelda.

"Those bastards would, if they could," muttered Gaaroll.

Dekkard smiled momentarily, then said, "They might all resign before they're transferred. I worry about some of them keeping their weapons. I just have the feeling that it won't be a smooth transition."

"How could you possibly say that, dear," asked Avraal sweetly.

"You're right," replied Dekkard, his voice as earnest as he could make it. "Those ever-so-loyal Special Agents would *never* engage in any illegal activity, such as breaking and entering, sabotaging gas pipes, or shooting councilors. How could I possibly believe that?"

"The way you said that," replied Avraal, "if you weren't an isolate you might actually have a future as a courtroom legalist. Didn't Councilor Baar say something like that?"

"But he meant it as a compliment," protested Dekkard, mock-plaintively.

All three women laughed.

43

QUINDI morning found Dekkard awake early, thinking about the correlation between the absence of would-be assassins and Minz's absence from Machtarn, even though he well knew that correlation didn't necessarily prove causation.

Still, it is interesting. He also wondered just where Minz had gone. His gut instinct said that the former security aide had taken the ironway to Siincleer, to Siincleer Shipbuilding in particular. Minz had been gone for at least several days in the middle of the week, suggesting that he had gone on corporacion matters, while the fact that he was an influencer suggested that the matter involved the Council and affected both corporacions, and that Minz had gone in response to someone at Siincleer.

All of which tells you nothing. At that thought, Dekkard slowly eased out of bed and began to ready himself for the day, which would be long by the time services were over and they ate. After dressing, he picked up the envelope he'd prepared the night before.

Avraal was ready for breakfast and actually preceded him down the steps. She also carried an envelope.

"My envelope or yours first?" he asked.

"Yours."

When they reached the hall off the breakfast room, Dekkard said, "Emrelda, could I have a moment, please?"

Looking puzzled, Emrelda rose from the table and walked out into the hall.

Dekkard extended his envelope to Emrelda. "Happy birthday."

Emrelda looked at the envelope.

"Open it," urged Avraal. "Carefully."

Emrelda did so, easing out the black and gilt-edged card.

"Read it," said Dekkard. "It is for you."

Her mouth opened. "For me? This is an invitation to the Council's Yearend Ball."

"Each councilor has one, and only one, guest invitation."

"Steffan didn't ask me," said Avraal. "He told me."

"But, you could—"

"No," said Dekkard gently. "It's for you." He smiled. "I'm told you have several gowns that will be suitable."

Emrelda looked from Dekkard to her sister, and back to him. "Thank you." Her voice was uneven.

Dekkard eased back and let Avraal move closer to Emrelda.

Avraal extended her envelope to Emrelda. "Happy birthday. You already had your present, but you deserve something on the day itself."

"You didn't have to. The knives . . ."

"I wanted to, and it's from the heart."

Dekkard could see that both of them were close to tears and eased slightly farther away.

"You wrote?" Emrelda could barely get the words out.

"I did. I shouldn't have stopped."

Emrelda wrapped her arms around her younger sister.

After a long hug and more than a few sniffles, the two separated.

Emrelda cleared her throat. "You . . . two . . . this . . . it's special . . ." After another moment, she said, "I'll probably be late, but I don't care. Not too much." She hugged Dekkard and murmured, "Thank you." Then she embraced Avraal again.

Dekkard swallowed, glad he didn't have to say anything.

Some minutes later, and after Emrelda had left for work, he asked Avraal, "The envelope?"

"Just a birthday poem of sorts. I used to do that when we were younger. I haven't in a while. I should have. I told her we'd take her to dinner. She refused. So I said you and I would fix dinner."

Dekkard put his arms around her. "You're a good sister."

"I could have been better."

"You are now. You can't change the past. You're changing the present. That's what counts." He paused. "I didn't say anything about del Larrano and Venburg to Emrelda."

"Don't. There's no point in it until we know a lot more."

Dekkard nodded, then led her to the breakfast room, where Gaaroll was finishing a croissant, and then fixed their cafés.

After that, the only disruption to an otherwise uneventful breakfast and drive to the Council Office Building was when Gaaroll sensed strong feelings—and then death—which turned out to be an accident on Imperial Boulevard, where a small and battered Ferrum had turned in front of a massive steam lorry that flattened the much smaller Ferrum and its driver.

Avraal once more took the Gresynt, and Gaaroll and Dekkard walked the short distance to the building doors through the chill but comparatively light wind and from there up to the office.

"You have two messages, sir," said Margrit cheerfully as Dekkard entered.

"Thank you." Dekkard took both envelopes, then opened the envelope stamped "From the Premier" and began to read.

With votes on amendments on two major sections of the annual appropriations yet unaddressed, all councilors should plan on a full day of votes on Unadi, and possibly on Duadi and Tridi.

Dekkard just nodded and turned his attention to the second envelope, which bore only his name and title. Inside was a single card.

Steffan—

I appreciated very much your luncheon invitation and the engrossing conversation we shared. Your insights are, unfortunately, in advance of the information necessary to bring them before the committee at present, but I will keep you informed and trust you will do the same for me.

The signature was simply "Erskine."

Dekkard nodded, then looked back to Margrit. "I need to talk to Svard and Shuryn first or as soon as Shuryn arrives. Then I'll deal with the replies." He smiled. "I know you know that, but I feel better when I explain."

"I understand that, sir. I was always explaining to Anna and Karola."

Dekkard then walked to the door into the staff office. Bretta and Roostof were the only ones there, not that the others had to be. "Svard, just bring Shuryn with you when he arrives."

"Yes, sir."

Dekkard turned and entered his office, where he shed his overcoat and hung it on the hook on the back of the door to the small washroom and lavatory. Then he settled behind the desk. Because he'd thought about what Emrelda had said the night before, he quickly composed a message to Obreduur telling him that in the last week, Special Agents had not shown up in a number of patrol stations, but also saying he had no idea what that meant, only that Obreduur should know.

After having Margrit dispatch the message, he started reading and signing the replies awaiting him. A sixth passed before Roostof and Teitryn entered. Dekkard gestured to the chairs in front of the desk.

"Sir?" offered Roostof once he was seated.

"I have no complaints with either of you. I had lunch yesterday with Councilor Mardosh, the chair of the Military Affairs Committee." Dekkard looked to Shuryn. "In your research so far, have you come across the names of Juan del Larrano or Pietro Venburg?"

"I know that Juan del Larrano is the presidente of Siincleer Shipbuilding. I don't recognize the other name."

"Pietro Venburg is the vice-presidente for legal affairs at Siincleer Shipbuilding. I understand his purview extends to Siincleer Engineering. I need to know more about both, as well as any publicly available information on any contacts and associations. Again, it's vital that no one know I'm looking. I mean *no one* outside of this room—except Ritten Ysella-Dekkard. Is that clear?"

"Yes, sir." Despite his agreement, Teitryn looked uncertain.

"Neither individual likes others knowing more about him. If they find out that a councilor is looking for this sort of information, it could make accomplishing any reform of engineering contracting and construction much more difficult, if not impossible." Dekkard smiled pleasantly. "Our job is going to be hard enough without making it more difficult."

"Ah, sir?"

"How difficult? We finally accomplished Security reform, but in the process, three councilors were killed, as well as several regional councilors, a score of Special Agents, and several hundred others." Dekkard was exaggerating slightly, but he had the feeling that Teitryn didn't quite understand.

"If matters go wrong with trying to reform engineering contracting, it could be just as . . . messy."

The younger aide actually swallowed. "I see."

Dekkard doubted that. "That's all for that, right now. Svard, I have another matter for you. Shuryn, you can go."

"Yes, sir."

Once the door closed, Roostof smiled sadly. "He still doesn't quite get it. What was the other matter?"

"That was the other matter. In dealing with Security and the New Meritorists, Premier Obreduur was almost killed several times. So were Avraal and I. This won't likely be that obvious, but Shuryn's already aware of a good half score deaths likely arranged by the Siincleer corporacions. That doesn't seem to have made an impression on him. Take him to lunch at the staff cafeteria and see if you can get the point across."

Roostof offered an amused smile. "I can do that."

"Thank you."

After Roostof left, Dekkard went back to signing or changing replies. He even managed to read through the just-arrived letters and petitions before leaving for the Council Hall with Gaaroll.

"Moderately strong feelings coming toward us," murmured Gaaroll after they descended the staircase and walked toward the courtyard doors.

The only people approaching were Kaliara Bassaana and her two security aides.

"You mean the councilor?" asked Dekkard quietly.

"Yes, sir."

"We'll see what she has to say." Dekkard slowed his steps and, when Bassaana neared, said, "Headed to the Council Hall?"

"Where else, Steffan?"

Dekkard laughed gently and replied, "With you, I'd be reluctant to guess."

Amelya Detauran stepped ahead and opened the courtyard door for both councilors.

Dekkard followed Bassaana but stepped up beside her, while Gaaroll dropped back to keep pace with Amelya Detauran and Elyssa Kaan.

"You've been more social lately, Steffan, and it hasn't been just with Craft councilors."

"I knew no councilors, even casually, except Obreduur," replied Dekkard. "I'm just trying, bit by bit, to get to know people."

"Such as Yordan Farris."

"He was polite to me at committee meetings."

"And?" pressed Bassaana, with a hint of the sardonic in her voice.

"He was polite to me at committee meetings."

Bassaana laughed quietly. "You do have a way of making yourself clear without ever using derogatory terms."

"I try to keep those in reserve."

"I saw you eating with Gerhard Safaell the other day."

"He wanted to talk about the legal construction of the Security reform proposal."

"I could see that." Bassaana's tone conveyed a hint of doubt that legalese was the only topic discussed, and when Dekkard did not immediately reply, she went on. "You've lunched with quite a few councilors."

"Just to know them a little better and to get any advice they would like to share."

"Was there any common thread in their advice?"

"There was a certain emphasis on patience," Dekkard said dryly.

"Everyone sees patience as a virtue in others. Sometimes, it is."

"I'm still trying to sort that out."

As they approached the bronze doors to the Council Hall, Bassaana smiled. "It's always interesting to talk with you, Steffan, even for short periods of time."

"Thank you. I've learned from you as well."

For a fraction of an instant, Dekkard thought he caught an indication of surprise. He certainly hoped so, as he stepped back and let Bassaana enter the Council Hall first.

When Dekkard left Gaaroll and entered the councilors' lobby, Tomas Pajiin immediately moved toward him.

"What's on your mind, Tomas?"

"Lunch. I hope you'd join Julian and me."

"Julian? Julian Andros, from Zeiryn?"

"Is there another Julian in the Council?" Pajiin grinned.

"Not that I know of, and I'd be happy to join you both."

A few minutes later, Dekkard sat down behind his desk in the Council chamber and waited for Obreduur to reconvene the Council and for Haarsfel to bring up the next section of the appropriations—Security and Public Safety.

Even so, Dekkard knew that there would be more than a few amendments.

By the time the Council recessed just after midday, there had been votes on six amendments, four of them minor adjustments. The fifth amendment, offered by the Commercers, would have added funds to rebuild the destroyed regional Security offices. Dekkard voted against it, as did all the other Craft councilors, but all the Commercers voted for it, which surprised him, as did all but five Landors, which concerned him even more. While the amendment was defeated 32–34, the vote suggested a deep-seated desire by many for a stronger Security force than permitted under Dekkard's reform.

The last amendment would have appropriated additional funds to pay a healthy "severance" to Special Agents who chose not to accept investigative positions at either the Treasury or Justiciary Ministry. Dekkard felt it represented a blatant attempt to reward Special Agents. The vote there went along straight party lines, the nineteen Commercers for, and all the Craft and Landor councilors against.

After announcing the results of the last vote, Obreduur recessed the Council until first bell. Dekkard stood and left his desk. In moments, Pajiin and Andros joined him, and the three walked to the councilors' dining room.

After being seated, all three ordered the duck cassoulet and café.

Dekkard glanced around the dining room, catching sight of Schmidtz eating with Kuuresoh, hardly unexpected since they were two of the three Commercers on the Military Affairs Committee. Breffyn Haastar listened to Kharl Navione, while Kaliara Bassaana lunched with Harleona Zerlyon. *That has to be an interesting conversation.*

"Friggin' Commercers," muttered Andros. "How could they even offer that last amendment?"

"How could they not?" replied Dekkard sardonically.

Andros looked almost offended. "That was a payoff attempt. Nothing more."

"Exactly," replied Dekkard. "The Special Agents have been doing dirty work for the Commercers for years. Reforming Security stopped them from being paid by the Council for that, and the Commercers had to offer something to indicate support."

"That's the point," replied Andros. "Anyone with brains knows that. Why were the Commercers so blatant about it?"

"Because those who know won't support them anyway," Pajiin said, "and because they don't want disgruntled Special Agents going after them."

"They wouldn't do that. The Commercers and the corporacions are all that they've got behind them."

"All?" Pajiin imbued the single word with heavy sarcasm. "That's most of the marks in Guldor."

"Most of those marks are filthy," muttered Andros. "My brother's a patroller first, and Security headquarters ordered him and the others in his station to attack the Meritorist demonstrators last Summerend."

"What happened?" asked Pajiin.

"The captain claimed the orders arrived late. That's what Lendrew told me. No one got shot. The Specials were really pissed." Andros looked to Dekkard. "Do you know why the Premier didn't discipline the Specials who conducted those unauthorized raids?"

"The director who ordered the raids fled Guldor after ordering them. I imagine there'd be a problem in disciplining agents for following orders, even unauthorized orders."

"The Specials are all bastards. They did what they wanted. They all feel so superior to the regular patrollers. Be glad when they're all transferred." Andros paused. "When does that happen?"

"Sometime in the next two weeks. It has to be done before the tenth of Winterfirst."

"Should have been sooner," said Andros.

"That was the best Steffan could do," replied Pajiin. "He had to fight everyone to get a date that soon. The Commercers wanted three months."

"They would."

"We can't do anything about it now." Pajiin stopped as the server arrived with the three duck cassoulets. After the server left, he turned back to Andros. "How are things working out with Chairman Safaell and the Waterways Committee?"

"He knows the law. He should—he was a legalist for the Boatmens Guild. He's scheduled hearings on compliance with water safety laws. Don't know that it'll do any good."

"Hearings are a start," replied Pajiin.

From what Dekkard gathered from the rest of the meal, Pajiin's only purpose for asking Dekkard to join him and Andros was to get Andros and Dekkard together. If there was another agenda, that would come later.

Once Dekkard returned to the floor, the votes on amendments to the Security section of the proposed appropriations continued.

To his surprise, one amendment called for a substantial funding increase for the River Patrol, a separate agency originally under the former Security Ministry but now part of the new Ministry of Public Safety. Their mission involved patrolling the Rio Doro to halt smuggling and undesirables from illegally crossing the river between Atacama and Guldor.

The rationale for the amendment was that the combination of Guldor's unseasonably cold and wet autumn and Atacama's brutally hot and dry summer would increase smuggling and the numbers of "undesirable" people fleeing Atacama. Dekkard didn't pretend to understand all the dynamics or economics of smuggling across the southern border, but if more smugglers and people fled Atacama, then the River Patrol would likely need additional resources. The amendment passed with fifty votes.

Most of the other amendments were Commercer attempts to increase Public Safety funding in ways designed to preserve the previous structure. All those were defeated. Even so, by fifth bell, with another five Public Safety amendments to go, when Obreduur recessed the Council until fourth bell on Unadi morning, Dekkard felt exhausted, but since it was Quindi, he needed to sign the responses prepared by his staff.

He was about to leave the chamber when Obreduur motioned to him.

Dekkard immediately joined the Premier on the dais.

"I got your message," said Obreduur. "Do you know anything else?"

"No, sir. It just struck me as odd, and that the Special Agents might be up to something. I thought you should know."

"Thank you. I'll contact Minister Kuta and see what she knows." Obreduur offered a tired smile. "Have a good endday, Steffan."

"You, too, sir."

Dekkard turned and headed out of the chamber. Even going through responses or attending services was preferable to more votes. At least he thought it would be, provided that Jaime Minz hadn't returned to Machtarn.

44

BY the time Avraal and Dekkard went to sleep on Quindi night, after all the votes, services at the Hillside Trinitarian Chapel, and a late dinner, followed by a good bell of group speculation about what the next week might bring, and what the absence of Special Agents signified, he was more than ready for a good night's sleep. Because of a vague nightmare where unseen Special Agents kept shooting at him, he woke earlier than he needed to on Findi morning, a morning chill and blustery, but clear, or as clear as the sky over Machtarn ever was, with only a hint of coal smoke haze.

After breakfast, he took the Gresynt to run several errands. Despite the fact that Jaime Minz had apparently not returned to Machtarn, Dekkard asked Gaaroll to accompany him. The first stop was a hardware store on the east side of Erslaan, where he purchased a small can of putty. He thought about buying gray paint, but none of the paints came in less than bucket sizes. The second stop was the spirits shop, where he turned in the empty keg of Kuhrs for a full one and bought two cases of Silverhills white wine. Then came the grocer's, where he and Gaaroll followed the list that Emrelda and Avraal had jointly compiled, followed by the butcher shop.

After the two returned and unloaded everything from the Gresynt, Dekkard took the putty and prepared to go out to the garage and deal, on a temporary basis, with the bullet hole.

"What color is that putty?" asked Avraal.

"Pale gray. It was that or pale tan."

"Let me see."

"We'll have to go out to the garage. I need a screwdriver to open it."

"Fine. I'll come with you."

Once the two of them were in the chill garage, Dekkard used a screwdriver he'd found in Markell's toolbox to open the can of putty, and then a perfectly kept old plasterer's knife, also from the toolbox, to scoop out a glob of putty twice as large as what he thought he'd need. He held it up against the gray of the Gresynt and looked to Avraal.

"It's too light. It'll stand out even more," said Avraal. "Just wait here. I'll be right back." She turned and hurried out of the garage.

Dekkard wondered what she had gone to get, but knew that it wasn't the best idea to argue or question when she spoke in that tone of voice.

In less than a sixth, she returned carrying a small case no bigger than her hand, a small chipped plate that he'd never seen before in his recent weeks of washing dishes, and a tiny spoon.

"Put the putty on the plate," Avraal commanded.

Dekkard did so.

Using the small spoon, Avraal added a tiny bit of black from the small case. "Mix them together."

It took almost a third of a bell of minuscule additions of the black substance before Avraal nodded. "That should work."

After cutting and wedging a small piece of screen into place, Dekkard carefully filled the bullet hole with the now-dark-gray putty, then used a rag to wipe the excess off the painted metal of the steamer.

"It's a little duller than the lacquer finish," said Avraal, "but for now it will do."

"Except up close, you really can't tell," agreed Dekkard. "What was that you mixed into the putty?"

"Theatrical kohl. I knew Emrelda had some. And no, you don't want to ask."

Dekkard definitely decided not to ask. Instead, he sealed the can of putty, used the rag to clean off the plasterer's knife, and then replaced everything in the toolbox, setting the putty on the shelf next to the toolbox.

"What are you going to do now?" asked Avraal.

"I really need to write back to Naralta, and I might practice with the knives and give Gaaroll a lesson."

"Then Emrelda and I will go out for a bit. We'll fix something when we get back. We'll take her steamer."

A third of a bell later, Dekkard sat at the desk in the study, looking at a blank sheet of stationery, wondering how much to say in his reply to his sister. Finally, he began to write.

Almost a bell passed before he finished, and he reread the letter, his eyes especially taking in the parts where he'd tried to be careful about the uncertain state of affairs in Machtarn, and possibly in all of Guldor, without being misleading.

> . . . in time the Security reforms will reduce the ability of whichever party controls the Council, but at the moment, not that much has changed . . .
>
> . . . while former Minister Wyath and his temporary successor are now being tried, there's no way to hold to account all the individual Special Agents who followed orders clearly ordered without the approval of the Premier, and many of those agents are anything but pleased with the Security reforms enacted by the Council . . .
>
> . . . Avraal is splitting her time between her new position and helping to settle me into becoming a more effective councilor . . .

Dekkard shook his head, then signed the letter, and sealed it into the envelope he'd already addressed. Naralta would read between the lines. Hopefully, she'd get the sense of the current situation without being excessively alarmed.

For the next two bells, Dekkard took care of various neglected chores, such as polishing his boots and reorganizing his quarter of the large closet that he shared with Avraal, and practicing knife throwing with Gaaroll. After he put away the target and cleaned the knives, he was standing outside the kitchen, thinking about what else he needed to do, when he heard Emrelda's steamer come up the drive.

He moved into the hall, where he greeted his wife and her sister as they entered the house. "How was your outing? What did you do?"

Avraal smiled. "Not really much of anything, but we had a very good time."

"Just good girl-time," added Emrelda.

"I'm glad," replied Dekkard. "You two haven't had much time alone together in months."

"Longer than that," said Avraal, adding cheerfully, "Thank you, dear one."

"We'll have dinner in less than a bell," added Emrelda. "The chicken's been marinating all day, and it won't take that long for the rice and a salad."

"What's it marinating into?" asked Dekkard.

"Lime tarragon pepper cream chicken," replied Emrelda. "It's something new. I just hope it will be good."

"I'm sure it will be," said Dekkard.

"You haven't tasted some of my failures," said Emrelda wryly. "Now that you're family, you get to be experimented on."

"I'm sure it will be tasty."

"It will be edible," replied Emrelda. "As for tasty, we'll see."

Dekkard just smiled. As happy as the two seemed to be, edible would be more than good enough, although he doubted anything coming out of Emrelda's kitchen could be anything other than tasty.

45

WHEN he woke on Unadi morning, Dekkard hoped that he and Avraal could uncover enough to track down who was behind the attempts on his life. *It would be nice to sleep more easily.* Part of the problem was that he was now a councilor. If he didn't do that job, he wouldn't be a councilor long. But if he couldn't stop the attempts, his life expectancy was short.

He also hoped that the early risings would end or at least occur less frequently once the Council finished with the appropriations. *But something else will come up.*

With that less than optimistic thought, he eased out of bed, not without a more than fond look at Avraal, who was just beginning to rouse herself. He began his morning routine by drawing back the curtains and looking outside. The sky was dark and overcast, but the clouds were high, which meant no immediate rain.

When he reached the breakfast room, cafés in hand, he set them on the table, one at Avraal's place and one at his, then glanced at the morning edition of *Gestirn* on the side table.

"There's not much there," said Emrelda from where she sat. "The stories happen to be as gloomy as outside."

Dekkard didn't doubt Emrelda's summary, but glanced through the newssheet hurriedly, noting the brief article on the appropriations bill that only said the Council would likely send the measure to the Imperador by Tridi and another article on more crop failures caused by high winds and freezing rain in the southwest, particularly from Zeiryn to Encora and inland to the Silver Hills. There was a small article on the trial of Wyath and Manwaeren, but it didn't say much because, under law, trial proceedings couldn't be made public until both sides finished presenting their cases.

Breakfast was quiet and fairly quick, and before that long Avraal, Dekkard, and Gaaroll headed out in the Gresynt. All three were quiet and intent, given that there could be would-be assassins still trying to take out Dekkard, especially if Jaime Minz had returned to Machtarn. Even though Dekkard had no proof, he couldn't shake that feeling.

As he turned onto Imperial Boulevard from a side street north of Camelia Avenue, he immediately noticed a larger number of riders waiting for the omnibus, and as he drove closer to Council Avenue, the sidewalks looked more crowded than normal this early in the morning. Almost all the pedestrians walked north—the direction of the Imperial Palace. *Or the Council.*

"What can you sense about those people on the sidewalk? The ones in groups?"

"There are lots of feelings all along the boulevard," declared Gaaroll. "Some are strong, but not that strong."

"This looks like they're headed to the Council and the Square of Heroes," said Dekkard. "Probably another demonstration."

"There aren't any feelings that might be focused on Steffan, are there?" asked Avraal.

"I can't tell that. There are too many feelings." After a moment, Gaaroll added, "I can't sense any like a shooter."

Dekkard kept checking the mirrors, but no one seemed to be following, at least not close enough to take a shot. When he turned east on Council Avenue, people walked toward the Council buildings, but fewer, as if they were a vanguard. They all wore coats and jackets, and he didn't see any New Meritorist blue. *Under their coats until the last moment.*

Ahead on the right, about three blocks from the Council Office Building, he saw a steam lorry parked in the loading space in front of a nondescript building. One of the large rear doors to the van section was half open, and two men in brown coveralls and jackets appeared to be moving a pallet—or what looked like a pallet—toward the door, but Dekkard could barely make out what was on the pallet before he drove past the lorry. *Signs!*

With all those signs, it was unlikely the lorry contained weapons, because in most instances virtually all the demonstrators had been unarmed, with the exception of less than a handful of assassins at each of the Summerend demonstrations. Dekkard wasn't so sure that some of those hadn't been Commercer operatives. Still, a lorry with signs indicated marks and organization.

As they neared the Council buildings, Avraal said, "Just park. I'm staying close to you today."

"That'd be for the best," added Gaaroll.

As Dekkard pulled up to the guard post, and was waved into the covered parking, he commented, "I have to say I'm glad we had to be early today. That's going to be a large demonstration."

After getting out of the steamer, he could see more guards posted outside the Council Office Building than usual, indicating Guard Captain Trujillo's awareness of a possible demonstration. Dekkard had no doubt that the demonstrators would demand even more vigorously that the Council require the recording and public disclosure of the votes of individual councilors.

And when Obreduur declares that the Council is opposed, then what? Dekkard couldn't see the New Meritorists quietly fading away. So the question would likely be settled by force in some form, playing right into the hands of the Commercers. Except, if Dekkard happened to be right, the New Meritorists wouldn't have had dunnite and possibly even weapons without indirect aid from the Commercers.

He shook his head as he started across the side street to the Council Office Building.

"What are you thinking?" asked Avraal.

"That today isn't going to turn out well. Inevitably, the Commercers will make it worse. I just don't know how." He glanced toward the guards again. "Whatever it is, it will look obvious in hindsight, and that's going to reflect badly on the Council, Obreduur, and the Craft Party."

"Even if you knew, what could you do without evidence?" asked Avraal.

"If I knew, really knew, I might be able to think of something."

"And who would be willing to act without some proof?"

"I would, but without support, that would be futile, as we both know."

"Exactly."

Dekkard shook his head again, then nodded to the Council Guard as he neared the west doors to the building.

While the main floor corridor had a fair number of staffers, and a few councilors, headed one place or another, it felt too quiet to Dekkard. *But maybe that's just you.*

When he reached the office and stepped into the anteroom, Dekkard could see the look of relief on Roostof's face.

"Sir, in case you didn't know, there's likely going to be a demonstration outside the buildings this morning. We just got a message from the Premier's office."

"From the people we saw gathering, I got that impression."

"I didn't see any patrollers, sir, just Council Guards," replied Roostof.

"Neither did I." Dekkard didn't know whether it would be better—or worse—to have patrollers in addition to the guards. But he couldn't do anything about it, and it wasn't his responsibility. "Right now, all we can do is carry on. Are there any other messages?"

"No, sir," replied Margrit. "Not so far."

"I'll be out here," said Avraal quietly. "Do what you have to do."

That meant reading the incoming mail, and Dekkard entered his private office and settled into the chair behind the desk.

There looked to be close to fifty letters and petitions. Since he could do nothing about what might happen on Council Avenue, and since the letters weren't going to read themselves, he picked up the first letter, this time about the recent flooding on the Lakaan River northwest of Gaarlak and the need for higher levees.

Dekkard frowned. He hadn't heard about the flooding in his district, but with all the rain Naralta had mentioned, and the weather stories in *Gestirn*, that wasn't unexpected. The letter also pointed out that he needed someone in Gaarlak to keep him posted on such matters.

Something else you should have thought about earlier.

He continued through the stack, finding in the process three roughly similar letters, apparently with real names and addresses, asking him to consider the idea of greater personal voting accountability for councilors. They might have been New Meritorist plants, but how could he tell?

Dekkard had just finished going through the incoming mail when Avraal hurried into his office. "Gaaroll says that lots of people have been killed outside the Council. Shot, she thinks. Roostof went to find out more."

"Frig! I knew there'd be trouble." Dekkard stood and walked to the window, useless as he knew it would be because his office didn't overlook Council Avenue, and with all the windows closed against the cold, he hadn't heard anything either.

A good third of a bell passed before Roostof, breathing heavily, hurried into Dekkard's office. "According to the guards, several groups of uniformed patrollers appeared, then turned on the demonstrators and opened fire. The duty guard sergeant immediately ordered the guards to target the patrollers, but that took several minutes because the guards had to flank the patrollers to avoid shooting the demonstrators. Two guards appear to have been killed by the patrollers, and several others were wounded. The demonstrators are dispersing. The guard I talked to said that the guards killed at least two of the patrollers. There looked to be bodies everywhere on the sidewalks opposite the Council buildings."

"Thank you, especially for letting me know quickly." Dekkard turned to Avraal. "We're headed to the Premier's floor office—*now*." He started out the door, but instead of taking the main staircase, he took the staff staircase, thinking it might be faster.

There weren't any guards in the courtyard between the office building and the Council Hall, nor did he see anyone else. He heard muffled shouts, but nothing resembling shots. He looked toward Avraal. "How bad is it? Can you tell?"

"Too many wounded to count. I get the feeling there could be more than a hundred, possibly two hundred."

Two hundred? Dekkard winced but kept walking.

The single guard outside the Council Hall opened the door for the two of them and motioned them inside, clearly not wanting them in the courtyard.

When they reached the door to the Premier's floor office, the guard outside said, if deferentially, "The Premier's . . . rather occupied, sir."

"Tell him it's Councilor Dekkard with some information he needs to know now. It will take two minutes."

"Ah, sir . . . I can't do that. No one . . ." Abruptly, the guard blanched and staggered.

Dekkard knew why, but didn't look at Avraal. "Thank you. Now, if you'll excuse us." He stepped past the guard and into the outer office, looking at the secretary beside the door to the small private office. "Is he in there?"

"Guard Captain Trujillo's with him, Councilor."

"Excellent!" Dekkard walked past her, opened the door, and stepped inside.

Obreduur looked annoyed for a moment, then said, "What is it, Steffan?"

"The shooters were most likely Special Agents with the scarlet patches removed from their uniforms. They'll have killed enough unarmed New Meritorists to turn them against the new Council, either for being behind it or for failing to stop it. I don't know that for certain, but, as I messaged you on Quindi, no Special Agents were in patroller stations all of last week. If the Council Guards shot any, you could check their uniforms for signs of patch removal. There'd be stitching holes or unfaded fabric."

"Justiciary Minister Kuta didn't know about the missing Special Agents, and neither did the acting Security minister, but I haven't heard more. What else have you surmised?" asked Obreduur evenly.

"We haven't seen the last of the pilfered dunnite. I'd guess it will be used to maximum effect against the Council. How or when I couldn't say."

"Is that all?" asked Obreduur.

"That's all I know. There is one other unanswered question. How did the shooters know in advance about the protest? They couldn't have mustered them on the spur of the moment, or prepared the uniforms. I won't keep you. You have too much to do." Dekkard inclined his head, then added to Trujillo, "You do as well."

"Thank you, Steffan," replied Obreduur, his voice almost resigned.

Dekkard turned and left the small office, closed the door, and turned to the secretary. "I'm sorry. It was urgent."

"Unlike some, Councilor," replied the secretary, "you proved your loyalty long ago."

"Thank you." Dekkard hoped he'd proved more than loyalty, but he just inclined his head, then turned and left through the corridor door that Avraal had already opened. Once outside, he turned to the still-dazed guard. "I'm sorry. The Premier needed that information, and I didn't have time to argue."

"It's all right, sir." The guard smiled wanly. "You did say you'd be quick."

"We tried. Thank you."

Before Dekkard and Avraal started back toward the Council Office Building, he glanced toward the door to the Guard captain's office, then said, "I might as well just go to the councilors' lobby. We're scheduled to reconvene in a third."

"Will the Council even proceed after what happened?"

"It's scheduled to meet. Obreduur would have called the Council into session anyway to brief them on the massacre. We can talk just outside the lobby until fourth bell. Then you can wait a bit, and if you hear the gong announcing a vote, that means we're proceeding with votes on the appropriations. If you'd like, and I'd prefer it, we could meet for lunch in the dining room."

"I think that would be a very good idea. That is, if the voting goes on."

"It will, I suspect, although Obreduur might not be presiding. Haarsfel can handle that. The other thing I mentioned to Obreduur was that the shooters had to have known in advance. How? Unless they've infiltrated the New Meritorists?"

"That's another indication of a link between the Commercers and the New Meritorists," said Avraal. "It's also disturbing that some Special Agents knew about the protest and didn't let anyone in the government know."

"Or that someone near the top of Security kept Obreduur from knowing. Either way, it shows just how corrupt the Special Agents have become."

"You're surprised at that?"

"Not really, but it's still disappointing, and we have no direct proof right now."

The two stopped outside the councilors' lobby.

"I should have said something to Obreduur earlier," Dekkard said.

"What else could you have said or done?" asked Avraal. "You told me that a month for agent transfers was the shortest time you could get through the

Council. How the Council handled that in a month was Obreduur's problem, not yours."

Dekkard forced himself to take a long slow breath. "You're right, but it bothers me. Politically, Obreduur probably didn't have much choice. Wyath and Manwaeren are being tried, and so are the Special Agents sent against us. There's an arrest order out for Director Jebulon, not that he's likely anywhere in Guldor."

"He's probably in Noldar by now," interjected Avraal.

No doubt hoping that all this will result in the collapse of the government and new elections that will restore the "rightful" Commercer autocracy so that he can return. Dekkard kept that thought to himself and just said, "Or somewhere else from where he can't be extradited." He stopped short as he saw Hasheem, flanked by Erleen Orlov and Myrenda Lestiig, approaching.

"Have you talked to the Premier?" asked Hasheem.

"Only for a minute or two. He was with the Guard captain."

"What do you know? How could the patrollers do that?"

"They could if they were Special Agents who removed the scarlet patches from their uniforms. I don't *know* that, but that sort of thing isn't in any patrollers' interest, and the Special Agents have already proved to be an intransigent nasty bunch." Dekkard smiled pleasantly. "I originally made their transfer effective in two weeks."

"You were right, but we didn't have the votes to keep that, even in committee."

One of Baar's successful amendments. But Dekkard just nodded.

"Being right isn't enough in politics if you don't have the votes," Hasheem added.

"I've discovered that," replied Dekkard wryly. "Facts don't always convince people."

"People convince people," replied Hasheem. "Sometimes facts help."

Not when people don't want to believe them. "Sometimes."

"We might as well go on in," added the older councilor.

Dekkard turned to Avraal. "Until lunch?"

She nodded.

Once in the councilors' lobby, Dekkard looked around at the handful of councilors, hoping to see Villem Baar, but Baar wasn't in the lobby, and Dekkard made his way in to the Council chamber and took his place at his desk. Perhaps a dozen councilors were already present, most of them Landors. Breffyn Haastar smiled briefly and nodded to Dekkard, as did Navione.

Hasheem stood at the rear of the chamber, talking to Mardosh as the chamber began to fill and councilors moved to their desks.

Obreduur reconvened the Council at fourth bell, and took the Premier's lectern. "As most if not all of you know, the New Meritorists held a demonstration this morning outside the Council. No other demonstrations occurred anywhere else in Machtarn so far as we can determine. A number of men in patroller uniforms appeared and opened fire on the demonstrators. They killed ninety-one demonstrators, and wounded more than a hundred others, some of whom may not live. This is a truly horrifying act, and we're working on determining who was behind it. So far, it has been established that the shooters were not current patrollers. The five uniforms recovered from the shooters killed by the guards suggest that they were wearing uniforms that belonged to Special Agents, with the scarlet patch removed. Whether the shooters were in fact all former or present Special Agents has not been determined. I will keep you all informed as we learn more."

Obreduur paused. "The Council will resume consideration of the appropriations."

Dekkard wasn't certain that was wise, but then, most of the population wasn't that sympathetic to the New Meritorists. *Not yet.* And without knowing more, what could the Council do immediately? It made sense to finish off the appropriations act so that the Council could deal with the massacre of the New Meritorists, but Dekkard knew that people weren't always sensible.

As Haarsfel took over, Dekkard noticed that Obreduur left the chamber, most likely to deal with more aspects of the shooting.

From what Dekkard heard, the shooting had been well-planned. The only way to determine the guilty Special Agents' identities was to question them all before an empath. Whoever had planned the shooting knew that, and the guilty ones had likely already resigned, obtained guns elsewhere—or had them supplied—and would be out of Machtarn within bells, if they weren't already. While it remained possible that the shooters weren't former Special Agents, given the number in patroller uniforms, Dekkard thought it unlikely that the shooters had been anything but former Special Agents, especially given that they'd known about the protest.

But you don't know for certain, and the way things have turned out, it's unlikely that anyone will be able to prove it.

He turned his attention back to Haarsfel, who had finished describing the amendment to cut funding for the northern Mountain Patrol, on the grounds that, with the long period of stable relations between Argental and Guldor, there was less need for as many mountain troops.

By the time Haarsfel recessed the Council just before noon, the Council had finished with the Security section of appropriations, the only successful votes having been in favor of cutting funding for the Mountain Patrol and approving the Security and Public Safety section. Dekkard had been one of the few Craft councilors to vote against cutting Mountain Patrol funding.

Avraal was waiting for him in the dining room entry. "How did it go?"

"Obreduur announced the shooting. They verified that at least the shooters who were killed were wearing Special Agent uniforms with the scarlet patches removed."

"Did he mention you?"

"No, thank the Almighty."

The maître d'hôtel seated them at a table between two others already occupied, one by Harleona Zerlyon and Elyncya Duforgue and the other by two Commercers, Marryat Osmond and Maximillian Connard, who'd succeeded Maastach as the councilor from Aaken. Both Commercers focused on Avraal longer than Dekkard would have liked. Neither Zerlyon nor Duforgue offered more than a passing glance and a nod.

Dekkard didn't see Villem Baar anywhere, nor Mardosh or Kaliara Bassaana.

Once they'd ordered, he looked at his wife and said, "I think we're running out of time. Are you up for a bit of a gamble?"

"So long as it doesn't involve unjustified violence and mayhem."

"Excellent. If, sometime in the next day or so, we can catch a certain councilor away from others, I'll need you to concentrate on reactions."

"Are you going to tell me who it might be?"

"One who suggested a certain amendment."

"That's a gamble, but it could be interesting."

"Do you think our former occupational peer has returned from his travels?"

"He has. I went to check after they cleared Council Avenue. He parked his steamer hood out, rather than the way it usually is, as if he wanted to be able to depart quickly."

"Do you think that means more chances of 'you know what I mean'?"

"Don't you?"

"Of course." Dekkard would have said more, but the server arrived with their orders, and he caught sight of Pajiin with Eduardo Nortak, walking toward them.

Pajiin immediately slowed.

"Tomas," said Dekkard, standing, "I don't believe you've met my wife. Avraal, this is Councilor Tomas Pajiin, from Eshbruk, and Councilor Eduardo Nortak, from Encora."

"I'm pleased to meet you both," replied Avraal, with a warm smile. She looked to Pajiin. "Steffan's told me about you, and it's good." She then looked to Nortak and added, "But I'm afraid I don't know much about you, except about your district, because I grew up near Sudaen, not that it's that close."

Pajiin smiled. "You're a very fortunate man, Steffan."

"In respect to Avraal, I know that absolutely." After the briefest pause, Dekkard added, "You two looked very absorbed as you walked in. Has something else happened?"

"Not about the demonstration," said Pajiin. "We were complaining about the weather in our districts. There's too much snow too early in mine and too much rain in his."

"There's been more cold rain all over Guldor this fall, it seems," returned Dekkard. "And early snow in a number of places."

"We can't change the weather." Nortak nodded to Avraal. "A pleasure to meet you, Ritten."

"My pleasure as well in meeting both of you," replied Avraal.

"We won't interrupt your lunch further," said Pajiin, adding with a good-natured grin, "You lucky bastard."

Once the two had made their way to a table in the corner where Julian Andros already sat, Dekkard asked, "What did I miss?"

Avraal smiled. "Nothing. Their words matched their feelings. That happens, if rarely, and it's a relief."

"They both mentioned the unseasonal weather, and there have been stories in the newssheets as well. I worry that if we get food shortages on top of everything else, it's going to be a long winter and a worse spring."

"You may be right. Is there anything else about our gamble?"

"Only that we'll have to be opportunistic and lucky."

"You have been known to force luck."

"Not always successfully," replied Dekkard wryly, "especially in political matters." Belatedly, he turned his attention to the three-cheese chicken breast and golden rice before him.

The rest of the meal passed more quickly than Dekkard liked, and before long he was back in the Council chamber waiting for Obreduur to speak.

As soon as he gaveled the Council into session, Obreduur took the Premier's lectern. "In view of the horrifying and disturbing events that transpired earlier today, after conferring with all three floor leaders, and with their agreement, we have decided that all votes on the appropriations will be completed in this session of the Council, even if it takes until midnight or later. I have already sent word to your offices. There will be a short recess of half a bell at fifth bell." Then he turned to Haarsfel. "Floor Leader, I yield to you."

As he had earlier, Obreduur left the chamber, although Dekkard noticed that, during the morning session, the Premier had missed no votes, only returning long enough to cast his plaque.

"The first amendment to the Military Affairs section is to increase funding for overseas port bases for the Navy . . ."

Dekkard settled in for what he knew would be a very long afternoon, and a longer evening.

After four bells of seemingly endless amendments, all of which were proposed by Commercers and for unrealistic additions to obscure functions of the military, its contracting budget, the overseas operational budget, and other parts of military affairs that he'd never even heard of, Dekkard was more than ready for the short evening break. First, he went to the councilors' lobby to see if either Gaaroll or Avraal was there. Neither was.

He then went to the councilors' dining room, where he found Avraal seated at a table, where café and a half order of a duck cassoulet waited for him. A half order of three-cheese chicken was on her platter.

"I thought this might help you get through the next few bells. You could be here until midnight."

"It might be earlier. Haarsfel has been pushing the votes on all the amendments quickly." Dekkard took a sip of café, then a bite of the cassoulet. "What's happening outside of the Council?"

"Obreduur issued a statement that's in all the newssheets about the so-called patroller assassins being imposters and troublemakers, but he didn't say anything about them being former Special Agents."

Dekkard finished another bite of cassoulet before replying. "He's being cautious, even when he spoke to the Council."

"Roostof sent Gaaroll out for the afternoon editions of both *Gestirn* and *The Machtarn Tribune.* They both printed Obreduur's statement. Both also questioned his lack of forethought in not having real patrollers present. The *Tribune* also said that while the Council Guards acted gallantly, there were too few of them, and they were caught off-balance. There was even a hint that Obreduur hadn't contacted patrollers on purpose."

His mouth full, Dekkard shook his head. He finally said, "How was he, or anyone else, to know that a large number of former Special Agents would appear in uniform and open fire on the demonstrators, who were demanding that the Council change the Great Charter to require all votes be recorded by name?"

After a quick sip of café, he asked, "Can you be sure to meet me as soon as we recess, right outside the councilors' lobby? I know it might be a guess and a wait, but I'd like to see if we could try our gamble."

"I thought you might have that in mind."

"After this morning's shooting, I have a very strong feeling we're running out of time."

"You're also running out of time to finish your cassoulet, and you're going to need it, if we're going to do what you have in mind," said Avraal with a smile. "While you were suffering through amendments, I drove by a certain building. A certain steamer had been driven out and returned. That only means he's back."

Dekkard finished another mouthful, pushed aside the unfinished cassoulet, and said, "At least we'll be driving home in the dark. That's something." He looked at his watch. "I'd better be heading back."

"I'll be outside the councilors' lobby."

"Thank you." Dekkard stood, then walked around the table, bent down, and kissed her cheek. "I'll see you then."

He hurried toward the corridor leading to the Council chamber.

As he entered, Hasheem moved to his side.

"Your office has a message, but I wanted you to know that there will be an emergency meeting of the Security Committee at third bell tomorrow morning."

"Thank you for letting me know."

"Steffan, you've been ahead of most councilors on these issues. Is there *anything* that might help?"

"I wouldn't allow any Special Agent to transfer into either Justiciary or Treasury without an interview with a good empath present and a list of questions concerning their knowledge of and links to the raids, this morning's shooting, and the New Meritorists."

"Why the New Meritorists?"

"How did the shooters know in advance about the protest? Where and when it was going to be? At the hearings, Manwaeren professed to know nothing about the New Meritorists. Was he kept in the dark so that he could answer honestly that he never knew? Mangele committed suicide, or someone wanted us to think he did." The last was a thought that occurred to Dekkard as he recalled what Manwaeren had said, and what Mangele had not been asked.

Hasheem sighed. "Thank you. I'm supposed to meet with the Premier later. I'll convey your observations."

Obreduur will likely sigh, too.

As Dekkard headed for his desk, he realized, again, how much he had to learn about being a councilor, especially about questioning witnesses before a committee.

In the end, after Dekkard joined the majority in voting down another series of Commercer amendments designed to increase the contracting and procurement budget of the Guldoran military establishment, likely for the benefit of certain corporacions, at a third past the second bell of night, Haarsfel announced the passage of the appropriations act for the coming year.

Even before the announcement, Dekkard headed for the councilors' lobby, hoping Avraal would be waiting outside, since the voting had taken less time than he'd thought.

She was.

"I'm glad you're here."

"That was still a long session. Gaaroll's in the office, waiting. So is Roostof. He sent everyone else home at fifth bell."

"We need to see if we can catch Villem alone—now." Dekkard was hoping that with the length of the session Baar would be heading out by himself.

He turned and watched the archway to the councilors' lobby. Several councilors emerged, including Palafaux and Schmidtz together, neither of whom even looked in Dekkard's direction, followed by Navione and Haastar, who offered a smile and a quick wave.

Several minutes later, Villem Baar appeared, alone, and clearly lost in his own thoughts.

Dekkard moved toward him. "Good evening, Villem."

Baar looked up, clearly annoyed. "What is it, Steffan?"

"I have a question for you. When the Security Committee was marking up the Security and Public Safety Reorganization Act, you offered two amendments to the proposal to extend the transfer time—"

"For the Special Agents. I know. After today, I wish I hadn't."

"Was that your idea, or did someone suggest that the time was too short?"

Baar looked at Dekkard, then Avraal. "Steffan, you have me at a disadvantage."

Dekkard smiled. "That was the idea. And under most circumstances, your amendments would have made sense."

"I had difficulty believing—"

"I know. Was it Jaime Minz who suggested it? The influencer from Northwest Industrial Chemical? Or perhaps Oskaar Ulrich?"

"I've never even spoken to Ulrich. I'm not sure I'd know him if I met him. Is that all, Steffan?"

"That's more than enough, Villem."

"I commend your tactful ambush, Steffan."

"You didn't say a word, except that Ulrich never influenced your actions or amendments. You don't mention the ambush, and neither will we."

"Thank you. You're known to keep your word. So do I. Good evening, Steffan."

"Good evening, Villem."

Dekkard let Baar move away before he and Avraal resumed their walk toward the courtyard doors.

"Was it Minz?" he asked when he was sure no one was close by.

"From his emotional reaction, I'd say so. You know that's not proof."

"No. It's proof, but not admissible in any way. Besides, it's not illegal to merely suggest 'improvements' to a bill. But I can mention, if I need to, that Baar consulted with Commercer influencers. I'd rather not."

"What are we going to do next?"

"Find a way to link Minz to all of this. With hard proof." Dekkard laughed softly and harshly. "Don't ask me how. I have no idea."

When they stepped out into the cold evening and started to walk along the gaslit roofed walkway to the Council Office Building, Dekkard realized that fat snowflakes drifted down. "Snow and dark. We might just be fairly safe on the drive home."

46

THE snow and darkness made for a slow trip home. But Dekkard was right. Neither Avraal or Gaaroll sensed any danger. Late as it was by the time Dekkard and Avraal went to bed, he slept uneasily and woke early on Duadi morning. He showered, shaved, and dressed quickly before making his way downstairs, where Emrelda ate alone at the breakfast table.

"The snow melted," she said. "There's a cold drizzle that looks to last for a while, leaving some slushy or icy patches in places. How are you feeling this morning?"

"Worried." Dekkard went into the kitchen and fixed two mugs of café, then returned and set them on the table. "Did Captain Narryt have anything to say about yesterday? I should have asked last night, but I was a little tired."

"The captain's only real comment was that it had to be Special Agents. The Tacticals would have been more efficient and would have taken out the Council Guards first so that they could have massacred all the New Meritorists."

Dekkard shuddered at that thought. At least, he'd gotten the STF under Army control immediately.

"I need to get moving," said Emrelda, standing and heading toward the kitchen with her mug and platter. "With this weather, some patrollers might be a little late."

"Just be careful," returned Dekkard.

"I'd say the same to you, but I'm not certain being careful will help much," she returned wryly.

"Thank you so much." Dekkard shook his head and picked up the news-sheet, wondering how *Gestirn* had reported yesterday's events.

The lead front-page story was about the demonstration massacre, and the first part didn't differ much from the story in Unadi's late edition, but the third paragraph contained something Dekkard hadn't heard or seen.

> Late last night, the Premier issued an emergency Council order requiring all Special Agents on the agent roster as of the tenth of Fallend to report to their new assignment at either the Justiciary or the Treasury no later than midday on Tridi. Those who resigned after the tenth are to report to the Treasury. Failure to do so will be considered at the least dereliction of duty and may subject violators to additional and criminal charges . . .

Dekkard smiled wryly. One way or another that would likely identify most of those responsible, either by empath-monitored questioning or by their absence. *Most likely by absence.*

Another short story stated that the presentation of evidence in the Wyath and Manwaeren trial would likely be completed by Tridi or early Furdi.

At that moment Gaaroll entered the breakfast room. "Are we going in early?"

"Not quite so early as yesterday. There's an emergency meeting of the Security Committee, and there just might be a few other unexpected matters to deal with."

Gaaroll frowned. "If they're unexpected?"

"What he means," replied Avraal as she stepped into the breakfast room, "is when something like what happened yesterday occurs there are always unanticipated problems."

"Always," affirmed Dekkard.

Avraal seated herself at the table. Then she lifted her mug and took a sip of café.

As he watched his wife, Dekkard decided not to address another word to her, not until she finished the first mug of café. Instead he went to find the croissants.

Halfway through her second mug of café, Dekkard handed Avraal the newssheet, waiting for her to read and comment.

She set it aside and said, "It's what we expected, isn't it?"

"Except for the bit about the Special Agents reporting."

"He should have done that earlier. He knew about Baar's amendments to lengthen the time, and you warned both him and Hasheem."

"He couldn't, except by an emergency declaration. Until yesterday, there wasn't an emergency. As you might recall, he said there were 'political considerations.'"

"Well, he's paying a high price for those considerations."

"Shoulda listened to you," said Gaaroll.

"He listened. He just couldn't do anything about it, not with the law as written," replied Dekkard. "Until there was an emergency."

Gaaroll shook her head.

Dekkard returned his attention to his second quince-paste-filled croissant.

In minutes, the three had finished eating and dealt with dishes, then left the kitchen to ready themselves to leave for what Dekkard feared might be a long day.

He took one of the more indirect routes to the Council Office Building, absently wondering again why the assassin or assassins didn't concentrate on his approach to covered parking or the house, but the only answer that made sense was that whoever wanted Dekkard dead clearly didn't want any links to them. Both places had few locations for clear and clean shots from a distance beyond the range of Gaaroll and Avraal to sense someone. The large oak tree had been one of the few such locations.

As soon as Dekkard, Avraal, and Gaaroll entered the office, Roostof handed Dekkard a newssheet. For a moment, Dekkard wondered why, until the senior legalist said, "I thought you should also see what appeared in the *Tribune* this morning."

"Thank you." Dekkard began to read. The lead story was much the same for the first paragraph or so, but then the tone changed.

While the loss of life is indeed regrettable, far fewer would have perished or been wounded if the new Council had continued the practices of the former Council and shown a firm hand in dealing with the lawbreakers calling themselves, incorrectly, "meritorists." There is nothing to praise and everything to condemn in a group that wants to destroy a structure that has worked well for centuries. Nor is the Council serving the public good by catering to such misguided and lawless populists. Premier Obred-uur should be held fully accountable for his regrettable loss of perspective in catering to the rabble who are determined to undermine the very foundations of Guldoran government . . .

Dekkard finished reading and handed the newssheet back to Roostof. "Thank you. Like most misguided news stories, there's a little truth in it, such as condemnation of the goals of the New Meritorists. Their leaders use the worker discontent to support stupid ideas, and that plays right into the hands of the Commercers. If they regain power before we can make some changes, things will get worse." *Much worse.*

Margrit said quietly, "You have a message, sir."

"From Chairman Hasheem most likely."

"It's in a Security Committee envelope." She handed the message to Dekkard.

He read the message. "It's confirmation for an emergency meeting of the Security Committee at third bell. I suppose I'd better go through the incoming mail."

"I'll be out here with Margrit and Gaaroll," said Avraal.

"I'm not going anywhere," Dekkard replied with a wry smile.

Once in his office and settled behind his desk, he quickly read the letters and the four petitions. Even so, it was almost a third before third bell when he finished and sat back in his chair, thinking. There hadn't been a single letter expressing Meritorist sympathies. All told, he'd received little more than a half score of such letters. *What does that mean?* How much support did that indicate? How many others agreed, but were afraid to write? Were the letters he had received the result of a mere handful of activists? *How can you tell?*

Both Avraal and Gaaroll stood waiting when Dekkard stepped out of his private office to walk to the Security Committee meeting, and both wore coats, although Avraal's was unbuttoned. Given recent events, he hoped neither he nor Avraal needed to use their knives.

On the walk to the Council Hall, Dekkard glimpsed Schmidtz and Pala-faux ahead of him, although they didn't appear to be conversing, and farther ahead Sandegarde and Bassaana. He had to wonder if the Commercers would hold a caucus about yesterday's shooting. But why would Volkaar have called a meeting at the same time as a Security Committee meeting? *Or is something else going on? Possibly a meeting of senior Commercer councilors?* Three out of four had been committee chairs in the last Council, and Bassaana had been in line to become chair of the Transportation Committee.

When Dekkard followed the other four into the Council Hall he could see Bassaana and Sandegarde walk past the councilors' lobby and toward the committee rooms. Shortly, so did Schmidtz and Palafaux.

As Dekkard, Avraal, and Gaaroll neared the door to the Security Committee hearing room, he saw Rikkard and Baar approaching from the other direction, followed by Baar's empath and isolate.

"The taller councilor saw you," murmured Gaaroll, "and his emotions got a lot stronger."

"Thank you," said Dekkard quietly, wondering why Rikkard was the one angry or upset, and not Baar.

Avraal leaned toward Dekkard and whispered, "He's scared, really scared. Baar's just feeling resigned." After a moment, she added, "We'll just wait for you here in the corridor."

Dekkard motioned for Baar and Rikkard to precede him.

"Thank you, Steffan," said Baar politely, his voice neither warm nor cold.

Rikkard didn't even look in Dekkard's direction.

Before Dekkard entered the hearing room, he noticed that Baar's security aides appeared as though they'd wait as well. Hasheem already stood behind his chair in the committee room, talking quietly to Navione.

Dekkard made his way to his own chair and was joined within minutes by Pajiin. The last councilor to enter was Breffyn Haastar.

Once all the committee members were in their places, Hasheem seated himself and rapped the gavel once. "The committee will come to order." After a long pause, he declared, "The Premier has requested that the committee develop a set of recommendations for dealing with the New Meritorists. The first step in doing so is to discuss yesterday's events and what steps might be useful in dealing with future demonstrations."

In short, Obreduur told you to call the meeting so that he could say that the Security Committee was already looking into the matter.

"As we all know," Hasheem continued, "Guldor has never seen demonstrations such as those occurring these past few months. It's fair to call the situation unprecedented." He paused and cleared his throat. "We'll begin with a simple question. What do each of you think was the direct cause of yesterday's demonstration and the attack by those using patroller uniforms that had been worn previously by Special Agents?"

"Sr. Chairman," offered Baar deferentially, "might I ask a question of fact before we continue?"

"You may," replied Hasheem, "offer a question of fact." He emphasized just slightly the word "fact."

"How was it established that the uniforms belonged previously to Special Agents?"

"The uniforms of the attackers who were killed were examined. The fabric on the upper shoulders was darker in the shape of a Special Agent patch. Several uniforms still had traces of scarlet threads, suggesting that the patches had been recently removed."

"Thank you, Sr. Chairman. One other factual question, if you please?"

"Go ahead, Councilor."

"Has it been factually determined that any of the attackers were in fact former Special Agents?"

"That investigation is still in process, I've been told. We should know more by Quindi, possibly sooner. Those investigating have reason to believe that at least some of the attackers were indeed Special Agents or former Special Agents. Because that has not been proven officially, the government can only say that they were not patrollers from the Machtarn area."

"Thank you." Baar inclined his head.

"Since Councilor Baar has requested the opportunity for factual questions, does any other councilor have a question of fact?"

When no one else spoke, Dekkard said, "I do. It's my understanding that firearms issued to Security or Public Safety patrollers are recorded. Do you know if the attackers used such weapons?"

Hasheem smiled wryly. "The attackers used weapons identical to those used by Security forces stamped with serial numbers. It will take another day or so to determine if the five pistols recovered were issued and to whom. Are there any other questions?"

No one else spoke.

Hasheem turned to Navione. "Your thoughts on the cause or causes?"

Navione smiled wryly. "My thoughts are strictly speculation. The so-called New Meritorists appear to be led by populist agitators who see the road to power in appealing to those who contribute least to a healthy society. We've increased the use of steam power, and that has temporarily put many manual laborers out of work. The agitators take advantage of this. I have no idea why anyone attacked them, except that using patroller uniforms gave the shooters the advantage of surprise. It also indicates advance planning by another group that opposes the New Meritorists, and that they knew that there would be a demonstration. Other than that . . ." Navione shrugged.

Hasheem looked to Haastar. "Your thoughts?"

"I agree with my colleague. It's likely some of the attackers were in fact former Special Agents. It's clear from the deaths caused by the illegally authorized raids undertaken earlier by the Special Agents that some of those agents strongly oppose the New Meritorists. They may well have decided to take matters into their own hands before they lost the power to do so."

"Councilor Rikkard?"

"It's regrettable if, in fact, the New Meritorists' rebellious populism has inspired devoted public safety officers, or others, into overreacting to their demonstrations. But, we shouldn't forget that these populist power-seekers set off explosions in fifteen regional Security headquarters, and assassinated or tried to assassinate a score of elected officials, including councilors and our current Premier. They're not innocent."

"Councilor Pajiin?"

"I see two sets of lawbreakers. The Council should deal with both, as quickly and forcefully as necessary. Most important are the renegade Special Agents who have continued to abuse their positions for years. Exactly how the government can do this, I couldn't say, except that the regular patrollers may be more effective. If they're not, then the Army should be brought in."

"Councilor Dekkard?"

"I do not agree in the slightest with the tactics of the New Meritorists, but significant problems in Guldor have led to the resurgence of their ideas. As Councilor Navione pointed out, far too many able-bodied Guldorans are without work. Too many unsafe workplaces lead to worker injuries, leaving many unable to work. Smaller businesses encounter corporacion practices making it difficult to compete, putting even more out of work. Add to that weather-caused crop losses and higher food prices, and the poorer segments of Guldoran workers are hungry and unhappy. So far, neither the previous Council nor this one has addressed any of these issues. These difficulties fuel support for the New Meritorists. The raids conducted by the Special Agents and yesterday's shooting serve to make those people angrier and more militant." Dekkard paused to clear his throat, then continued. "Swift action to determine those behind the shooting and dealing with those individuals might minimize the impact, but without addressing the underlying problems, it will be difficult to put an end to the New Meritorist idiocy."

Hasheem nodded slightly, then said, "Councilor Baar?"

"I could only speculate. I'm afraid I don't know enough to do anything that might be useful at the moment. It would appear to me that at least some of the problem lies with the leadership of the Security Ministry during the previous Council, since the current Council leadership could not have organized any of the actions of the Special Agents in the time in which they have been in power."

Definitely throwing the responsibility on Wyath and Jebulon. At least some of it belonged there. Of that Dekkard was certain, but he was also certain that corporacions backed the corrupt Special Agents, many of whom likely saw nothing wrong with what they had done, because they'd done it in the name of some greater good, perhaps as a way to "restore" Guldor's greatness.

"Are there any further comments?" asked Hasheem.

None of the other councilors spoke.

"Very well. Since the Security Committee has been requested to come up with a set of recommendations to deal with maintaining public safety while dealing with the New Meritorists, the committee staff is drafting a rough set of recommendations. Each of you will receive a copy later this afternoon. The committee will meet at fourth bell tomorrow. I trust all of you will consider the matter and will be able to offer constructive suggestions." Hasheem rapped the gavel once.

Pajiin turned to Dekkard. "He's not giving us much time."

"Events and the Premier aren't giving him much time," replied Dekkard as he stood. "The New Meritorists certainly won't."

"More demonstrations?" asked Pajiin.

"Does it rain in Machtarn?"

Pajiin laughed, if harshly.

Dekkard saw that Baar and Rikkard had already left the committee room, and Navione and Haastar weren't far behind.

As expected, Avraal and Gaaroll waited outside the committee room. Dekkard didn't say anything until they exited into the damp chill of the courtyard. "How did the two Commercers feel when they left?"

"Baar was calm. Rikkard wasn't happy to see us, but he wasn't as upset as earlier."

"He got more upset the farther he got from us, though," added Gaaroll. "Well, his feelings were stronger. I'm not sure about why."

More upset after leaving the meeting? "Were he and Baar talking?"

"Not so far as I could tell," replied Avraal.

"I wish I knew where he was heading," said Dekkard. "Or what had him so agitated."

"Can't tell you that," said Gaaroll.

Avraal smiled, then asked, "What happened in the meeting?"

Dekkard told her.

Even wearing one of his new and heavier suits, Dekkard felt chilled by the time he entered the Council Office Building. Both sets of councilors preceding him were out of sight as well. "Can you sense Rikkard?"

"Not now," replied Avraal.

Some minutes later, Dekkard had just entered the office anteroom when Roostof appeared and, without speaking, handed him a broadsheet. Dekkard immediately began to read.

GULDOR NEEDS ACCOUNTABLE COUNCILORS
Corrupt Special Agents have killed 500 innocent Guldorans this year.
The corrupt "Specials" conducted raids that falsely arrested and killed scores! The Premier only charged three officials, and the Council gave the rest new jobs. The Premier and Council knew they were corrupt, but delayed acting. Is this accountable government?
New Meritorists for Better Government!

"Well," declared Dekkard dryly, "they got the corrupt Special Agent part correct." He paused, then added, "Unfortunately, the rest of it is factually accurate as well, if misleading." He handed the broadsheet to Avraal, standing beside the table desk she used, and waited until she read it. Then he looked to her and then Roostof. "We need to talk this over." He motioned to his office door, then followed Avraal in.

Roostof came last and closed the door.

Dekkard sat down behind the desk and took a deep breath. Then he looked at Roostof. "Svard, if you were Premier, what would you do?"

"Interview and interrogate every single one of the Special Agents with an empath present. Commend and retain the few that aren't guilty, and throw the rest in gaol for the next two years, or let them take permanent voluntary exile, say, after three months' imprisonment. That way, you don't have as many people getting in the way of the patrollers and Council Guards in dealing with the demonstrators."

"Then what?"

Roostof offered an embarrassed smile. "After that, it gets a lot harder. There's no one thing that will fix the problems. I'd do the sort of things you've talked about. Tighten up the laws so that the corporacions can't evade their intent. Maybe require freight rates be set by weight and not by cubage, or some combination so it's cheaper to ship food. Require all contracts with the government to be publicly available. It's no one thing."

"You're right about that." Dekkard turned to Avraal. "Your thoughts?"

"Concentrate on measures that improve what poorer workers are paid. A lot of women are the family breadwinners, but corporacions pay women less when they're doing the same job as men. Ingrella's won some legal judgments against some of the mills, but it might help to make it a criminal offense to continue that sort of discrimination . . ."

That discussion continued for almost a bell, with Dekkard occasionally jotting down notes.

After Svard left, Dekkard said, "That helped some, although Obreduur's likely thought of most of it."

"He probably has, but he may not have, and even so, if the committee recommendations agree with what he has in mind, it strengthens his political position."

"So now what?"

Avraal moved to the edge of his desk. "You catch up on your replies and reading correspondence, and then come up with a rough draft of what you'll recommend at tomorrow's meeting. I'll take the Gresynt and do some reconnaissance."

"It can't hurt, and you're doing better than I am right now." *At least, it feels that way.* He stood and walked with her to the door out to the main corridor.

"Just be careful."

"I'm always careful." She smiled. "Or careful enough."

By the time Avraal returned just after third bell, Dekkard had finally caught up on both reading incoming mail and signing or correcting the replies typed to that moment, and he was studying the Security Committee staff recommendations, shaking his head.

"Whatever you're reading, it can't be good," she said as she entered his office.

"The committee staff recommendations." He looked up from the two-page document. "It's all very sound advice, but it has a few problems."

"What do you mean?"

"The staff recommends capturing, incarcerating, and putting on trial those behind the New Meritorist bombings of the regional Security headquarters buildings. Excellent advice. Except that no one in Security seems to know who or where they are. That is, unless that information can be pried out of the Special Agents."

"So start with that."

"I will, along with a few other steps they've so conveniently skipped."

"You have half a bell to write those steps out. Then we're leaving."

"Why then?"

"Because it's a good bell before you ever leave and because your dear former colleague is in town and no longer at his office."

That unfortunately made sense to Dekkard.

"There's also another matter we need to discuss," said Avraal. "Not about us or work."

"What? Gaaroll or Emrelda?" Dekkard thought it had to be one or the other, given that Avraal had brought it up when they were alone and not in the house.

"Emrelda. It's only four days till Yearend."

"And three days to the Yearend Ball," said Dekkard. "Is she worried?"

"Not about the ball. House taxes are due by the seventeenth of Winterfirst."

Dekkard knew about property taxes and house taxes, which composed the largest share of the government's annual revenue. He'd certainly heard his parents complain about them, but since he'd never owned property or a house, he'd never had to pay those taxes, some of which went to the district government but most of which went to the Imperial Treasury. "Does she need help?"

"She wouldn't say, but I saw her looking at the notice, and she felt really worried. They bought the house for about five thousand marks, and generally the tax is around five percent of the value. I don't know the current assessment, but it's probably closer to ten thousand now with all the improvements that they've made and the way house prices have gone up in Hillside."

Dekkard swallowed. *Five hundred marks?* That was more than he'd made in a year as a security aide. But he'd collect about six hundred for his monthly pay as a councilor on Quindi. "I can do that."

"No. I was hoping you could lend me a hundred."

"I'm living there, too, dear, and I'm pretty sure I make more than you do. We'll split it."

"You're sure?"

"She's done so much for us. How could I not?"

Abruptly, she put her arms around him, then kissed him gently, then murmured in his ear, "In addition to being incredibly handsome, you're a really good man."

"I do try."

"You do more than try." She eased back from him. "You need to write out those steps. And tonight, we need to read more about Averra to get your mind off all this, at least for a while."

Dekkard smiled. That also made sense.

Averra is a city of hills, and likely always will be, for it has been, and I hope will remain, a city without pretensions, neither of greatness nor of false modesty, unlike Teknar, once known as the city of seven hills. As Teknar grew and prospered, it filled the dales and vales between the hills, the streams diverted or paved over so that the city now encompasses a vast artificial plateau encircled and supported by towering stone walls, above which rise gilded towers, overlooking gardens so large they have their own streams fed by massive and extensive aqueducts extending as far as the Nardian Mountains some five score milles to the north.

Whatever once was Teknar, and the honesty of its being, has long since vanished beneath that plateau, along with the wandering ways, the streams, and the hills, so that what remains is a confusion of walls, buildings, and artificial pleasure gardens created not by those who have always lived there, but by those with wealth enough to ignore and override the needs and desires of those who are forced by necessity to remain, ignored by and subservient to a smaller and smaller group of wealthier and wealthier men.

Averra has its men of wealth as well, but so far they have let the city reflect all who inhabit it, rather than using their golden dohleers to remake Averra for their pleasure or merely to demonstrate that they have the power to reshape an honest and ancient place.

AVERRA
The City of Truth
Johan Eschbach
377 TE

R EADING from *The City of Truth* did in fact distract Dekkard enough that he slept better, even if he started worrying again once he woke on Tridi morning and readied himself for a day that would include another Security Committee meeting. One that likely would accomplish little more than provide limited political cover for Obreduur and the Craft Party. Even if Obreduur and Justiciary Minister Kuta could prove that the shootings on Unadi had been carried out by renegade Special Agents, that would only convince most people that the new Council didn't have a firm grip on the government.

Which we don't. No new government would after forty-plus years of Commercer rule, but most people won't understand why or care what the reason is.

He mulled it all while he dressed after showering and shaving.

"You slept better last night," said Avraal, as she rolled over in bed and looked at him. "I like that suit, too."

"You should," replied Dekkard with a smile. "You picked it out. But I like it, too."

"Good."

Dekkard just looked appreciatively as she got out of bed.

"Go on and get the café ready. I'll be down shortly."

Dekkard grinned, but followed her suggestion.

Emrelda and Gaaroll were both at the table in the breakfast room when he arrived with the cafés he'd gotten in the kitchen.

"Some sun this morning. Cold, though," offered Gaaroll.

Dekkard glanced toward the copy of *Gestirn* on the side table.

"There's nothing new in it, except for more bad news from growers in the southwest."

"The storms wiped out the late crops there?"

"Mostly," replied Emrelda. "There's a short story saying that all five of the dead men in patroller uniforms were Special Agents. You knew that already."

Dekkard set one café at Avraal's place and one at his, then picked up the newssheet. The story was indeed short, but he knew Obreduur would appreciate the last few lines.

> . . . intent of the Security and Public Safety Act was to rein in the excesses of the Special Tactical Force, and the Special Agents. Unfortunately, Commercer amendments to the legislation extended the implementation date for Special Agents, which allowed renegade elements to conduct unauthorized raids and keep the weapons used in Unadi's shooting.

Dekkard doubted that those lines would appear in *The Machtarn Tribune*, given how tied that newssheet was to the Commercer point of view.

Another story noted that the trial of three former Special Agents charged with arson, attempted murder, and dereliction of duty had begun on Duadi. He turned to Emrelda. "Have they called you to testify at the trial of those agents?"

"No. The captain doesn't think that will happen. Some of the charges will be hard to prove, he says, and they'll likely plead guilty to lesser charges."

Unfortunately, Dekkard could see that. He just shook his head as he replaced the newssheet on the side table.

The remainder of breakfast was cheerfully unremarkable, and before that long, Dekkard, Avraal, and Gaaroll were in the Gresynt, ready to leave.

Even before he pulled away from the portico, Dekkard asked, "Any strong emotions anywhere?"

"Not that I can tell, sir," replied Gaaroll.

"Not yet," murmured Avraal.

Dekkard had the feeling that neither Gaaroll nor Avraal would sense the assassin who would finally shoot him. He pushed that thought away and concentrated on driving and trying to see if anyone was tailing them.

When they neared the Council Office Building, he asked, "You'll need the Gresynt today?"

"That might be for the best."

"Almighty straight," came from Gaaroll.

With that settled, Dekkard pulled up in front of the west entrance to the building, where he leaned over and kissed Avraal's cheek. "Be very careful."

"I will. You, too."

Then Dekkard got out, and Avraal slid into the driver's seat. Dekkard watched for a moment as she drove off, then turned and walked toward the bronze doors. He slowed as Julian Andros, coming from the covered parking, neared the door as well.

"Go ahead," said Dekkard. "We'll follow."

Andros smiled and opened the door, then waited for Dekkard and Gaaroll. "Would you mind if I walked up with you?"

"Not at all." After a minute, Dekkard asked, "What do you think of what's happening?"

"The frigging Commercers are trying to discredit Obreduur before he can do anything. They've got influencers talking to every newly elected councilor. You must know that."

"They seem to have avoided me," said Dekkard dryly. "Who's been to see you?"

"Who hasn't?" returned Andros. "The same's been true of Tomas, and even Chiram Ghohal and Elyncya Duforgue."

Dekkard had talked to some degree with all of the newly elected Craft councilors, but his interaction with Ghohal, the Crafter from Surpunta who'd replaced Jorje Kastenada, had been brief. "Who are these influencers, or the corporacions they work for?"

"Offhand, I don't remember all of them, but the latest one was Stoltz, Fernand, I think, and then there was Jaime Minz. Couldn't forget him. Big bear of a fellow. Cheerful, though. They both said that they'd been staffers here, and understood how new councilors needed good information in a hurry."

Andros stopped speaking as he started up the central staircase.

Dekkard waited a moment, followed, then asked, "Do you recall who Stoltz is working for?"

"A legalist firm that represents Eastern Ironway. I remember that. Minz represents some chemical corporacion. Northwest something or other."

"Northwest Industrial Chemical."

"I thought you said none of them came to see you."

"He hasn't. He told me he was going to work for them when I was still a staffer. Did he have anything interesting to say?"

"He mostly talked about phosphates and how theirs were the best for growers, and how important it was to retain the tariffs on phosphates shipped in from the countries in Sudlynd. Said a few words about how Northwest had the most modern and secure chemical facilities in Guldor, offered to provide any information I might need. That was about it. He said that he was visiting all the new councilors who looked like they'd be here for a while." Andros reached the top of the staircase and stepped to one side.

Dekkard nodded. "He'd say something like that."

A puzzled look crossed Andros's face momentarily. Then he smiled and said, "It was good to talk to you, Steffan. Until later."

"Until later," Dekkard replied warmly, but he couldn't help shivering as Andros walked away. Had Minz made that comment as another of his indirect messages? Or was it that he really didn't believe Dekkard would be around that long? Either way, it was unsettling.

When Dekkard reached the office, he immediately asked Margrit, "Any messages?"

"No, sir."

"That's good, I think." As Dekkard turned toward the door to his private office, Roostof hurried out of the staff office.

"Sir, have you read the *Tribune* this morning?"

"No, Svard, I haven't." Dekkard offered a humorous smile. "I rely on you for that."

"You might want to look at this." Roostof handed him the newssheet. "The lead story, but especially the lines below the fold."

Dekkard skimmed the first paragraphs, a slightly more critical summary of what had been in the first paragraphs of the *Gestirn* story, and concentrated on what followed.

> ... Although the aim of the Security and Public Safety Reorganization Act was understandable, what the Craft Party drafters and the Premier failed to take into account in passing the legislation, and in implementing it, was the impact it would have on the morale and behavior of the Special Agents, in particular, who felt betrayed and possibly even offered up to placate the rabble represented by the New Meritorists ...

In reading those words, Dekkard winced. *Indirectly portraying uniformed killers for hire as honorable public servants, rather than as the tool of corporacion interests.* "I see what you mean. I don't know there's much either we or the Premier can say that hasn't already been said. The *Gestirn* story explained the reasons, but those who are against us won't pay much attention."

"The Meritorists might not, either, sir."

"Not if it suits their purposes to ignore it," Dekkard agreed.

"Sir?" Roostof's voice was deferentially polite.

"What am I missing, Svard?"

"If you and the Premier don't point out that you tried to keep the Special Agents under control and were blocked by Commercers and old landed interests, who will?"

Dekkard laughed. "Well put, Svard. Write a short note to exactly that point, from me to the Premier, suggesting that it might be in his best interest to emphasize 'old landed interests' and Commercers in every statement he makes. I may have to present that point a little more politely in committee. Let me see the note as soon as you finish it. In the meantime, I'm going to try to catch up on mail and replies." He paused. "One other thing. I need to know what Shuryn's turned up on del Larrano and Venburg."

"Yes, sir."

Dekkard made his way into his office. He immediately tackled the replies drafted for his signature, absently noting that he had to make fewer changes as Colsbaan, Roostof, and even Teitryn, who drafted a few replies, were coming to understand what he expected.

Less than a third later, Roostof entered the office and laid a typed letter on the desk.

Dekkard read it carefully, then signed it. "You did an excellent job, Svard. Have Gaaroll deliver it personally to Karola."

"Yes, sir."

After Roostof left, Dekkard finished signing the replies and began reading through the incoming mail.

At a third before fourth bell. Dekkard turned over the replies and incoming mail to Roostof and motioned for Gaaroll to accompany him.

Once they were out in the main corridor away from the office and walking toward the central staircase, Dekkard said, "You delivered my message to the Premier's office. Did anyone say anything?"

"Karola just thanked me. They all looked awful busy."

"I imagine they were. Obreduur's been a councilor longer, and he has extra duties and commitments as Premier. He only gets a few additional clerks as Premier."

As they neared the grand staircase, Dekkard asked, "What can you sense now?"

"Mostly piles of normal feelings. A few . . . sort of spikes, here and there."

Dekkard recognized Marryat Osmond, the Commercer councilor from Machtarn, on the lower section of the stairs, accompanied by his security aides. "The councilor down there, how strong are his feelings?"

"Not that strong. They're mustardy gray, sort of."

"What would you say mustardy gray means?"

"It's a little disgust, I think, along with not caring very much."

Dekkard asked the same question about several others, all staffers, as they walked through the courtyard, which seemed even colder than it likely was because of the light wind out of the north. Then he said, "You sense more than the strength of feelings. You're just not sure what the colors mean." He opened the bronze door to the Council Hall and stepped inside.

Gaaroll followed. "Sort of a guess, really."

"We need to see if you can refine your senses. It'd be good for you, and for me, I'd have to admit."

As they neared the committee room, Dekkard saw Rikkard and Baar standing outside the door talking. When Rikkard saw Dekkard, he said something to Baar, then immediately walked through the open door into the chamber. Baar followed.

"What did you sense with the two councilors?"

"The one who went in first, his feelings got stronger when he saw you. They were black with a hint of purple. The second one's feelings didn't change. Black, not very strong."

Dekkard stopped short of the open door. "You'll have to wait outside because I have no idea how long the meeting will last. I'd guess around a bell, but it could be longer."

"I'll be here."

"Good." Dekkard offered a smile before turning and entering the committee room.

The only councilors not already present were Hasheem and Navione, but both entered by the time Dekkard took his seat.

Hasheem gaveled the meeting to order and immediately declared, "At the moment, I have no further new information, except that a number of current and former Special Agents have already reported to either the Treasury or Justiciary Ministry. I trust all of you have read through the staff recommendations. I'll ask each of you for your suggestions first. There will be no questions or debate about another councilor's remarks until all councilors have had a chance to offer comments on the staff recommendations and to propose any additional recommendations of their own." He turned to Navione. "Your thoughts, Councilor?"

"As I'm sure most of you have realized, the staff recommendations begin with the assumption that the New Meritorists responsible for the bombings have been caught. So far as I'm aware, they have not been apprehended. I'd be more interested in knowing what recommendations the staff might have for identifying and capturing those individuals. I'll defer to others for their thoughts."

"Councilor Haastar?"

"I agree with my colleague. I'd also like to see recommendations for more effective intelligence on subversive groups and organizations. We've recently seen large numbers of less than desirable individuals crossing the Rio Doro, and it might be useful to know their activities."

"Councilor Rikkard?"

"All these recommendations are a waste of time. We need to repeal the Security reforms and turn the STF on the New Meritorists. Nothing else will work. That's all I have to say."

"Councilor Pajiin?"

"It seems to me, Sr. Chairman, that the staff has concentrated exclusively on the New Meritorists and neglected the remainder of public safety. Between the unauthorized Special Agent raids and Unadi's shooting, it appears to me that far more people have been wounded and killed by Special Agents than by the New Meritorists. Maybe we should just concentrate on reforming public safety and leave the Meritorists alone for a while."

At those last words, Dekkard watched Rikkard, who looked like he wanted to attack Pajiin.

Hasheem didn't even blink. He just said, "Councilor Dekkard?"

"As my colleague indicated, we've skirted the problem with the Special Agents. I'd recommend that the Justiciary Ministry interview and interrogate every single one of the Special Agents with a criminal-specialist empath present to determine who was guilty and to what degree, as well as extract other information. The interviews should also concentrate on discovering who in the Security Ministry had infiltrated the New Meritorists. Someone in Security had to have done that. Since there's no record, it would be wise to investigate within the higher levels of the old Security Ministry. That's all I have."

Hasheem looked to the other side of the dais. "Councilor Baar?"

"Perhaps we should just ban public demonstrations and declare that anyone who participates is subject to exile." Baar smiled wryly and added, "I know that peaceful public demonstrations are enshrined in the Great Charter, but once we open it up to change, especially change as radical as that demanded by the New Meritorists, we could lose far more than we could possibly gain. Councilor Dekkard brought forth a comprehensive and well-thought Security reform measure, and the Council passed it. Yet even before it was fully implemented, the New Meritorists started demonstrating. They've scarcely given this Council a chance to get settled or to consider other changes we could make. They seem to be more interested in making trouble than in seeking workable improvements in government. We need to root out those behind the trouble so that we can address the problems without having to deal with riots and shootings. On that point, I agree with Councilor Dekkard."

Dekkard didn't exactly care for the way Baar had characterized his suggestions, but he and Baar at least agreed, seemingly, on the need to find out who was behind the New Meritorist movement.

"Are there any comments or questions?"

"Yes!" snapped Pajiin. "The most honorable councilor from Endor suggested we scrap reforms we haven't had a chance to let work and return to the old system. As I recall, under the old system, the Meritorists blew up fifteen buildings without Security even knowing what happened. Under the old system, the STF massacred innocent people, but never came up with a single important

Meritorist. The Special Agents shot loggers who protested unsafe working conditions. Those idiots couldn't tell a Meritorist from a deadfall."

Dekkard managed not to smile.

After another bell of "debate," which consisted mostly of Rikkard rejecting everything other than repealing all reforms, and Hasheem trying to extract concrete suggestions beyond the few already proposed, Hasheem rapped the gavel loudly.

"Thank you all. The staff has been taking down suggestions, and we will compile a revised set of recommendations for the Premier as a result of your efforts."

Dekkard suspected that few of the "recommendations" would be made public, but that Obreduur would praise faintly the Security Committee for offering recommendations.

"That's all?" muttered Pajiin.

"We're political cover," replied Dekkard. "Whatever the Premier does, he'll mention all those involved, the Security reform act and that it attempted to resolve the problems with corrupt Special Agents, and who knows what else. It won't mollify the New Meritorists, but it should put most of the blame on previous Councils. It might buy him a little time."

"You're cheerful this morning, Steffan."

"I'm always cheerful," Dekkard replied sardonically as he rose from his seat.

Surprisingly, at least to Dekkard, Villem Baar stood waiting outside the committee room, his security aides standing well back from him and from Gaaroll.

"Steffan, I just wanted to tell you that you made a very good point this morning." Baar paused. "Do you honestly feel that many of the Special Agents are not entirely to be trusted?"

Dekkard didn't answer immediately, trying to find a way to answer honestly without emotion. "It depends on how you define trust. I've personally seen Special Agents shoot unarmed students in the back. According to *Gestirn,* three Special Agents, one of them a subcaptain, are on trial for attempted murder through arson. I had to stop a Special Agent from shooting the Premier when he was a councilor. A great many Special Agents participated in the unauthorized raids. While they may have felt they had no choice, I seriously doubt that they had to shoot and kill as many suspected New Meritorists as they did. These agents could likely be called trustworthy in carrying out orders, but I wouldn't term them trustworthy in terms of public responsibility or adherence to the principles of the Great Charter. That's why I pushed to have the organization essentially dismantled. There didn't seem to be any other way to remove the idea that whatever they were ordered to do was in the public good, no matter how many others got killed."

"You've killed people." Baar's voice was even.

"I have. So far, those I've killed were trying to kill Councilor Obreduur or me, if not both, and had weapons out and had attempted to use them. There were witnesses in every case." The last sentence might have been a stretch, but it was still true.

Abruptly, Baar nodded. "Interesting. Thank you."

Then he turned and headed in the direction of the courtyard.

Gaaroll immediately joined Dekkard.

"What did you sense?"

"He wasn't feeling strong, not real strong, anyway. Small black pile. His empie was, though. Felt like he was looking more at you all the time. The isolate, though, he didn't look comfortable, but with isolates there's no telling."

"Thank you. We might as well head back to the office." He turned toward the courtyard doors, still wondering what Baar's questions signified.

The courtyard was warmer, but the sunlight felt weak, possibly because of the haze that had grown over the city since earlier in the day.

When he reached the office, Margrit immediately said, "You have a message. The messenger was one of the private services." She handed him the envelope.

"From a private messenger service?" Dekkard frowned, then opened the envelope and smiled as he recognized the writing. "It's from Avraal. She might be late this afternoon." He nodded to Margrit. "Thank you."

Then he headed into his office, realizing that, for the first time in days, he might have a chance to just sit down and think—until he saw the papers in his inbox. Warily, he picked them up to discover draft legislation and supporting documentation—Luara's work. He sat down and began to read the draft act—entitled "Legalist Representation for Unrepresented Working Women." Reading the proposed legislation didn't take long, although the preamble was the only part immediately clear to him, because all the other sections were insertions or modifications to existing statutes. One clause simply read, "Remove Section 4a(1)."

From the draft legislation, he turned his attention to the documentation which followed. It amplified and clarified—and in places corrected—what he'd outlined to Colsbaan about the need for working women of the streets to be able to seek legal representation through the Working Women Guild. While he had to trust her and Roostof on the technical changes, she'd clearly explained the need far better than he could have.

He stood, smiling, and picked up the papers. Then he walked out of his office into the staff room.

Colsbaan looked up as he approached. "Sir?"

Dekkard handed her the papers. "Excellent work, Luara. The supporting documentation is superb. For now, you keep the package, but have someone type up a copy of the supporting documentation so that I can study it in detail. I'm going to have to gather some support, so it will be a little while before I bring it up before the Workplace Administration Committee." He paused. "It could be longer, depending on what it takes to get Chairman Haarsfel's attention, but I'll keep at it." *Until I get it passed.* He had to keep that thought to himself because getting any legislation passed took far more than one junior councilor.

"Thank you, sir. I didn't do it all alone. Svard checked the legislation against the existing statutes and helped me with acceptable legislative phrasing."

"She did all of it," interjected Roostof. "I just proofed and checked it."

"Thank you both," said Dekkard, before looking directly at Colsbaan and adding, "and mostly you." He paused, then asked, "Are you ready for another project, one that might take years to get passed?"

"Yes, sir. What might that be?"

"For lack of a better name, the 'Equal Pay for Equal Work Act.' Something that will require equal pay for women doing the same job as men, or the other way around, although I don't know of any instances of that. There also has to be a provision disallowing the use of different names or classifications for the same job, and one that says the pay of a better-compensated position held by men cannot be reduced to achieve pay equality—and any other provisions that would make it stronger or more workable."

"Sir?" Colsbaan looked questioningly at Dekkard.

"I know. You're thinking that trying that would be an exercise in futility, aren't you?"

"I wouldn't say that, but—"

"Luara," interjected Roostof, "how many people would have thought a brand-new councilor would get Security reform passed in his first month in office?"

"She's right, Svard," said Dekkard. "Pay reform will be much harder, but I don't see any reason not to try. After all, no one thought the Silent Revolution would succeed, either. It also took years." Dekkard grinned. "That's another reason we need to start now." He looked back at Colsbaan. "Right?"

She smiled almost helplessly.

"You don't need to hurry, and you can fit it in as you can, but keep working on it."

"Yes, sir."

Still smiling, Dekkard turned and headed back to his office, where Margrit had left another set of responses to be read and signed.

By the time Avraal arrived at a third past fifth bell, Dekkard had actually caught up on all the correspondence, and only Roostof and Gaaroll remained in the office. While Dekkard had earlier strongly suggested that the senior legalist could leave, Roostof insisted he wouldn't feel comfortable until Avraal returned with the steamer.

Dekkard wasn't about to argue that point, but the moment Avraal arrived, he turned to Roostof. "She's here. Now, I will insist that you go."

Roostof smiled. "I'll turn off the last lamp in the staff room, get my overcoat, and depart. Have a pleasant evening."

The moment Roostof was out the door, Avraal said to Gaaroll, "Lock the main door. I need a few minutes with Steffan before we go."

"Yes, Ritten."

Dekkard followed Avraal back into his office and closed the door, then said, "You found something, didn't you?"

"I did. Rather one of Carlos's sources did. He wouldn't tell me who, but he or she came up with something on that clerk with the Atacaman fire pepper, your would-be assassin Sohl Hurrek . . . rather a 'someone.'"

"Who?"

"His fiancée. It turns out Hurrek was engaged, and she was the beneficiary of his new banque account. She's a typist at Faegel and Cardenaez, and until two years ago, was a committee typist for the Security Committee, when she got the better job at the legalist firm."

"Faegel and Cardenaez. Isn't that one of the legalist firms in that building?" Dekkard shook his head. "How did you find all that out?"

"I went and talked to her. She's very sweet and heartbroken. That's where I've been. Hurrek worried about keeping his job, and he'd lined up a position as a legal clerk in Endor. He planned to give notice, but they were short of marks to get married and move."

"Endor? That's about as far from Machtarn as you can get and still stay in Guldor. That's Rikkard's district." Dekkard paused. "Oh, but it *was* Ivaan Maendaan's, and *he* was the Security Committee chair and Hurrek was the holdover clerk. So he likely had contacts of some sort there, if only by mail."

"Hurrek told her about the banque account, and that she was his beneficiary. He didn't tell her how much it held. Imagine her shock when she found out how much was there. He only said he was doing work on the side. He wouldn't say for whom. Just that it was someone he trusted and had known through work."

"I have an idea where this is leading," said Dekkard dourly.

"She saw the man once, from a distance. Said he was big and burly, like a bear. He drove a blue steamer of some sort that looked new."

"That's a little more than suggestive."

"But it's still not admissible proof in a Justiciary proceeding."

"I take it that you needed to do some sympathetic emping?"

"Not much. She needed someone to talk to. She's from a little town west of here and would have had to marry an older man she couldn't stand. She left the moment she finished her typing training. The school gave her a recommendation, and she managed to get a junior typist slot in Machtarn Sanitation. Her family disowned her. Later, she got a committee typist's position. That's where she met Hurrek."

"What did you tell her?"

"Close to the truth. That I was trying to find someone who was supplying Atacaman pepper dust to people without warning them about how dangerous it was."

"She knew how he died, then?"

"One of the typists in Rikkard's office, who knew her and Hurrek, told her. I fuzzed her memory just a little. She'll remember that she talked to someone and vaguely remember the details."

Dekkard nodded slowly. "I can't believe you did all that, except I can."

"It still leaves a lot unanswered."

"Like who and what else is going on and why someone would pay so much."

"Why would they pay so much? Dear, what would it have been worth to the Commercers to have the Premier's former aide and the councilor shepherding the Security bill to have killed a clerk over a mere prank with Atacaman pepper? Ten thousand marks would be cheap for obtaining that."

Dekkard considered, then nodded. Another thought occurred to him. "They also would have gained a seat if I were expelled, because a disgraced councilor's seat is filled by the party who had the next most votes in the last election."

"As I said, cheap at the price."

"Along those lines, I also had an interesting conversation today, one with Julian Andros." Dekkard went on to relate what Andros had said.

"Circumstantial—and suggestive—again," Avraal said slowly.

"We need to go," Dekkard said, "and think about all this." *Not that thinking is going to resolve any of the problems.*

They both stood.

After putting on his overcoat, Dekkard turned off the wall lamp, then followed Avraal out into the main office, where Gaaroll waited.

49

THE drive back to the house on Tridi night was quiet and tense, but neither Avraal nor Gaaroll sensed anyone who might be a sniper. Even so, Dekkard let out a long breath when he stopped the Gresynt under the portico roof to let off Gaaroll and Avraal.

Avraal reached out and squeezed his hand before she got out of the steamer.

Dekkard garaged the Gresynt, checked the water and kerosene levels, and the acetylene tank and fittings, then closed the garage door and walked to the portico. For a moment, he stopped because he saw young Tomas hopping from place to place on the front walk.

The youngster stopped and looked at Dekkard.

"Just wave to the man, Tomas," said the nanny.

Tomas waved enthusiastically.

Dekkard smiled and waved back before he climbed the steps to the portico door. He'd no sooner entered the house than Avraal called, "Hang up your coat and go wash. Dinner's almost ready."

Although he hurried, Dekkard was the last one to the table, partly because he got the wine for Emrelda and Avraal, and the lager for Gaaroll and himself. He sat down and looked at the main serving platter, trying to figure out the dish, then asked, "Rabbit?"

"Oven-roasted rabbit with bacon and herbs, to be exact," said Emrelda.

Dekkard didn't need to ask about the cheesed potato slices or the spicy turnips, which he hadn't seen in years, not since he'd left home.

Once everyone's platter was full, Emrelda said, "What happened in your lives today?" She looked at Dekkard.

"Mostly routine matters and a rather subdued Security Committee meeting where a Commercer councilor declared that the only way to deal with the New Meritorists was to scrap the Security reforms, and send the STF and Special Agents after the whole lot. After that there were only a few constructive and workable suggestions."

"All of them yours?" asked Avraal with a mischievous smile.

"A few, and Navione and Baar each added one." Dekkard looked to Emrelda. "I suspect you had a more eventful day."

"I feared so, but Captain Narryt turned it into routine. I thought I might have to testify at the trial of those three Special Agents, until the captain told me that I wasn't needed because they all pled guilty to all the charges."

"All of them?" asked Gaaroll. "No way the bastards'd do that."

"They faced charges of attempted murder and the possibility of involuntary manslaughter," replied Emrelda. "If they pled guilty to all the other charges, the prosecutor agreed to drop the murder and manslaughter charges. They were sentenced to six years in the Jaykarh Mountain Work Camp, with the additional stipulation that any future felonious offense would result in involuntary exile."

"Six years isn't long enough for them," said Gaaroll.

"I still wonder why the prosecutor didn't want a trial," said Dekkard. "The trial would have revealed just how corrupt the Special Agents have become."

"Possibly," replied Avraal. "But if that gets revealed, a lot of people will question why the Council passed legislation that keeps them in good standing and gives them new jobs. It might also come out that the sponsor of that legislation lived in the house those three targeted. It could have gotten messy. I'm sure the legalists for the Special Agents made that clear to the prosecutor. Obreduur likely wants to keep things simple."

Once again, political imperatives are making it harder.

Gaaroll just snorted dismissively.

Dekkard decided to concentrate on the rabbit and the potatoes. He only ate a small portion of the spicy turnips, but Gaaroll had no difficulty finishing off the last of the turnips.

Later, once Dekkard and Avraal retired to their bedroom, he looked at her and asked the question that had been troubling him since she'd reported on her discovery. "What do we do now? Everything leads to Minz, and there's not a shred of hard evidence."

"He has us—you, especially—on the defensive. We need to put him where he's reacting, where he's a little uncertain."

Dekkard almost pointed out that such actions could be dangerous, then smiled ruefully.

"You're smiling. What's so amusing?"

"I was about to say that could be dangerous, but how much more dangerous could it be than already being targeted?"

"A bit more, but not so dangerous as doing nothing," suggested Avraal.

"I do have one thought. Can you get hold of Atacaman fire pepper dust?" asked Dekkard.

"No, but regular red pepper dust will do, if I'm guessing what you have in mind. If the grocers here don't carry it, I can make it. Either way, that should suffice, and, that way, it's clearly a prank and not a crime."

"How do you know how to do that?"

"We used to crush the seeds into flakes to keep the squirrels from the root crops in the garden. Father used making the flakes and the dust as a punishment when we didn't please him."

"Let's hope you can buy it and not have to make it. What else?"

"A new Realto shouldn't have loose acetylene fittings. Little things like that. We need to come up with more than a few."

"Except we don't even know where he lives—" Dekkard broke off the words as he saw Avraal smile. "You tailed him?"

"How else? He has a very stylish flat in Westpark, with covered parking that's disappointingly unsecure."

"I suppose you also discovered whether he's married?"

"He's not. He almost was once, but it didn't work out."

"Cherlyssa Maergan?"

"She's a bit of a bitch, but she's too smart to even think of it. No, Iferra Vonacht. She wouldn't talk about it, except to say that breaking off the engagement was the smartest thing she ever did. That was before you started with Obreduur."

"I take it that he made a pass at you."

"I never let him get that close. Besides, he knew I wasn't impressed. You might recall that he almost never approached you when I was around."

Dekkard hadn't thought about it, but that was definitely true. "You're also better at wordplay and double meanings."

"One of the few advantages of a Landor upbringing."

Catching the slight sardonic edge to her words, Dekkard replied, "But you can put them to better use now."

"I know," she said sweetly, "I do so well as a councilor's wife."

Dekkard winced.

"It's not you. I never wanted to be just an ornament."

"You never have been with me." *Especially since I'd already be dead without you.*

"Too many councilors look at me that way."

"Not the ones who count. Certainly not Obreduur, or Hasheem, Mardosh, Bassaana, or even Vhiola Sandegarde."

"That's a start, I suppose."

"It's only been a month and a half," Dekkard pointed out. "It takes a little while. Nobody thinks of Ingrella as an ornament. Or Delehya—"

"Delehya?"

"The Scarlet Daughter who married the Premier at the time."

"That's a comparison I can do without, thank you."

But Dekkard detected the hint of a smile, and he grinned.

Avraal shook her head, but there was amusement in the gesture. Then she said, "We need more ideas, but we've made a start."

"Sleep on it?"

"In a while." This time Avraal gave more than a hint of a smile.

50

DEKKARD slept soundly. He even woke with a smile on Furdi morning, despite the cloudy sky and the sound of wind stripping the already faded leaves from the maple tree outside the bedroom window.

He turned in the bed to see Avraal smiling at him.

"You definitely got a good night's sleep. So did I."

Dekkard found himself blushing, yet leaning toward her.

She laughed softly and pulled the sheet around her. "It's already later than it should be. Go get your shower."

Dekkard sat up and shook his head with what he thought was a doleful expression.

"You don't do mournful well, dear."

He laughed and stood.

"You are handsome, and it is too bad it's late, but you do need to take that shower. More important, I need you to take it."

Dekkard let himself be persuaded and headed for the bathroom.

Somehow, in less than a third, they were in the breakfast room, where Avraal sipped her café while Dekkard readied the croissants—and quince paste. Emrelda was long gone.

"You two don't usually sleep that late," observed Gaaroll.

"I was tired," said Dekkard.

Gaaroll did not quite smirk. Dekkard let it pass and picked up the morning *Gestirn,* intending just to glance at it until he read the headline—SECURITY MINISTER CONVICTED.

"What is it?" asked Avraal.

"They convicted Wyath on charges of criminal malfeasance in office, misfeasance, and high treason."

"High treason. Doesn't that carry a death penalty?"

"Usually."

"What about Manwaeren?"

"He was convicted on counts of misfeasance and criminal neglect of duties. The High Justiciary will hand down the sentences at first bell tomorrow afternoon." Dekkard leafed through the newssheet, finally locating a short story about the trial of the three Special Agents, which said little more than the three had pled guilty and been sentenced to six years at the Jaykarh Mountain Work Camp. He smiled wryly, relayed that information to Avraal and Gaaroll, and set the newssheet back on the side table.

"I'd hoped that Obreduur would have pushed his new Justiciary minister to make more of it than that," said Avraal.

"What else could they do?" said Dekkard as he sat down. "Wyath made the decisions and gave the orders, and he'll be executed. Manwaeren was an incompetent stooge who didn't know what was really going on. There's no real proof beyond that, just like there's no real proof of who ordered the Special Agents to attack the house, *and* no way to get it. Not that's acceptable in court, anyway."

"When you need the law," said Gaaroll, "it's not there."

"No," replied Dekkard. "The problem is that we're dealing with people who know how to exploit every weakness in the law, and they're very good at it."

"They also spent years changing the laws to their benefit," replied Avraal.

"More like changing the enforcement of the law to their benefit."

"Still means you can't count on the law," said Gaaroll.

"That's true. Sometimes you can't." *Like now with Minz.* Which meant that they'd have to go around the law, or find another way to use it to their advantage.

Dekkard ate quickly, and Avraal even consumed a whole croissant, and the three were soon on their way, later than on recent mornings, but still earlier than usual. The haze over Machtarn reduced the morning sunlight, as it often did in late autumn and winter, but the coal haze wasn't anywhere as bad as in Oersynt. Dekkard took another indirect route, modified slightly by Gaaroll's perceptions.

When Dekkard turned onto Council Avenue heading west toward the Council buildings, he asked Avraal, "You're taking the Gresynt, I presume?"

"Absolutely. Among other things, I have to pick up a few hard-to-find items, and I did promise Carlos I'd help with some meetings."

"Fourth bell or fifth bell this afternoon?"

"Closer to fifth bell, I'd think, but I could be there earlier."

Dekkard drove past the Council Hall and the walled courtyard and pulled up in front of the west doors to the Council Office Building, where he bestowed a parting kiss on Avraal before turning the Gresynt over to her. He carefully reclaimed his gray leather folder as well. He watched for a long moment as Avraal drove off.

Then he and Gaaroll made their way into the building, where he asked, "Any strong feelings?"

"Not yet, sir."

Gaaroll sensed nothing untoward on the walk up to his office, where Margrit smiled as they walked in.

"You got this from Premier Obreduur," said Margrit, extending an envelope. "Anna delivered it a few minutes ago."

Dekkard took and opened the envelope. The handwritten message was short.

Steffan—
   If it's convenient, I'd appreciate your joining Fredrich and me for a few moments at a third past third bell in my regular office.

Axel

Dekkard replaced the card in the envelope. "I've got a meeting with the Premier just after third bell." Then he walked into the staff office and to Teitryn's desk.

The young engineering aide looked up. "Yes, sir?"

"Later today, I'll need to know what else you've discovered, especially on del Larrano and Venburg. I'll let you know. I have an unexpected meeting this morning, and I don't know how long it will last."

"Yes, sir."

When Dekkard reached his private office, the morning mail awaited him, along with a neatly typed copy of Colsbaan's proposed legislation and the supporting documentation. He sat down to see how much of the incoming mail he could read before he had to meet with Obreduur and Hasheem. He not only finished reading through it all, but he had almost a sixth to begin to study the supporting information that Colsbaan had provided for the proposed changes to the Working Women's Act.

He and Gaaroll reached Obreduur's office at a sixth past third bell. Both Isobel Irlende and Karola smiled as he entered.

"Councilor," said Karola, "he said that you'd probably be early, and if you were to just go on in to his office."

"Is he there? I wouldn't—"

"He also said you'd try to not interrupt, but to send you in anyway."

Dekkard couldn't help smiling as he opened the door and stepped inside, closing it behind himself.

Obreduur didn't rise from behind the desk, but gestured to the chairs before it. "I hoped you'd be a bit early. I appreciated your note and your suggestions. I intend to use them, but not for a few days. I think it would be best to let Wyath's conviction speak for itself for a day or so." He paused. "I imagine you were surprised that the trial of the Special Agents was so quiet."

More like angry and disappointed. "Initially, I wondered, but when I thought about it, I could see that there might be a downside if you pressed too hard."

Obreduur nodded. "For better or worse, that was my thought. Are you still concerned about dunnite?"

"I still think it's going to be a problem, more than I initially thought."

"Is there anything else you're working on?"

"A small problem I learned about when we accompanied you to Gaarlak, Oersynt, and Malek. Myram Plassar in Gaarlak also raised it." That wasn't quite true, since Dekkard had raised it with her.

"I don't seem to recall that name." Obreduur frowned, which amused Dekkard, since Obreduur always seemed to recall everyone.

"The regional steward for the Working Women Guild of Gaarlak. It's about a way to get legalist representation—"

"For women who work the streets. I remember that issue now, but not the name."

Dekkard was the one to frown. Then he remembered. "Now that I recall, I don't know that you met her. When you had me speak in Gaarlak, she sat at my table, but the issue really came up when you met with the Working Women in Oersynt."

"What are you thinking?"

"It's as much a Workplace Administration issue as anything else. If even some of the street women join the guild, they'll get legal protection and learn better health practices. It seemed to fit in with what the committee has been doing since Chairman Haarsfel has been holding hearings on health and safety practices."

"Have you drafted anything?"

Dekkard nodded.

"Let me talk to Guilhohn. He might find that interesting. You could work on that until it's more opportune to deal with another Security issue."

Dekkard knew an implied trade-off when he saw one, and if Obreduur talked to Haarsfel about it, Haarsfel would at least listen. "If it wouldn't be a problem."

Obreduur smiled. "I've always appreciated your courtesy, Steffan, and it won't be a problem. How is Svard working out?"

"He's been outstanding."

"I thought he would be." Obreduur shook his head. "I couldn't have kept him much longer. Someone would have offered him a senior legalist position. He was better than most senior legalists years ago. I'm just glad it worked out for both of you."

"So am I."

There was a rap on the door, and then Fredrich Hasheem entered the office. Behind him, Karola eased the door shut.

"I'm sorry I was a little late," Hasheem offered as he took the other chair in front of the desk. "The presidente of Rio Doro Barge and Transport stayed longer than I anticipated."

"That's fine. It gave Steffan and me a chance to catch up." Obreduur straightened in his chair. "I wanted you both to know. Right now, out of the four hundred Special Agents posted in the Machtarn area, three hundred and fifty-seven are accounted for. That includes the three just sentenced to the work camp and the five killed at the demonstration on Unadi. All five killed were Special Agents, and the semi-automatic pistols recovered belonged to them. Justiciary Minister Kuta strongly doubts the remaining former Special Agents will be located any time soon. Do you have any thoughts on what we should do?" Obreduur looked to Hasheem.

"Fifty loose somewhere? It could be worse. Tie them to Mangele or Stuart Jebulon. Claim they were used as a private army."

"Steffan?" prompted Obreduur.

"How many of the three hundred and fifty-seven have been interviewed with an empath present?"

"Very few, if any, so far."

"I'd suggest all of them be interviewed with an empath present as a condition for continued employment by any ministry. I'd be amazed if two hundred could pass an interview asking about illegal activities and shooting unarmed demonstrators or shooting people without authorization." Dekkard smiled sardonically. "That might also reduce ministry expenses."

"Anything else?"

"I suspect many of them have performed 'favors' for corporacions, but asking about specifics would be pushing even the limits of the self-incrimination statute."

"It would be, Ingrella has informed me."

"Then you considered interviews?"

"Of course. Now I can say that they weren't just my idea, but came from influential members of the Council and appropriate ministries. I'm going to have to make a statement and let the newsies ask questions. They won't miss the chance to have an empath present."

Dekkard knew that the newssheets couldn't print an empie's conclusions, but they could make assertions based on those conclusions, which was why few politicians ever met with newsies. "You're doing that to show a form of accountability to blunt the charges of the New Meritorists?"

"It's worth a try."

"It's also a dangerous precedent," said Hasheem.

"If we don't show we're different from the Commercer governments of the past, Fredrich, we won't last that long."

Dekkard had to agree with that.

"Is there anything else either of you would like to know?"

"What are you going to do at the next demonstration?" asked Dekkard.

"What do you recommend?" returned Obreduur cheerfully.

"You can either let them demonstrate or break up the demonstrations by force. I'd let them demonstrate peacefully while you try to find out who's behind them."

Hasheem frowned.

"The demonstrations have been organized, and it definitely took organization to bomb fifteen buildings across Guldor on the same day." Dekkard paused, then added, "It seems rather unusual that Security knew nothing."

"The Justiciary Ministry has been questioning a number of demonstrators, following up with the families of those who were wounded or killed on Unadi." Obreduur added dryly, "Apparently, the previous leadership of the Security Ministry never thought to do so. If they did, there's no record."

"They were too busy trailing and tracking Crafters," returned Hasheem.

"I also wonder how they're funded," said Dekkard. "I saw a steam lorry filled with signs used in the demonstration."

"You never mentioned that," said Obreduur. "That's something else we can try to track down."

Dekkard thought about saying that it wasn't his job to do what the patrollers and Justiciary Ministry were supposed to handle, but only nodded.

"Is there anything else I should know?" asked Obreduur.

"I don't think so," replied Hasheem.

Dekkard just shook his head, given that there was nothing else he wanted to say with Hasheem present.

Obreduur stood. "Then I'll thank you both for coming and wish you a productive day."

Dekkard and Hasheem both stood as well. Dekkard let Hasheem lead the way from the office. In the anteroom, Gaaroll spoke quietly with Orlov and Lestiig, but all three immediately stopped and turned.

Hasheem and his aides left first.

Once Dekkard and Gaaroll were out in the corridor walking back toward his office, he asked, "Did you learn anything interesting?"

"Not really."

After a minute or so, Gaaroll asked, "Why is Councilor Hasheem the chairman of the Security Committee?"

"Because he's the most senior Craft councilor on the committee. That's usually what determines who is the chair. Why?"

"He's not that impressive."

"You don't have to be impressive to be a good councilor or a good anything. A number of people I know who look impressive are pretty miserable people." *Like Jaime Minz or Yordan Farris.* "What matters is what you do, not how you look." *Or, sometimes, what you don't do.*

Once he returned to his office, Dekkard called Teitryn in and asked, "What have you found out about del Larrano and Venburg?"

The engineering aide handed several sheets to Dekkard. "There's not much that's public. There are mentions of the corporacion every time they complete a ship, and great detail about the ship, and nothing about del Larrano. The biography is pieced together from several sources. For Sr. Venburg there's even less. I might be able to find out more by talking to people, but you indicated you didn't want anyone to know."

"That's right. Let me go over these, and see if I have any ideas." Dekkard paused. "One other thing: At some point we'll need to look at the contracts Siincleer has with the Navy. Find out who has access to them, but only ask about procurement contracts in general."

"Yes, sir."

Once Teitryn left, Dekkard began to read what he'd compiled on Juan del Larrano:

Presidente of Siincleer Shipbuilding since 1255. Corporacion founded by his uncle, interestingly enough. Born in 1205, graduated from the Military Institute in 1226. Served four years as a junior engineering officer in the Imperial Navy before returning to Siincleer Shipbuilding. Held various positions in engineering development and corporacion accounts: became director of corporacion accounts in 1240, vice-presidente of the corporacion in 1245. Married with four children. There was nothing else at all personal or even professional.

As for Pietro Alexi Venburg, there was almost nothing. Born 1215, graduated Imperial University in 1247 with degrees in engineering and law. Joined Siincleer Shipbuilding legalist department in 1248 and became vice-presidente for legal affairs in 1255. There were no personal details at all.

When you can't even find out general information about these people . . . Dealing with the Siincleer corporacions was definitely going to be a long process. *And then some.*

Dekkard spent the rest of the workday dealing with correspondence and studying the background material Colsbaan had provided because he wanted to have the information solidly set in his mind before he talked to Haarsfel.

Avraal returned to the office at just before fifth bell, about the time that Dekkard began to get uneasy, partly because he had the feeling Avraal just might have been doing things he might worry about if he knew. She slipped into the office with a smile, closing the door behind her.

"How did your errands go?"

"I actually found ground red pepper seeds, and a small package of ground Atacaman fire pepper and a few other things."

"You have that look. What else were you up to?"

"After shopping, when our former colleague went to lunch, I investigated the building. Well, a little more than that." She held up two keys. "It was tedious and took a little doing."

"Tedious?"

"I had to put the building supervisor to sleep, and keep him sleep dreaming while I went through the master key drawer. You need a key to the building and an office key, but there's usually a master key for all the offices for the cleaning staff. That way we can investigate his office."

"Breaking and entering, yet? There won't be any records of anything he shouldn't be doing, either in his office or home."

"I know that. These are for later, just in case."

"In case of what?"

Avraal smiled again. "We'll think of something. If we don't, the keys will just disappear." She paused. "There was one thing. The master key drawer was well-labeled, but the slot for Northwest Chemical had another name as well—Capitol Services. I assume that was what it meant. It was abbreviated 'Cap Serv.' So I went up and walked past the door. It was closed, but I could sense one person inside."

"A clerk or secretary, most likely."

"The name on the office door was just Northwest Industrial Chemical, though."

"Capitol Services. I wonder if our friend Jaime is running another business on the side."

"Maybe it's not on the side," suggested Avraal. "After that, I went back to Carlos's office and sat in on a few meetings and tried to earn some of what he's paying me."

"Did you?"

"Some of it, anyway. I also asked him, later, if he'd ever heard of Capitol Services. He said he thought he'd heard the name somewhere, but he wasn't sure. It's so generic. There must be a score of businesses that are Capitol something or other. He did say he'd ask around."

"You found something that just might help."

"Or not," she replied slightly sardonically. "Now, we need to head out of here and go home."

Dekkard was more than ready to leave, but he definitely wondered about Capitol Services, if that indeed was even the name.

51

WHEN Dekkard got out of bed on Quindi, one of the first things he did was to draw back the curtains and look out the window. The early morning looked cold and greenish gray, much more like winter than autumn.

But then, it's the next to last day of fall and of the year. It had definitely been quite a year, from falling in love and getting married to going from being a mere security aide to being a councilor—and the target for would-be assassins. He looked over to the bed.

Avraal began to open her eyes and smiled. "You look happy this morning."

"It's a short working day. Just until noon, and I'll be taking my lovely wife to a ball this evening. *And* we have two days off after that. Mostly, anyway."

Avraal stretched, then shivered. "It's cold in here."

"It's cold outside. Emrelda lit the furnace, but the radiators are barely warm." Dekkard went to the closet, pulled out a robe, and handed it to her. "I'll be quick in the shower."

"Don't use all the warm water."

"I wouldn't think of it."

Dekkard was as good as his word, then dressed and hurried downstairs, encountering Emrelda in the hall, where she donned a patroller's cold-weather jacket.

"What time will we be leaving for the ball?" she asked.

"I thought we'd leave the house at two thirds past fifth bell."

"I'll be ready."

"What are you wearing?" Dekkard grinned.

"That's a surprise. You'll see. Now, I need to go."

Dekkard shook his head as he entered the warmer kitchen, where Emrelda had clearly turned on the stove, which radiated heat. Dekkard checked the oven, but everything was off, except for the café pot. Then he poured two mugs and set them on the table and went to get the croissants.

When he returned, he noticed that Gaaroll had both hands around her mug.

"It's not that cold," said Dekkard.

"Not for someone from a family that spent generations surrounded by the eternal ice of Argental," declared Avraal as she hurried into the kitchen and stood close to the stove.

"Your café is hot," he said.

"Good." After a moment, she settled into her chair at the table, cupping her hands around her mug before taking a first sip of café.

Dekkard sat down across from her and split his croissants, slipping the quince paste into place before taking a bite of the first croissant.

The remainder of breakfast was uneventful, and little more than a third of a bell later, the three were in the Gresynt.

Dekkard was just about to pull out of the drive when Gaaroll declared,

"There's strong feelings on Jacquez, just up from Florinda. Might be an accident."

"We'll go another way, just in case it's not." Dekkard turned east on Florinda. He ended up taking the very long and winding way along the north side of the Imperial University grounds and eventually emerging onto Imperial Boulevard.

As he turned onto Council Avenue, he asked, "Are you going to Carlos's this morning?"

"Unless you need me."

Dekkard shook his head.

"Is a third past noon all right for me to come back?"

"That would be fine. Gaaroll and I can wait."

"Svard won't leave till you do," said Gaaroll.

"If he chooses," replied Dekkard, "Svard can wait a third as well." Minutes later, he brought the Gresynt to a stop in front of the west doors of the Council Office Building. He opened the door and stepped out, then smiled at Avraal. "I'll see you in a few bells." Then, he closed the steamer's door, and watched as she headed back toward Imperial Boulevard.

A moment later, he nodded, turned, and walked to the entrance. When he pushed the bronze door open and stepped into the building, he caught sight of two councilors on one side of the corridor, just outside an office door. They looked familiar, and after a moment, he realized that the two were Rikkard and Schmidtz. As Dekkard continued walking and watching, Schmidtz turned and walked swiftly toward the far end of the building, while Rikkard entered the office.

"That councilor walking quickly up there, can you sense any feelings?"

"Nothing real strong. Sort of ordered low piles. I'd guess satisfaction, but that's a guess. He's definitely not upset."

Schmidtz being satisfied after talking momentarily to Rikkard. Dekkard couldn't help but wonder what that had been all about.

When he stepped into his own office, he looked to Margrit. "Any messages?"

"Only two. One was from the Premier to office staffs. It was a reminder that the Council will close for business at noon and will not open until Duadi morning, the second of Winterfirst. All staff and councilors are expected to be out of the building no later than first bell. This is the other." Margrit smiled and handed Dekkard the envelope. "There also wasn't as much mail."

"How are you going to celebrate Yearend?" asked Dekkard.

"My family always gets together. We have a good time. I can play with my niece. My sister will tease me about still being unmarried. This year I can point out that Ritten Ysella-Dekkard is two years older than I am, and she just got married."

Dekkard smiled. "I was very fortunate that she agreed."

"We all wondered when you two would get around to it." Margrit flushed. "I'm sorry, sir. I didn't mean . . ."

"You don't need to apologize," replied Dekkard, trying not to laugh. "Sometimes, things are obvious to everyone but the couple themselves."

Dekkard was still smiling when he hung up his overcoat and opened the envelope from the Premier, containing a sheet about the ball, informing councilors that if they drove their own steamers, they could park in the spaces east of the Council Hall, and that outerwear could be left with attendants at the councilors' dining room.

With a nod, Dekkard sat down at his desk to read through the mail. When he finished less than a bell later, he was still in a good mood. There hadn't been any more New Meritorist letters and nothing of a nasty nature.

Since nothing demanded his immediate attention, he took out the background material Luara had prepared and began to go through it again. After that, he looked out the window intermittently while trying to figure out not only some way to deal with Jaime Minz, but also what might be done with the New Meritorists. Certainly, cutting off their financial support would help, but Dekkard hadn't the faintest idea of where to start. While he suspected some corporacions were funneling funds, he had no idea which ones or how much.

He was still puzzling over those questions when Avraal arrived shortly after noon.

"You look worried again."

He immediately stood. "Just thinking about everything."

"You might as well stop worrying for the rest of the day and see if we can enjoy the Yearend Ball. Worrying isn't going to change things, except to depress you."

"The ball might as well," Dekkard replied glumly.

She offered a wicked smile. "Between the two of us, we can make it much more interesting."

Dekkard couldn't help smiling as he donned his overcoat and then picked up his gray leather folder.

52

D EKKARD donned the dark, but rich, gray formal jacket, whose cut and style only allowed him space for a single throwing-knife sheath. He hoped he wouldn't need even that. Going without any weapons worried him, although he knew a single knife wouldn't be that much help against firearms. He had noticed that Avraal wore dancing boots under the near-floor-length gown, and that each had a knife sheath sewed to it. She had a blade in each.

"Fancy boots. The sheaths are a nice touch."

"I ordered them that way right before we were married. I knew I'd need them, because councilors get invited to formal events." She smiled. "You do look like a theatre idol."

"That's because you're enamored of me."

"Emrelda said the same thing the first time she saw you, and she didn't even know you."

Knowing that more protesting would change nothing, Dekkard studied Avraal's ball gown, the silk an intense jade, with wrist-length sleeves and a high neck. As Dekkard watched, she opened a long narrow black case, from which she lifted a chain and pendant, the pendant an elongated narrow diamond shape with a modest but brilliant red stone in the center. "I've never seen that before."

"We haven't been any place where it would be appropriate before."

"That's stunning."

"It's meant to be. The chain and pendant are electrum, and the stone is a red diamond. My grandmother gave it to me when I graduated from the Empath Academy. The stone was from a ring her grandmother had given her. Father was furious. He said it was an ostentatious way of quietly revealing that I was an empath. Grandmother told him that was the whole point and not ever to say a word about it again. I've never worn it in public, but I thought now would be a good time to start."

"Red diamond. It has to be . . ." *Worth more than most houses.*

"It is. That's one reason why I'm wearing it." She slipped the chain over her head and centered the pendant.

Dekkard just looked, once more marveling at the fact that he was actually married to her.

Then he frowned as she picked up a small leather pouch and slipped it into a slit pocket in her skirt. "What's that?"

Avraal offered an embarrassed smile. "A squeeze bag with red pepper dust."

Dekkard raised his eyebrows. "I don't intend to get that familiar on the dance floor or anywhere in public."

"It's a promise and a family custom."

"To handle unruly males? I doubt that will be a problem at the Yearend Ball."

"I know it won't, but I promised my grandmother that I'd keep it with me whenever I wore the pendant." Avraal smiled wryly. "I know, I know. But a promise is a promise, and it's not Atacaman fire pepper dust, just regular red pepper dust. Well, with a small touch of Atacaman pepper."

Dekkard shook his head, then asked, "Shall we go?"

"We should. I'm sure Emrelda's waiting."

Dekkard followed Avraal down the steps to the main hall, where Emrelda indeed waited, wearing a gown similar to the one Avraal wore, except Emrelda's was a deep magenta.

"You two put theatrical idols to shame." Emrelda's eyes went to the pendant. "So, you're finally going to wear it. Grandmother would be pleased."

"You're wearing yours as well," said Avraal, smiling.

Dekkard belatedly realized that Emrelda was also wearing a pendant on a chain, both of electrum, but the stone was a rich magenta.

"Hers is a magenta ruby," said Avraal.

"I've worn mine before," said Emrelda. "Avraal never has."

"Every man at the ball will be envying me," declared Dekkard, "coming in with two beautiful and bejeweled women." He glanced toward the side hall where Gaaroll stood, just looking. "We're the same people, Nincya."

"The Rittens look so different. Like top swells."

Dekkard laughed softly. "That's because they are and always have been. I'm the one still learning how to behave like one."

Avraal elbowed him in the gut, if not terribly hard. "Enough of the poor impoverished artisan act. You have more class than most Landors." Her voice held a mixture of amusement and exasperation.

Gaaroll grinned. "Have a good time."

"We'll have an interesting time, at the very least," returned Dekkard.

Then the three donned their outerwear, and made their way to the portico, where Avraal and Emrelda waited while Dekkard got the Gresynt and drove it up to the portico.

There was little traffic, and Avraal sensed no danger on the drive to the Council Hall. Just after sixth bell, Dekkard parked the Gresynt in the designated area east of the Council Hall, far closer than his usual space, and patrolled by at least four Council Guards, not counting the two at the lot entrance. At the entrance to the Council Hall, Dekkard had to produce the invitation for Emrelda and give her name, which he provided, as Ritten Emrelda Ysella-Roemnal.

Once inside, Dekkard glanced around, taking in the wide gold and green ribbons festooning the main corridor, but carefully strung away from the mantles of the bronze wall lamps. "It does look more festive."

"I can see that it would be rather somber otherwise," replied Emrelda.

"Almost ponderously depressing at times," said Dekkard.

"They've set up the main corridor outside the dining room as a ballroom," said Avraal.

Dekkard saw perhaps twenty people standing and talking near the sideboards that flanked the dancing area. A small orchestra, already playing light music, occupied the part of the corridor farther west. Dekkard didn't recognize the tune.

At the entrance to the councilors' dining room, they turned over their outerwear to a young woman whose eyes widened noticeably at the near-matching pendants worn by the sisters.

"Light refreshments are available in the dining room," said Dekkard, "and various wines and lagers at the sideboards. Shall I get you two Silverhills?"

"We'll come with you," said Avraal.

As the three moved toward the nearest sideboard, Dekkard could see that several people's eyes turned toward them. One of those was Jareem Saarh, who was talking to Saandaar Vonauer, the Landor floor leader, and an older woman who was likely Vonauer's wife. Saarh looked to be alone, which didn't surprise Dekkard, given that many Landor councilors had their wives manage their holdings.

Saarh looked away abruptly.

"Did you see that? With Saarh?" asked Dekkard quietly.

"He's heading this way," murmured Avraal. "I can't believe it."

"He always was a bit brazen," returned Emrelda quietly.

The three turned as the Landor councilor neared.

Saarh inclined his head politely. "Steffan, Avraal, *and* Emrelda. You look even more beautiful than I recalled."

Emrelda inclined her head politely. "You're too kind, Jareem. It's been a few years. I have to congratulate you on becoming a councilor. Your father would have been so proud. And how is Maelle?"

"She's well, and handling the lands, likely better than I would." Saarh smiled warmly, an expression clearly directed at Emrelda.

"I'm sure you'd do well also. You've always been very determined."

"Thank you." Saarh inclined his head. "I won't keep you. I just wanted to say hello."

"That's very thoughtful," replied Emrelda. "I trust you'll enjoy the evening."

"As Steffan will discover, it's an obligation. Good evening, Emrelda."

As Saarh returned to Vonauer and his wife, Dekkard shook his head, if with an amused smile, saying, "Rather condescending, considering it's his first Yearend Ball as well."

"That's Jareem," replied Emrelda.

"What was he feeling?" asked Dekkard.

"A hash of feelings—arrogance, fear, determination, and hatred."

"Poor bastard," murmured Dekkard.

"No," said Avraal. "'Bastard' itself is perfectly adequate, and I'd like a glass of Silverhills."

Dekkard and the two sisters moved to the sideboard, where he ordered and the server provided one beaker of Kuhrs, and two glasses of Silverhills. Then the three moved away.

Dekkard glanced around, then saw a stoop-shouldered, balding, and older councilor with a much, much younger red-haired woman moving toward the three.

"Councilor Safaell and his daughter, I'd wager," murmured Dekkard.

"Gerhard," said Dekkard once the two were nearer, "I'd hoped we'd see you. You may have seen my wife Avraal, and this is her sister Emrelda."

"And this is my daughter. Bettina, Councilor Dekkard, his wife Avraal and her sister, both Rittens in their own right." Safaell smiled. "I persuaded Bettina to come with me. She agreed—on the promise that I'd introduce her to you." Safaell looked to Avraal and added, "Am I not telling the truth?"

"You are, but you're worrying that I won't back you up," replied Avraal.

Bettina laughed softly. "I like that."

"You're in your last year of university, as a legalist, your father said?" Dekkard asked Bettina.

"Yes, sir."

"Waterways law or something else?"

"I haven't decided. There are so many interesting aspects to law. Some are even fascinating." Bettina dropped her eyes for a moment, then said, "I know I'm not yet a legalist, but I was very impressed by your Security reform bill."

"Thank you, but I only deserve part of the credit. My senior legalist, Svard Roostof, made certain all the legal language and terms were correct."

"But you came up with the provisions," Safaell pointed out.

"I did, but it took both of us. I'm incredibly fortunate that the Premier suggested that I make him an offer and let me take him as my senior legalist."

"He suggested it?" asked Bettina.

"I worked for Councilor Obreduur, up to the moment I became a councilor. I wouldn't have approached any of his staffers without his permission and knowledge."

"That's known as ethics," said Safaell dryly, "and courtesy. Traits not always found in councilors."

Bettina turned to Avraal, her eyes on the pendant. "The stone is . . ."

"Red, scarlet, if you will," replied Avraal, "but it was a choice of that or being deceitful."

"Oh, you're an empath? I'm sorry. I didn't know." Bettina glanced to her father.

"I'm sorry," replied Safaell. "I didn't tell you. Avraal and Steffan were a security team before they were married."

For just an instant, Bettina appeared disconcerted.

"Sometime, if you want to," said Dekkard, "you could stop by the office and talk to my legalists to get an idea of what it's like. They're both experienced, although Luara has most of her experience away from the Council."

"That's very kind, Steffan," said Safaell, with a warm smile. "She just might take you up on it. We won't take any more of your time."

"It was our pleasure," replied Dekkard.

As Safaell and Bettina moved toward the sideboard, Dekkard took a small swallow of his Kuhrs, then glanced around, noting that the number of councilors and their guests had more than tripled in the time since they'd arrived.

"Steffan," murmured Avraal, "I think that's Councilor Haastar approaching from behind you."

Dekkard turned immediately. A muscular but trim woman, who looked close to the councilor's age, accompanied the slender Haastar.

"Breffyn, you surprised me."

"I don't think you're ever caught off guard, not when you're with your wife, anyway. Since I've met your most capable and lovely wife, I wanted you both to meet Tatyanna, especially since she's not in Machtarn that often. She arrived earlier in the week. Dear, this is Steffan Dekkard and his wife Avraal Ysella-Dekkard."

"And Avraal's sister Emrelda," returned Dekkard, thinking that Tatyanna looked fairly refreshed, given that the ironway trip from Brekaan had to take two days of solid travel, if not longer.

Tatyanna offered an open smile. "I'm glad to meet you all. Breffyn's written about you two," and she nodded to Emrelda, "and I do know a little about your distinguished family."

"That's mostly in the past," replied Emrelda cheerfully.

"Not that much in the past," said Haastar. "My father still occasionally corresponds with yours."

"Oh?" said Emrelda. "Then your father's Balthasar."

"The same," replied Haastar. "The last time he wrote, he asked if Avraal was your sister. I wrote him back that you had to be. The name and the resemblance were too great for it to be otherwise. I'm glad that I was right. It would have been a bit embarrassing if I'd been wrong."

"Neither of you remained near home?" asked Tatyanna.

"That didn't suit either of us," replied Avraal brightly, "although our brother carries on the family traditions."

"Someone must," replied Tatyanna, "but that leaves you free to lead your own lives. I hope our daughters have that much sense and drive."

"How many do you have?"

"Two sons, two daughters." Tatyanna smiled wryly. "More than we planned. Our daughters are twins."

"How old are the twins?" asked Dekkard, managing not to wince at the thought of twin daughters.

"Fourteen."

"The age when they think they know better than you, but hopefully have enough sense not to say so," said Emrelda.

"So far they've had enough sense of self-preservation to be polite and tactful," said the councilor.

After a good ten minutes of warm but polite conversation, the Haastars took their leave.

Emrelda glanced to her sister.

"What you heard is what they are—basically good but traditional Landors," said Avraal. "She meant what she said about the freedom for her daughters to find their own way." She paused and looked at Emrelda. "There's something you're not telling me."

"The councilor's father approached Father about . . ."

"An arranged marriage with Breffyn?" asked Avraal.

"No, his older brother Baaltar. I was only seventeen at the time. Mother said there was too much of an age difference. One of the few times that we agreed on something. Even Father thought so." Emrelda immediately added, as if she didn't want to dwell on the matter, "Breffyn is much nicer than Jareem, but that's hardly difficult."

Dekkard and Avraal exchanged glances, and Avraal shook her head. Dekkard nodded back, just slightly, to signify that he wouldn't pursue the matter of Baaltar Haastar.

More and more people arrived and occupied the main corridor opposite the councilors' dining room, and Dekkard noticed a group that moved from the sideboard not all that far away. One of them was Villem Baar. Almost as soon as Dekkard recognized the other councilor, Baar moved away from the group with whom he'd arrived and walked toward Dekkard. That was a definite surprise, but Dekkard turned to greet Baar, as did Avraal.

"Steffan, Ritten Ysella-Dekkard." Baar inclined his head.

"Villem, might I introduce Avraal's sister, Emrelda Ysella-Roemnal? Emrelda, Councilor Villem Baar, of Suvion."

"A pleasure to meet you" offered Emrelda warmly. "Steffan has spoken of you."

"Not always favorably, I expect," replied Baar with a touch of humor in his voice.

"Personally," replied Avraal, before Emrelda could speak, "Steffan's been complimentary. He did not care for a few of the amendments you offered, but he's neither said nor intimated anything personally uncomplimentary."

Baar hesitated for just a moment. "That's kind."

"No," replied Avraal, her voice warm, "it's true."

"It is," added Dekkard, "and I regret the necessity of our abrupt questions the other evening, but since there have been a number of attempts on me since the one in the committee room, my patience was more frayed than I would have preferred."

Baar definitely looked surprised. "I had no idea."

"One doesn't like to spread information like that," said Dekkard, "true as it is, but you've been exceedingly courteous and professional, and you deserve an explanation."

"I can't tell you how much I appreciate that." Baar smiled more than politely. "I wondered . . . could I introduce you three to one of the few people I knew here in Machtarn before I arrived as a councilor?"

"I'd like that very much," replied Dekkard.

The three followed Baar toward the group that Baar had left. As they neared, Dekkard recognized Eyril Konnigsburg, the retired admiral and present councilor from Veerlyn, with a dark-haired older woman likely his wife, a silver-haired man with a younger woman, and, not totally surprisingly, Kaliara Bassaana.

Baar stopped slightly short of the group and half turned. "I won't do formal introductions. For those who don't know or aren't sure, the handsome councilor there is Steffan Dekkard, with his wife Avraal, in the jade, and Avraal's sister, Emrelda, both from the Ysella family of Sudaen. Over here are Haarden Hallaam, presidente of the Imperial Banque of Machtarn, and his wife Vincentia, and Admiral and Councilor Eyril Konnigsburg and his wife Emilya, and I think all of us know Councilor Kaliara Bassaana."

For a moment, there was silence. Then Konnigsburg said genially, "Most of you wouldn't know this, but Steffan and I share several—experiences—besides being new councilors. Can any of you think what they might be?"

Although Dekkard suspected he knew one of those experiences, he could see the amusement in the retired admiral's face as Konnigsburg surveyed the faces of the others in the group, including Baar.

The first to speak was Hallaam. "Might it be that you both graduated from the Military Institute?"

"That's part of one, but not all."

With that, Dekkard had a fairly good idea what the two similarities were.

"You know, don't you, Steffan?" asked Konnigsburg.

"Part of my answer would be a calculation, but I think so."

Konnigsburg smiled. "What do you think?"

"We were both Triumphing Tens and the top in the martial arts competition?"

The retired admiral nodded. "That's true, but there's one thing you wouldn't know. In the forty-one years that the Institute has kept records there are only three graduates who've accomplished that."

That shocked Dekkard. "I didn't know that."

"Vice-Admiral Hooraan was disappointed that you didn't opt for a line commission, but, as matters turned out, it's clear that you made the right choice. He was very pleased when I told him that you were a councilor, the youngest ever."

Baar looked long at Dekkard. "You've never said anything."

Avraal laughed. "He never told me about either. I found them out from other people."

Emrelda looked to Avraal. "You didn't even tell me about the martial arts."

Much as Dekkard appreciated what Konnigsburg had done, he had to wonder why. *Because that tie is important to him? Because he wants to point out what the Institute graduates do? Or does he want to build friendships or possible alliances across party? Or something else?*

Baar shook his head, then said, "One thing I found out about Steffan quickly. He doesn't boast, and he does his best to be completely prepared for whatever he undertakes. I discovered that when he shepherded the Security reforms through the Council."

Hallaam frowned for an instant. "That's where I heard your name before." He smiled, slightly more than pleasantly. "That was a mixed bag, it seems."

"Sometimes," replied Dekkard, "political realities make matters messier than they ideally could have been. In the long run," *if we survive the short run,* "we'll have a better public safety ministry."

"Do you really think so?" asked Hallaam.

Dekkard smiled as warmly as he could manage. "Once we shake all the bad apples out of the tree. It turned out that no one had control or oversight over the Special Agents. They'll be much more duty-focused in the Justiciary Ministry. And we won't need as many, which will reduce the costs to the government." Dekkard paused just an instant before saying, "You're in charge of the largest and most important banque in Guldor, if not in the world. What do you think is the most important task facing the new Council?"

"I don't know that there's ever just one important task for the Council or for a banque."

Dekkard kept on smiling. "What would you like to see the Council address?"

"It might be useful to put down the New Meritorist nonsense, rather than catering to it."

"I think we'd all agree on that," said Dekkard, "but shooting them seems to create even more unrest."

Hallaam's smile turned cooler. "Perhaps if the Council had gotten the Special Agents under control earlier."

"You're absolutely right," agreed Dekkard. "That would have been ideal." *Except too many councilors voted against that.* "But those messy political realities got in the way. Thank you for pointing out what should have happened."

Hallaam looked surprised.

"I forgot to mention," injected Baar smoothly, "that Haarden is my wife's uncle, and he's been invaluable in helping us make the move to Machtarn. I'd hoped that Gretina could have been here tonight, but it's taken longer."

Dekkard laughed gently. "Everything takes longer."

"And usually costs more," added Hallaam almost genially.

"I do hope we can meet your wife before too long," Avraal said to Baar.

"I'd hoped you could, too." Baar glanced past Dekkard. "I see the Premier's arrived."

Dekkard heard *something* in Baar's voice. Then he understood. "Has Sr. Hallaam ever met the Premier?"

"He hasn't had the good fortune."

"Then perhaps he should," said Dekkard, catching the tiniest nod from Avraal. He turned slightly and saw Obreduur speaking with Saandaar Vonauer, the Landor floor leader, but didn't see Ingrella anywhere near. "If you'd excuse us for a moment." Dekkard looked to the banker and said, "Sr. Hallaam, since you haven't met the Premier, let me introduce you."

"I'd appreciate that, Councilor."

As Dekkard approached, followed slightly by Hallaam and Baar, Obreduur turned.

Dekkard could see that the Premier didn't really want to be disturbed, but he frankly didn't care and escorted the banker to Obreduur. "Premier Obreduur, this is Sr. Haarden Hallaam, presidente of the Imperial Banque of Machtarn. Sr. Hallaam, Premier Axel Obreduur." Dekkard looked to Obreduur again. "Sr. Hallaam is the uncle of Councilor Baar's wife." Then he stepped back.

"Thank you, Steffan. I believe Ingrella had some words for you."

"Thank you, sir." Dekkard turned to Baar. "I need a word with you as well." He didn't give Baar a chance to protest, and escorted him back toward Avraal and the others. He noticed that Vonauer had also moved away.

When they were several paces from Obreduur, Baar said quietly, "Thank you." Then he offered an amused smile. "You also made a point with Haarden that he won't forget."

I sincerely hope not. "Time will tell."

When Dekkard and Baar rejoined the group, Konnigsburg smiled, knowingly, as did Kaliara Bassaana. Vincentia didn't even look away from her conversation with Avraal and Emrelda.

Emilya Konnigsburg said, "You're rather politely efficient, Steffan."

"He wanted to meet the Premier. I saw that the Premier had not yet been besieged. Why not?"

"Even after his comments on the Security reforms?" asked Councilor Konnigsburg.

"He was right about the Special Agents. The original draft had them being transferred within two weeks. That was too soon for all the Commerce councilors and most of the Landors."

"A month seemed reasonable to most," said Konnigsburg evenly. "There wasn't a floor amendment for a shorter period."

"The Security Committee wouldn't support a shorter period."

"Since you drafted the original proposal, you must have had a reason for a shorter compliance period."

"In my previous position as a security aide, I had a number of occasions to witness the conduct of Special Agents."

The retired admiral nodded.

"Hindsight," added Baar dryly, "is always so much clearer than foresight."

Dekkard couldn't help but smile, not at the comment, but at Baar's tone and delivery.

At that moment, the orchestra began to play more loudly, and a melody that sounded like a courteille, rather than the slightly faster waltz. Dekkard saw several couples immediately beginning to dance, among them Jaradd Rikkard and his partner, and Yordan Farris, presumably dancing with his wife, because Dekkard couldn't imagine anyone else who'd want to dance with Farris, not if they knew him at all.

He turned to Avraal. "A dance?"

She smiled mischievously. "I thought you'd never ask."

Dekkard took their glasses and put them on a tray offered by an attendant, and Emrelda did the same with hers. Dekkard couldn't say he was totally surprised to see Baar incline his head to Emrelda. He was surprised that she nodded assent. *But why shouldn't she enjoy a dance?* His second thought was to wonder what Baar wanted to find out.

Dekkard appreciated the orchestra's playing a courteille, rather than a waltz or the southern two-step, partly because he could hold Avraal and enjoy the dance and talk at the same time. After they joined the others dancing, he just enjoyed the moments that followed. When the music died away, and they moved to the side of the dancing area, he asked, "What did you sense from all of that?"

"The admiral favors you. I don't think he cares much for Hallaam. Villem Baar's harder to read. He respects you. He's uneasy with me. I wouldn't trust Hallaam in anything, but your ability to cut through everything and introduce him to Obreduur definitely made him wary. Did you notice that he tried not to come close to me?"

"I did. What about his wife?"

"Sweet, submissive, and actually in love with him. Almighty alone knows why. Emilya Konnigsburg strikes me as a lot like Ingrella, at least on first impression."

At that moment, Villem Baar appeared with Emrelda, inclined his head to her, and said, "Thank you. I very much enjoyed the dance."

Emrelda nodded in return. "So did I. You dance well, Villem."

Dekkard thought Baar flushed slightly.

"Not so well as you, but thank you." Baar nodded again and made his way back to the Konnigsburgs and Vincentia Hallaam.

"I know it's a ball," said Dekkard, "but we need to find Councilor Gerard Schmidtz or Mardosh."

Avraal smiled. "We can certainly do that, especially since you asked me to dance first."

Dekkard felt himself blushing. "I do know who's most important."

The three made their way toward another sideboard. Nearby, the square-faced Mardosh and a petite woman in a green gown with a short silver jacket chatted with Tedor Waarfel and a stocky woman in a teal gown who was likely his wife. With them was a muscular man in deep purple formalwear, his silver-tinged blond hair slicked back and his green eyes taking in everything.

As Dekkard and the two sisters neared, Mardosh smiled guilelessly. "Steffan, I see you brought your wife and another lovely lady."

"I did. This is Emrelda Ysella-Roemnal, Avraal's sister." Dekkard saw the slightest tightening of the eyes of the man in the purple formalwear, if but just for an instant.

"Yudorya and I are glad you're all here." Mardosh looked to Avraal. "I've seen you from a distance, but never had the pleasure of meeting you." His eyes then went to Emrelda. "And you're every bit as lovely as your sister."

Dekkard kept watching the man he didn't know, whose eyes had definitely taken in the pendants worn by the sisters, his eyes lingering slightly longer on Avraal's.

"The one in purple is an isolate," murmured Avraal.

An isolate, likely as Mardosh's guest . . . interesting. "I don't recognize him. Do you?"

Avraal shook her head.

"Steffan," Mardosh went on pleasantly, "I'd like you to meet Pietro Venburg. Sr. Venburg is the vice-presidente for legal affairs of Siincleer Shipbuilding. He usually doesn't travel that much. So we're fortunate to have him here."

An isolate and a legalist. Even more interesting and concerning. Dekkard smiled broadly. "I'm very glad to meet you, Sr. Venburg. Given the scope of Siincleer Shipbuilding and its subsidiaries, you must have a considerable workload. I'd like to thank you for coming."

"I'm very pleased that Erskine invited me. I'm well aware that such invitations are hard to come by and not given lightly. I intend to enjoy the evening to the fullest." His eyes flicked to Emrelda, who smiled politely, and then to Waarfel's wife, before returning to Dekkard.

"How do you find Machtarn?" asked Dekkard.

"Machtarn is so different from Siincleer."

The way Venburg spoke the last words gave Dekkard the impression that the differences didn't favor Machtarn, and he replied, "Siincleer has a warmer climate, one much more favorable to shipbuilding."

"It does indeed." Venburg looked to Emrelda. "Have you been to Siincleer, Ritten?"

"Several times over the years."

As Emrelda replied, Dekkard turned his head and murmured, "Keep sensing Mardosh."

"I'm afraid I don't see excessive warmth as an attraction," Emrelda continued, "although for some, I suppose, it has its appeal."

Venburg turned back to Dekkard. "You have a most interesting background, Steffan. That's what Erskine tells me."

"I was raised as an artisan, went to the Military Institute, graduated, took security training, worked for the Premier as a security aide and economic assistant, and found myself unexpectedly selected as a councilor. Everything's rather usual, except for the last."

"That's what makes it unusual and interesting."

Venburg's voice, while well-modulated and pleasant, somehow grated on Dekkard, but he wondered if that feeling was because he despised the entire Siincleer operation. "I suspect, by that token, the backgrounds of most councilors could be said to be interesting and unusual. How did you come to end up as the vice-presidente of legal affairs?"

"Where else would a legalist interested in shipbuilding and engineering end up?"

"A very capable legalist, that is," added Dekkard, pausing and then saying, "Erskine, we wouldn't want to take time from you and Sr. Venburg." Dekkard inclined his head to Venburg. "A pleasure meeting you."

"The same to you, Councilor, and to your wife and Ritten Ysella-Roemnal," replied Venburg.

Once they were away from Mardosh and Venburg, Emrelda said, "Can we go somewhere and sit down? Perhaps get some refreshments?"

"That's a good idea," replied Dekkard. "There are light refreshments in the councilors' dining room."

The three were almost to the dining room when Julian Andros appeared, accompanied by a woman in a gown of the identical shade, but not style, of Emrelda's.

"You have excellent taste," said Emrelda.

"So do you," replied the other in an amused tone.

"Julian," said Dekkard, "this is my wife, Avraal, and the woman who also has excellent taste is her sister. Avraal, Emrelda, this is Councilor Julian Andros."

Andros gestured. "My wife, Consuela." After a moment, he asked, "Do you know Ramon Griessler, the regional craft guild coordinator for the Southwest Coast?"

"I'm afraid I don't."

"He's my guest, and he was supposed to meet us here."

"I'm sorry I can't help."

"That's all right. Have a good evening." With that, Andros and Consuela hurried off.

Dekkard smiled, glad that his own guest was close at hand, and led the way into the councilors' dining room.

An array of various foods filled the table in the entry area of the dining room. Dekkard wasn't sure all of them were light, at least not if one ate even a small fraction of what was laid out. He took several of the basil-and-bacon-wrapped shrimp, some melon squares wrapped in paper-thin ham, a miniature quiche, and a small chocolate cream roll, then had the server at the adjoining sideboard pour him a beaker of Kuhrs.

He noted that both Avraal and Emrelda chose lighter items for the most part, except that Avraal did take a dark chocolate tart. Both chose white wine, and the three moved into the dining room, where about half the tables were taken, more than Dekkard would have expected so early. He immediately saw Ingrella Obreduur sitting at a corner table with Harleona Zerlyon and several others he did not recognize, but whose importance he had no doubt of, given their presence with Ingrella.

Avraal led the way to the only corner table that was free, and they seated themselves so that all three could survey the room. Emrelda took a small swallow of wine almost immediately.

"What was your impression of the honorable Pietro Venburg?" asked Dekkard quietly.

"A snake with poisoned fangs," said Emrelda. "The way he looked at me and Avraal."

"That's because he recognized your name," said Dekkard. "I shouldn't have used your full name, but I had no idea—"

"How did you know that?" asked Emrelda.

"His eyes tightened just a fraction when I introduced you."

"And he kept looking back to you," added Avraal.

"You didn't sense anything?" asked Emrelda.

"He's an isolate."

"That makes perfect sense," Dekkard pointed out. "Mardosh told me that he was the highest official in the Siincleer organization who would know the details of anything improper. He keeps that information from Presidente del Larrano, and he can't be sensed by empaths."

"If he knows my name," said Emrelda, "then he has to know about what Siincleer did to Engaard Engineering."

And to Markell. "I don't see how he couldn't," replied Dekkard, pausing as he saw Mardosh and his wife, along with Erich Kuuresoh and a woman who was presumably his wife, as well as Pietro Venburg, enter the dining room with beverages and plates and take one of the larger tables. Dekkard was happy that Venburg took a chair facing away from Emrelda.

"At least he's looking in the other direction," said Emrelda quietly.

"He didn't even look in our direction," Avraal pointed out. "He was busy talking to the other councilor."

"Kuuresoh," supplied Dekkard. "He's on the Military Affairs Committee."

"Venburg's definitely not wasting any time," said Avraal dryly. "Then, he wouldn't have accepted the invitation without calculating how to use it."

Dekkard still wondered if Mardosh had tendered the invitation or if Venburg had requested it. He'd thought about asking Mardosh, but decided that doing so at the ball wouldn't have been in the best of manners. Asking later would have to suffice.

"Typical corporacion type," murmured Emrelda.

"How was that pickled radish, or whatever it was?" Dekkard asked Emrelda.

"Hot. I thought it might get a certain taste out of my mouth, except it followed us."

"I could go back and get you one of those chocolate tarts like Avraal has. They have to be sweet."

"That's kind of you, Steffan, but no. I'm fine with what I have. The wine helps."

"I really didn't expect this," Dekkard said.

"How could you have known?" replied Emrelda.

None of the three spoke for a long moment, and Dekkard took the opportunity to try one of the shrimp.

"How is it?" asked Avraal.

"Much better than I expected. Here, try one. I got several."

Avraal took a shrimp and ate it. "You're right. Much better than it looked."

"What are those circles?" asked Dekkard.

"Miniature crushed broccoli and cheese pies."

"I think I'll pass." Dekkard took a swallow of his Kuhrs, and then ate the remaining shrimp. He looked to Emrelda. "Are you feeling a little better?"

"The refreshments help."

Several minutes passed. Then Dekkard saw that Ingrella and those at her table were getting up, but instead of moving toward the door, she and a pleasant-looking but not particularly distinguished man walked toward Dekkard's table.

When the two reached the table, Dekkard immediately stood. "Good evening, Ritten."

"You don't have to be formal with me, Steffan. I just wanted to introduce you two. Augustus, this is Councilor Steffan Dekkard, the young councilor I mentioned. Steffan, this is Augustus Oliviero, the presidente of Guldoran Iron-way. He's a longtime acquaintance."

"And sometime adversary," added Oliviero, looking momentarily to Ingrella. "Friendly adversary, I still hope."

"Unlike some, you've been an honorable adversary," replied Ingrella.

Dekkard wasn't quite sure what to say at that moment because Avraal left the table, and no one but him seemed to notice. After a brief hesitation, he said, "Would that all adversaries were honorable."

"I'm afraid you're asking too much with that, Steffan," replied Oliviero, "but it's a pleasure to make your acquaintance, particularly since we have quite a few lines running through your district."

"I know. In fact, about two weeks ago, I got a thoughtful reminder from your Gaarlak district manager."

"That would be Waaltar, Waaltar Haelkoch. One of the newer district man-agers. Very diligent. Thank you for letting me know. I'm sure you and Waaltar will get along. A pleasure to meet you, Steffan."

Ingrella looked around. "I thought Avraal was here. She must have slipped out to the ladies' room. Tell her she looks gorgeous, and so do you, Emrelda."

"Thank you," replied Emrelda, inclining her head.

"I'm sure we'll see you all again before that long."

Dekkard waited until the two turned and headed away before sitting down.

"Axel and Ingrella are good people," said Emrelda.

"But they don't let it get in the way of practicality."

"Sometimes, you have to be that way. I've learned that as a patroller."

"Do you still like being a patroller?"

"I can't imagine not being a patroller."

That wasn't really an answer, but Dekkard could understand why, given what Emrelda had been through in the last half year or so.

Less than a minute later, Avraal returned. She didn't seat herself, but looked to her sister. "I just had to take care of something. Did I miss anything?"

"Ingrella wanted to tell you that you looked gorgeous," said Dekkard, "which you do. And I got an introduction to the presidente of Guldoran Iron-way. Ingrella referred to him as an honorable adversary."

"From her, that's definitely praise of sorts." Avraal asked Emrelda, "Are you all right?"

"I'm fine. But could we go before Venburg comes back?"

Dekkard hadn't even seen Venburg leave, but then, he'd been preoccupied with Ingrella and the presidente of Guldoran Ironway. "We certainly can."

He immediately stood, then followed Avraal and Emrelda from the dining room out into the main corridor. When they reached the edge of the dancing area, he turned to Avraal. "Another dance?"

"I'd love one, but why don't you and Emrelda take this dance? I'll just wait here, and the next one will be mine."

Dekkard looked at her intently. He had the feeling his fears were all too jus-tified. "Are you all right?" he asked quietly.

"I just need a moment. That's all. Just dance with Emrelda."

Dekkard didn't press. Whatever it was, Avraal would tell him when she was ready. He turned to Emrelda. "Might I have this dance or what's left of it?" He smiled.

"You may." In return, Emrelda smiled.

As they slipped into the dance, a waltz, she said, "Thank you for getting me away from Venburg. I might be overreacting, but the way he looked at me I didn't want him to come back and see me again."

"I can understand that. I have the feeling that he's both calculating and ruthless." As he guided Emrelda into a turn, he thought he saw a Council Guard heading into the councilors' dining room, but everything seemed calm. *Let's hope it stays that way, at least for a little while.* He returned his attention to Emrelda. "Then again, I think most legalists for corporacions like Siincleer are cold and calculating. Well, calculating. The best ones are likely warm and calculating."

"Venburg projects a certain warmth," replied Emrelda, "but it's all superficial, at least to me. I suppose that skepticism comes from being a patroller."

"Maybe you have a trace of being an empath."

"A trace? Maybe. And only sometimes, if the feelings are really strong, but it's an effort, and I don't have enough strength and control to be even a low-level empath. I've tried, the Almighty knows."

"Was that one of the reasons you helped Avraal get training?"

"No one's talent should be wasted, especially hers."

Dekkard could definitely agree with that.

As the music died away, Dekkard guided Emrelda back to where Avraal waited.

"You two look very good together," said Avraal.

"Not as good as you and Steffan," replied Emrelda, who inclined her head to Dekkard. "Thank you."

The next dance was a courteille, which Dekkard preferred, and he smiled as Avraal stepped into his arms. "Feeling better?"

"I always feel better when I'm with you."

"Emrelda's worried about Venburg."

"I could see and sense that. She was right to be worried, not that I could sense anything from him."

"Having an isolate legalist as a buffer between the top management and anything shady makes sense, although I wouldn't have thought about that, given the restrictions on isolates who are legalists. I'm surprised that other corporacions haven't done that."

"How do you know they haven't?" she replied. "Neither of us has met any of them, except Venburg. That's not something that they have to reveal."

"He doesn't wear gray."

"That's a custom, not a requirement, and his formal jacket and trousers were trimmed in dark gray, rather than black."

"I didn't notice that."

"I did."

Dekkard laughed, softly. "You notice a great deal that I miss."

"You don't miss much, dear."

"More than I should sometimes." He paused. "Would you mind, if after this dance, we wandered and met people?"

"Isn't that part of what the Yearend Ball is all about?"

"It is, but . . ."

"I'm fine. We'll do what needs to be done for as long as needs be."

Dekkard didn't press. Even if his concerns about Avraal were valid, it was better that they didn't make an early exit from the ball.

When the music stopped, or, rather paused, before resuming as a waltz, Dekkard and Avraal rejoined Emrelda.

"Steffan needs to be social and meet and greet," Avraal said. "You don't have to come along."

"I wouldn't miss it," declared Emrelda. "When else will I ever get to meet some of these people, if only briefly?"

"What about next year?" asked Dekkard cheerfully. "At least if the Imperador doesn't call for new elections in the meantime?"

"I won't turn down an invitation, but by then you might have other obligations."

"Some obligations are more important than others," replied Dekkard.

Avraal just nodded.

The next councilor that Dekkard encountered was Tomas Pajiin, who was talking with Eduardo Nortak and, presumably, Nortak's wife.

"Steffan," said Nortak genially. "I'd like you and your wife to meet mine. Adryann, Steffan Dekkard and his wife Avraal."

"And Avraal's sister, Emrelda," said Dekkard. "It's good to meet you, Adryann."

Adryann, a brunette who appeared to be a good fifteen years older than Dekkard, addressed Avraal warmly. "Your dress and pendant are absolutely stunning. You two look more like models than a councilor and his wife."

"Youth has an advantage in appearance," returned Dekkard, "and the definite disadvantage in experience. With experienced colleagues, I hope to overcome that disadvantage."

Nortak laughed. "After what you've already done, Steffan, do you really expect me to believe that?"

Dekkard smiled in return. "I can hope."

"Adryann," added Pajiin, "don't let those young innocent looks deceive you. Before Steffan became a councilor, those two were the best security aides in the entire Council. That's what Guard Captain Trujillo told me a couple of days ago."

"He never makes idle conversation," observed Dekkard. "What did he want?"

Pajiin looked slightly embarrassed. "Some of the other councilors wondered how good you two were. I figured he'd know. So I asked him."

"That's Tomas for you," said Nortak. "Always wanting to make sure."

Pajiin offered an expression of long suffering, then shook his head.

"How else would he have lasted as a guild steward and gotten elected?" returned Dekkard. "Especially in Eshbruk."

After another few minutes of banter, Dekkard eased the two sisters away and toward Hansaal Volkaar, who talked with a small group that included several people Dekkard didn't know, as well as Maximillian Connard and Marryat Osmond. He hadn't planned to approach or join the group when Volkaar gestured. "If you have a moment, Steffan?"

Dekkard wasn't about to ignore the invitation of the Commercer floor leader, and he and the sisters moved to join Volkaar and his group.

"Sir, I don't believe you've formally met my wife Avraal, or her sister Emrelda."

"I can't say I have, but I've definitely heard of their family. The Ysellas of Sudaen, if I'm not mistaken. I'm glad to meet you."

Both women inclined their heads.

"Now, Steffan, you know Maximillian and Marryat, but I suspect you haven't met Jan Vandenhoff, the presidente of Uldwyrk Systems." Volkaar gestured to one of the few men considerably taller than Dekkard.

"I'm afraid I haven't had the pleasure, Sr. Vandenhoff. I'm well aware of your corporacion and its accomplishments."

Vandenhoff smiled pleasantly. "In what regard, might I ask?"

"We studied your turbines in engineering at the Military Institute. Because I went security instead of line, I have to admit that, after graduation, I never served on a ship powered by them."

"You definitely missed an experience, Councilor, but not everyone can be that fortunate. A pleasure to meet you." Vandenhoff inclined his head and turned back to conversing with Osmond and Connard.

Dekkard smiled at Volkaar. "Thank you for the introduction, Hansaal. I do appreciate it." *If in a useful manner.*

"Are you enjoying the ball, Steffan?"

"I've found it interesting and enjoyable." *Limited enjoyment and valuable interest.*

"Good, good." Volkaar paused, then said, "Enjoy the rest of the evening, you three."

"I'm sure we will," replied Avraal.

"Who is he?" murmured Emrelda as they moved away.

"The former majority floor leader and the current Commercer floor leader." Dekkard turned to Avraal. "He didn't even recognize you."

"Of course not. He didn't really notice me when I was a lowly security aide for a Crafter, even though we were with Obreduur when he encountered Volkaar on more than a few occasions."

"I'm definitely less than impressed," said Emrelda.

For the next two bells, Dekkard and the sisters mixed and mingled, although he did dance twice more with each of them.

At a sixth after the third bell of night, Dekkard turned to Avraal. "I've had more than enough. What about you two?"

"More than enough," agreed Avraal.

"Spoilsport," said Emrelda, with a wicked grin.

Avraal grimaced at her older sister. "You never forget, do you?"

"Of course not. I'm an Ysella, just like you."

Dekkard shook his head, then turned back toward the councilors' dining room.

In less than a sixth, the three had their overcoats and walked toward the east doors of the Council Hall. Less than a sixth passed before they were in the Gresynt, where Dekkard had to wait slightly for the flash boilers to heat up to full power. "We never finished talking about Mardosh. What did you sense?"

"He was concerned when you appeared, even worried."

"Because he told me that Venburg didn't travel, and there he was with him? Or something else?"

"I couldn't tell. He was relieved when we left, though."

"Interesting." *Because I didn't ask who invited Venburg or for some other reason?* "What haven't you told me about those we met this evening?"

"I wasn't that impressed with Haarden Hallaam," said Avraal. "He never realized who or what I am—other than your supposedly submissive spouse."

"Did you sense anything of interest from him?"

"He wasn't terribly impressed with either you or the admiral. He was not quite dismissive and more than ready to move on to meet Obreduur. You didn't say much about the presidente of Guldoran Ironway."

"There wasn't much to say. It was a pleasant introduction, nothing more. Ingrella seemed at ease with him. I have the feeling that I'll hear from him at some point, likely sooner than later."

"Why sooner?" asked Emrelda.

"Because he'll want more funding for rail maintenance in next year's appropriations, and he'll want to establish at least some relationship before he comes back to ask for something."

"You mean he didn't want to get to know you for your outstanding qualities and capabilities?" Emrelda's tone was only slightly sarcastic.

Dekkard had difficulty not laughing. "Not just for those anyway." He eased the Gresynt out of its parking space and then out onto Council Avenue, heading east.

"I can't believe that Hansaal Volkaar is the Commercer floor leader," said Emrelda. "The only thing important about us was our family lineage. Does he treat the women councilors like that?"

"All five of them, you mean?"

"There are five? I only saw one."

"Two Commercers, and three Crafters. No Landors."

"What a surprise."

"Who's the third woman Crafter?" asked Avraal.

"Traelyna Treshaam. She's from Jeeroh. She's on the Transportation and Health and Education Committees. She was elected this past election. Our paths don't really cross."

"How does Volkaar treat them?" repeated Emrelda.

"He has to give some deference to the Commercer women. Kaliara Bassaana and Vhiola Sandegarde are each individually extremely wealthy, and Kaliara could probably personally pound him into the ground. The three Crafters . . . are Crafters, and they don't have money or family."

"I like him even less," said Emrelda.

"He also thinks he'll be majority floor leader again before long. He as much as told Obreduur that after the election."

"I'm glad you're a Crafter," said Emrelda.

Dekkard forced himself to concentrate on his driving, worried as he was about what he feared had occurred.

53

ONCE they reached the house, Gaaroll stood waiting and wanted to hear about the ball, and the three spent a good third summarizing who they saw. Emrelda also made a point of telling Gaaroll how well Dekkard danced.

When Dekkard and Avraal were alone in their room, Dekkard turned to his wife. "You killed him, didn't you?" He barely murmured the words.

"What choice did I have? What else could I have done?" Avraal's voice trembled. "Venburg didn't know who she was until—"

"I stupidly introduced her." He shook his head. "I had no idea that Venburg would be there. Mardosh told me he seldom traveled. I didn't even think it could be him, especially when you said he was an isolate."

"I couldn't risk it," Avraal went on, her voice low and uneven. "The two people I love most in the world are you and Emrelda. If he left the ball tonight, you'd both be in even more danger. I couldn't let him tell anyone else at Siincleer. I couldn't . . . I just couldn't." Her eyes glistened, and tears seeped from them.

"I think Mardosh must have told him something, but I never mentioned anything about Emrelda. Obviously, trusting him even a little was a mistake."

She smiled sardonically, blinking away tears. "I just might have diverted attention away from you, or us, at least a little."

Dekkard had more than a few questions, but he asked the simplest one. "How?"

"I waited until no one was in the men's facility but him, then I walked up behind him as he washed his hands. He turned. He was surprised enough at seeing a woman, or maybe me, that he froze for an instant. I squeezed the pepper dust into his nose and eyes. He could barely see and was choking, but he grabbed for his pistol. I knocked it aside. Then I slit his throat. I left the pistol and slipped out when no one was near the door."

"That was quite a risk."

"Not really. Not until I slit his throat."

"But doing that the first time without practice. On the throat, I mean . . ."

"I had plenty of practice. On pigs and hogs I got very good at it. I hated getting blood on my clothes." The short sound she uttered was between a laugh and a sob. "Father didn't want his daughters to be squeamish. Never ask the workers to do something you wouldn't, he always said. Venburg wasn't any more than a pig, not after what he ordered or allowed to happen to Markell." She swallowed several times. "I couldn't say anything to anyone but you. That way, if it does come back, you'll both be safe. Or safer. You can't tell Emrelda anything." She paused again. "I still don't see why there wasn't some sort of outcry or uproar."

"That's because Obreduur is a careful and political man. The last thing the Council would want is an uproar at the ball. He might not even suspect that we had anything to do with it, because the murder took place in the men's room. Also, Venburg has to have more than a few enemies, some of them highly placed. Ingrella and even the presidente of Guldoran Ironway were with me, and everyone around saw that I never went to the men's room. I'm not sure anyone saw you either. Neither Emrelda nor Oliviero really noticed."

"I created a little distraction, emotionally, both for her and the presidente, and for those at the other table with Venburg."

"How?"

"I created the sense and feel of an intense scent. It was honeysuckle last night. People focus on that."

"Still, Ingrella noticed your absence."

"I doubt that she'll say anything." After a moment, Avraal added, "I hope Emrelda won't remember that I was gone. I fuzzed her recollection."

Thank the Almighty for that. "I'm sure that Guard Captain Trujillo will be involved, and he'll doubtless notice the red pepper. That might confuse matters, since I was attacked with Atacaman fire pepper dust."

"It wasn't Atacaman fire pepper. Well, there was a little in there with the regular red pepper dust."

Dekkard was the one to swallow. All he could do was put his arms around her as she quietly sobbed.

54

D EKKARD did not sleep well, and woke early on Findi, while the morning was still greenish gray. He just lay there, not wanting to disturb Avraal.

Then she turned toward him and kissed his cheek. "You don't have to lie there so you don't wake me. I've been awake for a while."

"So have I."

"Then we might as well face the day. There will likely be a story in *Gestirn*."

"We'll also have to attend the Advisory Committee reception this afternoon, and someone's bound to ask."

"We tell them that we talked briefly to Sr. Venburg and never spoke to him again. We saw him briefly in the dining room when we got refreshments and something to drink, and then we left. Whatever happened must have occurred sometime after that." Avraal sat up and swung her legs over the side of the bed.

"Nice legs," said Dekkard.

"Steffan, you're impossible."

"No. I'm very possible." He managed a grin that quickly faded and stood. "But Siincleer Shipbuilding is well known for its dubious practices, even if it's managed to avoid getting caught, and it's not surprising that Sr. Venburg created enemies who took an opportunity to strike back. Since those enemies could date back years and could involve corporacions or others we know nothing about, there's little point in speculating until more is known."

Avraal nodded. "That's all we say. To anyone. Different words, but the same story."

She took a deep breath. "We also have to give Emrelda marks for the annual house taxes."

Dekkard turned and fumbled through his top drawer for his chequebook, the new one he'd been issued when he'd become a councilor, not that he'd written any cheques since then. Once he had it in hand, he turned and asked, "How much?"

"I sneaked a look at the tax bill. Half is two hundred sixty-two marks."

"I can do more than that."

"No, you can't. You need to save your marks. We'll need at least a small house in Gaarlak, remember? And furniture."

If we survive until then. "I remember." He found his fountain pen and wrote out the cheque, leaving it on the chest of drawers for the ink to dry while he got ready for the day.

After he showered and dressed, he made the bed and waited for Avraal. Then they went downstairs together. Avraal had both cheques in an envelope.

When they entered the breakfast room, Gaaroll looked up. "You all missed the big news."

"What big news?" asked Dekkard. "Were there more storms in the southwest?"

"No. At the Yearend Ball. Some big swell corporacion type got spouted."

"Spouted?" asked Avraal.

"It's in the newssheet."

"Sr. Venburg," said Emrelda. "It's rather gory, from the story. I can't say I'm surprised. Not that he didn't deserve it. More than deserve it, in fact."

Emrelda didn't seem that worried or upset, and Dekkard couldn't tell if she really didn't remember Avraal's absence or if she was a good actress, but he wasn't about to test those waters. Instead, he picked up the morning edition of *Gestirn* and began to read.

He reread one part twice.

> The murderer apparently approached while Sr. Venburg was washing his hands. Venburg most likely attempted to use a pistol for self-defense, but was disarmed and his throat slashed in a single cut . . .

No mention of red pepper. Dekkard handed the newssheet to Avraal. "You should read it, too. I get the impression that they think he was killed by a strong professional assassin, but they're still investigating."

"How could that happen in the Council buildings?" asked Gaaroll.

"It wouldn't be that hard if it were planned ahead," said Dekkard. "All he'd need would be a Council Guard's uniform. They were posted throughout the Hall. Just act as though he belonged. Using a knife can be messy, unless the killer was very experienced, but it's quick and doesn't make noise. The killer could get far enough away before someone found the body. Besides, no one really notices the Guards. They're almost part of the furniture." Dekkard shrugged. "That's just speculation, though. Siincleer's made a lot of enemies. Mardosh told me that neither the presidente nor Venburg travel that much. Those enemies might be why."

"You two are dressed for work," said Gaaroll. "Why?"

"Because part of the day will be work. We need to attend the Guilds' Advisory Committee reception this afternoon." Dekkard went into the kitchen, emerging shortly with two cafés, one of which he set on the breakfast table before Avraal. "There you are."

"Thank you."

"Do you have any idea who asked Venburg to the ball?" asked Emrelda.

"I don't *know,* but it likely was Mardosh. Conceivably, it could have been Kuuresoh. Konnigsburg's also on the Military Affairs Committee, but I don't see him tendering an invitation with all the trouble the Navy has had with cost overruns on projects handled by the Siincleer corporacions."

"Do you think Venburg requested an invitation?" asked Avraal.

"I'd thought about that, and I was going to ask Mardosh, but not at the ball. I'm not about to ask Kuuresoh." Dekkard went to get the croissants, returning shortly with two for himself and one for Avraal. He sat down, as usual, across from his wife.

"Can't believe you were there and didn't see anything," said Gaaroll.

"We talked with him earlier," said Dekkard. "But then we talked with a lot of people, even the councilor who wanted to marry Emrelda years ago. I still can't believe he actually approached you."

"I was polite, and so was he."

"That's sometimes for the best," said Avraal.

"I meant to ask you last night, Emrelda," said Dekkard, "but did Villem Baar have anything interesting to say?"

"Not really. He told me I danced well, better than he did, and asked whether I was enjoying the ball. I said I was and asked him how he liked being a councilor. He said that it was rather different from what he'd expected and that being a legalist wasn't as helpful as he'd thought it would be. He also asked about our pendants. I just said that they were gifts from our grandmother. That was about all. He was very polite."

"He always is," said Dekkard. "Even when he's unhappy."

The remainder of breakfast was quiet, and before long, Gaaroll stood up. "Will you need me for the reception this afternoon?"

Dekkard looked to Avraal, who shook her head, then said, "Not today. Do you have any plans?"

"No. Feels good to have marks, though."

Dekkard had half forgotten that yesterday had been the last Quindi of the month. He smiled, recalling when he'd gotten his first pay. "Don't spend it too quickly."

"Don't intend to spend any of it, not for a while, anyway." She smiled and slipped out of the breakfast room.

Once Gaaroll had gone, Avraal handed the envelope she'd brought down to Emrelda. "This is for you. It should cover the year-end taxes."

Emrelda extended the envelope back toward her sister. "You don't have to do that. I can manage."

"Emrelda," said Dekkard quietly, but firmly, "you've made it possible for us to be married and to live in a wonderful house. You wouldn't let us pay rent—"

"You've paid for most of the groceries and all of the wine and lager."

"We should have. There are three of us and one of you," Dekkard pointed out. "Since you haven't let us pay rent, this is the least we can do. Please."

"I offered. You're family."

"Exactly," replied Dekkard. "Families split things. This is our share."

"It's really not even enough," added Avraal, "considering you didn't let us pay full value for the Gresynt."

"And that you're paying for all of the gas and water bills," said Dekkard.

Emrelda smiled wryly. "You're as stubborn as Avraal. But only this time."

"No. Each year as long as we live here. Otherwise we'd be freeloading. Fair is fair."

Emrelda slowly opened the envelope and looked at the cheques. "That's five hundred twenty-five marks. How did you—"

"I snooped," declared Avraal. "If I'd asked, you would have lied about the amount." She paused, then asked, with the hint of a grin, "Wouldn't you?"

"You two." Emrelda shook her head. Then she smiled. "Thank you. I can't say how much it means. Not so much the marks."

"You can stop worrying about it now," said Avraal.

"I can't keep much from you, can I?"

"Not when I'm worrying about you."

Emrelda stood. "I'm going to have another mug of café."

After a moment, Dekkard murmured, "That was the easy part of the day. We still have the Advisory Committee reception."

"When do you want to go?" asked Avraal.

"How about going early and leaving early? Stay long enough that we're not seen as rushing in and out unless we discover a reason to remain longer."

"That might be best."

Dekkard shrugged. "Who knows?"

"Who knows what?" asked Emrelda as she returned and sat back down.

"When would be the best time to go to the Guilds' Advisory Committee reception this afternoon."

"Go early. No one notices when you leave while others are still arriving. At some point, they'll realize you're gone, but most people won't remember when."

"You're absolutely right," Dekkard said.

"My slightly greater age is of some value."

In the end, the three sat and talked in the breakfast room for almost a bell, mainly about family experiences from past Yearends.

Then Dekkard checked the Gresynt, since it had been late when they returned the night before, and he'd certainly been in no mood to do so then.

As he did, he thought over the events at the ball. He couldn't dispute Avraal's decision, not after he'd seen Venburg's reaction to Emrelda. Besides, what was done was done. The immediate question was what, if anything, to do next. Both Obreduur and Mardosh had effectively told him not to pursue the Siincleer corporacions, Northwest Industrial Chemical, or Suvion Industries at present, and trying to pursue them would lead nowhere except angering both of them at a time when that would be counterproductive, to say the least. *Even when you* know *who's behind it all, you can't do anything.*

Obreduur knew of his and Avraal's connection to the Siincleer corporacions, but based on what Dekkard had observed, Ingrella would have said little except where Dekkard, Avraal, and Emrelda were sitting, and those at Venburg's table had never even glanced in Dekkard and Avraal's direction. At least, that was all Dekkard could hope. While he had mentioned his interest in Siincleer and contracting abuses to Mardosh, it had to be obvious that neither Dekkard, Avraal, nor Emrelda had ever met Pietro Venburg before.

As he finished adding water and kerosene to the Gresynt, Dekkard decided that any further immediate action would likely implicate rather than conceal. Sometimes, doing nothing was better than anything. He closed the garage door and walked back to the house.

Before Dekkard fully realized it, the clock in the hall chimed first afternoon bell, and he needed to finish getting ready to go to the reception.

Little more than a third later, wearing one of his new and heavier gray suits, he stood by the portico door, waiting for Avraal. Several minutes passed before

Avraal appeared in a stylish deep blue afternoon dress and jacket. One modest gold lapel pin with the small scarlet starburst proclaimed she was an empath, the other that she was a councilor's spouse.

Once they were in the Gresynt, headed for the Machtarn Guildhall, Avraal asked, "Do you think we need a side trip to a certain office?"

"What do you think?" returned Dekkard.

"I think it's unwise and unnecessary, but I thought I'd ask."

"I agree with you. Besides, Minz wouldn't keep Atacaman fire pepper dust anywhere, let alone in his office anyway, and he could claim it was planted. There's also a risk of being seen, and for what? Trujillo's aware of the red pepper, I'm sure, but he'll certainly be puzzling over who would want both of us dead."

Dekkard did take another indirect route to Imperial Boulevard and came out north of Camelia Avenue, and turned south. When he reached the Avenue of the Guilds, he turned right off the boulevard toward the river. Five blocks later, he pulled into the parking area of the Machtarn Guildhall, recalling that the last time he'd been there, unknown parties had tried to attack him and that he'd never discovered who might have been behind it.

The locked side door that Dekkard had used before meant that they had to walk around to the main front door, where two young aides stood.

"Councilor, Ritten, the reception is in the main hall, straight ahead."

"Thank you."

As Dekkard had suspected, while there were a number of people already present, most looked to be guild functionaries, likely guildmeisters, assistant guildmeisters, or guild legalists. Dekkard did see Eduardo Nortak and his wife talking to several people, and on the other side of the room, Tedor Waarfel and his wife.

Avraal and Dekkard had only taken a few steps into the hall, which featured tables with hors d'oeuvres in the center of the chamber and sideboards near the walls with lagers, ales, and wines, when a dark-haired man moved quickly toward them with an expression that suggested he knew either Avraal or Dekkard.

It took a moment for Dekkard to recall the other's name. "Guildmeister, I don't believe you've met my wife. Avraal, this is Raoul Carlione, the head of the Artisans Guild of Machtarn."

"I'm pleased to meet you, Ritten."

"And I, you," returned Avraal.

"You might recall, dear," said Dekkard, "Councilor Obreduur assigned me to look into tariff inspectors who wrongfully underassessed imported artworks in order to put artisans out of business."

"The councilor here—"

"Steffan, please."

"Steffan was the one who did most of the work," said Carlione.

"No, I started it, and then after former Minister Munchyn tried to assassinate Premier Obreduur, Obreduur issued an order." Dekkard paused, then said, "How is that working? I'm sorry I didn't have a chance to see it through because of, well, strangely getting selected as a councilor."

"It's going much better. We're still working with the Treasury Ministry, but the worst abuses have stopped. Don't be sorry. All of us in the guild are more than happy that we got a real artisan as a councilor. There hasn't been one for some time." Carlione gestured to the nearest sideboard. "Something to drink?"

"Yes, thank you."

"I'd introduce you to my wife, but she had a bit of a cough, and she's not all that enthused about receptions." Carlione turned to Avraal. "As I recall, you were also an aide to the Premier."

From there, after both Dekkard and Avraal had beverages in hand, the conversation continued on the basis of who had done what and when, while other Craft councilors and spouses slowly entered. Then Obreduur and Ingrella entered the hall.

"If you'd excuse me," said Carlione apologetically.

"Of course," said Avraal warmly.

Carlione had barely left when an older man, sandy-haired with a weathered but clean-shaven face, moved toward them. "Mind if I join you, Councilor, Ritten?" His voice was rough but not gravelly. "Konrad Hadenaur."

"The head of the Sanitation Guild," said Dekkard. "This is my wife Avraal."

Hadenaur frowned, then nodded. "You were an aide for Obreduur, too, weren't you? I thought you were too good-looking to be an empath."

"A lot of people made that mistake," said Dekkard.

"Since you married her, you didn't. Anyway, I thought I'd thank you. You were the one who wrote up everything over the beetle salary problem."

"I just did the paperwork for what you and the councilor worked out."

"You did a good job. You should have seen the district sanitation manager when we dropped that opinion from the Health minister on him." Hadenaur smiled.

"I'm glad it worked out."

"So are we. Just wanted to welcome you and thank you."

"You going to talk to the Premier?"

"I'll get around to it. It's not like we haven't known each other for years." With a last smile, the Sanitation guildmeister turned and walked toward the sideboard.

"Well," said Dekkard, "that takes care of the only two guildmeisters I know. Do you see anyone you know?"

"Right now, I haven't seen anyone from Seamstresses Guild or the Women's Clerical Guild." Avraal looked past her husband, then murmured, "Here comes Councilor Mardosh. By himself."

"Can you sense him?"

"Determined, but not immediately angry. That's from what I can tell."

Dekkard turned, smiling pleasantly.

"Good afternoon, Steffan, Avraal."

"Good afternoon, Erskine. Is Yudorya with you?"

"Alas, no. She was feeling under the weather. The unpleasantness last night unsettled her."

I can imagine, especially if Venburg was your guest. "You mean about Pietro Venburg? I read about it in *Gestirn* this morning. It must have happened late. We never saw any sign of disturbance, and we didn't leave the ball until after third bell."

"You don't seem terribly disturbed, Steffan."

"That's because I'm not. As I've conveyed to you, Siincleer has been involved in a considerable number of affairs involving strange deaths, improbable occurrences, and massive cost overruns blamed on others. We both know that there's never been enough evidence even to bring charges. Or if there was, those who had it were afraid to provide it. When I read the story, it seemed to me that likely someone else came to that conclusion as well and took matters into their own hands. In some ways, that's regrettable because Venburg won't ever have to answer to anyone—except possibly the Almighty. If the Council does get around to investigating the matter, Presidente del Larrano and the others involved can claim it was all Venburg's doing. In some ways, del Larrano may have the most to gain from Venburg's death."

For an instant, Mardosh looked surprised. Then he fingered his chin. "I must say I hadn't even thought about that."

"I have. I brought the matter to your attention and to the attention of the Premier. All of a sudden Pietro Venburg, who seldom travels, appears at the Yearend Ball, then turns up murdered."

"Still, few of those accusations and events are new," Mardosh pointed out.

"No, they're not," replied Dekkard, "but one other thing is. There's a new Council, a Craft Council far more likely to be less sympathetic to corporacions, especially given that the Premier's wife happens to be a noted legalist who has been most successful in opposing them. Also, a noted and political legalist heads the Justiciary Committee." Dekkard shrugged. "I'm only speculating."

"Hmmm, what you've said raises some interesting aspects to the matter." Abruptly, Mardosh nodded. "Thank you, Steffan." He looked to Avraal. "I apologize for the interruption, Ritten."

Almost as soon as Mardosh had left, another man approached, a graying figure Dekkard was quite certain he'd never met. "Councilor Dekkard? I'm Helmer Vardian, chairman of the Advisory Committee."

"I'm pleased to meet you. My wife, Avraal Ysella-Dekkard."

Vardian inclined his head. "My pleasure, Ritten. I'm so glad you're here as well."

Dekkard had the feeling that more than a few wives of councilors had found themselves "indisposed."

"I wouldn't wish to be anywhere else this afternoon," Avraal replied. "You've gone to quite the effort, and it would be a shame not to enjoy it."

"That's most kind," replied Vardian, pausing as he saw Ingrella Obreduur walking toward the three.

"Helmer," said Ingrella warmly, "you and your people have outdone yourselves."

"You're most kind, Ritten."

"I'm never kind with incompetence. Polite, perhaps, but not kind. You should know that by now."

Vardian laughed softly. "Most aren't like you. But then, most aren't like the Premier, either."

"I doubt that either you or the Premier," said Avraal, "would be happy if either of you were like most people."

"That's true," replied Ingrella with an amused smile. "It did take Axel a while to realize that." She turned to Dekkard. "You were a bit like Axel in that. I wondered how long it would take you to see what was right in front of you."

"It took a while, but I think I appreciate Avraal more because it did."

"If you will excuse me?" offered Vardian.

"Go, Helmer," Ingrella half ordered, if humorously, "you have rounds to make, and I haven't really had a chance to talk to these two in weeks." She turned back to Dekkard and Avraal. "Besides, Axel's a little temperamental today. He was up rather late with Guard Captain Trujillo and with Justiciary Minister Kuta and the acting Minister of Public Safety."

"About the killing of Pietro Venburg?" asked Avraal.

"Exactly. I don't know why anyone bothers. He was a terrible man, and everyone's known it for years. It's a wonder someone didn't do it earlier."

"From what Erskine Mardosh told me," said Dekkard, "it might be because he seldom left Siincleer, where the corporacion essentially owns the patrollers." Mardosh hadn't said all of that by a long way, even if it happened to be true, but Dekkard wanted Ingrella's reaction.

"I can't believe he told you that much. He never says much about the Siincleer corporacions."

"He didn't exactly say it. Part of those were my conclusions from what he didn't say."

"And from your own knowledge as well, I'm certain."

"That, too." After the briefest pause, Dekkard asked, "What do you think?"

"Criminal law is hardly my specialty, Steffan, but there's apparently little evidence from what Axel has said, other than the murder wound itself and the semi-automatic pistol on the floor. There was just a single precise slash, perfectly placed and deep enough that he didn't have a chance. As for suspects, the list appears to be endless, and none of them were anywhere near. No one heard anything, and Venburg had been dead a good third or more before anyone found his body. That means a professional killer, likely hired through intermediaries. Because Venburg was prominent, if hated quietly, there will be an investigation, but unless the killer is foolish enough to make a mistake, I don't see much happening beyond the initial investigation. That's just my opinion, though. What Axel and Minister Kuta do is up to them." Ingrella frowned. "He really was an evil man, and I don't say that often." She shrugged. "I'd prefer to talk about more cheerful matters. Have you two made plans to go to Gaarlak yet? Axel was fortunate that I already owned a house in Malek. You two don't have that advantage, but I understand dwellings in Gaarlak are reasonable."

"We'd thought we'd go during the Midwinter Recess," said Dekkard. "That's assuming that the New Meritorists don't cause more trouble or something else doesn't come up."

"Something else always comes up," replied Ingrella cheerily. "Unless it's major, don't let it get in the way." Then she focused her eyes on Dekkard. "Make certain she's happy about whatever place you choose."

"Did Axel ever object to your choices?" Dekkard couldn't help grinning.

Her smile was mischievous. "It never came up. I owned the house in Malek, and I bought the one here."

Avraal laughed.

As Avraal's laugh died away, Ingrella said, "Here comes Axel, doubtless to escort me to meet with someone."

Obreduur reached the three within moments and looked to his wife. "I thought I might find you with these two."

"That's because we don't see them very often anymore, or I don't." Ingrella's words were delivered warmly. "I encouraged them to go to Gaarlak during Midwinter Recess. I also told them that I thought Pietro Venburg was an evil man."

"Evil men deserve justice as well as good men," Obreduur said mildly.

"As we both know, dear, sometimes the machinations of the law fail to deliver justice."

He smiled. "Sometimes, they do."

Ingrella shook her head. "He's not the legalist, and he says things like that." But her tone was that of amusement.

"Now's not the time for serious matters," said Obreduur, looking at Dekkard almost casually, "but you should know that Guard Captain Trujillo will be calling on every councilor who was at the ball."

"I imagine that's necessary," replied Dekkard.

"You always understand, Steffan." Obreduur gestured toward the far side of the hall. "And you'll understand that I need to have Ingrella meet several people."

"We will do another dinner before long," said Ingrella, before turning and leaving.

Dekkard and Avraal didn't even have a chance to look at each other before another couple appeared.

"There she is," declared the shorter woman to the taller one.

"Who are they?" murmured Dekkard.

"I have no idea," returned Avraal quietly.

"You may not remember me," said the shorter woman. "Ciella Lefraise."

"She's the guildmeister of the Women's Clerical Guild," added the taller woman.

"I came in late when you talked to the guild earlier this year. Then I heard from Carlos Baartol that you'd married a councilor and were working for Carlos. I just wanted to tell you that what you said to the younger women really inspired them. And that you're a security empath who helped catch criminals."

"Actually, Steffan and I were a security team for several years. We got married right after the elections where he became a councilor."

After the guildmeister of the Clerical Guild, the guildmeister of Metalworkers appeared with his wife, and then came another guildmeister, from the local Ironway Maintenance Guild, and then someone from the Stevedores Guild.

When he and Avraal left the Guildhall at a third before fifth bell, Dekkard doubted that he'd remember all of them.

"So much for leaving quickly," he said wryly as he opened the steamer door for Avraal.

"That just might be why most councilors come later," pointed out Avraal.

"You have a point, but then you always do." He closed the door and walked around the Gresynt to the driver's side, where he got in and lit off the boiler, then when there was enough pressure, he eased the steamer out of the parking area and headed east on the Avenue of the Guilds. "Do you think Ingrella suspects?"

"Not from her emotional reaction. She also really doesn't want the killer caught, and given what we've seen of her legal expertise and views, that suggests that Venburg was worse than we thought."

"With either of them, you really can't tell."

"Obreduur wasn't cold and calculating like he sometimes feels."

"That's a good sign." *We hope.* "What do you want to do for the last bells of the year?"

"Have a quiet evening at home with Emrelda, and then read some of *The City of Truth* with you."

"And then?" Dekkard grinned.

"We'll see. If you behave." Except she smiled.

55

At times, the fine spray of the Fountain of the Seasons veils the statuary from which the jets of water issue, creating a curtain between that momentary aetherial beauty and the solidity of Averra which surrounds the fountain. At such moments, I find myself of two minds, thinking of art as it is created and as it exists in the world without the hand of the artisan. The Fountain of Seasons is artistic, and far from pretentious, as much of what is said to be art often is. Streams of water rise from stone flowers, climb into the air, and gracefully arc into the stone basin. Those contained sprays cool that corner of the Plaza in late spring, summer, and early autumn. Winter finds those waters absent and thus mute, which is fitting, because winter needs no further cooling or, were the waters there, ever-increasing ice.

Yet those aerial arcs will continue only so long as artisans maintain the pipes and nozzles, only so long as those in Averra support those artisans, and only so long as one generation of artisans begets another of equal or greater skill.

Infrequently, I ride west to view the Three Nymphs, where one cascade forms a white flowing ribbon down to the next, and that ribbon of white water to the third, which in turn veils the black wall of Turmin as it drops into the River Restless. Those three cascades will long outlast the Fountain of the Seasons, which pales against the majesty of the Nymphs. Yet all remark upon the artistry of the Fountain of the Seasons, while comparatively few so praise the Three Nymphs. The fountain, being made of stone, will doubtless outlast the words I put to paper, but the Three Nymphs will likely endure when Averra is not even a memory.

AVERRA
The City of Truth
Johan Eschbach
377 TE

56

BETWEEN being tired and relaxing after reading more of *The City of Truth,* Dekkard went to sleep without difficulty, but woke sweating on a chill and damp Unadi morning after a series of disturbing nightmares, where he tried to defend Avraal from snipers and Special Agents. In the nightmares, he hadn't been all that successful, no matter what he did. As he slowly sat up in bed, he shuddered.

"Are you all right?" asked Avraal.

"Not the best of dreams," he answered. "Averra looks better and better, if it even existed."

"In some fashion, it likely did. Otherwise, why would Ingrella have given us the book?"

"To learn something from it, but that doesn't mean Averra existed." Dekkard finally stood.

"Does it matter? It raises points we need to think about."

"You mean points I need to think about," said Dekkard dryly as he got out of bed. "I definitely need a shower."

"So do I."

"I'll be careful not to take all the warm water."

"Thank you."

Dekkard quickly shaved and showered, dressed while Avraal showered, and then made his way downstairs.

When Dekkard entered the breakfast room with two cafés, one of which he put at Avraal's place, the other at his, Emrelda looked up soberly from the breakfast table. "You'd better read the newssheet."

Dekkard swallowed.

"It's not about Venburg. Well, there's a story about him, too."

Dekkard picked up the newssheet. The headline seemed to glare at him.

GUILDHALL BOMBED

Early yesterday evening an explosion tore through the Machtarn Guildhall toward the end of the traditional Yearend Reception held by the Advisory Committee of the Guldoran Guilds. Fifteen people were killed, with more than two score injured. Most of those killed were Guild staff members. The center of the blast was located on the first level of the building, just below the entrance to the main hall where the reception was being held.

... materials found around the Guildhall were linked to the extremist group known as the New Meritorists ...

... among the injured were Artisans Guildmeister Raoul Carlione and Councilor Chiram Ghohal ... Premier Obreduur and his wife escaped injury, as did several other councilors ...

Dekkard read through the story again. There was something, but he couldn't recall what it might be.

"Fortunate you left early," said Gaaroll. "Real fortunate. Friggin' Meritorists."

"I'd wager they had nothing to do with it," replied Dekkard, looking for the other story, the one about Venburg. The heading on that article read: MURDER COMMERCIAL REVENGE?

> Siincleer Shipbuilding Vice-Presidente Pietro Venburg was murdered at the Council's Yearend Ball, mystifying both Council Guards and Public Safety Patrollers. The comparatively young professional was athletic and strong. He was in a highly guarded area, but was overpowered and killed by a single deep slash across his throat. No one saw the killer, and the killer left almost no traces . . .

Dekkard nodded. *The one trace being red pepper, which no one is about to tell the newssheets.*

> . . . what has come to light is that Sr. Venburg's actions as the legalist mastermind of recent acquisitions have been surrounded with controversy that the corporacion had successfully minimized until now. Several knowledgeable and reputable sources informed *Gestirn* that Venburg's death wasn't entirely unexpected, given the number of questionable circumstances surrounding the Siincleer corporacions' acquisitions in recent years and its methods for acquiring lucrative military contracts . . .

The newssheet story went on to intimate that Venburg's death might have come, if through a third-party agent, from someone victimized by the, often, ruthless tactics of the corporacion. When he finished reading the story, Dekkard started to lower the newssheet.

"There's one more story. Page two," said Emrelda.

"Thank you." Dekkard turned the page. The second story held Juan del Larrano's reaction to Venburg's killing. Most of it was praise about the dead man's legal and organizational skills, but del Larrano was quoted as saying, "While Sr. Venburg will be greatly missed, the organization and procedures he established will assure that the Siincleer corporacions will continue in the tradition he established." *A hardly veiled declaration that nothing will change and more people will die if they get in the way.*

Dekkard shook his head and set the newssheet next to Avraal's place.

"What do you think?" asked Gaaroll.

"I don't know what to think." Which was true, if not in the way that Gaaroll or Emrelda would likely take those words.

"It looks like more people are willing to talk now that the bastard's dead," said Emrelda.

Or Obreduur and/or Mardosh are doing their best to give that impression. "Strange how that happens," said Dekkard ironically as he headed for the croissants in the pantry cooler. When he returned with three croissants, Avraal had settled into her chair and was taking a sip of café. Then she set down her mug and began to read.

Her eyes widened, and she looked to Dekkard. "The Meritorists?"

"I don't believe it. It's an attempt to turn the guilds and the Craft Party against them. A lot of guild members were sympathetic to some of the Meritorist positions. The Meritorists had nothing to gain and everything to lose by bombing the Guildhall."

"That's true," said Avraal, almost musingly.

"Read the story about Venburg and the one on page two as well," Dekkard said as he split his croissants.

Only after she'd set aside the newssheet did she speak. "No one wanted to say anything while he was alive."

"Even now," replied Dekkard, "they'll only speak if their names aren't used. Del Larrano still will have ways to make their lives uncomfortable."

"Do you think Mardosh will be more interested in looking into the abuses by the Siincleer corporacions?" asked Avraal.

"I don't see it. He might look at changing contracting procedures, but I don't see that happening anytime soon. He'll want to see what happens, especially after the bombing of the Guildhall. Del Larrano will likely be more careful for a little while. After that, who knows?"

"So nothing will change?" said Emrelda.

"For a while, Siincleer will likely only use economic pressure on competitors, without the unsavory practices. But that won't last unless the Council looks into matters more deeply."

"What are you two going to do today?" asked Emrelda.

"We aren't going shopping or out to eat," said Dekkard dryly, an easy statement to make because almost no commercial establishments of any sort were open on Firstday, the first Unadi of the new year. "If I wanted to punish myself, I'd go practice with throwing knives, but I'm not feeling that masochistic today."

"Even if you were," replied Avraal, "you'd be doing it alone." She turned to Emrelda. "What about—" She stopped. "I almost forgot. You have duty this afternoon."

"Just from noon to fifth bell. We split shifts on holidays."

"Then we'll have dinner ready when you get home."

Dekkard smiled wryly. That told him what he'd be doing in late afternoon, while trying not to worry too much, not that he could do much about any of it, especially not on Firstday.

57

ON Duadi, Dekkard and Avraal woke early, looking at each other. Dekkard smiled sardonically. "I'm not sure I even want to look at a newssheet this morning."

"I can't imagine why."

"I tell myself that no one else should have gotten killed, and no other buildings exploded, but there's this voice that asks, 'Are you certain?' And I really can't say that I am."

Avraal said simply, "Then assume something else terrible happened, and you won't be surprised if it has, and you'll be relieved if it hasn't."

"That's very good advice. I hope that little voice in my head will take it." Dekkard eased himself out of bed, glad for the carpeting, but he knew the tile floor in the bathroom would feel like ice. "Compared to what's going on right now, the Kraffeist Affair was simple." He paused.

"What is it?" asked Avraal, sitting up, but drawing the covers around her.

"Remember how I said that Premier Grieg's statement about the Kraffeist Affair sounded as though he wanted the Imperador to request his resignation?"

"I remember. Go on."

"What if he really did? What if he had just a shred of ethics and wanted out in a way that didn't look like he was running?"

"Why would he do that?"

"What happened to Kraffeist?"

"He 'accidentally' fell down his stairs to his death."

"What if Grieg worried about the same thing? If he gets dismissed, it doesn't look like he's running out and Ulrich becomes Premier, which he clearly wanted. Ulrich uses his own committee to hold hearings and hush up everything. Everything is cleaned up—over." He shrugged. "I'll have to think about it."

"Don't think in the shower and use all the warm water."

"I won't. I promise."

True to his word, Dekkard hurried through his shower, dressed quickly, then made his way downstairs to the kitchen, definitely warmer than their bedroom. After making two cafés, he entered the breakfast room and asked, "What disaster is in the newssheet this morning?"

"Nothing new," replied Emrelda. "No one's been arrested for the Guildhall bombing. There's nothing more about Venburg. That's likely because the New Meritorists make better copy. Oh, there was another large fire, this time in Woodlake, at the brewery there. Bunch of out-of-work laborers broke into the warehouse. They tied up the night watchman, and drove off with a delivery lorry loaded with kegs of lager. Looters from Woodlake showed up after that. When the patrollers followed them, the looters set the warehouse on fire. Then they fled. The fire spread to the brewery and burned three blocks' worth of cold-water row houses, likely rat traps."

Wondering how *Gestirn* knew who the thieves were, Dekkard had to read the story. He set the cafés in place, then picked up the newssheet. He shook his head to read that they'd just parked the lorry behind an abandoned tannery and tapped the kegs there. They were still drinking when the patrollers arrived. Dekkard just took a deep breath. "They stole a lorry to get a keg of third-rate lager."

"They just wanted to celebrate Firstday," said Gaaroll. "Idiots."

Desperate idiots. But Dekkard just nodded, set the newssheet down, and went to the pantry cooler for croissants. When he returned, Avraal was seated and sipping her café.

All four ate quickly. Dekkard, Avraal, and Gaaroll left the house right after Emrelda. Neither empath sensed any danger nearby, but Dekkard still varied his route to the Council Office Building.

As he brought the Gresynt to a halt opposite the west doors of the building, he asked, "Lunch or later?"

"Later. How much I don't know."

"That's fine. I'm likely to be busy." He smiled wryly and added, "Answering various questions posed by assorted authorities." Then he opened the driver's door and got out.

Avraal slipped behind the wheel and replied, "Enjoy yourself."

"Thank you, dear."

Dekkard was still smiling wryly when he opened the bronze door and stepped inside the building. He didn't see anyone near Saarh's doorway, nor any other councilors in the corridor as he and Gaaroll made their way to the office.

"Good morning, sir," offered Margrit brightly. "It's good to see you."

"It's good to be here. Shall I say that it was an interesting two days?"

"Were you in the Guildhall?" offered Roostof from the doorway into the staff office.

"No. Fortunately, we'd left just before that. We went early, hoping to leave early, but we were there longer than anticipated." Dekkard looked back to Margrit. "Any messages?"

"Just one from the Premier. Shalima brought it. She's my replacement."

"I haven't met her."

"She seems very nice." Margrit handed Dekkard the envelope. "There's not much mail."

Once inside his office, Dekkard opened the envelope and read the short message.

Steffan,
  I'd appreciate it if you could stop by my councilor's office at third bell this morning. It won't take long.

Dekkard set the card on the desk beside the small pile of letters. He definitely wasn't looking forward to that meeting. Obreduur would likely have more than a few questions, and Dekkard would have to be careful about his answers. The Guildhall bombing had to be the work of some corporate operative. And it had to have been set up earlier, possibly months earlier.

Abruptly, he stiffened, recalling the men working on the wall in the lower level of the Guildhall when he'd gone there to meet with the Artisans Guild about the undertariffing of fine art imports. They'd been working just about where the newssheet placed the explosion. At the time, he'd thought they were just there to see when he would leave—to set up the attack that had followed. But that had been four months ago. It had to be coincidence. *Didn't it?*

No one could have planned that far ahead. *Except they already had.*

After several moments, he sat down behind the desk and looked at the letters. A crimson-edged envelope stood out from the others in the neat stack, as Dekkard suspected it was meant to do. He eased the envelope out of the stack, removing the single folded sheet and reading it. He read it twice, just to make sure what he thought he'd read was indeed what he had.

Councilor Dekkard—

This notice is to inform you that, unless the Council immediately passes legislation to require all votes to be recorded, with the vote made by each councilor being made public on a weekly basis, we will take whatever action is necessary to assure that change is embodied in the political structure of Guldor. You and the Council have until third bell on Furdi, the fourth of Winterfirst.

All councilors are receiving a similar notice. This is not a negotiable matter.

The Committee for Personal Accountability.

Dekkard checked the postmark—from Machtarn and dated the thirty-fifth of Fallend.

That doesn't make sense. Why would the New Meritorists send such an ultimatum and then set a bomb in the Guildhall? *To prove they're serious?* They had proved that by destroying fifteen Security buildings. Or was it to remind the new Council? Or had they done it at all?

The remaining letters were far more mundane, and Dekkard had no trouble in reading them and then handing them off to Roostof before he and Gaaroll left the office to walk to Obreduur's office.

As soon as they entered, Karola smiled and said, "Go right in, Councilor."

After saying "Thank you," Dekkard did just that, closing the door and taking a chair after Obreduur gestured. "Good morning, sir, not that it's been that good, I suspect."

"Sometimes, Steffan, you can make things difficult, but you often come up with possibilities. What do you think about the Guildhall bombing?"

For the first time, ever, Dekkard could hear the weariness in Obreduur's voice. After a moment, he said, "I assume you got their letter this morning. I'd originally thought the Commercers might have been behind it to turn the guilds against the New Meritorists, because a lot of guild members had some of the same concerns as the New Meritorists about working conditions and corporacion dominance. And the letter would seem to support that idea. The New Meritorists have gone out of their way to avoid alienating the guilds, but that's likely what will happen. It's also going to make things harder for you, which I suspect is the goal for both the Meritorists and certain Commercer interests."

"You've always thought there was a Commercer presence involved with the New Meritorists. Do you know anything else besides what you told me earlier?"

"You may know this, but I didn't. Lukkyn Wyath was director of security at Suvion Industries before he became Deputy Minister and later Minister of Security. You know about Ulrich and Jaime Minz. Erik Marrak, from Suvion, offers a veiled threat, and then that night five Special Agents try to blow up my house. Marrak gets replaced by a legalist who throws every possible legal obstacle against the legislation, several suggested by Jaime Minz, and after that I get attacked by a staffer whose fiancée believes Minz paid him to do something."

"You didn't mention that."

"It's new, and not solid. She never met Minz. She said Hurrek did work for someone, and she saw a man like Minz driving a steamer like his drop Hurrek off."

"As you've pointed out," replied Obreduur, "none of that constitutes proof."

"It's proof, just not legal proof," replied Dekkard. "I had one other thought. How trustworthy are the empaths monitoring the interviews with former Special Agents?"

"Interestingly enough, Justiciary Minister Kuta had the same question. Some turned out to be compromised. Consequently, the interviews will continue, and a number of the former Special Agents have been sent to the work camps, as disciplinary assistants, for now."

Very astute. That gets them out of Machtarn and under supervision. "There's also something Ingrella might be interested in. The legalist firm of Wheitz and Groebel represented the three former Special Agents who attacked our house. Given the location of their offices, they can't be cheap. So who paid the legalists?"

"The Justice minister looked into that. There's no way to obtain that information. Serapha did discover one interesting fact. Jakob Wheitz is an isolate."

"That means he can't appear as legalist in court."

"Braeden Groebel represents clients in court, but apparently Wheitz talks to the clients and prepares the brief and arguments."

"So that's what they say." Dekkard shook his head. "That's the same barrier the Siincleer corporacions used. Mardosh told me that Venburg was the highest official who knew the dirty details, and he was an isolate as well."

"How did you—? Oh, Avraal was with you when you met him at the ball."

"Did you know he was an isolate?" asked Dekkard.

"No. Ingrella did say that there was no record of him ever appearing in a Justiciary proceeding."

"That explains why. It also brings up another matter of interest. Erskine

Mardosh told me that Pietro Venburg almost never travels, and days after I mention some of the dubious takeovers and other actions by the Siincleer corporacions, Venburg appears at the Yearend Ball with an invitation, likely from either Mardosh or Kuuresoh. Add to that the fact that Mardosh sought out me and Elyncya Duforgue, and we're likely to be the most involved of the new councilors in wanting to eliminate, or at least rein in, corporacion abuses."

"Erskine obviously cannot be too openly aggressive in such matters."

Dekkard just looked at Obreduur.

After a long moment, Obreduur offered an amused smile. "The Council can be a very interesting place at times, as you're discovering." The smile vanished. "You've made some good points about Commercer corruption, but they're not enough. How would you suggest that we proceed to find out more?"

"Is Johan Grieg still in Machtarn?"

"I believe so. Why?"

"Grieg, as you intimated, wanted to be dismissed. Why? He knows a great deal, and since he was never questioned or charged, he's still vulnerable. Why don't you use your considerable charm to invite him to dinner at your house, as well as a certain junior councilor and his empath wife?"

"Charm won't get him to come, Steffan."

"I know that, but I suspect you've tried everything you can think of, or we wouldn't be having this conversation."

"You know he won't come, unless . . ."

"I know that, too, but he at least had enough sense, and possibly a hint of ethics, to want out of the mess. You're known to keep your word, but I assume you never promised not to look into the matter."

"Steffan, you do have interesting ideas. I'll have to think about it." Obreduur rose from behind the desk. "Thank you for coming on such short notice."

Dekkard stood as well. "I hope my thoughts were useful."

Obreduur smiled warmly. "They're always insightful. Until later."

Dekkard inclined his head and left, closing the door.

Outside, in the anteroom, stood Harleona Zerlyon.

Dekkard smiled broadly. "Good morning, Harleona."

She smiled in return, an expression both amused and sardonic. "Do I have to tiptoe in after you?"

Dekkard laughed. "I doubt you've ever tiptoed. Politely entered, but not tiptoed."

"Then I'll enter politely."

Before Dekkard left the anteroom and stepped into the main corridor, Karola had the door to Obreduur's office open.

As he walked back to his own office, Dekkard considered the fact that Obreduur had asked nothing about the ball. *Because he's waiting for the results of Guard Captain Trujillo's investigation?* That was certainly likely. Obreduur never liked to muddy the waters. That meant Obreduur's questions would come later.

Guard Captain Trujillo arrived in the office at a third before noon, but that timing didn't matter because Dekkard had no intention of walking over to the councilors' dining room to eat alone or with anyone except Avraal. The Guard captain sat down in the chair closest to the window and turned it slightly to face Dekkard.

"I understand you met with Sr. Pietro Venburg twice at the Yearend Ball."

Dekkard shook his head. "Just once." He then related the entire meeting, except for his observation of Venburg's reaction to the mention of Emrelda's full name. When he finished, he just waited for Trujillo's next question.

"You were seen in the councilors' dining room at the same time Sr. Venburg was there. Who was with you?"

"Just my wife and her sister."

"Did you talk to Sr. Venburg in the dining room?"

"No. He and his party—I didn't recognize all of them but Councilor Kuuresoh was with him—they came in later, after we'd been there awhile. They sat several tables away, and Sr. Venburg sat with his back to us. I don't think he even saw us. We were at the corner table. As we were just about to leave, Ritten Obreduur came to our table, and introduced Augustus Oliviero, the presidente of Guldoran Ironway. We talked for a bit, and then he and Ritten Obreduur took their leave. Immediately after that we left."

"What did you talk about?"

"The ironway and the Gaarlak district manager who had contacted me. That was all."

"Was Sr. Venburg at his table during this time?"

"He was at his table when Ritten Obreduur and Presidente Oliviero appeared at ours. He must have left during the time we talked, because he wasn't there when we got up to leave."

"Did you see which way he went?"

"I didn't even notice him leaving."

"Where did you go then?"

"We went out into the corridor where everyone was dancing. At my wife's hint, I asked Emrelda to dance, and then I asked Avraal to dance. After that, we mixed meeting people with dancing."

"You never saw Sr. Venburg again?"

"No. I wasn't particularly impressed with him, and there was no reason to seek him out."

"Are you sure Sr. Venburg didn't know you were in the dining room?"

"I have no idea what he knew. He didn't look in our direction when he came in, and I wasn't following what he did, except to notice, almost in passing, that he appeared to be talking to Councilor Kuuresoh."

"Appeared to be?"

"His back was to us."

For the next sixth, Trujillo repeated variations of the questions he'd already asked.

Dekkard replied patiently.

Finally, Trujillo nodded. "Thank you, Councilor. What you've told me matches everything else I've heard so far. Do you have any ideas who killed Sr. Venburg?"

"If the newssheets are correct, he had quite a few enemies, but I wouldn't know. I do know that the Siincleer corporacions have a reputation for practices which are unethical at best."

"You don't know anyone personally who hated Sr. Venburg enough to kill him and who could have?"

"No. I can't say I do." Technically, that was an accurate answer to the question as asked. Emrelda certainly hated Venburg, but she couldn't have killed him in the way he'd been murdered. And Avraal hadn't acted out of hate, but to protect her sister and Dekkard.

Trujillo said nothing.

Neither did Dekkard.

Then Trujillo smiled politely. "I'm sorry to have taken so much of your time, but the Premier insisted that I be thorough."

"I understand completely." Dekkard stood, knowing Trujillo wouldn't leave without being dismissed.

The Guard captain stood and inclined his head.

"I wish you well in the investigation," Dekkard added warmly. *Just not too well.*

"Thank you."

Dekkard moved toward the office door, following Trujillo, and stood in the open doorway while he left the office.

When the corridor door closed, Margrit offered an inquiring look.

"The Guard captain has been ordered to interview every councilor about the death of Sr. Venburg. I don't envy him."

Margrit shook her head. "That could be very uncomfortable. Do you think he'll discover anything?"

"Probably, but I doubt that he'll discover the killer. A good number of councilors or their guests might theoretically have had an opportunity, but I'd wager that all of them can prove that they didn't."

"Then why?"

"The Premier has to be able to report that there's no evidence that anyone in the Council did it. Most likely, the evidence for motivation lies with the Siincleer corporacions, and they aren't about to open those records, assuming that they exist. If the presidente of Siincleer discovers who it is, he'll likely deal with that individual in the corporacions' usual way." Dekkard half turned. "I need to get back to work."

Once back behind his desk, Dekkard spent several bells trying to figure out possible ways to identify links with the New Meritorists. He was still at it when Avraal arrived just before fourth bell.

"How was your day?" she asked.

"I had a meeting with Obreduur." After describing that, he added, "He just might ask Grieg and his wife to dinner. He's sounding rather tired."

"Do you really think that will help?"

"Grieg knows something, but whether it will lead to anything is another question. Then I underwent an interrogation by Guard Captain Trujillo. I have no idea what he's thinking, except that he doesn't want to do it, and he's determined to be methodical." Dekkard shrugged.

"He's very methodical, it appears. I wonder . . ."

"You wonder what?"

"I was just thinking about how to use that methodical diligence. I'll need to think more about it."

When Avraal didn't volunteer more, Dekkard asked, "What about your day?"

"Carlos has some banking contacts. He did find out that Capitol Services actually exists, on paper, anyway. It has the same street address, and same suite number, as Northwest Chemical and a commercial account at the Banque of Machtarn. Finding out more might be harder, but Carlos is making other inquiries."

Dekkard frowned. "That means that it's at least semi-legal."

"Or that it's a semi-legal front for less legal operations," suggested Avraal.

"That's likely, but Minz probably has a legal way to handle the finances for whatever Capitol Services does. It's likely he's receiving payments for what seem to be legitimate services and subcontracting them to others, while those others actually undertake less legitimate services. As an isolate, he could be the buffer between the corporacions and the less savory element."

"Like Venburg, on a smaller scale," said Avraal.

"That would fit, but it's only a speculation. But what if he was running Capitol Services when he was still working for the Security Committee? If he was doing it alone, and wasn't employed by anyone else *and* wasn't selling whatever services he provided to businesses and not to the Council or government ministries, that would skirt the conflict-of-interest rules."

"I can ask Carlos if that's ever come up before. Since we're talking about Minz, I drove by his building on the way here, and his Realto was parked there. Not that it means anything."

So much doesn't seem to mean anything right now. Dekkard stood. "I can't do any more here. We might as well head home."

"That would be a good idea. It's getting colder, and we might be getting sleet."

"Just what we need." Dekkard pulled on his overcoat and motioned for Avraal to precede him.

Neither empath detected anything focused on them on the drive home, but Dekkard felt relieved after garaging the Gresynt, partly because he still worried about assassins and partly because the sleet had indeed begun to fall before they reached Florinda Way.

Dekkard was, as usual, the last one into the house and he'd just hung up his slightly damp overcoat when he saw that Avraal and Emrelda stood in the hall, looking at him. "What is it?"

"I have a package," said Avraal. "I suspect it's really for both of us."

"Oh?"

"It's from a C and F Ysella in Sudaen."

Dekkard immediately moved to join the sisters, who were looking at a flat paperboard box roughly a yard long and half that in width sitting on the bench by the front door.

"Open it in the breakfast room," suggested Emrelda.

Dekkard picked it up and carried it in to the breakfast room table.

Avraal looked at the box. Finally, she took a kitchen knife and began to cut the paper tape. Inside the outer box, surrounded by what looked to be old towels, was an oblong package wrapped in paper with a design of interlocking green and gold circles, tied in green ribbon topped with a large bow. Tucked under one part of the ribbon was an envelope with the name "Avraal" on it.

"Letter or package first?" Avraal looked to Dekkard, then to her sister.

Dekkard didn't respond immediately. He had no idea.

"Letter first," suggested Emrelda. "If it's good, then you don't have to worry. If it's not, you can take consolation in the package. Whatever Fleur chose to send will be in good taste."

Avraal extracted the envelope gingerly, then opened it, taking out the flat card inside, reading it and then handing it to Dekkard. Even before he read the words, he was struck by the elegant penmanship.

Avraal and Steffan—
May your life together be rich and fulfilling
and may your shared dreams sustain you.

Cliven and Fleur

"It's all Fleur," Avraal said. "Nothing of Cliven."

"I didn't want to say anything, but it was that way when . . ." Emrelda swallowed, then went on, "Cliven did write later and still does, if infrequently."

"Why don't you open the gift, dear?" said Avraal. "It is to both of us."

"You're sure?"

"Please."

Dekkard suspected what was coming. He unfastened the ribbon and eased the paper away, only to discover that the oblong object beneath was enclosed by a large green felt cloth bag. One end was sealed, and the other consisted of a flap folded inside, which Dekkard unfolded. Then he eased out the silver tray and set it on the table away from the box. "It's beautiful, I have to say."

"Of course," replied Avraal, "it would be. Fleur arranged for it."

Belatedly, Dekkard saw the engraving in the middle of the long side of the wide rim:

RITTER AND RITTEN STEFFAN DEKKARD

Surprisingly, Avraal offered an amused smile as she saw the engraving. "Definitely Fleur."

"Cliven will come around," said Emrelda.

"Only after Father does." Avraal turned to Dekkard. "If you'd put the cover over the tray. We need to help Emrelda with dinner."

"There's some space in the dining room sideboard," said Emrelda. "I'll show you."

Dekkard replaced the tray in the felt bag and followed Emrelda.

58

AS was often the case in early winter, the sleet that had fallen the night before melted by the time Dekkard and Avraal rose on Tridi morning, but the bedroom was definitely cold. Dekkard shaved and took a very quick shower. When he returned, Avraal had wrapped herself in a heavy robe.

"Last night, I didn't want to say much about the tray and the note."

"You didn't have to say anything, dear. I saw your face. You understood as soon as you read the card and saw the tray."

"Your brother's wife . . ."

"Fleur does the best she can. She'd like us all to be closer, but not if it costs her Cliven."

"The perfect Landor wife?"

"No. She's better than that. I feel so much for her." Avraal paused. "Cliven's sweet in his own way, especially to Fleur. He just can't imagine life in any other way."

Dekkard nodded, although he couldn't say he understood.

Avraal smiled. "I'd much rather be here with you. Go fix us some café. I won't be long."

Dekkard mostly dressed, except for his cravat and jacket, and hurried downstairs just in time to wish Emrelda a good day before she left. Knowing Avraal would be longer than she had said, he immediately picked up the morning issue of *Gestirn*.

One of the front-page stories was about the New Meritorist demand for a vote to change the Great Charter and how unrealistic it was, especially after the bombing of the Machtarn Guildhall on Firstday. The paper quoted Obreduur as saying that "the Council will not be dictated to by an extremist group given to bombings and public demonstrations."

A smaller story noted that the High Justiciary had set the execution date of former Security Minister Lukkyn Wyath for Quindi, the eleventh of Winterfirst. Dekkard recalled Obreduur's words when Wyath had resigned, even before his resignation had been requested.

Wyath had said that anyone who followed him wouldn't have the option of doing much differently from what he'd done. Obreduur had pointed out that while Wyath couldn't see anything but what he believed, at times everyone acted that way. Which was why it was vital to listen to those whom you trusted but didn't think the same way, because the more power anyone had, the more easily they could shut out what they didn't want to hear.

Is that why Obreduur listens to you, rather than because you're often correct?

Dekkard got on with fixing cafés, including another mug for Gaaroll.

Because he and Avraal had overslept, they had to hurry through breakfast, although Dekkard wondered why he felt he had to be precisely on time, given that nothing was scheduled for Council or committee action.

Habit or misguided sense of duty? As he walked to the garage, he decided he had no idea which drove him. In just a few minutes, he had the Gresynt out of the garage, the door shut, and the steamer waiting under the portico for Avraal and Gaaroll. Once they seated themselves, before he eased the Gresynt from under the portico, he asked, "Any strong emotions anywhere?"

"I don't sense any, sir," replied Gaaroll.

Dekkard said nothing more until he approached Council Avenue from the east. "Your schedule today?"

"If you don't need me, I thought I'd come to the office around fourth bell."

"That's fine. It should be a quiet day."

After getting out of the Gresynt and turning it over to Avraal, Dekkard, accompanied by Gaaroll, entered the office anteroom just as the two bells chimed. After seeing the small pile of mail on his desk, he wondered why he'd been in such a hurry. He slipped the gray leather folder into the second drawer and sat down.

Or are you worried that you'll miss something? He pushed the thought aside and began to go through the letters and petitions. The second letter came from Augustus Oliviero, a short handwritten note on an engraved card proclaiming him as the presidente of Guldoran Ironway.

> Councilor Dekkard—
> It was indeed a pleasure to meet you at the Yearend Ball of the Council. I look forward to getting to know you and your charming and accomplished wife over the years ahead.
> My best wishes to you both for this coming year.
>
> Augustus

He definitely didn't waste any time. But then, that was likely why he was presidente of the largest ironway in Guldor.

Dekkard continued through the mail, noting that Haarden Hallaam hadn't sent a note or card, not that Dekkard would have expected it.

Abruptly, Dekkard took out one of his own note cards and wrote a short message for Eyril Konnigsburg, asking if he'd be free for lunch today or tomorrow and apologizing for the short notice. Then he dispatched Gaaroll with it, telling her that, if the councilor happened to be there, to wait for a response.

He just finished reading a letter complaining about heliograph message charges when Margrit knocked on the door and then opened it. She said quietly, "There's a young lady here. A Bettina Safaell?"

Dekkard immediately stood. "She's Councilor Safaell's daughter, and I'll see her. She's really here to see Svard and Luara, although they don't know it yet. I just forgot."

Margrit nodded.

Dekkard followed Margrit out into the anteroom, where he smiled at the red-haired young woman and said, "I'm glad you took us up on the invitation, Bettina."

"I didn't want to impose so soon, but my father said that I should visit today."

"He was right." He gestured toward the staff office. "Let me introduce you to my legalists."

Dekkard led the way, stopping in the open space in the middle of the room. Everyone looked up, including the two typists.

"Svard, Luara, this is Bettina Safaell. She's in her last year at Imperial University in law, and I hoped you two would talk to her about your experiences. Bettina, Svard Roostof, there, is senior legalist, and this is Luara Colsbaan, who has a solid legalist experience away from the Council, but is relatively new here." Dekkard paused, then turned to Bettina. "They can explain what they do and why far better than I can. I'll leave you in their hands."

"Thank you, Councilor Dekkard."

"You're welcome." Dekkard turned and slipped back to his own office.

He'd read through most of the mail when Gaaroll returned and handed him an envelope.

"Councilor Konnigsburg was there, sir. He sent this back with me. He was very pleasant. He's imposing."

"He should be. He's a retired admiral." Dekkard smiled. "Thank you." After Gaaroll left, Dekkard opened the envelope.

Steffan—
   Thank you for the kind invitation.
   I'd be happy to join you for lunch tomorrow. If just before noon at the dining room is acceptable, you don't need to reply.
                                                                    Eyril

Dekkard still drafted a short and polite confirmation and sent it off with Gaaroll.

Then he went back to the mail.

After he finished going through it, he carried it out to Roostof. "Thank you both for taking the time to talk to Councilor Safaell's daughter. I hope it wasn't too much of an imposition."

Luara laughed. "Svard definitely enjoyed explaining to her."

"She's extremely bright," Roostof said.

"And very attractive," added Luara.

Roostof flushed.

Dekkard couldn't help smiling. "I just wanted to thank you. I'm sorry I didn't inform you both in advance. I've been a little distracted the past few days."

"From what we saw, she'll make an excellent legalist." Luara grinned and added, "And I don't think Svard minded the distraction in the slightest."

"She'll make an excellent legalist," replied Roostof.

"I think we agree on that," said Luara blandly.

Roostof flushed, then said almost stiffly, "We do."

"Thank you both again." Dekkard turned. He was still smiling when he went back to his office. That warmth faded as he tried to come up with questions for Johan Grieg, in case Obreduur asked the former premier to dinner. When Margrit bought in a stack of responses drafted by the legalists and Teitryn, he turned his attention to those. He finished with them slightly before Avraal arrived at a third before the fourth afternoon bell.

She smiled as she entered the office.

"You look happy," said Dekkard. "How did your day go?"

"Well enough. I sat through two empath interviews. One of them might actually work out for Carlos. I wrote up my thoughts. He likes them on paper. Then we discussed what the New Meritorists might do next."

"They'll likely plant a bomb in the Council Office Building," said Dekkard dryly.

"Not the Council Hall?" Avraal's tone was a mixture of humor and sardonicism.

"They keep talking about reforming the Council, not destroying it. An explosion in the office building is more directed at councilors than the idea of the Council."

"You know, you might send a quick message to Obreduur to that effect."

"That's a very good idea. Thank you."

"You're welcome, dear."

Dekkard immediately took out another note card and his fountain pen and began to write. When he finished, he put it in an envelope and took it out to Gaaroll for her to deliver to Obreduur. When he returned, he sat back down behind the desk and asked, "What else did you do?"

"More paperwork and delivering a message on my way here. How has your day been?"

"About as exciting as yours, but Bettina Safaell did take up the invitation. She must have spent well over a bell with Svard and Luara. I think Svard was smitten."

"Wasn't that one reason you tendered the invitation?" asked Avraal.

"It was. From what I could tell, they're both sweet people. If it leads to something, good. If it doesn't, Bettina has some contacts and learned a bit."

"And Safaell will be appreciative."

"I honestly didn't think about that."

"I know." She smiled. "Are you ready to head home?"

Dekkard nodded, then stood, retrieved the gray leather folder, and went to get his overcoat.

59

O N Furdi morning, Dekkard woke early—and worried—wondering when the next Meritorist demonstration and/or explosion would come. He showered and dressed quickly, then headed downstairs.

When the three left the house after breakfast, the air over Machtarn not only neared freezing, but was also hazy and smoky, with the acrid odor of coal, as usual on cold winter days when there was little wind. Not hazy enough, Dekkard reflected, to hamper an experienced assassin. But with his choice of route to the Council Office Building and the guidance of Gaaroll and Avraal, he pulled up in front of the west doors without incident. There he turned the steamer over to Avraal, and he and Gaaroll made their way to the office.

"You have a message from the Premier." Margrit handed Dekkard a sealed envelope.

"Thank you. Is there anything else?"

"Nothing besides the mail on your desk," she replied with a smile.

Dekkard returned the smile and entered his office, where he shed his overcoat, then opened the message envelope from Obreduur. The note inside was brief.

Steffan—
 I appreciated your insightful observation. Thank you!

Axel

Only the exclamation mark indicated that Obreduur's reply wasn't just perfunctory.

With that, Dekkard devoted himself to the mail, after which he continued to think about how to deal with former Premier Grieg, something that was turning out to be more difficult than he'd initially envisioned. *Much like everything these days.*

He felt he'd finally made some progress by the time he had to leave to walk to the Council Hall to meet with Eyril Konnigsburg.

When Dekkard stepped out of his office, not wearing his overcoat, Gaaroll was waiting, wearing her security-blue jacket.

"Ready to brave the cold of the courtyard?"

"Yes, sir. My parents didn't come from the Ice Mountains."

"My suit's heavier than your clothing, and it's a relatively short walk between the two buildings."

On the way down the main staircase, Dekkard saw Julian Andros on the lower level, walking toward the courtyard doors, possibly heading to the dining room as well. He didn't see anyone else as he and Gaaroll crossed the courtyard.

When they reached the councilors' dining room, Dekkard looked to Gaaroll.

"Plan to be back here by a sixth past first bell. It might be a little longer, but I won't be going anywhere without you."

"Yes, sir."

Dekkard waited less than a sixth before Konnigsburg appeared. Not surprisingly, the former admiral wore a suit of the same dark blue as Navy winter blues, but with a tie of councilor red.

"Steffan, I do so appreciate the invitation."

"I appreciate your acceptance." Dekkard nodded to the host. "Two."

Once seated, Dekkard noticed that other councilors filled half the tables. The three seated closest to Dekkard were Andros, Ghohal, and Dholen. On the other side sat Vhiola Sandegarde and Felix Quellar, the Commercer who'd replaced Antony Devoule after Devoule's assassination in the Summerend demonstrations. "Apparently, a few others had the same idea."

"It's a chilly day, and nothing's scheduled."

"Not near as cold as in Veerlyn right now."

Konnigsburg chuckled. "That's one of the few things Emilya appreciates about Machtarn, at least for now. She also admits that it's far better than Port Reale."

"You were posted there?"

"Isn't every senior officer, sooner or later? That's the Southern Fleet headquarters."

"I should have remembered that. I was only there once."

"Summer duty when you were at the Institute?"

"What else?"

Before Konnigsburg could respond, their server arrived. The former admiral nodded to Dekkard.

"The white bean soup, with café."

"I'll have the same." Konnigsburg turned back to Dekkard. "Good weather for that soup. What did you think of the Yearend Ball?"

"It ended far more eventfully than I knew when we left that night."

"Someone wanted Venburg dead, I could definitely see, but it was a shock that it happened at the ball."

"I wondered about that. During the last days of the previous Council, I heard that the Navy had trouble with the new night heliographs, and I later found a significant cost overrun that Siincleer Shipbuilding blamed on the corporacion that they'd acquired."

Konnigsburg snorted. "More than significant. So far as I could figure out—it came to light just after I retired—Siincleer ruined the other company, then bought it, and blackmailed the Navy into paying more by saying they didn't buy the liability associated with failure to deliver in a timely fashion. The High Justiciary agreed. First Marshal Bernotte scalded the Navy general counsel for agreeing to such a flawed procurement contract."

"Not the first time, I heard. You're interested in looking into that, I take it?"

Konnigsburg smiled wryly. "My Commercer colleagues aren't that interested, and the chair wants to proceed methodically. The Premier is new to the committee, as is Councilor Ghohal, although both of them are certainly intelligent, and then there's Councilor Nortak."

Dekkard frowned, but then recalled that Military Affairs was the largest committee, with ten members, instead of the more usual seven. "I think I understand, but it may get better."

"In time—" Konnigsburg paused as the server returned with their cafés, soups, and a bread tray. "Just how did you manage to get Security reforms passed so quickly?"

"The apparent incompetence of the Security Ministry in dealing with the New Meritorists helped greatly. Then several of the councilors had firsthand experience in Security overreach. It just worked out."

"Steffan, I may be new here, but nothing just works out."

Dekkard laughed softly. "Then let's say that the chair backed my efforts to persuade the majority of the committee that the legislation was in their interests."

"I understand neither Commercer councilor was exactly in favor of the legislation."

"Dealing with Villem Baar definitely required my best efforts."

"He said the same thing about you. What do you think of him?"

"I don't agree with many of his positions, but I respect him."

"Might I ask why?"

"Because he seems to believe in and respect the law as written, not as something to be contorted to fit into a political agenda."

"Shouldn't all councilors feel that way?"

"They should, I believe, but so far as I could tell Marrak didn't, and neither did former Premier Ulrich. Some commercial legalists don't, either, I've discovered."

"Many, unhappily. What happened to Marrak was rather strange, don't you think?" mused Konnigsburg.

"He likely offended someone very much." Dekkard took several spoonfuls of the soup. "Whoever did it risked quite a bit, stealing an armored Security steamer and then ramming Marrak. I understand he comes from a wealthy and well-connected family."

"About as well-connected as one can be. They hoped politics would keep him occupied."

"Junior and undirected son?"

"That's what I gathered. No one said so. If I might ask, why did you go out of your way to introduce Haarden Hallaam to the Premier?"

"Because Hallaam's arrogant and because I wanted to make things easier for Villem. Hallaam had clearly leaned on him through Villem's wife. Had you met Haarden Hallaam before?"

"I never had that pleasure," replied Konnigsburg dryly. "I take it you hadn't, either?"

"A former security aide from the Craft Party? Who's not in the leadership?"

"Your point is well-taken. Hallaam could have used a few years at the Institute, except he appears to be the type who leaves when they discover that what matters is ability and determination, not wealth or position."

"I learned that quickly there."

"From what Vice-Admiral Hooraan told me, you knew that from the day you arrived."

"You obviously did as well."

Konnigsburg laughed softly. "It took me about a month, maybe a bit longer, but I definitely didn't want to be a physician like my father."

Most of the rest of the meal was casual, but Dekkard had to admit that he enjoyed it, and from what he could tell, so did Konnigsburg.

Gaaroll was waiting when he left the dining room at a third past first bell.

"I'm sorry I'm a bit late," Dekkard said.

"Wasn't that long, sir. I spent the time practicing determining the colors of the emotion piles of people as they passed."

"You might become a certified empath yet." Dekkard turned and began to walk toward the courtyard doors.

"Not likely. I have to figure it out. Good empies like the Ritten know right then."

"Don't sell yourself short, Gaaroll. Keep at it, and you'll see."

"I'll keep at it anyway."

When he entered the anteroom of his office, he made it halfway to Margrit's desk before she said, "There's another message from the Premier, sir."

Now what's come up? Dekkard couldn't help being worried about messages from Obreduur, but he just said, "Thank you," and took the envelope.

Once he was in his office, he opened the envelope and read the card.

Steffan—
    You and Avraal for dinner this coming Findi at fourth bell.
    Dress is what Ingrella calls "winter casual."

Axel

Dekkard replaced the card in the envelope and the envelope in his gray leather folder, in the same pocket as the letter from Jaime Minz, which he'd kept there because he didn't like leaving it anywhere. Then he wrote a quick reply to Obreduur confirming that he and Avraal would be there at fourth bell on Findi, and dispatched Gaaroll.

With that done, he settled behind his desk. He definitely needed to work on questions for Johan Grieg.

Avraal appeared slightly before fourth bell. "How did your lunch with the admiral go?" She sat down in the chair closest to Dekkard.

"Well, I think. It was also enjoyable, and instructive. He definitely wants changes in military contracting, and he's anything but fond of the Siincleer corporacions." Dekkard related the conversation, as close to word-by-word as he could recall. Then he waited for her reaction.

"That's another strong indication that you can't trust Mardosh, either because he's afraid of del Larrano or because he's just too cautious to really do anything."

"Or likely both. It also may be that he wants to be able to claim that the committee members forced any reform legislation on him." Abruptly, another thought occurred to him. "Frig!"

"What?"

"When I had that lunch with Mardosh, I wondered why Obreduur had deferred and let Mardosh become chair. It wasn't deferral at all. Obreduur didn't want to be chair. He probably didn't even want to be on the committee. He took that seat to keep watch on Mardosh. I should have realized that."

"How could you have known? You know now, but that's because you told Mardosh a bit too much." Avraal smiled sardonically. "Sometimes, the only way you can learn is to make mistakes, and it's painful."

"But if I'd known, you—"

"You don't know that. Venburg still might have been there, and you still would have introduced Emrelda. Mardosh could have been misleading you about Venburg all along."

Dekkard forced himself to take a deep breath. "You're right. It still bothers me that I didn't see it."

"The good side is that you'll likely question matters like that in the future."

"There's one other thing. We're having dinner with Obreduur and Ingrella on Findi at fourth bell and with former Premier Grieg and his wife. Dress is winter casual."

"He took your suggestion." She frowned. "He's either close to desperate or doesn't have any better ideas."

"That means matters are worse than we know, or soon will be. I've been working on leading questions for Grieg. You need to go over them."

"Is there any reason you can't bring them home?" She smiled warmly. "We could go over them in front of the fire."

"Not at all." Dekkard rose to retrieve his overcoat.

In less than a sixth, he and Avraal walked down the central staircase, followed by Gaaroll, and before that long, all three sat in the Gresynt, headed for Imperial Boulevard.

When they reached the house, Avraal said, "Just drive to the garage. We'll get out there."

Dekkard didn't argue. After Avraal and Gaaroll exited the Gresynt, he picked up his gray leather folder and followed, closing the garage doors. He'd just entered the house and closed the portico door when he heard Emrelda call out from the kitchen.

"There's a letter from Sudaen on the front table."

"Thank you," replied Avraal.

"Cliven?" asked Dekkard as he hurried up to his wife.

"That's not likely. Not if Fleur had to pick out the tray and send it."

"Your mother?"

"I almost hope not."

"Why do you say that?"

"If it is, you'll see." Avraal took off her overcoat and hung it in the hall closet. While Dekkard hung up his overcoat, Avraal took the envelope from the table and studied the handwriting, then said, "It's from Mother." She looked to Dekkard, adding, "In the sitting room."

The two settled on the settee, and Avraal opened the envelope and then held it so that Dekkard could read it as well.

Dear Avraal—

Your announcement of your marriage took us all by surprise, your father most of all, but that might be because you had never even hinted that you were serious about anyone, let alone someone you worked with in the councilor's office, except that he's now the Premier, for now, anyway. We had all hoped, once you saw how politics worked, that you'd be more inclined to return to Sudaen and settle down.

I am so glad that Steffan is a councilor. That way you won't have to explain why you're a Ritten, and he's not a Ritter. Emrelda wrote that he was exceedingly handsome as well as quite intelligent, but as we all know looks and intelligence only can take one so far. You mustn't mind your father's past statements about political Ritters. A good many councilors are much better people than some we know with the traditional Landor title. With Steffan having been made a councilor at such a young age, he certainly could make an even greater mark in the years to come, especially with you at his side. Of that, I have no doubt.

Your father does hope that you won't put off having children for too long. Life is most uncertain, as your poor sister has discovered.

At that point Dekkard shook his head and took a deep breath. "I can't believe . . . except you told me."

"Do you see what I meant?" Avraal asked quietly.

"I do. I also see why you left Sudaen." He put his right arm around her, then returned his attention to the letter, much as he dreaded reading the lines to come, and knowing Avraal dreaded them even more.

60

W HEN Dekkard woke on Quindi morning, he was still half thinking about the letter from Avraal's mother and its mixture of condemnation, condescension, and lack of empathy or understanding. Coming from a different way of life simply didn't explain it. Both Emilio Raathan and Breffyn Haastar were Landors, and Dekkard doubted that either would have written a letter like the one Avraal had received. From what Avraal and Emrelda had said, neither would Cliven's wife Fleur.

He wondered if he'd really ever emotionally understand. At the moment, all he could do was be supportive to Avraal and Emrelda, and that didn't feel like enough.

When she opened her eyes, he just held her tight.

"Are you all right?" she asked sleepily.

"I'm fine. I'm worried about you and wanted you to know that."

"I can't change my parents and Cliven. Only they can change themselves, and I don't see that happening."

"We can do what we can and hope."

She kissed him on the cheek. "Thank you for saying 'we.' It's getting late." She smiled. "Save me some warm water."

Dekkard made sure that he did and had her café ready for her when she reached the breakfast room. They ate quickly, finished dressing, and made their way to the Gresynt.

When Dekkard turned onto Council Avenue from the east, a route he'd chosen just in case the New Meritorists decided on another demonstration, he asked, "Any strong feelings ahead, Nincya?"

"No, sir."

"Good." Dekkard still wondered what the New Meritorists would do next— and when. *Riot? Explosion? Something else?* He did know that the timing would catch everyone off guard.

After he pulled up before the west doors of the Council Office Building, he turned the Gresynt over to Avraal, and he and Gaaroll walked to his office.

No messages awaited him, not that he expected any, and a few more letters than on recent mornings were neatly stacked on his desk. Not a single one expressed Meritorist sympathies or strident criticism of the Council. One complained about ironway freight rates, and another that Northern Industrial Chemical charged flax growers in Gaarlak more for phosphates than it did cotton growers in Encora, which made no sense, since Encora was more than twice as far from Chuive as Gaarlak.

I wonder what Minz would say about that?

With that fleeting thought, Dekkard went back to reading the mail.

He'd only read three more letters when Margrit knocked on his door.

"Sir, Guard Captain Trujillo is here. He hoped you could spare him a few minutes."

Trujillo? What now? More about Venburg? Dekkard stood. "Show him in. He can have whatever time he needs." *Since he'll politely take it, in any event.*

Trujillo stepped into the office and inclined his head. "I hoped you wouldn't mind, Councilor, but we're following another lead, and I thought you might be helpful. If you wouldn't mind?"

Dekkard felt more puzzled than worried, given Trujillo's almost apologetic approach. "If I can help, certainly." He gestured to the chairs, then reseated himself behind the desk.

"Does the name Antonette Talirano mean anything to you?"

Dekkard shook his head. "I'm fairly sure I've never heard the name. I certainly don't know her."

"She's a typist for legalists. Apparently, she was Hurrek's fiancée. Could you have met her without knowing who she was?"

"Only if she worked here in the Council, but I don't really know any of the typists here by name, except those in the Premier's office or mine." Dekkard paused. "I'm a little confused. What does a typist or Sohl Hurrek have to do with the death of Sr. Venburg? I'm assuming that's what you're following up on."

"We're not sure, but there's certain evidence that might link Hurrek to Venburg's murder. Bear with me, if you would."

As if I have a real choice.

"According to Councilor Hasheem, the only members of the Security Committee staff from the previous Council that you knew personally were Sr. Jaime Minz and a legalist."

"Frieda Livigne," Dekkard supplied.

"The chairman also said that, days after you asked her a few questions, she resigned. Might I ask the nature of those questions?"

"There was nothing secret about the questions. When the committee started looking into the abuses by the Security Ministry I went to look through the committee records from previous Councils, except I discovered most of the committee records had disappeared. Frieda was the only legalist left, and I asked her who ordered the removal or destruction. According to her, Minz said that Premier Ulrich had ordered it. She didn't know why."

"Why did you want to see the records?"

"Being new to the committee, I was trying to find out as much as I could."

"Have you talked to either Sr. Minz or Legalist Livigne recently?"

"The last time I talked to Frieda was when I asked her those questions. It's been much longer since I've talked to Minz. It was right before the elections."

"And you haven't seen or heard from him since?"

"I haven't seen him at all, except at a distance. Right after the election he sent me a letter telling me he'd become an assistant director of security for Northwest Industrial Chemical and congratulating me on becoming a councilor. He assured me that Northwest Industrial Chemical's records accounted for all the dunnite they had produced, or words to that effect."

"Do you still have that letter?"

"I do." He reached for the leather folder, on the second shelf of the side table, opened it, took out the letter, and handed it over to Trujillo.

The Guard captain took his time reading it, almost memorizing it, before handing it back to Dekkard. "Why would he mention dunnite?"

"Because when he said where he'd be working before the election, I told him that the dunnite used by the New Meritorists had to have come from either his company or Suvion Industries because the Navy munitions plant is guarded to the teeth."

"From the overly polite tone of the letter, it would seem that Sr. Minz was not terribly fond of you."

"After the Imperador called for new elections, it became rather clear that neither he nor his boss—Premier Ulrich—were terribly fond of Premier Obreduur, and I worked for the Premier."

"Do you know if Sr. Minz knew Sohl Hurrek?"

"I don't know. I'd guess that Minz did, simply because he worked for the Security Committee for more than two years, and he must have known the clerks at least a little."

Trujillo posed different versions of the same questions for another sixth. Finally, the Guard captain smiled, almost sadly. "You've been most patient, Councilor. Thank you."

"I appreciate all your efforts, Guard Captain." *If not quite in the way you might think.* "If there's anything else I can do." Dekkard stood.

Trujillo stood and stretched slightly. "You've added a few pieces to the mosaic. We'll just have to see where they fit."

After Trujillo left, Dekkard wondered how the Guard captain had found out about Hurrek's fiancée and if he'd be able to find out more. That was certainly possible. At the same time, Dekkard had always had the definite feeling that Trujillo discovered more than he'd revealed about Hurrek's attack.

Dekkard shook his head. There wasn't anything that he could do.

He went back to the mail, after which he turned to possible questions for Johan Grieg.

Much to Dekkard's unexpected pleasure, Avraal appeared just before noon. "I thought we could have lunch."

"I'd like that. You know, you're the second surprise today."

"What was the first?"

"*Who* is more accurate. Guard Captain Trujillo was here." Dekkard recounted the low-key interrogation. "What do you make of that? How did he find out?"

Avraal offered a smile both apologetic and mischievous. "I arranged for him to find out. Very indirectly. Carlos doesn't even know, but it's one of the tricks I learned from him. Trujillo will think it came from a city patrol station. He'll likely thank them afterward, and they'll accept the thanks, but quietly wonder what it was all about."

"You didn't tell me?"

"I thought it would be better if you didn't even know her name."

"I'm that transparent?"

"Not to most people."

"Trujillo's more perceptive than most people," Dekkard concluded, adding wryly, "You're probably right."

"I also thought it wouldn't hurt to have the Guard captain looking into our friend. At the least, it might make Minz a bit more cautious."

"If anything will," replied Dekkard.

"You sound like you need to eat. It's going to be a while before you'll get another chance." She paused. "We didn't go to services last Quindi."

Dekkard thought about sighing, but Presider Buusen generally offered an insightful homily, and kept his services thankfully short. Instead, he stood, surveying Avraal. "I can't believe you did that, but I can."

"I wouldn't want you to think I'm totally predictable." Her smile was definitely mischievous.

61

FINDI dawned cold, with a light frost. After a tardy breakfast, Dekkard and Avraal took the Gresynt and Gaaroll and ran errands for the next several bells. Then, after returning to the house, Dekkard spent time cleaning and checking over both steamers. Following a light, late lunch, he and Avraal retreated to the sitting room, where they pored over his proposed leading questions for Johan Grieg.

Then they dressed. Winter casual for men, Dekkard discovered, meant complementing but not identical jacket and trousers, and a dress shirt in a color other than white without a cravat or a vest. Dekkard had to make do with a gray dress shirt, dark gray trousers, and a light gray coat. Avraal was far more stylish, in a calf-length not-quite-formfitting dark green dress with a lighter silvery green jacket, and dark gray boots. As almost always, she also wore her small gold lapel pin with a crimson starburst.

"This outfit doesn't scream 'isolate,' but it definitely shouts it," he said to Avraal as they were about to leave the bedroom.

"Good. That way, Grieg will be worrying about you."

"He'll be worrying about me anyway. I'm sure I'll be asking most of the questions, but if you think of one that's important, interrupt me."

"You didn't think I was going to ask your permission, did you?"

"I didn't mean it that way. Sometimes I get carried away."

In an amused tone, Avraal replied, "I've noticed that."

"I'm sorry. Shall we go?" *To this dinner that could turn into a personal and professional disaster?*

"We should. We need to be there before the Griegs. The wine for the Obreduurs?"

"I already put the basket in the Gresynt." Dekkard opened the bedroom door and gestured. Then he followed her to the stairs and down to the main floor, where he saw Gaaroll and Emrelda coming from the breakfast room.

"Looking like swells again," commented Gaaroll from the side hall to the veranda door.

From beside her, Emrelda offered an amused smile.

"I'm looking like one," replied Dekkard flippantly. "She is one."

Avraal elbowed him in the gut.

"You deserved that," said Emrelda. "Like it or not, you're a swell."

Gaaroll just grinned.

"In that case," declared Dekkard pretentiously, "the swells shall depart."

This time, he blocked the elbow headed toward his midsection, then helped Avraal into her overcoat before donning his, after which he escorted her to the portico. "I'll get the steamer."

"I can walk to the garage, dear Ritter," she said sweetly. "After all, my first Ritten is complimentary, and the second is due to you."

"You, impossible imp, get the last word. I'm conceding. Not out of condescension, but out of the realization that, if you want to, you will always have the last word. And neither of your Rittens is complimentary, certainly not the second because I'd never have gotten where we are now without you. Now, please let me get the steamer for you."

Avraal smiled innocently. "Since you said that all so nicely, I can do that." Then she grinned.

Dekkard shook his head, stepping out into the chill wind, and walking to the garage. He got the steamer out, closed the garage doors, and then drove to the portico, where Avraal waited on the bottom step.

He took yet another route to the Obreduurs', where he ended up approaching their modest mansion from the east on Altarama Drive. Since the gates stood open, he drove up to the portico and beyond so that the Griegs could park under the portico roof.

Dekkard and Avraal almost reached the side door when Obreduur opened it.

"You're a bit early, as we expected." Obreduur smiled warmly.

Dekkard handed him the basket containing the two bottles of Silverhills Red Reserve.

Obreduur glanced at the bottles. "Steffan, you didn't have to."

"It was my idea. At least I can try and soften the imposition."

"I didn't have to agree, but come in. There's no point in standing out here."

Avraal and Dekkard followed Obreduur into the house, where they shed their outerwear, giving their coats to Rhosali, then followed the Premier to the front parlor.

Ingrella rose from an armchair as they entered the room. "You two always look so good together."

Dekkard noted that Obreduur wore a brown tweed jacket over solid brown trousers and a tan dress shirt, while Ingrella was in dark purple, with a light gray jacket. Before he could say anything, Avraal did.

"As do you and Axel."

"They brought excellent wine, again," said Obreduur. "I think we should have it for dinner."

"Then we will." Ingrella gestured vaguely in the direction of the settee. "Do sit down."

Then she reseated herself. "It's been a rather eventful week for everyone."

"More so for you two, I imagine," replied Dekkard.

"Certainly for Axel," said Ingrella, "and the Advisory Committee. They lost almost half the staff. Most of the younger staff, and that's so sad."

"Raoul Carlione suffered a broken arm," added Obreduur.

"What about Konrad Hadenaur?" asked Dekkard.

"No injury that I know of."

"Have the patrollers discovered anything?"

"The explosive used was dunnite," said Obreduur. "One way or another, it couldn't have been anything else."

"How reluctant was Grieg to come tonight?" asked Dekkard.

"Slightly resigned, but it might be better for him this way," replied Obreduur.

"Anything said in a private conversation is hearsay and can't be used," said Ingrella, "but if it leads to physical evidence, the evidence is admissible unless he can prove entrapment."

"And you'll make certain I don't do that?" asked Dekkard.

"I'm sure that won't be necessary."

That was more of a command than an observation, Dekkard knew.

"Do you think Johan will actually bring his wife?" asked Ingrella.

"He'll want a witness, but one he can control," replied Obreduur.

Dekkard couldn't mistake the looks that Ingrella and Avraal exchanged.

"I hear someone." Obreduur stood and headed for the side door, returning shortly with another couple.

The former premier had sandy-blond hair, high cheekbones, a square jaw, and, at first glance, the slightly muscular and easy good looks of everyone's best friend, an impression bolstered by the warm smile he bestowed on Ingrella, and the tailored garments he wore—dark green jacket, pale yellow dress shirt, and light gray trousers.

His wife wore a deep maroon dress with a cream jacket, her blond hair in a bob. Her eyes went straight to Avraal.

"Johan, Maryanna, you know Ingrella," said Obreduur. "These two young people are Councilor Steffan Dekkard and his wife Avraal."

"We're pleased to meet you both," replied Grieg in a mellow baritone.

As Dekkard looked closely at the former premier, he noticed the hint of dark circles under the green eyes that moved constantly and quickly from person to person. Although Dekkard doubted that Grieg was even as old as Obreduur, Dekkard got an impression of weariness. "And we're happy to meet you."

"Would anyone like some wine or lager or a hot rum punch?" offered Obreduur.

Johan Grieg opted for red wine, as did Ingrella, while Maryanna and Avraal chose white, and Dekkard asked for lager.

"Make yourselves comfortable while I get the drinks." With that, Obreduur left the front parlor.

"Dekkard, you're the young councilor behind the Security reforms, aren't you?" asked Maryanna.

"I have that dubious distinction," replied Dekkard.

"Long overdue," commented Grieg. "If I could have done that, there might not have been a need for elections."

"Was Ulrich the principal opponent to Security reform?" asked Dekkard.

"Along with Ivaan Maendaan and Gerard Schmidtz. Maendaan and Ulrich really."

Maendaan? Dekkard had overlooked Maendaan, one of the three councilors killed by the New Meritorists in the Summerend demonstrations. "But Ulrich was the most opposed to Security reform?"

"They all were. When you have four committee chairs opposed to anything . . ." Grieg shrugged.

Four? Who might have been the fourth? "Palafaux was the fourth?"

"Who else?"

Before Dekkard could ask another question Obreduur returned with a tray and the drinks.

There was one hot rum punch among the wines and the sole lager.

"You're the one fond of the hot rum punch in this house?" Dekkard asked Obreduur.

"He'll have Hyelda make it at any pretext," replied Ingrella cheerfully. "With lots of cinnamon."

"It sounds like Ulrich wanted to set the agenda for the Council." Dekkard addressed Grieg.

"Oskaar certainly had his opinions on everything," replied Grieg.

"He was a serpent," said Maryanna, "and he still is."

"Why do you think that?" asked Avraal.

"He was the one who pressured Jhared to sign those coal leases," replied Maryanna, "and he had something to do with Jhared's death. Linaya told me that after the memorial service."

"We don't know that, dear," said Grieg in a placating tone. "Linaya was upset."

"Do you have any idea why Linaya thought that?" asked Avraal.

"She said she overheard part of a conversation in Jhared's study. He was talking to Oskaar. Oskaar had come over right after Johan had resigned to demand Jhared's resignation. Jhared refused to resign and told Oskaar he had the right to dismiss him, but he wasn't going to resign, not when Oskaar had gotten him into the mess. Oskaar told Jhared that he'd have to pay the price if Oskaar had to dismiss him."

"That doesn't mean Oskaar arranged his death," Grieg said quickly, still holding the glass of red wine he had yet to even sip. "It likely meant that he'd never get another decent position in government or a corporacion."

"Jhared told Oskaar that all the marks the corporacions had poured into his services business wouldn't save him if word about the coal leases got out. Oskaar told Jhared that it was up to him to make sure they didn't or his life wouldn't be worth a half mark. That's what Linaya said."

"The two just let her listen in?" said Obreduur. "Isn't that a little unusual?"

"She was worried. They had adjoining studies with a connecting door. She went into her study and listened at the door."

"It's still hearsay," pointed out Ingrella, "even if Linaya were willing to testify."

"So," said Dekkard slowly, "Ulrich effectively runs Capitol Services." Dekkard hoped that the mention of Minz's shadow operation might get a reaction.

For just an instant, Obreduur looked surprised, as did Grieg, but the former premier covered the look with a quick lazy smile. "I don't know if he does now that he's a vice-presidente of Suvion."

"How much did you have to do with Capitol Services?" pressed Dekkard.

"Nothing," replied Grieg immediately. "That was his and his alone, except I had the feeling one of his committee aides did most of the work."

"Jaime Minz?"

"The Security isolate, the one built like a bear? I got that impression, but I didn't know, and Oskaar never said anything."

"What sort of services did that side business provide?"

"I'm sure that some of the services were, if you will, dubious. That's why I never inquired."

"Rather interesting," said Obreduur, almost dismissively, as he stood, "but I do believe it's time for dinner." He gestured in the direction of the dining room.

Once everyone was seated, with Obreduur at the head of the table, with Avraal on his left and Maryanna on his right, and Ingrella at the other end, with Grieg on her right and Dekkard on her left, Ingrella declared, "Since we're being casual, we're getting salad and entrée at the same time."

"And the excellent Silverhills Red Reserve is courtesy of Steffan and Avraal," added Obreduur.

In moments, Rhosali had served each diner with a mixed winter salad and truffled beef tenderloins with mushroom risotto and green beans amandine. She then brought in a basket of hot dinner rolls.

"For a casual dinner," said Grieg in an amused tone, "this is rather elaborate."

"Only the dessert," replied Ingrella, lifting her fork.

After several bites, Grieg said, "I beg to differ. This is excellently elaborate, which brings up the question." He turned to Obreduur. "Why did you ask me and not Oskaar?"

"It might be difficult to get Oskaar to come all the way from Suvion for dinner. You showed common sense and attempted to avoid, as best you could, the unethical and likely illegal tactics Oskaar employed. I'm assuming that your statement about there being no evidence that Jhared did anything illegal was technically correct as well as a way to give the Imperador a reason to dismiss you, both as Premier and as councilor, so that you wouldn't have to deal with Oskaar."

"That is your assumption," Grieg said lightly.

"Of course."

While Obreduur and Grieg had been talking, Dekkard had been eating, and especially enjoying the truffled beef tenderloins and the mushroom risotto.

"And you're again letting someone else do the digging and pursuing, I see," said Grieg, looking at Dekkard.

Dekkard swallowed his latest mouthful and was about to reply when Obreduur held up his hand.

"Not exactly. The councilor here persuaded me to do it this way. I have my doubts, but so far he's been right more often than I have, and with what we've already heard . . ."

Grieg was silent for a moment. "That might be your greatest strength, Axel." He turned to Dekkard. "Why did you want to drag me back into it?"

"Because your statement about Eastern Ironway was totally incompetent, and no one who gets to be premier is that incompetent. You clearly wanted out as soon as possible. But why? I didn't know then. I became more skeptical when Ulrich covered up the whole mess by confining the hearings to the Military Affairs Committee and convinced there was much more when former Minister Kraffeist had his unfortunate accident."

"Most people suspect all of that," Grieg pointed out. "What's the point of dragging it out now and in detail?"

"Because Ulrich and others did much more than that," said Dekkard. "And so did Capitol Services, and they're both continuing to do so."

"Johan had nothing to do with what Oskaar did," declared Maryanna. "Absolutely nothing at all."

Obreduur smiled pleasantly and said, "I don't believe that Steffan ever even intimated that." He turned to Ingrella. "This is an excellent dinner."

Dekkard broke the momentary silence by asking Grieg, "Was Ulrich the one who quietly backed you for premier? Possibly because no one trusted him?" The last was a guess.

Grieg looked to his wife, then at Avraal, and shrugged. "That's not exactly a secret."

"Did Ulrich suggest Lukkyn Wyath to be Security minister?"

"He did. It was a reasonable nomination. He'd been the deputy minister under the previous Council."

"Did you know that Wyath had been director of security at Suvion Industries?"

"I believe that was mentioned."

"What do you make of Ulrich becoming vice-presidente at Suvion Industries?"

Grieg glanced to Avraal, then replied, "I imagine that was Suvion's way of repaying Oskaar, but that's only a supposition on my part."

"Repayment for favorable military contracts?"

"That would have been too obvious," Grieg replied dryly.

"Then perhaps for less stringent oversight by the Military Affairs Committee?"

"That would be a good assumption."

"What sort of information and services operation did Ulrich run or control through Capitol Services?" asked Dekkard.

"I knew he was involved in something shady, but I couldn't see that getting involved or even asking about it would do anything but implicate me."

"So you knew that Palafaux and Schmidtz were involved?"

"That was my suspicion, but I never asked."

"What else did you know about Capitol Services?" For the first time, Dekkard thought, Grieg looked uneasy. "What corporacions used them?"

"I was under the impression that it handled errands and the like for a number of corporacions."

"Did it transfer funds?"

"I have no idea, one way or the other."

"Did you ever meet anyone working for Capitol Services?"

"Not to my knowledge, except Sr. Minz."

"Was one of the corporacions using Capitol Services Suvion Industries?" asked Obreduur gently.

"Most likely, but I don't know that for a fact."

"What about Siincleer Shipbuilding?" asked Dekkard.

"Since Pohl and Oskaar were quite close, it's possible. Again, I don't know for sure."

Dekkard could tell from Avraal's lack of reaction that Grieg told the truth, but Grieg also had made a concerted effort to avoid getting entangled with Ulrich except where absolutely necessary on Council matters.

"Was Fernand Stoltz the Council legalist involved in negotiating with Eastern Ironway?"

That was a total shot in the dark, but Dekkard felt he wasn't getting enough from Grieg.

Grieg offered his lazy smile, then looked at Avraal, and shook his head, almost ruefully. "Gerard Schmidtz insisted on it as his price for relinquishing Public Resources Committee jurisdiction over the coal leases. Gerard wanted to make sure Ulrich didn't cut him out. Oskaar did tend to be secretive."

"What did Jaime Minz do for Ulrich besides his committee duties?" That was another long shot, Dekkard knew.

"I have no idea, except possibly for Capitol Services. Once, when one of the accountants questioned a travel payment for ironway fare for Minz to Chuive, Oskaar said it was a mistake and repaid it out of his own personal account."

"Then you saw Jaime Minz upon occasion?"

"Oskaar only used a security aide when he traveled to inspect Navy facilities. We went on two such trips together, once to Port Reale and once to Siincleer. Sr. Minz seemed quite competent. Those were the only times I interacted with him."

"How did Minz end up as an assistant security director at Northwest Industrial Chemical?"

"I don't know, but I imagine Oskaar arranged it. He's rather good at arranging matters, I discovered." There was definitely a sardonic edge to Grieg's words.

"Do you have any idea who Amash Kharhan is?"

"No. Neither did Jhared."

"I do believe it's time for dessert," said Obreduur, "as well as time for less-taxing conversation."

"That would be nice, Axel," said Maryanna coolly.

"Dear, I've found this taxing conversation far more pleasant than most of those I had with Oskaar in the last months of my time as premier." Grieg's words were almost gentle.

"I did say he was a serpent."

"That's perhaps too kind," said Ingrella. "Dessert is much sweeter and lighter, however."

"And the conversation will be much lighter as well," promised Obreduur.

Once Rhosali cleared away the salad plates and main course, she returned with dessert, presenting each diner with a plate containing a slice of a lemon chiffon cake, lightly frosted, and a small scoop of lemon sherbet.

"How are you finding the life of a retired premier?" Obreduur asked Grieg, adding with a smile, "Sooner or later, I'll face that."

Hopefully later. But Dekkard knew it could well be sooner if Obreduur and the Council didn't deal successfully with both the abuse of power by Commercer and corporacion interests and the New Meritorists.

Grieg smiled. "It's far less stressful, and Maryanna sees a great deal more of me, sometimes more than she wishes, I fear."

"Hardly, dear. You have years to make up."

"Axel won't have that problem," said Ingrella, "since I'm gone as much as he is."

"No, you'll keep being a legalist, and I'll have to take up gardening or something," replied Obreduur.

"You two have quite a few years before you need to think about that, though," said Ingrella, turning toward Dekkard.

"I might have to go back to university and get certified as a legalist," said Dekkard lightly, knowing that eighteen years was the maximum time a councilor could serve, and few lasted that long.

"If you're successfully reelected," replied Grieg, "by the time you leave the Council, that might not be so appealing."

"You won't have to worry about that for a while," said Obreduur.

"That's a very stylish outfit you're wearing, Avraal," observed Maryanna. "Where on earth did you find it?"

"In the back of my closet. I bought it in Siincleer years ago."

"You don't look old enough to have bought anything years ago."

"I am, unfortunately. Steffan and I look younger than we are. That's a mixed blessing. Good for me, and not quite so good for him."

"I can see that," agreed Grieg.

The comparatively light banter continued for a third of a bell, but it was another third before the Griegs departed and Ingrella, Obreduur, Avraal, and Dekkard sat down in the front parlor.

"Where did you discover Capitol Services?" Obreduur looked to Dekkard.

"I didn't. Avraal did. She found a reference to it when she was tailing Jaime Minz."

"I asked Carlos if he could find out more," added Avraal. "He found that it does exist and has a banque account and the same address as Minz's Northwest Industrial Chemical address."

"That surprised Johan," said Ingrella. "So did the question about Fernand Stoltz. Was Grieg telling the truth?"

"He was," replied Avraal. "I think he suspects more than he revealed, but I got the feeling he doesn't know, and didn't want to. I'd guess because of Ulrich."

"Maryanna certainly doesn't care for him." Dekkard looked to Avraal. "Did she believe what she said about Jhared Kraffeist's death?"

"With complete certainty."

"That doesn't mean it's true," said Ingrella. "I'd wager it's so, but tying a death already ruled accidental to Ulrich would be close to impossible."

"Do you know what legalist firm represented Wyath and Manwaeren?" Dekkard asked Ingrella.

"It's no secret that Barthow, Juarez and Whittsyn represented Wyath and Manwaeren. The firm has offices in only two cities—Suvion and Machtarn. I was a little surprised. They don't usually take criminal cases. Most times they refer those to Wheitz and Groebel."

"That's the firm that represented the Special Agents who attacked the house," said Dekkard. "And Villem Baar was a junior partner in Barthow, Juarez and Whittsyn."

"I'd forgotten that," admitted Obreduur.

"There are also two things about Jaime Minz," Dekkard added. "First, that ironway fare to Chuive. Chuive is the headquarters of Northwest Industrial Chemical, and Minz is now an assistant director of security for Northwest. Second, he often visits the building housing Wheitz and Groebel. I have to ask why, because the only tenants in the building are legalists. His position with Northwest Chemical Industries shouldn't have him dealing with legalists, unless Capitol Services is paying for the defenses of Special Agents, with funds supplied by various corporacions."

"That's possible." Obreduur looked to Ingrella.

"I'll see what I can do."

"The other aspect of this is that Fernand Stoltz is now with Paarsens and Alvara, who represent Eastern Ironway here in Machtarn, and he's continuing to meet with Councilor Schmidtz." Dekkard shook his head. "It's all suggestive, maybe more, but none of it's proof."

"It may not seem like it, Steffan," said Obreduur, "but you and Avraal did some good work tonight. Let us see what we can find."

Do we have any choice? Dekkard nodded and said, "I wish you luck. Solid evidence is hard to come by."

"Until enough hints amount to probable cause," said Ingrella. "Now, you two need some rest. You've obviously been spending a lot of time on these matters. Some things can't be forced."

"There are times when patience trumps action," said Obreduur as he stood, "especially rash or ill-considered action."

Ingrella stood as well.

Dekkard managed a smile as he rose. "Thank you both for the dinner."

"You're more than welcome," replied Obreduur. "Thank you for the idea and for your questions and the wine."

Obreduur eased them toward the portico door, and Ingrella retrieved their overcoats.

"Just be careful on the drive home," admonished Ingrella as Dekkard and Avraal left.

"We will," replied Avraal.

Dekkard definitely felt discouraged when he eased the Gresynt down the drive and onto Altarama Drive. It seemed as though, no matter how much he pointed out to Obreduur, Hasheem, Mardosh, and others, no one seemed to see just how dangerous the combination of Ulrich and his associates and the New Meritorists could be. When he'd been a security aide, he could act against a known threat to Obreduur. Now, as a councilor, he couldn't even act directly against those behind personal attacks. He didn't say anything until he turned the steamer onto Imperial Boulevard. "Now what do we do?"

"We've stirred everything up. We just survive and wait."

"Will that change anything? Really?"

"Obreduur has a great deal at stake, and he'll have even more at stake after the next act by the New Meritorists. He knows that, and so does Ingrella. She has something in mind. I'm sure of it. Just remember she's the one who forced the Imperador to call new elections by bringing Graffyn's petition on revising leasing procedures to the High Justiciary."

Dekkard couldn't help but smile wryly at that thought.

62

O N Unadi morning, Dekkard and Avraal woke up to the patter of sleet on their bedroom windows, and that eventually resulted in a slow, indirect drive to the Council Office Building.

When they neared the west doors, Avraal said, "Just park the steamer. I'd feel better staying here today."

"The weather?"

"I'd rather not drive to and from Carlos's office. Too many chances for an accident."

Dekkard felt that wasn't the only reason, but he didn't ask. He just drove the steamer to his assigned space in the covered parking, and the three walked across the street in the sleet.

Despite her winter jacket, Gaaroll muttered, "Frigging cold out there," once she was inside the building. Then she looked up to Dekkard and added, "Begging your pardon, sir."

"It's cold," Dekkard agreed. *But not that cold.*

"We're from warmer places than you are," Avraal pointed out.

"Oersynt isn't that much colder than Machtarn."

Avraal just shook her head at Dekkard's deliberately obtuse response.

Once the three entered the office, Dekkard smiled as he saw Margrit. "You made it through the sleet, I see."

"Svard and I did. Bretta's here, but not Luara, Illana, or Shuryn. They all come in from the east, and the omnibuses are running slow there, I heard."

"That's where the storm's blowing in from," Dekkard said.

"There's one message, but no mail yet." Margrit handed Dekkard an envelope.

"Thank you. Not surprising with this weather." Dekkard looked to Avraal. "Since you're here, and there's no mail, I'd like you to read over something and give me your thoughts."

"I could read it out front."

"You can read it in the office." He gestured to the inner office door, then followed her in.

There, he took her coat, and hung up both his and her coat, and set the leather folder on the shelf of the side table before taking the draft legislation and background material out of his second desk drawer and handing both to her. "The would-be working women's legal representation act."

"You think you can get it passed?"

"I can get it considered by the Workplace Administration Committee." He shrugged. "Beyond that, who knows?"

Avraal took the papers, sat down in the chair nearest the window, and began to read.

Dekkard opened the envelope, which turned out to be a reminder from

Guilhohn Haarsfel that the Workplace Administration Committee would be holding another oversight hearing beginning at the second bell of the afternoon on Tridi, dealing with iron casting and finishing processes in stove works and foundries.

While Avraal continued to read, Dekkard went out and informed Margrit of the hearing.

"Luara just came in and so did Shuryn."

"Thank you." Dekkard returned to his office and waited until Avraal finished reading the background materials.

"This is well thought out."

"That's mostly Luara's doing. I told her what I wanted the legislation to accomplish and asked her to find the best way to do it. After she finished, I had Svard look at it. He said he didn't have to do much. Then I went over it all. I didn't find any problems."

"You were fortunate to get her." Avraal smiled. "Except fortune had nothing to do with it."

"Well, the fortune of having Ingrella recommend her."

A few moments later, Margrit knocked on the door. "I've sorted the mail, sir."

"Just bring it in."

Once Dekkard had the mail on his desk, Avraal stood and said, "I'd like to wander around the building, if you don't mind."

"Not at all. You might even strike up an interesting conversation or two. Lunch, though?"

She nodded.

"Until then," Dekkard said with a smile.

Once she left, he returned to the mail, which contained the usual range of issues and complaints, including several letters demanding that the Council deal firmly and immediately with the New Meritorists. All of those letters clearly had been written by professionals or corporacion managers. When he finished reading through it all, he noted no letters supporting the Meritorist positions.

Just coincidence? Most likely, but Dekkard was getting less and less certain about anything. *Except that the New Meritorists are going to do something drastic before long.*

Despite Avraal's observation that there was little they could do but wait and survive, he struggled to find other options until Avraal returned to the office a third before noon.

"Did you run into anyone interesting?" he asked.

"I did, surprisingly. Kenalee Foerstah."

"She got another position here?"

"She's now the senior legalist for Felix Quellar, from Chuive."

"Considering Chuive's the headquarters for Northwest Industrial Chemical, that's very interesting. Did she have very much to say?"

"Neither she nor Quellar care much for Minz, but Councilor Quellar feels he has to be polite and cordial to him, given how many people work for the corporacion. Minz has met with Quellar several times, but so far hasn't asked or pushed for anything."

"So far. Anything else?"

"Not much. She did see Minz having lunch in the staff cafeteria with Fernand Stoltz and Cherlyssa Maergan."

"Cherlyssa was a Security Committee empath. If they were in the staff cafeteria, she has to be working for someone else now."

"She is. Pohl Palafaux. Again, quite suggestive, but hardly proof."

Dekkard smiled sourly, then said, "We might as well head over to the councilors' dining room and see if anyone accosts us. Besides, I'm hungry, and I suspect you are as well, since your breakfast was one mug of café."

"I could use something to eat."

Dekkard opted not to wear his overcoat, since it looked as though the sleet had almost stopped, but Avraal decided to wear hers. The courtyard was chill and windy, leaving Dekkard very glad to step inside the Council Hall.

When they reached the councilors' dining room and were being escorted toward a table, Harleona Zerlyon appeared.

"Could I persuade you two to join Elyncya and me. We just sat down."

Before Dekkard could say a word, Avraal said, "We'd love to."

In moments Avraal and Dekkard were seated, with Dekkard across from Zerlyon and Avraal across from Elyncya Duforgue.

"You looked absolutely stunning at the Yearend Ball, Avraal," said Duforgue. "Well, both of you, really."

"I just attempted to provide a tasteful backdrop for Avraal," said Dekkard, offering a playful smile.

"You're never a backdrop, Steffan," declared Zerlyon, "even if you try, and I've seen you try. Other councilors watch you all the time."

Most likely to stay out of my way when I do something stupid. "I'm almost the most junior in the entire Council," Dekkard said. "I'm definitely the youngest, and I have a lot to learn."

"If that's so, the Almighty help the rest of us when you do," replied Zerlyon.

"What are you two plotting?" asked Dekkard.

"Plotting?" asked Duforgue innocently.

"When the two best Crafter legal minds get together . . ." Dekkard smiled.

"Rumor has it that a certain councilor has an interest in an expansion of certain rights for certain women," said Duforgue.

"That's quite a rumor," said Dekkard.

"The majority floor leader asked me what I thought about the idea. He didn't mention who was behind it, but it had to be a Crafter, and it wasn't any of the three women. That left the men, and none of the others would even consider it."

"And?" asked Dekkard.

"How far along are you?"

"There's a solid draft and supporting documentation."

Duforgue looked to Zerlyon. "I told you."

"Could we look at it?"

"Well . . ." Dekkard drew out the word. ". . . since it's obviously not a secret anymore, I don't see why not. It was suggested that I not rush things."

"We're working on a broader bill," ventured Zerlyon.

Avraal turned and looked at Dekkard—pointedly.

"So am I," said Dekkard. "Or rather, Luara is. One of my legalists. It deals with pay discrimination."

The other two exchanged amused glances.

Then Duforgue said, "Why pay discrimination?"

"There are a few other provisions, but marks are power. If the Council ensures equal pay for equal jobs, and makes certain that the same jobs don't have different names for men and for women, then that increases the power women have. I'm sure you two have thought of that."

"We have," replied Zerlyon. "It's more interesting that you have." She looked to Avraal.

Avraal laughed. "I had nothing to do with it. I didn't even see the draft legislation for those 'certain rights' until earlier today."

"I can have another copy typed up," volunteered Dekkard. "Which one of you gets it?"

"Send it to Elyncya," said Zerlyon.

At that moment a server appeared and took their orders. Dekkard went with the three-cheese chicken, as did Avraal. Both legalists ordered the white bean soup. All ordered café.

Then, Duforgue asked, "Does either of you know any more about the murder of the Siincleer vice-presidente?"

"I haven't heard anything new," said Dekkard, which was certainly true. "Have you?"

"No," replied Duforgue. "Not since Guard Captain Trujillo talked to me. Because you're closer to the Premier than we are, I wondered if he'd said anything new."

"If he has, I'm certainly not aware of it. He can be very closemouthed."

"Has the Security Committee held any meetings or hearings on it?"

Dekkard shook his head. "He hasn't said, but I'm assuming that Chairman Hasheem feels that it's a case of murder having nothing to do with the security of Guldor. If he did, we'd have had hearings."

"That sounds like Fredrich," said Zerlyon.

"Has either of you been approached by a Fernand Stoltz?" asked Dekkard. "He used to be a legalist for the Public Resources Committee, but he's now working for Paarsens and Alvara, the firm that represents Eastern Ironway."

"I know of the firm," replied Zerlyon, "but I never heard of Stoltz."

"He's fairly close to Gerard Schmidtz and Pohl Palafaux."

"Why do you want to know?" asked Duforgue.

Dekkard smiled. "Because I'm curious. I've seen Schmidtz with Stoltz a number of times, and once Avraal and I saw Schmidtz, Palafaux, and Jareem Saarh having dinner together at a rather expensive restaurant."

"How expensive?" asked Zerlyon.

"Estado Don Miguel."

"That's definitely expensive," replied Zerlyon. "What were you doing there?"

"I took Steffan there to celebrate our first month anniversary," said Avraal.

"She tricked me," said Dekkard. "We went shopping for some winter clothes, and after that, she lured me in."

"Oh, poor man," said Duforgue.

"But we happened to see those three, and it seemed a little odd," Dekkard added.

"That's definitely an odd combination," agreed Zerlyon. "How was the dinner?"

"Excellent," replied Dekkard. "It was quite a treat."

"Do you two go there often?" asked Duforgue.

"No," said Dekkard firmly, "but the Premier did take us once."

"He can afford to," said Zerlyon. "His wife makes more than he does."

While Dekkard hadn't realized that until several months ago, he definitely agreed.

"By the way, was the other woman with you at the ball related?" asked Zerlyon.

"That was my sister Emrelda."

"She's lovely. Not quite as lovely as you, though."

From there on, the conversation became pleasant and superficial.

After leaving the dining room a good bell later, Dekkard and Avraal stepped out into the courtyard. The clouds had passed, and the sun struggled to break through the mist and haze that hung over the city. A ragged lacework of sleet intermittently covered the grass, but not any of the stone walkway.

"Back to work," said Dekkard, "or at least to checking and signing responses and having someone type up a copy of Luara's draft legislation."

"Not the background information, I hope?"

"I only promised the legislation."

63

ALTHOUGH a high haze hung over Machtarn, Duadi morning dawned warmer and drier than Unadi. When Dekkard turned off Imperial Boulevard heading east on Council Avenue, he scanned both sides of the avenue, taking in the variety of buildings, looking for anything that seemed out of place. For the most part, everything appeared normal, although he took a second look at a large stake lorry, its dull brown paint battered and scratched, with a patched canvas top covering the rear cargo area. His first thought was that it looked like the type of lorry used by renderers. It was also parked near where he'd seen the lorry holding the signs for the demonstration disrupted by the renegade Special Agents.

"Is there anyone around that big brown lorry?"

"No, sir," declared Gaaroll. "No strong feelings, either."

"I don't sense anyone nearby," added Avraal.

"Thank you both."

Dekkard continued to wonder about the slightly out-of-place lorry when he and the other two neared the Council Office Building more than a third before second bell.

"There don't seem to be quite so many people out and about this morning," said Dekkard as he eased the Gresynt to a stop opposite the west doors of the Council Office Building.

"That just might be because we're earlier," Avraal pointed out.

Dekkard certainly hoped that was the case and that he was just being overcautious. "I take it I won't see you until this afternoon."

"Since I didn't show up at Carlos's yesterday, I thought putting in a full day might be a good idea."

"I can see that." Dekkard opened the steamer door and got out, picking up his gray leather folder, while Avraal moved behind the wheel. "Fourth bell?"

"I'll send a message if I'll be much later than that."

"Have a good day, and give Carlos my best." Dekkard closed the steamer door, then stepped to the sidewalk and watched for a moment as Avraal drove off toward Imperial Boulevard, before turning toward the bronze doors of the building.

"Do you have any meetings today?" asked Gaaroll once they were inside and walking toward the central staircase.

"Not that I know of. I don't know that the Council will be that busy between now and the Midwinter Recess, but that could always change, especially depending on what the New Meritorists do."

"You think they'll do something so soon after the explosion in the Guildhall?"

"They'll do something. When is another question. Usually, there's been time between their demonstrations." *But what if there's not?*

He shook his head. "We're going to Guard Captain Trujillo's office."

"Sir?"

"The lorry we saw this morning? The last time I saw one there was when there was a New Meritorist demonstration."

Less than a sixth passed before Dekkard and Gaaroll were in the very small chamber adjoining the Premier's floor office.

"Councilor? What can I do for you?" asked Trujillo as he turned from the filing cabinet and closed it.

"It might be nothing, but there's a brown stake lorry parked across the street some two blocks west of the Council Office Building. There was no one in it, but the last time one was parked there . . ." Dekkard explained briefly, then finished, "It might be nothing, but I wanted to let you know."

"We'll look into it, and I'll pass the word to the outside guards and the sentries, just in case."

"Thank you."

Trujillo smiled. "No. Thank you. Your insights have always been useful."

After leaving the Guard captain, Dekkard wondered if he was being too sensitive. *But if it's a problem and you didn't let Trujillo know . . .*

Once he and Gaaroll were back in the Council Office Building, he saw several staffers on the way to the central stairs, but they weren't people he recognized or knew closely.

When Dekkard neared the top of the stairs, he saw another councilor—Chiram Ghohal, who appeared to be waiting for him. "Good morning, Chiram. How are you doing?"

"Acceptably. The newssheets exaggerated my condition." Ghohal paused. "Could I have a moment of your time?"

"Certainly." Dekkard glanced to Gaaroll, who immediately stepped away. "What is it?"

"Chairman Mardosh had scheduled some hearings on procurement. With Navy officers from Uldwyrk. He canceled them. I asked him why. He said the timing was impolitic. I suggested that it was very politic, since all sorts of mentions about contract irregularities appeared in the newssheets. He chuckled and said that someday I'd understand."

Dekkard wanted to sigh. He didn't. "Chiram, Councilor Mardosh was assistant guildmeister for the Shipfitters Guild in Siincleer. Siincleer is his district. Siincleer Shipbuilding is not only the biggest corporacion in Siincleer, but one of the largest in all of Guldor. Sr. Venburg was the head of legal affairs for the corporacion. He was likely the guest of either Councilor Mardosh or Councilor Kuuresoh—although that's just a guess—"

"Someone requested the chairman to ask Sr. Venburg. He told me that."

Dekkard managed a polite nod. "How would it look to the presidente of Siincleer if, right after a senior corporacion official was killed here in the Council Hall, the Military Affairs Committee held hearings on procurements involving Siincleer? How might the presidente feel about Councilor Mardosh? Or the Council?"

"He might be upset, but isn't it our job to fix things?"

"It is, but if the chairman feels the time isn't right, it becomes more difficult. He has to have the votes, and right now it can be hard to get Commercer and some Landor votes."

"You got the Security reform bill through."

"That was easier. The Commercer councilors opposed it, but everyone else wanted reform after all the abuses. Right now, the abuse occurring in military contracts outrages only a few people." Dekkard paused. "I take it there have been some egregious examples in Surpunta?"

"You wouldn't believe." Ghohal smiled sheepishly. "I expect you would after dealing with Security."

"I'm sure that Chairman Mardosh will revisit the hearings when he thinks the time is right." *Whether he'll do more than hold hearings is another question.* "If he doesn't within a few weeks, or if you think something isn't quite right, I'd appreciate your letting me know."

"I certainly will. I appreciate your thoughts, and thank you." Ghohal smiled, then turned, presumably heading to his office.

Dekkard started toward his own office, and once they were well away from Ghohal, he asked, "What did you sense about Councilor Ghohal?"

"Low purple piles. He's scared-like of you. Not a lot, but some."

"Did he feel puzzled?"

"I don't think so. Light blue is puzzled. I know that."

Because Ghohal hadn't ever sought out Dekkard before, he couldn't help but wonder if Mardosh, or someone else, had suggested that Ghohal talk to him. *And if not Mardosh, who?*

Obreduur likely wouldn't have, nor Nortak, and Ghohal wouldn't have confided in any of the Commercers. But then, it could have been someone not on the Military Affairs Committee, possibly Julian Andros or even Pajiin.

After Dekkard and Gaaroll reached the office, Dekkard hung up his overcoat, put the folder on the side table shelf, and settled behind the desk, thinking over the events of the past few months, especially the past few weeks. Life had been so much simpler as a security aide—identify the possible threat, almost always an individual, and neutralize it. The threats were different as a councilor, and his ability to do anything rested not merely on seeing the threats, but on convincing others.

Dekkard thought he'd been moderately effective at seeing threats, and less effective at convincing others. *Is that you . . . or the nature of politics . . . or some of both?*

Finally, he began to go through the mail, reading each letter, some quickly, when he could get the gist of the writer's purpose, and some more slowly. Even so, he felt uneasy, and after a time walked to the window, looking out to the north, where he could see the upper reaches of the Imperial Palace. A story below the window stretched a wide hedge, bordered by a stone walk, and then a swath of lawn extending some twenty yards to a stone wall a little more than two yards high. Beyond the wall was a narrow street used mainly by vehicles servicing the Council Office Building and the Council Hall.

A steam lorry headed west on the service road, but continued past the

Council Office Building without slowing or stopping. Dekkard smiled wryly and walked back to his desk. After reading for another half bell, he found himself again uneasy, and he walked to the door, opened it, and asked, "Are there any messages?"

Margrit smiled. "Not yet, sir. Are you expecting any?"

Dekkard managed a smile in return. "I can't say that I am. Thank you." He closed the door and walked to the widow, looking out once more at a few steamers headed east on the service road. He shook his head and went back to his desk. Less than a third later, he came across another almost aimless letter.

> . . . here in Gaarlak, the early flax grows well, and that's good, but not so good, because there's lots of it, and we can't get a good price for it, but when there's too much early rain, it washes out the seeds, and then those that are left spread too much so that the fibres are too short and the seed yield is down . . . but if it's too dry early we can't get enough water because it all goes to the mills . . .

Dekkard read the letter again, but the writer wasn't asking for anything, at least not so far as Dekkard could determine.

He shook his head, trying to shake the uneasy feeling that had never really left him. Finally, he stood and walked to the window, where he looked again at the Palace on the heights that overlooked Machtarn. It was a good view.

Movement on the service street caught his eye, and he concentrated to make out what crept eastward. From what he could tell, it was a large stake lorry, the same brown-painted one he'd noted on the drive to the Council Office Building. The lorry slowed, then stopped a little short of a point opposite the middle of the building.

Two men at the back of the cargo area began rolling back the canvas, revealing an odd-looking device that they swiveled toward the building. As they did, Dekkard also noted that the side pointed toward the building presented a flat metal front that shielded the two men.

Armor plate . . . or something like it? Frig!

In instants, the two had the device pointed at the building. A blast of steam issued from a small gap in the plate protecting the device, and something flew toward the second story of the building.

Frig! Frig!

Dekkard turned and dashed into the outer office. Before he could say a word, a massive CRUMMPTT reverberated through the building.

"Everyone out of here! Leave everything! Run! Take the east staff stairs to the basement! Go!"

Roostof came running. "What—"

"They're using a steam cannon to shell the building! Go!"

Dekkard had to drag Illana from her desk, but the two of them weren't that far behind the others, scrambling down the steps. He just hoped they could make it to the basement before the gunners targeted the east end of the building. He'd been in the basement enough to know that nothing fired from the makeshift steam cannon could penetrate the heavy stone foundations, and possibly not even the heavy outer walls, but the windows on all floors would allow shells or whatever the steam cannon was launching to reach into the offices before exploding, and the shrapnel and fragmented internal masonry could easily make the center hall a killing ground. *If there's enough dunnite or whatever in the shells.* But whether there was Dekkard had no way of knowing.

Dekkard had barely entered the staircase when there was another explosion, followed by another . . . and another. In the few minutes it took him and his staff to reach the basement, Dekkard thought he heard close to a half score explosions.

"Stay inside the stairwell!" he ordered as he reached the basement floor.

Roostof turned to him. "Now what?"

"The moment the explosions stop we go up to the first floor and get out of the building. One of those explosions could rupture a gas line. There are supposed to be surge-cutoff valves, but who knows?" As he finished explaining, he realized he hadn't heard any more detonations. But then there was a single, larger explosion, somehow more muffled, but continuing for much longer than the others.

"That might be it," Dekkard found himself saying. "We'll wait and see for a minute or two."

Several minutes passed with no further explosions. Then Dekkard could hear yelling and shouts, and someone screaming. Somewhere, a steam whistle screeched out a distress signal. As Dekkard started up the steps, amid the dust sifting down the stairwell, he could hear others coming down the steps from the second floor. He emerged from the stairwell archway into a haze of dust and grit.

"Everyone out of the building! Out of the building!"

Dekkard had no idea who was calling out the orders, but suspected it was a Council Guard. He looked back to see Roostof, then Colsbaan, following him, then Teitryn, Bretta, Illana, and finally Gaaroll and Margrit. Once she was through the archway, Gaaroll hurried forward so that she was beside Dekkard. He looked back toward Roostof and called out, "We're going to the Council Hall." He kept moving toward the courtyard doors, held open by two Council Guards, obviously to make it easier for people to leave the building.

Once Dekkard had his staff out of the Council Office Building, he glanced back. While he couldn't see the north or south side, a mixture of dust and smoke wreathed the entire building, although it seemed heavier around the upper floor. The attack had been made with only one steam cannon, and it had been directed at the offices on the north side, in the middle.

Dekkard swallowed. *Obreduur! And Macri, Karola, Anna, possibly Isobel Irlende or even Ingrella.*

Then again, Obreduur might have been in the Premier's floor office. *But that leaves all the others.* He thought about heading back, then shook his head. There was absolutely nothing he could do. He wasn't a physician, or even a nurse.

It had to be the same stake lorry! Why hadn't Trujillo done something?

Or had the lorry been moved? Dekkard couldn't do anything about that now. "Just keep close together," he said to the staff.

"Sir," said Roostof, "all you said was that someone was shelling the building with a steam cannon. How did you know that?"

"I was wondering about a letter, and I walked to the window. I saw an old steam lorry, a covered stake lorry, stop on the service road. Two men rolled back the canvas and turned this odd-looking device toward the building. There was a gout of steam. That was when I realized what it was. I hurried toward the staff office, and then the shell or bomb exploded. You know the rest."

"You don't know any more?"

"No. It all happened so fast. I just wanted to get everyone out. I'd guess that the last long explosion was when the guards destroyed the cannon, or it destroyed itself. Otherwise, I think the shelling would have lasted longer."

Dekkard glanced back again. People poured out of the Council Office Building. Some milled aimlessly around the courtyard. Others seemed to be following Dekkard and his staff. He turned his attention back to the covered portico and the walkway ahead, where just a few handfuls of people preceded him and his staff. He had no real idea of what to do next, but it seemed to him that any sort of direction or information would more likely be found in the Council Hall and there was little sense in standing around in the courtyard and getting chilled.

"Who was it, sir?" asked Roostof. "Was it the New Meritorists? Could you tell?"

"I couldn't, but the odds definitely favor the New Meritorists." Dekkard found his thoughts going back to Obreduur and those he'd worked with. *Maybe they missed his office.*

But he had a cold feeling that the gunners hadn't missed, and the only question was who had been in Obreduur's office and who had died.

In the few minutes it took Dekkard and his staff to reach the Council Hall more guards appeared, most of them hurrying toward the Council Office Building, but two remained by the Council Hall doors, being held open by wooden wedges.

"Councilor, sir, all councilors are requested to go to the Council chamber."

"Thank you." Dekkard nodded, then stepped inside the Council Hall. After several steps he turned and said, "Svard, we need to get everyone to the staff cafeteria before it fills up and no one has a place to sit. I don't think they'll be allowing anyone back into the office building anytime soon."

"Yes, sir."

Behind him, he could hear the guards repeating, "Councilors to the Council chamber, please." Ahead of them, the corridor wasn't at all crowded, but Dekkard knew that would change.

Once they reached the staff cafeteria, Dekkard made sure that Svard ushered everyone to two adjoining tables, then headed for the councilors' lobby. He'd no more than stepped in when Breffyn Haastar hurried over.

"Steffan! What do you know? I came over from the banque, and the guards insist that the Council Office Building has been bombed and may be unsafe. They're not letting anyone go back."

"The building wasn't bombed. It was shelled, most likely by the New Meritorists. Where's your office?"

"On the lower level on the south side just to the east of the main staircase."

"They shelled the north side, and it didn't last that long. I'd guess your staff is probably all right. The Council Guards sent everyone here. You might take a quick look at the staff cafeteria. That's all I know."

"Thank you." Haastar rushed off.

Dekkard just stood there, possibly for several minutes, before he slowly walked into the Council chamber and toward his desk.

Then, before Dekkard could sit down, Haarsfel appeared. "You're here! How did you escape? Your office was one of those totally destroyed. There's no trace of your staff."

"They're all right. I happened to be looking out my window when they fired the first shell. I ordered my staff out of the office and into the stairwell. We made it just in time."

"You *saw* what happened?"

Dekkard shook his head. "Only the first shell. I didn't need to see any more."

"Shells? They had a cannon?"

"I didn't know what it was until the two men fired it. I think it was a makeshift steam cannon. One side had metal plating. The side closest to the building."

"Guard Captain Trujillo will need to talk to you. Stop by the Premier's floor office in two bells or so."

"What about the Premier? His councilor's office?"

Haarsfel shook his head. "It doesn't look good, Steffan."

Dekkard just shuddered.

"Nothing like this has ever happened," said Haarsfel. "Never."

There's a first time for everything. But what Dekkard said was, "Nothing like this past year has ever happened." He paused. "They didn't hit your office?"

"It's on the first floor, on the south side, and I was here in the Council Hall working with the committee staff on tomorrow's hearing. Do you have any thoughts or suggestions?"

"Don't let anyone interfere with Trujillo or advise him except you, and see if someone can determine which corporacion manufactured the dunnite."

"Dunnite?"

"Guilhohn, the Premier was certain that the New Meritorists had more dunnite stashed away. I'm guessing that's what they used. The smoke would have been darker if they'd used black powder, and the explosions not as powerful."

"You know a lot—"

"I'm a Military Institute graduate, remember? You might ask Admiral Konnigsburg. He'd likely know even more."

"Oh, I should have thought of that. Thank you."

With that, Haarsfel hurried off.

Dekkard couldn't but wonder how Haarsfel knew about Obreduur's office, except that the Council Guards would have briefed him in Obreduur's absence. *Could Obreduur have been elsewhere?* Dekkard could hope, but he had sinking feelings and great doubts. The New Meritorists wanted to strike at the Council, and some corporacion agents would have been more than glad to suggest that targeting the Premier would be a perfect way to do just that.

Dekkard shook his head. He'd worried about bombs being smuggled in and planted, but he hadn't even thought of a targeted strike at Obreduur with a frigging steam cannon. *But it makes sense. Afterward.* And any group with the ability to destroy fifteen Security buildings certainly had enough expertise to make a single steam cannon. No one would even look twice at a compact steam device, even if one side happened to be plated. Various steam engines were everywhere. Making a score of shells out of large copper tubing with lead azide fuses wouldn't be that difficult, and they already had the dunnite.

You knew that lorry wasn't right. But what else could you have done besides tell Trujillo? There wasn't anyone around, and you and Avraal couldn't physically search all the nearby buildings.

Around him, other councilors filed in, most of them talking in lowered voices.

Dekkard was still sitting at his small desk, trying to sort it all out, when someone approached. He looked up and saw Eyril Konnigsburg.

"How are you doing, Steffan?"

Dekkard stood. "Personally, I'm fine. A little shaken. No, more than a little, but— What about you?"

"There are advantages to being a junior Commercer. My office isn't that far from the west doors on the main level. The New Meritorists targeted the second level somewhat east of the office. The building is rather solid, except for the windows. Floor Leader Haarsfel said your office was destroyed. Your staff?"

"I got them all out." Dekkard provided a quick explanation.

Konnigsburg nodded. "That's what Haarsfel said. Did you have any idea?"

"I told the Premier that the New Meritorists would do something drastic and unexpected, and that it would be soon, but I had no idea. A frigging steam cannon in the cargo area of a stake lorry?" After a moment, he asked, "What do you think?"

"The plating was enough to keep the roof guards from being able to take them out while they targeted the part of the building where the Premier has his office and where there are more Crafters. Then they targeted your office. They even had to move the stake lorry some to do that, and they could have done more damage if they hadn't."

"I didn't know that."

"Haarsfel told me that. He wanted my thoughts. By the way, I agree with your conclusion that they used dunnite as the explosive agent. The blast smoke is distinctive. Do you have any thought on where they obtained it?"

"My thought was that they got it more than a year ago from a source at either Suvion Industries or Northwest Industrial Chemical, because dunnite was what they used to destroy the Security buildings, and frankly, because the only place where they could get it in bulk from the Navy was at the munitions works, and the Navy has tight safeguards."

Konnigsburg offered a wry smile. "We agree on that. Why would anyone do that?"

"The one thing that makes sense is that someone wanted to make the New Meritorists more of a threat than they otherwise would have been in order to build a case for strengthening the Security Ministry. The STF was on its way to becoming a military unit under the control of the Security minister."

"Steffan, you were made for Naval Intelligence, but right now . . ." The retired admiral shook his head. "What else can you tell me?"

"Former Premier Ulrich is now a vice-presidente of Suvion Industries and his former security aide, one Jaime Minz, is an assistant security director, here in Machtarn, for Northwest Industrial Chemical. I find that interesting, but exactly what that means . . ." Dekkard shrugged.

"It's a bit more than interesting. Thank you." Konnigsburg looked past Dekkard toward the dais, and the session bell chimed. "It looks like the majority floor leader will be addressing us." He nodded to Dekkard and then moved away, presumably toward his desk.

A bit more than interesting? Dekkard also wondered about the reference to Naval Intelligence. Had that been Konnigsburg's command? He looked up to the front of the Council chamber, where Haarsfel approached the lectern.

The conversations and murmurs died away, but Haarsfel was silent for several moments before speaking.

"Little more than a bell ago . . ."

Has it been that long? Dekkard found that hard to believe.

". . . a steam lorry stopped on the north service road. In minutes, two men turned a makeshift but armored steam cannon on the north side of the Council Office Building and began to fire shells of some sort at the second level of the building. The first shells hit the windows of the Premier's office and those on each side. It appears that the Premier and most if not all of his staff were killed. In addition to the Premier's office, the offices of Councilors Marryat Osmond, Tedor Waarfel, Quentin Fader, and Steffan Dekkard were totally destroyed. Councilor Dekkard's office was the last targeted, and he managed to escape with all of his staff. The other four and most of their staffs were not so fortunate. We have not had time to identify any others who may have been killed. There are well over a score who were wounded but who are expected to survive.

"The perpetrators are believed to be members of the group calling themselves the New Meritorists. Those operating the steam cannon did not survive an explosion that largely consumed the lorry and the weapon. That explosion sent shrapnel through various windows on the north side of the building. That is all the information that I have at present. The Council Office Building will be closed until it is fully inspected and determined to be safe to reenter. All water and gas lines have been secured, and the water damage has been held to a minimum.

"The Council will meet tomorrow morning at third bell to receive additional information and to discuss the next steps. Following that session, the Security Committee will meet at first bell of the afternoon. All other hearings scheduled for the remainder of the week are postponed. The councilors' dining room and lobby will be open from second morning bell until fifth afternoon bell for the immediate future."

With that, Haarsfel turned and left the lectern, heading for the Premier's floor office. As majority floor leader, Dekkard knew, Haarsfel was acting temporary premier, at least for the present, but that wasn't likely to last. According to what Obreduur had told Dekkard, Haarsfel preferred being floor leader to premier, and Dekkard began to see why.

As the other councilors began to leave, Villem Baar walked toward Dekkard.

"Are you and your staff all right, Villem?"

"One of my legalists was cut by flying glass, but not badly. How in the world did you escape?"

"Sheer luck." Dekkard went on to explain briefly.

"Not just luck. Most of us don't think that quickly, Steffan. Your staff should be grateful."

Dekkard managed a wry smile. "I'm just glad I could save them from the effects of whatever it was, but I don't see why they targeted my office."

"The Security reform act. You removed the cause of a lot of anger against Security and the government. That makes the job of revolutionaries that much harder. You and Obreduur set a moderate course. You concentrated on solving the problems of the workers without destroying the productive side of Guldor. Extremists and ideologues don't care for moderates." Baar smiled sympathetically. "You're going to have your work cut out for you."

"What do you mean?" asked Dekkard. "Maybe it should be obvious, but I'm probably not thinking as well as I could be."

"That's understandable. Most of us probably aren't at the moment, and we weren't affected as directly as you. Something unthinkable yesterday happened this morning. What I meant was that the Craft Party and the Council lost a strong leader, and that's going to make dealing with the New Meritorists and other problems even more difficult. The Crafters need new ideas, and from what I've seen, outside of the Premier, most of the new ideas were coming from you and a few other very junior councilors. Without Obreduur, getting them considered, let alone implemented, is going to be much more difficult."

"That makes sense," Dekkard agreed. "I knew that the older Crafter councilors tend to be rather cautious." *But you'd never considered that Obreduur would be assassinated in the way it happened, or what that will mean.* "I appreciate the insight, and now I need to go and brief my staff."

"I do as well. You have my best wishes, Steffan."

Baar hurried off, and Dekkard followed him to the councilors' lobby. From there, Dekkard walked to the staff cafeteria, making his way through the crowd of staffers, not that difficult a task because the staffers saw the councilor's pin and moved aside.

Roostof and the others looked at him expectantly as he stopped at the end of one of the two tables. He could also see and sense that the staffers of other councilors or committees nearby were listening, and he realized that he'd have to be careful with every word.

"First off, before you leave today, you need to give Svard your message address. Yes, I know that administration has them and so did Svard, but I've been informed that our office was destroyed, not the walls likely, but the windows and everything else, and it may be days before the Council Office Building is safe to reenter. We need your messaging address so that we can inform you when and where to return to work. You still have positions, and you'll be paid. I suspect, but I don't know, that you'll get your pay on schedule or close to it."

From there, he went on to repeat, as accurately as he could, what Haarsfel had said. Then he asked, "Do you have any other questions?"

Margrit asked, the tracks of tears on her face, "The Premier's staff?"

"It's unlikely that any of them survived, unless someone was out of the office at the time, and it may be several days before we know, because of the number of people injured and missing." Dekkard was just hoping that Ritten Obreduur hadn't been in the office, although that would have been unlikely. Losing both Obreduurs would be an even greater blow, something Dekkard would never have seen even four months ago.

Margrit nodded, but did not speak.

Roostof just looked stunned.

Dekkard understood. Both of them had worked for years with Obreduur before coming to work for him, and they'd been close to those staffers almost certainly killed.

"Do any of you have any questions?"

Shuryn Teitryn cleared his throat. "Sir, how did you know so quickly?"

Once again, Dekkard explained.

"How long do you think it will take to repair the building?" asked Luara.

"I don't know, but some of the offices on the main floor were scarcely damaged. They got the water and gas off quickly so the water damage has been contained and there was no fire. It all depends on the amount of damage on the second floor. I'd say a good week at a minimum, but that's just a guess." Dekkard paused. "Any other questions?"

No one spoke.

"Then I'll need to speak to Svard and Nincya. The rest of you are free to go, after you leave your messaging address with Svard. I'd strongly suggest you at least leave the Council buildings. I don't think there will be any more violence, but it's likely to be crowded and confusing, and there's nothing else you can do here at the moment."

While Roostof began to take down messaging addresses on scraps of paper, Dekkard turned to Gaaroll. "Nincya, I need you to do something for me." He handed Gaaroll two ten-mark bills. "Find a steamhack and go to Carlos Baartol's office. Tell my wife what happened and come back here with her. If she's already left, take a steamhack back here. I'll either be here, in the councilors' lobby or the dining room, or maybe in the Premier's floor office."

"Yes, sir." Gaaroll immediately hurried off.

Almost a sixth passed before Roostof had jotted down the various addresses and all Dekkard's remaining staffers had left the staff cafeteria. Then Roostof turned to Dekkard.

"I don't know that there's anything else you can do today," Dekkard said. "Tomorrow, I might know more."

"Should I meet you before the Council convenes tomorrow morning, then?"

"I think afterward would be better. I doubt I'll know any more until then. Just take a table in the staff cafeteria, and I'll find you."

"Sir, I'd feel better if I stayed until Ritten Dekkard returns."

"I appreciate the thought, Svard, but I'll wait for her in the councilors' dining room. You really can't do much right now, and tomorrow could be a very busy day."

"Are you sure?"

"I'm sure, but you can walk there with me."

As the two made their way to the councilors' dining room, they had to navigate around various groups nearly filling the main corridor, largely of staffers, from what Dekkard could tell. He saw several councilors, each talking to their staff, among them Julian Andros and Jareem Saarh. Once he said goodbye to Roostof and entered the dining room, he saw that most of the tables were taken.

Then Kaliara Bassaana gestured, insistently, and Dekkard walked to her table and sat down.

"I was hoping I'd have a chance to talk to you. Are you all right?"

"Other than having my office destroyed, discovering that I was a target, and learning that the councilor I respected the most has been killed, along with apparently all of his staff, I suppose I'm dealing with matters as well as could be expected." As he finished speaking, Dekkard realized that his tone had been sharp and bitter.

"Considering all that, and likely more, you look to be holding up remarkably well."

"What about you?"

"I was fortunate to escape injury."

"Was your office damaged?"

"We lost a window, and several staffers have cuts. One suffered a deep slash across her upper arm. What about your staff?"

"I got them out without injury."

"Might I ask how?"

Dekkard explained quickly, ending with, "I was just lucky to be looking out the window."

"It wasn't luck, Steffan."

"Then what was it?"

"I suspect you're one of those very rare individuals who can sense danger, even when it's unexpected, or perhaps you're just more attuned to it. You also react quickly and decisively to danger once it presents itself."

"I've had the benefit of excellent training."

A server approached. Bassaana stopped him and said, "A café for Councilor Dekkard."

"Yes, Councilor."

"What do you expect next?" asked Bassaana.

"In a day or two, perhaps a week, there will be a letter or a broadsheet demanding that the Council immediately amend the Great Charter to require the recording and publication of all votes."

"How would you react to that?"

"Denounce it. The only thing worse than a Council moved by marks or popularity would be a Council intimidated by violence."

"That's easy enough to say, but how would you stop the violence?"

"I suspect that Premier Obreduur already set in motion some of the steps to do that. That's only a guess on my part, and that may be why this morning's attack was so unexpected."

Bassaana didn't bother to hide her surprise or her interest. "What exactly do you mean? What else do you know?"

"It's barely more than a week since the explosion in the Machtarn Guildhall. They've never created this kind of havoc this close together. They rushed to do this attack, clearly targeting Obreduur. Other demonstrations had a much wider focus. The Summerend demonstrations were aimed at the Security Ministry, not at Minister Lukkyn. The more recent demonstrations were against the Council and the Crafters. But this one?"

"Was aimed at Obreduur, and at you."

"It was certainly aimed at him. They took out his office and those on each side. I was almost an afterthought." *Or they were just slow.* But Dekkard wasn't about to say that. He waited for the oncoming server to deliver his café, then took a small swallow.

"Why you at all?" asked Bassaana. "You were the one who pushed through the Security reforms."

"That's a very good question, Kaliara. It does suggest that the New Meritorists or whoever is grouped together behind that name have more in mind than reform, or that reform is merely a façade."

"Out-and-out revolution, you're saying."

"That's certainly the most obvious possibility. I wouldn't discount others. I couldn't say what they might be, but it appears that nothing about the New Meritorists is quite as it once seemed. That's why"—*one reason, anyway*—"I don't want to jump to premature conclusions."

"Conspiracies within revolution, yet." Bassaana's voice was both sardonic and sarcastic. "Isn't that a bit extreme?"

"My judgment could easily be in error. That sort of thing happens when people try to blow up you and your staff."

"I can see that from almost anyone but you."

"I'm just as human as anyone else." Dekkard took another swallow of café. "And it has been a very long and violent morning."

"You mentioned that you thought Obreduur might already have taken steps. What do you think they might have been?"

"I don't know. Since I became a councilor, we've been much more distanced, and in our few interactions, he cautioned me in one way or another not to push for anything for a while."

"You have other legislative proposals?"

"A few. But after all this, who knows if anything along those lines will be possible for some time. What about you? I can't believe you don't have some ideas for improving transportation, especially concerning the ironways."

"We'll have to see who becomes the new chair."

For a moment, Dekkard was confused, then realized that with Waarfel's death in the morning's attack, Haarsfel would have become the chair, but since he was already chair of Workplace Administration, he'd have to step down as chair there if he wanted to chair the Transportation Committee. If he didn't take the Transportation chair, then either Elyncya Duforgue or Traelyna Treshaam, both just elected, would have to be the next chair. "Haarsfel may have to take it."

"That would create some interesting possibilities."

"These days," replied Dekkard dryly, "everything creates interesting possibilities."

"Whom do you think Haarsfel will propose as a candidate for premier?"

"I haven't even thought about it," replied Dekkard frankly and bluntly.

"The most senior Craft councilors besides himself are Mardosh, Safaell, and Hasheem."

"He might have to put himself up, or the others might insist," suggested Dekkard.

"Guilhohn has never wanted to be premier."

"Then we'll have to see what happens." Dekkard did know one thing, and that was that he didn't want Mardosh as premier under any circumstances.

"That we will." Bassaana smiled and then stood. "I enjoyed talking with you. Take care of yourself, Steffan. The Craft Party—and the Council—need you."

Dekkard continued to ponder his conversation with Kaliara Bassaana when Avraal hurried into the dining room. Dekkard stood as she headed for the table.

Relief flooded across her face. "You're all right!" Both her arms went around him, and she just held him tightly.

Dekkard held her firmly, if not quite so strongly. "I just wanted to get word to you so you wouldn't worry. Nincya did reach you, didn't she?"

"She did, but I still worried. I gave her some marks and told her to get something to eat in the staff cafeteria and to wait there. I said it might be a while." Avraal gradually released him. "I can't believe about Obreduur. Shouldn't we see if we can help Ingrella?"

"If she wasn't in the office. She almost never is, but still." Dekkard frowned. "I've been requested to meet with Guard Captain Trujillo, since I'm apparently the only one who saw what happened—or at least I'm one of the few." Dekkard gestured. "We might as well sit down. I probably should have something to eat. It could be a long afternoon, although that's just a guess. If you think it's necessary, you could go see about Ingrella."

"Right now, I think I'll stick close to you."

Dekkard eased out the chair across from him.

"Was someone here earlier?" asked Avraal.

"Absolutely. Kaliara Bassaana wanted to pick my brain. I tried to give her just the bare details of what happened. After that, she wanted speculation. I demurred. She left, pleasantly. She did tell me to take care of myself, because both the Craft Party and the Council needed me."

"That means she needs you now that Obreduur isn't here."

"Most likely."

"What else did she get from you?"

"I did hint at the fact that some other party might be influencing the New Meritorists."

"Was that wise?"

"I think it was necessary."

Avraal frowned for a moment, then nodded. "I can see that. Now tell me everything that happened, every little detail."

"I will in a moment." Dekkard gestured toward one of the servers. "After we order."

Dekkard was slightly surprised that she ordered what he did—the white bean soup—although she asked for a cup and he ordered a full bowl. Then he told, yet again, except with every detail he could remember, what had happened all the way through his briefing his staff.

Halfway through, their soups arrived, and he paused and took a sip of the fresh café before continuing, more slowly, as he occasionally took a spoonful of soup.

When he had finished the recounting of the morning—and the soup—he said, "I needed to eat. So did you."

"I did. I admit it. When are you supposed to meet with the Guard captain?"

"Whenever he shows up between first and second bell in the Premier's floor office."

"We have another third."

"We?" asked Dekkard.

"I'm coming with you."

"That's a very good idea." Dekkard frowned. "I told Trujillo about that brown lorry this morning. He said he'd look into it."

"Maybe they moved it." She paused. "We didn't sense anyone around. What else could you have done?"

Dekkard shook his head, then said, "Did anything interesting or new show up with Carlos?"

"Nothing good. One of his leads for Amash Kharhan was found murdered last night. His people have been trying to locate the man for weeks. A contact in the central Machtarn patrol station sent him a message that he'd been murdered. Oh, I did send a message to Emrelda at her station saying that you were all right."

"That was another good thought, of which you have many."

Roughly a sixth later, Dekkard and Avraal left the dining room, but Dekkard led the way to and through the Council chamber and then into the Premier's floor office. The two clerks and the secretary looked up in surprise.

"Floor Leader Haarsfel told me to come here to meet with Guard Captain Trujillo. I really didn't feel like coming by the main corridor. Ritten Ysella-Dekkard is acting as my empath security aide. I'm certain you understand."

"Yes, sir."

From the way the two reacted, Dekkard had the definite impression that Avraal had reinforced his words.

"We haven't seen the Guard captain, but Councilor Haarsfel was with him when he left. That was more than two bells ago."

"We'll wait."

"Ah, sir, I don't think anyone would mind if you waited in the inner office. It's a bit more comfortable."

"Thank you. We'll leave the door open."

Dekkard and Avraal settled into the two chairs in front of the bare desk, the way Obreduur had kept his desk except for whatever papers he was immediately working on.

Almost a third passed before Dekkard heard the door to the main corridor open. Moments later, Haarsfel entered the Premier's inner office, followed by Trujillo, and said, "I'm glad you're here, Steffan. Guard Captain Trujillo very much wants to talk to you." Haarsfel looked to Avraal. "Ritten."

"She stays," Dekkard said firmly. "I'll tell her anyway, and, as a trained security empath, she just might be able to add something."

"Oh, I'm sorry. I'd forgotten. I'm sure you understand." Haarsfel actually sounded sorry.

Avraal smiled. "I do understand. I believe I'm the first spouse of a councilor who's been a Council security aide."

"Just a moment." Haarsfel stepped out into the main office and immediately returned with a straight-backed wooden chair, which he set at the side of the desk, half facing Dekkard and Avraal. Then he sat behind the desk.

As Trujillo took the straight-backed chair, Dekkard could see traces of dust and grit on his uniform.

"Before we start," said Dekkard, "what about the Premier and his staff? Was Ritten Obreduur there when it happened?"

Trujillo shook his head, which could have meant anything, then said, "The Premier was in his personal office. No one else was. There were seven other bodies. Ritten Obreduur was not one of them."

Dekkard swallowed. "That sounds . . . like . . . the whole staff."

"We'll know for certain in a while," replied Trujillo, his voice slightly hoarse. He coughed several times. "Councilor Haarsfel said you saw the beginning of the attack. Would you please tell me exactly what you saw?"

Dekkard cleared his throat and began. "I told you the first part of it already, when I drove up Council Avenue and saw the stake lorry—"

"When the guards got there, it was gone," said Trujillo. "I passed the word to all those on duty. Please continue."

Dekkard went on to relate exactly what he had witnessed, then waited for the questions that would surely come.

"How did you know that the lorry you saw was the same one used to attack the building?"

"To my eyes, the brown scratched paint and the patched canvas cover of the cargo area looked the same. I'd be very surprised if there were two like that."

"You said they were using shells. How did you know that?"

"I didn't know that. The steam device—or cannon—conveyed something so fast I couldn't see anything beyond the steam it released. Whatever it released exploded inside the building. That suggested an impact fuse and a military explosive. I called it a shell because it was fired like a shell and it exploded like one. I thought that they might have used copper tubing, maybe annealed it, because it would be easy to work. At the time, all that was a guess. I wasn't about to stay around and subject my staff to what seemed to be coming—or myself, for that matter."

"You didn't think about warning others?"

"No. I didn't. I could say that I knew it would be useless, which it would have been, but at the time I was just concerned with getting my staff to safety."

"You react quickly. Are you sure of that?"

"I am, but you need to remember one thing. I didn't know what the device was. I saw it being pointed. I saw the steam after something was released. I didn't know it was an explosive until I heard and felt the impact."

"I understand you told Premier Obreduur that the New Meritorists would likely attack the Council Office Building. What was your basis for that statement?"

"The rhetoric of the New Meritorists, and their emphasis on reforming the Council and changing the Great Charter. Their acts never seemed designed to overthrow the entire government, but to force councilors to vote for what they wanted. In the past, they targeted individual councilors. With that mindset, I felt it was far more likely that they'd target the Council Office Building, rather than the Council Hall. It was a feeling as much as anything. But I did tell Premier Obreduur they might place bombs in the building. I never even thought that they might shell it."

Trujillo nodded, then asked, "Do you believe that Sr. Jaime Minz is involved in some way with the shelling of the Council Office Building?"

"If he is, I'd think it would be in some very indirect fashion." Dekkard paused, then said, "He's involved in some fashion with a business called Capitol Services. I believe, but I have absolutely no proof, that various corporacion funds are funneled through Capitol Services to pay for other services, ranging from payoffs and bribery to worse."

"Why do you think Sr. Minz is linked to this Capitol Services?"

"Because the business addresses are the same, and because the only people in his office are Minz and his secretary."

"That would indicate some linkage." Trujillo smiled briefly. "The Premier mentioned that someone had suggested former Premier Ulrich might have had a connection to Capitol Services. Is that correct, and were you that person?"

"I believe it to be correct, given that Sr. Minz worked for years for Ulrich. I'd guess, and it's only a guess, that Minz is the bridge between Ulrich and Capitol Services, especially given that Minz is an isolate. I'm not whoever that person is, but if the Premier said someone suggested something, someone did indeed suggest it."

"Can you say who that person might be?"

"I cannot." *Not without revealing more than I essentially promised.*

"Are you particularly friendly with Sr. Minz?"

"No. We've never been more than casual acquaintances in the same profession. We exchanged words occasionally, but, as I told you earlier, I haven't seen him since before the elections."

"Do you think it's possible he was behind the Atacaman pepper attack on you?"

"I can't think of anyone else it could have been. I just don't know why, unless it had something to do with Premier Obreduur, but that doesn't make sense because, once I was elected, we seldom saw each other."

"Would you define seldom?" asked Trujillo in a slightly amused tone.

"We've had dinner with them three times in about two months, and I've had three or four brief meetings in his office, usually about either legislation or my thoughts on the New Meritorists."

Haarsfel laughed harshly, if softly. "Steffan, that makes you one of his closest confidants, especially given that you're not part of the leadership. That alone might explain why the New Meritorists went after you."

"The Premier indicated that you felt Sr. Minz was involved in how the New Meritorists obtained the dunnite used in the various explosions. Is that accurate?" asked Trujillo.

"The dunnite had to come from either Suvion Industries or Northwest Industrial Chemical. They're the only manufacturers. Ulrich paid for an ironway ticket for Minz to go to Chuive well before the Summerend explosions. Chuive is nowhere near Ulrich's district, and Minz was a security aide, not an investigator or a legalist, but the Premier found out he charged his ticket to the committee, and Ulrich said that was a mistake and paid for it."

"Why would a corporacion even think of supplying dunnite to revolutionaries?" demanded Haarsfel.

"The corporacion might not even know," Dekkard pointed out. "All it would take would be one official at the right level."

"That still doesn't explain why," said Haarsfel, almost querulously.

"That part is simpler," replied Dekkard. "Someone might have wanted to make the New Meritorists even more of a danger in order to justify increasing the power of the Security Ministry. The New Meritorists were happy to have the dunnite to attack Security. It probably would have worked except for the Kraffeist Affair, which forced Premier Grieg's resignation. Then when the Summerend explosions occurred, it was Ulrich who got forced out, and not

Grieg. Since it was the second major problem for the government, that led the Imperador to call new elections."

"That's all speculation," said Haarsfel.

"Not entirely," said Trujillo. "Those events occurred just as Councilor Dekkard pointed out. While there's no evidence at present, I doubt that the New Meritorists were unhappy to obtain the dunnite, however that transfer occurred. So far, there is no evidence about who might have facilitated the illegal transfer of the dunnite or any proof of a specific motive. There is recent evidence that Sr. Minz may have committed some other offenses. The Ministry of Public Safety and the Council Guards are also looking into certain 'irregularities.' I trust all of you will remain silent about that. By the way, Councilor Dekkard, your leather folder is outside. I retrieved it from the remains of your furniture when we inspected your office. I thought you might like to have it, since it will be several days at the least before the Council Office Building will be open."

"Thank you."

"Now, how were you certain that the explosions had concluded?"

"There was a larger explosion, but none followed that. I thought that either the Guards had managed to do something or that the device malfunctioned and a shell exploded in the device and set off others."

"The roof sentries were warned to look for the brown lorry, but it took several minutes for them to get into a position to fire around the metal plating. They believe they wounded or killed one of the men and that led to the explosion."

Trujillo's subsequent questions, most of them attempts at expanding Dekkard's earlier explanation, went on for another third of a bell before the Guard captain said, "Thank you, Councilor Dekkard. I appreciate your patience."

Haarsfel immediately asked, "When do you think we'll know more?"

"When we find more, sir," replied Trujillo, standing.

"Guard Captain," said Dekkard, "I'm sure that you've thought of it, but when repairs begin—"

"We have thought of it, sir. We'll have guards watching closely."

"Thank you."

"Now, if you'll excuse me, there's a great deal more I need to attend to." Trujillo inclined his head, then turned, opened the door, and left the inner office.

"Just what else do you know, Steffan?" demanded Haarsfel.

"I've told you what I know." *Just not quite all of it.*

"Do you really believe the Commercers would stoop so low?"

"No. I believe Ulrich and a few others would. Grieg couldn't stop them without risking getting killed, and that's why he got himself dismissed." Dekkard paused, then smiled, but only momentarily.

"What are you smiling about?"

"Just about how strangely things sometimes turn out." Dekkard stood. "Since there's nothing else I can do here, I'll see you in the morning."

"I have the feeling you've done more than enough, Steffan." Haarsfel's voice held a mixture of anger and resignation.

"Guilhohn, most all of that happened when I was a mere security aide, and you were the Craft Party floor leader. We're just the ones left picking up the pieces that resulted from Ulrich's lust for power, while he's a highly paid vice-presidente of Suvion Industries. If you want to blame anyone for Axel's death, blame Ulrich. Unlike you, Avraal and I put our lives on the line time after time to protect Axel."

Abruptly, Haarsfel shut his mouth. After a moment, he said quietly, and apologetically, "I'm sorry. It's just . . . this shouldn't have happened."

"No . . . it shouldn't. I told him there would be an attack. I just didn't foresee that kind of attack—shelling from behind with a frigging steam cannon. I wish I had, but I didn't. I owe him for so much . . ." Dekkard found himself swallowing and unable to speak. Finally, he shook his head, blinking back the tears he hadn't even realized were flowing from his eyes.

"Steffan," said Haarsfel kindly, "you did all you could. No one else could have done more. You need to go home and have a stiff drink or four. I'll see you tomorrow."

Dekkard just nodded.

Avraal took his arm and guided him out. She did not look at Haarsfel.

Dekkard did remember to pick up his leather folder, scuffed in places, before they left the outer office.

By the time they neared the staff cafeteria, Dekkard could speak. "We need to see Ingrella."

"If she'll see us."

64

AFTER meeting Gaaroll at the staff cafeteria, Dekkard and Avraal had to walk along the outside front wall of the courtyard and then past the front of the Council Office Building toward the covered parking. Although several second-level windows had been blown out—all of them in the middle of the building—Dekkard saw no other damage. But then, the stone-walled Council Office Building had been solidly constructed.

As they neared the covered parking, Avraal said, "I'll drive."

Dekkard didn't protest. He still felt stunned by everything that had happened, that he was imagining the shelling—except he knew he wasn't.

Once they were out of the covered parking and heading west on Council Avenue, Dekkard said, "Nincya, how are you doing?"

"Most likely better than you, sir." After a slight pause, Gaaroll asked, "Why were the Meritorists after you, sir?"

"I think they tried for me as a favor to whoever arranged for them to get the dunnite. That's a guess, and I'd appreciate your keeping it to yourself."

"Yes, sir. Would that be whoever's been after you before?"

"I'd guess so, but I don't know." Dekkard paused. "Are you sensing any strong feelings?"

"Not now, sir. I don't know that it makes any difference now, but I didn't sense any before the explosions. Not until you ordered us out of the office."

"None?" asked Avraal.

"None. Real quiet for feelings."

"I wonder if the gunners were isolates," said Dekkard. "Then, it would be hard to come up with that many without drawing notice, especially if they needed training. What about susceptibles?"

"They'd still have feelings," said Avraal.

"Could they have been persuaded that they were just doing target practice or something like that?"

"It's possible, I suppose," said Avraal as she turned south on Imperial Boulevard. "It would take a strong and talented empath to do that, though."

"The other possibility is combat-trained veteran troopers," mused Dekkard, "men who knew that, if they did their job right, there was little risk to them."

"That sounds more likely to me," said Avraal.

"Whatever the reason for the lack of feelings, I'll need to bring that up to Guard Captain Trujillo."

Before that long, Avraal turned the Gresynt east on Altarama Drive, then turned again on the next cross street before heading east for several blocks so that she could return to Altarama heading west in order to come up directly in front of the small mansion. When she brought the Gresynt to a stop, the gates to the Obreduur drive were closed, and two Council Guards were posted by the pedestrian gate to the side.

"You'll have to wait here with the steamer, Nincya," said Dekkard. "That is, if we're even allowed to see Ritten Obreduur." He got out of the steamer and walked toward the guards.

"Sir, the Ritten isn't seeing anyone," began the younger-looking guard.

"Look at his pin. That's Councilor Dekkard. He's the one," said the older guard.

"My apology, sir," said the first guard. "The Ritten said she'd see you and Ritten Dekkard. She thought you'd be here a little earlier."

"It took longer than we realized," said Dekkard.

"Much longer," added Avraal as she joined Dekkard.

The older guard opened the pedestrian gate.

Dekkard inclined his head. "Thank you."

"My pleasure, Councilor, Ritten."

Nellara stood waiting on the side portico as Dekkard and Avraal walked up the drive toward the house. When they neared her, although her face was blotchy and her eyes were red, she said, if unsteadily, "I knew you'd come. I'm so glad you're here. Gustoff just paces back and forth, and it will be days before Axeli can get home. He may not even know yet. We sent a heliogram a while ago, but . . ." She half turned and opened the side door. "Mother's in the sitting room."

Avraal and Dekkard followed her, and Dekkard shut the door behind himself.

Ingrella immediately stood when Avraal and Dekkard entered the sitting room.

Avraal hurried forward and hugged Ingrella. "I'm so sorry."

"Thank you for coming," replied Ingrella when Avraal stepped back. "I thought—and hoped—you would."

"I'm sorry we're so late," said Dekkard, "but I had to stay to brief Guard Captain Trujillo on what happened. It turned out that I was one of the few who saw it."

"You saw it?"

"A little too late," said Dekkard. "We might as well sit down. It's not a short story."

"You, too, Nellara." Ingrella gestured to one of the side chairs.

Avraal and Dekkard took the settee across from Ingrella.

"The attack all started with a letter that was frustrating me," Dekkard began, debating whether to mention his earlier sighting of the lorry, but deciding to. From there he carefully told everything about the shelling, then about the brief Council meeting, and his wait for Trujillo and Haarsfel. He summarized the meeting with Trujillo. "That's why we were late in coming."

"You came as soon as you could, and we appreciate your letting us know what happened. You couldn't have done anything else. You warned Trujillo, and you warned Axel. I know. He told me."

"I never thought that they'd shell the Council Office Building. I considered that they might plant explosives or even storm the building—but not that."

"Steffan, no one can foresee everything," said Ingrella quietly. "Axel couldn't, and you can't, either. Reproach for what we didn't do or couldn't do is use-less. We need to get on with what's important. That's what Axel would have wanted."

"That sounds like something he'd say," replied Dekkard. "Or did he learn that from you?"

"As you two have begun to discover, we learned from each other. I think it's fair to say that we accomplished more together than we ever could have alone. That doesn't mean I'm about to quit. I couldn't now. Especially after what happened today. You understand that, I'm certain."

Just from her tone of voice, Dekkard definitely did.

"Axel shared your belief that certain corporacions have given aid to the New Meritorists. Will you keep me informed about that, and about anything else that bears on . . . what happened today?" Ingrella swallowed again after she spoke.

"I will. One thing that I do know is that Guard Captain Trujillo is looking into the activities of the Machtarn office of Northwest Industrial Chemical and that he's working with the Ministry of Public Safety. I suspect he's doing more than that, but when Guilhohn Haarsfel pressed him, he just nodded and left, saying that he had a lot more to do. From what I've seen, he's very methodical."

"Axel thought well of him."

"From what I've seen, so do I, but Axel certainly had more knowledge of and insight into the Guard captain. As he did about many things."

Ingrella smiled, if sadly. "He did." Before either Avraal or Dekkard could respond, she added, "Thank you, again, for coming. I appreciate all both of you have done. Axel did as well, I know."

Dekkard understood and immediately rose. "We won't take any more of your time now. But we'd like to call on you later."

"I'd like that. So would Nellara, I'm sure." Ingrella stood, gracefully.

Nellara also stood, if not so gracefully as her mother.

"Would you mind," asked Dekkard cautiously, "if, in the future, not now, we asked for your legal and political advice?"

Ingrella gave an amused and brief smile. "You only have to ask, Steffan."

Avraal walked over to Ingrella and gave her a gentle hug. "In the meantime, if you need us?"

"I know where to find you. Thank you."

Then Nellara escorted them to the portico door, where she said quietly, "Thank you. It means a lot to Mother, and to me."

Avraal reached out and hugged Nellara, who hung on to her for a time.

On their walk down the drive, Dekkard said, "I'd like to drive home."

"That might be best, just in case," replied Avraal.

"No strong feelings near," said Gaaroll, "except some in the house."

Dekkard stopped, for just a moment, realizing that the only time Avraal had shown overwhelming emotion had been when she'd seen him. *But she and Gaaroll have sensed overwhelming emotions—and deaths—their entire lives.*

"Are you sure you're all right?" asked Avraal.

"I can drive. I just realized something, really realized it."

"What?"

He smiled apologetically and said, "How many deaths and how much grief you've sensed and endured in your life."

"We learn to live with it, dear. Those who can't become recluses. Now's not the time for you to dwell on it."

Dekkard nodded, then opened the steamer door for Avraal, before closing it after she seated herself. Then he walked around the Gresynt, took a long look at the Obreduur house, and got into the steamer. The drive back to Hillside was quiet.

When Dekkard turned up the drive to the covered portico and the garage beyond, he saw that both garage doors were closed, and that meant that they'd arrived before Emrelda.

"Since we're home early," said Avraal, "I'll see what I can fix for dinner."

Dekkard drove straight to the garage, where he got out and opened the doors for both Gresynts, while Avraal and Gaaroll disembarked and walked toward the house.

Once Dekkard garaged the Gresynt and got out of the steamer, he remembered that he'd put his gray leather folder on the second-row seat, and he opened the middle door to get it. The folder was slightly scuffed in a few places, but not dusty, even inside, when he opened it. The copy of the letter Emrelda had received from the anonymous patroller in Siincleer was still there, as was the letter from Jaime Minz, both neatly in place.

Dekkard frowned. The last time he'd looked at the letters had been when he'd shown a copy of the Minz letter to Trujillo, and he was fairly certain he hadn't been that neat in replacing the letter. Even if he had, the folder had clearly been tossed around by the explosion in his office.

So Trujillo had likely read the letter from the anonymous patroller in Siincleer. Dekkard paused, even though there was nothing in the letter that directly connected it to Emrelda or Dekkard. However, it would tell Trujillo that Dekkard had an interest in unexplained deaths of senior patrol officers in Siincleer. *And that's bad enough, given Venburg's death.*

He closed the folder, then shut the one garage door, and made his way to the house and inside. Absently, as he shivered in a gust of chill wind, he wondered if his new overcoat had survived the blast, or if it had been shredded, since it had been on one of the hooks beside the door to the small washroom and toilet.

That's the least of your worries.

Once he entered the house and set down the folder on the hall side table, he joined Avraal in the kitchen, where she started some sort of chicken casserole. Dekkard just followed her directions for the next bell, until the casserole went into the oven.

A good bell after that, while he and Avraal were still sitting at the breakfast room table, Emrelda arrived home and hurried to join them.

She looked to Avraal. "Thank you so much for the message. When we got the word about the explosions at the Council, I was worried—a lot."

Dekkard suspected Emrelda had feared that both he and Avraal could have been involved.

"I was fine," said Avraal. "Steffan almost wasn't." She stood and looked at him. "I'll finish getting dinner ready. You tell her what happened at the Council."

"You might as well sit down," said Dekkard to Emrelda. "It's not a long story, but it's not short, either." He waited until she sat down across the table before he began. "I'm likely still alive because of a rambling and confusing letter." From there he launched into what had occurred, including the first sighting of the brown stake lorry, ending with his questioning by Trujillo, which he touched on only lightly, except for saying that the interview or interrogation lasted almost a bell for an event that had taken less than a sixth of a bell.

When he finished, Emrelda said, "I can see why the Guard captain wanted every detail. You're one of the few who saw what happened, and you were one of the targets. He wanted every detail he could dig out of you, just in case something happened to you." She paused. "Do you think whoever was behind the shelling was the same person who's been after you?"

"I have no way of knowing, but I believe there's some sort of link."

"After that," added Avraal, from the kitchen, "we went and saw Ingrella. She was glad to see us. Nellara was especially glad. We didn't stay that long, but it was good that we went."

"What will she do now?" asked Emrelda.

"What she always did," said Avraal. "She's a top legalist, and she's likely why they could afford the house in East Quarter."

"She also said that we could ask her for advice," added Dekkard. "In the future, not now."

"Dinner will be ready in about a third," said Avraal, "if anyone wants to wash up."

"I really need to." Emrelda immediately stood. "I'll let Nincya know, too."

"Thank you," said Dekkard, standing and walking into the kitchen to see how he could help Avraal. That help turned out to be setting the breakfast room table, getting out plates, and then getting drinks for everyone.

Avraal served the casserole in the kitchen, and Dekkard carried the plates to the breakfast room table, followed by a basket of fresh-baked rolls.

"It smells wonderful," declared Emrelda, once everyone was seated.

"It's just a vegetable and chicken casserole with a few additions, and rolls on the side," protested Avraal. "Nothing compared to what you fix."

"Food always tastes better when someone else fixes it," replied Emrelda.

"No," declared Dekkard firmly. "If I fixed dinner, you wouldn't say that."

"Or if I did," added Gaaroll.

The sisters exchanged glances, and both smiled, but only briefly.

"Go ahead," declared Avraal. "Eat while it's hot."

After several bites, Emrelda took a sip of wine, then asked, "What will happen now with the Council?"

"For the moment," replied Dekkard, "Haarsfel is acting Premier. The Craft Party will have to choose a possible successor, and the Council will have to vote. Then the Imperador will have to confirm the choice."

"Will Councilor Haarsfel try to be premier?" asked Gaaroll.

"I have no idea," replied Dekkard. "I heard that he's never wanted to be premier, and I'm beginning to understand why." His last words were wryly dry.

"Then who else could be?" asked Emrelda.

"It would have to be one of the senior Craft councilors. Hasheem, Mardosh, Safaell . . . Nortak's senior enough, but . . ."

Avraal shook her head. "No one would support him or Dholen. Of that group, I'd favor Hasheem."

"I'd favor Safaell, I think," said Dekkard, "but if Haarsfel refuses, it's likely to be a choice between Mardosh and Hasheem. I'd take Hasheem any day over Mardosh. We'll just have to see."

"As with so many things," said Emrelda sardonically. "When will this happen?"

"I don't know," confessed Dekkard. "I'm sure there's a precedent somewhere, but I don't even know the last time a sitting premier died in office."

"The Silent Revolution, most likely," said Avraal.

"I might find out tomorrow, but I'm not sure of that, or anything else at the moment," said Dekkard.

"By the way," interjected Emrelda, "this casserole is really good. I'm not just saying that. I'd like some more."

"So would I, if there's enough," said Gaaroll.

"There's definitely enough," said Avraal.

From there, after everyone had an extra serving, the conversation was sparse, and largely about food.

Once the four cleaned up dinner, Emrelda and Gaaroll went to the dining room, where from the bottom of the large sideboard Emrelda took out what looked to be an almost antique wooden box and then retrieved an equally antique game board. "Nincya, you're going to learn to play crowns."

Gaaroll looked almost helplessly toward Dekkard and Avraal.

"Avraal won't play with me, and Steffan won't play board games with anyone."

"I won't be very good."

"Not at first, but you're smart. You'll learn."

Dekkard and Avraal eased out of the dining room and made their way to the sitting room, where Avraal took one of the armchairs and Dekkard found himself pacing back and forth.

Avraal offered a sympathetic look. "You have a few things on your mind. Sit down and tell me."

Dekkard eased into the other armchair, leaning forward slightly. "A few thoughts I wanted to share with you. I've been thinking about Grieg. I don't think I gave him enough credit. He wanted to be dismissed, not just to avoid the difficulties arising from the Kraffeist Affair, but to set up Ulrich to be dismissed, both as premier and as councilor. He must have had some idea about the dunnite going to the New Meritorists."

"Of course! He knew that the Commercers couldn't take two large scandals without the Imperador calling for new elections."

"But he didn't realize how badly the Summerend demonstrations hurt the Commerce Party and how much Obreduur had built up the Craft Party. He just thought that there would be yet another, if slightly weaker, Commerce Party government. That's my guess, anyway."

"That's also why he willingly admitted the information about Ulrich and Minz," said Avraal. "Do you think Guard Captain Trujillo can tie anything to Minz and Ulrich?"

"I don't know. He and the Council Guard, or the patrol, will have to come up with more hard evidence than we've ever had. Minz is more likely." Dekkard debated whether to mention his folder, then said, "I think Guard Captain Trujillo looked through my folder."

"What was in it?"

"The letter from Minz, but I told you I'd shown him that. There was also the copy of the anonymous patroller letter. Nothing linking it to any of us personally, but the fact that I even had it?"

"That could be a problem, but you showed it to Mardosh, and told him you wanted to investigate irregularities in military procurement contracts. I'm just glad you let me know that he might know. Also, because he didn't have your consent, unless he finds something else, he'll be reluctant to bring that up."

Dekkard nodded. "That's true."

"What else were you thinking about?"

"About the frigging stake lorry. I *knew* something about it wasn't right when I saw it the first time. I just couldn't imagine . . ." He shook his head.

"You thought that because you'd seen another lorry used by the Meritorists there, not because you expected to find a steam cannon in it." Avraal frowned. "I'd wager there wasn't one in it when we passed. They wouldn't have left it unattended. Not with shells in it, anyway. What else is bothering you?"

"I still worry about Minz, and how long I'll have to have you and Nincya looking out for me." Dekkard paused. "There's one other thing that I just realized. The gunners knew which office was Obreduur's, and when he was most likely to be in it. The Council Office Building isn't open to many."

"But Minz or former aides would know that, and where your office is, and that ties in with your suspicions. Also, if Minz was partly behind the bombing maybe that was why the attempts on you stopped."

"Because he passed the word that I needed to be removed as well as Obreduur?"

"That way, the blame is all on the New Meritorists. It certainly makes sense."

"What happens now? He's likely already found out that I escaped the shelling."

"We'll keep watching. I'd think he'd wait a while before trying anything else. The patrol and the Council Guards and even the Justiciary Ministry are looking into the attack on the Council Office Building. Trujillo might very well pay a visit to your friend Jaime, since he officially knows about the dunnite letter

Minz sent. That alone might suggest to Minz that it might be better not to act immediately. After the way Trujillo questioned you, I don't see him leaving any possibilities uninvestigated."

Dekkard certainly hoped so.

"In the meantime, we should read a little more in *The City of Truth*. It might help."

Dekkard certainly hoped so.

65

Some time ago, for I am to the point in life where most events of personal consequence occur in memory, a traveler boasted of the resplendent Residence of Art in his home city of Teknar, and then inquired as to why Averra had no museums to display significant art from the past, asking almost condescendingly if that might be because there was no art worth displaying.

Rather than reply directly, I took time from my day to escort him through the galleries of the Artisans Quarter. When I concluded that tour, which occupied much of the day, the traveler became even more puzzled, conceding, if grudgingly, that at least a few of the artists of Averra were the equal of any in Teknar. He pressed me for an answer, but I demurred, saying only that art and its display reflected the city of its creation and those who commissioned and purchased it.

I did not tell him, for he would not have understood, as most do not understand, even those who live here in Averra, that the city has no need for museums to display art. For those who understand, all art is a combination of appeal—appeal to the senses, to the mind, and to emotion—and of function. For those who do not understand, it is a display, either of wealth and power or of a perceptive presentation of what others find appealing. The understanding purchasers of art feel it; those who do not feel the art they have purchased display it as a means to create feelings in others. Very few do both, and the more costly the artwork, the more likely it will be used to manipulate the feelings of others.

In Averra, art is considered personal, and respected as such. To publicly display personal art to anyone would be a violation of personal feelings and to display manipulative art would be an imposition upon others. I have visited the grandiose Residence of Art in Teknar, although I did not mention that to the traveler, and found what was displayed there to be masterfully manipulative. I was also quietly reassured by the fact that then, and to this day, Averra has no museums of art.

AVERRA
The City of Truth
Johan Eschbach
377 TE

66

READING from *The City of Truth* made it easier for Dekkard to get to sleep. It didn't prevent the disturbing, yet inchoate, nightmares that plagued him for most of the night, or so it seemed when he woke to the cold and drizzle of Tridi morning.

"You had a restless night," said Avraal quietly.

"I can't imagine why." Dekkard eased himself out of bed. "We need to get moving. Haarsfel is convening the Council at third bell."

"You mentioned that last night."

"I'm sorry. I don't mean to repeat myself, but I told the same story so many times yesterday."

"I understand. Go take your shower."

Dekkard did just that, then dressed in one of his warmer new suits before making his way down to the kitchen, where he fixed two cafés.

"It's all in *Gestirn*," said Emrelda as Dekkard stepped into the breakfast room with a mug of café in each hand. "Not as much as you told us, and nothing new."

Dekkard set the mugs on the table, then picked up the newssheet and looked at the headlines.

COUNCIL BUILDING SHELLED
PREMIER AND COUNCILORS KILLED

He read the long story quickly, but, as Emrelda had said, the story contained nothing new, only mentioning by name Obreduur and the other councilors who had been killed, as well as Haarsfel as acting Premier. Dekkard, however, found two sections interesting. One was a line that said, "While the perpetrators appear to be associated with the group calling itself the New Meritorists, there is reason to believe they received assistance from others."

Dekkard couldn't help but wonder about why that had been included. *To provoke a reaction somewhere?* He couldn't see that getting a reaction from either Ulrich and Suvion Industries or from Northwest Industrial Chemical, although it might make Minz a bit more cautious. Other than that, he didn't see the purpose, but whoever informed the newssheet had a reason, and it was likely Trujillo. Dekkard couldn't imagine Haarsfel saying anything like that.

The second interesting section read:

> The New Meritorists have advocated reform, and Premier Obreduur pressed for and obtained a complete overhaul and reform of the Security Ministry in little more than a month. His reward, apparently, was to be assassinated for not doing more.

Dekkard could only imagine what the *Tribune* had published on that matter.

When Avraal arrived, Dekkard gestured to the newssheet.

"Does it say anything new?"

"Only that someone believes the New Meritorists had help. It doesn't say who. And that they didn't do their cause much good by assassinating the premier who gave them a major reform in little more than a month."

"The first was Trujillo's doing." Avraal picked up her mug and took a sip. Gaaroll just nodded.

"I'll see you later," said Emrelda, rising and then leaving the breakfast room.

The three in the breakfast room finished their respective breakfasts quickly, although Avraal ate an entire croissant, and they were in the Gresynt in less than a third of a bell. Neither Avraal nor Gaaroll sensed anything that felt dangerous along the way to the Council Office Building.

When Dekkard turned onto Council Avenue, heading west, he said, "There's nothing you can do here, and you might find out more from Carlos."

"I don't like leaving you, but you're right." Then Avraal turned in her seat. "Nincya, if you sense anything—anything at all—that seems even slightly unusual, let Steffan know immediately."

"Yes, Ritten. I will."

"Fourth bell? Councilors' dining room?" suggested Dekkard.

"I'll be there."

Just before turning in to the drive to the entrance for the Council Hall, Dekkard glanced east, where he saw scaffolding in the middle of the Council Office Building. "Haarsfel didn't waste any time in getting repairs underway."

"I'd wager your office is one of the first repaired, or should be," said Avraal.

"Why do you think that?" asked Gaaroll.

"Because I'm still alive," said Dekkard dryly, "and I doubt that replacements for those who died will be made for at least a few days." *And possibly because Haarsfel and Trujillo don't want me walking around for any longer than necessary.* With that thought, he pulled up in front of the east doors to the Council Hall, stopped the Gresynt, and got out.

Then he turned to Avraal, who'd eased into the driver's seat. "I doubt the Security Committee meeting will last longer than a bell, possibly two. After that, I'll be in the dining room."

"Try to pick a companion other than Kaliara Bassaana this time." Avraal offered a mischievous smile as she finished speaking.

"Your wish is my command, dear." Dekkard smiled back, stepping away from the steamer and watching as Avraal left and turned east on Council Avenue. When she was out of sight, he and Gaaroll made their way into the Council Hall, Dekkard noting that there were more guards than usual. *After the fact, of course.*

As they neared the councilors' lobby, Dekkard said, "Nincya, I'd like you to wait outside here. When the session is over, and I imagine it won't be that long, I'll come out and tell you anything you need to know, and you can tell me if you've noticed anything unusual."

"Yes, sir."

"Oh, one other thing, Svard is supposed to be in the cafeteria. When the Council has been in session for about a third of a bell, see if he's there, and tell him to meet me with you when the session's over."

Gaaroll nodded.

"Thank you. I'll talk to you later."

As soon as Dekkard entered the lobby, Gerhard Safaell moved toward him. "Steffan, I'm so sorry. I know how close you and Axel were."

"Thank you, Gerhard. The whole mess hit me pretty hard."

"Guilhohn said when the impact really struck you, you couldn't even talk."

"That's about right. Avraal had to drive. Well, she insisted on driving."

"Smart woman. Like Elizabeta . . . and Bettina. She takes after her mother. She really appreciated your taking the time and introducing her to your legalists." Safaell frowned. "She seemed very impressed by your senior legalist."

"Svard Roostof." For a moment, Dekkard wondered about the frown; then he smiled. "In case she's interested, he's unattached, never married, owns his own flat, and I've always found him dependable and reliable, both when I worked with him and since he's worked for me."

Safaell offered an embarrassed smile. "Fathers do worry, you'll discover."

"When it comes to that, I'm sure I will."

Safaell half turned. "Here comes Tomas Pajiin. I won't keep you."

"When matters are less unsettled, we need to have lunch," Dekkard said.

"We should. I'd like that." Safaell smiled sympathetically before leaving.

"Steffan," began Pajiin, "how by the Almighty did you manage to escape that attack *and* save your staff?"

"By luck. Because of a frustrating letter." Dekkard went on to give a brief summary of what happened.

"Why were they after you, do you think?" asked Pajiin when Dekkard finished.

"Villem Baar thinks it's because the New Meritorists are mad about the Security reform act, because it removed a lot of their grievances and might have cost them supporters. I have my doubts, but I won't discount his thoughts."

Over the next bell, he retold that summary to several others, beginning with Julian Andros and ending with Kharl Navione, just before Haarsfel called the Council into session.

"The first order of business is the official recognition of the death of Premier Axel Laurent Obreduur as a result of yesterday's shelling of the Council Office Building. The other councilors who died as a result of the attack were Marryat Osmond, Quentin Fader, and Tedor Waarfel."

From there, Haarsfel gave a short biography of Obreduur and each councilor who had been killed and finished by saying, "On Unadi, the thirteenth of Winterfirst, the Council will hold a memorial service for those councilors and for all staff who were killed. Attendance in the chamber and galleries will be limited to immediate family."

After an explanation of the memorial service, Haarsfel paused, cleared his throat, and continued, "In the event of the death of the Premier, according to the provisions of the Great Charter, the Council must select and present to the Imperador a successor no later than two weeks after the day of death, during which time the majority floor leader assumes the duties of the Premier. Given the damage to the Council Office Building and other necessities, including the memorial service, the floor leaders of each party have agreed that the Council vote on the successor to Premier Obreduur will take place next Duadi, the fourteenth of Winterfirst.

"Repairs to the Council Office Building, as you may have noticed, are already underway. We believe that most offices in the building can be reoccupied by Duadi or Tridi. If that changes, each of you will be notified."

Haarsfel continued with various other details until well past fourth bell, after which Dekkard was rising to head out of the Council chamber when he saw Haarsfel moving toward him.

"Steffan, might I have a few minutes?"

Haarsfel's courteous tone immediately made Dekkard wary. "Of course."

"In the Premier's floor office, if you would." Haarsfel gestured, then turned.

Dekkard followed the older councilor, half expecting to see Guard Captain Trujillo waiting for him, but the only ones in the outer office were two clerks. The inner office was empty.

"If you'd close the door, Steffan, please."

Dekkard did so, still wondering what Haarsfel had in mind as the acting Premier sat down behind the desk. Dekkard took one of the two chairs and waited.

"You're likely one of the closest councilors to Axel, particularly on a personal basis."

"I've gathered that, although it hadn't occurred to me until you pointed it out."

"Sometimes, the obvious is hard to recognize, especially in an unexpected context," declared Haarsfel. "As you would know more than most, someone has to be appointed to succeed Axel as councilor from Oersynt. With the current uncertainty, such an appointment needs to be made expeditiously. Do you have any thoughts about such a successor?" Haarsfel offered a crooked smile. "I've already had several offers to serve and a recommendation."

Dekkard raised his eyebrows, although he supposed he shouldn't have been surprised. "Might I ask who?"

"Among others, Jens Seigryn, Jareld Herrardo, and Leon Foerrster."

Dekkard didn't bother to hide his wince.

"That was my reaction as well," said Haarsfel. "Do you have any thoughts?"

Dekkard paused. He definitely did. "What about Ingrella Obreduur? She was an established legalist in the Malek/Oersynt area. She's personable and brilliant, and her selection would be far less controversial than most."

"It likely wouldn't be controversial at all," mused Haarsfel. "But would she accept?"

"Do you want me to find out?" asked Dekkard, knowing very well that was what the other wanted.

"If you wouldn't mind."

"I wouldn't, but I'll need the use of a Council steamer. Avraal has ours."

Haarsfel smiled wryly. "We can manage that."

"And I'll need a moment to tell my senior legalist and gather my empath-in-training."

"I'll have the steamer waiting at the east doors. But there's one other matter. Your senior legalist. He came from Axel's office, as I recall."

"He did."

"Would you ask him if he would do the eulogy at the memorial service for Axel's staff? I know you could do it, but I'm not having councilors speaking, except about councilors. No more than two or three sentences for each person."

"I'll ask him. I would think he would."

"Thank you, Steffan."

"You're welcome." Dekkard wasn't so sure that either Ingrella or Roostof would be that pleased, but she would be the best pick for councilor, and Roostof was likely the only one besides Dekkard or Avraal who knew Obreduur's staff well.

He left the Premier's floor office by the door to the main corridor. He didn't get more than twenty yards before Roostof and Gaaroll hurried toward him.

"We wondered what was taking you so long," declared Roostof when he reached Dekkard.

"The acting Premier cornered me," said Dekkard. "That means Gaaroll and I have to take a ride. He also had a request of you. Why don't you come along, and I'll explain."

Less than a sixth later, the three rode in the back of a black Gresynt limousine with the Council insignia on the front hood that had been waiting at the east entrance to the Council Hall.

"Where are we going?" asked Roostof quietly.

"Somewhere on Council business," replied Dekkard. "I'd rather not give the details right now, but I will on the way back. And keep your guesses to yourself. The other matter is short eulogies for the Premier's staff." Dekkard went on to explain, then waited.

"Why did he ask me and not you, sir?"

"It's political. No councilors are speaking about staff at the memorial service."

"I'll do it." Roostof gave a forced smile. "There really isn't anyone else if you or Ritten Dekkard can't speak."

"Thank you."

When the limousine came to a stop in front of the Obreduur house, two Council Guards remained posted there. Both looked at the limousine even before Dekkard said to Roostof and Gaaroll, "Just wait here. I shouldn't be too long."

Then he got out.

The guards looked at Dekkard.

"Councilor Dekkard with a message from the acting Premier for Ritten Obreduur."

"He's on the list," said the shorter guard, who opened the pedestrian gate.

This time, when Dekkard reached the portico door, Gustoff was the one who met him.

"Good morning, sir."

"Good morning, Gustoff. I need to see your mother."

"She's in the study." Gustoff turned.

Dekkard followed him.

Ingrella looked up from where she sat behind the desk. "Steffan, what brings you here alone? Not that I'm not glad to see you."

Dekkard turned and shut the door, then seated himself across from her. "I have a favor to ask of you."

Her brief smile displayed amusement. "What might that be?"

"To consider fully what I'm about to tell you."

"It must be serious."

"It is. Haarsfel would like you to consider being appointed as councilor from Malek and Oersynt."

Ingrella nodded slowly. "I thought that might be why you're here. Why do you think Guilhohn asked you to come?"

"If you choose not to accept, I'll keep it quiet. I hope you don't, but I will respect your decision one way or the other."

"I know that." She smiled again, sadly. "I suspect you understand that, given who Axel was, and who I am, I have no choice. You can tell Guilhohn I will accept."

"Thank you." Dekkard tried not to exhale too hard in relief.

"By the way, your papers in the vault are still safe. Just let me know when you need them."

"I appreciate that. With all that's happened, it may be a while."

"I understand. Just have Guilhohn let me know where and when I'm supposed to be sworn in."

"I'll convey that to him." Dekkard decided against saying more, although he was fairly sure that it would be on or before next Duadi, when the vote on the new premier was scheduled.

"Does Avraal know this?"

"Not yet. She's at work with Carlos right now. That's why I arrived in a Council limousine."

"You don't have any security?"

"My emotional-pattern sensor and empath-in-practical-training is in the limousine."

"Be careful, Steffan. Very careful."

"I'm doing my best." Dekkard paused. "About Axel. I know it's sudden."

"He requested no ceremonies and no memorials, even family ones." She smiled wryly. "Under the circumstances, we can't do anything about the Council memorial service. But thank you for asking."

"I understand, but if—"

"I appreciate your concern, but he was very firm."

"I understand, but I didn't want you to think we didn't care."

"We all know that and *thank you*." She paused. "Now go tell Guilhohn."

"Yes, Ritten."

"Ingrella from here on."

Dekkard grinned then stood. "I'll try hard on that as well."

She smiled and gestured. "Go."

Dekkard left. He didn't see Gustoff; so he let himself out and walked down the drive to the pedestrian gate.

Once he was back in the limousine as it pulled away from the house, Roostof and Gaaroll looked at him expectantly.

"I had to deliver a message from the acting Premier and take back her response. Even that has to stay between us for now." He looked at Gaaroll. "Do you sense any strong feelings?"

"No, sir."

"That's good."

Then he began to tell the two what had happened at the morning session of the Council. When he finished, he asked, "Any questions?"

"No, sir."

"I'm sorry to have to keep you both standing around today, but until after the Security Committee meeting I won't know if I'll even need you tomorrow, Svard." Dekkard paused. "You might ask around and see if anyone knows about replacing or repairing the desks and typewriters, and anything else you can think of, but not until after I meet with Haarsfel. Then you two can get something to eat. Nincya, you'll meet me at the entrance to the councilors' dining room at a sixth before first bell to escort me to the Security Committee meeting."

Once the limousine pulled up to the east entrance to the Council Hall, as Dekkard got out, he said to the driver, "Thank you."

"My pleasure, Councilor. Much better than sitting around waiting."

Dekkard could see that.

A few minutes later, Dekkard entered the Premier's floor office from the main corridor.

One of the clerks said, "Someone's with him, Councilor, but it shouldn't be long."

"Thank you." Dekkard sat down in the straight-backed wooden chair to wait.

After less than a sixth, the door to the inner office opened, and Guard Captain Trujillo stepped out. He nodded to Dekkard and said, "Your help is proving to be very useful. I never really thanked you."

"You had a great amount to deal with in very little time."

"So did you," replied Trujillo, "and I wasn't dealing with explosive shells."

"There's one other thing that I didn't think about."

Trujillo stopped. "Yes?"

"As I told you earlier, Ritten Dekkard and Gaaroll didn't sense anyone in the lorry or nearby. But I realized later that it's improbable they would have left the lorry unattended if both the steam cannon and the shells, whatever they were, had already been loaded. I'm sorry, but that didn't occur to me until last night."

"With what you went through, that's understandable," said Trujillo sympathetically, "but we came to that conclusion as well. We also discovered some interesting materials in the building. You'll pardon me if I'm not more specific at present."

"I understand. I just didn't want to leave that insight to chance."

"You seldom leave anything to chance, Councilor. I'm grateful for that." Trujillo smiled, then nodded again before leaving the outer office.

"Steffan," said Haarsfel, "please come in."

Dekkard entered the inner office, and Haarsfel motioned for him to sit down.

"She accepted your offer. She just asked that you let her know where and when she should appear."

Haarsfel nodded. "I hoped she would. I'll have the selection papers ready by tomorrow. We'll have a brief Council session on Quindi for her and Osmond's successor. I haven't heard from Vonauer about Fader's successor or from the Craft Party leadership in Aloor."

"You thought she would, didn't you?"

"Especially if you made the offer for me. Duty runs strong in that family. I suspect it does in yours as well."

"It does, but my parents would call it responsibility."

"What do you think the New Meritorists will do next and when?"

"Some other attack on the Council, but I'd be surprised if it's soon. It took time to build that steam cannon and maybe longer to make the shells. Then again, Unadi's attack was much sooner than I'd thought any New Meritorist action would be."

"Guard Captain Trujillo thinks that's because they wanted to remove you and Axel as soon as they could."

"Me? I could understand Axel's removal, but not mine. Did the Guard captain indicate why?"

"No. He said he didn't want to say anything because it was still largely speculation. He did say he hoped he'd know more by next week." Haarsfel paused. "Do you have any idea?"

"I'm guessing that it all has to do with how the New Meritorists obtained all that dunnite, but that's speculation as well. I've been trying to figure that out, but . . ." Dekkard shrugged. He wasn't about to say that Hasheem and Obreduur had both shut down the idea of holding hearings on the matter.

Haarsfel merely nodded, then said, "I appreciate your talking to Ingrella. I'll let you both know when your offices are usable. Most of the damage was to windows and furniture, and to the wall and floor surfaces." He paused, then said, "The other matter, the staff eulogies?"

"Svard will do it. He's very capable."

"Excellent. There will be a brief meeting at second bell of the afternoon on Quindi, in the Security Committee chamber. We'll go over the order and the procedures for him and the other staff speakers." Haarsfel stood after speaking. "Thank you, again."

Dekkard immediately stood as well. "I was glad to do it. There won't be a Council meeting until Quindi?"

"Not unless there's another emergency."

"Have you decided on the time?"

"Fourth morning bell."

Dekkard inclined his head and left, still wondering about what both Trujillo and Haarsfel had said. *Something's definitely happening.* But it could be anything, and Trujillo was definitely no fool. He'd figured out the reason for the Atacaman pepper attack on Dekkard, even if he hadn't determined who. *Or he hadn't said who he suspected because he had no proof.*

When Dekkard left the office, both Roostof and Gaaroll immediately joined him.

"I have half the answer," said Dekkard cheerfully. "Svard, it's likely I won't need you at all tomorrow, but there will be a Council session on Quindi. In addition, there will also be a Quindi meeting of the staff speakers at the memorial service at second bell in the Security Committee room. Now, I'm going to have something to eat, and I suggest you two do as well."

"After we walk you to the dining room," said Roostof.

"Was there more about your meeting with the acting Premier?" pressed Gaaroll.

"He *says* he'll select Ingrella Obreduur as her husband's replacement, but don't say anything to anyone until it's announced. Sometimes, people change their minds."

"Or have 'em changed," replied Gaaroll sourly.

"He also believes the Council Office Building will be habitable for most councilors by next week. They targeted very few offices, and the others were untouched or only suffered minor damage. He's not sure about when our office will be repaired. He gave the impression it won't be that long."

"That could mean anything," muttered Gaaroll.

"It could, but I hope it won't be more than another week."

When Dekkard entered the councilors' dining room, he glanced around to see who was already there. Pajiin sat with Andros and Ghohal, while Elskar Halljen and Jareem Saarh occupied another table. Immediately, Villem Baar, who was alone at a table, gestured for Dekkard to join him.

Wondering if Baar had something to say or ask, or was merely lonely, Dekkard sat down across from the other junior councilor. "Has your wife managed to join you yet?"

"Not yet, but we found a modest house in Hillside to lease for at least a year, and we'll be able to move in after the eighteenth. We're both looking forward to it. If nothing's scheduled for tomorrow, I'll go shopping for some furniture."

"Do you have a house in Suvion?"

"We do. I'd thought about selling it, but with the requirement of a district tie, we'll likely be renting it out. Whatever happens, we wouldn't move back into it. Even with just two children, it was getting cramped. Hillside seems like a nice area. We couldn't afford East Quarter, even to rent." Baar shook his head.

"Hillside is a nice area. We moved in with Avraal's sister. She lives there."

"She's charming and a very good dancer." Baar paused. "I don't mean to pry, but there's a touch of sadness there."

"She's not exactly widowed, although it's likely her husband is dead. He was an engineer for a rising construction business. He vanished under unusual circumstances, and when the head of the firm went to investigate, he reportedly suffered a heart attack, but the investigations couldn't find anything definitive."

"I'm sorry to hear that." Baar frowned. "That sounds rather sinister, almost like a plot in a mystery novel."

"It happened, believe me. Those sorts of things have occurred with other rising small corporacions. One of my staff has been looking into that."

"That's right. You're on Workplace Administration. How common are such occurrences, do you think?"

"Far more common than the corporacions who commit them would have the Council believe and far less common than the New Meritorists would likely claim."

Both looked up as a server appeared. "Are you ready to order, Councilors?"

Baar looked to Dekkard, who nodded. Then Baar said, "The three-cheese chicken and café."

"The duck cassoulet—just a half order. Café as well."

Once the server left, Baar looked back to Dekkard. "Who do you think Haarsfel will select to fill the two vacant Craft seats?"

"I know he has some names under consideration, but I'm not aware that he's officially selected anyone."

"You worded that very much like a legalist, Steffan." Baar's tone voiced amusement. "You should have been one."

"If I'd been a legalist, I'd never have become a councilor. I also don't think I'm temperamentally suited to being a legalist." Dekkard laughed softly, then added, "I'm not sure I'm temperamentally suited to being a councilor."

"You could have fooled me, Steffan."

"One learns patience as a security aide, but reluctantly resigning yourself to it doesn't mean accepting it."

"Are you saying that too many senior councilors are too accepting of past practices that don't suit the present situation?"

"I'd say that anticipating the need for change is far better than being forced into it, as the present circumstances seem to prove."

"What if your anticipation is wrong?"

"Then you have time to change it," Dekkard said, "which you may not, if you wait too long."

Baar laughed. "You do have a point there."

Dekkard managed to keep the rest of the conversation light, and after their meal they walked to the Security Committee room, followed by Baar's two security aides and Gaaroll.

Breffyn Haastar was standing next to Hasheem, and the two were talking quietly, while Jaradd Rikkard sat at his place behind the long, curved desk, simultaneously looking bored and indifferent. By the time Dekkard seated himself, Navione and Pajiin arrived, and Hasheem took his place in the center and gaveled the committee to order just as first bell chimed.

"The acting Premier has requested that this committee meet to discuss the impact of the shelling of the Council Office Building in order to formulate recommendations assuring that another such event does not occur. The chair will ask each councilor for brief thoughts on the matter. After all councilors have commented, I will ask for recommendations. Councilor Navione?"

"I don't have much to say, Sr. Chairman, except that the New Meritorists have gone too far and that the Council needs to deal firmly and quickly with them. They initially appealed to real grievances to enlist supporters and then moved to violence. That's totally unacceptable."

Hasheem then nodded to Haastar.

"I have doubts that most of the New Meritorists are that violent. As my colleague suggested, most are likely peaceful. I'd prefer an approach that deals with the real troublemakers, the ones who shot people and blew up buildings. If we attack or incarcerate anyone who's even a sympathizer, we'll just make matters worse, because we'll turn more of them against the Council. That won't end well."

"Councilor Rikkard?"

"They're all the same. You're right about not executing or incarcerating them all, but they don't believe in what Guldor is and stands for. Anyone involved ought to be exiled. Those proved to be involved with the violence, death, and explosions should be executed."

For Rikkard, Dekkard thought, those words were almost moderate.

"Councilor Pajiin?"

"I agree with Councilor Haastar. Get rid of the troublemakers and criminals, and the patrollers can take care of the rest."

"Councilor Dekkard?"

"I agree about the troublemakers, but I'm concerned about who they actually are. There may be another group involved besides the New Meritorists. According to all testimony before this committee, for more than two years, the New Meritorists did almost nothing but meet and talk. They showed no real ability in publicity, no interest in weapons or explosives. Then, in some fashion that no one has yet been able to explain, they obtained a large amount of dunnite, somehow managed to inflict significant damage to fifteen Security buildings, including the headquarters, and began a technically sophisticated attack, first on Security, then on the Palace, the Craft Guildhall, and lastly on the Council. Yet none of the few people interviewed, incarcerated, and interrogated had any of those talents. All they had was a manifesto.

"Interestingly enough, although it may be coincidence, none this occurred until *after* the disclosure of the Kraffeist Affair. In addition, the New Meritorists only used weapons in the first demonstration against the Council when a handful of them shot at Council Guards. That suggests that weapons and explosives were in the hands of a very few individuals. I see two possibilities. Either a more militant group infiltrated the New Meritorists or they allied with them. Either way, I agree that the Council, the Ministry of Public Safety, and the Justiciary Ministry need to focus on finding that group or those individuals."

Hasheem nodded, then said, "Councilor Baar?"

"Councilor Dekkard and the other councilors make very good points. The problem remains—what can this committee do? It seems to me that, as Councilor Dekkard indicated, it's really a problem for the Ministry of Public Safety, and its patrollers, the Justiciary Ministry, and its investigators, and possibly the Council Guards. Until we know the causes of the violence, we can't act effectively. Some workers face real grievances, but everyone has grievances, and this committee only has jurisdiction over security issues. With the passage of the Security reform measures, we have done all that we can."

Except for looking into the question of where the dunnite came from and who provided it. But Dekkard knew that, certainly at the moment, especially with Obreduur gone, there was no possibility of such hearings even being held, and even less point in bringing up the matter. *Especially since the records of both Northwest Industrial Chemical and Suvion Industries will show no irregularities whatsoever.* Of that, Dekkard was equally certain.

Hasheem looked from one end of the committee dais to the other. "Although I believe that Councilor Baar has succinctly addressed the question of recommendations, are there any other recommendations or comments?"

Since no one else seemed inclined to do so, Dekkard spoke. "I would suggest that the committee reserve the right to investigate the source of the dunnite obtained by the New Meritorists. While that would be premature at present, I believe the committee would be derelict in its duty if ongoing efforts by the Ministry of Public Safety and the Justiciary Ministry do not uncover how that quantity of explosives ended up in the hands of the New Meritorists."

Surprisingly to Dekkard, Navione said, "I second that reservation."

"Is anyone opposed?" asked Hasheem. "Seeing no opposition, the reservation will be entered into the provisional future schedule of the committee."

After a few more words, Hasheem adjourned the committee.

Pajiin looked to Dekkard. "You always have interesting insights. I'm not sure that Rikkard likes them, but Baar nodded."

"He thinks more," said Dekkard quietly.

Roostof and Gaaroll waited outside the committee room to meet Dekkard.

As they walked back toward the councilors' dining room, Dekkard said, "Svard, take the day off tomorrow, at least from being here at the Council. There's nothing else you could do tomorrow that you can't do on Quindi, and you'll need to work on those short eulogies. Once the office is repaired, you'll likely have to work longer bells to get everything organized, or reorganized."

"Luara will have to redo all that work on that legalist proposal."

"That depends on the damage. Even if it was destroyed, she won't have to redo everything. Remember, we sent a copy to Councilor Zerlyon. Bretta or Illana might have to borrow it back and retype it. And I have a copy of the background document."

"I'd forgotten that."

"There's nothing you can do here this afternoon. I'll meet you at the councilors' lobby on Quindi just before the session, and we'll meet again afterward. It will begin at fourth bell and won't be that long, maybe a bell." Dekkard paused, then added, "Gaaroll and I will be fine."

"You're certain?"

"I'm not certain of anything, but anything she can't warn me about, you couldn't do anything to stop, either." Dekkard paused. "But, just in case, I don't have your address here. If you could write that down."

Roostof grinned and produced a card. "I thought these might come in useful."

"Thank you." Then Dekkard smiled. "Did you give one to Bettina Safaell?"

Roostof flushed. "Ah, as a matter of fact."

"Excellent," said Dekkard. "I'll see you on Quindi."

After Roostof had left them, Dekkard looked to Gaaroll. "Was he as surprised as he looked?"

"More, I think."

Dekkard saw Baar and Rikkard standing outside the councilors' dining room.

"What are those two feeling?"

"The shorter one is calm, low black piles. The taller one has bigger piles. They're grayish red."

"Anger and disgust?"

"I think so."

Both Baar and Rikkard walked into the councilors' dining room.

Dekkard didn't want to follow them. "Let's just walk awhile, back and forth here in the Council Hall, and you tell me what you sense about each person we see. Quietly, of course."

After nearly two bells of walking, with Gaaroll sensing, and explaining, Dekkard caught sight of Avraal walking toward the dining room.

She frowned as they approached.

"We've stayed in the Council Hall. Nincya's been working to get a better feel of what she's sensing."

"Is it helping?"

"Yes, Ritten."

"We can go now," said Dekkard. "I have some interesting news for you, once we're in the steamer."

"That interesting?"

Dekkard nodded.

Once they were outside and walking toward the covered parking, he could see that the few shattered windows on the south side of the Council Office Building had been replaced.

When they were in the Gresynt, even before Dekkard could pull out of the covered parking, Avraal asked, "Your news?"

As he drove, Dekkard explained the coming days' schedule, the committee meeting, his brief conversation with Trujillo, his longer conversations with Haarsfel, including the request of Roostof, and his trip to see Ingrella.

Avraal sighed. "I thought that might happen. She'd be the best choice. I wasn't sure Haarsfel would do it."

"With the alternatives he faced, what else would make sense?"

"Sometimes even the smartest people don't do the sensible thing."

Dekkard wasn't about to say a word. He'd understood very well the look she'd given him when he'd explained about what he and Gaaroll had been doing.

67

FOR the first time in weeks, if not longer, nothing of apparent import or interest occurred on Furdi. Dekkard went to the Council Hall, but very few councilors were there, most of them senior Commercers who shied away from him, but then, except for the one brief encounter with Gerard Schmidtz weeks ago, that was scarcely new.

He saw no sign of Haarsfel or Guard Captain Trujillo, or Pajiin, or even Safaell. Villem Baar was likely out furniture shopping. And so, after more than a bell, he and Gaaroll took a steamhack to Carlos Baartol's office, where he met Avraal. She drove them home and told Dekkard to stay there so that she didn't have to worry about what he might be doing.

Dekkard knew better than to argue, since the possibility remained that Minz or whoever else it might be could still be targeting him.

After he changed into older clothes, he and Gaaroll spent more than a bell practicing with knives, despite the chill wind out of the northeast. Then he sharpened all his throwing knives, swept out both sides of the garage, and checked the kerosene and water tanks, after which he cleaned the filters as well. Various other somewhat neglected chores occupied another bell or so, partly because he didn't hurry.

After that, he was even tempted to read more in *The City of Truth,* but since he and Avraal read that together, he refrained. Instead he took a book off the shelf in the study entitled *History of Engineering in Guldor.* It had to have been Markell's, or at least he thought so, because he couldn't imagine Emrelda purchasing or reading it, but then, he'd never thought he'd be reading something like *The City of Truth.* He settled into one of the armchairs in the sitting room and began to read . . .

> The first engineer documented as such was Denoidre of Teknos, who designed and built the Veritas Palace in ancient Argo, the one structure remaining after the Autarchs leveled the center of the city . . .

He was still reading when Avraal returned, but quickly replaced the book, and helped her fix dinner.

He couldn't help wondering where the day had gone when he fell asleep.

68

WHEN Dekkard and Avraal woke on Quindi, he glanced outside, only to see a thin layer of frost, a definite rarity in Machtarn, unlike Oersynt, where he'd grown up. Then he looked over at Avraal, who had the blankets wrapped around her.

"Go take a shower. Please make it quick."

Dekkard grinned. "I thought a long, hot—"

A pillow thrown hard and accurately at his face cut off his teasing, but he was still smiling when he headed for the bathroom. He did take a very short shower.

He finished dressing well before Avraal and made his way to the kitchen, where he fixed two cafés and carried them into the breakfast room.

"Put down the cafés, and look at the newssheet," said Emrelda. "Then tell me what it means."

Gaaroll immediately looked at Dekkard.

He took in the front-page headline even before he picked up the newssheet. Then he read it twice, frowning.

SUSPECTED COUNCIL HALL KILLER CAUGHT

Who have they caught and why do they think he killed Venburg? Dekkard just stood there and began to read.

> Justiciary prosecutors announced late on Furdi afternoon that a team of investigators from the Ministry of Public Safety, the Justiciary Ministry, and the Council Guard took Sr. Jaime Minz into custody. Minz has been charged with one count of murder in the death of Pietro Venburg, the Vice-Presidente of Legal Affairs for Siincleer Shipbuilding, one count of manslaughter in the death of a Council clerk, and several violations dealing with felonious financial practices involving a consulting and services firm that he managed . . .
>
> . . . the prosecuting legalists indicated that additional charges might be added as a result of an ongoing investigation . . . Sr. Minz is currently an assistant director of security for Northwest Industrial Chemical and alleged to be the manager of Capitol Services . . .

The rest of the story focused on Venburg and his murder.

How by the Almighty did Avraal manage that? If she did. But that wasn't a question he was about to ask anyone but her, especially since she might only have had a small part.

"What do you think?" asked Emrelda.

"They must have a solid amount of evidence," replied Dekkard. "There's no way they're going to charge a former Council aide unless they're sure. I always suspected he was behind the Atacaman pepper attack, and from what we've learned recently, I'm not surprised that what he did with Capitol Services was shady, if not out-and-out illegal, but we could never come up with enough solid evidence to make a complaint."

"Complaint?" questioned Avraal as she entered the breakfast room.

"You have to read this." Dekkard managed not to thrust the newssheet at Avraal, but to hand it to her carefully.

She read it quickly, then nodded. "He deserves it. I wonder how many other bodies they'll discover in his backyard."

"You think that he had something to do with Mathilde Thanne's vanishing?" asked Dekkard, thinking back to the "disappearance" of Mardosh's empath.

"I'd guess so. He's also the one who made sure you knew Mathilde vanished. He's an isolate. She'd never have sensed his intent."

"Mardosh never replaced her," Dekkard mused.

"What would be the point now that Mardosh is chair of the Military Affairs Committee?" replied Avraal. "He got the message, probably conveyed from Venburg to Minz for the arrangements. Why do you think you've had such trouble getting Mardosh to look into military construction contracts?"

Dekkard thought about that, then shook his head. "I don't like the idea of targeting staff to threaten councilors."

"I like it even less than you, dear." Avraal set the newssheet on the side table, sat down, and took a sip of her café.

"What will happen now?" asked Gaaroll.

"We'll just have to see." Dekkard could see the possibilities, and none of them looked good for Minz, but he wasn't about to speculate. *Not now.*

"What do you think those other charges against Minz are?" asked Emrelda.

"One of them will likely be illegal employment while holding a position as a Council aide. Aides can work for themselves, but there's an income limit, and they can't be employed by anyone else. I suspect he violated one of those categories. He also likely hired assassins, but they won't find proof." *Because they were hired to take you out, and they didn't succeed, no one knows that but Minz and the assassins, one of whom is dead.* Since Minz was an isolate, it would be difficult to discover who he might have hired, and anyone he hired—and was still alive—wasn't about to come forward.

"He couldn't have been doing that on his own." Emrelda snorted.

"Of course not, but there won't be any paper trail to Ulrich, who has to be the one directing Minz's activities with Capitol Services. If the Craft Party hadn't won the last election, they could have kept doing it for years because they controlled Security through Lukkyn Wyath."

Wyath! Dekkard reached for the newssheet and began leafing through it until he found the small story.

> The execution of former Security Minister Lukkyn Wyath took place two bells before dawn this morning. Wyath was convicted of criminal malfeasance in office, misfeasance, and high treason.

"What are you looking for?" asked Avraal.

"I found it. The notice of Wyath's execution. He was executed this morning. That's very convenient for Ulrich. Wyath's dead; Manwaeren knows nothing; Mangele officially committed suicide while incarcerated; and Stuart Jebulon fled Guldor for lands unknown."

"That leaves Minz."

"For now," said Dekkard. "And there's nothing we can do about it." *One way or another.* He replaced the newssheet on the side table and went to get the croissants. He brought three back.

Avraal looked at the croissant he put before her.

"You'll need it. I assume you'll come to the Council session this morning to see Ingrella sworn in."

"Oh, you told me, but . . ." Avraal offered an embarrassed smile.

"We've both had more than a few things on our mind."

"Now that you're both here," announced Emrelda as she stood, "I need to be on my way. Services tonight?"

"Definitely," said Avraal before Dekkard could have lodged an objection.

Once Emrelda left the breakfast room, Dekkard split his croissants, added a thin layer of quince paste to both, and then began to eat. He finished both before Avraal had eaten half of her single croissant. But he just sat across from her, nursing his café until she finished.

Then the three took their time cleaning up and finished dressing in an unhurried fashion, since there really wasn't much he could do once he got to the Council Hall, except wait for the session to begin. He wanted, however, to be somewhat early, just in case anything turned up.

At a third before third bell, Dekkard drove the Gresynt under the portico a minute or so before Avraal and Gaaroll arrived.

"Sense anything, Nincya?" he asked.

"Not so far."

Neither empath sensed any danger bearing on Dekkard on the drive to the covered parking area. After parking the steamer and starting across the street, Dekkard glanced toward the Council Office Building. Although he couldn't see the north side, he could see construction lorries, as well as workers loading debris into several lorries.

"Haarsfel certainly has them working," Dekkard said. "I just hope Trujillo's guards keep watching closely."

"They'd better," said Gaaroll.

"I was thinking," began Dekkard, "about Ingrella. If I can, and if she accepts, I'll ask Ingrella to have lunch with us. That way—"

"I would have suggested it, if you hadn't," replied Avraal. "We can offer some support, and it would allow councilors to offer sympathy and greetings without it being lengthy or overwhelming. *But* leave it up to her."

"I wouldn't think of pressing her."

After Dekkard, Avraal, and Gaaroll entered the Council Hall and neared the entrance to the councilors' lobby, Dekkard saw Svard standing there waiting, along with several other staffers. He smiled and said, "I told Svard to meet me outside the councilors' lobby before the session, but he didn't have to be here this early."

"He's very conscientious, and you like that," Avraal pointed out.

"Svard, what brings you here so early?"

"Sir, when I read *Gestirn* this morning, well . . ."

"It occurred to you that Sr. Minz was the one behind the Atacaman poisoning in the Security Committee?"

"It *seemed* like the story was the same."

"No one's contacted me, but I'm guessing that it's the same, because I don't know of any other deaths of Council clerks."

"But he was a security aide."

"He was a security aide to Premier Ulrich," Dekkard pointed out. "Ulrich managed the appointment of the recently deceased Lukkyn Wyath and the other office directors in Security."

"You knew that?"

"Not all of it. Some of it came out in the Security Committee hearings. I never trusted Minz, but I never had enough proof to bring the matter to the Council Guards or the patrol. Obviously, they found that proof that we were unable to find."

"Could he somehow be linked to the New Meritorists?"

"I wouldn't put anything past Minz, but I don't know of anything that would tie him to the New Meritorists."

"Also, there wasn't anything in the newssheets about Ritten Obreduur."

"I'm sure acting Premier Haarsfel wanted to keep that quiet until it is a fact. I'm sure there will be a story this afternoon and tomorrow morning. Now, is there anything you've found out that I should know?"

"I've asked around, and they already have masons replacing the damaged and missing stone and brickwork. They've removed almost all the debris, and the broken windows have been replaced, except for the offices where the brickwork has to be finished first."

"Like ours."

"I asked about that. Ours wasn't as bad as some, but it's going to be a while."

"Anything else?"

"No, sir."

Dekkard looked to Avraal, to see if she had any questions.

"Nincya and I will stay here with Svard."

Dekkard got the message—he was to check out the councilors' lobby and find out what he could. "Then unless I learn something of immediate import I'll meet you in the dining room after adjournment."

Avraal nodded in return.

When Dekkard entered the lobby, he immediately saw far more councilors than usual, but that made sense, since no one had an office in which they could wait. Tomas Pajiin stood in a group with Dholen, Andros, and Ghohal, but he smiled at Dekkard. Kharl Navione and Breffyn Haastar talked with the Landor floor leader, Saandaar Vonauer, while Villem Baar, Jaradd Rikkard, and Erich Kuuresoh gathered in the far corner, but didn't seem to be conversing.

Dekkard turned to his left in time to see Vhiola Sandegarde moving toward him.

"Steffan, it's good to see that you escaped, especially that you appear unharmed. What about your staff?"

"I got them all out safely."

"Good." Sandegarde paused, then said, "I'm so sorry about Axel. You and your wife were quite close to him, I know."

"We were. It was quite a shock."

"The Council is going to miss him more than many councilors realize yet." Sandegarde lowered her voice slightly. "Do you know who might succeed him?"

"No. I haven't heard anything at all. When I left yesterday, Haarsfel hadn't even called for a Craft Party caucus."

"He's called for a Council vote on Duadi. That doesn't leave much time. Do you have any suggestions?"

"I haven't been a councilor long enough to know all the senior Craft councilors—besides Premier Obreduur—well enough to make an impartial recommendation."

"What about a partial one?" Sandegarde smiled coolly.

"From a junior councilor?" Dekkard smiled in return. "I think not."

"You know, Steffan, you're a strange mixture of the impulsive and the calculating."

"It might be because I've seen enough not to be young, but not enough to accumulate all the experience to be truly wise."

"I doubt any of us learn enough to be truly wise. How well did you know Jaime Minz?"

The abrupt change of subject caught Dekkard off guard, but he said, "We were both isolate security aides. We talked occasionally, but not often. Probably not a score of times in the past half year. Certainly not since he went to work for Northwest Industrial Chemical."

"He didn't pay you a courtesy call?"

"No. He just sent me a letter telling me he was an assistant director of security for Northwest. I was totally surprised to read that he was taken into custody."

"You haven't heard?"

"Heard what? That they've filed more charges against him?"

"No. They were taking him to court for the initial hearing. He was shot, a little before third bell. One of the patrollers was shot as well."

"What? How?"

"Minz was killed by a sniper, it appears. No one even saw the shooter. That's all I know. Gerard Schmidtz told me just a few minutes ago."

And he asked you to tell me and get my reaction, I'm sure. Dekkard shook his head.

"You're surprised, but not that surprised."

"I've suspected for a long time that he's been involved in something shady, and I was fairly sure he orchestrated the Atacaman pepper incident. I honestly never knew why he'd go to such lengths. I never did anything to offend him."

"Except, after a little more than two years as a security aide, you became an economic assistant and then a councilor. That was doubtless hard for him to accept."

"Personal jealousy?"

"You're also talented, handsome, and have a beautiful wife. Jealousy causes more crimes than politics, Steffan, far more."

"I have to say that I still find it hard to believe."

"Trust me," replied Sandegarde. "That's the way it is, and it's certainly what any investigation will conclude."

Dekkard shook his head. "I still can't believe it."

"That's because you hold on to the illusion of honor. Or at least, the illusion of rationality. Now, if you'll excuse me, I promised Gerard I'd tell Erich."

"Thank you for letting me know."

"My pleasure." Sandegarde smiled pleasantly. "I never cared much for him, either." Then she turned and walked toward Kuuresoh, Baar, and Rikkard.

Dekkard had the feeling Sandegarde's news wouldn't displease Kuuresoh at all. He also felt stunned, almost numb, as he turned and walked out of the lobby, hoping Avraal and Roostof had remained.

Avraal stepped forward, well away from Roostof and Gaaroll. "Did Vhiola Sandegarde tell you—about Jaime Minz?"

"She did. She got the news from Gerard Schmidtz."

"That follows," replied Avraal, lowering her voice and saying, "You look a bit stunned."

"I am," replied Dekkard quietly. "We'll have to talk alone later, although I suspect you already thought it through. I need to get back to the lobby, but I wanted to make sure you knew."

"Vhiola Sandegarde was so sweet," said Avraal, quietly, but acidly, "that she wanted to be the one to tell you."

"Of course." Dekkard leaned forward and kissed her on the cheek. "I'll see you after the session."

When Dekkard returned to the councilors' lobby, Pajiin immediately hurried over.

"What was that all about? Sandegarde talked to you, and you left. Then she talked to Kuuresoh and Rikkard, and they left."

"Did you read *Gestirn* this morning?"

"You mean about that influencer? Oh, the manslaughter charge came from the pepper attack."

"Exactly. Vhiola told me Minz was shot and killed when they took him to the court for the initial hearing."

Pajiin frowned. "Someone didn't want him talking, sounds like."

"That's my impression. I wanted to let Avraal know because he was a security aide when we were. I didn't want her surprised."

"I can see that. You think he was tied to the New Meritorists?"

Dekkard shrugged. "It looks like we may never know that now." *Which is what Ulrich likely wants.* "We should go into the chamber now."

"Good idea."

Once inside the Council chamber, Dekkard glanced around, noting the presence of almost all the councilors, possibly because of the vote on the expense resolution to follow.

The lieutenant-at-arms moved to the center of the dais as the chimes died away and thumped the ceremonial staff.

Then Haarsfel stood and declared, "The first order of business for this Council session is the swearing in of Councilor-select Ingrella Obreduur of Malek and Councilor-select Emile Hebersyn of Machtarn. Lieutenant-at-Arms, please escort the councilors-select to the floor."

Looking around the Council chamber, Dekkard saw several surprised looks, as well as several nods, one of which came from Kharl Navione.

The same uniformed figure who had opened the Council session walked to the door from the Premier's floor office and opened it, then led Ingrella and Hebersyn to the dais. Ingrella wore dark mourning green, while Hebersyn had donned a dark blue suit with faint white pinstripes. His cravat was red.

Dekkard wondered what Hebersyn's political connections happened to be, because he'd never heard of the man before. *But then you'd never heard of most of the councilors when you first joined Obreduur's staff.*

Haarsfel read the oath of office, phrase by phrase, as both councilors-select repeated each phrase. Ingrella's voice was clear and firm.

After the swearing in, Haarsfel said, "Congratulations to both of you."

Both moved to the floor of the chamber.

Then Haarsfel spoke again. "Before we take up the second order of business, I would like to remind all councilors that, for the memorial service on Unadi, spouses will accompany councilors into the chamber, where additional seats will be placed. That will allow more space in the galleries." He paused for almost a minute before continuing. "The second order of business is a Council resolution appropriating an additional four thousand marks to the expense allowance of those councilors, or their successors in office, whose offices suffered major damage from the shelling of the Council Office Building, and an additional five hundred marks for all other councilors."

That vote took less than a third and passed unanimously, after which Haarsfel announced that the Craft Party would caucus at third bell on Duadi morning, and that the Council would meet at fourth bell on Tridi morning for a vote on the election of a new premier, rather than on Duadi as previously scheduled. Then he adjourned the Council until Unadi.

Dekkard immediately moved to Ingrella. He could see that her eyes were bright, possibly with unshed tears, but she offered a faint smile.

"Would you like to have lunch with us? Although I'm certain others will stop by."

"I would appreciate that very much, Steffan."

"I should have asked you sooner," he said apologetically, "but today has been a bit disconcerting."

"I read about Jaime Minz. Axel also mentioned him. We should talk later."

Dekkard nodded, then stepped back slightly as Fredrich Hasheem appeared and inclined his head.

"I'm so sorry, Ingrella, but I appreciate your willingness to carry on."

Dekkard just stood there as various other Craft councilors came to greet her and to offer condolences, among them Safaell, Mardosh, and Harleona Zerlyon, who offered extended thanks and appreciation. Both Vonauer and Volkaar made brief appearances.

Then Dekkard escorted Ingrella to the dining room, where Avraal had a table waiting.

"This is very thoughtful of you two," said Ingrella as she seated herself.

"You've always been thoughtful to us," Dekkard pointed out.

When the three ordered, Dekkard and Avraal both chose the three-cheese chicken, while Ingrella opted for the onion soup.

Then Ingrella said, "Being a councilor is not something I ever even thought about." She shook her head. "Axel wanted so much to make Guldor a better land. I don't have his skills."

"You have yours," Avraal pointed out.

"They're not the same. I'm a legalist, not a leader." She looked to Dekkard. "You have those skills. Axel saw that in you. He wanted you to have more experience, but the Craft Party in Gaarlak forced his hand. At the time, he worried, but I'm very glad that matters turned out as they did for you. Now, I've said that piece, and we should try to enjoy lunch. We can talk about politics later."

"Since that's the decision," said Dekkard, with a smile, "does Nellara still practice with the throwing knives?"

"I couldn't stop her if I tried. She goes to the garage and practices. She says she can get most every throw within a digit of where she wants, and hard enough that they stick firmly. She wants to carry her knives the way you do, Avraal. I told her she couldn't do that until both of you approved. I trust you don't mind."

"We can do that," said Dekkard, "but it should be in a while, and when you're ready to have us look at how she's throwing."

"Perhaps during Midwinter Recess," said Ingrella.

"It might have to be a bit after or near the end of the recess," replied Dekkard. "We've put off making a trip to Gaarlak. There's the matter of establishing a permanent tie there, like a house."

"That's right." Ingrella nodded. "We were fortunate that I already had a house in Malek."

"We'll have to find something rather modest," said Dekkard, "although I understand that houses there are considerably less expensive than here in Machtarn."

"Spend on the basic house and the location," advised Ingrella. "You can decorate and improve later."

Lunch conversation from that point on dwelt upon houses and what was necessary—or not—with Ingrella offering amused advice primarily to Avraal. Dekkard largely listened.

As lunch was drawing to a close, a server came to the table. "Councilor Dekkard, this is for you." He extended an envelope.

"Do you know who it's from?"

"The Guard captain, sir."

Dekkard took the envelope. "Thank you."

The server immediately withdrew while Dekkard studied the envelope, which bore only the words "Councilor Dekkard."

"You might as well open it, dear," said Avraal.

Dekkard did, taking in the short message.

"What is it?" asked Avraal.

"He'd like a few minutes of my time in the next bell, if it's convenient, of course."

"Gaaroll and I can walk Ingrella to her steamer, and then we'll wait for you. Where are you meeting him?"

"In the Premier's floor office."

"Then we'll be waiting."

"I'll go through the Council chamber," said Dekkard. "That will make it easier." But he still escorted Avraal and Ingrella out of the dining room before retracing his steps and making his way to the floor office.

One of the clerks looked up. "Guard Captain Trujillo is using the Premier's private office. You can go in."

Dekkard entered and closed the door.

Trujillo was sitting in one of the two chairs in front of the desk. Dekkard took the other.

"Thank you for entertaining my request, Councilor."

Not that I have a real choice. "I'm happy to help."

"I do appreciate it. I take it that you had a chance to read this morning's newssheet?"

"About Jaime Minz, you mean? I did. And Councilor Sandegarde told me that he'd been shot and killed on the way to a preliminary hearing."

"That's correct." Trujillo smiled pleasantly. "What are your thoughts about the shooting?"

"It was a cover-up. I certainly can't prove it, but I believe Minz provided a link between corporacion officials who ordered shady actions or outright illegal ones. Because he is an isolate, there's no way to determine the veracity of any response to questions. But since he faced possible execution, he might have bargained for exile by revealing what corporacions he acted on behalf of, or at least the individuals from whom he received 'suggestions.' That's only my belief, of course."

"That was Premier Obreduur's as well. Do you think Sr. Minz had anything to do with Premier Obreduur's death?"

"Again, I don't *know*. I *suspect* Minz somehow facilitated the ability of the New Meritorists to obtain the dunnite they used. How and to whom, I have no idea. There's something else that occurred to me as well. How did the gunners know which offices were Obreduur's and mine? Or when Obreduur was likely to be in his office? That's not information that's readily available, except to former or present councilors or staff."

"We considered that as well."

"It's so obvious that I didn't even think about it until last night."

Trujillo nodded.

"You didn't find anything else?"

"No. After looking at the banque records, I doubt that anyone will." After the briefest pause, Trujillo asked, "How do you think Sr. Minz managed to kill Sr. Venburg?"

"If anyone knew hidden ways to enter the Council Hall, or even overt un- noticed ways, Minz would have. He could have posed as a Council Guard or a server from the councilors' dining room."

"Why would he have used Atacaman pepper?"

"He did?"

Trujillo nodded. "We also found traces of the same pepper mix linked to him."

Dekkard frowned, then said, "If he surprised Venburg, a shot of pepper would keep Venburg from being able to shout for help. I could barely talk after the Security Council incident. Minz was a security aide for much longer than I was."

Trujillo actually looked slightly surprised. "I hadn't thought of that, and no one else mentioned it."

"I didn't think of it, either, until you asked."

"Do you have any idea *why* Minz might have attacked Venburg?"

"That would be another guess."

"I'm open to guesses, Councilor."

"Ten thousand marks is a great deal of money. Siincleer Shipbuilding has a reputation for having been involved in some less than savory practices. Cap- itol Services may, *just may,* have provided those services. I can't believe any corporacion would spend ten thousand marks to remove a junior councilor, especially in such an indirect way. Perhaps he diverted funds Venburg pro- vided for other services? Siincleer Shipbuilding isn't exactly known for being forgiving, and if Venburg pressed Minz?" Dekkard shrugged. "That's just my best guess. There wouldn't be any way to prove or disprove it. But, if he did use Atacaman pepper, I always considered Minz as the likely one behind the Atacaman pepper incident at the Security Committee, but I never saw any way to tie him to it with nothing but a very great deal of circumstantial evidence."

"We found a witness. I mentioned that to you earlier. She identified Minz as the man who hired Hurrek for side work. We discovered that Minz had withdrawn ten thousand marks from the Capitol Services account, in mark notes, three days before Hurrek opened an account with the Imperial Banque of Machtarn, with ten thousand marks in cash."

"Rather an unlikely coincidence, I'd think."

"We also discovered that every large deposit to the Capitol Services account was either in cash or by banque cheques with no notation as to the source. Very few by personal or corporacion cheque, and those tended to be smaller and local."

"I take it that there were no cheques from either Northwest Industrial Chemical or Suvion Industries?"

"Not a one. Premier Obreduur and acting Premier Haarsfel both found that interesting, but as you said, there's certainly no evidence. Thank you for talking to me, again. I'm sorry to bother you. You've already been through a great deal this past week."

"I just hope I've been helpful."

"You have been. So have others. Without all of you, I'm not sure we'd have gotten to the bottom of this."

"I just wish we could find out how the New Meritorists obtained all that dunnite."

"I'm still working with the Ministry of Public Safety and the Justiciary Ministry on that. We have a few leads on who received it, but we will have to see. Thank you, again."

Dekkard had the definite feeling that Trujillo was done. So he stood. "Thank you for everything." He inclined his head and then made his way out of the Premier's inner office and then out into the main corridor.

Roostof, Avraal, and Gaaroll were all waiting for him.

"He had a few more questions about Jaime Minz. Nothing that we haven't talked about before. He gave me the impression that, while they may never discover where the dunnite came from, they're still looking into where it went and who might have whatever's left. He'd only say that they were looking into it."

"Who is 'they,' sir?" asked Gaaroll.

"The Council Guards, the Ministry of Public Safety, and the Justiciary Ministry." Dekkard looked to Roostof. "Have you discovered anything new about the office?"

"They'll begin on new windows tomorrow. The administrative offices are working on replacement furniture and typewriters."

"Good. Anything else I should know?"

"I can't think of anything, sir."

"Then I'll see you just before the memorial service on Unadi. After your meeting this afternoon, go home and try to enjoy Findi."

Roostof smiled. "I'll do my best." He turned and walked toward the staff cafeteria, likely just to have a place where he could sit and wait for his meeting.

"How's Ingrella?" Dekkard asked quietly.

"Composed, but grieving."

"She will be for a long time," predicted Dekkard. "They were close."

"They truly loved and respected each other."

Dekkard swallowed, then said, "We might as well head home."

Avraal reached out, took his hand, and replied, "We should."

69

B Y the time Dekkard, Avraal, and Gaaroll reached the house and Dekkard had garaged and checked over the Gresynt, it was nearly third bell.

Avraal waited for him. "Let's go into the study."

The study had a door that closed, unlike the sitting room, which connected to the front hall through an archway. Dekkard made sure that door was closed, then turned to Avraal.

"What did Trujillo really say?" she asked.

"I'll tell you exactly what he said, or as close as I remember. Do you want to sit down?"

She shook her head.

"He started off by asking me if I'd read the morning newssheet . . ." Dekkard went on from there, ending with Trujillo's comments about still looking into where the dunnite might have gone, and then adding, "He really seemed like I'd told him all he wanted to know, and that he was as grateful as he said he was."

Avraal frowned. "The one time I listened and watched him, he was very direct, and there weren't any contradictory or subconscious feelings. Do you really think he feels Minz killed Venburg?"

"I don't think he cares. He *knows* that Minz's scheming killed Hurrek and might have killed or dishonored me. He knows that Minz handled dirty marks, or more properly, carefully laundered marks, and he as much as said that there's no way to discover where those marks came from. I also got the impression that he doesn't have a favorable impression of the Siincleer corporacions."

"You think he'll leave it at that?"

"Unless concrete evidence to the contrary comes up, and there isn't any. There was one thing he said that surprised me. He said that they'd also found traces of the same Atacaman pepper mix linked to Minz." Dekkard raised his eyebrows.

"That makes sense."

"There wasn't any breaking and entering, I hope?"

She shook her head. "I imagine they found it in his brand-new blue Realto."

"Someone wanted to make sure—very sure."

Avraal looked directly and evenly at Dekkard. "No one gets away with killing or trying to kill people I love."

70

WHEN Emrelda got home on Quindi, the three decided that, after services, they'd all go to Elfredo's for dinner, since no one wanted to cook, and since they hadn't been in a while. Presider Buusen's homily was not unreasonably long, and not especially theological, dealing as it did with the subject of trust, and how trust was the basis for both faith and society.

Dekkard wasn't so certain about trust as the basis for faith or religion, but he'd definitely seen what untrustworthy individuals could do to undermine government.

After a cheerful dinner at the taverna, they returned home, where the four settled in the sitting room and discussed the day's events, after which Dekkard and Avraal repaired to their bedroom. Although Dekkard wondered how he'd sleep, he was so tired that, when he woke on Findi morning, he said, "I don't remember falling asleep."

Avraal smiled sheepishly. "Neither do I."

"Yesterday wasn't that hard physically, either," Dekkard pointed out.

"But it was emotionally hard, with the news, the lunch with Ingrella, and your interview with Guard Captain Trujillo."

"That's true. What should we do today?"

"As little as possible that's stressful."

"Then we should enjoy breakfast."

"Go take your shower."

Dekkard smiled, but he got up and headed to the bathroom, where he quickly showered, careful to leave enough warm water for Avraal, since it wasn't any warmer than Quindi morning had been, and then dressed and headed downstairs, wearing an older, gray shirt and trousers, and a dark gray sweater his mother had given him when he'd started to work for Obreduur. Both Emrelda and Gaaroll sat at the breakfast room table.

"There's a short story about the death of Jaime Minz and a very nice article about Ingrella becoming a councilor," said Emrelda.

Dekkard picked up *Gestirn*. There was nothing new about Minz's death. He turned to the story about Ingrella.

NOTED LEGALIST SUCCEEDS HUSBAND
AS COUNCILOR

The Craft Party chose the noted legalist Ingrella Irsian Obreduur as councilor to replace her late husband, Premier Axel Laurent Obreduur. The Premier was killed earlier this week in the attack on the Council Office Building. The new Councilor Obreduur has been distinguished by her success as a legalist, particularly in successfully litigating cases expanding the rights of women in the workforce . . .

The story went on to list several of her more notable cases, most of which, Dekkard had to admit, shamefully, he'd never heard of. Even so, he couldn't help but smile as he replaced the newssheet on the side table and went into the kitchen to get cafés for himself and Avraal. After carrying those out to the breakfast room and placing them on the table, he went to fetch croissants.

By the time he had the croissants, and his most necessary quince paste, on the table, Avraal had seated herself and was reading the newssheet. When she set it aside, she took a sip of café, then another, before she spoke. "That was actually a good story about Ingrella. Except for the part about Axel's death, it was all about her accomplishments, rather than his, with him as a footnote."

Dekkard couldn't help wondering how the story had been portrayed in the *Tribune,* most likely picturing her as a dangerous legalist whose legal career had been based on forcing corporacions to pay unreasonable wages, "unreasonable" never being defined, but being understood as equal wages for women.

"I'd wager that the Landors don't pick a woman to replace Quentin Fader," said Emrelda.

"Did you know him?" asked Dekkard.

"No, but I've never heard of a woman Landor councilor. Even the Commercers had one or two."

"Two," replied Dekkard. "Both wealthy and unmarried."

"The Craft Party isn't much better, dear," said Avraal. "Unless I'm mistaken, out of the four women who are Crafter councilors, the only married one is Traelyna Treshaam."

Dekkard almost pointed out Ingrella, before realizing that Ingrella wouldn't have ever sought election while Axel was alive, unless he'd been in office long enough to be forced to stand down. *And now she's not married, if not by choice.* "You're right. We do need to do better."

"Try to avoid Axel's example, dear," added Avraal with a mischievous smile. "It'd be a waste. I can't succeed you."

Because you're an empath. That was just another reminder for Dekkard of the barriers for Avraal. Empaths couldn't be elected officials or ministerial appointees, while isolates could, but neither could appear as legalists in legal proceedings, although there was no prohibition on meeting with clients or writing briefs or other legal documents.

"Would you really want to be a councilor?" asked Emrelda. "With all you've seen?"

"No, but I'd like to see more women. Even ones like Kaliara Bassaana are preferable to about half the Commercers and two-thirds of the Landors."

"What about the Crafters?" asked Emrelda, with a smile that was almost evil, Dekkard thought.

"Most of them aren't that much better. I just happened to be married to one of the few that is."

"About the only one," murmured Gaaroll.

Both Avraal and Emrelda laughed.

So did Dekkard.

At that moment, there was a knock on the door, followed by the chime of the door pull.

"I'll get it," said Dekkard, rising from the table and walking to the front door.

When he opened it, he saw a messenger in the gold and black of Guldoran Heliograph standing there. "Yes?"

"I have two secure messages. One for a Ritten Emrelda Ysella-Roemnal and one for a Ritten Avraal Ysella-Dekkard."

"You have the right place," said Dekkard.

"I'll need some verification of identity."

"Just a moment. I'll get them." Dekkard walked back halfway to the breakfast room and called, "Emrelda! Avraal! You each have a secure message. The messenger needs something to verify you are you."

Dekkard walked back to the door and stood there for what seemed several minutes before both sisters appeared. Emrelda presented a patroller badge and a patrol identity card, while Avraal presented her Council credentials. The messenger didn't even blink. Then each had to sign a log sheet. In turn, each received a thick envelope.

Once the messenger left and Dekkard closed the door, he said, "That's strange. I've heard of secure messages before, but I've never seen or received one. Where are they from?"

"Sudaen," said Avraal, with an indrawn breath. "I hope there's no problem."

"Surely, we would have heard sooner if something had happened to someone," finished Emrelda.

"I wouldn't wager on that," said Avraal. "I actually got that letter from Mother a little over a week ago. I've *never* had two letters from her in a month, let alone two letters in successive weeks."

"Let's go into the study," said Emrelda quietly, almost fearfully, Dekkard thought.

Once the three were in the study, Emrelda and Avraal exchanged glances.

Then Avraal said, "I'll go first." Taking a letter opener from the desk, she slit the large envelope, only to find two envelopes inside, one bulky, and one clearly a letter.

Dekkard looked over her shoulder, but the letter envelope was addressed to Avraal, and the return address was from Sudaen. The bulkier envelope only bore her name.

Avraal opened the letter and began to read. Her eyes widened, and she turned and held the letter so that Dekkard could read it as well.

Dear Avraal,

I'm so sorry that my initial response to the announcement of your marriage was less than enthusiastic. It did take us very much by surprise, since you'd only mentioned Steffan as a solid and brilliant man with whom you worked. You neglected to mention just how brilliant and accomplished when you said that he was an excellent security specialist.

Your father and I have come to realize that you were never meant to follow the path we have. What we have been slow to understand was just how much you have accomplished and how much more you and Steffan have already accomplished together.

You may recall Balthasar Haastar. He's somewhat older than your father, but they've been friends for years. It turns out that his younger son is the councilor from Brekaan. Balthasar sent us several clippings about you and Steffan's accomplishments, because young Breffyn said that you hadn't even seen them, and certainly wouldn't have been able to let us know. Apparently, even Emilio Raathan and Patriana were also quite impressed.

The lines about the Raathans also reinforced for Dekkard just how tightly the old Landor families were connected, even over long distances, but then Georg Raathan had known who Avraal was just by her name.

Because it's clear that your destiny does not lie in Sudaen, or likely anywhere close, the enclosed bond is your wedding gift. Knowing you and reading about Steffan, I'm sure you'll use it wisely.

Our Love,

There were two signatures.

Dekkard read it again, then looked at Avraal.

She swallowed. "You open it. I'm afraid to."

Dekkard understood. The bond could mean anything, from an effective dismissal to a belated acceptance. He took the letter opener and carefully opened the envelope, extracting the heavy paper of the elaborately printed document. As he read it, his eyes widened, and he handed it to Avraal. "It's definitely safe to read."

She read it, twice, then looked to Emrelda. "Yours should be safe to open."

Both Dekkard and Avraal waited as Emrelda read her letter, then opened the second envelope. She shook her head, as if unbelieving, then handed the bond to Avraal.

Dekkard took in the numbers. Each bond was to a sister, and each was for fifteen thousand marks.

Avraal looked to Dekkard. "I think it's safe to make arrangements to go to Gaarlak over the Midwinter Recess."

"I just wish . . ." murmured Emrelda, her eyes bright.

Dekkard understood that unspoken wish. *Late is better than never, but there's still a cost. Sometimes a terrible one.*

71

DESPITE the fact that the Council's memorial service wouldn't begin until late morning, Dekkard woke on Unadi as the first hints of gray light began to seep into the bedroom. For a time, he just lay there, thinking so many thoughts: why he hadn't been able to predict the method of the sneak attack on Obreduur; why Minz had seemingly hated him so much; why Venburg and del Larrano were so vicious to smaller businesses, so much so they destroyed lives, like Markell's, depriving Emrelda of the love and joy she'd struggled so much to obtain; or why Avraal had needed to kill Venburg to save her sister—*and possibly you.*

He was still thinking when Avraal turned to him. "You're so quiet, you haven't moved."

"I've been thinking."

"Do you want to talk about it?"

"Not all of it." He smiled. "I still need to think out more than a few things."

"Then what do you want to talk about?"

"Your mother's letter, if you're ready. You were really quiet, after the surprise. You said you wanted to think."

"I've thought."

Dekkard opened his mouth, found he didn't quite know what to say, and closed it. Finally, he said, "I can't believe it . . . but I can. And I don't want to."

"It's not that bad. They are who they are. The one thing that galls me—they couldn't take my word for anything. No, newssheet clips from Breffyn Haastar to his father, and his father tells my father, and the light floods over them."

"I can see that. I definitely do. Why do you think I never said much about the Military Institute accomplishments?"

"Oh, they're not artisan accomplishments?"

"I knew that they were only academic honors, but they were hard to come by. My parents were pleased, but they never even told Naralta, and then they forgot." He paused. "Your situation is worse. But I do understand."

Avraal laughed, a combination of humor and bitterness. "I appreciate what Breffyn Haastar did because it got through to them somehow, but . . ."

Dekkard nodded, then reached out and drew her closer, holding her tight.

Eventually, they got up and readied themselves for the day. Dekkard wore the darkest gray of his winter suits, with a dark green mourning sash and matching green cravat. Avraal donned a gray winter dress with dark gray boots and a dark green jacket.

By the time they got downstairs to the kitchen, Emrelda had left for work, and Gaaroll sat there alone.

"Took your time this morning."

"There wasn't any hurry," replied Dekkard. "Is there anything in the newssheet?"

"Not much. Short story about the memorial service."

"I'll get the café," said Avraal. "You get the croissants. I'll have one."

They ate quietly. Since Dekkard finished before Avraal, as he almost always did, he took a quick look at the newssheet, only to find that Gaaroll's succinct analysis was correct.

On the drive to the Council Hall, Dekkard found himself taking another indirect route, even though he'd told himself that it wasn't necessary, that Minz was dead. *But there still could be someone else.* Neither Avraal nor Gaaroll sensed anything untoward.

After Dekkard pulled the Gresynt into the covered parking and the three got out, Avraal adjusted the mourning-green headscarf. As the three walked toward the Council Hall, Dekkard could see more Council Guards posted outside both the office building and the Council Hall. All of them wore sashes of mourning green. As they neared the entrance, Dekkard almost stopped in his tracks, shaking his head.

"What is it?" asked Avraal.

"It's been almost a week since the attack. So far as I know, there's been no statement from the New Meritorists. No more demands. Nothing. There were letters or broadsheets soon after all the other demonstrations and attacks."

"It's only been five days, and one was an endday," Avraal pointed out.

"I still wonder."

"Wonder what?"

"What if the attack wasn't a planned Meritorist attack, but one set up on the side by corporacion operatives working with the Meritorists?"

"That figures," muttered Gaaroll. "Kill the only guys in power who understand workers. Let everyone else mess it up, and put the Commercers back in charge. Except they missed you, sir."

"I also don't have much power."

"There's power and there's power," said Avraal, quietly, but firmly. "You got the Security reform bill through committee without any help from Obreduur. You also persuaded councilors to vote for it."

"It's going to take a lot of persuading to accomplish any reform." *Or to stop Ulrich and his corporacion terrorists.*

"You and Ingrella will manage just fine."

Dekkard was about to reply when she gestured to the Council Hall doors ahead. "We can talk later. You need to find Svard."

"He'll be waiting near the councilors' lobby."

Once inside the Council Hall, Avraal just eased the headscarf off her hair and around her neck.

As the three walked down the main corridor toward the Council chamber, Dekkard saw that the corridor wasn't close to crowded. That wasn't surprising, since the entrance to the galleries was through an outside door on the north side of the building.

He turned to Gaaroll and handed her a five-mark note. "Wait for us in the staff cafeteria. We'll find you."

"Yes, sir." Gaaroll grinned and headed toward the cafeteria, while Dekkard and Avraal approached the councilors' lobby.

Dekkard didn't have to look far for Roostof, because he hurried up to them before they got close to the lobby.

"Good morning, sir."

"Good morning, Svard. Are you ready to speak?"

"As ready as I'll ever be. I've been checking with maintenance people, and there's a chance they'll be done with the repairs and painting in our office by the end of the week."

"That would be good, but I don't think I'll hold my breath." Dekkard paused. "I don't think we should even try to meet after the service. How about outside the councilors' lobby tomorrow a little before third bell? Unless you have a better idea."

"No, sir. I'll be there."

"So will I." Dekkard smiled. "I'm looking forward to hearing you speak today."

"Don't judge me harshly."

"You'll do fine," said Dekkard cheerfully.

After Roostof hurried off, Dekkard turned to Avraal. "Since spouses are allowed in the chamber and the councilors' lobby for the service, we might as well go in and see who's here."

"Will we be able to see Ingrella?"

Dekkard chuckled. "Since she's now the most junior Craft councilor, besides me, her desk is my old one, and I've been moved to Pajiin's. They're next to each other."

When they stepped inside the councilors' lobby, Dekkard immediately looked around. From what he could see, not that many councilors had brought their spouses.

Schmidtz, Palafaux, and Rikkard stood together, but didn't seem to be talking, and the same appeared to be true of a Landor group, Navione, Halljen, and Saarh. Villem Baar stood talking with Eyril and Emilya Konnigsburg. Another small group consisted of Maximillian Connard, the councilor from Aaken, and his wife and Emile Hebersyn and his wife.

In another corner Dekkard caught sight of Ingrella, Harleona Zerlyon, and Elyncya Duforgue. *The best legalists in the Council, most likely.*

Beyond them, Mardosh talked with Safaell and Daffyd Dholen, but when Mardosh caught sight of Dekkard, he turned and started toward Dekkard, then abruptly moved to one side to talk to Eduardo Nortak, who was accompanied by his wife, Adryann, Dekkard recalled.

"He was going to talk to you, then he saw me," said Avraal quietly.

"He's wary of you," replied Dekkard.

"He *should* be, the bastard."

Dekkard decided he and Avraal wouldn't head in that direction. "Why don't we join Villem and the Konnigsburgs?"

"That would be lovely."

As they neared, Eyril Konnigsburg half turned. "Please join us." He smiled wryly. "I would have said, 'Good morning,' or the equivalent. But . . ." He shrugged.

"It's not exactly a good morning or a good week," agreed Dekkard.

"You both look so stylish," said Emilya warmly.

"So do you two," returned Avraal. "Are you settled yet?"

Emilya smiled. "We're renting a small place in East Quarter. We don't need much now that Margueritte and Daensyn are out of the house and on their own, and my mother's happy to take care of our house in Veerlyn."

The house in Veerlyn suggested to Dekkard that Konnigsburg had definitely been in Naval Intelligence, since the intelligence headquarters happened to be there, and they likely wouldn't have purchased a home there if he'd had a fleet command.

"Recent events have suggested," Emilya added, "that with all the unrest, and the possibility of frequent elections, councilors may not remain in office as long as in the past."

"If the Council doesn't manage to deal successfully with a few of its problems," Dekkard replied, "you may be right. I'd hope, for everyone's sake, that you're excessively pessimistic."

"Steffan's a very careful optimist," said the retired admiral.

"Then maybe the two of you can restore some order and common sense," suggested Emilya. "Or is that too much to hope for?"

Dekkard smiled. "We'll have to see, but since the Council hasn't had two councilors like us in some time, if ever, who knows what we might accomplish together."

"That might be interesting," said the admiral.

"Do you think we should let them conspire together?" Emilya asked Avraal.

"Why not? Conspiratorial cooperation might actually work."

"So long as we don't call it that," said Dekkard dryly.

"What would you call it, then?" asked Baar cheerfully.

"How about 'mutual professional respect'?" replied Dekkard.

"An excellent term," admitted Baar.

Before that long, councilors and spouses began to drift into the Council chamber, and, as Dekkard had predicted, his "new" desk was next to his old one, where Ingrella had already seated herself.

Rather than sit in the back in one of the temporary chairs, Avraal stayed with Dekkard, and said, "I'll just kneel when the service starts."

"We can share the desk chair. It's wide enough."

"We'll see."

As the last of the five bells chimed, Haarsfel stepped to the Premier's lectern and waited for quiet to settle across the chamber and the galleries. "Presider Geoffryn Garryen from the Machtarn Trinitarian Grand Chapel will say a few words to begin this memorial ceremony to remember and to honor those brutally and suddenly wrested from us in such an untimely manner. Presider?"

The silver-haired Presider Garryen strode to the other lectern. He just stood there for several moments, then said, "We all know our days are but fleeting threads in the fabric of time, our rocks of solidity but grains of sand on the beaches of eternity, washed hither and thither by the storms of fate and chance. In this time of mourning, we turn to the Almighty, for only the Almighty grants life, and the blessing of existence, the joy of breath, and the depth of understanding, empathy, and compassion. As we the living share and experience these blessings, we mourn and remember those taken from us. In this time of trial and deprivation, we ask that the Almighty bless and comfort their souls and enfold them into the eternal bliss of the Trinity."

After a slight pause, he declared, "Thanks be to the love, power, and mercy of the Almighty."

Those in the chamber repeated, "Thanks be to the love, power, and mercy of the Almighty."

Standing at the Premier's lectern, Haarsfel waited for the murmured chorus to die away, before he began to speak. "On Duadi, the eighth of Winterfirst, the unthinkable happened. For the first time ever in the history of Guldor, a premier, three councilors, and thirty-four dedicated staff members were killed by shells fired into the Council Office Building. While the Council will hunt down and deal with the perpetrators, the moments that follow this morning are to recognize all those taken from us, their past, their achievements, and their future."

When Haarsfel finished his short address, he stepped back, and Fredrich Hasheem stepped forward to give the eulogy for Obreduur. He waited for several moments, then surveyed the floor of the Council chamber and then the galleries, packed with relatives of those who died in the attack.

"Axel Laurent Obreduur was Premier for two months. He engineered the greatest shift in political power in more than a generation. More important than that was the way in which he accomplished it. There were no backroom deals, no veiled or direct slanders, nor anything else sordid. Always careful about the promises he made, if he made one, he kept it. Two present councilors are here because he promised not to override district Craft Parties, even when he would have preferred another candidate. His word was more than good. It was gold.

"In the end, he would have wanted the Council to continue under the best precepts of the Great Charter, making necessary improvements through law and careful legislation that recognizes the rights under law of all men, women, and children. He never wanted what was best for one party or another, but what was best for *Guldor,* and that is how he should be remembered."

After the eulogy for Obreduur came those for the other three councilors, in order of seniority, beginning with Marryat Osmond, followed by Tedor Waarfel, and then Quentin Fader. The eulogies of staff members were arranged by the seniority of the councilor for whom they had worked, and that meant that Svard Roostof spoke first for the fallen staffers.

"This is especially hard for me," began Roostof, "because I worked with the staff in Councilor Obreduur's office for nearly five years, and then he recommended me for my current position. His staff was close, and everyone not only liked each other, but they respected each other as well.

"Ivann Macri knew more about law than any legalist I met, but he never mentioned it. He could correct a horrendous mistake in a way that made you feel better, not just then, but all day.

"Felix Raynaad was quietly fearless, but so well-mannered that he could show a corporacion director that the director was lying and that Felix knew he was lying without the director even getting uncomfortable.

"Karola Mayun brought sunlight into the office, but was sharp enough that the Premier never was scheduled wrong, and that visitors felt as though they were the most important people in Guldor . . ."

As Roostof went on, Dekkard felt his eyes burning. *They were all such good people.*

But he also knew that neither the Meritorists nor Ulrich and his corporacion allies cared. Collateral damage, the price others paid, didn't matter at all to them.

But there's always collateral damage from every attempt to change things. Or was the real difference between the reformers, like Obreduur, and the extremists, whether revolutionaries like the Meritorists, or reactionaries like Minz and Ulrich, that reformers tried to balance the possible improvement against the costs, while the extremists seldom considered the costs, either in marks or deaths?

Dekkard felt more than a little wrung out when the service concluded just after the first afternoon bell and he stood. Sharing his chair with Avraal, although he was more than glad that she'd stayed, had left him slightly stiff.

He immediately turned to Ingrella. "How are you doing?"

"Surviving, Steffan."

"Don't you think that Fredrich captured some of the essence of Axel?"

"He's a nice man, a good man, and he did his best. I just hope he'll listen to you more, Steffan."

Ingrella pitched her voice so low that Dekkard had to strain to make out all the words. "You think Haarsfel will put him up for premier?"

"Who else?" Ingrella smiled sadly. "Mardosh isn't totally trustworthy, and Safaell isn't nearly forceful enough."

Although Dekkard liked Safaell the best, he could see what she meant. "Would you like to join us for lunch?"

"I'd love that, but I agreed to eat with Harleona and Elyncya. Why don't you two join us?"

"If it wouldn't be an imposition."

Ingrella laughed softly. "Hardly. Elyncya suggested it."

"I feel honored." Dekkard grinned. "The only man, and the only councilor who's not a legalist."

"The way you worded that was suspiciously like a legalist," replied Ingrella.

"Exactly," agreed another voice.

Dekkard turned to see Elyncya Duforgue standing beside Avraal. Both of them were smiling.

Then Elyncya said, "I already told Harleona to get a table for five."

"I'm not only honored," replied Dekkard, "but clearly outnumbered and overwhelmed."

"Never the latter, dear," said Avraal dryly. "Let's just join Harleona and have lunch."

Dekkard nodded, deciding that silence was the better part of valor. *At least for the moment.*

In less than a sixth, the five seated themselves at a large corner table in the councilors' dining room. Since there was no other Council business scheduled, Zerlyon and Dekkard each had Kuhrs, and the other three had Silverhills white.

"Svard did very well at capturing the sense of Axel's staff," said Ingrella, "even the two he didn't know that well."

"He's very talented and diligent. I'm so fortunate to have him and Margrit, and that was because of Axel's generosity."

Ingrella smiled. "Not totally generosity. He would have lost both of them before long because he couldn't pay them more. He recommended them to you. That way everyone benefitted."

"Just because he was practical didn't mean he wasn't generous," replied Dekkard, "and that applies to you as well."

Ingrella turned to Avraal. "In some ways, I like Steffan even more as a councilor."

Both Zerlyon and Duforgue laughed.

Then Duforgue asked, "Why?"

"He was exceedingly polite and deferential, at times more deferential than he should have been. Now I'm seeing more of who he really is, and I like that."

"Don't let that go to your head," Avraal immediately said to Dekkard.

"I don't dare," he replied with a grin. "You'd let me know immediately, as you just did."

A hint of a smile crossed Ingrella's lips, but before anyone else spoke, their server reappeared with their entrées, with Zerlyon and Ingrella each having onion soup, Duforgue and Avraal the three-cheese chicken, while Dekkard once more settled for the white bean soup.

Once the server departed, Duforgue spoke. "On a more serious note, does anyone know who might be nominated for premier tomorrow?"

"Any Craft councilor can nominate," replied Zerlyon, "but that seldom happens. Usually, the Premier, or the floor leader, suggests someone, and then asks if any other councilor has a nominee. If there is another nominee, his name is usually offered by one of the senior councilors."

"So who will Haarsfel offer as a possible premier, or will he offer his own name?" asked Duforgue.

"I doubt that Guilhohn wants to be premier," said Ingrella, "unless the entire Craft Party demands it."

"I don't see that happening," said Dekkard. "If it doesn't, the premier candidate will likely be one of the senior councilors. Besides Haarsfel, the three most senior Craft councilors are Hasheem, Safaell, and Mardosh."

"What about someone a little less senior," asked Zerlyon, "like Leister Milyaard or Paarkyn Noyell?"

Dekkard had had no interaction with either of the two Craft councilors Zerlyon mentioned, except he knew that Noyell hailed from Oost and served on the Waterways Committee, while Milyaard came from Nuile and was on the Transportation Committee. *Except, with Waarfel's death, Milyaard is now chair.*

"Anyone who gets the votes can be presented to the Imperador as a premier candidate," said Ingrella evenly.

From that evenness, Dekkard definitely felt that Ingrella was not impressed with either, and that likely meant that Axel Obreduur hadn't been either.

"Oh," uttered Zerlyon. "I suppose that leaves us with the choice of those three."

"Hasheem or Safaell," suggested Dekkard politely.

"Mardosh is a bit more forward," suggested Zerlyon.

"Except when it comes to reining in corporacion abuses," Dekkard countered.

Elyncya Duforgue nodded. "I've gotten that impression as well."

Ingrella nodded.

Zerlyon said quietly, "Your thoughts, Ingrella?"

"They're both good men. Fredrich is more resistant to pressure."

"I think that settles it for me," declared Zerlyon.

Duforgue nodded as well.

"How is the chicken?" Dekkard asked after several minutes.

"The same as always," said Avraal. "Better than decent and less than outstanding."

From there the conversation turned to food and restaurants, followed by comments about clothing, comments that Dekkard merely observed, occasionally nodding.

It was close to third bell when the five finally left the dining room, and from there Avraal and Dekkard accompanied Ingrella to the covered parking, with a brief stop at the staff cafeteria to find Gaaroll.

After seeing Ingrella drive off in the Gresynt that Dekkard had used to chauffeur her husband for more than two years, Dekkard looked to Avraal. "I almost wish I were still driving Obreduur."

"Dear, that could never have happened. If you hadn't been selected as councilor, likely one or both of us would be dead. Sometimes, the best outcome is still terrible."

Dekkard knew her words would linger far longer than the drive back to the house.

72

ONCE Dekkard, Avraal, and Gaaroll arrived home, Avraal immediately set to making dinner, in a methodical fashion that suggested to Dekkard that she was just as quietly concerned and upset as he was.

Gaaroll obviously sensed that, because she said, "I could peel the potatoes, the turnips, and the carrots."

"Thank you," replied Avraal. "That would be a help."

Dekkard peeled and chopped the onions, while Avraal dealt with the lamb and put everything together. After that, he mostly cleaned up and fetched. Between the three of them, they had the shepherd's pie in the oven and almost ready by the time Emrelda walked into the breakfast room.

"This is a treat," she said with a smile.

"Don't say that until you taste it," replied Avraal. "The service wasn't short, and we had lunch with Ingrella and two other councilors. It was too late for me to go back to work at Carlos's, and Steffan doesn't have his office back. So it made sense for us to come home and fix dinner. It's anything but elaborate."

"It smells wonderful. It was a long day. A very long day."

"Trouble of some sort?" asked Dekkard. "I mean larger trouble than usual. Southtown?"

"Where else? They called me in to deal with a group of angry women. A grocer gimmicked his scales. Not a lot, but those people need every coin's worth. The grocer will probably get off with a citation and a fine. Who knows how long he'd been doing it? He had the nerve to blame the women for causing trouble." Emrelda shook her head. "I need to wash up. Then I'll be back."

After Emrelda left the breakfast room, Dekkard looked to Avraal.

"The way she feels, it was worse than she's saying."

Gaaroll just nodded.

"You're getting better at sensing what people feel, aren't you?" said Avraal.

"Some, anyway."

"More than some, I think," suggested Dekkard in an amused tone.

"You keep at it, and in a while, you might be able to be certified at least as a provisional empath," added Avraal.

"You think?"

"I do," affirmed Avraal.

Before that long, Emrelda returned, and Avraal served up dinner.

After a single mouthful, Emrelda said, "I don't care about your demurrals and your claims that the dinner isn't fancy or elaborate. It tastes good, and it's filling."

"I agree," added Gaaroll.

Dekkard just grinned.

"Not a word," Avraal said to him. "Not one."

Dekkard kept grinning.

Emrelda tried to keep from smiling, then giggled. "I love it."

Avraal glared at her sister, but ended up shaking her head and smiling.

After that, the conversation was mostly about the memorial service and about the continuing problems facing patrollers in Southtown and Rivertown.

Later, well after dinner, Dekkard and Avraal remained in the sitting room long after Emrelda and Gaaroll had retired to their rooms.

"You've been very quiet," said Avraal. "Do you want to talk about it?"

"I don't even know where to begin."

Avraal just waited.

"If I've recalled correctly," mused Dekkard, "in about half a year, nine councilors and a premier have been killed, and yet, with everything that's happened recently, no one's even noticed. At least, I haven't heard anyone say a word, not even Volkaar or Haarsfel."

"Maybe they haven't thought about it that way. The deaths have been strung out," replied Avraal. "That hasn't happened before, except for the Silent Revolution, where the deaths were even more spread out."

"Half of them were Commercers, too."

"What else would you expect? The New Meritorists were behind most of the deaths."

"Were they, really?" asked Dekkard. "Freust was likely killed by a Commercer-paid assassin, and we know Marrak wasn't killed by the Meritorists. But they certainly killed Aashtaan, Maendaan, Haaltf, and Devoule. That leaves the four killed in the shelling. If Minz was behind that . . ."

"It was still likely agreed to by the New Meritorists. Even if it wasn't, they killed at least four councilors and tried to kill several others."

"But three of the five targeted in the shelling were Craft councilors," Dekkard pointed out. "I'd say that suggests a certain Commercer influence."

"It doesn't make any difference. Almost all the deaths wouldn't have happened without the New Meritorist demonstrations."

Dekkard took a deep breath. "That's exactly what Ulrich and Wyath wanted, to make them a threat so that they could use the Council to increase Commercer influence. There's already unrest in the poorer parts of Guldor. That can only grow over the winter, what with the poor harvests and the rising costs of food. Without Obreduur as premier . . ."

"Then you and Ingrella, and some others, will have to keep the pressure on whoever is premier."

"How do we do that? Most of us are junior."

"Dear, I'm sure that you can find a way, especially if you and Ingrella work together."

Dekkard took another deep breath. "I hope so."

"You will." Avraal rose, then took his hand. "Sitting here and worrying won't solve anything. A good night's sleep might help."

As he stood, Dekkard took consolation in the fact that she hadn't emphasized the word "sleep."

73

DEKKARD woke on Duadi morning in a cold sweat from the last of several dreams in which he and Avraal kept trying to change what had happened. No matter what he tried, Obreduur died.

"You were restless last night," said Avraal as Dekkard sat up and blotted his forehead.

"I was working hard trying to change the past."

"I wish you could, dear, I do, but we both know it doesn't work that way."

Dekkard knowing didn't help much with the feeling that there should have been something he could have done. *But how could you have known?* All along, the problem had been that neither he nor Obreduur had ever had enough information.

Trying to concentrate on the day ahead, he made his way to the bathroom.

A little more than a bell and a third later, he eased the Gresynt down the drive. "Any sense of anything, Nincya?"

"No, sir."

Dekkard turned right on Florinda, but soon ended up on Jacquez, finally turning west onto Council Avenue, heading toward Council Hall, realizing that it was only a third past second bell. "How about meeting me for lunch and then driving us home, assuming no disasters arise?"

"If you'll promise to be good."

"I should—"

"*Promise,* not try," Avraal said firmly.

"I promise."

"Just before noon in the dining room, then?"

"I'll be there. If something comes up at the last moment, I'll leave a message. I don't know of anything, but after all that's happened?"

"I understand."

Dekkard brought the Gresynt to a stop opposite the east doors to the Council Hall, then leaned over and kissed Avraal on the cheek, before getting out. "Until lunch."

She smiled and closed the steamer door.

Dekkard watched until she turned west on Council Avenue. Then he and Gaaroll walked into the Council Hall.

As Dekkard neared the Premier's floor office, the Council Guard on duty there spoke. "Councilor Dekkard, the acting Premier would like a word with you, sir."

"Thank you." Dekkard opened the door and motioned for Gaaroll to enter, then followed her in. Once inside, with the corridor door closed, he said, "The acting Premier wanted a word with me?"

"I did," called Haarsfel from the inner office, the door of which was open. "Just come in, Steffan. I thought you might come through the east doors."

Dekkard entered the inner office and closed the door, then seated himself and waited for Haarsfel to speak.

"What are your thoughts about possible candidates for premier?"

"You're by far the most experienced and senior," Dekkard pointed out.

"That's something that I cannot and will not do, Steffan. I would not be a good premier. I wouldn't even be a mediocre premier."

"I find that hard to believe."

"You'll have to trust me on that. I will say that Axel agreed with me on that." Haarsfel's words were deprecatingly wry.

Since Obreduur had mentioned something along those lines, Dekkard nodded and asked, "So who does that leave? Who'd be at least competent?"

"Fredrich Hasheem would be competent, as would Gerhard Safaell, but I fear Safaell would be too retiring."

"What about Erskine Mardosh?" Dekkard definitely had his own ideas, but he wanted to hear what Haarsfel might say.

"You've talked to Mardosh. What do you think?"

Dekkard smiled politely. "I know what I think, but you've known him far longer."

"Let's just say I have reservations. More important, Daffyd Dholen will likely offer Erskine as a candidate for premier."

"That means you'll propose Hasheem, I take it?"

"I will, but I'd prefer not to oppose Mardosh directly. Some of the councilors who would like to be committee chairs would prefer him."

"Someone like Paarkyn Noyell or . . ." Dekkard had to struggle for another councilor of middling seniority. ". . . Lewell Contiago?"

"Lewell wouldn't be that foolish," replied Haarsfel mildly.

"You're suggesting that Hasheem doesn't excite some of the newer Craft councilors all that much."

"Quiet maturity and judgment are often lost on those who prize appearance or calculated image."

Dekkard nodded. "There's not much time."

"I'll be a little late."

"I'll see what I can do."

"I appreciate it, Steffan." Haarsfel stood.

So did Dekkard, inclining his head, before turning and leaving the inner office.

Once outside in the main corridor, he said to Gaaroll, "Things are getting complicated. After I go into the lobby, you're free until the caucus ends. Wait for me outside the councilors' dining room."

"Yes, sir."

As Dekkard knew would be the case, Roostof was waiting outside the councilors' lobby.

"Good morning, sir."

"Good morning, Svard. I want you to know that you did a wonderful job of capturing the essence of each staff member. Ingrella Obreduur was moved by what you said, and found your ability to portray the spirit of each in just a few sentences amazing. I agree with her. I also know that it had to be difficult."

"Thank you, sir. I know it was hard for you, too."

Dekkard smiled wryly. "But I didn't have to talk about them. You did, and I just wanted you to know how well you spoke."

"Thank you, sir."

Dekkard didn't know what else to say, not immediately, but, finally, he spoke. "On a much more mundane matter, is there any news on our office?"

"Nothing new, sir."

"Then do what you can. I've some unexpected matters to take care of before the caucus vote. If you could be outside the dining room once the caucus is over?"

"I can do that."

"Thank you." With that Dekkard made his way into the lobby, casually glancing around. Since he saw Pajiin and Andros talking, he joined them.

"What do you think about who's up for premier?" asked Pajiin.

"The most senior are Haarsfel, Hasheem, Safaell, and Mardosh," replied Dekkard.

"Heard that Haarsfel won't take it," said Pajiin. "That true?"

"That's what I've heard," replied Dekkard.

"So, what about the others?" asked Andros.

"I've worked with Hasheem. He's often quiet, but he's solid. Safaell's solid, too, maybe a bit too retiring."

"I was thinking about Mardosh," said Andros. "What do you think?"

"I've only talked to him twice, but he said one thing, then later did something that invalidated all that he'd said. That makes me nervous. Hasheem doesn't promise much, but in all the maneuvering on the Security reform legislation, he never played games or deceived me."

Andros frowned. "Daffyd likes him."

"He's very likable," agreed Dekkard.

"I'm concerned about councilors who are reserved," said Andros.

Pajiin laughed. "You didn't hear what Steffan didn't say, Julian."

"What do you mean?"

"Daffyd's outgoing. He likes likable. Too many likable types bend their principles to be likable. Hasheem doesn't. I saw that on the Security Committee. Sounds like Safaell doesn't, either." Pajiin eased Andros away from Dekkard and gave a quick look in the direction of Chiram Ghohal, who entered with Elyncya Duforgue.

Dekkard eased his way toward the two newcomers.

Duforgue smiled warmly, almost in a relieved fashion. "Steffan, join us, if you would."

Ghohal looked surprised, almost annoyed, for an instant, but managed a pleasant smile, and said, "Good morning, Steffan."

"Good morning to both of you."

Ghohal looked directly at Dekkard. "Did you and Elyncya plan this encounter?" His tone of voice was edged, but humorous.

"I wouldn't plan anything involving another woman, Chiram, without the consent of my wife. I also have no intention of forcing my views about who should be the Craft Party candidate for premier upon anyone. I will simply say that I'll support Fredrich Hasheem. I'll do it because he was effective at getting the Security reforms through committee and through the Council. He didn't put off hearings, and he didn't promise things and then go back on his promises because of powerful corporacion interests in his district or elsewhere in Guldor."

"You said Mardosh was justified."

"I explained why he did what he did. That was what you asked. You didn't ask me if I approved. I didn't. I can understand those pressures. Most councilors face them. That's not the question. The question is whether a councilor who defers to corporacion pressure as a committee chair can be counted on to resist such pressures if he's elected premier. It's an important question, given the negative corporate actions already revealed." Dekkard smiled pleasantly. "I wouldn't think of trying to make that decision for you."

"You make it sound so easy, Steffan."

"It's not," Dekkard replied. "Councilors are often put in a position where they must make a choice: whether it's better for themselves or better for Guldor as a whole, or better for the party or for the country. I try to base my judgments on what others have done rather than on what they promise to do." He shrugged. "We'll just have to see what happens."

At that moment, another voice came from behind Dekkard. "Good morning, Steffan."

Dekkard turned to see Harleona Zerlyon, who had spoken, along with Ingrella Obreduur and Traelyna Treshaam, and he inclined his head to all three.

"Shall we see what the leadership has to offer?" asked Zerlyon, gesturing toward the Council chamber.

"We might as well," agreed Ghohal, in a tone bordering on resignation, stepping forward as if he wanted to get away from Dekkard and Duforgue.

Dekkard just hoped that facts would prevail over empty promises in Ghohal's decision about whom to support.

Duforgue slowed her steps, so that they entered the Council chamber behind the others, at which point she said quietly, "You made more of an impression than I did."

"He might just vote against Hasheem because I pressed him too hard."

"He might, but he definitely would have supported Mardosh if you hadn't."

Dekkard wanted to shake his head. He knew he wasn't that good at flattering people into doing the right thing. *Especially when you're not completely sure it's the right thing.* From what he'd seen Mardosh wasn't always to be trusted, but that didn't necessarily mean that he wouldn't be a better premier than Hasheem. *You can only go on what you know, and what those you trust might know.* But Dekkard also knew that, more than a few times, what others he trusted had "known" hadn't been accurate.

Less than a sixth passed before Guilhohn Haarsfel appeared on the dais. "Good morning, everyone. Today, we have the duty of selecting the Craft

Party candidate to replace Axel Obreduur. Before I begin the proceedings, I wish to make it clear that I have no interest in becoming premier, and that I will refuse to accept any nomination if offered. So please don't offer it. Is that clear?" After that question, Haarsfel surveyed the room, then continued. "As Craft Party floor leader, it is my prerogative to first offer my nominee, with my reasons for that nomination. After I state my reasons for supporting that nominee, the floor is open for other nominees. Either the councilor offering another nominee or the one seconding that nominee, but not both, may offer a statement of support."

Again, Haarsfel paused before continuing. "As Craft Party floor leader, I propose that the Craft Party nominee for premier be Fredrich Alois Hasheem. As both councilor and Security Committee chair, Fredrich exemplifies the mixture of insight, quiet determination, and leadership needed for a premier. Excessive aggression and bold unfounded talk only make reaching working solutions harder. Fredrich's firm but non-antagonistic leadership is especially necessary for this time in the history of the Council and of Guldor. Fredrich guided through the reform legislation sorely needed to remedy the years of abuse of power by the Security Ministry. He was highly instrumental in working out the necessary changes to the annual appropriations. These are acts, not rhetoric or promises."

In less than three minutes, Haarsfel finished outlining Hasheem's qualifications for the position of premier. Then he paused again before asking, "Is there another nomination?"

"There is!" boomed out the voice of Daffyd Dholen. "I nominate Erskine Mardosh as the Craft candidate for premier."

"Is there a second?"

"I second the nomination of Erskine Mardosh."

Dekkard didn't recognize the voice and turned to see that it was Paarkyn Noyell. *Haarsfel had that right.* But then, Haarsfel had always been known for foreseeing the likelihood of how votes would turn out.

"Which of you will offer a statement of support?"

Dholen immediately moved to the dais, where he turned to face the assembled Craft councilors. "Erskine Mardosh is the best suited to be premier in these times. He's determined and knowledgeable. Patience and reserve are not the qualities we need now, not with Commercer abuses continuing and the New Meritorists killing a premier and three other councilors just last week. We need a more aggressive spokesman, one who will revitalize and rejuvenate the Craft Party."

Dekkard noted that one of the clerks had begun to write as soon as Dholen began to speak, and wondered why, then realized he was creating cards containing Mardosh's name.

Dholen continued for several more minutes in the same vein before concluding, ". . . and that's why we need Erskine Mardosh."

"Now that the honorable councilor from Actaan has concluded the campaign speech," said Haarsfel dryly, "are there any other nominations?" He waited. Finally, he said, "Seeing none, we will commence voting in a minute or so. At present, there are twenty-eight Craft councilors eligible to vote, since the Craft Party of Aloor has not yet submitted a recommendation to fill the seat of Tedor Waarfel. For those of you new to a caucus vote, go to the clerks' table. There you will receive three cards, one with the name of one candidate, the second with the name of the other. The third card is blank. You are to place the card that holds the name of the candidate you support into the voting box. If you support neither candidate, place the blank card in the voting box. Then deposit the two cards you did not use in the null box. You have one third in which to vote."

Haarsfel immediately walked over to the clerks' table and received his three cards, followed by Dholen, and then by Noyell.

Dekkard waited several minutes, then followed Ingrella and Safaell to the clerks' table. When he received the cards, he checked them carefully, then voted for Hasheem and deposited the other two cards in the null box.

When the clerk signaled that all councilors had voted, the count began, with Haarsfel and one clerk counting the cards in the voting box, and Dholen and one clerk counting the cards in the null box. As the tallies were written down, Dekkard watched Dholen. He didn't look happy.

Haarsfel walked to the front of the dais with the written tallies. "The tallies from both boxes match. Sixteen councilors voted for Fredrich Hasheem, eleven for Erskine Mardosh, with one abstention. Fredrich Hasheem is hereby declared as the Craft Party selection for premier. That vote will take place at fourth bell tomorrow morning. If the Council receives the names of those individuals chosen to replace Quentin Fader and Tedor Waarfel before that vote, they will be sworn in prior to the vote."

Haarsfel stepped down from the dais and walked over to Dekkard. "When you're finished here, Guard Captain Trujillo is in the floor office. He has some information for you."

Then he added in a lower voice, "Thank you, Steffan."

Dekkard replied quietly, "I just did what I could, and so did several others."

Haarsfel just smiled, then walked toward Hasheem.

Dekkard followed, but stood back and waited while Haarsfel and several other senior Craft councilors offered congratulations, followed by Ingrella Obreduur. After Ingrella spoke for several minutes, she motioned for Dekkard to join her.

"Sometimes, Steffan," she said with a smile, "you're still too deferential." Then she looked to Hasheem. "Just so you know, Fredrich, Steffan was very instrumental in helping secure your nomination."

"I appreciate that, Steffan. I did have a sense of your involvement, and I do and will welcome your thoughts. Axel told me he never dismissed your insights."

"Sometimes, unhappily, my insights were correct, but not specific enough to be useful except for explaining matters after the fact."

"And sometimes," said Ingrella, "they were correct enough to prevent more deaths and destruction."

Just not in the case of Axel.

"Please feel free to share insights," said Hasheem, "incomplete as you may believe them. I'll need all the insights possible."

"I'll do that and congratulations."

"Thank you. I do wish matters were otherwise."

"That's kind of you, Fredrich," said Ingrella, "but matters are as they are, not as we wish them to be. All we can do is our best for as long as we can."

"I'll do my best at that, and to follow Axel's example."

Dekkard stepped away with Ingrella as Tomas Pajiin stepped up to congratulate Hasheem.

"Where are you headed now, Steffan?"

"For a meeting with Guard Captain Trujillo. According to Guilhohn, he has some information for me. Later, around noon, Avraal's joining me for lunch. Would you like to—"

"I've imposed on you two enough—"

"It wouldn't be an imposition at all. I'm still a very junior councilor, and I have much to learn. Besides, we enjoy talking to you."

"You're very kind."

"No, I'm being selfish. We both value your knowledge and advice, and I was foolish not to ask you about more things earlier."

Ingrella laughed softly. "I like it when you're politely insistent. I'd be delighted. A bit before noon in the dining room?"

Dekkard nodded. "Now for the Guard captain. Wish me good fortune."

"I will, but I doubt you'll need it."

That was a feeling Dekkard didn't share. There were far too many things that could go wrong, too many aspects of what had happened unresolved. He pushed those thoughts out of his mind for the moment, knowing that they'd return.

Trujillo stood as Dekkard entered the floor office, hopefully soon to be Hasheem's, unless Mardosh and his supporters defected to a Landor or Commercer candidate, which seemed unlikely, but theoretically possible.

Trujillo gestured toward the inner office. "Floor Leader Haarsfel said we could use the office."

Dekkard led the way, and Trujillo followed, shutting the door before taking one of the chairs in front of the desk. Dekkard took the other.

"Again, I'd like to thank you, Councilor. Without your observations, I don't think it would have been possible for us to discover what we have."

Since Dekkard didn't know what they'd discovered, he simply said, "I'm glad you found my observations helpful, but I haven't the faintest idea of what that might be, except for the fact that Jaime Minz was deeply involved."

Trujillo nodded. "He was more deeply involved than we initially believed. Your observation of where you saw the stake lorry proved to be one of the keys. We found an empty storage room in the basement that had been temporarily leased by someone calling himself Amash Kharhan, but the building owner wanted a co-signer, even though the rent was paid in advance and in mark notes. One of the conditions of the lease was that all copies of the lease be returned to the lessor when the space was returned to control of the building owner. Fortunately, the owner recalled the co-signer's name—Elise Reed, of Capitol Services."

"Was that Minz's secretary?"

Trujillo nodded. "Of course, she vanished when the Justiciary Ministry took Sr. Minz into custody, but the trail goes back to him. Although the room had been swept and seemed empty, we found some small fragments of annealed copper in floor cracks. They match the fragments we found in the Council Office Building and in and around the wreckage of the stake lorry. It took almost a week, but we tracked down who supplied the copper tubing from which they made the shells. You were right about that, as well. The tubing was delivered to a small machine shop in Rivertown, which was also rented by one Amash Kharhan. The shop was empty, but we found small traces of dunnite there. From what we could determine, it had been empty for several weeks. We tried to track down the stake lorry, but it was purchased with mark notes from someone who wasn't very particular about documentation."

"Was Minz Amash Kharhan?" asked Dekkard.

Trujillo shook his head. "That's one thing we're sure of. Everyone described Kharhan as very average in height, and that's one thing that Sr. Minz definitely was not. The person who most closely fits the description of Kharhan is Sohl Hurrek."

Dekkard's mouth opened, and he shook his head. Hurrek had died more than a month before the shelling. *Minz or Ulrich had to have planned the shelling almost immediately after the election.* So it couldn't have been recently decided. *Except possibly for the idea of targeting you.*

"You see?" said Trujillo. "Sr. Minz didn't just pay Sr. Hurrek to deal with you. He also set up Hurrek from the beginning so that there wouldn't be any witnesses."

"And, with his death and the disappearance of his secretary, there aren't any left."

"There's one other thing about Sr. Minz. He had two banque accounts, one for Capitol Services, and a personal account. The greatest balance ever in the Capitol Services account was slightly over sixteen thousand marks. The personal account had two thousand marks in it, payable on death to Elise Reed. She didn't claim it."

"She must have thought she'd be tied in to the attack."

"That was our feeling."

"What about the New Meritorists?"

"We have strong indications that the three men who died in the explosion of the steam cannon and the remaining shells also developed and built both. It appears that while they and Minz had links to the New Meritorists, they operated almost separately."

"From what you've discovered, it would certainly seem so."

"There's doubtless more there, Councilor, but the basics aren't likely to change. We've traced the manufacture of the weapons, and there's no doubt of what Sr. Minz did."

"You're right about that," *mostly,* "but there's one aspect," *if not several,* "of it all that still bothers me. I have to wonder if there's more dunnite out there."

"Since no one knows how much the New Meritorists originally obtained," Trujillo pointed out, "there's no way to tell if they've exhausted their supply, or if there's more. Right now, we have no way of knowing, and no way to proceed. But we have resolved who physically accomplished the attack on the Council Office Building, and your observations were invaluable. I did want you to know that."

"Thank you very much for letting me know. I can't tell you how much I appreciate it." Dekkard paused. "I just wish I'd known more earlier."

Trujillo's soft laugh had a bitter edge. "Don't we all?" After a moment, he added, "You have nothing to apologize for, Councilor. Sometimes, the worst is beyond our control."

Dekkard nodded, then slowly stood. "Thank you again, Guard Captain."

Trujillo stood as well. "It was my pleasure."

Dekkard could hear the sincerity in the officer's voice. "Let's just hope we don't need any more meetings like this." His voice held a touch of wry humor.

"We can certainly hope." Trujillo spoke with a certain dubious optimism.

With a parting smile, Dekkard turned and left the office, making his way through the Council chamber to the councilors' dining room. He couldn't help wondering about the dunnite in copper tubing. The picric acid reacted badly with most metals over time. Just how long had the dunnite been in those tubes? Could that reaction in one of the makeshift shells have been the cause of the explosion that destroyed the lorry prematurely? Or an oversensitive lead azide fuse? He supposed he'd never know, not for certain.

As he expected, given that it was barely fifth bell, Avraal wasn't there. Roostof and Gaaroll, however, were waiting outside.

"Sir?" asked Roostof.

"The Craft candidate for premier is Fredrich Hasheem. The other candidate was Erskine Mardosh. Mardosh had some enthusiastic supporters, but not enough in the end, thankfully. The full Council vote will be at fourth bell tomorrow morning." He paused. "The office?"

"They'll start painting this afternoon. They *think* we should be able to return on Furdi. That's when everyone else will probably be allowed back in the building."

"That would be good."

"Have you heard any more about the attack?" asked Gaaroll.

"I've heard some," admitted Dekkard. "I just met with Guard Captain Trujillo." He went on to give a brief summary.

"So everyone they could find is either dead or disappeared?" asked Roostof.

"Mostly dead. I have suspicions about some others, but there's no way to link them to the attack, let alone to the New Meritorists."

"So, that's it? After all the deaths?"

Dekkard shook his head. "That's it for now. The New Meritorists will likely be very quiet for at least a little while. So will those others, I suspect. If or how soon things will heat up again I couldn't say." *Only that they will, so long as*

Ulrich and a few others you don't even know are still around. Especially if the Craft Party continued to hold control of the Council.

"What will you do now, sir?" asked Roostof.

"Do the best I can as councilor, while keeping an eye out for trouble. What else?" Dekkard managed a grin. "That means I'll need all the help I can get from you and the rest of the staff. Is there anything else I need to do?"

"No, sir."

"Then just take care of yourself, and I'll see you tomorrow morning before the vote."

Once Roostof left, Dekkard handed Gaaroll a five-mark note. "Here's your lunch money. I'll be eating with Ritten Dekkard and Ritten Obreduur, and it's likely to last past first bell, how much past I don't know."

"I'll be here outside the dining room."

"Practice your sensing while you wait."

"Yes, sir."

As Gaaroll headed for the staff cafeteria Dekkard made his way into the councilors' dining room, obtained a table, sat down, and ordered café. He was still nursing the same mug when Avraal arrived at a third before noon, followed almost immediately by Ingrella.

"Was Hasheem selected?" asked Avraal.

"He was, despite rather enthusiastically misleading comments for Mardosh and equally misleading implications about Hasheem by Daffyd Dholen," replied Dekkard, standing and gesturing to the chairs.

After everyone was seated and had ordered, Avraal said, "I'm certain that there was more than that to it."

"Not much or not during the caucus," replied Dekkard. "Most votes were likely decided beforehand."

"Some of which were strongly influenced by your husband," said Ingrella to Avraal. "Enough to make the difference."

"I wouldn't say that," replied Dekkard.

"I would, and I do," said Ingrella, a glint in her eye. "You can be very persuasive."

"I have the feeling I pressed too hard on one councilor."

"Chiram Ghohal, you mean? Anything less wouldn't have worked. Elyncya's fairly certain he voted for Hasheem." Ingrella paused. "What did you tell him?"

Dekkard told them both.

Avraal shook her head, but she was smiling. "Only you."

"Very effective," said Ingrella. "You insisted that the choice was his, to vote for a man who had not only kept his word, but acted to support those words, or for one who hadn't done either. You would have made a good legalist."

This time Dekkard shook his head. "I didn't plan those words. I just said what I felt. I could easily have said something stupid."

"Axel often said words similar to what you just said. You're likely correct. You have the chance to do more as a councilor than you could as a legalist."

The three paused as the server approached with their orders. Dekkard had ordered the onion soup, partly out of a desire for something different and partly because he wanted something lighter. Avraal had a cup of the white bean soup, while Ingrella had a half order of the three-cheese chicken.

After several mouthfuls of soup, Dekkard said, "I had a short meeting with Guard Captain Trujillo right after the caucus."

"Good or bad?" asked Avraal.

"I'll let you decide." Dekkard related what Trujillo had told him, as precisely as he could recall.

"Most of that makes sense, especially about Hurrek," said Avraal.

"And some of it doesn't," replied Dekkard. "The issue of where they got the dunnite remains buried, and I have very strong doubts that Hurrek was the original Amash Kharhan. I don't think Minz was either, for that matter. He didn't have that many marks in his personal banque account, and the Capitol Services account never held over seventeen thousand, according to Trujillo. I think Minz used that name just to confuse matters or possibly to get Hurrek in more trouble if, by chance, he survived."

"Why would they ever sign a lease revealing the involvement of Capitol Services?" asked Avraal.

"They'd already left the machine shop, and they wouldn't have wanted to travel all the way across Machtarn from Rivertown on the day of the attack, especially with all those explosives. They might have also planned to wait longer before attacking. Either way, they needed a storage space close to the Council. They cleaned everything, so that they could all disappear. If Trujillo hadn't discovered the links to Minz, then all traces would have vanished after the attack one way or another, and Minz would still have been operating Capitol Services." Dekkard paused.

"What is it?" asked Avraal. "You had the strangest look on your face."

"For some reason, I just remembered something that Axel said when we dropped in the night the house was attacked. He said, 'In both law and politics, the more personal you make it, the higher the cost.' That's where Minz got himself in trouble. He went after me personally. The red pepper attack on me got Trujillo involved in looking at Minz, and that was the beginning of the end for him."

Ingrella nodded. "Axel often said that it was dangerous to get personal in politics or war."

Dekkard didn't remember Obreduur saying anything about war, but that addition certainly made sense.

"What I still wonder about," said Ingrella, "is why Jaime Minz had to kill Pietro Venburg."

"According to Trujillo, Minz only had two thousand marks in his personal account," said Avraal. "He had to use marks from the Capitol Services account to bribe Hurrek into using the Atacaman pepper on Steffan. What if the marks came from Siincleer Shipbuilding? Given the way corporacions funded Capitol Services, most likely Venburg would have been the only one who knew that."

Ingrella frowned, then nodded. "That clears that up, I think. At least, until or unless something else comes up."

"What still worries me is that the investigation never got to the bottom of things," said Dekkard. "I still think that Ulrich and someone high at Suvion Industries, as well as Venburg and a few other corporacion types, were behind the violence of the New Meritorist attacks, and the way this ended has cut off any way to tie them to Minz."

"Until they try something else," said Ingrella dryly, "and they likely will, because you and Fredrich will clean up as many of the abuses as you can, and that will reduce their power."

"You, Fredrich, and Steffan," corrected Avraal.

"You're kind, dear," replied Ingrella. "Too kind."

Dekkard just smiled.

74

T HE remainder of lunch with Ingrella and Avraal was cheerful, and uneventful, after which Dekkard and Avraal gathered up Gaaroll and drove
back to Erslaan. There they visited the grocer and picked up several items, including a chicken for roasting, a matter which Avraal addressed almost as
soon as the three entered the house.

Dekkard changed into security grays, and despite the chill of the afternoon,
set up the target for knife practice. He spent time working with Gaaroll, and
a little later, with Avraal when she joined them.

Emrelda arrived home slightly after four bells and found the other three in
the sitting room. "I can't believe it. Three dinners in a row, and roast chicken
tonight."

"Enjoy it," declared Avraal. "Once Steffan's office is repaired, we go back
to working later. Carlos has been very forgiving, but I don't want to take advantage of him."

"Your expenses aren't that high. You haven't even bought any more clothes."
Emrelda's last words contained amusement.

"For now, I have enough. We're saving. We'll need it all," replied Avraal.
"Remember, we have to buy a house in Gaarlak . . . and we'll need to fur-
nish it."

"You'll manage."

Avraal got up from the armchair. "We need to go into the kitchen. I need
your help. I can't remember how you do that apricot glaze."

The sisters left the sitting room, and Gaaroll looked to Dekkard. "You have
to buy a house in Gaarlak?"

By the time Dekkard explained that and several other questions, it was time
for dinner.

The apricot-glazed chicken with cheese-drizzled mashed potatoes and late
beans was delicious enough that no one spoke for a time.

Finally, Emrelda did. "Avraal explained most of what happened with the
New Meritorists, but she almost made it sound like the New Meritorists
would just disappear. From what I've seen, none of what happened addressed
their problems. Five or six key people died, but there were hundreds, maybe
thousands, on the streets, and we're having more problems in Rivertown and
Southtown, even in the old river harbor area."

"You're right," said Dekkard after swallowing another morsel of the moist
and tasty chicken. "The New Meritorists aren't going away. At least the renegade Special Agents are largely gone, and those that are left can be prosecuted
as common criminals. That will reduce a lot of the violence, at least for a
little while. Shutting down Capitol Services makes it harder for Ulrich and
his peers and their backers to funnel marks to either the New Meritorists or
other troublemakers. I'm hoping that the patrollers will be more effective with

the removal of the Special Agents and with a Public Safety Ministry focused on public safety and not on harassing Crafters and others. How does Captain Narryt feel about that?"

"He says it's better that way. We're not getting as many street conflicts with people now that the SAs and the STF are gone, but a lot of people are getting hungry, and there are more domestic-violence complaints—and accidental deaths of women that weren't accidental."

Dekkard nodded. "Poor harvests all over Guldor haven't helped, and the tariffs on Sargassan swampgrass rice and emmer wheat-corn keep prices high."

"It'll be worse by late winter," added Emrelda.

"I know. I'm hoping that with less interference from corporacion agents provocateur we can make legislative changes that will blunt the appeal of the New Meritorists and improve life for the less-skilled working people."

"At least you and the Crafters see the problems and are trying to address them."

"We are," agreed Dekkard, "and the new premier understands that." *Most of it anyway.*

Later that night, when Dekkard and Avraal remained in the sitting room after Emrelda and Gaaroll had retired—or departed to give the couple space—Dekkard turned to Avraal. "You know I still worry. We've gotten rid of the worst evils in the old Security system; Venburg's not around to threaten or do worse to your sister; Minz isn't a problem anymore—"

"I can't believe how that worked out."

Dekkard snorted. "I'm certain Ulrich had Minz assassinated. His death meant nothing could be traced back to him and Suvion Industries. Northwest Chemical can claim they never knew, and, as Minz wrote me, their books will show nothing."

"Hiring an assassin to do in a trusted former employee who was doing your dirty work." Avraal shook her head.

"We got a little time, a little space," *and more than that for Emrelda,* "but the problems are still there."

"They'll always be there, but we can try to make them smaller." Avraal held up a certain leather-bound volume. "Enough of problems for the night."

Dekkard agreed.

A poet long since forgotten by most wrote of how the Autarchs of Argorn turned from "truth's terrible spare beauty" in constructing Argo and instead relied upon mere additive artifice to curry the favor of those anogenic autodidacts, suggesting not even indirectly that the Autarchs were so naïvely narcissistic that they equated great art with greater masses of artistic forms and objects.

Truly great art as sometimes, but not often enough, manifested in Averra, occurs when no element of a building, object, or representation stands out from any other, and, when the whole is considered, any addition would detract from the impression, rather than improve it. That forgotten poet also observed that too few words, no matter how accurate and how powerful, are often bombarded into obscurity by a barrage of banality, while too many words bury their meaning in blandiloquent boredom.

All too often, in the misuse of words, men brandish their "truth" like a weapon, claiming that it is the only one, a talisman or touchstone that will reveal all to those who believe, a blandishment that blinds rather than reveals, just as the sprawling pleasure gardens of the Autarchs and their ever-higher walls left them unable to see beyond the confines of their creation.

Words create walls as well, barriers in the perceptions of the mind built on meanings ascribed to those words not supported by the world beyond. How and what we name limits what we perceive, yet, without naming, we cannot communicate, and in that paradoxical observation lies the importance of words and naming and the need for great care in the use of names and descriptions, particularly when describing or seeking the "truth."

How many men and women have sought the "truth," creating verbal and theological structures of imposing weight and verbosity? How many have sought it in the form of the unseen supernatural? Or laid it out in the imprisoned confines of logic?

"What is truth?" ask so many.

Truth is simply what is. Truth is a single perfect rose or a jumbled myriad of wildflowers at the edge of a wood. A dead soldier with an arrow through his eye. A carelessly stacked woodpile. A ruined and burned villa. Averra as it is at this moment.

Those, and a million other examples of what is, are truth.

Nothing more and nothing less.

AVERRA
The City of Truth
Johan Eschbach
377 TE

OR whatever reason, perhaps indeed the near-forgotten words of *The City of Truth,* Dekkard slept soundly and well, and woke to find Avraal looking fondly at him.

"That's the best you've slept in weeks."

"The past month has been a bit stressful."

Avraal laughed. "Just a little understatement there."

"I presume you're going to be there for the vote."

"Of course, even if it's a formality. I wouldn't get much done, anyway, thinking about it."

"An important formality, though." Dekkard stretched and then sat up. "I suppose I should get moving."

"Go take your shower." But she smiled as she spoke.

In the end, breakfast was leisurely.

When they left the house Dekkard wore one of his new winter suits, with the brightest of the red cravats. He was glad it wasn't quite so cold as it had been several days earlier, since he hadn't replaced his presumably destroyed overcoat. He could always hope, and perhaps the overcoat could be repaired.

When they neared the Council Hall, Dekkard asked simply, "Nincya?"

"No strong feelings, sir."

"Very quiet emotionally," added Avraal.

Once he parked the Gresynt and got out, Dekkard studied the Council Office Building, but the scaffolding on the north side had vanished, suggesting that the outside stone and brickwork and the outside window trim painting had been completed. The walk to the Council Hall took longer, as it had ever since the attack, because they had to walk along the south side of the Council Office Building, the walled courtyard, and the south front of the Council Hall.

Once they entered the Council Hall, Dekkard started looking for Roostof, but found the legalist waiting outside the councilors' lobby, looking a little downcast when Dekkard, Avraal, and Gaaroll approached.

"Problems, Svard?" asked Dekkard.

"Not severe ones, but it's looking like we won't have the office until Quindi."

"That's disappointing, but we can deal with it." Dekkard grinned. "Take some time off and take Bettina Safaell to lunch or dinner."

Roostof blushed.

Avraal smiled.

"Have you asked her?"

"We're having dinner tonight. Well, she asked me to dinner at her house, her father's house, that is."

"Just be yourself." Dekkard paused. "I didn't mean to intrude. You're not the only one who gets unexpected advice. About the time I finally realized how special Avraal was, another security aide bluntly asked me if I was going to let her slip through my fumbling fingers."

"Someone said that?" asked Gaaroll.

"A woman did, in fact," Dekkard admitted.

"That had to be Amelya Detauran," said Avraal.

Dekkard nodded. "Who else?"

"Was she, oh, forget I said that, sir."

"No. She's involved with someone else. She likes Avraal and didn't want me to botch it. Which I could have." Dekkard smiled. "I have a question for you. Is there anything you really need to do here today?"

"I could—"

"Could doesn't count."

"No, sir."

"Good. Take the day off. Take Furdi off as well. If I need you, I'll message you. We'll meet at the office on Quindi, or in the corridor outside, if the work isn't done. Have Margrit come in at the regular time, the others at fifth bell."

"Yes, sir."

"Enjoy yourself, Svard."

"Thank you, sir." Roostof smiled broadly before turning and walking swiftly toward the east doors.

"He's definitely interested in Bettina Safaell," said Avraal.

"I could be wrong, but I think they just might fit together."

"More than a chance, at least from Svard's side."

"Was I that obvious?"

"Not until the end." Avraal smiled.

"You were better at not showing things." Dekkard grinned. "Until the end."

Avraal shook her head ruefully, then said, "You'd better go in and make sure that everything is without surprises."

"I haven't been doing that well, lately."

"Stop asking for compliments. You've done better than anyone else for the past year."

Dekkard winced. "You're right on both points." He paused and added cheerfully, "Especially the first."

Then he made his way into the councilors' lobby, where he saw Ingrella speaking with Mardosh. After just a moment, he decided to move toward them. Surprisingly—*or perhaps not so surprisingly*—Mardosh beckoned for Dekkard to join them.

"Good morning, Ingrella, Erskine."

"It is a good morning," agreed Mardosh. "Although the circumstances are tragic, they're also almost unprecedented. So far as I could determine, it will be the first time ever that a Craft premier succeeds a Craft premier. That's assuming the Imperador doesn't do the unthinkable, of course."

"It's highly unlikely," agreed Ingrella, "but we'll have to see. If there are no surprises, what are you planning in the way of hearings in your committee?"

"I haven't heard of any major changes in committee membership. Does that mean you'll be on the Military Affairs Committee?"

"That's what Guilhohn and Fredrich have told me."

"It's a shame they didn't put you on the Justiciary Committee," said Mardosh thoughtfully. "With your expertise . . ."

"Oh, instead of a regular second committee position, they decided that I should be an ex officio member of the Justiciary Committee. It's been done before. Not often, but it's not unprecedented. I won't be able to vote, but I'll be able to contribute in every other way."

"Hmmm," reflected Mardosh, "I can see the appeal of that."

Dekkard wagered he could. "You were going to comment on possible hearings?"

"The strange death of Pietro Venburg and then the shelling of the office building meant we had to postpone hearings on possible improvements in the current military contracting process, and we'll need to look at funding for western and river defenses. There's a great deal of internal unrest in Atacama."

Dekkard smiled pleasantly as Mardosh went on until the warning chime sounded.

"Thank you, Erskine," said Ingrella warmly. "I do appreciate the insights and notice."

"My pleasure, Ingrella, and since you're not on the committee, Steffan, we should talk about some of your thoughts when the time comes."

"Whenever you think it's appropriate, Erskine, I'd be more than happy to."

Dekkard let Mardosh and Ingrella lead the way into the Council chamber.

Just as Dekkard stepped into the chamber, Villem Baar motioned, and Dekkard joined him, standing by Baar's desk, also in the back row, as was Dekkard's.

"How are you holding up, Villem?"

"Much better. Gretina and the children arrived yesterday, and we'll be moving into the house on Findi. Once we're settled, I hope we'll be able to get together."

"Avraal and I would like that very much."

"Excellent! I won't keep you."

Dekkard smiled, then made his way to his desk, nodding to Ingrella as he seated himself.

When the chimes struck four bells, their echo was followed by a single echoing deep chime that seemed to reverberate through the Council chamber, as Dekkard knew it had been designed to do.

The lieutenant-at-arms in the green and black dress uniform of the Council Guards strode to the middle of the dais, directly before the desk behind which Haarsfel now stood, and struck the floor with the gold and black ceremonial staff. Then he declared in a deep voice, "The Council is now in session," after which he pivoted and marched off the dais.

After a long moment of silence, Haarsfel declared, "The first order of this Council and of this session is the swearing in of two new councilors, duly selected as members of the Council of Sixty-Six. After a lengthy debate, the Craft Party of Aloor recommended Kastyn Heimrich as the replacement councilor for the Aloor district. The Landor Party of Silverhills has recommended, and the Landor floor leader has affirmed, the selection of Ellus Fader as the replacement councilor for the Silverhills district.

"Lieutenant-at-Arms, please escort the councilors-select to the floor."

Kastyn Heimrich was a dark-haired but balding and wiry man almost a head shorter than Dekkard, and he looked to be a good twenty years older. Ellus Fader didn't look that much different from his predecessor, blond and darker-skinned than most, a sign of a long Landor heritage, round-faced and slightly chunky, although slightly taller than Heimrich. Dekkard had the distinct feeling that Ellus Fader was either a sibling or a close cousin of the late Quentin Fader. Given what he knew and had learned about Landors, that was most likely so.

The entire Council stood as Haarsfel read the oath of office, phrase by phrase, as the two selected councilors repeated each phrase.

Having completed the swearing in, Haarsfel smiled briefly, offered congratulations to each, and waved them to the chamber floor, where a clerk directed each to a desk, although the seating would be changed—for Landors and Crafters—before the next Council session. Most of the councilors seated themselves.

"The Council now stands ready to conduct its necessary business," declared Haarsfel. "The Craft leadership has proposed, and the Craft Party caucus voted to support, Fredrich Alois Hasheem as its premier-designate. The vote is for or against the candidate. All councilors have a third in which to register their vote and deposit a plaque."

As he finished speaking, Haarsfel gestured, and the deep gong rang once.

Dekkard watched as the senior councilors began to vote. As he kept watching, he found himself sitting on the edge of his chair, and that he was moistening his lips, even though it was unlikely that Hasheem would fail to gain a majority. After most of the senior councilors had voted, he stood and made his way to the Craft Party plaque box, where he picked up the two tiles, and then walked to the two boxes, careful to put the affirmative tile in the voting box and the negative one in the null box.

When he sat down, he looked sideways at Ingrella. She offered a calm smile.

Finally, the deep chime rang again.

"The vote is closed," declared Haarsfel. "Floor leaders, do your duty."

Haarsfel joined the other two floor leaders to watch as each voting tile was removed from the ballot box and placed in one of two columns in the counting tray. Each column was also separated by party. Then the clerk wrote the vote totals on the tally sheet, and each of the three floor leaders signed the sheet. As the floor leader of the party with the greatest number of councilors, Haarsfel carried the tally sheet as he stepped onto the dais.

"Those councilors approving Councilor Fredrich Alois Hasheem as the Council's selection for Premier of this Council—twenty-nine Craft councilors, five Landor councilors, and three Commerce councilors, for a total of thirty-seven. The Council has selected Fredrich Hasheem as Premier."

The applause from the councilors and from the gallery was modest and brief.

Haarsfel was smiling broadly as he gestured to Hasheem. "Premier-select Hasheem."

Hasheem stepped to the Premier's lectern. "Thank you. All of you. I'll be following the long-established precedent. I won't offer my first address to the Council until I am officially accepted, and, if accepted, I will address the entire Council on Quindi. Thank you, again."

Haarsfel stepped forward. "There being no other pending matters before the Council, the Council stands adjourned until noon, Quindi, the seventeenth of Winterfirst."

Dekkard took a deep breath, then looked up to the spouses' gallery, where Avraal looked down at him, smiling.

EPILO·GUE

NEW PREMIER VOWS CONTINUED PROSPERITY FOR ALL
After the Imperador, Laureous XXIV, confirmed Fredrich Hasheem as Premier and successor to the late Premier Obreduur, Premier Hasheem reaffirmed the policies set forth by his predecessor. In the first Council session after his confirmation, Premier Hasheem declared that his priority and that of the Council would be "prosperity for all, not just the wealthy and fortunate." He went on to declare that, along with the need to pursue prosperity, the Council's priority was also to take all steps necessary "to maintain stability and order," especially after the violent attacks on the Council Office Building and the Craft Guildhall. He lauded the combined efforts of the Justiciary Ministry, the new Ministry of Public Safety, and the Council Guards to capture Sr. Jaime Minz, one of the masterminds of the violence.

Premier Hasheem asserted that, while such violence was "totally unacceptable," the unrest that had fueled support for demonstrations and violence was the direct result of the failure of recent Commerce governments to understand that destroying Guldoran jobs to increase short-term corporacion profits only meant that most Guldorans suffered immediately and that such increased profits would be short-term and temporary, and that such shortsightedness could only fuel more unrest.

Gestirn, **17 Winterfirst 1267**

ABOUT THE AUTHOR

L. E. MODESITT, JR. is the author of more than seventy books, primarily science fiction and fantasy, including the long-running, bestselling Saga of Recluce and Imager Portfolio series, as well as a number of short stories.

lemodesittjr.com